ELIZABETH WAITE OMNIBUS

A London Lass

Time Will Tell

W0007922

sphere

SPHERE

This omnibus edition first published in Great Britain in 2007 by Sphere
Elizabeth Waite Omnibus copyright © Elizabeth Waite 2007

Previously published separately:
A London Lass first published in Great Britain in 2001 by Little, Brown
Published by Time Warner Paperbacks in 2002
Copyright © Elizabeth Waite 2001

Time Will Tell first published in Great Britain in 2000
by Little, Brown and Company
Published by Warner Books in 2001
Copyright © Elizabeth Waite 2000

The moral right of the author has been asserted.

A CIP catalogue record for this book is available from the British Library.

ISBN 978-0-7515-4016-1

Papers used by Sphere are natural, recyclable products made from
wood grown in sustainable forests and certified in accordance with
the rules of the Forest Stewardship Council.

Printed and bound in Great Britain by Clays Ltd, St Ives plc
Paper supplied by Hellefoss AS, Norway

Sphere
An imprint of
Little, Brown Book Group
Brettenham House
Lancaster Place
London WC2E 7EN

A Member of the Hachette Livre Group of Companies

www.littlebrown.co.uk

A London Lass

Chapter One

South London, 1920

'DID YER SEE what's going on over at the Castle?' Jimmy Bradshaw asked as he and his mate Ronnie Brown approached the men grouped around the coffee stall which stood on the island in the centre of Tooting Broadway.

Wally Simmonds, manager of Tooting Markets, put his mug of tea on the counter, looked at the two lads and grinned good-naturedly.

'It's Saturday night, son, and turning-out time for the pubs usually means trouble of one sort or another.'

'But this woman's taken one 'ell of a bashing by the looks of 'er.' Sixteen-year-old Ronnie's voice held not only concern but a hint of fear as well. 'We saw 'er being dragged off by 'er hair.'

'Yeah, screaming blue murder she was.' Jimmy put his twopennyworth in; after all, he was older by two years and wasn't going to be outdone.

'All right, lads, I'll take a look.' Wally sighed as he picked up his mug and drained the last of his tea. He was ninety per cent sure that it would be Mickey Jeffrey having a go at his long-suffering wife Alice.

From where he stood outside Lyons tea rooms, Wally had only to look across the main road to see that the forecourt of the Castle pub was being cleared rapidly due to the presence of two policemen.

'Mickey must have scarpered pretty quickly,' he murmured to himself. 'Anyhow, I may as well go home down Selkirk Road, it's not much out of my way.'

Truth was, he had a lot of time for Alice Jeffrey; she didn't have much of a life. In a nutshell, she'd an eight-year-old daughter, a three-year-old lad, no regular income and persistent beatings from Mickey whenever he thought the world wasn't treating him right.

Wally crossed over the main road, walked a few yards and turned left into Selkirk Road. It was gone eleven but the street was well lit, and the pie and eel shop on the left and the fish and chip shop on the right were still doing a roaring trade. Young lads and even a few younger kiddies were sitting on the high kerbstone, their feet dangling in the gutter, eating their pennyworth of chips out of greasy newspaper or spooning eel liquor into their mouths from what was known as a penny basin, which consisted of mashed potatoes and a thick green soup. Meanwhile, their parents were inside the shops, seated at marble-topped tables having their supper off china plates. Loads of people were still about, of course there were; within yards of where he was walking there were four pubs which had just turned out: the Selkirk, the Fox, the Angel and the Castle.

Saturday night, and the locals were having what to most of them was their only weekly treat. Never mind that the landlord would be wanting his rent come Monday, this lot were living for the moment. Again Wally sighed; folk round these parts never seemed to look further than the nose on their face.

Could he blame them? Not really.

Two years ago, in 1918, when the Armistice had been signed, the wounded and the crippled had been left to fend for themselves, and those few men who had returned whole had long since given up looking for the land fit for heroes that they had been promised.

Why did he stay around these parts? Wally asked himself that same question time and time again. Too lazy to seek pastures new? No, that wasn't true.

He'd been born and bred in Garrett Lane, gone to school in Broadwater Road and then Defoe Road School for Boys. You could say he was one of the lucky ones, but maybe privileged would be a better word. His parents had met when they were in service, his mother a parlourmaid, his father a stable lad. It was the training in working with horses that his father had received that had gained him entry into a crack cavalry regiment when he'd answered Lord Kitchener's call to fight for his country.

A blessing in disguise, his mother had said, when a bad bout of pleurisy had prevented Wally himself from being called to the colours and sent to France.

His father had risen through the ranks to become a lieutenant. An office that was short-lived; he'd been killed in France on the Western Front in 1916.

The only good to come out of that whole episode was the fact that his mother received an officer's war pension.

It hadn't made them rich, but at least they hadn't wanted for the essential things in life. They had a neat little house, and they had each other. It had been enough. Though if the truth be told, since his mother had passed away two years ago, Wally had often admitted to himself that he felt the need of a woman in his life. Still, he was only twenty-one, and some day he hoped he might meet the kind of woman he could settle down with.

When he'd first left school, aged fourteen, he'd had high hopes of getting a job in Fleet Street; he'd always wanted to be a reporter. More than willing to start on the bottom rung, he'd have run errands, made the tea, whatever, but no such luck. Too many lads chasing too few jobs.

He'd been lucky to get taken on with the co-op that ran the markets. He'd started off as a van boy, up at four o'clock every morning and off with a couple of stall-holders to Covent Garden or Spitalfields to bid for fruit and vegetables. He'd learned to love the life. The noise was always deafening. The chaos of porters carrying great quantities of boxed fruit dashing about all over the place, while costermongers piled their push carts. By the time they were ready to go to the café for a hearty breakfast, they had to be careful how they trod, because the floor of the great hall would be littered with cabbage leaves and squashed tomatoes.

Now, seven years later, the fact that they had given him the title of manager didn't alter the fact that he was still a dogsbody. Apart from being responsible for collecting the rents, and having eyes out the back of his head where the barrow boys were concerned, he was also caretaker and nightwatchman all rolled into one. Still, there wasn't a trader that he couldn't call his friend, and by and large he was his own boss. Except for his Monday-morning call to the main offices, when if he hadn't the full amount of rent money, he'd have to have a very good reason as to why a certain stall-holder was falling behind in his dues.

The street door of number twenty-three was wide open, the light from the unshaded single bulb in the passageway streaming out. Wally heard a woman scream and he broke into a run.

It was worse than even he would have thought. Mickey

hadn't waited to get his wife inside the house; she was lying in a crumpled heap on the damp pathway that led up through the small front garden. Suddenly Mickey straightened up, took a deep breath and kicked his wife viciously in the stomach. He was laughing; a drunken beast he might be, but he was well aware of what he was doing. Again his leg was raised and his booted foot caught the side of Alice's head.

He was unfastening his belt when Wally reached him.

He heard the crunch of knuckles against bone as he shot his fist out and whacked it straight into Mickey's face.

'You . . . you . . . bastard.' Mickey was having a job to get his words out as he clenched his hand tight up to his chin and felt the blood trickle between his fingers.

Wally watched in horror as Alice struggled to get to her knees. Her moans were so pitiful, he felt he had to help her. Mickey blocked his way. Wally, being at least three inches taller and far more thick-set, could have swatted him like a fly, but for the moment that wasn't what was bothering him. Peering into the darkest corner of the front garden, he felt the vomit rise in his throat.

Janey and Tommy, Alice's two youngsters, were huddled together. Wally felt so sorry for them. Dare he interfere? At times little Jane was the sweetest child one could imagine. A baby face that would look great on an expensive china doll, clear blue eyes and soft silky hair that hung in natural ringlets to form almost a halo around her head and shoulders. But upset her and she had the temper of an alley cat. She was cuddling Tommy, her baby brother. Most folk thought of Tommy as an adorable child. His hair was several shades darker than his sister's, his face plump and dimpled, with the biggest dark brown eyes you could imagine. Both children were shivering; all they were wearing was very thin nightclothes, and they looked dirty and bedraggled.

With Wally's attention focused on the children, Mickey started his battering again. Having managed to get up on her knees, Alice was sent sprawling once more. Both the children winced as they heard the thud of their mother's head hitting the pathway.

Wally breathed a sigh of relief as the police van screeched to a halt. He hastened to put his arms around the kiddies and the three of them watched as two uniformed coppers pulled their father away from their mother. Mickey sealed his fate for the night as the policemen dragged him to his feet. He hadn't the sense to go quietly and did his utmost to boot one of them between his legs. He hadn't managed to raise his foot high enough, but all the same his boot made contact with the copper's shin, causing enough pain to ensure that some form of retaliation would soon be forthcoming.

Wally, Janey and Tommy watched as Mickey was practically thrown into the back of the van and the door slammed shut.

'I'll see to the kids.' Mavis Owen's voice was harsh as she stepped over the low fence that divided the two houses. 'Disgusting, ain't it, Wally? The way Mickey carries on, an' gets away with it every time.'

Wally heaved another great sigh, 'Living next door all these years, Mavis, you know more about it than I do. Right now, I think I'd better see about getting Alice indoors, though she probably ought to go straight to the hospital.'

'No, me mum don't never want to go t' St James'.' Jane's voice held a note of authority which belied the fact that she was so young.

By now Wally had bent and picked Alice up from the ground, cradling her gently in his arms he walked into the house.

Neighbours were standing at their doorways; it was nothing new for them to see Alice Jeffrey get a bashing, but it was a strange twist to see Wally Simmonds get involved.

'Best thing that could 'appen, if you ask me,' Hannah Watkins chuckled. 'I've lived all these years across the road with me front door facing theirs and I've seen so much of it. It's about time someone took Alice's side.'

'Who said anything about him taking sides?' John, her husband, asked. 'I'd say Wally will be sorry he came along when he did.'

Inside number twenty-three, Wally had set Alice down in a big shabby armchair, and his one thought was that she looked like death. Mavis had taken coats down from a hook on the back of the kitchen door and was helping young Tommy to put his arms into the sleeves, while Janey had already shrugged herself into hers.

'By God! Will yer look at her face, she'll 'ave a massive black eye come the morning,' Mavis murmured half to herself. 'Are you going to stay for a cup of tea?' she added, looking up at Wally.

'I'll put the kettle on,' Janey piped up. 'It won't be a minute.'

Wally glanced sideways at Mavis as Jane went through to the scullery, and remarked, 'That girl has an old head on her young shoulders, more's the pity.'

'Yeah, you're right there. Been a case of 'aving t' grow up. Ain't been an easy life for her so far, an' it don't look as if things are going to improve with time, does it?'

Janey came back into the room holding out a wet face flannel and a striped towel, and asked Mavis, 'Would you mind wiping me mum's face while I get the tea?'

Wally swore beneath his breath. This shouldn't be happening. A decent women knocked nearly senseless and an eight-year-old girl left to care for her. Mickey was probably sleeping off his drunken stupor in a warm police cell, and like as not they'd let him out first thing in the morning.

Then he had to quickly smother a grin. The thought had come to him that maybe, just maybe, the copper Mickey had kicked might have been mad enough to give him a good going-over. It would be no more than he deserved.

Janey brought in two steaming mugs of tea for Wally and Mavis, and a few minutes later she knelt down in front of her mother, saying quietly, 'I've made you a cup of tea, Mum, I've put loads of sugar in it.' As Alice struggled to sit up, she stared into her daughter's face, and what she saw there hurt her more than all the beatings that her husband ditched out.

Wally was at his wits' end to know what to do for the best, and Mavis had three children of her own next door to see to. Whatever they did tonight to help Alice and her children wouldn't make the slightest bit of difference to the way they lived.

They both knew that, though neither would admit it.

Chapter Two

JANE'S BABY FACE looked very different this morning. Her huge blue eyes showed she was in a temper, and with good reason, she would have told anyone who cared to listen.

Her dad was home. She could hear him shouting.

When finally she had got into bed last night she had said her prayers, remembering that her Sunday school teacher had told her that the dear Lord Jesus would always be there for her.

So why had her dad come home?

She'd wanted him to be sent to prison. And kept there, for ever and ever. Where he couldn't hurt her mum nor her. She'd told Nancy about the times he'd hurt her, and old Nancy had been ever so angry but all she'd said was, 'We have to make allowances for him.' What did that mean? No one ever answered that question. Sometimes she felt that she was the cause of all the things that went wrong for her father. She tried hard to keep out of his way whenever he was in a bad mood. She knew the signs. When he'd lost money at the bookmaker's. When the Labour Exchange had made him go after a job. Jobs he made sure he never got.

Helping out at the markets, touting on the racecourse, all for money in his hand, so her mum said, was all he was willing to put himself out for.

If he'd had a bad day, it was always Jane he picked on. If she were lucky she'd manage to slip out of the house and run up to Nancy, who lived in the end house of this road. Nancy was a smashing lady. Kind. Oh yes, kind to everyone. Short and dumpy, with a head of dark frizzy hair which Mum always said was Nancy's own fault because she was always burning it with hot curling tongs. You could always be sure of a kiss and a cuddle from Nancy, and even more to the point, something nice to eat, because she was ever such a good cook.

'I suppose I'd better go downstairs,' Jane muttered to herself.

'Sit up to the table, luv, I'm just making you a bit of porridge.' Her mother's voice sounded shaky and it was only when she turned round that Jane saw just how dreadful she looked. Her face was a mass of bruises; she had a big black eye, her lips were swollen and a patch of dried blood seemed to be covering her right ear.

'Oh Mum! You should be in bed.' Jane managed to get the words out before she burst into tears.

'It's all right, pet, really it is. Come on, sit down, Tommy's had his breakfast and he's gone next door to play with Mavis's lot.'

Jane sensed her father's closeness and knew she'd have to pass him to get to the table. She hung her head, making sure her eyes looked only at the floor.

Suddenly he lunged out at her, grabbing both of her arms and almost yanking her off her feet.

'You're a crafty little bitch, you are. It's you that's the cause of more than 'alf the goings-on in this 'ouse, an' I've just about 'ad enough of it. Bad enough I took yer mother on; didn't bargain for all the trouble she was bringing with 'er.' He flung her from him with such force that her right leg smashed against the side of the table and she wasn't able to stop herself from falling.

'Mick, Mick, you promised!' Alice beseeched him, her voice little more than a croak.

'Me promised? Don't come that old lark with me. What about you? You ain't exactly come across, 'ave yer? When did you ever bring so much as one pound note into this 'ouse? Go on, tell me that.'

'Oh Mick, you know I try. I take in washing, I do dressmaking, or I did till you took it in your 'ead to smash me sewing machine.'

'Pennies, that's all. Yer said she'd never be a burden to me. Well let me tell yer, you an' she are a bloody great burden t' me day in day out. You could get out there an' earn a few quid a couple nights a week; most wives round 'ere do. But not you. Oh no. Too damned lah-di-da, or so you think.'

Alice ached from head to foot, felt tired out, beaten, but she made one more attempt to get her husband to see reason. 'Mick, that's not true. There's not a woman in this street that I know would do what you ask me to.'

Jane knew things were beginning to turn nasty again, and all she wanted to do was slip away from the room and out of the house. She'd almost made it to the door when her father took two strides and grabbed hold of her.

'You mind what you're saying, young lady. What goes on in this 'ouse is between yer mum and me. It ain't got nothing t' do with you. And certainly not the damn neighbours.

You got that?' He was still raging mad and gave her a hefty slap around her head as he let her go.

Alice was crouched up against the fireplace, the tears trickling slowly down her poor bruised face. What Mick did to her was bad enough, but what he did to young Janey went beyond cruelty. It was evil. How could she stop him? If she interfered, especially today, she'd more than likely make matters even worse.

But she had to do something!

She had allowed this situation to go on for far too long, and at this rate it was never going to get any better. She didn't have any choice now. She had to act before Mickey did something terrible.

Something they would all live to regret.

Jane dragged her feet but kept walking. She wished she knew what she could do to make her father like her. Well, not so much like her as be a bit kinder to her. She felt the side of her face with trembling fingers; it was stinging, and her head really hurt. Sometimes she managed to duck when she saw a blow coming, but this morning her dad had really caught her a hefty blow. Her mum had to suffer terrible things and it wasn't fair, because she was kind and gentle really. Though there were times when she wished Mum would stand up for her a little bit more. She could see what was happening, but she never did anything to stop it. There was the time that Tommy had knocked their dad's tobacco tin off the side of his chair and it had burst open, spilling all the tobacco over the lino.

It was me, Jane was ranting to herself, that got down on my hands and knees and did my best to scrape the tobacco into a little pile. Me dad never said thanks. He kicked me halfway across the room and I had a pain in my side for ages after that.

There was the time when her teacher had asked why she was limping so badly. She had thought about telling her the truth: that her dad had kicked her shin and stamped hard on her foot. But she'd tried that with Nancy and it hadn't got her anywhere. If Nancy couldn't help her, then no one could. So in the end she'd just said that she had fallen over.

She gave a sad little sigh. She couldn't walk any further, her head hurt so and her mouth was bone dry. She wished she'd had a drink of tea before she left the house. Turning off the main road, she stumbled on to Garrett Green, making her way to the bench that was set beneath a huge tree. Thankfully she sat down, lifting her legs up to stretch them out in front of her. Leaning back, she clutched her arms around her chest, wondering what she had done this morning to set her father off. She tried so hard, she really did. But there was no pleasing him, no way that she could think of to stop him clouting her. She had known all her life that he didn't love her. More than that, he didn't even like her. But why was he always so angry with her?

She knew her mum had seen her dad shake the life out of her this morning and then bash her round the head, but as ever she'd not tried to stop him. Though perhaps today Jane ought not to feel that way, because Mum looked so ill. Last night had been terrible, with Mum lying on the ground in the front garden, and Dad kicking her ever so hard.

It wasn't fair. Why couldn't he pick on someone of his own size?

Then she remembered. Mr Simmonds had whacked her dad in the face. Good job too. Perhaps that was why he was still in a bad temper today. But what did I do? Jane asked herself. Nothing, except try to keep Tommy warm. Her dad loved Tommy. She was glad about that, he was such a lovely little boy. Still, it didn't seem fair. Not all the time. She wondered what the difference was: why he was always so angry with her and never with Tommy.

She began to cry. Her leg hurt where she'd knocked it against the table, the side of her face was stinging and her head really hurt. She tried to think of nice things, like going to school; she liked her teacher a lot. Eating bread pudding that Nancy had brought out of the oven steaming hot and sprinkled with lovely brown sugar. She wished she could live with Nancy.

Her head drooped down on to her chest. She'd have to stay where she was for a while; she couldn't walk any further.

It wasn't long before this lonely little girl thankfully drifted off into a state of unconsciousness.

It was three o'clock in the afternoon and Alice was getting worried. Where the hell had her daughter got to? Mickey had just come back from the pub and the first thing she'd asked him was if he'd seen Janey.

'No I ain't, but I suppose it would be too much t' 'ope for that she's disappeared for good.'

'Mick, sit down. It's about time that we 'ad a talk. I know you did me a favour by marrying me when I was pregnant, but by God you've made me pay for it over the years. You use me as a punching bag whenever the mood takes you, and maybe I've only got myself to blame for that, but I think it's about time you laid off Janey.'

He'd had more than a few pints of beer and he stood there gently reeling, his face showing nothing but amusement.

'Aren't you afraid you'll hurt her real badly one of these days?' Alice's voice held a plea.

'Maybe she won't end up in the pudding club like you did if I knock a little sense into 'er now. Told me you were doing a neighbour a favour, minding 'er kids, when their father came 'ome an' raped yer. Nobody was daft enough to believe yer. Except me! Yer don't want yer daughter taken in like that, do yer? So it stands t' reason someone should knock a bit of sense into her. She might even thank me for it later on.'

Alice sighed heavily. 'The worst of it all is, Mick, I think you actually believe that. You've lied to yourself for so long.'

'Oh, so now you're telling me I'm too hard on you an' the kid?' Mickey said, visibly angry at being told a home truth.

'Too hard? *Too hard?* Do you ever bother t' look at her bruises, not t' mention how you leave me looking.'

'Don't be ridiculous. You ask for everything you get, and as for the kid, you should be grateful that I put a roof over 'er 'ead and food in 'er belly. She's a cheeky bitch, gets away with murder just because she looks like butter wouldn't melt in 'er mouth. You make 'er worse, all the time yer spend on those bloody curls an' telling 'er what beautiful big blue eyes she's got.'

'You're drunk, Mick. But not too far gone t' know that what I'm saying is the truth. I'm just really sorry that I held on to her. I was only just fifteen when I was raped, and not even sixteen when Jane was born.' Alice paused and stared at the state her husband was in. 'I should have gone into a home for unmarried mothers and let the baby be put up for adoption. Even leaving her on the steps of a church would have given her a better chance than she's had here. She doesn't deserve the life she has to lead, with you on at her all the time.'

Mickey wiped a hand across his face as if trying to pull himself together. 'If you're doing yer best t' make me feel guilty about her, don't bother. I've been pretty good t' that kid.'

'Really? You believe that?' Alice asked sarcastically. 'You give her a clump practically every day, but mostly you're dead clever. The worst you do to her can never be seen.'

'Don't know what yer talking about.'

'Oh, you know right enough! Like a few weeks ago when the poor kid couldn't sit down properly because you'd pinched her backside so badly. She didn't let on for days, and when I did find out she'd got a festering sore. Your fingernails had drawn blood and the dye from her navy-blue kickers had got into it. You're damned lucky she didn't tell her teacher about you.'

'Yer want t' mind what you're saying or I might just give you a taste of me belt, because I'm warning you, Alice, I'm master in me own 'ouse, always will be or I'll know the reason why. Jane knows she's a little bitch at times, an' she never answers back when I chastise 'er 'cos she knows she deserves it.'

'She's too afraid of you to argue with you, and you know it.'

Alice watched in wonder as Mickey took a quart bottle of brown ale from the dresser and poured himself a glassful. Talking to him was like pouring water over a duck's back. Seeing what he was doing to her daughter, day in day out, had made her begin to really hate him.

But not enough to stand up to him. She had done in the beginning and ended up black and blue herself. Now she cringed whenever he raised his hand to Janey and winced as she watched the blows rain. Yet she could never summon up enough courage to try and stop him. She hadn't the guts to do that.

In her own way she was as frightened of Mickey as Jane was, so she stood by and let it happen.

And for that she hated herself.

Chapter Three

LES BANISTER, THE local policeman, looked at his watch. It was seven thirty on this cold November night. Another hour and a half before he could report back to the warmth of the station. I deserve a fag, he said to himself. Drawing his tobacco tin from his overcoat pocket, he walked across the grass of Garrett Green, making for the wooden bench, all the while telling himself that he might just as well take the weight off his feet for a few minutes.

There was no one about to hear his gasp of horror when he realized that the heap of clothing that lay on the end of the bench was actually a small child. He shone his torch and cautiously moved the arm that was covering her face. Her long blonde curls were stained red and matted to her head. As far as he could tell, the bleeding had been coming from around her ear.

He talked to her, saying anything that came into his head, but got no response. For one terrifying moment he thought she must be dead. 'I have to get an ambulance,' he said aloud, and heaved a sigh of relief that not far away, on the main road, a green light shone over the doorway of a doctor's surgery.

He blew three long blasts on his whistle to summon assistance. With fumbling fingers he undid the buttons of his coat and swiftly but gently wrapped it around the small body, then stared down at her for a moment. How on earth did such a small child happen to be out on her own at this time on a winter's night? And more to the point, how come she was injured, because there was no mistaking that she was.

And badly so.

He heard footsteps approaching, turned and ran to meet his colleague. Shouting loudly, he gave his orders. 'Get to that doctor's surgery and tell them we've a badly hurt child here on a park bench and we need an ambulance.'

'Right,' the constable called back, sizing up the situation right away

'Thanks, mate. I'll stay here with the child.' As he retraced his footsteps he thanked God that professional people had telephones now.

The time that he sat holding the cold little hand and saying over and over again, 'You'll be all right, pet, you will, I promise,' were the longest minutes he had ever had to live through. He was allowed to ride in the ambulance with her. The ambulanceman had put an oxygen mask on her small white face and smothered her in blankets, but even he hadn't been sure at first that she was still breathing. On arrival at hospital she was placed on a trolley and rushed away, surrounded by nurses.

He felt dazed and bewildered as he made his way back to the station, where his sergeant was waiting to take his report. 'No name, no identification whatsoever?' the portly, red-faced officer asked in disbelief.

'No, Sarge. I felt sure someone would have reported the child missing by the time I got back here.'

'No such luck, son. Still, you sign off, get yerself a cup of tea in the canteen and I'll ring the hospital, ask them to let us know when the child is able to talk.'

'*If* she's able,' Les Banister said softly to himself. He was relieved to think that he had found her, but had he been in time? What if she had lain there all night? And the state she was in! God, he'd like to get his hands on whoever had treated a small child so cruelly. She could so easily have died.

When Jane woke up in the early hours of the morning, she began to cry. She didn't know where she was or how she was going to get home. If she was ever so late her dad would surely have a real go at her.

The nurse who had been sitting beside the bed got to her feet and, bending over the tiny figure, spoke softly. 'There, there, pet, no need for tears. You're safe and warm now. I'll just let Sister know you're awake and I'm sure she'll give you something nice to drink.'

'Please don't go, I don't know where I am.' Jane's fingers fluttered and the nurse took hold of her hand.

'You're in hospital and everyone is going to take such good care of you, you'll see.'

Jane managed to get the young nurse's smiling face into focus. She wanted to ask if her mum and dad knew where she was, but she was afraid. She tried to sit up but fell back; she was giddy, her head hurt so and the side of her face stung and felt funny.

'Try and lie still.' The nurse had seen her wince. Poor child, she had a concussion, and had suffered a terrific blow to her ear. The damage had not yet been assessed because there was still blood being drained from it. Also, the doctor had said he was appalled at the amount of bruises they had found on her body.

The sister came, raised her gently and held a feeding cup to her lips. Jane drank, then gratefully felt herself being lowered down against soft white pillows, and soon she closed her eyes and slept. The nurse went off duty and a young doctor came to watch over her. It worried him that she cried in her sleep, and as he stared at this young child's face he knew that she had been treated badly over a long period of time. There were questions that would have to be asked. But would they get any answers? Any true answers, that was. He had seen injuries like this before and very rarely were they the result of an accident. Something would have to be done to protect this child from further harm. But what?

It would be a wise man that could answer that question.

That same night, Wally Simmonds met up with Alice Jeffrey.

Having checked on all the neighbours, and Nancy in particular, and found no trace of Jane, Alice, now half out of her mind with worry, had been wandering the streets.

'Wally, you haven't come across Janey, 'ave you?'

'No, luv, I 'aven't, but surely she's not out on a cold night like this. An' look at you, you look 'alf frozen t' death, come on t' the coffee stall and I'll get you a hot drink.'

'Thanks, Wally, but I can't. I 'ave t' keep looking for 'er. I think she's probably afraid to come home.'

'You are going to 'ave that drink and I'll take no argument,' he said, taking hold of her arm very firmly. 'While you're drinking it you can fill me in on what has happened and we'll take it from there.'

'Sometimes I think Mickey has hated Jane from the day she was born,' Alice told him sadly, 'and yet she's so wonderful, a terrific kid, always trying to please everyone. So pretty, that's been more than half the trouble; she's been the little girl everyone fell in love with. Except Mick. I know he resents her and I do believe he's actually begun to hate her.' Then it all became too much for her and she started to cry.

Wally was very moved by her tears but he could do nothing except stand and stare at her. He had always had great admiration for the way this woman coped. He knew full well her life had never been a bed of roses, but he hadn't until very recently had any idea that Mickey might be ill-treating the little lass.

Holding out a steaming mug of cocoa, he insisted that she wrap her hands around the mug and sip it slowly. 'How long has she been missing?' he asked, his eyes blazing when he heard the truth as to why Janey had gone off.

'Since this morning, about half past ten or maybe eleven o'clock. It's not fair, Mickey is so jealous, it's mad really, she's only a little girl, and yet . . . all our troubles, no matter what, he lays the blame on her, says she's responsible.'

'We'll find her,' Wally said firmly. 'But first I think I'd better see you home, it's too cold for you to be out. Then I think I'll call in at the police station just in case she has been in an accident.'

'Oh my God! Let me come with you,' Alice implored him.

'No,' he said, even more firmly. 'You go home, wait indoors in the warm and I'll come and tell you the minute I find out anything.'

Sergeant Bolton was very relieved when Wally Simmonds put in an appearance and was able to tell them that he was a hundred per cent sure that the little girl the constable had found injured on Garrett Green was Jane Jeffrey from Selkirk Road.

'Can you tell me how badly she was hurt?' Wally asked, showing great concern.

'Not exactly, we haven't had a full report yet. The doctor did tell our constable that the child had concussion, two broken ribs and quite a bit of damage to her ear. However, I'm sure she's in good hands now and the hospital staff will take care of her.'

This statement didn't do much to reassure Wally. It had finally become crystal clear to him that Mickey Jeffrey not only knocked his wife about but his young daughter as well. He felt such revulsion that he had to clench his fists and make sure that he kept them to his sides. But with knowledge came the resolve to put a stop to it, in as much as he was able. No child should have to suffer at the hands of a no-good waster like Mickey.

Speaking quietly and choosing his words carefully, Wally made his suspicions known to Sergeant Bolton.

'My God!' the sergeant exploded. 'Has there been no one to protect her?'

'I think the mother lives in fear of her husband and feels if she intervenes it will only make matters worse. She did admit to me some time ago that her husband is not Jane's real father and that most of the time he not only resents her but hates her.'

'So he thinks that gives him the right to use his fists on the child? Come to that, how can a grown man hate a little child?'

'Who knows what goes on in the mind of men like Jeffrey?' Wally answered sorrowfully.

'Well I'll tell yer this, after this night and the facts that have been brought to our attention, he'll find things will be a damn sight hotter for him. Oh yes.' The sergeant paused, held out his hand to Wally and thanked him profusely for having come into the station. 'You leave this to me. You can rest assured he won't abuse that child ever again, I'll make it my business to see t' that. He'll be sorry for it, you mark my words. Whatever excuses that man comes up with for hitting her won't wash with me. He'll find this time it was once too often.'

Alice wasn't totally surprised when she answered the door to find a uniformed constable standing on her doorstep. As she listened to the policeman telling her they had found Jane and that she had been taken to St James' hospital, she felt emotionally and physically drained. She had reached the end of her tether.

'It's only me, Alice.'

Mavis Owen's voice was loud as she walked in through the back door. She stepped into the kitchen and was in time to see Alice doing her best to wipe away her tears.

'I saw the copper leaving. 'Ave they found Janey?'

Alice nodded her head. 'Yeah, it was a policeman on his beat what found her. She was lying on a bench on Garrett Green.'

''Ad she bin 'urt, d'you know?'

'According to the copper she was 'alf dead, would 'ave bin by morning if he hadn't come across her.'

'She 'adn't been in an accident, 'ad she?'

'No, I told you earlier when I went out to look for her, she was afraid t' come 'ome. As she tried to pass Mick this morning he gave her a right bash round the 'ead.'

'Good God, does he never let up? I think it a bloody disgrace the way he picks on Janey, and what about you? You don't look the picture of 'ealth. Look at the state of yer face. I wouldn't let my ole man treat me the way Mickey does you.'

Alice went to shake her head but winced as it started to throb again.

'Sit down before you fall down, gal, I'll put the kettle on. Any idea what set him off again this morning?'

'Well, a night in the cells didn't do that much for him, and I don't suppose they treated him too kindly. After all, he did kick one of the coppers on the shin . . .' Alice paused and did her best to pull her swollen lips into a smile.

'What's tickled you all of a sudden?' Mavis asked as she struck a match to light the gas under the kettle.

'I shouldn't be laughing, I know, but Mickey got more than he asked for in more ways than one last night.'

'Well go on, 'urry up, tell me about it,' Mavis chipped in.

'You know Wally Simmonds came along when Mick was bashing the life out of me. Well, I don't think he would 'ave interfered but for the fact that he saw Tommy and Janey shivering an' huddled up in the corner of the front garden, an' like any decent man would, he went to get to get t' them.

'And?' Mavis said hastily.

'Wally punched him straight in the face. I didn't dare t' look too close this morning, but I'd lay money his nose is broken.'

Mavis crossed the room and gently put her arms around her friend. 'Damn good job too! Pity you ain't 'ad someone t' take your part long before this.'

'Oh, I don't think he was taking *my* part exactly; he was thinking of the kids more like.'

'If you say so,' Mavis grinned, 'but I'd never be surprised to 'ear that Wally 'as a soft spot for you.'

'Oh Mavis, don't say that! Ain't I got enough complications in my life as it is?'

Mavis laughed out loud at that, saying, 'We'll see.'

Five minutes later she brought two steaming cups of tea to the table and the two friends sat opposite each other, deep in their own thoughts. While Mavis sipped her tea and thanked God that her Joe had a regular job and that he wasn't a bad father to their three children, Alice was trying to reason with herself as to how she could carry on living with Mickey. What she had allowed to happen to Jane was nothing short of sheer wickedness on her own part. As to Mick: well, the police were involved now, so she probably wouldn't have any say in the matter.

She chided herself again: you should have acted before.

She sighed heavily. It was too late to turn the clock back now.

For most of the next few days, Jane slept fitfully. Her mother came to see her every day and tried to explain to the doctors that Jane's injuries had been caused by her continually falling over. They knew she was lying, but they sympathized with her and told her over and over what a sweet little girl her daughter was. The nurses would have done anything for Jane. She was so good. She cried, often, but only quietly, always sobbing beneath the bedclothes. She seemed so grateful for everything they did and sighed with pleasure when they gently gave her a bedbath and finished off by covering her with sweet-smelling talcum powder. She never had much to say, even when her mum was there. She just lay still, watching, sometimes sighing, but when she did smile it lit up her pretty face and tore at the hearts of those who attended her, making them ask, 'How on earth could anyone bring themselves to hurt such a dear little defence-less child?'

One afternoon her mother was very talkative. She told Jane that she must be brave, that where she was going would be a very nice place, so much better for her than coming back home.

'What do you mean, Mum? Aren't I coming home when the doctors say I'm better?'

'Well . . . not for the time being.' Alice was whispering. 'I have t' tell you that I won't be able t' see you for a while.' She got up from her chair and sat down gently on the side of the bed. With trembling fingers she smoothed the soft hair from her young daughter's forehead.

'You'll be with other children, it won't be so bad, I promise you it won't.'

'Why can't I come home? Where are you going, Mum?'

'Oh pet, I'm not going anywhere. I came today to say goodbye. It really is for the best that you don't come home.'

Jane struggled to sit up, her face showing the terror that was running through her mind. 'Where will I live, when will I see you, and what about Tommy?' With wisdom beyond her years, she knew that whatever happened to her from now on, the arrangements would not include her father.

'Please, darling, you're not to get upset.'

A nurse who was hovering near by felt she wanted to scream out: 'She's not to get upset! What do you expect her to do?' The child's headache seemed to be a lot better but her poor little ribs were still strapped up with tape and still no one knew for sure how much damage had been done to her ear. Now here was her mother quietly telling her they weren't going to have her home ever again. All the staff knew that the relieving officer had been in touch with the lady almoner of the hospital and that the police had been involved. The outcome of it all was that the father was to be charged, if and when they found him; for the moment he had thought it best to disappear. And the little girl was being taken into a council home.

'Do you mean it, Mum, I'm not coming home, not ever?'

Alice didn't answer. She hung her head, fighting her own tears.

Jane needed no telling that her father didn't want her. Did her mother not want her either? Suddenly she felt very frightened. Was this all happening just because her father didn't like her? Perhaps now her mum had had enough of her as well. Could that be right? After all, she'd heard Mum say to Nancy that Janey was the cause of all the trouble.

And when she thought about it, her mum had never stopped her dad from hitting her. She'd never helped her, and now she was telling her she couldn't come back to live at home and that she wouldn't be seeing her for a while. So in other words, thought Janey, she really doesn't want me and is getting rid of me.

That was what all the talking was about. That was the reason her mum had come today. She had said she wasn't going anywhere, she was going to stay and look after Tommy, but she'd come to say goodbye to Jane. Jane was trying so hard not to cry, but she couldn't help herself. Was she being given away, and if so, who to? Who would want her? There had been a family in the next street to them that were put in the workhouse, and all the neighbours had cried and felt sorry for them because they'd heard the workhouse was such a terrible place. But they had all gone together. Would she be put in there all on her own?

Now she wasn't just frightened; she was terrified.

Alice bent down and gently kissed her on the cheek. 'I'm sorry . . . about your dad . . . and everything. Be a good girl an' always remember that I do love you.'

Jane wanted her mum to know that it wasn't her fault and that she loved her too, but she didn't know what to say. Alice straightened up and stood there looking at her for a few moments, then she pulled the bedclothes up round her, tucking the sheet beneath her chin, and turned and walked away, without saying another word.

Jane burrowed down in the bed, pulling the clothes over her head, and sobbed as if her heart was breaking.

Chapter Four

SISTER WALKER HELD out her hand to Mrs Elsie Rogers, a child welfare worker from Sussex who had become involved in this case. She was not only thoroughly pleased that it was this woman who had come from the children's home to pick up Jane Jeffrey, but intensely relieved. The poor child had suffered enough. It had torn at her heartstrings and those of her nurses as they'd listened to Jane's small, breathless sobs become uncontrollable after she had watched her own mother walk away from her. That drama had taken place over two weeks ago. Jane had hardly spoken a word since. Much as she would dearly love to keep the child here, where she was safe, Sister Walker knew it was impossible. A hospital was not what Jane needed now.

But if anyone could console the child it would be Elsie Rogers.

Widowed at an early age and having no children of her own, Elsie had given her life over to caring for children who were placed in the care of the authorities. She was a remarkable woman with a sweet smile and piercing blue eyes that seemed to see everything that went on. She kept her finger on every situation and did her best for each and every child.

Elsie had visited the hospital twice in the last fortnight to discuss the arrangements that the court had ordered for Jane Jeffrey. But she hadn't expected the child to be so frail-looking, nor so upset.

'Has she been told that I'm coming for her today?' she queried.

'Yes,' Sister Walker answered softly, feeling that never before had she been invovled in such a sad case. 'She's all ready, waiting for you in my office . . .' She hesitated. 'You won't believe how sweet she looks; most of the staff clubbed together and bought her a coat. You could have shot peas through the one she was wearing when she came to us.'

They walked the corridor in silence, and when Sister opened the door to her office Elsie Rogers stepped in first. 'Hello, Jane,' she said solemnly. 'Remember I told you I was coming for you today? We're going to travel by train, and then when we get to the right station there will be a lovely surprise waiting for you.'

Jane made no reply; she merely looked at Sister Walker, her eyes pleading to stay here in the safety of the hospital where, for the first time in her young life, she had felt wanted and safe; even more than that, she'd felt everyone in the whole place had loved her.

Elsie was staring at the child, and what she saw tugged at her heartstrings. Janey did look so sweet, almost unreal, dressed in a blue coat that reached the top of her well-worn buttoned boots. Her little matching hat had an upturned brim that showed off the fair ringlets hanging down to her shoulders.

'My, my,' she exclaimed quietly. 'Haven't the nurses done you proud? You really do look a very pretty little young lady.'

Jane wasn't used to being spoken to so kindly, and the colour rose in her cheeks, which only served to made her look even more doll-like.

Sister Walker had great difficulty in swallowing the lump in her throat, which was threatening to choke her. 'Come along, pet, there's a lot of people who want to say goodbye and wish you well.'

Jane didn't speak but walked slowly out into the corridor, stopping within an arm's length of the nurses and doctors who were standing in a group.

Sister watched her hesitate, and when the first nurse put her arms around the child she saw her eyelids close and the tears trickle down from beneath them. 'Oh, don't, Janey, don't cry. For God's sake, don't cry, you'll set us all off,' she murmured.

When finally all the goodbyes had been said, the young doctor who had been in charge of her throughout her stay picked Jane up and wrapped his arms about her. His action was very gentle, and he held her as if she were fragile and could easily break. The kiss he placed on her cheek was tender, and there was a tremble to his lips as he said, 'Be happy, Jane, and if you ever need us, you come back here and find us.'

Elsie Rogers looked around. There was no suitcase, only a brown paper carrier bag that held a nightdress, washing things and two picture books, all of which had been provided by the staff. Outside the main entrance a taxi was waiting to take them the short distance to the railway station.

Jane stared out of the rear window until she could no longer see the mass of waving hands. She had no idea where she was going or what kind of reception awaited her. Just one thing she was sure of. She had never before been treated with such love and kindness as she had received whilst in

St James' hospital. She looked into Mrs Rogers' eyes; they looked kind, but that didn't tell her much, so she looked down at her feet so that the lady wouldn't see just how frightened she really was.

After the quietness of the hospital, the railway station was alarming. A porter opened a carriage door for them, and having assisted Mrs Rogers up the high step, he lifted Jane and set her down safely within the carriage, saying, 'It isn't every day I get to see such a pretty little girl.'

That was twice already that someone had told her she was looking pretty. For an instant Jane smiled the smallest smile. Elsie Rogers was pleased; the smile had made such a difference to that pinched little face. She wanted to do her best to keep this child from further hurt, and everything she wished for Janey showed in the way she took her in her arms and held her. Jane looked up at her, half afraid that she had imagined something, and yet she didn't know exactly what. Suddenly she realized with amazement that this lady actually cared what happened to her!

And from that moment a bond was established.

Settled in a corner seat, Elsie undid the ribbons of Jane's bonnet, held out her arm and nestled the child in close to her side.

With a great swoosh, several jerks, and a lot of steam, the train pulled out from the station. Where were they going? Who exactly was Jane going to live with? Would she ever see her mum again? And how about little Tommy? It was she that mostly looked after him. Was he wondering where she was? Would he miss her? So many questions and no answers. And when Jane heaved a little sigh, Elsie hugged the child tighter and kissed the top of her head.

Safe for the moment in these kind and caring arms, all the fighting and arguing, the slaps and the punches and the disappointment that had lately been inflicted on her didn't seem quite so bad. And whatever happened when they got where they were going, she knew with wisdom beyond her eight years that she had found a true friend in this lady who was sitting beside her, holding her gently but safely.

Jane missed the spectacle of the changing scenery, because hardly had they left the soot-riddled buildings of London behind than she had fallen fast asleep.

No matter, Elsie mused to herself as the train rattled on into Sussex. The trees outside the window were a mass of bare branches, but the fields were fairly green, and there were plenty of beautiful black-and-white cows and shaggy sheep to be seen. Had not Jane fallen asleep she would have been utterly enthralled by the countryside. There was no doubt in Elsie's mind that the child had never been far from the city of London, and she had made it her business to know that she had never experienced the joys of a family holiday.

When the notes on this case had first been handed to her, she had felt utterly helpless. Sorry for the mother, married at sixteen and already breast-feeding a baby of only a few weeks old. The poor lass had grabbed at straws. Turned from her own home because of the disgrace she had brought on her hard-working but God-fearing father, she'd had no choice but to accept the offer of marriage to a man ten years older than herself.

Reading between the lines of the report, written by the relieving officer who had been appointed to supervise this case, Elsie had uttered to herself, 'By God, the lass didn't know what she was letting herself in for!'

But the real victim in this nasty affair had been the child herself. Although the woman had gone on to give her husband a son, whom he apparently adored, he had never let her forget that she had come to him with another man's child. Never once, it would appear, did he take into consideration that the mother had been little more than a child herself, raped by a brute of a man that the courts had sent to prison for two years' hard labour.

Still, Elsie sighed softly, God works in a mysterious way his wonders to perform.

Having been asked for help because of the difficulty her colleagues were experiencing in placing the small girl, she had agreed to read the case history. No stone had been left unturned, but the fact was that every charity-owned children's home within the London boundary had been full to capacity.

It was then that Elsie had called upon two dear friends who had been a tower of strength when she herself had needed comfort.

Dorothy and Richard Stuart were an elderly couple, quite comfortably off, who since retiring had devoted most of their spare time to good causes. It was through them that she had come to know of the charity that went under the name of the Guardians of the Poor, and of the children's home set in Sussex of which the Stuarts were directors.

She firmly believed that if it were necessary for a child to be taken from its parents, for whatever reason, or if a child were to be orphaned with no relatives to be held responsible for its upbringing, there was no better place for that child to be sent than Winchelsea Lodge.

She had come to understand that, with only a few exceptions, the staff at the home did not regard their work as a mere job but as a vocation. When Elsie herself had been widowed after only eighteen months of what had been a truly happy marriage, she had gone to pieces, ranting as to why she was not only widowed but childless.

When Richard Stuart had suggested that she take a post
as house mother at Winchelsea Lodge, it had taken her some
time to enjoy the job, because it often involved her in court
cases, some of which made her feel so helpless. And even
more time to realize that she had been called by God to be
of service in special work and in special conditions all to do
with underprivileged children.

It had been her salvation.

It had also been a great relief when Richard and Dorothy
Stuart, having listened to her account of the ill treatment
of Jane Jeffrey, had agreed to put it to the board that the
child be given a place at Winchelsea Lodge.

Making soothing noises, Elsie now gently shook Jane until
she was wide awake. 'Only a few more minutes and the train
will be pulling into our station. Sit up so that I can put your
bonnet on.' Jane yawned and gave a gasp of utter surprise
as she looked out of the window to see nothing but fields,
with not a building in sight.

The train slowed its speed down to a crawl and slid along
the platform. A large sign in the centre of the platform
proclaimed that they had arrived at Rye. The day was very
cold, but a weak sun was shining and it did a lot to lift
Jane's spirits as she held Mrs Rogers' hand and walked along
the short platform towards a funny-looking man who was
dressed differently to anyone she had ever seen. He was
wearing a corduroy jacket, a bright waistcoat and a highly
coloured neckerchief, and grinned down at her as he held
open a rickety wooden gate. Ted Grimshaw was a big, bluff
man, his face puffed and red from drinking too much cider.
He'd lived in the village of Winchelsea all his life, and
although he had several irons in the fire when it came to
making a few bob, he was never too busy whenever the staff
at the children's home asked him to help out.

Jane was struck dumb with astonishment when the jolly man indicated that she was to put her foot on to a step, take hold of a hand rail and heave herself up into an open carriage that had a huge horse standing between its shafts. She was thrilled at the prospect of riding in this horse-drawn vehicle, but looked shyly up at Mrs Rogers to gain her permission before she put her foot on the high step.

Elsie Rogers couldn't help herself: she threw back her head and roared with laughter. 'Oh Ted,' she said, clutching at his arm, 'isn't the look on Jane's face a picture to behold?'

Ted agreed that it was, his gaze observing every detail of this frail-looking little girl. 'Let's be 'aving yer, missus,' he said as he caught hold of Elsie's arm and helped her into the carriage.

Once settled in the front seat, Ted flicked the reins and the horse moved forward. As they went down the narrow cobbled high street, Jane looked at the houses and shops in utter perplexity. They were nothing like the buildings where she came from. Some of them were so crooked they looked as if they were falling over. Many didn't even have proper roofs; they were thatched, but Jane didn't know that. She was still staring wide-eyed at the small, funny-shaped windows, most of which had red and green banners stretched above their doorways wishing their customers A HAPPY CHRISTMAS.

A postman on a bicycle went whizzing by, shouting, 'Morning, Ted, see yer t'night.' Two kindly-looking elderly women, each carrying a wicker basket, stood on the narrow pavement, and as the carriage drew near they each raised a hand in salute and called out a greeting to Ted and Mrs Rogers.

'See you both soon,' Elsie Rogers called back over her shoulder as they passed by.

How come everyone seemed to know each other and was so friendly? Jane was asking herself.

At the bottom of the main road, Ted steered the horse to the left. They were now passing alongside what looked like a river, with many different kinds of boats moored along the bank. Mrs Rogers bent her head and whispered, 'We are only two miles from the sea; what you are looking at is Rye Harbour.'

When Jane made no reply, she added, 'Where you are going to live is a place called Winchelsea, and it even has its own beach. Come the summer, you and all the other girls will spend many a happy hour down by the sea.'

Jane had no idea as to how she was supposed to react. She had never seen the sea. At school they had read about it, and there were some pictures of seaside places pinned up on the wall in the main hall, but to be told that not only would she be able to see it soon, but would spend days on a beach . . . It couldn't be true. Not really.

Soon it became a bumpy ride. Jane didn't know where to look next, there was so much to see. Holding tightly to the hand rail, she twisted from side to side as the horse clip-clopped through the country lanes.

Then, out of the blue, they were approaching a huge crowd of people, and the sight and sounds had Jane reaching for Elsie Rogers' hand.

'It's all right, pet, what we're looking at is the pre-Christmas horse fair,' Elsie laughed.

Horse boxes were lined up at one end of the field. There were a few horses on show and several lovely little ponies. Farmers, trainers, breeders and owners milled around. At the other end there was a fair. Jane knew all about that, because on bank holidays her mum had often taken her and Tommy to the fair on Clapham Common. Here, there were gaily painted gypsy caravans and lots of stalls.

'Buy a sprig of lucky heather for the young lady, missus?' A dark-skinned young woman with hair the colour of a raven and a beautiful curly-haired baby in her arms ran beside their horse and cart.

'Course I will.' Elsie Rogers grinned as she fished in her handbag to find a couple of pennies.

Smiling broadly, showing a gold tooth, the young gypsy reached up for the coins and handed over the lucky sprig, saying, 'Thanks, missus. Gawd bless yer, an' you too, missy.'

Elsie gave the purple heather to Jane and, watching the delight on the child's face, felt it had to be a good omen.

They left the noisy scene behind and Jane remained quiet, deep in thought, until Ted turned the horse into the yard that led up to Winchelsea Lodge.

As if it knew they were almost home, the horse neighed, scattering a flock of chickens and hens and making two dogs bark.

Ted turned his head, and there was a triumphant gleam in his eye as he said, 'I live over there, missy.' He pointed to a cottage some way away. 'Matron up at the lodge gives out the jobs, but maybe you'll get t' come down 'ere an' gather up the hens' eggs from time t' time.'

Elsie laughed. 'Give her time to settle in before you have her working, Ted.'

Jane was having mixed feelings. She had seen live chickens before, because one of their neighbours had kept a couple in his back yard. But there were an awful lot of them here, and she didn't know about going amongst them to get at their eggs. Besides, there were those two dogs. Ever so pretty they were, their silky coats all black and white, and from where she was sitting, high up in the cart, they were all right. But to go near a dog! Oh no, she couldn't do that. Dogs frightened her.

When Ted Grimshaw finally lifted Jane down, she couldn't have described how she felt, not even to herself. Everything that had happened today was becoming too much for her to take in, and at that moment she would have given anything for her mum to appear, put her arms around her and say, 'Come on, Janey, I'm going to take you home.' If that were to happen, at least she would get to see Tommy. He had to be wondering where she was after all the time she'd been away.

A sob rose in her throat and she shuddered as she tried hard not to cry.

Rye railway station she had thought looked like a castle. A huge great red building with ever so many windows and such a lot of nice grounds around it. Now, as she stared up at Winchelsea Lodge, she knew she had never before gazed on such a lovely house, but the whole of the outside looked so big and so different. It wasn't made of bricks; it had been built with what to Jane looked like huge stones.

Elsie Rogers sensed the child's confusion and gave her a moment to get her bearings. Then, taking the small hand within her own, and without saying a word, she drew her forward and felt Jane's grip tighten as they walked side by side up the wide stone steps. At the top she had to let go of Jane's hand because it took all of her strength to push open the heavy oak front door.

Janey couldn't believe the length of the entrance hall, nor the roaring fire that was burning in the wide fireplace. 'Cor, look at that,' she exclaimed out loud, pointing at the high window set in the far wall. The wintry sun was shining through it, causing its gentle blues and reds to fill the hall with colour.

'That's really lovely, all those colours,' she murmured.

'It is beautiful, isn't it?' A soft voice had come from behind her, and Jane turned quickly. What she saw was a kind of nurse, but not quite like the nurses who had looked after her in the hospital. Dressed in a navy-blue dress with long sleeves and a white collar and cuffs, Lillian Cooper wore sensible low-heeled lace-up shoes and dark stockings. Above average height, she had short shiny dark hair and deep brown eyes, and looked just what she was: capable and efficient. If asked, the powers-that-be would all agree that she managed Winchelsea Lodge and its occupants just fine.

'It is known as a stained-glass window,' she told Jane, then paused. When no reply came, she said, 'You must be Jane; we are very pleased to have you staying with us. I am what is known around here as Matron.' Lillian's voice was full of fun as she bent her knees and looked into Jane's pale face, adding, 'I shall see you later, and we will all do our best to see that you are happy here.'

Still Jane hadn't uttered a word.

Elsie Rogers nodded to this confident, kind woman as she straightened up, and holding out her hand she said, 'Come along, Jane, we have to go up this big staircase to get to where you'll be sleeping.'

Jane took the outstretched hand and Elsie gave the small fingers a squeeze of reassurance.

The first-floor landing was broad and long. There were three bedrooms, the doors to which were propped open, showing that each held six single beds, three on either side of the room. Elsie passed the first two, but at the entrance to the third she stopped and ushered Jane inside. 'The middle bed on the right will be yours for now,' she smiled. Beside each bed stood a tall locker, and she was about to tell Jane that she could put her things away in what was to be hers when she remembered that there was no case to unpack.

'Take your coat and hat off, Jane,' she said softly, doing her best to conceal her embarrassment. Removing a padded coat hanger from the narrow cupboard, she took the coat from Jane and hung it up for her. 'I'll show you where the bathroom is. You can wash your hands and then we'll go back downstairs.' Glancing at her watch, she added, 'We shall just be in time for tea.'

So many wonders! A great big white bath set on iron claw feet had pride of place in the centre of the room, and a toilet with a polished wooden seat was set in the corner. What was more, there were two taps fixed to the end of the bath. Surely you didn't just turn them on and water came out into the bath?

'There is also a toilet next door if the bathroom is occupied, and another downstairs near to the eating quarters,' Mrs Rogers quietly told her.

Three toilets. All inside the house! This place must belong to someone very, very rich!

Back downstairs, through a huge kitchen, and there was the eating quarters. Three long tables and about thirty girls, mostly older than herself, all smiling a welcome at her. At a nod from Matron, a girl seated about halfway down the first table rose and came bustling to where Jane was standing. Tall, fat, with fair hair tied back into two short plaits, Connie Brown was all smiles.

'Jane, this is Connie. She will be around at all times to look after you and show you the ropes,' Matron smiled.

Although neither girl made a move to put out a hand or take a step towards the other, their eyes met and held. 'We'll be friends, you'll see,' Connie whispered as they walked side by side to sit at the table.

Jane lowered her eyes and bit her lip, wondering if this Connie really meant what she said. Not many people had ever wanted to be her friend. At least not for long. Once they discovered the terrible names her dad called her, or heard him hollering and swearing, they never spoke to her much. Not even at school.

Still, her dad wasn't here, was he?

Connie, being fourteen years old, felt Jane's doubts, and once they were seated side by side at the table she said again, 'I'll be your friend, you'll see.'

'I . . .' Jane's voice was barely more than a whisper, 'I hope so.'

Having eaten a slice of bread and jam and a rock cake, and drunk a mug of milky tea, they were all ordered to stand before filing out and returning to their allocated jobs.

'I've already been told that you are to be with me, at least for the next few days,' Connie told Jane as she half pushed her through another door. 'Normally I work outdoors – well, most of the year I do – but as it's getting near Christmas there's not a lot that can be done. Ground is too hard. Still, makes a change.'

Jane counted. There were six other girls in this sitting room besides herself and Connie.

'We've all got some needlework to finish,' said a fresh-faced young lady with creamy fair skin, red hair and huge green eyes that looked as if they were laughing. 'But you will be excused, Jane. There are plenty of books on the shelves over there; find one you like and go sit by the fire.'

Jane squirmed. She didn't know what to say. Sensing this, the redhead said, 'I'm Fran, short for Frances, and I'm captain of this team. There are four in the house; you'll be told which one you'll be in when Matron decides to give you a badge.'

Jane couldn't take her eyes off this Fran, who was easily the prettiest girl she had ever seen.

Connie tugged at her arm. 'Come on, I'll see you settled with a book before I start on my work.' When the choice had been made and Connie was about to turn away, she hesitated, then, seeing Jane look so frail and vulnerable, bent over the arm of the chair in which the younger girl was sitting and spoke softly. 'There's no need to be so frightened, really there isn't. By an' large this is a great place to be sent to. Mind, not everyone is as nice as Fran, and when it comes t' some of the staff they're not all of the same kind nature as Matron. But you'll find out for yourself who you can trust, and like I said, I'll be around whenever you want me.'

Everything was beginning to overwhelm Janey. It was all too much. And Connie's kindness broke the dam. Pulling a handkerchief from up her sleeve, she nestled right into the corner of the winged armchair and held the cotton square tightly across her eyes while she quietly cried her heart out.

Later, with all her tears spent, she rubbed hard at her eyes and stared into the fire. Standing to the side of the hearth was a large tapestry, mounted on a polished wood screen. A colourful peacock was the centrepiece, surrounded by lovely flowers and greenery. It was so real-looking that Jane was tempted to lean forward to smell and even touch the small petals. Nancy did a lot of needlework and knitting, selling her finished articles on Tooting Market. Jane had often watched her sew, but her work wasn't anything like this. While she was fascinated by it, she was equally sure that this screen must have taken a very long time to make.

Frances O'Brien came to the side table to fetch a new reel of cotton. Seeing the look of intense awe on the face of this new little girl, she knelt down beside her chair.

'Every stitch is a work of art, isn't it?' She spoke softly.

Janey nodded her head.

'The sisters come here every Wednesday and they are responsible for work of that kind. You could join one of their classes if you think that's what you'd like to do.'

Jane raised her eyebrows. 'I couldn't do nothing like that!'

'How do you know if you've never tried?' Fran was laughing as she spoke. 'I've spent many a happy hour being taught how to patiently sew smaller tapestries than that one. You get to use fine silks and wools in every colour of the rainbow. Anyway, we'll see. If you don't like your book, have a little sleep. Connie will wake you up when it's time for supper.'

Jane's first hot meal at Winchelsea Lodge was an eye-opener. A hot meal for supper was not something she was used to. The shepherd's pie with rice pudding to follow absolutely filled her up. Connie told her it was the only time of the day when all the girls and staff sat down together, and that when everything was cleared away prayers would be said. Jane had been startled to see how many of them there were. Forty-two all told, Connie informed her.

At eight o'clock, along with nine other girls, the youngest in the home, Jane climbed the stairs, undressed and got into the strange single bed. She wanted her mum. She wanted her to cuddle her and to kiss her good night. Not that she ever did if her dad was at home at bedtime. She wanted to say good night to Tommy, to feel his chubby little arms round her neck. Oh, she wanted to be at home.

Suddenly five small voices were calling out, 'Good night, Jane. God bless you.'

In a tight voice she managed to answer, 'Good night,'

before she tucked her head down beneath the bedclothes.
Then, in the darkness, the questions came flooding back.
Why was she here? Why hadn't she been able to go home
when she came out of the hospital? Why didn't her mum
want her any more? Was she to stay in this home for ever
and ever?

The day had taken its toll. She was too tired even to cry.

At last her eyelids began to droop and merciful sleep took
over.

Chapter Five

THE VERY NEXT day Jane was initiated into the more normal routine that would be her life for the foreseeable future. She was also quick to learn that not everything in Winchelsea Lodge was going to be as nice as it had been during the first hours of her arrival.

Woken at seven o'clock, she washed and dressed in a room that was totally different to the main bathroom in which she had washed her hands yesterday. This room was sparse and cold. A line of metal basins stood in a long zinc-lined trough, with cold-water taps placed at three-foot inter-vals and slabs of hard yellow soap held in racks above.

Jane shivered, standing barefoot and wearing only a clean pair of navy-blue knickers which she'd found laid out with other items of clothing on the foot of her bed. She washed her face and neck, then dried herself using a harsh towel that had to be shared with the girl standing next to her. Watching the other girls, she saw that they were cleaning their teeth with a toothbrush which they dipped into a bowl containing a grey powder. When told to do the same by a girl standing opposite her, Jane found the taste absolutely horrible.

'You'll get used to it, and by the way we do get hot water on bath nights,' Connie whispered.

When Jane had brushed her teeth, the older girl helped her to put on a vest, then a fawn jumper and over that a thick brown pinafore dress. Black woolly stockings held up by a piece of white elastic, and a pair of black plimsolls completed her outfit.

'They haven't got any shoes small enough for you at the moment,' Connie informed her.

Breakfast, at a quarter to eight, consisted of thick oatmeal and a slice of fried bread.

From the top table Mrs Rogers watched Jane carefully as she ate her breakfast. She looked so small, the youngest in the home at the moment, and she was such a shy child. Or perhaps a better word would be withdrawn. In some respects she seemed very frail, yet in other ways there was a quiet strength about her, and a knowing that belied her age, and then there was the cautious way she had of approaching people. Connie Brown was a good choice for the task of taking Jane under her wing. She had been orphaned at the age of ten and had been at the home ever since. She was a friendly girl who chafed a bit at the restrictions of Winchelsea Lodge and dreamed of going out into the big wide world.

'Normally we'd be getting ready to go to school as soon as breakfast is over.' Connie grinned at Jane. 'But we've broken up for the Christmas holidays. It's not all good news though,' She added when she saw Jane smile. 'Some of us have to attend classes here. Only those in their last year, nearly sixteen, are excused; they have jobs to do.'

'So will I have to go to a classroom?'

'Yes, you will, but first I've been told to take you to Matron's office.'

They walked down the long entrance hall and stopped outside a door marked OFFICE, where Connie turned to leave, saying, 'I'll see you at lunchtime.'

Jane was wondering what was going to happen to her now as she stepped into Matron's office.

'Did you manage to get any sleep?' Lillian Cooper asked, smiling, doing her best to put Jane at her ease.

'A bit,' Jane answered quietly.

Why did the child look so frightened? There were a great number of questions Lillian would have liked to ask, but it was too soon for her to do such a thing. Instead she said, 'We are putting you in the blue team. Frances O'Brien is the captain, and you must have made a good impression on her yesterday, because she particularly asked to have you.'

Jane stood silent, her eyes downcast.

'I thought you'd be pleased. Didn't you like Frances?'

Jane looked confused. 'Yes, but . . . why have I got to be in a team? An' why must I go t' school?' The words finally came out in a rush.

'All children have to go to school. Don't you want to learn?'

'Yes, an' I like my own school an' my teacher.'

Lillian Cooper took a long, slow breath, wanting to choose her words with the utmost care and not upset Jane more than was necessary.

'You are going to stay here with us for a while, and of course it would be too far for you to travel every day to attend your old school.' She smiled warmly at Jane, 'We're very pleased to have you.'

'Oh,' was all Jane said.

Matron waited. She knew the hard part was yet to come.

Suddenly Jane blurted a question out bluntly: 'How long am I going to stay here?'

There was a pause while Matron again weighed her words carefully, never taking her eyes off Jane's sad face.

'Your mother isn't well. You know that, don't you?'

Jane nodded, then again blurted out, 'But she'd be all right if me dad didn't keep hitting her.' Realizing what she had said, she flushed a deep red and covered her mouth with her hand. Several moments passed before she added, 'I didn't mean t' say that.'

'Never mind, Jane. A doctor has seen your mother and he's going to be taking care of her from now on. But . . . your mum thinks you will be a good deal happier staying here with us. Besides, you'll have lots of other girls who will want to be friends with you.'

Jane took her time considering what Matron had told her. Then, drawing in a deep breath, she said, 'I'm never going home, am I?' Her big blue eyes looked straight into Lillian's.

The question was so direct that Lillian knew she could not lie to this frightened child. It took her a while to form an answer.

'I honestly don't know. I don't think your mum does either. Maybe you will when things get better at home.' It was as honest as she could make it without telling the girl that it was out of her mother's hands and that it was the authorities who would make the decisions as to what happened to her from now until she reached the age of sixteen.

In an effort to ease the child's pain she said quickly, 'Jane, you must never forget that your mother loves you. You know that she does, don't you?'

Jane nodded silently. Then, a second later, she said, 'I think she does . . . sort of . . . though she never . . .' Her eyes filled with tears as she remembered all the times her mum had watched her dad hit her. Later Mum would always say, 'I'll kiss it better,' but kissing hadn't made it better, had it? And Alice had come to the hospital to say goodbye. Why hadn't she said she was taking Jane home? She hadn't seen Mum since then. Was she ever going to see her again? Does she even know where I am? she wondered. It was hard to say whether she still loved her mum, but if not her, who else was there for her to love?

Finally she whispered, 'I love her too, and Tommy.'

Matron had read in the notes that Jane had a younger brother, but now was not the time to go into that. The child had more than enough complications to cope with as it was.

'Come along,' she urged, rising from her seat behind her desk. 'I'll take you along to the class you will be in for the next few weeks until we can sort out what standard you are up to and find a suitable school for you to attend.'

Matron held her hand as they walked, which was a great comfort to Jane, and she was very reluctant to let go as a classroom door was opened. There were ten girls in the class. Jane was startled as they all got to their feet, and even more mixed up when the teacher said, 'One by one, starting at the back row, introduce yourselves to our newcomer.'

Peggy . . . Lizzy . . . Hilda . . . Mary . . . Jean . . . Pauline . . . Maggie . . . Doreen . . . Ann . . . Kathleen.

Jane was by now thoroughly flustered. Was she supposed to remember all their names?

Matron said a few words to the teacher, then, having patted Jane on the head, she took her leave, saying, 'Miss Paterson will take care of you.'

Jane wasn't too sure about that!

Miss Paterson was a formidable sight. She was a big woman, with mousy-coloured hair cut short like a man's.

She wore a heavy tweed skirt topped by an equally heavy Fair Isle twin-set, the outfit finished off with grey lisle stockings and heavy brogue shoes

'So you are Jane Jeffrey,' Miss Paterson barked. 'How old are you?'

'Eight,' Jane mumbled.

'Speak up, girl. And I'd say you're almost nine, seeing as how your papers say you were born on January the first, 1912.'

Jane couldn't have said whether that fact was true or not. Birthdays had never been a source of celebration at home.

'Turn around.'

Jane did as she was told.

'Not too bad. Quite neat really,' Miss Paterson said kindly, in a much softer voice.

Jane was about to give a sigh of relief when the bark returned, making her jump.

'My goodness, this hair is really dreadful.' Miss Paterson lifted a few strands of Jane's long blonde hair and let it run through her fingers, grimacing as she did so.

Jane was aware that her hair was not looking its best. The nurses had washed it gently because of her bad ear, and the night before she left the hospital one of them had done it up in rags, just as her mother had loved doing, so that her ringlets had looked really pretty. But the journey had helped to tangle her curls, and though Connie had made an attempt at brushing them while they had been in the washroom this morning, time had been short and a monitor had told them to hurry up.

'No matter,' Miss Paterson stated. 'When class is finished for the day I personally will see to your hair.'

Jane saw the girl sitting nearest to her wince. She kept her eyes low as she made her way to the vacant desk that was allocated to her. She didn't like the sound of Miss Paterson saying that she would personally see to her hair.

Come to that, she didn't like Miss Paterson very much either.

The lesson went quite well. Much better than Jane had imagined. Miss Paterson was pleased to learn that she could do joined-up writing and was able to recite her times-tables.

At the end of an hour, the rest of the girls were told that they could leave the class, but Jane Jeffrey should remain behind. Miss Paterson held tightly to her hand as they went out through the front door and down the stone steps. 'You see those three sheds over to your right?' she said to Jane, pointing with her forefinger. Jane nodded. 'Well, they are the toilets you will use when working or playing outside.' They went on past the lavatories and stopped outside a much larger and more solidly brick-built building. Miss Paterson pushed open the door.

Inside a man in his shirt sleeves was sitting at the far end of a table, with a smallish woman with a head of thin white hair at his side. The two of them were apparently sorting out a pile of clothing.

The door closed with a slam behind Jane, making her jump slightly. Then Miss Paterson pushed past her, saying, 'I'm told an assignment of clothing has arrived. This is our latest arrival, Jane Jeffrey. I thought you might like to meet her, she badly needs to be kitted out.'

'Oh!' The exclamation had come from the man, and he repeated, 'Oh! Well, it would 'ave been nice, Miss Paterson, if you'd given us a bit of notice. We 'aven't got 'alfway through the 'amper yet.'

'Still, needs must when the devil drives,' the small woman said, getting to her feet and smiling at Jane. 'Did you bring any clothes with you at all, my dear?'

'Do they ever?' Miss Paterson cut in before Jane had a chance to reply. 'She needs from the skin outwards; gymwear can wait for the time being.'

Having by now sorted out the situation in her own mind, Jane spoke up. 'I've a lovely brand-new coat. The nurses at the hospital bought it for me and it wasn't second hand.'

The man rose slowly to his feet, all the while staring at Jane. Then he pushed a chair towards her, saying, 'Sit you down, my love, my missus 'ere will fit you out, you've no need to fear, an' as for being second hand, you wait and see. We get clothes given to this home which come from some of the finest families in the land.'

Jane was surprised at how soft and kind his voice sounded.

'I'm Patrick Carter, and that's me wife, Emma. We're always about somewhere, 'cos we live in a cottage down by the gate, so if ever you need us, you won't have far t' look.' He bounced his head with almost every word, as if to emphasize that he meant what he was saying.

'You're a bit smaller than most of the girls we have to deal with.' Emma Carter spoke quietly as she began sorting things out of a great big hamper. She nodded towards Miss Paterson. 'What d'you think of this?' she asked as she took out a navy-blue raincoat. 'It does have a very thick lining, so it might do her for school.' She laid the coat across the table, and Miss Paterson looked at it, feeling the material between her finger and thumb.

'It will have to be shortened quite a bit, but it is a very good quality,' she said eventually.

'Well, we'll only turn the hem up, we won't cut it, then it can be lengthened again as she grows,' Emma Carter said, nodding from one to the other now. 'Come along, child, try it on.' When she saw Jane in the coat she looked pleased, even though the hem was touching her ankles. 'Yes, my dear,' she murmured. Then, falling to her knees, she pinned up the hem. 'Now that's better. That's much better. What do you think, Miss Paterson?'

The teacher looked solemnly at Jane and agreed, adding, 'It really is good quality.'

Jane took the coat off and it was handed to Mr Carter, who drew lines round the hem with a piece of tailoring chalk.

Next two skirts were brought out. One of them was far too big, but a navy-blue one was deemed to be fine. Two blouses followed, which Jane was told would be suitable for school, and a jumper and a cardigan. 'There's plenty of warm underwear over at the house, in the cupboard on the first floor.' Emma Carter spoke more to herself than to anyone in particular.

Miss Paterson seemed pleased with the result and was preparing to lead Jane away when she turned her head towards Patrick and asked, 'No chance of any footwear, I suppose?'

'I was just glancing at the child's feet. Did she arrive wearing those plimsolls?' Patrick asked, although he suspected that he already knew the answer.

'No, she has a pair of boots but they've seen better days. Plimsolls were all Matron had that would fit.'

'Um . . .' Patrick grunted. 'Umpteen of the lasses could do with a decent pair of boots or shoes, but as you know, it's what we get least of. We've nothing for her, even to be going on with. But I'll tell you what, send her boots over an' I'll do what I can to repair them.'

'Thanks, Patrick,' Miss Paterson said quietly.

Jane's feelings were mixed as she wondered just how long she was supposed to be staying here. All these different clothes they were giving her! And as for this Miss Paterson!

One minute she was jumping down your throat and the next she was being ever so kind.

As if to prove a point, Miss Paterson turned to Jane now, saying, 'Come along and let's see what I can do about that hair of yours.'

Patrick Carter placed an arm around Jane's shoulders. She smiled up at him, but his face was straight. And what he said next Jane was to remember for the whole of the time she would spend at Winchelsea Lodge: 'I meant it, lass: if and when you need a friend, or just feel like a chat, you come and find me or me missus.'

Miss Paterson nodded, first to him and then to Emma, then turned and led Jane quickly from the room.

Once back inside the main house, Jane was ushered into what appeared to be a cloakroom. A chair was pulled forward and she was told to sit down, then Miss Paterson flicked a towel around her shoulders, tucking it in all round her neck and under her chin. When Jane saw that she was holding a comb and a pair of scissors, her face crumpled.

Miss Paterson held her by the shoulders as she explained quietly, 'It wouldn't do to let you keep this long hair. No child is allowed to. We haven't the time to keep it clean, let alone tidy.'

Jane felt so sad. Her hair was the only thing that made her look pretty. It made people take notice of her. Besides, what would her mum say when she saw her without her ringlets? But then a thought struck her. When was her mum likely to see her? Never, probably. So what difference did it make anyway!

There was dead silence in this small room for a moment, and then Miss Paterson got to work.

Head down, eyes glued to the floor, Jane watched as the long, fine, silky strands of hair fell around her feet. The towel was whipped away and she felt the soft bristles of a brush go around her neck, then Miss Paterson said, 'All done. There's a mirror on the wall over there. Go take a look at your new self.'

Her face looked smaller, clean and white, as if she had just washed it. What hair she had left was straight, barely touching her ears. She ran her hand around her neck. It felt cold, and utterly bare.

Her mum wouldn't recognize her.

But then she'd already worked that one out. Her mum wasn't likely to see her, was she? Jane was no longer her responsibility.

Chapter Six

THERE WAS LIGHT streaming from all the windows at the front of the house as the crocodile of girls walked up the steps to the front door.

They had all taken off their woolly hats and unwound the long scarves from their necks, and were trying to take in the effect of the surroundings. The huge Christmas tree had been standing in one corner for two days. Now decorated with baubles made by the girls themselves from silver paper, it looked beautiful.

The hall, too, looked lovely, adorned by paper chains and with holly draped around the top of the picture rail.

'So you've all come back now everything is almost finished,' a big booming voice called from the far end of the hall. 'Well, at least it will save me getting up and down these steps; some of yer come an' hand the holly up to me.' Ted Grimshaw was perched halfway up some standing steps.

Elsie Rogers turned her gaze to Jane, who was standing with a look of amazement on her face. Elsie, along with two other members of staff, had just taken the girls to a carol service in the local church. She had watched Jane throughout the entire service and had come to the conclusion that this was probably the first time in her young life that the girl had experienced the true meaning of Christmas.

When Matron came down the stairs it was to a babble of voices all exclaiming how wonderful the decorations were looking.

A cluster of girls were handing all sorts of greenery up to Ted Grimshaw, and when he almost overbalanced and was saved by several pairs of hands grabbing at the steps, the whole room seemed to rock with laughter. Ted, wiping his hands down his apron, said, 'I think I've earned a drink,' before muttering, 'You'd think with all the females in this house one of them would be capable of making a man a cup of tea.'

With laughter rumbling in her throat, Lillian Cooper didn't answer him for a moment, then she said, 'Well, by the time you've finished off up there I shouldn't be a bit surprised if hot drinks and even mince pies aren't laid out on the table for everyone to partake of.'

To herself Matron was saying, 'Oh, I hope each and every girl that is here in my care has a happy Christmas. And all my staff. They work so hard, never seem to let up.' Then she smiled broadly. Their cook was a gem, even if she did rule the kitchen with a rod of iron. These past few days she had come up trumps. With almost a full week ahead during which there was to be no schooling, she would have her work cut out feeding this lot. It would be a happy time, though. Lillian would make it her business to see that it was. Fifty per cent of the girls here had come from broken homes and the rest had either lost their parents through tragic circumstances or been abandoned. The board of directors had been generous in making an additional allowance this year, and she and her staff had between them decided as to how it should be spent. There was not enough money to go mad, but each child would receive a small present and a stocking, which would be hung on the end of their beds on Christmas Eve.

'Clear a space,' Nellie, the cook, called out, coming into the hall carrying a heavy tray. She was followed by Daisy and Minnie, her two assistants.

Willing hands poured tea, and there was hot milk for those who preferred it. Slices of Madeira cake and hot mince pies were being handed round by the senior girls. Elsie Rogers was still watching Jane. She loved to see the different expressions of surprise and sometimes delight which flickered across the child's face. During the short time Jane had been at Winchelsea Lodge there had been a marked improvement. She didn't jump now when spoken to, neither did she back away from physical contact. Elsie gave a short laugh as she listened to what Ted Grimshaw was saying to the girl.

'These pies are as good as my Maggie makes. Must be Christmas, 'cos they don't often feed me when I'm working up here.'

Stepping closer, Elsie said, 'He does go on, doesn't he, Jane? You know we wouldn't starve him, don't you?'

Jane smiled happily. 'I think he's only teasing, don't you, Mrs Rogers? He likes coming up to the house really, he told me he does.'

Ted looked a bit embarrassed and mumbled, 'Suppose I'd better go an' do me own clearing-up if I want it done properly.' Then, turning to Jane, he said, 'Me an' me missus has been invited up here for tea on the great day, so I'll see you then if not before.'

A while later they were all saying goodbye to Ted as he pulled on his overcoat when the door bell rang and Matron called out, 'Whoever is nearest please open the door.'

Frances O'Brien stepped forward and quickly called out, 'There's two woodmen here, Matron, they say they have a load of logs to deliver.'

'Well I never,' Matron was heard to mutter. 'I certainly wasn't expecting them, but never the less they are so welcome. Ask them to come in.'

In all, six sacks of logs were brought in and stacked to the side of the great fireplace. When one of the woodmen casually remarked, 'Did you know it has started to snow?' girls turned their faces to each other and then there was a general rush to the windows. It was only four o'clock in the afternoon, but already the night was drawing in. The white flakes were floating silently down, turning the paths into a white trail and decorating the bare branches of the trees in a Christmas magic all of their own.

'May I be allowed to know who has so generously sent us this most welcome gift?' Matron asked after she had seen that both men were handed a big mug of tea and a hunk of Cook's Madeira cake.

'Don't know as how we can answer that, mam, 'cos we wasn't informed.' The taller of the two men scratched his head before adding, 'But we can tell yer that we loaded up the sacks ourselves from Mr Stuart's grounds, and after that it were himself that asked us if we'd make the delivery.'

Lillian looked across to where Elsie Rogers was standing and they both nodded knowingly. Their thoughts were running along the same lines. What great friends were Dorothy and Richard Stuart, and such good benefactors to the occupants of Winchelsea Lodge.

One way and another it was going to be a very nice Christmas.

★   ★   ★

The next seven days were an eye-opener to Jane. Spending Christmas in the happy safety of Winchelsea Lodge, it was as if she had been transported to a different world. If only Tommy could be here to share it with me, was her constant thought. She no longer asked herself if or when her mother was going to come and take her home. She had been rejected by her family. It was only too plain that she was unwanted by them. Her thoughts did often run to dear old Nancy, who had been like a grandmother to her. Not that she knew much about having grandparents; only what the girls at school had told her. In fact she couldn't remember her father ever having mentioned his parents. She had had a gran, her mother's mum, and she had been real nice, but she had stopped coming to the house a long time ago and her dad had told her that Gran had died. What puzzled Jane was that her mother wouldn't talk to her about her gran. She had stopped asking questions about her, because Alice got ever so upset.

Even though Christmas had been such a happy time, Jane had missed her brother Tommy. How she would have loved to have shared with him all the things that she had been given. Wished that he could have seen the big Christmas tree, been there when they toasted chestnuts on a long-handled shovel over the big log fire. How he would have laughed when the chestnuts popped and jumped off the shovel. She hoped that he too had had a nice time.

She had been fast asleep when the church bells had rung in the new year.

She was woken up by cries of 'Happy birthday, Jane.'

Sitting up and rubbing her eyes, she took the small crepe-paper-wrapped parcel which Connie was holding out to her and stared at it in disbelief. 'Go on, open it up,' Connie urged her. The wrapping tore away easily to reveal a small comb and a pale-blue enamel hairbrush with an edging of silver paint.

As Jane sat turning both items over and over in her hands without saying a word, Connie asked softly, 'Don't you like them? Your hair will grow again soon and I thought they would be useful.'

'Oh,' was all that Jane uttered, but Connie could hear the sob in her voice. It took a couple of minutes before she was able to say, 'I think they are so lovely. Thank you, Connie, for buying them for me.'

'That's what birthdays are all about. Friends always give little presents,' Connie reassured her.

'Not to me, nobody ever did before,' Jane said sadly.

'Well, today will be different, you'll see. So get up quickly, we don't want to be late, not on the first day of the year.'

It was a day Jane would always remember. There was a card signed by all the girls and members of staff, as well as one from Matron and one from Mrs Rogers. Cook said she was saving her surprise until tea-time, and it turned out to be a huge sponge cake with nine lighted candles. When it was time for Jane to blow out the flames of the candles she had to have help, because her big blue eyes weren't able to focus properly. They were filled with tears.

Then, with the new year eight days old, Jane set off with ten other girls all under the age of twelve to start her first day as a pupil at Lion Street School for Girls in the old town of Rye. The school was a collection of solidly built one-storey stone cottages. Collectively they had the appearance of being a church. There was no rule as to uniform, but it had become normal for all the girls to wear blouses and a gymslip, and on Jane's first day she looked no different from any of the others who attended the school, thanks to the efforts of Patrick Carter and the sewing ability of his wife Emma.

The classroom was not at all like the one Jane had been used to in London. It was heated by a round stove. At regular intervals, even while a lesson was in progress, the caretaker would enter and feed the stove with coke, then make sure that he replaced the guard that stood around it. After prayers had been said and hymns sung, Jane watched as small bottles of milk were placed around the base of this stove so that they might thaw out on this frosty morning. Then, at playtime, each girl was given a bottle of milk to drink, absolutely free. Milk had been available at her London school but only if a child had a halfpenny to pay for it. Which Jane had seldom had.

During the morning she was given an exercise book, on which she was told to write her name, plus a pencil, a rubber, a pen and two pen nibs. There was an ink well in the top right-hand corner of her desk. The tall girl who sat next to her leaned across and said, 'It will cost you dearly if you lose any one of those things.'

Jane was puzzled. She had no money, so how would she be able to pay? She decided that she had better take very good care not to lose a single one of them.

As time went on she was taught other things rather than just lessons. Each class took it in turn to clean the main hall. Some pupils washed the windows while others dusted and polished the pews. All cleaning cloths then had to be washed and hung out on a line in the yard behind the main building.

Jane's school terms became reasonably happy. She was a bright pupil, quick to learn, but was given no advantages.

Scholarships and suchlike were not for children who lived in charity-run homes. She had to take a lot of ribbing from local children, who never let her forget that she had no proper family. But at least she had the comradeship of the other girls who were in the same boat as herself.

And so the pattern of her next five years was set.

She settled down at Winchelsea Lodge and became very adapt with a sewing needle, taught by the Sisters of Mercy from the Church of England, who gave their services free to the girls of this home every Saturday afternoon. It was Jane's ambition to start and finish a fire screen as beautiful as the one that stood in the hearth of the small sitting room. She would do it before she left. She'd made up her mind on that. Some girls left the home when they reached the age of fourteen; that was, if they were lucky enough to find employment that offered them accommodation as well. Others found employment but still returned daily to the home, using most of what they earned to pay for their keep. No one, however, was allowed to remain under the care of the home after they reached the age of sixteen. It was from then on that a girl was on her own.

Over the years, Jane was to become part of many a tearful goodbye. The worst was the day that Connie Brown walked through the front door to live her life in the outside world. She had kept her promise to Jane and had been her friend, a fact that was greatly appreciated by Jane, who realized that in the beginning it was Connie who had made life a whole lot easier for her, cushioning blows that otherwise would have floored her.

Jane tried hard not to think about the day when she herself would no longer be allowed to stay at Winchelsea Lodge. She never heard from her mother, not so much as one letter, but she still thought of her. Especially when the lights were turned off at night and she lay in her narrow bed and no one came to kiss her good night. There weren't many days that she didn't think of her brother Tommy. What school was he going to, and what kind of a life was he leading?

As to her father . . . She still had the odd bad dream when she was at her wits' end to know what to do to please him. These dreams became less frequent, but the terror he caused her was still there in the back of her mind.

Mrs Rogers had long since told her that her father had got over the trouble he was in with the police, and she had firmly assured Jane that he had not been sent to prison. So was he still at home? Did her family still live in Selkirk Road?

As Jane neared her fourteenth birthday, Elsie Rogers made her report to the Guardians of the Poor. In her view, she told them, Jane was still shy, but not so withdrawn now. Over the years she had learned to trust those she lived with. Strangers were a different matter. Especially males. The only two men that Jane really trusted were Ted Grimshaw and Patrick Carter. She had grown into an attractive girl, though she herself did not seem to sense it. No one could accuse her of being vain. She still wore the second-hand clothes that were given to the home. Not a single letter or a parcel had she received from her parents in all the time she had been at Winchelsea Lodge, yet she never complained. It was Elsie's considered opinion that Jane Jeffrey was still far too insecure to be turned out of the home to fend for herself.

At the end of her report she added a reminder that Jane was entirely without family or any known relatives who would offer her a home. She also stressed that were Jane to be allowed to stay on at Winchelsea Lodge for a further two years, she felt sure the girl would do any task asked of her, and do it willingly.

It was a month before Matron received the official letter.

The board's written decision was that Jane be allowed to stay on at Winchelsea Lodge for a further two years. During that period she was to work as an assistant to Nellie Matthews, the cook, who was reaching the age when she needed full-time help. Two local girls from the village were employed on high days and holidays, and though only paid a few shillings they were still a drain on Matron's expenses. Jane would work in return for her board and lodging.

Those two years were to stand Jane in good stead for the rest of her life.

Nellie Matthews liked Jane, and the feeling was mutual. Therefore Nellie shared her knowledge, taking the time to teach Jane not only how to cook everyday substantial meals, but also how to make a little go a long way. She taught her too how to make bread and cakes that would cost a fortune if bought at a baker's shop.

The two years passed all too quickly. There wasn't a person, male or female, associated with Winchelsea Lodge who wouldn't be sorry to see Jane leave.

The thought of leaving the safety of the home and all the friends that she had made had Jane feeling really sick as she sat facing Matron. Did she but know it, Lillian Cooper wasn't feeling all that good about it either, but her hands were tied and there was nothing she could do. As Matron, she was trying to convince herself that Jane's time spent here at Winchelsea Lodge had been a godsend to the child. She had been fed, given warmth and shelter. But much more than that, she had been taught to value her own worth. She had been loved and had loved in return. The skills she had learnt while under this roof were endless. She had no worries that Jane wouldn't be able to work and earn her own living. It was the fact that no one had ever laid claim to her in the entire seven years she had been here.

Loneliness was the biggest problem Jane was going to have to contend with. And what could possibly be worse than that?

Heaving a sigh, Lillian sat up straight and, using her Matron's voice, began: 'Well, Jane, a lot of loose ends to tie up. First, Mrs Rogers has found you a place to live. It is in Chestnut Grove in Balham. The trustes have voted to pay your first month's rent to give you a chance to find a job and get on your feet. They will also be giving you six pounds, which should be enough to tide you over until you receive your first week's wages.'

The colour had drained from Jane's face, and Matron felt she couldn't bear to look at her. Meanwhile Jane had just about grasped what she had been told. First week's wages? Where was she going to work? Who was going to give her a job?

'I don't want to leave here.'

It was a cry for help rather than a statement, and it tugged at Lillian's heartstrings.

'I do understand, Jane. The very fact of going out into the world must seem terrifying to you. But you are grown up now. You'll have Christmas with us and then start the new year off as a sixteen-year-old. You know we aren't allowed to keep any girl here after they reach the age of sixteen, which if you think about it is only fair. There are so many young girls who need our help, just as you did seven years ago.'

'Why do I have to go and live in Balham?'

'Most of us thought it best to let you go back to a neighbourhood near to where you lived the early years of your life. Balham is not too far from Tooting, and more than likely, once you get settled, you might even look up old friends and relations. You can't have forgotten everyone.'

Jane felt she wanted to scream. No, she had not forgotten, but then again she didn't want to be reminded. Her family had made it quite clear that they wanted nothing more to do with her, so why should she go seeking them out?

Matron felt she had to try a bit harder.

'There are so many things that you can do. You'll go along to the Labour Exchange, have a talk with the people there, and I'm quite sure they'll have no difficulty in finding you a job. Think about it, Jane. You'll be earning money of your own. Meeting girls your own age, making friends.'

Jane stared at her, her eyes brimming with tears.

'What you're telling me is I'm old enough to be taking care of myself. That I should be out there earning a living, making my own decisions. Well, Matron, I know you're right. I am old enough. But it doesn't feel like it. I just don't know how I'll cope.'

It would have been hard to tell which of these two females were feeling worse at that moment.

Jane left Matron's office feeling she was carrying the worries of the world on her shoulders. She had so much to sort out in her mind. When I first came to Winchelsea Lodge I was in a terrible state, terrified, she reminded herself, but this is ten times worse. She had learned to feel safe here. Everything she needed had been provided, plus love from kind, caring people, and suddenly all that was to be cut off.

From now on she had to fend for herself. Find new friends.

It was a daunting thought, but she knew with utter certainty that whatever happened in the future, she would never find better friends than she had at Winchelsea Lodge.

Chapter Seven

MRS ROGERS AND Jane stood side by side on Rye railway station, staring into space for what seemed an eternity. For Elsie Rogers speech was almost impossible; she was too choked up. For seven years she had watched this child grow, seen her become more confident and less frightened. I know I should never have got myself involved so heavily, she was telling herself. But at the same time she was asking how anyone could have resisted the pinched face of the small child she had picked up from that London hospital seven years ago. Especially someone like Elsie herself! No husband, no children of her own; what else was to be expected? There had been many a sad story that she had had to deal with since she had become implicated in court cases. But never a one where she had felt the child was so vulnerable.

Jane broke into her thoughts by saying, 'Matron said I'm old enough to take care of myself, and I told her it doesn't feel like it.'

She sounded like a small child again, and Elsie couldn't

stop herself from taking her into her arms and holding her close.

Several minutes passed before she could bring herself to say, 'Jane, I'll always be there for you. I shall treasure my fire screen, and every day, when I look at the neat stitches that you learned to do, I shall think of you. We'll write to each other, and meet as often as possible.' She meant what she said. She wouldn't just cut this girl off as a job well done. Jane had become a whole lot more than just a case number. There was a bond between them that had come about through love.

The screech of a whistle announced that the train was coming down the track. Time for one last long, lingering hug.

The train stopped. Someone opened the door of the nearest carriage and Jane, carrying a mackintosh over one arm, an attaché case and two brown paper carrier bags climbed the high steps. She dumped everything down on a seat and went to stand at the window. She wasn't sure that she believed that Mrs Rogers would keep in touch with her, but she dearly hoped she would.

The idea that this might be the last time she would ever see this dear friend – for that was what Mrs Rogers had become over the years – was something that she just did not want to think about.

Jane managed to smile and lift her hand to wave, and when finally the train gathered speed she sank down into her corner seat and buried her head in her hands. All she could think of was what she was leaving behind her: safety, warmth, friends, food and clothing. The enormity of what she was going to have to face suddenly hit her, and out loud she murmured, 'God help me!'

Then, taking a grip on herself, she said, 'There may be

many things that I'll be sorry for in the future, but I'll never be sorry that Mrs Rogers came into my life and made it possible for me to be taken into Winchelsea Lodge.'

Jane came out of the railway station and stood in Balham High Street feeling at an utter loss. So many people. So much noise. Everyone in such a hurry. Old men and women, young women with babies in prams, even they were all rushing along. Each and every person, except herself, seemed to have someone to talk to and somewhere to go.

She caught sight of herself in a shop window and realized that she not only felt different, she *looked* different. Thanks once again to Patrick and Emma Carter, she was well turned out. She was wearing a dark-grey skirt that was perfectly straight, the hemline finishing just below her calves. The jacket was a work of art. A darker shade of grey, it had been very much too big for her the first time she had tried it on, but armed with a pad full of pins and a tape measure, Emma Carter had gone to work.

'Don't make her look like a flapper,' Matron had pleaded as Emma nipped the jacket in at the waist.

Jane had seen pictures of flappers. Some girls managed to get hold of magazines, and these were handed round so often that they became dog-eared, especially the fashion pages. They did, however, give the girls an inkling of what was going on in the big world.

The material of the jacket was quite thick, but seeing as how this was January and some days were bitterly cold, Matron had herself provided a thick, long-sleeved jumper in the most cheerful shade of red. Jane loved it. It went so well beneath the grey jacket. As a special treat Jane had been allowed to have her hair cut in a ladies' hair salon in Rye. Though it had been kept short during her stay at Winchelsea

Lodge, the blonde assistant who had seen to it this last time had been very encouraging.

Having washed it with real shampoo, she had remarked on the beautiful natural colour of Jane's hair: no longer quite so fair, but a rich shade of dark gold. Jane had been astounded at the finished result. It was still cut short at the back, but the young lady had used the length at the sides to finger-pinch it into waves that covered Jane's ears.

Elsie Rogers had sighed deeply when first setting eyes on the new Jane.

'She's no longer a little girl, is she?' she had commented to Matron.

And the answer had been: 'No indeed, they are so young when they arrive here, but how the time flies by.'

Well, this won't do, Jane chided herself, and so she picked up her attaché case and started walking. She knew from the drawing that Mrs Rogers had given her that Chestnut Grove was only a few minutes' walk from the station. A tram stopped in the middle of the road; the destination board on the front said TOOTING BROADWAY. It awoke such memories from the back of her mind that for one crazy moment she was tempted to get on that tram, go to Tooting and try to find her mother. She had no idea if Alice still lived at the same address, let alone if she would be glad to see her should she turn up on the doorstep after seven years.

She found Chestnut Grove and was surprised at the spacious houses with their own large gardens. This area was nothing like Tooting! At least not how she remembered it. There were no children playing in the street and no women standing gossiping on the doorsteps. These properties looked as if they belonged to very rich people. Tall, with high windows and massive front doors. Surely the folk who lived in this kind of house did not rent out rooms. She glanced again at the slip of paper. 'Walk on down past the field that is used as a park, cross over and you'll find a blind alley in which there are only four houses. The one you are looking for will be the last one on your right.' Mrs Rogers had certainly been explicit.

Having found the house, Jane let out a sigh of relief. 'Oh, it does look nice,' she murmured. It was a much less impressive building than those she had just passed, and for that she was grateful. The windows were sparkling and the lace curtains were starched and pure white. She opened the gate, walked up the path, which had evergreen shrubs on each side, and rang the bell. In no time at all the door was opened and a neat little woman in a hairnet, wearing carpet slippers and a wraparound pinafore, was saying, 'I watched you from my sitting room window, thought for a moment you weren't going to come in. I had been notified to expect you today, you must be Jane Jeffrey. I'm Mrs Forrester, come along in.'

The hall smelt of lavender and furniture polish. There was a gate-legged table on which stood a bronze plant pot with an aspidistra in it, and underneath the pot a white lace crocheted mat had been placed. The narrow stair carpet was held in place by brass stair-rods so shiny that it almost dazzled Jane to look at them.

Jane decided her new landlady was a pleasant, very clean, very proper lady.

'I'm afraid the only room I had vacant is right at the top of the house,' Mrs Forrester said, as she motioned for Jane to follow her.

'Has Mrs Rogers found you a job?' she asked, pausing for breath when they reached the first landing.

'No . . . not yet . . .' Jane said apologetically.

'What kind of work are you going to be looking for?'

'Anything I can get,' she answered honestly. 'I hope they will have something for me at the Labour Exchange.'

'I'll get me hubby to save his evening paper for you. You never know, you might find something in there.'

'Thank you, I'd be very grateful,' Jane said as they reached the third floor.

'Anyhow, there's one thing you've not got to worry about: your rent's paid up for a whole month. That's a blessing, isn't it?'

Jane nodded her head in agreement and was rewarded by a smile from her new landlady.

The room Mrs Forrester showed her into was low-ceilinged and had only two very small windows, but it was cheerfully furnished and seemed cosy, and on looking round, Jane found it to be surprisingly large. There was a narrow single bed, covered with a patchwork quilt, a wickerwork armchair that held two blue cushions, and a low chest of drawers on top of which stood a two-burner gas cooker, a saucepan and a tin kettle. Placed at an angle was a black iron-framed gas fire, beside which stood a gas meter.

'I have put a shilling in the meter,' Mrs Forrester said. 'That will keep the fire going for this evening, and after that you must put your own money in.' Seeing Jane's worried look, she quickly added, 'It does take pennies if you haven't always got a shilling to hand.'

Jane thanked her, though she wasn't feeling very thankful at the moment. Then, turning round, she saw that Mrs Forrester was holding open the door of a cupboard. Inside, a rail ran from side to side holding four coat hangers, and below it were several shelves.

'I hope you will be happy here, lass. You'll find a few bits and pieces of china there, in that small cupboard on the wall,' the landlady said warmly. She had decided that all

Mrs Rogers had told her about this girl was true. She was quietly spoken, clean and tidy, and very polite, and she didn't look as if she was going to be much trouble. Mrs Forrester liked having the rent from the rooms she let, it made a difference to both her and her hubby, but she never wanted to get involved in the comings and goings of her lodgers. If once she started to feel sorry for this young girl – because by the look of her that was all she was – who knows where it would end.

Shaking her head, she made for the door, saying over her shoulder, 'I forgot t' show you where you'll wash. If you'll come back down to the next floor I'll give you a couple of towels and point out which rooms you share the bathroom with.'

Back in her own room, Jane placed the two towels on a shelf in the cupboard, then plonked herself down on the bed.

For several minutes she just sat there, staring at nothing in particular. She couldn't ever remember feeling so lonely. She wanted to cry, but she stopped herself, muttering aloud, 'What good would it do? No one is going to help me. From now on I am on my own and the quicker I get used to the idea the better off I shall be.'

With a heavy sigh, she opened her attaché case and hung her one dress and one skirt up on the rail, placing her underwear, two blouses and a cardigan on the shelves. She had certainly left Winchelsea Lodge with a lot more than she had gone there with.

Daylight was gradually creeping through the curtains and Jane was thankful that the first night was over. She had tossed and turned, going over and over in her mind what she might do. She decided there weren't many options. Top of the list was to find a job. The very thought scared her half to death.

Washed and dressed, she realized she was starving. There wasn't a thing to eat in her room, and not even a spoonful of tea with which to make herself a cuppa. She had heard people moving around and her first attempt to use the bathroom had been unsuccessful because the door was locked.

'That's right.' She was muttering to herself again, for who else was there for her to talk to? 'If you want to eat and drink from now on, you have to go shopping.' Mrs Forrester had said there was a corner shop if she turned right at the top of the road, but she hadn't felt like going out again last night. Now she'd have to; it was either that or starve. God! Going into a shop to buy food, and she'd have to find a dairy if she wanted milk! That was something that had never even entered her head!

By eight thirty she was in Balham High Street. Passing a café, she sniffed, and although she was frightened of spending too much of the money she had been given, she couldn't resist. As she opened the door, the heat hit her. The whole café seemed full of steam, though she could see at a glance that several men were seated at the tables. After hesitating for just a moment, she made her way to the counter and ordered a cup of tea and a bacon sandwich.

'Large tea?' the man who owned the place asked. He was a stocky man in his fifties who was thinking that this young lady was very different from his usual customers.

'Yes please.' Jane smiled her answer.

From a huge brown enamel teapot he filled what looked like a pint pot with scalding strong tea and pushed it across the counter, saying, 'Find yourself a seat, I'll bring your sandwich over when it's ready.'

Jane lingered over the food, enjoying every mouthful, then

finally drained the remains of her tea and went back to the counter to pay her bill.

'That'll be eightpence,' he told her, watching with interest as she produced a florin from her purse.

Giving her her change he held on to her hand much longer than was necessary. He felt sorry for her; she looked frightened, and he wondered why.

'Please could you direct me to the Labour Exchange?' Jane asked.

Ah! So that was it. She was new to these parts and needed a job. 'Course I can, my luv. I'll come to the door and point you in the right direction.'

Jane was grateful. She felt very much better for having eaten something, and it was right what Matron had told her: there were some kind people around who would help her if she could only pluck up enough courage to ask them.

There weren't many applicants in the exchange, and within a quarter of an hour Jane found herself in a wooden cubicle, sitting opposite a middle-aged woman whose hair was dragged back from her face and twisted into a tight bun, which made her look a lot more stern than she probably was.

So many questions! But Jane knew she had to answer them truthfully because she badly needed a job. From her bag she pulled out a letter that Lillian Cooper had had the foresight to write.

'This will explain where I've been living and tell you something about me.' She spoke quietly as she leaned across the counter and handed in the letter.

There was complete silence as the lady clerk read the page and a half of Matron's neat handwriting.

'Hmm. Going to be a bit difficult to place you!' she muttered when she had finished. Then, pulling a long, narrow wooden box in front of her, she quickly ran her fingers through the endless cards that it contained. Only two cards had she pulled out by the time she reached the end of the box. She cleared her throat before settling back in her chair and saying to Jane, 'I've only found two possibilities. The first is for the Sunlight Laundry, in the bag-wash section; then again, maybe not, you don't look particularly robust, and at the end of the day it would mean heaving sacks of damp washing back on to one of their delivery vans.'

Jane looked as bewildered as she felt. She'd never heard of a laundry that did bag-wash! The lady clerk picked the second card up.

'This client is requesting a maid of all work.' She smiled knowingly at Jane. 'That title could cover a multitude of jobs. But I think we'll give you a green card and send you along for an interview. It states that interviews are given between two and three o'clock. It's a big house just off Wandsworth Common, you'll have plenty of time to find it.'

Jane was twisting her hands in her lap and her eyes were lowered.

'Well?'

The one word, barked at her like that, made her jump. 'I'm sorry, I was listening,' Jane said.

'Well, answer me. Are you willing to go along for an interview?'

Doesn't seem as if I've got much choice, was what Jane felt like saying. Instead she softly said, 'If you think I will be suitable.'

'That's for the employers to judge. I'll make you out a card, and to be on the safe side I think you should take this letter along with you. Matron Cooper has been very explicit and it will save you a lot of explanations.'

Once outside the Labour Exchange, Jane decided to take her time and walk towards Wandsworth Common. It was still only a little after eleven o'clock in the morning and the day stretched endlessly before her. Once again she looked at the people in the street, all well wrapped up against the biting-cold wind, hurrying along, no doubt anxious to get home where more than likely someone would be there to greet them. Just watching them made her feel so lonely; yes, that was the word, lonely.

She was sixteen years old. On her own and feeling lost.

She sighed heavily, pulled the belt of her mackintosh more tightly around her waist and slowly began to walk. Thoughts were going round and round in her head, What on earth was she doing here? She knew no one. In fact she couldn't think of a single soul to whom she could turn. Why was she so alone? For almost nine years of her life she had had a mother, father and brother. Sometimes she hadn't been exactly happy, but that didn't seem to matter so much now. At least then her mother had loved her, and Tommy had been such a lovely little boy. Then, almost without warning, she had become the responsibility of the Guardians of the Poor.

Again she asked herself why.

Not that she wasn't grateful to them. Oh, she was. Life had been good at Winchelsea Lodge, once she had accepted the fact that her family had turned their backs on her. But now, no matter which way you looked at it, the same thing had happened all over again.

She agreed with Matron that it wouldn't be fair to let girls stay on in the home once they reached the age of sixteen. Not when there were so many other youngsters needing protection.

But being right didn't make it feel any better for her.

If only she had someone to talk to. It felt rotten to have been turned out. As if, once again, folk were saying, we've done all we're going to do for you. You're on your own from now on. For the second time she had been abandoned. Was that the word? Or was rejected a better one? What did it matter? It all boiled down to the same thing.

No one really wanted her.

When she found the address that was written on the green card, the house was nothing like she had expected it to be. This was a huge building made of red bricks. Not friendly and warm-looking like Winchelsea Lodge. Silly thing to say, but to her it looked cold. It was so plain, no bow windows. Just three large, straight windows on each side of the front door. The second-floor windows were smaller than those on the ground floor, but even these looked enormous. The top row of windows were quite small and Jane guessed these to be the attic rooms, probably only used for staff. The roof was made up of grey slate tiles, with huge chimney pots rearing up almost as if they were turrets on a castle.

A brass plaque on the outside wall noted that the trade entrance was round to the left.

'I suppose I'd better use that door, seeing as how I'd not exactly be classed as a visitor,' she murmured aloud. Then she stood still and added, 'This is getting to be a bad habit, talking out loud to yourself.'

She found a flight of flagstone steps leading down to a heavy oak door that held a black painted lion's-head knocker. Having raised it and knocked quite hard, she stood well back, doing her best to stop her teeth from chattering. It wasn't so much that she was cold, just plain scared as to what would happen next.

A couple of minutes passed before she heard a bolt being

shot and the door was opened. Standing there was a gentleman with a thick head of white hair. She knew he had to
be a gentleman by the good suit he was wearing and the
leather shoes he had on his feet.

Without a word, Jane handed him the letter that Matron
had so thoughtfully provided and the green card which she
had been given at the Labour Exchange.

He glanced only at each side of the card but did not
remove the letter from its envelope. He didn't speak for a
moment but stood looking her over, then said, 'Have you
been in service before?'

'No, sir. Well, not exactly.'

'Either you have or you haven't,' he said, but the voice
was amused and Jane felt herself relax just a little.

'If you would kindly read the letter, sir, it will explain
things properly.'

He laughed. 'Well then, if we are going to do things properly, I had better introduce myself.' He paused, glanced again
at the card, then said, 'Miss Jane Jeffrey, I am Mr Harris.
You had better come in.'

As she followed him down a short passage, her first impression was how dark and cold the house was. The first
room they entered was obviously the kitchen. It was only
half as big as the one she and Nellie had had the run of
at Winchelsea Lodge, yet she was pleased to see that the
black-leaded range was much the same, with a huge oven
to the side and on the top lots of space for kettles and pots
and pans. Then, having found that she was smiling to see
that a good fire was roaring away in the grate, she chided
herself: don't run away with the idea that they'll let you do
any of the cooking even if you do get the job. Maid of all
work it said on the card. And, as the clerk had half insinu-
ated, that would probably mean that she'd be doing all the

hardest and dirtiest jobs that nobody else would stoop to.

'Sit yourself down there.' Mr Harris pointed to a high-backed wooden chair

When she was seated, he stood in front of her, removed the letter from the envelope and read it. 'You've never worked with a family.' It was an observation, made more to himself, and Jane gave no answer. He pursed his lips, half turned away from her, then, quickly swinging back to her again, said, 'You might as well meet the lady of the house, but never let it be said that I didn't warn you: she's not the most even-tempered person you'll be likely to meet.'

Jane swallowed deeply and stared at him. She was surprised when he quickly added, 'It's my sister I'm talking about. Her husband died two years ago, and having just returned to England after working abroad for five years, I made the mistake of coming here to live with Marjorie.'

Jane was even more taken aback now. Should Mr Harris be talking to her like this?

He must have read her thoughts, because he said, 'Sound ungrateful, don't I?' Then he muttered a few more words, but he now had his back to her so Jane didn't quite catch what he said. He half smiled. 'Take your coat off and I'll take you upstairs, you can at least judge for yourself.' Then, as an afterthought, he asked, 'Could you do with a cup of tea?'

Jane didn't know how to answer. She hadn't had a thing since she left the café early this morning. The walk had been far longer than she had expected and every now and then she had sheltered in a shop doorway to get out of the biting wind. So yes, she would love a really hot cup of tea, but it didn't seem right for her to say so.

Mr Harris was no fool. He watched the different expressions flick across the young girl's face and quickly said, 'Of course you could, and so could I. And seeing as how Cook is lying down, we can lay claim to her kitchen.' Whilst saying all this he had been walking round the room, gathering cups and saucers from the dresser, and before very long he had not only made the tea but had produced a Victoria sponge cake from the larder.

They ate and drank in silence, but somehow Jane now felt very much at ease with this strange but friendly gentleman.

'Would you like another slice?' he asked, at the same time sliding a wedge of the sponge cake on to her plate.

She looked at him and they both laughed as he said, 'The strawberry jam inside is very nice, isn't it? I think I will have a second piece too.'

Then, with their plates cleared and their cups drained, he said, 'Well now, I think I'd better go and see if Mrs Bonneford will see you.'

In his absence Jane felt the silence. Winchelsea Lodge was never this quiet. It always rang with the sound of children's voices and laughter. Oh yes, there weren't many days when laughter wasn't heard, and how she was missing it!

A short while later the kitchen door opened and Mr Harris came back into the room and beckoned to her. He led the way down the dark passage and up a narrow flight of uncarpeted stairs into what she presumed was the main entrance hall.

Now this area was cold! There was a stone floor with just a couple of rugs placed one each side of a big round table. There was a fireplace, a huge one with a marble surround, over which hung an enormous gilt-framed mirror. How long since a fire had been lit in that grate? Jane was asking herself. Many a long day, she decided, because there were no dead ashes, just dust. In fact everywhere she looked could do with a good clean-up.

Mr Harris was crossing the hall now, and Jane followed him up the staircase. Halfway up, she stopped to get her bearings. It was a beautiful staircase divided into two, with one flight branching off to the left and the other to the right. She had never before seen anything like this.

They had reached the first landing now, and what a difference!

Mr Harris opened a door and stood back, allowing her to enter the room first. Her breath caught in her throat. It was a beautiful room. Light, airy and best of all warm. And why wouldn't it be, for a brilliant log fire was crackling away, sending sparks flying up the chimney. The furniture was old, but even at first glance Jane knew that whoever was responsible for keeping this part of the house clean was doing an excellent job. The chairs and sofas were all the same colour, a kind of dove grey, with cushions and curtains being pale blue. The carpet on the floor was so thick that Jane felt her feet would sink in it. She was still standing just inside the doorway and hadn't noticed there was a woman sitting near the window, until the lady rose and turned to look at her.

Just looking at her face was a surprise, because if, as Mr Harris had said, she was his sister, then she must be years older than he was. She could easily have been mistaken for his mother!

'Marjorie, this is Jane . . . Jane Jeffrey.'

His manner and even his voice sounded stiff. Not at all like the friendly gentleman he had been when they were downstairs in the kitchen.

'I gave you the letter to read, it tells you quite a lot about her.' He stepped right back as he finished speaking, as if he wanted to get out of his sister's way.

'How old are you?' The words were said sharply. But then everything about this lady seemed kind of sharp. Her mouth was small, her face long and thin, her nose pointed. The nicest thing about her was her hair. It hung loose down her back, long, jet black and very silky. Oh, her clothes were also beautiful. A long pale-lilac dress with a soft loose matching coat that was left unbuttoned to reveal the embroidery adorning the hem of both dress and coat.

'Sixteen.' Jane got the word out eventually.

'Sixteen what?' Sharp words again.

Jane was puzzled, almost frightened, and she made no answer, but dropped her gaze to stare at the floor.

'When you speak to me you will address me as madam. So what you should have answered was, "Sixteen years old, madam."' Now she had a finger stretched out straight, pointing at Jane, and she added, 'Or you could use my title, which is Mrs Bonneford, do you understand?'

'Yes . . . madam.'

'That's better. They haven't taught you much, this home where you've been cared for for the past seven years.'

It was a long time since Jane had lost her temper, but right now she was very tempted to answer back. However, as she bit her tongue, she turned her glance to see that Mr Harris was gently shaking his head at her and half smiling. That kind gesture was enough to put the brakes on.

And then she was glad she hadn't been cheeky, because suddenly the lady smiled and said quite nicely, 'Well now, we know where we stand, don't we? I'm still not sure that you are up to doing the rough work that will be required of you, but we'll give you a month's trial. Can you start straight away? Would you like Mr Harris to show you where you will be sleeping?'

Panic bells were ringing in Jane's head. She hadn't referred to him as her brother, only as Mr Harris. What did that tell her? And again, if she were to give up the room in which she had only spent one night and things did not work out here, where would she go? It would be like burning her bridges.

'Please . . . madam . . .'

'Well, girl, what is it? Didn't the Labour Exchange tell you the hours, and that the wages are six shillings a week paid monthly, and on top of that all your food will be provided?'

'Yes, they did . . . madam, but it's about the room. Arrangements were made for me, at least for the time being. I only moved in yesterday and my rent has been paid for a month.'

'That's no problem if it's what you prefer. Just remember you have to be here by seven o'clock in the morning.'

'Yes, madam, thank you.'

As she said those four words, Jane felt, at least for the time being, that her fate had been sealed. She should be feeling grateful. She had a job and all her meals would be provided. So why were her lips trembling, and why did she still keep getting the urge to cry?

'Very well, you can start the day after tomorrow; that will give you a little time to get yourself sorted.' Mrs Bonneford turned from Jane and glanced at her brother.

'You can outline the tasks we shall expect her to do, and fix it up with Ada about her uniform, her day off and such-like. Oh, and by the way, give her sixpence to pay her tram fare back to her lodgings. Can't expect her to walk, it will be quite dark soon.'

Jane was flabbergasted!

That woman certainly was a mixture!

Out on the landing, they had moved away from the door before Mr Harris stopped and, looking her straight in the face, said, 'My sister can seem very kind at times, and at others she will appear hard. Just remember, whatever her mood, she very rarely allows anyone to be fully aware of her true colours.' He stared at her for a moment longer before starting down the staircase.

Jane shook her head.

Now what was she supposed to make of that?

Chapter Eight

BY THE TIME Jane was back in Balham High Street, it was gone four o'clock. Mrs Bonneford had been right: already it was almost dark. She longed to get back to her rented room and light the gas fire, for it was not only cold now, it was actually snowing. But before she could turn her footsteps towards Chestnut Grove, she had to tackle the problem of buying some food. She didn't think she was likely to find a dairy around these parts, but there were several grocery shops. The first one to hand was the Home & Colonial. Having taken a deep breath and pushed open the heavy door to the shop, she knew immediately that she had made a wise choice. The man who stood behind the polished wooden counter was in his forties, thin, with a balding head and a waxed moustache on his upper lip, and he was wearing a navy-blue and white bibbed apron.

His welcoming smile and enquiry as to how he might help her went a long way towards making Jane feel a little more secure about what she was going to purchase.

'Please,' she began, but then had to clear her throat before saying, 'May I have a quarter of a pound of tea and . . . do you sell milk?'

He looked curiously at this slight young lass who seemed almost at a loss for words. In the normal way of things he would have asked a customer which type of tea she preferred. But not in this case. He sensed the girl was not used to shopping and he placed a packet of the most popular tea on the counter before saying, 'No, miss, I'm sorry, we don't stock fresh milk. We leave that to the dairyman, who does two rounds during the day, but we do sell condensed milk, Funnels is a very good make,' he added, placing a small blue and white tin beside the the packet of tea.

Jane thought that would do very well – Nellie always kept condensed milk in the cupboard as a standby at Winchelsea Lodge – but then a thought struck her. Would there be such a thing as a tin-opener in her room? Well, she'd soon find out, wouldn't she?

'Can I get you anything else, miss?'

Jane felt she would have like to say, yes please, something for my dinner, but she didn't dare, so she said, 'Just some crackers and a small piece of cheese, please.'

While she watched the man cut into a huge round of Cheddar cheese, using a very thin wire with a wooden handle on each end, her thoughts were running along the lines that at least she had found herself a job without too much trouble, and that from the day after tomorrow she would have her food provided and wouldn't have to worry about what she was going to buy or how she was going to cook it.

'May I suggest a small pat of butter?' The enquiry broke into her thoughts.

'Yes . . . Thank you.'

Now he smiled at her and made a great show of dipping his two wooden butter platters into a bowl of water. He eased a small amount of butter from a large mound and deftly shaped it into a neat round, then pressed what looked to Jane like a silver letter-opener against the pat that he had formed. Laying the pat of butter on a sheet of greaseproof paper, he held it out for Jane's inspection.

He was rewarded by a wide grin. For in the centre of her butter was the impression of a perfect Scotch thistle.

'Will that be all?' The grocer smiled back at her, and when she nodded her head, he totted up the five items and told her the total was one shilling exactly.

Jane offered him half a crown and he gave her one shilling and sixpence change. As he did so, another thought came to her mind. She quickly held out the sixpence and, with her cheeks flushing red, blurted out, 'Please could you spare me six pennies.'

He took the sixpence from her cold fingers and his heart went out to her. His fears were confirmed when she said, almost beneath her breath, 'I need them for the gas meter.'

The grocer was so touched, he did something he did not normally do. Picking up the brown paper bag in which he had packed her few bits of shopping, he came around to her side of the counter and held the door open for her.

When she said, 'Thank you very much,' he answered her, 'You're more than welcome. Good night, miss.'

He did not turn and go straight back into his shop, but leant his head forward and watched as Jane, head down, battled her way along the high street. He shivered, for the snow was coming down so thickly now that it blotted out everything only a yard or so in front of him.

'My God!' he muttered to himself. 'Me wife and I have a lot t' be thankful for. On a night like this, that lass is going home to crackers and a bit of cheese, and how long will her six pennies last in a gas meter?'

Life wasn't fair, he mused as he closed the shop door. It really wasn't.

Jane was frozen to the bone by the time she walked into the house in Chestnut Grove. Mrs Forrester waited while she stamped the snow from her shoes before asking, 'How did you get on today?'

Jane untied her scarf, which she had been forced to tie over her head to keep her ears warm, and rolled it into a ball. She was frightened it might drip on to her landlady's polished lino, because it was sopping wet where the snow had soaked through.

'I got a job,' she said, her teeth chattering. 'I'm to be a maid of all work in a big house near Wandsworth Common.'

'I don't much like the sound of that,' Mrs Forrester said, pulling a face. 'Do they want you to live in?'

'Yes, they did. But as they were taking me on a month's trial, I said I would prefer to stay here in my room, seeing as how the rent has been paid for me.'

'You've a good head on your shoulders, lass, that was a wise decision. Don't do to burn yer bridges till you've crossed over.'

While talking, Jane was edging towards the stairs. She didn't want to stand here talking, not that it wasn't nice and warm in the hall, but her legs were aching and she really wanted to make herself a cup of tea.

Reaching the second floor, she noticed the door to the bathroom was wide open, so she went in, closed the door and took off her mackintosh, which was soaking wet. She shook it over the bath and hung it up behind the door. Then, having used the toilet, she went on up to her room. Two minutes later she was back down with her tin kettle, which she half filled from the cold tap over the washbasin.

Back upstairs she struck a match, lit one of the jets on the small gas stove and placed the kettle on to boil. Now another match had to be struck and held against the flimsy gas mantle in order to give herself some light in the room. With a third match she lit the gas fire, thinking to herself: at this rate my six pennies aren't going to last for long. Only now could she close the door to her room, because she no longer needed the light from the gas jet on the landing to shine in and allow her to see what she was doing.

Now, one cup and saucer, one plate and a knife, and was there . . . She fumbled around at the back of the small drawer, and heaved a great sigh of relief as her fingers closed around a metal tin-opener.

Thank God she wouldn't have to drink her tea without any milk!

One thing she was determined on: as soon as she had eaten her biscuits and cheese, she was going to get into bed. At least there she would be able to stretch her legs out and hopefully get warm. She was feeling very tired now, exhausted in fact, yet in an odd sort of way she felt she had achieved a lot today. Despite all her misgivings she had found herself a job. Whether she would suit her new mistress was another matter!

She'd have to wait and see, wouldn't she?

It was midday before Jane decided to venture out. She had sat near the window of her room for more than an hour. Sitting down, she couldn't see below into the street, but she did have a good view of house tops, and in the distance the spire of a very old church rose high towards the grey sky. The snow lay thick, making everything seem not only a brilliant white but silent. Dead silent from where she was sitting in this top room all on her own.

Having wrapped herself up warmly, she came down the stairs and let herself out of the front door without seeing a soul.

She was going to be very brave and very extravagant!

She was going back to the café where she had had breakfast yesterday, and she was going to buy herself a hot dinner.

Oh, the pavements and the roads were treacherous. It must have frozen after the snow had stopped falling, and folk were having a job to keep upright, because every surface was so slippery. With difficulty she made it to the café, but as she opened the door she stumbled and actually fell in through the doorway. There was no shortage of men to help her; they left their food and came to her aid. Her right leg had buckled under her and was hurting badly as these kind, willing hands did their best to help her to her feet and on to a chair.

After a few minutes in which she took several deep breaths, she went to rise and go to the counter, but when the proprietor who had been so kind to her yesterday called out, 'Sit where you are, I'll bring you over a large tea,' she obeyed him without a murmur. Minutes later, he handed her a mug of tea and said, 'Let me 'ave a look at that leg,' and she made no protest as he straightened out her leg, lifted her foot and placed it on a second chair.

'Your shoes, that's the trouble, just look at this one.' He flapped the sole of her shoe, which had broken loose from the upper. 'You ought t' be wearing boots on a day like this,' he muttered, shaking his head and slipping her shoe off her foot at the same time. 'I'll see what can be done about this.'

'What? . . . Oh, thank you.'

'Were you intending to have something to eat?'

'Yes, I was. To tell you the truth,' her voice dropped to a whisper, 'I'm ever so hungry.'

'Well you've come to the right place. We've two specials today, me missus 'as gone mad. You can 'ave toad in the 'ole, or steak an' kidney pudding.'

Jane's mouth watered as she quickly said, 'May I have the steak an' kidney pudding, please?'

The proprietor went off grinning to himself and taking Jane's shoe with him.

She sipped at her tea. If it had been anywhere else that she had slipped because of her shoe she would have been embarrassed, but this café owner was a very nice man. Footwear had been a problem the whole time she had been at Winchelsea Lodge. Only once had she ever had a brand-new pair of shoes, and that was in the summer when she had been twelve years old. Even then they hadn't been real shoes, just sandals.

The tea was great, much stronger than she was used to, but it was warming her through right down to the soles of her feet. She let her mind wander.

If this job did turn out to be any good she knew what she was going to buy as soon as she had managed to save enough money. A pair of boots. Yes, a brand-new pair of boots!

Her dinner was placed in front of her and she ate every morsel. It reminded her a bit of the big stews that they used to have at Winchelsea Lodge, which made her long to be back there. At this moment she would have given anything to see Mrs Rogers again. And how about Matron? Just a glimpse of her hurrying down the stairs but never in such a hurry that she hadn't got time to smile and give a cheery wave. A sight of any of the other girls would be so nice. What were they all doing at this moment? At least they had company, which was a lot more than she had.

Would she ever get used to being lonely?

'Good girl,' the café owner said as he picked up Jane's

empty dinner plate. 'Now, what would you like for yer pudding?'

Jane was flustered by the question. She hadn't intended to have anything else to eat because she didn't want to spend too much money. There was at least four weeks to go before she would receive any more. And then only if she lasted that long in this new job.

'Look, lass, the price of the dinner is one an' tuppence, and that includes yer cup of tea and a pudding, so you might as well 'ave the lot,' he told her, sensing straight off that she was counting her pennies. 'There's college pudding an' custard, or apple pie an' custard.'

Jane hesitated, then, seeing he was smiling broadly, she too smiled and quickly said, 'I would love some apple pie and custard, please.'

When he came back and placed a bowl that was brim full in front of her he casually remarked, 'By the way, Sid the totter has just come in our back gate; he buys an' sells everything, 'as a scrap yard not far from here. As luck would 'ave it, he saw me trying t' mend your shoe and said he took on board several items from one of the big 'ouses this morning an' he thinks he's got a pair of button-up boots that might just fit you.' He saw the embarrassed look that came to Jane's face and added quickly, 'That's if you ain't too proud to . . .'

He didn't have to finish the sentence, because Jane was clutching at his hand and doing her best to tell him how grateful she was.

She was in no hurry to go out again into the bitter weather. She took her time eating the apple pie, savouring every mouthful, and it was nearly half an hour later when from behind the counter the café owner beckoned for her to come and join him.

'I'm Harriet, his wife.' A thin woman who was standing at the door of a large kitchen nodded her head towards the proprietor. 'And if he ain't told yer already, he's Jack. Come in, come in.' The woman was bending towards Jane, her face showing a great big smile. 'Sit yerself down . . . Aw lass, I forgot you've hurt yer leg an' you've only got one shoe on.'

Harriet hurried to give Jane a hand as she hobbled further into the kitchen and sat down on what appeared to be the one and only chair. Then she nodded towards a man who looked so very much like herself that Jane thought they must surely be brother and sister. 'Sid 'ere 'as found that pair of boots, if yer want to try them on.'

Sid was a weedy-looking man, red-faced, with thinning grey hair, but as he caught Jane's glance he gave a such a nice smile that she at once felt at ease. ''Ere yer are, me dear,' he said in a true cockney accent, holding aloft a pair of brown boots that to say the least looked as if they could do with a jolly good cleaning. Before Jane had the chance to say a word he was on his knees in front of her and very gently easing off her remaining shoe. His hands were grubby but they worked swiftly as he loosened the long laces of one of the boots, pulled back the leather tongue and helped her to put her foot inside. Then he did exactly the same with the other boot.

'Can yer stand up, gal?'

Jane did just that, and as she waggled her toes about inside the boots she grinned. 'Oh my goodness,' she said beneath her breath, 'they feel gorgeous. The lining is so soft and warm.'

She took a few steps, and Sid, Harriet and even Jane herself laughed. It was obvious the boots were at least two sizes too big for her small feet.

'Never mind that,' Harriet said, and pulling a dresser

drawer open she rummaged inside for a few minutes and came up with two inner soles. They were not a matching pair but what did that matter! Jane wouldn't have cared if one had been green and the other sky-blue pink.

'They won't make that much difference,' Sid said mournfully.

'Hold yer 'orses, you. Time I've given 'er a pair of Jack's socks to wear, she'll manage all right. I'll find a real thick pair and she can lace them boots up nice and tight. And you, me lad, can set to and give 'em a damn good clean.' This last remark was fired straight at Sid, who was looking very pleased with himself.

Jane couldn't believe it. She looked from one to the other and did not know what to say. She was smiling. For the first time since she had left the safety of Winchelsea Lodge, she was talking to people who were acting as if they had known her for a long time; as though they really cared about her. And that was a very good reason for her to be smiling.

'Well now, what are you going to do with yourself for the rest of the day?' Harriet put the question kindly to Jane, and when the answer was slow in coming she added quickly, 'Jack has mended your shoe, but it won't stand up to this weather, and Sid will be a little while cleaning up yer boots. Would yer like t' stay here an' give me an 'and? I can let yer 'ave the lend of me fluffy slippers. And I'll find yer a pinny.'

Jane looked anxiously at her benefactor and very quietly said, 'You don't have to do all this for me.'

'No, I know we don't, gal, but 'ave yer never 'eard it said what goes round comes round? Who knows when me or Jack, or even Sid, come t' that, is gonna need an 'elping 'and?'

'But Sid . . .' Jane hesitated at having used the man's

Christian name, 'he hasn't told me how much he is selling the boots for.'

''Ave you decided to stay here for a while and get stuck in on that sink full of dishes?' Harriet asked, pointing a finger towards a wooden draining board piled high with dirty plates.

'Well . . . yes.'

'Then we'll call it payment in full.'

At that moment Jack put his head round the door and was more than pleased to see that his missus and this little waif and stray that they seemed to have taken under their wing were laughing happily together.

For the rest of the day, Jane stood with her hands deep in soap suds washing an endless stream of crockery that kept coming from the café. Yet she was happy. Happier than she had been for the past two days.

Sharp at three o'clock she was ordered to sit down. Two huge toasted teacakes and another large tea were set in front of her, and this time she ate in the kitchen with Harriet for company. All Jane could think of was that she had landed on her feet.

She wouldn't have any need to go shopping today. She'd eaten more than enough to keep her going until tomorrow, when she would start her new job.

It was getting dark and the snow was starting to fall again as Jane said goodbye to her benefactors. She looked down at her now well-shod feet: shiny brown leather boots, high boots that came right up her leg to just below her knee, with a double row of buttons and laces which criss-crossed from one side to the other. A few yards on she turned her head quickly and glanced over her shoulder, and who was still standing in the doorway of the café but Jack and Harriet. Until yesterday she had never set eyes on either of them.

Now, because of their kindness and generosity, she had been well fed and kept warm all day, and was walking away wearing a pair of boots that would have taken her a whole year of Sundays to save up enough money to buy.

And to top that, her feet were warm inside because she was wearing a thick pair of socks that had belonged to Jack.

Unbelievable, wasn't it?

Life was strange.

Even funny, if you stopped to think about it.

Chapter Nine

IT WAS A nervous and subdued Jane that knocked on the heavy oak door at ten minutes to seven in the morning. She had lost the sparkle that had come so readily to her eyes yesterday.

'I'm Clemmy Morris.' A big-boned, wide-shouldered girl spoke in a friendly voice to Jane as they walked down the dark passage. 'I'm really pleased that you're starting here today. We've been without below-stairs help for three weeks now and a lot of the heavy work has fallen to me.'

That statement didn't do much to cheer Jane up. If this big girl thought the work was heavy, how was she herself going to cope?

The kitchen door was pushed open and the heat hit Jane immediately. She felt so thankful. She had left Chestnut Grove at five minutes past six and by the time she'd got here she was frozen to her very bones.

'This is Mrs Stratton, Cook to most of us in the house,' Clemmy said as she took Jane's mackintosh and hung it up in a cupboard. Mrs Stratton looked the typical cook:

short, dumpy, with a big bosom and rosy cheeks.

'Suppose yer could do with a cup of tea,' Cook said, and without waiting for an answer she pushed a big cup across the scrubbed tabletop, then, turning swiftly to the fireplace, took up from the hob a big enamel teapot. The tea in the pot must have been boiling, because it spluttered out of the spout as she poured it into the cup. Then she handed Jane a sugar basin, saying, 'Help yerself, you'll need to fortify yerself before you go upstairs to see 'er ladyship.'

As Jane sipped her tea, she was thinking that Mrs Bonneford had mentioned that it would be a person named Ada who would see to her uniform. It seemed that there were quite a number of people working in this household. She wondered how many family members there were besides the missus and her brother, Mr Harris.

'You won't get your uniform until Mrs Daniels comes in tomorrow,' Clemmy said, getting to her feet and indicating that Jane should follow her. 'She's left you an overall which will serve you for today.'

Seeing Jane hadn't quite understood, Clemmy explained: 'Ada Daniels is a widow. She comes here twice a week to do the washing and the ironing, sometimes three days if there are visitors staying in the house. I was told to set you on cleaning the main hall as soon as you arrived, so I'll show you where the the cleaning materials are kept.'

Jane followed Clemmy through the dark passageway, up the uncarpeted stairs and into the dreary-looking cold hall. She was certainly being thrown in at the deep end, was what she was thinking as she donned a dark-brown coat-like overall and wondered where she should start. The first thing she would have liked to do was light a fire in that massive hearth, but she supposed that was too much to ask for.

★　★　★

It took Jane a full week to get into the swing of things, and each day the tasks she was given seemed to be harder and dirty than the previous ones. From the minute she arrived in the morning until she left in the evening she was on the go all the time, with the exception of the thirty minutes allowed for her lunch. Her one consolation was Mrs Stratton, the cook. Though she presented a rough exterior and a loud voice, they covered a heart of gold, or at least they did where Jane was concerned. She put in front of Jane meals that were fit for a king. She also saw that there was a kettle of hot water at the ready so that Jane could have a good wash before she left for home.

Jane did most jobs without a word of protest. After all, she had known before she came here that she was to be a maid of all work. Yet her first task each morning was one that stuck in her gullet.

She had to attend Mrs Bonneford in her bedroom, which meant lugging a huge can of hot water all the way up the main staircase, then pouring it into a china bowl which was placed on a side table in order that her mistress could wash herself while remaining in bed. Meanwhile, Jane emptied the slop pail before going about whatever other tasks had been allotted to her for the day.

Then, when Clemmy blew a whistle, she had to come back up the stairs and carry the now dirty water back downstairs. All right, she was getting paid to do these tasks. But the fact was that Clemmy, being Mrs Bonneford's personal maid, was in the room all the time, always in full uniform: neat black dress, white starched apron and cap. Sometimes she would walk beside Jane in her drab grey uniform as she struggled either up or down the stairs with the water can, but never once did she offer to take a turn at carrying it.

Jane hadn't seen very much of Mr Harris, but the few

occasions they had met had reinforced her impression that he was a kind man. A true gentleman. Whereas his sister had never once uttered the words 'thank you'.

It was on the Thursday of the second week that Jane began to feel she was being asked to do too much. The minute Ada Daniels had arrived she had put what she called the white washing in to soak while she lit the fire beneath the copper. Then, calling for Jane to help her, they had dragged the long tin bath into the outhouse and all the coloured things had gone into that, together with a handful of soapflakes that had been grated off the big bar of yellow soap.

'All right, Jane, I'll manage nicely on me own now, you get yerself back indoors. I'm sure you've more than enough t' cope with.' Ada Daniels spoke kindly, for her heart went out to this young lass who she felt was being put upon rotten. Still, so far the lass seemed to be coping pretty well. But wait till the missus lost her temper. If Jane should be anywhere near when that had happened, then Gawd help her. The missus in a temper was not a pretty sight. In fact, if it were left to me, Ada was thinking, I'd say outright she should be put away in an asylum for some of the terrible things I've seen her do over the years. Jane walked thankfully back into the house. She was working in a bedroom on the first floor, doing her best to remove a stain from the carpet and not making a very good job of it, because she thought it was red wine which had probably been spilt the night before and allowed to soak in. Just as she had straightened up to take a breather, that was when she heard the scream and the commotion that followed.

She let it pass over her head and got on with what she was doing. Until she heard three sharp blasts on the whistle and knew she was being summoned.

Ada Daniels had slipped on the cobbles and banged her head hard and hurt her back.

Mrs Bonneford, dressed in full finery, stood several feet away from Jane and stared at her with a very odd smile on her face. Her weird expression had Jane feeling something was about to happen. It wasn't that she was afraid of her mistress. But she certainly was wary of her. Whenever Mrs Bonneford spoke directly to Jane, which wasn't very often, her words were always sharp, and although Jane tried to tell herself that it was just the woman's way, she knew it wasn't. She treats me like dirt and that's the truth of it, Jane admitted to herself.

'Jane, hurry and finish what you were doing and then take over from Ada. The washing has to be done, come what may, so don't be making any bones about it.' All this was said quickly before Mrs Bonneford made a dramatic departure from the room.

Jane just shook her head. This woman could not be civil if she tried.

She didn't think she would ever come to like her mistress.

As if reading her mind, Mr Harris, who had been standing behind his sister, said, 'Don't let her get to you. If she thinks she's got you cowed, she'll always be on at you.' He paused and smiled broadly at her as he added, 'But somehow, Jane, I think given the chance she might find she's met her match in you.'

Jane didn't answer, because if she had said what was really going through her mind she would surely have been shown the front door there and then.

Having been told by Cook what needed to be done, Jane got started.

Using the big ribbed wooden board, she scrubbed and then boiled the entire mass of washing that had been put in to soak. The steam from the copper was awful as she leant over, using a thick stick to lift each item out of the boiling water and then drop the next lot in. Every now and again she had to get down on her knees, open the little door at the base of the copper and feed into it more kindling in order to keep the water at boiling point.

Her hair was stuck to her head, her clothing to her body. She wasn't damp, she was soaking wet!

Now for the next stage, and by God, she murmured, that was the worst of the lot. Outside in the yard, especially after the heat of the outhouse, it was freezing cold. But it was out here that the great ugly-looking mangle stood. She took the oilskin cover off and stared in horror at the enormous wooden rollers and the mighty iron handle that she had to turn and keep on turning in order to squeeze all the water from the washed linen. It should be a job for two people, Jane was thinking to herself, as she did her best to fold the sheets and feed them between the rollers. 'God knows how I'm going to get this lot dry,' she muttered out loud, and nearly jumped out of her skin when Mr Harris's voice answered her.

'I've got a couple of lads coming in from the gardens to put up some clothes lines, one here in the outhouse and two in the big shed. I'll also get the gardener's wife to come and help you peg them up.' He patted her shoulder, saying, 'You've done a good job,' before turning and going back towards the house.

Jane sighed heavily. That was kind of him, yet it hadn't made her feel much better. Why? Because Cook had been out to tell her that Ada had been taken home on one of the carts because she couldn't straighten her back and so she wouldn't be turning up for work for some time.

When finally Jane left the house that evening, her legs

felt they could hardly carry her and every bone in her body ached.

Cook had said, 'Good night, luv, see yer tomorrow.'

Tomorrow! That held a lot of promise. A huge mountain of damp washing that would need to be ironed, and there wouldn't be any prizes for guessing who would get the job.

At ten o'clock the following morning, Jane was in the outhouse, and she didn't know how she was still standing on her feet. She had had an awful night. Before going to bed she would have given anything to have lain in a hot bath, but she had no idea how to work the geyser in the bathroom. She had put a shilling in the gas meter in her room and hung her clothes on the back of a chair because they had still felt so damp. That hadn't done much to improve things; the room had merely become very steamy.

It had taken a real effort to get herself to work this morning, and Cook had kindly said that she could tackle the ironing in the kitchen. That was fine. Heating the flat irons on the range, it was quite a pleasant task. But, feeling nicely warm, she had to make regular trips to the outhouse in order to fold the linen and bring it back into the house. Outside it was still freezing, and the outhouse was not only very cold but thoroughly damp.

Now she couldn't understand what was happening to her. It felt as if a tight band was wrapped around her chest and that two or three hammers were beating away inside her head as she moved the flat iron backwards and forwards across the surface of a linen sheet.

Clemmy had taken Mrs Bonneford's breakfast up on a tray some time ago, and although she was half expecting it, Jane jumped when she heard the shrill whistle.

She up-ended the iron on the corner of the range and

limped out of the kitchen, dragging herself up the stairs and into her mistress's bedroom. Mrs Bonneford was sitting up in bed, a pale-pink bed-jacket trimmed with swan's down draped around her shoulders, but it was Clemmy who said, 'You may remove the mistress's tray and bring the hot water up now.'

Going towards the bed to lift the tray from the bedside table, Jane glanced at Mrs Bonneford's face. The look on it was one of sheer disgust.

Jane took a step backwards, looking down at herself. Oh my goodness! she thought. She had forgotten to remove the sacking apron she had tied around herself in order to keep her body from coming in direct contact with the damp washing.

'How dare you come into my bedroom dressed like that!' Mrs Bonneford's voice was loud and harsh.

They stared at each other for a moment. Then her mistress was screaming at her: 'Get out, you're little more than a slut. Go on, do as I tell you, get out.'

Jane was so flustered, she dropped the tray.

The clatter it made was deafening. All hell was suddenly let loose.

Mrs Bonneford was using her fists to beat on the bedside table, emphasizing every word. Jane was pleading that she had come quickly in answer to the whistle and hadn't thought to get changed.

Mrs Bonneford would have none of it. 'Who do you think you are talking to, girl? I knew we should never have offered you employment. Dragged up, that's what you've been, in a home for unwanted children, but even they turned you out.'

How she got out of the room Jane never knew. She stood at the top of the stairs, blinded by tears, and didn't know how she was going to get down them. What that awful woman had said was so hurtful. She had not been dragged up. Everyone at Winchelsea Lodge had loved and cherished her. And from them she had learned about decency and kindness, dignity and courage. They had become her family. She *had* been wanted. They had truly loved her.

She tried to take a deep breath but the pain in her chest was too much.

She must get back downstairs. She lifted a foot, but her leg was so stiff she failed to find a step. She was going forward, falling, tumbling, and then suddenly she didn't care.

She felt her body go limp and then there were no more aches or pains.

Cook had heard her fall and came running immediately. She knelt beside her on the floor, trying hard to get her to open her eyes, to say something.

It was a few minutes before Jane did open her eyes. Cook breathed, 'Thank God,' as she touched the girl's face, but was troubled when she felt how dry and hot her cheeks were.

'You'll have to go home, Jane, no one can expect you to work, not the state that you're in,' she was saying when, looking up, she saw that Mr Harris was there.

'Let's get her up and into the kitchen,' he said, putting his hands under Jane's shoulders and endeavouring to get her up on to her feet.

'Is she going t' be all right? What ever happened upstairs? I could hear the mistress shouting from down here. Hadn't we better call a doctor?'

Jane was too dazed and too tired to even bother to answer.

Finally they had got her into the warmth of the kitchen and settled into a big armchair, which Mr Harris had drawn up close to the range. 'Cook, make her a hot drink and put lots of sugar into it. I'll be back as soon as I can.' At the doorway he paused, saying, 'Make sure she drinks it.'

When Cook offered Jane a cup of hot chocolate, she couldn't even hold it. She was shaking from head to foot. She felt so ill, but it no longer mattered to her. She was tired. All she wanted was to go to sleep and she didn't care if she never woke up again!

Cook supported her with one arm as she held the cup to Jane's lips.

'Come on, dearie, sip it for me, it will help to make you feel a whole lot better.'

Jane did her best to smile, but at this moment she couldn't think of a single thing that would make her feel any better.

She closed her eyes and slept.

She wasn't even aware that a doctor had bent over her and confirmed Mr Harris's fears by saying, 'This young lady has influenza and should be put to bed straight away.'

Cook cried as she listened. Too much had been asked of the lass!

'We can't keep her here.' Mr Harris voiced the words out loud.

Mrs Stratton had every sympathy with him. There was no need for him to explain further. If he were to attempt to keep Jane here and attend to her needs, he would be answerable to his sister. And the good Lord knew what that would mean. His own life would be made intolerable. She had seen it all before!

But that didn't alter the fact that Jane did have to be put to bed.

Mr Harris was shrugging himself into his overcoat and had reached for his hat before he spoke. 'I'll walk along to the corner and flag down a cab.' Then, seeing the astonishment on Cook's face, he heaved a great sigh and asked quietly. 'Do we have any alternative?'

Slowly she shook her head.

'Well, I'll give the cab driver her address and tip him enough to see her to the door.'

Cook heaved up her bosom and was about to say something when Mr Harris held up his hand and again spoke in little more than a whisper. 'Whatever it is you are thinking about me can't make me feel any worse than I already do. So, please, wake her up, get Clemmie to help you put her coat on, and between you get her to the back door.'

Cook woke Jane very gently and tried to get her to take a few more sips from her hot drink. Jane had neither the the desire nor the strength to swallow. She looked ill and her eyes were glazed . . .

'I have to get out of this house,' was all she managed to croak through dry lips.

Cook held her hand when she and Clemmie finally got her to the door. Looking at Jane sadly, she said, 'I wish there was some way I could take care of you, but if I lose this job I've nowhere to go. I will say one thing, though, you're well out of it here. You'll get better and find a much better job. You will, you'll see. Goodbye, lass.'

Jane did her best to squeeze Cook's hand.

She was too emotional to say anything.

Chapter Ten

WHEN THE CAB drew up at the corner of the street, it was raining hard, more like a freezing sleet and was still bitterly cold. Jane struggled to put one foot in front of the other. Only a few yards and she would be home. She tried to fix her eyes ahead; she had to get into the house.

The sight of Mrs Forrester coming towards her, holding a big umbrella, was enough to reduce Jane to tears.

It was to be many days before Jane realized just how good a friend her landlady had turned out to be.

Not only had Mrs Forrester helped her up the stairs, undressed her and got her into bed. She had also packed a hot-water bottle on each side of her, fed enough coins into the gas meter to keep it burning continually, and sat with her throughout the night. Jane had been delirious the whole time, shouting unintelligibly and muttering about things and people that Mrs Forrester had no knowledge of. The girl was running a high temperature, there was no doubt about that, and the landlady had been at her wits' end, not knowing what to do for the best. The minute it was daylight she had urged her husband to fetch a doctor.

The doctor had suggested that poultices be applied to Jane's chest and back at regular intervals, and had left a bottle of horrible bitter-tasting medicine to be given three times each day. It had been an almost impossible task to get Jane to swallow even a few drops; as Mrs Forrester spooned it into her mouth, it dribbled down her chin.

It was now the third day and Jane did not seem to be improving. Mrs Forrester decided she could not bear the responsibility on her own any longer. What if the child should die? Her own question frightened her. As soon as the doctor walked through the front door, she handed him a sheet of paper on which she had written the address of Winchelsea Lodge and the name Mrs Elsie Rogers.

'Please,' she begged. 'Will you get in touch with her? It was Mrs Rogers who came here and inspected the house and who paid a month's rent in advance for Jane. I do feel she should at least accept some of the responsibility.'

'Calm down, Mrs Forrester,' the doctor urged. 'You've coped remarkably well. Done your very best. Over and above the call of duty, I would say. So yes, you leave it with me.'

She offered him her heartfelt thanks. It would be a relief to have someone else involved in the girl's welfare.

Elsie Rogers did not waste any time. It was late in the evening of the same day when she appeared on Mrs Forrester's doorstep.

'How is she?' Elsie asked gently, fearing the worst, because she could tell from the look on Mrs Forrester's face that Jane couldn't be any better.

'Come an' see for yourself. I'm at me wits' end. I just can't think of anything else that we could do for her.'

But even that statement did not lead Elsie to expect to find Jane looking so dreadful. In these few days the illness seemed to have really taken its toll. Her face was grey, her cheeks sunken, and she was burning hot. As the two woman leant over the bed, the front door bell rang.

'It's all right, my husband will answer that,' Mrs Forrester said, straightening up. 'More than likely it is the doctor, he said he would call back this evening.'

Minutes later the bedroom door was pushed open and Mrs Forrester was making the introductions.

Elsie Rogers was greatly relieved to see the doctor, and murmured how grateful she was that he had contacted her. She was still so upset over the way Jane looked that she scarcely noticed what he was doing.

The two women stepped back from the bed, and it was some time before the doctor turned his attention to them. 'Her temperature is still very high, and she is dehydrated,' he told them, his face showing a dismal expression. 'I'm afraid you already know what I'm going to say . . . don't you?' he said, sounding deeply sympathetic.

'Please . . .' Elsie Rogers could say no more. She covered her face with her hands, for the moment too upset to cope. When she had composed herself she looked at the doctor seeking for him to reassure her.

He understood only too well. 'There isn't any thing else that I can do,' he said honestly. 'I will see if I can get her into a hospital, but the chances are very slim. This influenza has spread so quickly, there are not enough beds. All you can do is try to keep her temperature down by bathing her forehead with wet cloths, and if only you could get her to take liquids, as much as you can get her to swallow, that would help a great deal.' His tone was kind, but he didn't feel he could lie to these women.

He stayed a while, talking to Mrs Forrester while Elsie was already applying wet cloths as he had recommended.

Then, as he was taking his leave, he asked, 'Have you contacted her parents?'

Elsie sighed. 'I've reason to believe that I am the only person who really cares about her, but come tomorrow I will try to track down members of her family.'

Tomorrow may be too late, was what he was thinking, but what he actually said was, 'I wish there was more I could do for her . . . and for you . . . I can see how distressing this is for you.'

'For the last seven years I've been involved in her life, and to tell you the truth I've come to look upon Jane as the daughter I never had. There isn't anything that I wouldn't do for her.'

There was no answer to that, and the doctor felt utterly helpless as he followed Mrs Forrester down the stairs.

It was a long and lonely night for Elsie Rogers. She sat quietly by Jane's side, speaking softly to her, forcing water between her dry, cracked lips, making sure that the cloths on her forehead stayed wet and checking her pulse from time to time. And finally, as the morning light crept in, she felt that Jane was almost gone.

Mrs Forrester brought a tray of tea and offered to stay with Jane while Elsie went to the bathroom to freshen up. She also suggested that Elsie use her bedroom to try and get some rest. Elsie accepted the first offer but refused to leave Jane for any length of time.

At four o'clock that afternoon the doctor came again. The atmosphere in that big attic room was already one of despair, but as the doctor examined Jane she moaned and stirred uncomfortably, as though she were in pain. When he had finished, he straightened the sheet across Jane's chest, turned to the two women and gave them a weak smile.

'One can only marvel that she has hung on so long,' he said. 'Really it's remarkable. Has to be put down to the fact that she is so young, and that her physical condition is so good. But,' he sighed heavily, 'I have to say that she is nowhere near out of the woods yet. Not by a long chalk, I'm afraid.'

Two more days passed without much change

Elsie Rogers had given in to Mrs Forrester's plea and taken herself off for a walk. It was the first time she had been out of the house since her arrival. Having written three letters, she took this opportunity to post them. The most important was to Lillian Cooper, explaining why she had not yet returned to Winchelsea Lodge and urging Matron to use every power she had to trace Jane's mother and make her aware of just how ill her daughter was.

It was on her return, as she leant over the bed, that she heard Jane whimper. Then, quite suddenly, 'I'm so thirsty,' she muttered, in a voice that sounded ravaged.

'Oh, Jane, I'll get you a drink straight away,' Elsie said soothingly. She couldn't stop the tears from trickling down her face as she held Jane's head a little way off the pillow and placed a glass to her lips. The relief was overwhelming as Jane managed to swallow a few sips.

'Who are you?' Jane asked in a hoarse, ragged voice as her head rested once again on the pillow.

'Everything is all right, Jane. It's me, Mrs Rogers,' Elsie said, humouring her.

'Oh,' Jane murmured, sounding puzzled. Then she closed her eyes tiredly. 'No you're not,' she whispered. 'I haven't got her any more.'

These last words were spoken so sadly that they tugged at Elsie's heartstrings. She understood what was going through Jane's mind, but she couldn't let her continue to believe that once again she had been abandoned. She had to convince her that she was in safe hands. That there were people who cared very much about her and what happened to her. 'Everything is going to be fine,' she told her quietly. 'It is me. I'm here, and I'm going to stay here until you are really fit and well.'

Jane opened her eyes again.

'I don't believe you . . . Mrs Rogers said I had to be on my own,' she said, thrashing her arms frantically. Then she closed her eyes yet again, almost burying her head in the pillow.

The fact that Jane did not recognize her scared Elsie, but at the same time she felt pleased and relieved that at least the girl was able to mutter a few words.

When Mrs Forrester was told the good news, she urged Elsie not to celebrate too soon.

'But she is back with us,' Elsie insisted. 'It's just that her poor eyes are so sore she can't see properly and her mind hasn't yet grasped what has happened to her.'

'Well, she certainly seems to be a whole lot more peaceful. Maybe she'll sleep for a while now. Best thing that could happen if she does,' Mrs Forrester said, not wishing to dampen Elsie's hopes.

It was late afternoon of the next day when the doctor came again. He beamed at Elsie Rogers as he told how amazed he was at the vast improvement there was in Jane.

'How do you feel?' he asked the girl.

'Terrible,' she whispered.

'Of course you do,' he laughed. 'You're going to feel weak for some time to come, young lady, but you are going to be fine,' he reassured her. 'You're going to have rest, though, sleep a lot if you can and drink plenty,' and with that he held a glass of water to her lips, and this time her hands went around the glass and she held it and took several sips.

'Thank you,' she said, smiling wanly up at the doctor.

'I think it is these two ladies that you should be thanking. They've done a great deal more for you than I have.'

Elsie went to the top of the stairs with the doctor, closing the bedroom door behind her. 'What can we expect now?' she asked.

'Well, as you can see for yourself, she's as weak as a kitten, she won't recover that quickly,' he answered her honestly. 'She'll be surprised herself when she first tries to put a foot to the floor. She'll have to be patient, it will take time.'

'I understand,' Elsie said gratefully, racking her brains as to what provision she could now make for Jane's welfare. She shook hands with the doctor and walked slowly back into Jane's room. She looked down on this young girl she loved so much; she was sleeping, looking little more than a child. If Elsie had her way she would bundle her up in blankets, take her back to Winchelsea Lodge and look after until she was truly well and fit again. But that was not possible. The home belonged to the Guardians of the Poor, and they had already done their best for Jane, as they did for every child who came within their care. To single Jane out for preferential treatment would not be allowed. Yet there had been no response from Lillian Cooper about Jane's mother, or indeed any other living relative, so who, apart from Elsie herself, was there who would be willing to accept responsibility?

She could find no answer to that question.

She stayed two more days, until she was quite sure that Jane was out of danger. Then, very cautiously, she approached Mrs Forrester and asked her if she would be able to provide meals for Jane until she could fend for herself.

'My dear, that's the very least I can do. I'll take her on

willingly,' was the quick response, and Elsie heaved a great sigh of relief. 'Really, I mean it. I know you have to get back to your work, but please, rest assured I won't let her want for anything. At least for the time being, I promise you, I will do what I can for Jane.'

From her own pocket Elsie left enough money to cover Jane's food and toiletries, and she also passed over another month's rent for the bed-sitting room. When these arrangements had been completed, she stood up and held out her hand. 'I know Jane will be all right with you, but if she should slip back or seem at all unhappy, you will let me know, won't you? I'll be back just as soon as I can.'

'Jane will be fine now,' Mrs Forrester said with a warm smile. 'I promise. We've surely become good friends by now, good enough for you to trust me.'

'Of course.' Elsie returned the smile. 'I really don't know how to thank you. I shall always be grateful to you.'

'I keep telling you, no need for thanks. You just go back to you job and try not to worry, or else it will be you who is looking for somewhere to live.'

Elsie held out her arms. It was a special moment as the two women who had hardly known each other before Jane had been taken ill thought back over the nightmare of the past days. They hugged each other in silence, relieved, knowing how near they had come to losing Jane. A minute or two later they each had to wipe tears away from their eyes, but they were smiling as they did so.

'I'll just go back upstairs and have half an hour with Jane before I set off,' Elsie said from the doorway of the Forresters' comfortable living room, thinking how lucky she had been when looking for a room for Jane. This landlady had proved not only to be very kind, but a friend in need.

Poor Jane had been rejected by her own mother but had

had what Elsie hoped were several happy years at Winchelsea Lodge. To be turned out on her own to face an unknown world seemed so unfair. And yet somehow Jane had survived.

But what now?

Elsie sighed deeply, her heart aching, as she put her arms around Jane to say goodbye. The girl looked desperately unhappy, but not nearly as unhappy as Elsie herself was. She felt so responsible and at the same time so helpless.

'Bye-bye, Jane,' she said again, in a voice filled with regret.

Jane felt her knees wobble as Elsie let go of her. She had to sit down; all she could think of was that once again she would be on her own, and the prospect of having to find another job was absolutely terrifying.

'I'll see you again just as soon as I can,' Elsie said from the doorway.

Jane managed to raise a hand and wave, but words were beyond her.

All the way back to Winchelsea Lodge, Elsie could think of nothing other than what was to become of Jane. Whichever way she turned it over in her mind, there was no simple answer.

Life for Jane was going to be anything but easy.

Chapter Eleven

'I'VE BROUGHT YOU a nice piece of fish for your lunch,' Mrs Forrester said, looking carefully at Jane, knowing her suspicions had been correct. She was looking really mournful. 'I said to me 'usband, it's not a bad day, if we wrap up well we might take Jane for a short walk this afternoon. You've been cooped up here long enough and I got the idea you might be feeling lonely.'

'I was,' Jane confessed sheepishly. 'I just can't seem to get used to the idea that I have to live on my own. I suppose you think I'm daft.'

'Of course I don't,' she said, setting the lunch tray down in front of Jane, pulling a chair up next to her bed and sitting beside her. 'For years you've been living in a community of young girls, it's only natural that you're going to miss them all. It was like throwing a non-swimmer into the deep end of a swimming bath when they sent you out all on your own. If you don't feel like going out just yet, will you come downstairs every day and sit in our front room? At least there you can see people going by and tradesmen making their deliveries. What d'you say?'

'Thank you,' Jane said gratefully. 'I'd like that, and perhaps tomorrow we can go for a walk.'

'Well, eat your dinner,' Mrs Forrester insisted, removing the plate that covered the meal, 'and when I come back for the tray you can come downstairs with me.'

And so began a pattern that was to put new heart into Jane and help a great deal towards her recovery.

As Jane's strength returned, her mind turn to her everyday problems. She had been told that it was Mrs Rogers who had settled her immediate money matters, which left her feeling under an obligation and determined to do something about it as soon as possible.

With so much time on her hands, her thoughts had turned to other subjects. Most importantly of all was her family. If they still lived in Tooting, she was only a penny tram ride away. Should she visit? Would they be pleased to see her? She hoped her mother would be, but as to her father, she wasn't at all sure. She was a coward, she knew that much. They say absence makes the heart grow fonder, she mused. Would that apply in her father's case? There was only one way to find out what their reaction might be!

And wouldn't it be lovely to see her mum and Tommy? He'd be a grown lad by now. Her last thought before she fell asleep that night was that her mind was made up. She was going to do it.

It was just turned ten o'clock the next morning when she alighted from the tram at Tooting Broadway.

Nothing much had changed. For a moment she stood still on the pavement, comparing her surroundings with those of Rye and Winchelsea. Women were out doing their shopping, barrow boys were shouting their wares, the streets was strewn with litter and the smell was vastly different. There was a strong wind blowing, but it wasn't coming fresh off the sea.

She crossed the road and walked until she came to Selkirk Road. Down past the pie and eel shop, the fish and chip shop on the other side of the road, the oil shop where she had so often gone for paraffin and candles for her mother. Now she was passing the turning that led to Graveney Road and on past several houses until she reached number twenty-three, the house in which she had been born.

Her heart was beating nineteen to the dozen as she looked at the front gate, which was hanging on only one hinge. The paintwork of the front door was badly scarred, as if someone had tried to kick it in. The curtains at the windows were tatty and the steps, which her mother had always kept so white, hadn't seen hearthstone in many a long day.

It took a great deal of courage, but eventually Jane went down the path and lifted the knocker. The door was opened by an adorable little boy whose hair was a mass of golden curls. 'Is . . . your mummy in?' Jane asked bending her knees to be on his level.

'Mum, a lady wants yer,' he shouted back down the passage.

A young, tired-looking woman appeared, holding a baby in her arms. 'Yes, what is it?' she asked.

'I've come to see Mrs Jeffrey, but . . . it doesn't look as if she still lives here.'

The young woman stared at Jane for a moment, then said, 'I ain't never 'eard of her. I've lived here for four years and it was a Mrs Chapman that moved out when me an' me 'usband moved in. Sorry I can't 'elp yer, I've got t' go,' and with that she tugged at the boy with her free hand and kicked the front door shut.

Nancy! That was the thought that came into Jane's head, and she clung to it as a drowning man would cling to a piece of driftwood.

Last house in the street, she repeated to herself over and over again as she walked the length of Selkirk Road.

She had to knock three times before the door was opened. Then she was looking at an enormous body that almost filled the narrow passageway, but she couldn't believe this was her dear friend Nancy, because she hadn't remembered her being this size. The face was the same, though. 'Thank God,' Jane murmured, then the words came tumbling out. 'Nancy, oh Nancy, I am so pleased that you're still here.'

The woman was bending forwards, her huge breasts almost bursting out from her blouse. She tugged her cardigan more tightly around herself and stared hard at Jane. 'Is it? It can't be . . . Is it you, young Janey? In the name of God! It is.'

The next minute she had her arms round Jane and was holding her tight, not saying a word, just holding her close.

Now she was pulling Jane into the house and closing the door behind her.

'Come in. Come on, lass, come in.' She was now using both her hands to haul Jane along the passage and into a room where a young woman sat beside the fire with two crying children beside her and a baby on her lap.

'Be quiet, you kids,' Nancy bawled at them, and they all looked towards Nancy and Jane.

Now their mother got to her feet, lifted the baby on to her hip and, with a sweep of her hand, pushed the two boys across the room. Then, turning to Nancy, she said, 'I'll get out of yer way now you've got a visitor, I'll see yer later.'

'They live upstairs,' Nancy said by way of explanation. 'Worst day's work I ever done when I let me rooms to that tribe. But never mind about them just now. What about you? Sit yerself down an' I'll get yer a cup of tea.'

While Nancy busied herself out in the scullery, Jane sat still and took stock of her surroundings. This living room was bringing back such memories! The same faded wallpaper, damp patches in several places, crowded with large furniture. Then suddenly there was a banging and a shouting coming from overhead. Foul swear words were being hurled. Jane shuddered. Hurtful memories came flooding back. She felt she knew exactly what was going on up there.

There would be the young mother, who hadn't looked very clean, trying hard to cope with three children; probably the eldest of them wasn't even four years old. The father was in a temper from the sound of it, lashing out in desperation, feeling useless because five of them were living in two rooms.

Nancy came back with a steaming cup and handed it to Jane. 'Shut yer ears t' that lot,' she said, raising her eyebrows and nodding towards the ceiling. 'She's nineteen years old, already worn out 'cos that last baby never stops crying day or night. Her 'usband's a local lad, Ron Berry. Used t' be a decent lad; at least he married her when she found she was in the family way. His parents ain't badly off, took them in first off, but things went from bad t' worse and when he lost his job and just 'ung about the 'ouse all day they chucked 'em out. Can't say I blame them. Poor Ron only 'as t' lay his trousers on the end of the bed and she's pregnant again.'

She stopped talking, let out a great belly laugh and put her plump arm across Jane's shoulders. 'Now, how about telling me what's been 'appening to you all these years, 'cos yer know, I've never forgiven yer mother for going off the way she did without so much as a goodbye.'

Jane smiled weakly. 'I went to the house first. I was hoping my mum and dad might still be living there, and I did so want to see Tommy. When did they move?'

Nancy plonked herself down on to a chair and rested her elbows on the table before she said, 'Drink yer tea and I'll fry yer a bit of breakfast in a minute, when I get rid of some of these.' The last statement referred to a couple of mugs and a few greasy plates that were lying on the table. All the time thoughts were running through her head that were making her feel terrible. Surely someone must have told this poor lass what had gone on in her so-called family? Suddenly she raised her head and looked straight at Jane. 'Ain't you 'ad any contact with yer mum at all since the authorities put you away?'

'No, Nancy. Not a word. I did write a couple of times when I first went to Winchelsea Lodge, but I never had a reply.'

'Well, lass . . .' Nancy considered for a moment. 'I hate t' think that I've got t' be the one to set yer straight, but it don't seem like there's anyone else in line for the job.' She lumbered to her feet. 'I'll get you another cup of tea before I start.' She placed a hand on Jane's silky hair, adding, 'You've grown into such a beautiful young lady, very much like I remember yer mum looking when she first came to live here.'

When Jane had drunk her second cup of tea, she looked to where Nancy had seated herself and said, 'You were going to tell me about my mother.'

Nancy turned her head and looked towards the fire, saying, 'I'm trying to decide where to start.' Then, wetting her lips, she went on, 'I suppose first off it's best if I tell you, Mickey Jeffrey was not your father.'

The silence in the room was deafening.

Nancy heaved a great sigh before beginning again. 'That's

the reason he saw to it that you were never given any favours. In fact he was downright mean to you. Well, now you know why he acted as he did, not that that's any reason to make excuses for him. He knew when he married yer mother what he was letting himself in for. Yer mum was pregnant by another man.'

Jane didn't look at Nancy. Was she troubled by what she'd just heard? Difficult to say really. At the moment relief might be a better word. At least the knowledge went a long way to settling so many unanswered questions.

"Twas a long time ago, I know, but yer mum paid over an' over again for something that was not her fault. During the time when Mickey was going heavy on the booze, he led her a dreadful life.'

From the odd things that Jane could remember from her early childhood, she knew that her mother had indeed led a terrible life: bleak, without love or even affection; in fact it always seemed as if she lived in fear. But of what, Jane had never known. Now at least she had some idea. She closed her eyes tightly and her fingernails dug into her palms.

'It's no good, lass, I can't stop now,' Nancy said reluctantly. 'There's so much more you need to know, and like it or not, it seems that I 'ave t' be the one t' do the telling. There's no way of wrapping it up. Are you all right?'

Jane just couldn't bring herself to look at Nancy. In her mind's eye, she could imagine the beatings her mother had taken, and now she realized that it was because Alice had given birth to her that her husband had been so cruel to her.

Nancy waited for an answer but there was none forthcoming. She thought that Jane looked as if she were overcome with weariness and sadness. I have to tell her the rest, she decided sadly. Heaving her bosom high, she took a deep breath.

'About a year after you was taken away, young Tommy was admitted to the Grove 'ospital. He died three days later. Scarlet fever, they said it was.'

Nancy paused, giving Jane time to take in the terrible news that her little brother was no longer alive.

'Your mother was distraught. Mickey was calm enough until after the funeral, and then he let fly. Oh my God! What he did t' yer mother doesn't bear thinking about. She almost died. In fact, when the ambulancemen arrived they thought at first she was dead. She never came back to this street . . . but from what I've learned since – an' maybe it's only hearsay – it was Wally Simmonds that took her out from the 'ospital. What I can tell yer, lass, is that neither of them 'ave ever been seen in these parts from that day t' this. I've 'oped an' prayed that the pair of them 'ave made a new life together somewhere an' at last yer mother may 'ave found a bit of 'appiness. God knows she deserves it.'

In these last few minutes Jane felt she had lost everything.

Her young brother dead! It was more than she could bear. Tommy . . . oh, she had loved him so much. And he had loved her. She had felt she was on her own before now, but always at the back of her mind was the fact that somewhere she had parents and a brother. Now even they had been taken away from her.

Her father had never been her father! That fact didn't worry her too much. But she was never going to be able to see her beloved brother ever again. Her mother had been beaten half to death and no one knew where she was now.

If she hadn't been sitting down, she would have fallen down. She felt weak and slightly sick.

She leaned her head back against the chair. It began slowly, the tears just welling up in her eyes and dropping

down from her lashes on to her cheeks. Then like a swollen
river it became a torrent. She fell forward, buried her face
in her hands and sobbed as though her heart was breaking.

Nancy let her be.

She emptied the teapot and stood it on the hob; she'd
make a fresh brew later. Then, bending down, she took a
hearth brush and swept the loose ashes under the grate
before turning once more to the table and the sad figure of
Jane. She's nothing but a slip of a lass, she thought sadly,
and she must be feeling that the whole world is against her.

'Aw, lass,' she whispered, taking one of Jane's hands
between both of her own and squeezing it gently. 'I wish it
'adn't 'ad t' be me what told yer all this. I'm gonna get us
a bit of a meal now, but before we leave the subject I want
yer to listen to me. Will you do that?'

Jane sniffed and raised her head. Her bright-blue eyes
looked straight at Nancy and the sadness in them tore at
Nancy's heartstrings. What I wouldn't give to be able to
make life a lot easier for this young girl, she said to herself.
They say God makes the burden to fit the back: well, all I
can say is he got it bloody well wrong in her case. Still barely
more than a slip of a girl, she's had more troubles in her
young life than most kids have had hot dinners. And what
can I do about it?

The answer was not a lot, and sadly that was the plain
truth of the matter.

Nancy lumbered off towards the scullery again and came
back with a wet face flannel. Gently taking Jane's face in
one hand, she washed it, all the while softly murmuring:
'It's been a rough old morning for yer, 'asn't it, my love?
But I want you to remember that you're welcome here each
an' every day that yer feel like coming. Wasn't it always t'
me that yer ran when yer dad . . . sorry, lass, yer know what

I mean . . . when Mickey was in a temper? Well, I'm still here an' always will be for yer.'

With a clean towel she dried Jane's face, and her voice was low when again she began to talk. 'There's one thing yer mum did tell me after you went away, and that was that she thought she had done the best thing possible for you. I know for a fact that she lived in fear that Mickey would do you a terrible injury one day. And as things turned out, she wasn't far wrong. She took her time making up her mind, yer know. It wasn't an easy decision. It almost broke her heart to let you go. In the end it was only after she had been told that the home you would be sent to was a very good one, and the folk that ran it had assured her that you'd be well cared for. I saw yer mum the day she came back from saying goodbye to you at the 'ospital, an' believe me, she was in a terrible state. Was it true that the people in the home were good to you?'

Jane nodded her head slowly. 'Yes, that's perfectly true. And you know, Nancy, you're the first person I've heard talk about my mother in all these years. I know now that she did do what she thought was best for me at that time. What I can't understand is why she didn't keep in touch.'

Nancy didn't answer for a moment. She had heard rumours, but that was all they were. She had no way of knowing if there was any truth in them. So all she said was, 'Maybe she was still very ill when Wally Simmonds took her out of the 'ospital. Don't know exactly where they went: some say to Australia, others say Canada.'

Still looking at each other, they both held out their hands and, taking hold, Nancy said quietly, 'Give yerself time, Jane, get some order into your life, and then perhaps you can start making a few enquiries.'

Nancy bustled about frying sausages and making mashed

potatoes, but when she put her head round the door and
saw that Jane had slipped down in the armchair and was
fast asleep, she sighed thankfully and placed their two
dinners in the oven.

Food could wait, she decided. Sleep would do the girl far
more good.

It was late in the afternoon as Nancy stood on her
doorstep watching Jane walk away. They had talked for ages.
She knew all about the disaster of Jane's first job, and hoped
and prayed that she'd have better luck next time.

When Jane reached the corner of the street she turned
round to see that Nancy was still standing there waving to
her. 'I'll see you again soon,' Jane called loudly.

For answer Nancy nodded enthusiastically.

You can't go by appearances, Jane was saying to herself
as she walked towards the tram stop. She'd learned that
much today. Nancy might still look a bit untidy, and she
was most certainly very fat, but beneath all that she was still
the loving, caring person Jane had known as a child.

At least there was one person who was still there for her.

Chapter Twelve

THERE WERE TIMES during the next three weeks when Jane felt she was never going to be able to find a suitable job. She had been taken on at the Merton Box Factory, but after only three days they had told her she wasn't quick enough and not to come back.

If it wasn't for the fact that she had Nancy to call in to for a chat, she didn't know how she would have filled her days. It seemed most of the jobs on offer were for secretaries, but shorthand and typing lessons had never been available to children who were being educated by the Guardians of the Poor.

On her way home from another fruitless trip to the Labour Exchange, her mind was on money matters. Mrs Forrester had turned out to be such a good friend. Each and every day now she insisted that Jane have her evening meal with her and her husband. That was all very well, and Jane was very grateful, but it could not go on for ever. There was also the matter of the rent. It was about time that she stood on her own two feet, but how or when she was going to be able to do that she had no idea.

When she reached home to find Elsie Rogers standing in the hall talking to Mrs Forrester, she was overwhelmed with joy. Having been hugged and listened to a hurried whisper, 'Can't wait to tell you some really good news,' Jane was filled with excitement. No matter if she hadn't seen Mrs Rogers for a few weeks or merely a couple of days, it was always the same. Relief and a feeling of being loved.

Today was no exception.

Hardly inside Jane's room, Elsie could contain herself no longer. 'I'm staying the night here and tomorrow I am taking you to see a beautiful house where I am almost sure a job is waiting for you.' She blurted the words out.

'Oh, really?' Jane managed to mutter. Thinking, I've had one experience of working in a big house and I didn't come off too well. Then she smiled and leaned forward to kiss Elsie's cheek. 'You always manage to put in an appearance when I need you most. I have a lot to tell you but I'm not too sure about this job, even if it is in a beautiful house. Where is it?'

'Hold your horses,' Elsie laughed. 'Let's have some tea and then we can talk to our hearts' content. By the way, it's an early night for you because we have a car coming for us tomorrow. The driver will be here by eight o'clock and we must be ready.'

Now Jane was really intrigued. She had so much to tell and so much to find out.

Talk they did. Until a very tired but very excited Jane climbed into bed.

Even Mrs Forrester was impressed as she stood in her doorway and watched as a uniformed chauffeur held the door of his shiny black car open while Jane and Mrs Rogers settled themselves in the back seat. Jane's feelings were mixed.

Having told Mrs Rogers the sad news that Tommy had died and that her mother had disappeared, probably with Wally Simmonds, she had been heartened by being informed that there were ways and means by which people could be traced. With a firm promise from Mrs Rogers that she would do everything in her power to help, Jane had brightened up. Now her worry was where were they going and what kind of job was facing her when they got there.

As the scenery changed and London was left behind, Jane's mood ran from eager to impatient, at times excited, and finally, as she felt the area was strangely familiar, worked up. She knelt up on the back seat and stared out of the window before saying:

'Mrs Rogers, our chauffeur has just driven through Rye!'

'I thought you might notice once we hit the cobbled high street.' Elsie laughed loudly.

'But surely we're not going back to Winchelsea Lodge, are we?'

Jane half wanted to be told that yes, that was where they were going, but the other half of her was very apprehensive. It would be such a wrench to see the dear place and all her friends, knowing that it could only be for a fleeting visit.

'No, Jane, we've already passed the road that leads to Winchelsea. The next village on our route will be Peasmarsh and the one after that is Northiam. The house we are making for is about halfway between the two.'

When they had set out, a thin mist had masked London, but now they were in Sussex the sun had come out and the countryside was really showing signs of spring. There were new-born lambs in the fields and Jane stared at them, her face showing how delighted she was.

Now the car was turning into a wide lane.

'Nearly there. Are you all right?' Mrs Rogers asked her.

'Yes, I'm fine,' Jane smiled. 'I'd almost forgotten how lovely the countryside can look.'

'A good view of the house is just coming up,' Elsie said as the car turned a corner.

Adelaide House stood in front of them, tall trees to either side. The sun reflecting light from every pane of the many windows gave the impression that the whole house was glowing with warmth. The chauffeur brought the car to a halt in front of this magnificent house.

They crossed the numerous flagstones in silence. The massive front door under its stone arch was already standing open. A tall, grey-haired gentleman waiting at the top of the entrance steps smiled a greeting, saying, 'Good morning, Mrs Rogers, Miss Christy is expecting you. She is in her small sitting room on the first floor.'

'Thank you, Mr Wilson. Elsie smiled as they passed through into the large hall and made for the staircase.

There was a faint smell of lavender, and as a shaft of sunlight from the high window at the turn of the stairway struck across their heads, Jane looked upwards. The walls were wood-panelled and there was the dull gleam of gilt picture frames. A huge chandelier was suspended by three chains, and there were many beautiful curtains, all tied back with heavy tasselled ropes.

In a voice that was little more than a whisper, Jane said, 'It's beautiful.'

She thought the house in which she had worked for Mrs Bonneford had been lovely, but now she saw how different Adelaide House was.

Its old-world beauty was timeless and majestic.

Mrs Rogers tugged at her arm and she followed obediently into a room whose French doors gave a view of never-ending gardens. The curtains and the covers for groups of chairs were made from a rich yellow brocade, but they had obviously had a lot of use, as had the big comfortable sofa. On small side tables there were tall crystal vases full of fresh flowers, the scent of which filled the air. The room as a whole had a feeling of old-world elegance and luxury from a bygone age.

Almost as if time stood still within these walls.

As she took all of this in, looking around her wide-eyed, Jane was scared. Yet she was filled with a curious kind of excitement, such as she had never felt before.

She really had no idea why she was here, except that Mrs Rogers had said there might be the possibility of a job. What kind of a job? What on earth was she capable of doing in such a beautiful place? She crossed her fingers behind her back, praying that she hadn't been misled and that whatever the job entailed she would get it.

And more to the point, be able to do it!

A lady who appeared to be in her late forties rose to her feet as they crossed the room, and Jane immediately thought that never before had she encountered anyone more elegant. Her thick fair hair was coiled up, she wore a dress and loose-fitting coat of palest-pink flimsy material, and her shoes were a soft grey leather worn with sheer grey silk stockings.

'Jane, this is my dear friend Christine Dennison.' Elsie Rogers made the introduction after she and the woman had kissed each other lightly on the cheek.

Mrs Dennison's hand, as Jane shook it, felt soft to the touch, and the smile she gave lit up her face and was enough to make Jane feel that not only was this person beautiful, but a true lady.

'Please come and sit by the window. Very soon now all

the green slopes will be covered in daffodils. Do you like gardens?' Mrs Dennison asked.

Jane stared at her, then, finding her voice, quickly said, 'Oh yes, very much.'

When they were all three seated, Mrs Dennison said, 'I'll ring for some refreshments and then I'll explain to Jane why I asked you to bring her here today.'

While they were waiting, Elsie and her friend spoke in low tones, catching up with each other's news, both business and personal. Jane didn't mind. She moved her chair nearer to the window. One part of the ground was covered in crocuses, and some trees were already leafy green while others were only now awakening from their winter rest. In the distance a lake could be seen, so large that Jane wondered how it came to be in someone's garden. It looked like a vast patch of silver as the water glistened in the sunshine.

There was a tap at the door and a maid entered, pushing a trolley. Behind her walked a man. The very sight of him had Jane catching her breath.

'Hello, Mother,' he said, putting his hands on Mrs Dennison's shoulders and kissing her on both cheeks. Then, turning, he did the same to Mrs Rogers.

Elsie looked a little flustered as he stood back and glanced at Jane.

'This is my ward that I have spoken of so often,' she told him, then, turning her head, added, 'Jane, this is Charles Dennison.'

Jane made to get to her feet, but he gently pushed her back down. Then, taking her hand in both of his, he said, 'I am really pleased to meet you and I truly hope things will work out well for both you and my mother.'

Jane couldn't understand what he was talking about, but decided to let events take their course rather than start asking questions. But her mind was racing. The moment she had stepped through the doorway of this house she had known it was a very special place. Even the people were different.

Charles Dennison was twenty-five years old but looked thirty, maybe because he had that worldly look about him. He certainly was a good-looking man with a great deal of personal style. He appeared self-confident and very composed.

There was no mistaking he was his mother's son. The same thick fair hair, eyes such a bright blue and a wide mouth that seemed to have a smile about it at all times.

He half smiled at everyone, turned on his heel and headed towards the door, saying, 'I'll see you tomorrow, Mother.'

'What? You're not staying for lunch, Charles?' Mrs Dennison sounded surprised.

'Sorry, Mother, things to do today.'

For a few minutes after he had left there was complete silence in the room. Then, very sadly, Christine Dennison lifted her head and, staring at Elsie, said, 'I think maybe Charles has met his Waterloo.'

Elsie leaned back against the soft cushions of the sofa. 'He hasn't had much luck with the ladies since Maureen died, has he?'

'No. I'm afraid you've never said a truer word, Elsie. Maureen was exactly right for him. Such an untimely death. I still feel for her parents. One doesn't expect one's children to go before oneself. To die at the age of twenty-one doesn't seem fair. There was no meaning in it. None at all.'

Jane felt uncomfortable. Should she be listening to this conversation?

'And now?' Elsie left the question up in the air.

Mrs Dennison turned to face Jane, who by now was

making a great pretence of sipping the cup of coffee the maid had poured for her. 'I'm so sorry, my dear, we did not intend to exclude you from our conversation. Charles's affairs are the reason you are here. So, very briefly, my son has left home. He has set up with a married lady and her teenaged daughter. Which rather restricts my way of living.' Christine paused, obviously upset.

Elsie got to her feet. 'Would you like me to outline the situation to Jane?'

'I'd be grateful,' Christine said.

'Jane, you probably haven't noticed, but Mrs Dennison cannot see very well. She is fine whilst she is in familiar surroundings, but at a loss when it comes to going out, and for her to read at the moment is an impossibility. That's where you come in. After I opened up my heart to her as to what a trying time you have experienced since leaving Winchelsea Lodge, she came up with the suggestion that you might like to come and live here with her and act as her companion.'

Jane's fingers flew to cover her mouth, otherwise she would have let out a few loud words in utter astonishment.

'You would of course receive a salary.' Christine Dennison spoke kindly.

If they dangle any more carrots I shall think I've died and gone to heaven! was what Jane was saying to herself. Come here to live! Even Winchelsea Lodge didn't bear any comparison. And it certainly was a different world to Tooting. Only yesterday Nancy had said that as soon as she got rid of her lodgers Jane could come and live with her in Selkirk Road. In fact, Nancy had gone to great lengths to point out that Jane would be doing her a big favour. 'I'd be right glad of yer company,' was how she'd put it.

Back in the street where Jane had been born, probably

with a job up the market or helping out on one or another of the street stalls.

Yesterday that kind offer had seemed like a lifeline.

Now this!

'Please don't look so alarmed,' Christine implored. 'You wouldn't have any rough work to do, nor anything really personal for me. I manage fairly well. Mainly I would love to have someone who wouldn't mind reading to me. Even the daily newspaper is denied me now, and a trip to a book-shop is a long-gone pleasure. Elsie has told me so much about you. Please, at least say you will think about it.'

Jane looked at this elegant lady in total disbelief.

'You want me . . . to come here . . . live in this lovely house . . . just to read to you?'

'Oh, I think we shall be able to find you a few more duties than that.'

Jane spread her hands out wide as if she were clutching at the chance, 'This can't be true, it can't be happening.'

When Elsie had first spoken about Jane and the desperate situation she was in, Christine had felt she wanted to help, though at the same time she'd been sceptical, wondering what type of girl she'd be. But she'd taken an instant liking to Jane.

'It would be beneficial to both of us,' she assured her.

Elsie Rogers' hands were clenched tight in her lap. She had worried herself sick from the day that Jane had left Winchelsea Lodge. The girl was so young, so innocent to be out in the world entirely on her own. God knows she hadn't had much of a life so far. She deserved a break, and when Christine had suggested she came here as her compan-ion it had been an answer to Elsie's prayers. Looking across at Jane now, her pale cheeks flushed and her eyes sparkling, Elsie thought that she was growing into a lovely young lady, and she hoped and prayed that those looks would not be her downfall in life.

Finally, Jane pushed herself up out of her chair, glancing first at Mrs Rogers and then at Mrs Dennison. She saw again the flawless complexion of this attractive lady and just could not believe that her beautiful big blue eyes were almost sightless.

Very hesitantly she murmured, 'I would love to come here to live, but there still doesn't sound as if there would be very much for me to do.'

Both Elsie and Christine burst out laughing.

A few minutes ticked by before Mrs Dennison said, 'Well, Jane, if that is the only objection you wish to make, may I take it that my dear friend Elsie has solved my problems by finding me a charming companion?' She asked the question very slowly and very quietly, giving Jane even more time to realize that she truly wanted her to become her companion.

Jane turned to face Mrs Rogers. My God, she thought, you've done me some favours since I was eight years old, but this goes beyond all comprehension. Having got a nod and a wide smile from her benefactor, she walked slowly to stand in front of the lady she hoped would be her employer for a long time to come, and in a voice she hardly recognized herself said, 'I'd be more than happy to work for you.'

'And I,' Christine smiled, 'will be happy to have you as a companion. Now, I'm sure you would like to see over the house. There's just about enough time before we go down to lunch, I'll have Mary take you round.' She raised an arm, felt along the wall and tugged at a bell-rope. A different maid from the one that had brought in the refreshments appeared within minutes, and when she was asked to show Jane over the house, her rosy cheeks broke into a big grin and she said, 'Twill be my pleasure, Miss Christy.'

* * *

Jane followed Mary obediently through a long gallery, looking out at another view of the gardens beneath the windows. Another maid came out of a bedroom; it was the same girl who had brought the coffee, her arms now full of bed linen. She stopped and smiled, and Mary introduced her as Sarah. Jane looked at them both with interest, noticing their short hair and their calf-length skirts. She felt dowdy and plain. Her blonde hair had darkened to a rich golden colour and grown almost to shoulder length. It seemed such a long time ago that she had had it done at the hairdresser's in Rye, the one and only time it had been cut professionally. Her blue skirt reached almost to her ankles and was very faded. Her boots, for which she had been so grateful when it had been snowing, now looked worn and heavy as she glanced down at them. How she envied the pretty shoes the two maids wore. They were shiny black with little heels, rounded toes and a thin strap over the instep. They looked so light and so comfortable. She promised herself that one day she would walk into a shoe shop and buy herself a pair of shoes like that. It would be the first brand-new pair she had ever owned.

There were family rooms as well as formal ones. Mrs Dennison's bedroom was so feminine, with pretty curtains and a bedcover that matched. Her son Charles's room looked very orderly, with silver-backed brushes laid out on top of the tallboy. At the end of the corridor there was a nursery with a well-used rocking horse and shelves of children's books and games. Mary saw the curious look on Jane's face and explained, 'Mrs Dennison's sister comes to stay quite often, and she has five children. Or at least she used to; the children are like Master Charles, mostly grown up now.'

They wandered the rooms together, even the very top

floor, where the female staff shared rooms. Mary told Jane that the cook and the butler were a married couple, and they lived in the lodge which stood to one side of the house, near to where the stables were. Stables? That meant horses, and Jane wasn't too sure that she would want to come into close contact with those great creatures.

As Mary continued to talk about the house, her love for it and the family showed clearly and it went a long way to calming Jane's nerves.

They came back to the ground floor by the back stairs, and threaded their way through what seemed to Jane a warren of stone-flagged kitchens. Finally, they walked along a narrow and rather chilly corridor and then into a large cheerful kitchen. It smelt of roasting meat and savoury pies. There were two people there, a large, plump but happy-looking woman and a girl Jane judged to be a couple of years younger than herself.

Mary said, 'This is Jane Jeffrey.' Turning, she added, 'This is Mrs Wilson, our cook, and that young lass is Daisy, she's our tweeny, used to be our scullery maid but she was good and so she got promoted.'

Jane blushed as they stared at her.

Mrs Wilson got up from her chair. 'So, you may be coming to live here as eyes and ears for Mrs Dennison?'

'Oh, nothing is settled yet,' Jane hastened to assure her. Then she added, 'But hopefully.'

'Well, lass, you could travel much further and fare a whole lot worse than coming here to live.'

Jane was saved from having to answer by the ringing of a bell.

'That's to announce that lunch is ready,' Mrs Wilson smiled. 'Mary, take Jane to the dining room, for it's as sure as eggs are eggs she'll never find her own way there.'

When Jane was seated next to Mrs Rogers she felt nervous. There were only three places set but the table was so long and the room so grand.

Elsie leant nearer, patted her knee and gave her a reassuring smile. At one end of the room there was a stone hearth with an open basket filled with burning logs. There were family photographs clustered together in silver frames, and many pictures of English landscapes. Books and magazines were scattered around on side tables and there was a pipe rack beside a big leather armchair.

As Jane ate her delicious chicken soup she was thinking that for all its size and grandeur, this room had a lived-in feeling. It felt as if there had been many a happy family meal served and eaten around this big table.

She still couldn't fathom out how or why she was being offered the chance to come and live here. So far every person she had met had treated her with respect, had been kind, had even smiled at her. Did they know that she had been brought up in an institution? That she had no proper family? Only her mother, as far as she knew, was still alive, and she had made it quite obvious that she wanted nothing more to do with her. Funny she should be thinking about her mother while sitting eating in this posh dining room with a lady who had said quite clearly that she wanted her as a companion.

Her mother had more than likely made a new life somewhere with Wally Simmonds and it was more than possible that both of them would regard her as an embarrassment if she should ever turn up on their doorstep.

The meal was over. Elsie and Christine had moved to two armchairs by the fire and were lingering over their coffee. Jane had said she didn't want anything to drink and was filling the time by sitting staring out of the window.

She hadn't heard anyone move and jumped when Mrs Dennison came up behind her, lifted a hand and smoothed her hair. 'You're thinking that this will be a totally different life to what you have been used to. Does it frighten you?'

'Yes, it does,' Jane answered quickly, 'but on the other hand it is an unbelievably generous offer. I just can't understand. Why me?'

Christine stood very still. She moved her hand to rest on Jane's shoulder, a gesture that said they were already friends. 'I have never wanted for any material thing in my life. I do not know what it is to be unwanted or unloved. So, I count my many blessings. Now I need someone to be my eyes. What better person could I pick than a young lady who has so much love to give but no one to share it with? Tell me, Jane, what were you thinking as you gazed out of the window?'

Jane hesitated before answering.

'I was wondering what it would be like to live and work in a place as beautiful as this. To be able to see these lovely gardens every day. To be warm inside the house and when the sun shines to be able to be outside in the grounds. To be able to dig my hands into that rich earth, to plant my own bulbs. Oh, so many things. Most of all, Mrs Dennison, could I do what would be expected of me? Would I prove to be satisfactory?'

'Well,' Christine said, smiling her delight. 'Well. We'll have to see what we can do for each other. But first off, could you please get used to calling me Miss Christy, it sounds far less formal than Mrs Dennison.'

'If that's what you prefer, ma'am.'

Jane still couldn't believe her good fortune and suddenly blurted out, 'I'll do my very best, ma'am! I really will. I'll do anything you ask, fetch and carry, see to all your needs, you'll only have to ask.' By now she was on the verge of tears. She'd never expected anything like this. 'I just don't know how to thank you, ma'am.'

Christine smiled, and, doing her best to put Jane at ease, said, 'I expect you found the house to be a bit rambling. It will take some time to get used to it, but I'm quite sure we shall suit each other very well.'

Jane hoped and prayed that she was right.

Later, when the car was taking them back to Balham, Elsie took Jane's hand and squeezed it tight. Her eyes sparkled merrily. 'Oh, hasn't the day gone well? You and Christine took to each other, I could tell. Isn't the thought of the future now so exciting?'

Yes, it was, but it was also scary.

Chapter Thirteen

IT WAS BARELY eight o'clock the next morning when Nancy opened her front door to find Jane standing there.

'Gawd love us, where 'ave you sprung from?' she asked in surprise as she ushered Jane down the narrow passage. 'You ain't given the streets time enough t' get aired.'

Jane laughed as she took her coat off. 'I couldn't wait any longer to tell you what's happened. Honest, Nancy, you aren't gonna believe half of it! I still can't take it in myself.'

'Well, I've only just this minute washed an' dressed meself an' I can't be doing with surprises till I've 'ad at least three cups of tea. So, move yerself, fill the kettle and make a pot while I brush the tangles out of me 'air.'

Jane needed no second bidding. She hadn't bothered to get herself anything to eat before setting out to come to Tooting, knowing full well that she wouldn't be in Nancy's house for very long before the big black frying pan would be pulled to the centre of the hob and a smashing fry-up would be produced.

Half an hour later, Jane pushed her plate away declaring

that she couldn't eat another morsel, and as Nancy poured her third cup of tea she announced, 'I'm going to be a paid companion.'

Nancy's mouth dropped open and she spilled some of her tea over the tablecloth.

'Who in God's name is gonna give you a job like that?'

Jane began at the beginning, telling Nancy how Mrs Rogers had turned up, and the posh car that had taken them to Sussex for the day.

'So what's the name of the lady you're gonna work for?' Nancy asked.

'Mrs Christine Dennison. Her and Mrs Rogers have been friends for years but they said they became closer when they were both notified that their husbands had been killed in the war.'

'An' you're telling me this Mrs Dennison has a butler, a cook and three girls working in the 'ouse?'

'Yes, that's right, and two men, so I was told, to work in the grounds.'

'You said the poor woman was going blind. Surely if she'd that well off she could afford an operation to make her eyes better?'

'I don't know about that. I never asked no questions.'

'Shame.' Nancy tutted sympathetically. 'All I 'ope is that she treats yer better than that other mad woman did.'

'Oh, I hope so too. But I'm sure she will. All the staff speak ever so well of her.'

'Ain't she got no family?' Nancy wanted to know more.

Jane grinned. 'Only one son, and he's the reason I've been offered the live-in job?'

'What d'yer mean? Is he the skeleton in the cupboard? Got sent to prison, 'as he?'

Jane gave Nancy a playful push. 'Go on with you, they're

not that sort of family. It's just that Mr Charles, he's her son, has fell in love with a married lady. She's left her husband and they've set up home together. Which leaves his mother very much at a loss. Oh, and this lady has a teenage daughter who has gone with them.'

'Cor blimey, I don't like the sound of that. A married woman *and* 'er daughter! Two on the go, so t' speak.'

'Oh, Nancy! Trust you!' Jane couldn't help but laugh. She was so glad she had Nancy to come to. She was a real tonic and she couldn't be kinder if she were a true relative.

She said as much to Nancy, who straight off replied, 'Well, yer know what they say, gal. God gave us our relations, thank Christ we pick our friends.'

'Trust you to come up with a saying like that. But Nancy, will you tell me really honestly if you think I should go ahead and take this job? One minute I can't believe I should be so lucky, and then the next I keep asking myself, what if it all goes wrong again? There really didn't sound as if there were going to be much for me to do.'

'Huh,' Nancy scoffed. 'Wait till you get there before you believe that! I'll lay ten t' one the missus will keep you busy.' She took a sip of her tea and set the cup down again. Then she turned and stared hard at this young girl who had come to mean so much to her. She had felt so guilty for the years that she had lost touch. But even if she had known where Jane had been sent, what could she have done about it? Half the time she didn't have two pennies to rub together for herself, never mind trying to provide for a child. The authorities would never have allowed her to look after Jane. Then suddenly her face creased in a huge grin.

'Since you've asked my opinion, I'm going to tell yer, lass, t' grab this chance with both 'ands. Life's a gamble whichever way yer look at it. Whoever said life is what yer

make it ain't never wanted like most of us 'as. 'Cos if that
were true then we'd all be living in bloody palaces. No, my
luv, life is what you make of the circumstances you find
yourself in at any given point in time. As I said, you come
to a crossroads and you gamble on which road t' take. An'
if yer too yellow-livered to take a chance, then you stay put
an' get nowhere.'

'My, my, quite a well of wisdom this morning, aren't we?'
Jane teased.

'Yes, well, I ain't finished yet. If this job turns out t' be
all that you're 'oping for, then that's fine, but just you
remember you've always got a home with me, so no putting
up with things that ain't right 'cos yer think you've nowhere
t' go. You understand me?'

'Yes, Nancy,' Jane said, getting to her feet and putting
her arms around Nancy's broad shoulders.

'Now, now, don't start slobbering all over me. And let's
get one more thing straight. You might be gonna live in
Sussex, but I expect a penny postcard once a week and a
visit at least once a month. That's if you can tear yerself
away from this life of luxury that you'll be living in.'

'I shall ask my new employer to have all your rules and
regulations written into my contract. Will that satisfy you,
madam?'

'You cheeky whelp!' Nancy went to box her ears but Jane
was too quick for her. 'For that you can do the washing-
up, and when it's dinner time you and me will toddle off t'
the Selkirk pub where we will get ourselves a hot pie and
drink to you moving into wealthy society.'

'Now who's taking the mickey?' Jane asked, but nodding
her agreement she added, 'Maybe if we buy a drink and tell
the landlord of my good fortune he'll give us each a pie for
nothing.'

'And pigs might fly,' Nancy laughed as she began to clear away the remains of their breakfast.

While they were doing the washing-up Jane was feeling that perhaps her life really was taking a change for the better. Maybe she was going to work in a big house with servants, but it was this woman who had been there for her when life had seemed so bleak, and even offered her a home. It was true, Nancy was kinder than any relative. Jane wouldn't forget her; she'd visit just as often as it was possible and if she managed to save any money then she would help Nancy in any way she could.

Mrs Forrester's feelings were very similiar to those of Nancy as she listened to a very excited Jane tell her about the house and the offer of a job that Elsie Rogers had obtained for her. In one way she was thrilled for the girl, but on the other hand she was going to miss her terribly.

She admitted to herself that that feeling was full of irony!

The very first day that Jane had arrived at her house, she had been so determined to have as little to do with her as possible. After all, the girl came from an institution, and how was she supposed to know what her background was? Any help the landlady had given first off had been given grudgingly. It wasn't until Jane had been taken ill and she had been more or less forced into helping her that her attitude had changed.

Now, as she listened to a smiling Jane thanking her for her love and kindness, Mrs Forrester had to close her eyes to stop the tears from spilling out.

This young girl was something else!

Thick blonde hair, blue eyes, soft silky skin. Full of good humour and laughter, sprightly and energetic, she faced whatever life threw at her and was never heard to moan.

No wonder she had come to love her. Oh, please God, give her a break this time, she silently prayed. If anyone deserved it, this sixteen-year-old girl did.

Chapter Fourteen

CHRISTINE DENNISON TURNED her head towards where Jane was sitting and couldn't help thinking that the way this young girl had settled into her household was remarkable. Six months now she had been here, and to say that she had endeared herself to everyone she came into contact with would be no exaggeration.

Jane herself was far happier than she had ever thought possible. It was such a contented, orderly house that she couldn't feel otherwise. Both Mary and Sarah had become her friends, while Daisy, the tweeny, was at everyone's beck and call and did every job asked of her with a broad smile on her face. Jane's own tasks were varied, according to how Miss Christy was feeling. Sewing and darning took up a lot of her time, and Miss Christy was pleased to learn that she did her jobs well. The household linen went to a laundry but Jane washed Miss Christy's fine underwear and blouses by hand, and on the odd occasion that Mr Charles stayed in the house it was she who washed and ironed his shirts. She was mostly given an hour to herself after lunch but she was never idle. She would use the time to write letters to Mrs Rogers, Mrs Forrester and of course to dear Nancy.

She would read book reviews in the daily papers amd magazines which were delivered to the house, and then describe and suggest which books Miss Christy might find interesting. Her favourite task was reading them to her. At the moment they were reading Charles Dickens' *David Copperfield*, following the life of David through his many sufferings and misfortunes. Jane could hardly wait to read the next chapter. Though she had the distinct feeling that Miss Christy knew this story off by heart. One of her most enjoyable trips out was when they visited bookshops. Miss Christy never failed to make a purchase, which in turn opened up a whole new world to Jane.

She had wondered why the staff always referred to their employer as Miss Christy. Mrs Wilson explained that her husband had been in service to the family ever since he was a young lad, and that that was how Christine had always been referred to as a young lady growing up. The habit had never changed, even when she had become Mrs Dennison, and as each new member of the staff joined the household that was what they were instructed to call their mistress. Jane thought it was a nice idea. Not so stuffy as madam.

Today she had a tedious task but one that she hoped would be well worth all the trouble in the end. She was sewing seed pearls on to a velvet head-band for Miss Christy to wear on Saturday evening. She gave a small sigh which didn't go unnoticed by Christine.

'Is any thing troubling you, Jane?' she asked, showing concern.

Jane was sorry she had let that sigh escape and quickly said, 'No, it's just that I dropped a pearl and they are so hard to find if they sink into the carpet.'

Christine's instincts told her that wasn't the truth. 'The main topic of conversation in the kitchen is Saturday's party.' It wasn't a question, it was a statement. 'Tell me, Jane, what is being said?'

Jane had no option. 'Well, everyone is thrilled that Mr Charles will be home for his birthday, and Mrs Wilson is in her element, cooking enough for an army.'

'That was not what I asked you, Jane.'

'I know.' Jane hesitated before saying quietly, 'I think both Mr and Mrs Wilson are a bit uneasy because Mr Charles is bringing his lady friend.'

'They are not the only ones, and her name is Mrs Harman, Frieda Harman.' It was Christine's turn now to sigh, then very quietly she said, 'If we want to have my son to stay then we must accept that he and Frieda are . . . well, for want of a better word, an item.'

'Oh, miss, I didn't mean no disrespect, and neither do Mr and Mrs Wilson, it's just that, well . . . none of us are quite sure how to carry on.'

'I know, Jane, and it will be particularly hard for you, but I want you to treat Mrs Harman as if she were Charles's wife. I will speak to the rest of the staff myself. It's not that I approve of their relationship, but neither am I going to judge. Sarah will prepare a double bedroom and also the room next to Charles's own bedroom, then their sleeping arrangements will be up to them. However, Jane, I would appreciate it if you would see to the final touches, such as fresh flowers. I know I can count on you to use your discretion.'

Jane took a deep breath and let it out slowly. 'I'll certainly do as you ask.' She wouldn't dream of passing one iota of this conversation on downstairs, but she was afraid it would all come out over the weekend.

She continued with her sewing but half smiled as she thought of what Nancy would have to say if she were in her shoes.

Never trouble trouble till trouble troubles you!

Saturday had arrived.

Every member of staff was kept busy for the early part of the day. After Miss Christy had taken her nap and than bathed, it fell to Jane to help her dress. And it was such a pleasure. She stood back and gazed at her mistress. Elegant was the only word that Jane could think of. Her long evening dress, the palest shade of blue, was trimmed with silver, as were her high-heeled shoes and evening bag. The pearl headband had been woven into the high curls that the hairdresser had come to the house to do. Normally Jane did Miss Christy's hair, but not today.

Come evening, Sarah, Mary and Jane were all kept on the trot as the guests arrived, taking ladies' cloaks while Mr Wilson saw to the gentlemen's coats, hats and canes. It was taking Jane some time to get over her nervousness, for after all this was the first big party that she had ever been involved with. Suddenly she found she had a few minutes in which to breathe out, and she began to take more interest in what was being discussed and noted the different evening dresses all the ladies present wore.

She couldn't believe they owned so many jewels, and the various hairstyles must have taken their hairdressers hours to create.

She was quite shocked to see some of the young ladies smoking cigarettes in long tortoiseshell holders; there was even one using a gold holder. She had seen poor women in the streets of London roll their own cigarettes, but never anything like this.

There was no need to ask which lady was Frieda Harman. Jane looked across the room and could tell why Mr Charles had been captivated by her. She was truly beautiful. Small and dainty, even though she must be nearing forty, because she had a daughter who was seventeen years old. She looked so graceful in a deep-red velvet dress with a diamond choker sparkling in the light. Around her head was a band of the same velvet as the dress to which was attached two pale-pink feathers. That alone made her stand out from the others, Jane thought as she watched Charles lower his head and say something into her ear.

Then her heart thumped. He had looked up and seen her watching them. Now he was coming towards her and there was nothing she could do to escape without pushing her way through the throng of people, so she stood still, her eyes fixed on the tray of drinks she was holding.

'Jane, how are you?'

'I'm very well, thank you, Mr Charles.'

'Well, I'm glad to hear it, and I'll take this opportunity to thank you for all you do for my mother. She sings your praises. Says she has no idea of how she would cope without you.'

'It's very kind of her to say so, but it works both ways . . .'

Jane paused, startled, as she heard Miss Christy say from behind her, 'Is my son tormenting you, Jane?'

She blushed, unable to form an answer.

'She's still a little wary of us all,' Christine said kindly.

'Mr Charles was telling me that you were pleased with my work,' Jane finally managed to reply. Then she cast her eyes down and said, 'I'd better continue round with these drinks.'

All through the meal and the dancing which followed she felt jittery and on edge, often wondering how she came to be here. This was not her world. These were not her kind of people. She should feel privileged to be here. And she did. But at the same time she felt afraid.

Of what?

She didn't know.

The four-course meal seemed to take for ever, but finally everyone was moving into the drawing room. The room had been stripped of the big furniture, and small tables and chairs were set around the walls. The carpet had been taken up and the floorboards polished. A group of four musicians, all in black evening dress, sat in the window alcove.

Mr Wilson had been right in his prediction about late nights, Jane thought. It was after one o'clock when the last guests departed and the house fell silent.

Miss Christy came down to the kitchen on the arm of her son. 'She looks as tired as we all are,' Mary whispered to Jane.

'Mr and Mrs Wilson, I'd like to thank you both for all your hard work that went to make this evening such a success. Also, I am not forgetting all you girls, because each and every one of you has worked terribly hard and must be very tired. My thanks to all of you.' She smiled at them before adding, 'My son has something he wants to say.'

'Yes.' Charles grinned. 'I certainly won't be wanting an early-morning call, and since Mrs Harman is the only other house guest, and I'm sure she will agree, we shan't require breakfast before ten thirty, so please leave all the clearing-up until tomorrow, or later on today, I should say. Get yourselves to bed. Good night and, once again, our thanks to all of you.'

Christine nodded her head and took hold of Charles's arm again.

'Will I come up with you now, miss?' Jane asked.

'Thank you, Jane, but no. For one night I'll manage. I will leave all my clothes on a chair for you to see to in the morning. You must be worn out.'

As mother and son left the kitchen, Mrs Wilson nodded her head approvingly.

Mr Wilson said, 'Now that's what I call a real lady and gentleman. Many employers would have insisted on us clearing up tonight.' Then, smiling broadly, he said to Daisy, 'Put the kettle on, lass, and tonight you can all have a choice, tea or cocoa.'

When they were all seated with a hot drink, Mary looked at Jane and asked, 'What did you think of Mrs Harman?'

'A very nice lady, I thought, and you only had to see the way Mr Charles looked at her to know that he thinks the world of her.'

'Really? I never got much chance to observe them except when they were dancing, and then I thought, like you, that they looked smashing together. Did you know they are staying on here for a week or ten days?'

'No, Miss Christy never said.'

'Well, I only know because I heard Mr Wilson tell Sarah not to strip off their beds but to put out clean towels when she does their rooms.'

'We'll all have our work cut out in the morning,' Jane said, nodding to the stack of dishes and glasses piled high on the the big wooden draining board.

'Yeah, an' you'll have your work cut out upstairs, Jane. Best we go up now and at least get a few hours' sleep. Really lovely do, though, wasn't it?'

Jane sighed happily. 'It truly was. All those lovely dresses, and that wonderful food.'

'Opens our eyes as t' how the other half live, though, don't it?' Mary said, sounding really envious.

Jane didn't answer. She still felt very privileged to be here in this house and at this party, even if it was only as an employee. It certainly beat working in a factory, or even on a market stall, and living in a bed-sitting room with no real family of your own.

At least in her book it did.

It was Wednesday morning and Jane was having breakfast in the kitchen with the other female staff. When the house was running normally she would take her meals in the dining room with Miss Christy. Since Saturday, the day of the party, nothing had been what one would describe as normal. Miss Christy had been out and about far more than was usual, and there had been no need for Jane to go with her. Charles and Mrs Harman had insisted that everywhere they went Christine was to accompany them.

The companionable silence around the breakfast table was broken by a loud knocking on the door of what was known as the tradesmen's entrance.

'Who in heaven's name can that be at seven o'clock in the morning?' A very disgruntled Mrs Wilson put down the heavy brown teapot from which she had been filling Sarah's cup, and, giving Daisy a push, said, 'Get yerself up an' go see who it is, an' if it's either of them gardeners tell them to buzz off and come back when Mr Wilson has finished his breakfast.'

Daisy was none too pleased to have to leave her hot porridge, but did as she was told. Having walked along the narrow passageway, she struggled with the heavy iron door. When she had it opened, she panicked as she saw two police-men standing there.

''Ere, there ain't been an accident, has there?' she said, because it was the first thing that occurred to her.

'Nothing for you to worry yer pretty little head about,' the taller of the two constables said kindly. 'But we do need to see your master, Mr Charles Dennison, isn't it?'

Daisy looked at him fearfully. 'Mr Charles don't live 'ere no more. Well, not all the time he don't, ain't done so for a long time now. But what I'd better do is tell Mr Wilson you're here and let him see what yer want.'

She didn't wait to hear what the policemen had to say about that, but turned on her heel and ran, yelling as she went, 'There's two coppers 'ere say they want t' see the master.'

'What the hell is all the noise about?' Mr Wilson demanded as he came out into the passageway.

Daisy just pointed, ran into the kitchen and sank down thankfully on to her chair.

By the time Mr Wilson returned with the constables, he was aware of most of the facts.

'Send the girls about their normal duties,' he advised his wife. 'I have to go upstairs and wake Mr Charles, that is, if he hasn't already heard all the commotion. I will also have to make Miss Christy aware of what is happening.'

Mrs Wilson looked bewildered but knew better than to ask questions, especially in front of the staff.

The two policemen stood against the wall, helmets held in their hands. They were having a job not to smile as they listened to the cook shoo the girls off and mutter to herself, 'Be a godsend if someone were to tell me what's 'appening, but then I only work 'ere.'

Forty minutes had passed before Mr Wilson was showing the constables out, this time through the front door.

Meanwhile his wife had washed her face and hands and tidied her hair, expecting at any minute to be called up to the drawing room.

'Put the kettle on again, love, an' I'll do me best t' tell you what's going on,' her husband said as he came into the kitchen and sat down thankfully. 'Miss Christy said she'll ring when they're ready for their trays to be sent up. Poor woman, she's beside herself. She'll live to rue the day her son got himself mixed up in all this.'

'Bert!' Mrs Wilson yelled at him. This was a most unusual way for her to address him; in this house, it was always Mr Wilson. 'Bert,' she repeated, 'will you please stop talking in riddles and tell me what on earth has happened that's bad enough to have brought two coppers round here at this time in the morning.'

He heaved a great sigh, put his elbows on the table and indicated that his wife should sit herself down opposite him. 'To begin with, Mrs Harman's daughter has been arrested.'

'Oh my God!' Mrs Wilson's fingers flew to cover her mouth.

'I know, love, an' she not yet seventeen. She's been formally charged on two counts, shop-lifting and drunk and disorderly. They are bringing her before the magistrate this morning.'

'But why have they come here? Where's her father? And now I come t' think about it, didn't someone say she was still at school? Some kind of finishing college?'

Mr Wilson looked at his wife. He loved her dearly, but he made a point of never telling her half of what he knew that went on or was said above stairs in this house. He had been in this job a good many more years than she had and had learned that women loved to gossip. They were well set up in this house. He had brought her here as his young bride, and to be given the lodge for their own living quarters had been an extra bonus. He knew when he was onto a good thing and guarded it jealously.

But now was different! If he told her the events as he had learned them it would save a lot of speculation, and so, taking a deep breath, he began: 'Mrs Harman's husband is very much older than her, so I've been led to believe, and was retired. But when his wife took up with Mr Charles he applied to the Government to be given another job and has actually gone back to his old post in India. And as far as I can tell you, his daughter is, or should be, at an expensive boarding school.'

'He must have plenty of money.' Mrs Wilson was thinking out loud. 'Don't they have that great big house out on the other side of the Romney Marshes, with loads of ground?'

'Yes, you've got that much right, but I'm fairly sure he leases off most of the land to sheep farmers. He wouldn't be hard-up. Although he was young to have retired I wouldn't mind betting his pension is colossal.'

'What about our Mr Charles? He's bought that lovely old cottage in Rye where he and Mrs Harman live now, or do you think Miss Christy paid for that?'

'We don't get paid to think, my dear, and remember, you have to keep your thoughts to yourself. I have been wondering, though, about Mr Charles's businesses. There's the offices he has here in the village, but his main earner I always thought was up in London. He himself is a fully fledged chartered accountant, but having inherited the firm which has been in this family for a few generations, I suppose it is a safe bet to say he can leave the daily running to his regular staff. There was a time when he travelled daily up to the City.'

The shrill clanging of the bell brought their conversation to an abrupt ending. At the same moment, Jane appeared. 'Miss Christy said to tell you that Mary is laying up the dining room and that I am to help you bring the tea, coffee and toast up; they won't be wanting anything cooked this morning.'

'How is she?' Mrs Wilson asked quietly.

Jane twisted her hands together before answering. 'I'd say she is very fearful. Mostly worried about the effects this will have on Mr Charles.' Then quickly she turned to face Mr Wilson and added, 'I can't help feeling sorry for Mrs Harman. You felt the same, I know you did. She's blaming herself for what her daughter has done and at the same time she is feeling utter despair. Mr Charles is going to the court with her. Poor Miss Christy doesn't know what to think.'

Mr Wilson looked into Jane's face and saw that it was filled with concern.

It wouldn't only be Mrs Harman and her daughter who would be affected by this.

No, not by a long chalk.

And the worst thing was that he knew damn well things were going to get a darn sight worse before they ever started to get better.

Chapter Fifteen

JANE STOOD IN the open doorway and gazed wonderingly at the change in the beautiful gardens. The fields beyond were empty of crops. All the harvest had been safely gathered in. Her mind wandered back over the lovely church service she had attended with Miss Christy to celebrate the Harvest Festival. The summer was over, she thought sadly. The hours of daylight were getting shorter. There was a nip in the air, and in the mornings, mist hung over the fields and hedgerows. The air was full of the earthy smell which came from falling and decaying leaves. Oh, but it was still nice to live in the country.

The past months had been so good for her, she mused. A time of new experiences. A time during which she had learned to adapt to a way of life so very different to that she had known. And now, with winter fast approaching, she would not have to dread the cold or wonder where her next meal was coming from.

The only thing that was worrying the whole household was this business about Glynis Harman. It would be a relief when Mrs Harman learned exactly what was going to happen to her daughter. And as for Mr Charles, he walked about looking as if he'd got the worries of the whole world on his shoulders.

Anyway, today was Jane's day off, and as soon as breakfast was over she was going to see Nancy. This would only be her second visit to Tooting in all the months she had been at Adelaide House, but she had kept her promise and written every week, even if sometimes it was only a postcard.

She felt light-hearted as she got off the train at Balham station and walked towards the tram stop. It would be such a change to have Nancy to talk to. Although they all tried to skirt around the subject of Glynis Harman, the coming court case seemed to have put a shadow over the whole household. And none more than Miss Christy.

Which, when you thought about it, was only natural. Charles was her son, her only child, and she had bent over backwards to understand and accept the fact that he was in love with another man's wife. The husband seemed to have washed his hands of the whole affair once his wife left him. The worst part was that he wasn't even in the country. He didn't have to deal with the shameful mess his daughter had got herself into.

When Nancy opened the door and flung her arms around her, Jane sighed happily. She loved living at Adelaide House: the rich furniture and curtains, the high ceilings, the marvellous wallpapers, and the paintwork such a pale cream which helped to make the rooms seem even larger than they really were. She especially loved the smaller sitting room which Miss Christy and herself used daily because it opened on to the gardens. Here in Selkirk Road, Nancy's living room window looked out on to a back yard and an outside toilet. Nevertheless, it was a joy to be here. She wasn't paid to come here; she came because she loved Nancy and Nancy loved her. This was her home should she ever have need of it, and Nancy was all the family she had. The only person in the world she could turn to should she ever lose her job.

'I knew there was something up by the tone of your letters,' Nancy said when they were settled with the inevitable cup of tea in front of them.

'Well, I wouldn't dream of writing the whole story, but it is a relief to be able to talk sensibly with someone.'

'Don't you talk to this Mary and Sarah that yer work with?'

'Well, yes, of course I do, but it's difficult. You see, Nancy, I'm upstairs most of the time and I hear Miss Christy talking to her son and even some of her friends when they call. I was there when Miss Christy discussed the case with her family solicitor. I do my best to keep my head down, not to deliberately listen but to get on with whatever it is that I am doing. Often I suggest to Miss Christy that I go into another room, but she won't even hear of it.'

'I see what yer mean. Privileged position is what you're in, although it does put you between the devil an' the deep blue sea. Must make life 'ard.'

'Not hard, Nancy, more awkward like. Even Mrs Wilson tries to question me. Anyway, I've got a bit of good news.'

'Well, let's be 'aving it,' Nancy urged.

'I'm to stay the night if you'll have me.'

'Oh, pet. That's real cracking, that is. Yer know God works in a mysterious way.' She nodded her head towards the ceiling. 'I got rid of my tenants only about a fortnight ago, and you know Hannah an' John Watkins who live opposite, well, they wanted to rent my two rooms for their married daughter but I told them I thought you might be wanting to come and stay with me quite soon but I'd let them know. The back bedroom is nice and clean and the bed all made up for you. Now what d'yer think of that?'

'That you are either a white witch or you've been practising a bit of telepathy.'

An answer to which Nancy merely nodded her head knowingly.

Happiness was flowing through Jane. She had been so grateful when Miss Christy had said that visiting for the day did not give her and her friend much time together and suggested that Brownlow, the chauffeur, drive her to the station and meet her from the train tomorrow evening.

They talked, going from one topic to another. And when Nancy related some of the things the neighbours had got up to since she'd last seen her, Jane found she was laughing fit to bust, something she hadn't done since the police had called about Mrs Harman's daughter.

'Tell you what, Nancy, I'm not letting you cook dinner for us. I'll go and fetch fish an' chips for us both, my treat.'

'Oh, Miss Money-Bags are you now?'

'Well, I do get paid twelve an' sixpence a week, or rather fifty shillings a month, and to be honest, there is nothing I need to spend it on. I mostly save it, since everything I need is provided for me. But if you pass me my bag I'll show you what I have brought.'

As Nancy handed the bag across, Jane stuck out her legs and added, 'Look, new shoes, brand new, and while I was in the shop I got these for you.'

Nancy was too choked to comment as she took the poshly wrapped parcel and gingerly tore at the wrapping paper. 'Good God!' she exclaimed, putting a hand inside a fur-lined slipper. 'I ain't never 'ad anything like these before.'

'I wasn't sure of your size so I got a seven. The lady assistant said better too big than too small and that you could always put an inner sole inside if they were too big. Go on, try them on, please.'

They were made of a bright-red plush material, designed to come up high around the ankles and fully lined. Nancy now had one slipper fitted over each hand.

Jane laughed, got down on her knees in front of Nancy, eased off her well-worn black shoes and slipped the new slippers on.

Nancy was choked. It was ten months since Jane had turned up on her doorstep after spending eight years in an institution because there wasn't a soul who was willing to take the responsibility for bringing her up. But it was a very different Jane who was sitting at her feet now. She would be seventeen this coming January, no longer a waif-like little girl, but a beautiful young woman whose features showed no trace of the suffering she had been put through.

She was kind and considerate, and it put joy in Nancy's heart to know that Jane continued to regard her as a close friend. She herself had no relatives left alive; she had good neighbours but it wasn't the same, and sometimes she felt lonely. Not now though; she was proud of Jane, in her heart regarding her as the daughter she had never had, and was thankful that she had been able to tell her that there was a home here with her if she should ever feel the need.

'Jane, luv, I don't know what t' say, they are lovely. They'll keep me feet as warm as toast.'

'Now don't go all soft on me,' Jane murmured, sensing that Nancy was near to tears. 'I've just had a better idea. I won't go and fetch us fish and chips; we'll go to Harrington's and we'll eat it there. That way you won't be able to make me do the washing-up.'

'As if I would,' Nancy protested. 'But it costs about a tanner each extra to eat in the café bit of the shop.'

'So what? Today I'm splashing out, so start getting yourself ready.'

'All right, no need to bully me.' Then as she crossed the room, Nancy turned, tilted her head and slyly said, 'I might even walk up the street in me new slippers.' The kitchen door had closed with a bang before Jane could think of an answer.

They had had a lovely day. Stayed up until turned midnight, both of them talking nineteen to the dozen. But now it was nearly time to go. Nancy was coming to Balham station to see Jane off on the train.

'You will let me know what 'appens to that young lass, won't you, Jane?' she asked as the tram rattled on through Tooting Bec.

The question had come out of the blue and Jane wasn't quite sure how to answer it, so she responded with a question of her own. 'Could they send her to prison, do you think?'

'Most certainly they could. But whether the magistrate will see fit t' do so is another matter,' Nancy replied knowingly.

'And what's that supposed to mean?' Jane was flabbergasted.

'Well, if it were the likes of you or me there would be no two ways about it. With no money for legal 'elp we'd be a dead loss. We'd get a sermon on the severity of our crime, probably get told that we lacked morals, the police wouldn't 'ave a good word to say on our behalf and before you know it we'd be locked away in 'Olloway.'

Jane stared at her in horror. 'I've heard about Holloway,

it's a women's prison, isn't it? Do you really believe they will send Glynis Harman there?'

Nancy grinned. 'Now I never said that! I said that's what would more than likely 'appen if it were you or me up in that dock. No, love, for one thing she ain't being tried in London, so I ain't got a clue as to where she would go if she were to be given a prison sentence. I'd take a bet, though, that she'll get off with a caution. Oh, the magistrate will add strings to it just to make it look as though he is un-biased, but you mark my words, money talks all languages. And breeding comes into it an' all.'

The tram had stopped again and Jane jumped to her feet, crying, 'Come on, you've nearly made us miss the station.'

It was only Jane's skilful shepherding that got Nancy's great bulk down from the high platform step from the tram to the road and then safely on to the pavement. It also took a bit of manoeuvring for the pair of them to cross to the other side of the main road. This was largely due to all the traffic, but the fact that Nancy decided to have an argument with the policeman on point duty because he had held them up so long before waving them across didn't help in the least!

Once Jane had shown her return half of the ticket, a porter pointed to which platform the train would arrive at and told them they had twenty-five minutes to wait.

Nancy fished in her bag, found two pennies and waddled off towards the sweet machine. Jane had to laugh as she watched her place one of the coins in the slot, thump the handle, then tug the drawer open and take out a bar of Nestlés milk chocolate, all neatly wrapped in its red and gold paper. Then she did exactly the same again.

''Ere yer are, me pet,' Nancy smiled, offering one of the bars to Jane. 'Let's sit down over there an' eat these while we wait.'

When Nancy was seated and munching happily at her chocolate, Jane said, 'Nancy, were you implying that money or breeding or even both would make a difference to whatever sentence a magistrate might decide was appropriate?'

'Course I was, luv. Like I said, no two ways about it.'

Seeing Jane staring at her in disbelief, Nancy put an arm across her chest and heaved her ample bosoms higher. 'Look at it like this, Jane. On the one hand you 'ave the father of this young girl living in Government 'Ouse in India as a representative of His Majesty our King. You 'ave 'er mother attending a glamorous party with 'er live-in lover who is young enough to be 'er son, while this poor lass who should be safely tucked up in some posh academy takes it in 'er 'ead to go for a late-night stroll an' maybe 'ave a drink or two. Which one of this group of people who should be looking after the girl do you think is going t' take the blame for her going off on 'er own?'

Jane was appalled!

It was almost as if Nancy had been at Adelaide House and heard everything that had been going on. She hadn't realized that she had given her so many details. In fact she was sure she hadn't. But Nancy was sharp. She had lived a long time and seen some goings-on. She'd certainly been shrewd when it came to putting the pieces in place as regards Mrs Harman's daughter.

Whistles were blowing, the train was approaching. Nancy took Jane's hand. 'Keep yer spirits up, pet. It's not your worry. It will get sorted and your Miss Christy will find out she's been worrying 'erself needlessly.'

They hugged each other tightly, and from the window Jane blew kisses as the train pulled away.

When she could no longer see her dear friend, Jane sank back into her corner seat. Her thoughts were going round in endless circles. She had never even met this Glynis Harman, and yet she and Nancy had spent hours talking about her. Funny, they both felt sorry for her. One thing she was very glad about, and that was that Miss Christy hadn't been around to hear Nancy describe Mr Charles as Mrs Harman's live-in lover, or the fact that he was young enough to be her son.

The first time the police had called at Adelaide House, Mrs Wilson had shown how very upset she was. 'A nice carry-on I must say, and for a respectable house such as this to be involved is just too much,' she had declared openly. Adding, 'Mr Charles should never have got himself tangled up with that Mrs Harman.'

Mr Wilson had grabbed her by the shoulders and told her to keep her thoughts to herself. Defiantly she had told him, 'Sometimes the truth hurts.'

Thinking back to that time, and now all of what Nancy had had to say, it was all too much for Jane to cope with. She shook her head, but was unable to clear her thoughts.

Had Nancy been right in her prediction? She hoped the part about Glynis Harman not having to go to jail would turn out to be true.

She also wished with all her heart that this affair hadn't affected Miss Christy so much. She was such a nice kind lady. Always thinking of others. She lived in a beautiful house and wanted for nothing, except for her eyesight to improve, though you never heard her complain about that. Now, instead of being happy, one only had to look at her to see that she was feeling despair.

As for Mr Charles, he seemed different, which was only to be expected. He had always been nice to Jane and she hoped for his sake that the court would be lenient towards Glynis Harman and that not too much scandal would rub off on him. The entire staff liked Mr Charles, and there wasn't one who didn't wish him the best of luck.

'God knows he'll need it,' Jane muttered aloud as the train took her nearer to Adelaide House.

Chapter Sixteen

THE ROOM BEGAN to spin sickeningly and Christine tried to grasp her son's hand, but there was a great rushing sound in her ears and everything was receding into darkness.

When she came to, she was lying on the floor, her head in Charles's lap and he was staring sadly down at her.

Mr Clarkson, the family solicitor, remained standing, looking down at her, unable to disguise the fact that he was worried. He had asked to speak to Charles in private, but Charles had insisted that there were no secrets between him and his mother.

'Don't worry, Mrs Dennison, I'll move heaven and earth to get this sorted,' he said softly, as he and Charles helped her up.

When Christine was seated he turned to face Charles. 'The young lady is clutching at straws, and not only that, she sees this as a way of paying you back for taking her mother away from her father.'

Charles sighed heavily. He was still holding his mother's hand, and she looked at him, her eyes brimming with tears, and asked, 'Why would she be so wicked?'

Charles shook his head. 'I know she has never liked me, and she was very rebellious the whole time she spent her half-term holiday with us. But this!'

Silently Mr Clarkson was thinking, who could blame the girl? Her mother had left the family home to live with a much younger man, and instead of the father doing his best to be there for her to make up for the loss of her mother, he'd upped sticks and taken himself back to India. A truly selfish reaction. It couldn't be counted as unnatural that the girl hated Charles and was out for revenge. But to name Charles as the father of her unborn baby was taking things to the extreme!

It had all been too much for Christine to take in. She shook her head dazedly before asking Mr Clarkson if he would outline the court's decision once again.

The solicitor looked to Charles, and, having received his nod of approval, once more took a sheaf of papers from his briefcase and began to explain.

'There was great weight set upon the fact that this was Glynis Harman's first offence. The extenuating family circumstances and the fact that the medical officer had found the young lady to be pregnant were also mentioned. A probation order of twelve months was made and conditions were set. In principal, Mrs Harman has agreed to return to the family home and to reside there and be responsible for the well-being of her daughter.'

Slowly Christine got to her feet and stared at her son. He looked ghastly. Her heart ached for him. She looked from him to Mr Clarkson, whom she had known and trusted for so many years. 'You will be able to prove that she is lying?' Her voice was a hoarse whisper.

'This terrible accusation will be sorted out in no time,' he assured her with as much conviction as he could muster.

'Folk will believe what she's saying. They will. They won't believe me.' Charles sounded scared.

'I think they will, Charles. You are a man of some standing.'

'Yes, and Glynis Harman is the daughter of a diplomat.'

'Charles,' Mr Clarkson quickly interrupted, 'we shall set the wheels in motion immediately. There are many ways to prove parentage; you are not to worry, leave it to me.'

'That's all very well, but mud sticks, and proving that Glynis is lying may take weeks, months even. In the mean time, what am I supposed to do? Hide myself away?'

'I'm sorry,' was all that Mr Clarkson could manage to say. Then he nodded sympathetically and shook hands with Charles. To Christine he said, 'Keep your spirits up, my dear. We'll sort it all out.'

Charles said he would walk with Mr Clarkson to his car.

When they'd gone, Christine sank back against the cushions and buried her face in her hands. Oh why on earth couldn't her son have found a decent young lady to fall in love with? It was tragic that Maureen, his first love, had died when only twenty-one, but to go from her to a married woman, causing the break-up of a whole family, was beyond her comprehension.

And now! To be accused of having made the woman's young daughter pregnant!

Poor Charles! What a state he had got himself into. And for what?

Where on earth was it all going to end?

God help us if the local press get hold of this story, thought Christine in despair. Or even, God forbid, the national newspapers.

'How are you feeling now?' Charles asked as he came back into the room.

Christine did her best to smile, but it didn't ease his

concern. 'Mother, I am so sorry to have brought all this trouble on you.'

'It can't be helped, not now.' She looked up into his hand-some face, and her heart was heavy. She still felt dizzy but was determined to get the answers to a few questions. 'Let's hope this question of parentage will be over and done with before the birth. Meanwhile, what do you propose doing with yourself?'

'I'm going back to work full-time. If I travel up to the City every day, at least . . .' He didn't finish the sentence.

'I was asking more about your living arrangements now that Mrs Harman has returned to her own home.'

'Having bought the cottage in Rye, I shall live in it on my own,' he said with chilling finality.

His mother looked anxious. 'You could close it up for a while. Let the dust settle and give yourself time to think. You know you've always got a home here.' There was a moment of silence before Christine spoke again, and when she did it was a cry of anguish. 'Oh Charles, please come home. I shan't have a moment's peace thinking of you living in that cottage all on your own. Besides, you won't want to get back from the City each night and start cooking for yourself. Have you thought about that?'

Charles's face broke into a grin and for a moment his mother saw the old carefree, happy young man that her son used to be. 'I was going to call in here each evening to have dinner with you. You know, I really have missed Mrs Wilson's cooking,' he said, sounding almost cheeky.

'So, if we are to have the pleasure of your company, it won't be because you want to see me, but just to satisfy the inner man?'

When no reply was forthcoming, she teased, 'Have I got that right?'

'Of course not, Mother. All right, if it will please you I will move back in – come home, I should say – but I think I shall hang on to the cottage. I don't feel I want to sell it at this point in time.'

'Oh Charles, this is the first good bit of news you've given me in days. And I think you are right to keep the house in Rye. There will be times when you will want to be on your own, even do some of your office work down there.'

'Well, I'm glad we've got that settled,' Charles agreed, then added quietly, 'It upsets me, the thought that Frieda is having to cope with Glynis all on her own. I couldn't blame her if she believes what her daughter tells her, though I hope against hope that she knows me a darn sight better than that. I tried to explain that I never for a moment thought about Glynis in that way. In actual fact, I have never really spent any time alone with the girl. But instead of the two of us discussing it rationally, it turned into a really ugly scene.'

'Well, I suppose the poor woman is torn between the two of you. However, I can't feel too sorry for her. The daughter's the one who is in the wrong, not you.'

Christine was also thinking to herself that Frieda hadn't been much of a mother. Leaving home like that, her daughter away at boarding school, she had acted as if she were a free woman. Shaking her head, she dismissed the thought, because if her mind ran along those lines then she would have to admit that her own son didn't come out of all this exactly snow-white.

Aloud she asked, 'What kind of a young lady is this Glynis?'

'A rich, spoiled one. And a girl who is out for revenge,' Charles answered sadly.

Chapter Seventeen

JANE STARED AT the rain as it beat against the window pane, then impatiently threw down the needlework that she was doing. November was drawing to a close; it would soon be Christmas. It was supposed to be a happy time. The smells which daily came from Mrs Wilson's kitchen were enough to make anyone's mouth water. We should be thinking about getting the house decorated, getting the gardeners to select a tree and bringing in armfuls of holly, she reflected miserably. Instead a cloud still hung over the whole household.

It was two weeks since Mr Charles had learned that he was no longer being named as the man who had made Glynis Harman pregnant.

Not that the girl herself had finally told the truth.

It was a young man from a neighbouring college who had finally owned up and confessed that he and a couple of other students had made a habit of meeting girls in the woods after lights-out. The lad had been brave enough to offer to marry Glynis, even though his parents were dead set against the idea. When told that he was willing to under go tests to prove that he was telling the truth and in all probability was the father of her child, Glynis had no option but to admit that she had lied about Charles.

The air had seemed to clear for a while, and all the staff were pleased that Mr Charles was back home living with his mother. Still, Miss Christine was not herself.

Not by a long chalk she wasn't!

She's lived in a highly agitated state of nerves ever since this business with Glynis Harman had come to light. More so at weekends, when she needed no telling where Charles had taken himself off to.

Voicing her thoughts aloud to Jane, she would complain, 'Why does he go to her house? It's as if he is asking for more trouble, walking straight into the lion's den.' That was the question she'd asked Jane so many times. Always adding, 'Why doesn't he just cut the woman out of his life and be done with her?'

Of course Jane had no answers for her. If the truth be told, she herself was as impatient and frustrated as Miss Christy was. She thought Charles deserved so much better. His life had been almost ruined because of that spoilt young lady.

It had come as no surprise that both the local and the national press had run the story. Both Mrs Harman and Charles Dennison had some standing locally, and that kind of news sold newspapers. Charles's denial hadn't been given much coverage, and when the truth had been brought to light it was the young man who was made out to be a hero, while hardly a hint of an apology was forthcoming to Charles.

It was all so sad, for everyone concerned. There was no brightness about Charles any more. And now, when everything appeared to be sorted and the dust should finally be settling, there had been another turn-up for the books. This morning the police had arrived at Adelaide House for a second time and Charles had gone off with them, telling his mother not to worry.

Don't worry! He couldn't have said anything more daft if he had tried.

'Jane, will you please come and sit down. You pacing up and down isn't going to solve anything.' Christine smiled weakly.

'If you insist, Miss Christine.' Jane really wanted to fly downstairs to find out if Mrs Wilson was any wiser than they were as to why Charles had gone off with the police.

As Jane seated herself there was a tap at the door and Mr Wilson entered, his expression serious, his manner very formal. He was followed by an elderly grey-haired man in clerical garb.

'The Reverend Leonard Shepherd would like a few words with you, Miss Christy,' Mr Wilson announced in a deep and respectful tone.

Before Mr Wilson had closed the door, Jane watched as Christine rose to her feet, walked forward and held out her hand. 'Leonard, it is so good of you to call. I heard from your young replacement that you had not been well and I have missed you at morning service.'

'I am feeling a whole lot better, not quite ready to be pensioned off,' he laughed as he guided Christine back to her chair. 'I only wish I were the bearer of better news.'

Christine sighed, already anticipating that this visit was to do with Mrs Harman and her daughter. 'Come and sit beside me. Will you have a drink or a cup of tea?'

'I think a glass of your excellent sherry would be nice. It seems ages since I've been in this lovely old house.'

Jane stood up and went to fetch the decanter and glasses, while the Reverend took off his overcoat. She poured them a glass each, placing Miss Christine's to her right hand at three o'clock, as she had become used to doing, and then went to sit in the window alcove.

'I should be coming here full of congratulations that Charles has been cleared of that awful accusation which must have caused you so much unhappiness. Instead . . .' The Reverend paused, and Christine knew from the tone of his voice that something was wrong.

'Leonard, I guessed something had happened when the police came and asked Charles to go with them. Has Mrs Harman been involved in an accident?'

'Well, I suppose one could say that.' Again he seemed loath to come to the point. Eventually he said, 'I was visiting an old friend at the hospital when both Mrs Harman and her daughter were brought in by ambulance. I considered it my duty to stay long enough to see to which wards they were going to be admitted, and also if I could be of any help.' The silence hung heavily and Leonard Shepherd had no option but to continue. 'The daughter is probably going to lose her baby, but it is Mrs Harman who is causing the most worry.'

Christine gasped and dropped her head in her hands. A minute or two passed before she asked, 'What happened, do you know the details?'

'Well,' he sighed, 'only the bare outline. I have been told that mother and daughter were having an argument, that one or the other lashed out and in trying to avoid the blow they both fell. Unfortunately they were standing at the head of the stairs and they finished up in the hall, which as I know from having been in Ashford Manor is a very long way to fall.'

Jane had heard every word – it was impossible not to – but it was Miss Christine that she was worried about.

Christine had got to her feet. Now she walked towards the fireplace and stood with her back to it.

'Will this business with the Harmans never end? God knows, Charles won't walk away now. It is as if that woman has him tied to her with an invisible rope.' She stood for a few seconds, her almost sightless eyes staring across the room. She was shaking with temper, but her eyes were brimming with tears at the shock of it all.

The parson had been taken completely off his guard by her fury, but now he had gathered his wits about him and turned to Jane with raised eyebrows.

'Don't worry about her, she'll be all right. I'll keep my eye on her,' Jane promised.

Christine had sat down again, her anger quickly lessened, to be replaced by utter dismay, and she was quietly crying.

Jane came and put her arms around her. 'It won't help much, but I feel as if I want to cry with you.'

Christine dabbed at her eyes with her handkerchief and managed to give Jane a watery smile.

Jane had listened in a state of silent horror for most of the time, but now she looked at Mr Shepherd and asked, 'Do you know why the police fetched Mr Charles?'

'No mystery there, my child. Mrs Harman has no near relatives, and I'm sorry to say, but it's common knowledge that Charles Dennison and Mrs Harman have been more than just good friends.'

'You mean he'll have to be responsible for her *and* her daughter?' Now it was Jane who was showing signs of a temper.

'I think that will be a matter for Mr Charles to decide for himself when all the facts are out in the open. Till then . . . well, we can only wait and pray.'

Jane pulled a face.

The elderly parson got to his feet and placed a hand on Christine's head. 'Your son is a good man, he'll do the right thing. Now, before I leave you, shall we say a prayer together? For both the mother and the daughter, and for Charles, that the Lord may be with them and let his mercy and blessing shine upon them.'

'Oh, Holy Mary, Mother of our Lord Jesus Christ, look after my son,' Christine whispered quietly.

'God bless and keep us all,' the parson added.

Then, reluctantly, he took his leave, urging Christine to send for him if there was any way in which he could help.

The minute the door closed behind him, Christine gave vent to her true feelings.

'Just as Charles was getting his life organized, this has to happen! It's almost as if she's planned it. She'll have him tied to her good and true now, and knowing my son he'll stay linked to her like glue. And if I were to raise any objections I know exactly what his reply would be. What would you have me do, Mother? Desert a sinking ship?' She shook her head sadly. 'Oh Jane, what a mess.'

Jane gripped Christine's hand tightly. She knew what *she* would like to say to Mr Charles. Get on with your own life. He was such a lovely man. The whole house seemed brighter and happier when he was around. Mrs Harman and her blessed daughter had already sent him halfway to hell and back as a result of Glynis's malicious allegation, so why should he go running to help them now?

She knew the answer to her own question.

Because he was a decent man. Well, she wished that just this once he would think of himself and let that pair do what the hell they wanted without involving him.

Christine's senses told her what Jane was feeling and she

swiftly said, 'Come on, Jane, we'll have a cup of tea and some biscuits while we wait for more news from the hospital.'

'You stay here in the warm, I'll go downstairs and fetch us a tray,' Jane told her, patting Christine's hand, which rested on the arm of her chair.

Christine raised her head and smiled tiredly. 'What would I do without you, Jane? I dread to think.'

It was said so sadly that it prompted Jane to ask, 'Are you going to be all right?'

'Let's see. My son left home to live with Mrs Harman, a much older married woman. Her daughter accused him of having fathered her baby.' She heaved a sigh. 'The courts told the woman to come to her senses and take responsibility for her daughter, and Charles accepted that and came home to where he belonged. Now, at the first sign of trouble, the police come for my son. And if anyone should ask, Mr Harman has washed his hands of the whole affair and left my son to deal with it all as best he can. How does the saying go? If you have the sweets you have to put up with the sourers. Well, my poor Charles is certainly being made aware of that fact. Apart from that, everything is fine, wouldn't you say so, Jane?'

Jane had to smile. 'I'm glad you're not still in a temper and that you still have a sense of humour.'

'Only on the outside, Jane, believe me, only on the outside. Inside I am all churned up.'

Chapter Eighteen

MISS CHRISTY WAS in bed, and Jane was sitting in the garden room, as she had decided to call it. At the end of a long, tiring day it was real bliss to be able to sit in here with a cup of hot cocoa and relax a bit before she too went to bed. In her mind's eye she was making two lists. One consisted of good things, and the other of bad.

Forget the bad for the moment, she chided herself, and count your blessings. And she had to admit there were many. Only five days to go now till Christmas, and she was ready. Organized very well, really. She, Mary, Sarah and even Daisy had been given an afternoon off and had been driven into Hastings by Brownlow, the chauffeur, to do their Christmas shopping. They'd had a great time. They'd all bought Christmas cards and small presents for their relatives.

Buying gifts had brought a lump to Jane's throat. She had chosen well, though. Lavender-scented soap and talcum powder for Nancy and for Mrs Forrester. Prettily packed and finished with brown paper, those two parcels had already been posted. She had found the most exquisite lace handkerchiefs to give to Miss Christine and Mrs Rogers, because that was the biggest bonus of all: Elsie Rogers was coming as a house guest for two whole weeks! Oh, it was going to be such a wonderful time.

Jane had settled on small boxes of chocolates for her three workmates. The four of them had pooled their money and very extravagantly had bought half a bottle of whisky for Mr Wilson and a small bottle of port for Mrs Wilson. They had thought it would be presuming too much to buy a gift for Mr Charles.

Add all that excitement to the fact that the house was looking absolutely wonderful. Like a Christmas wonderland, had been Jane's thought as she wandered around the house after the gardeners had put the decorations in place.

Sighing softly, she turned to her not so happy thoughts. While out on her buying spree, she had been aware of how lucky she was to have money to spend on gifts for others, but oh, how wonderful it would have been were she able to buy something for her own mother.

Knowing that her brother Tommy was dead and that Mick Jeffrey had not been her father, she had, to her knowledge, only one real relative. She would give her eye teeth to be able to see her mother, or even to write to her, if it were true what Nancy had heard: that Alice and Wally Simmonds had left England together and had gone to live abroad.

She certainly did not want to appear ungrateful, but if she got a chance during the Christmas holidays she was going to broach the subject with Mrs Rogers. It was she who had said that there were ways and means of tracing missing relatives.

Living here in Adelaide House was like a dream come true. More than that! Because Jane had never known or even imagined that such an elegant way of life existed. Never would she take her job for granted. Nor the privilege of caring for Miss Christine. No, she'd never do that.

Every day was still a source of amazement. When she let her mind wander back to the time when she had had to leave Winchelsea Lodge, she would shudder. Sometimes she wondered how she had survived. She had felt so utterly alone, and there had been times when she'd been so cold, chilled right through to her bones, and even hungry. If it hadn't been for Mrs Rogers and Mrs Forrester, she probably wouldn't have made it. And there had been other caring people. She smiled as she remembered the café owner and his wife who had given her such heart-warming meals *and* provided her with a pair of boots to keep her feet dry.

Now her life was so very different and she was terrified of change. What if she should have to find another job, and go back to living all on her own in a bed-sitting room? It didn't bear thinking about!

The other thing on her bad list was the everlasting problem that Mr Charles had to face. Miss Christine did her best to hide the fact that still she worried over her son, but there were days when Jane knew her mistress was really sad.

Glynis Harman had suffered a miscarriage due to her fall down so many stairs. But she was young and fit and apparently had not sustained any lasting damage. According to the rumours that Mrs Wilson picked up from the delivery men who called at the house from the village shops, the girl could not wait for her probation order to be completed. Instead, her legal advisers had applied to the court for permission for her to leave the country to live with her father, on the grounds that her mother was now incapable of caring for herself, never mind her daughter. The court officials had agreed it was the best way out of a bad situation.

One had to feel sympathy for Frieda Harman. The fall had done her untold damage. If there were any truth in the stories floating around, she was practically paralysed from the waist down. Charles played his cards close to his chest. He never had a word to say on the subject. In fact he made no reference to Frieda Harman whatsoever.

Miss Christine had made it her business to find out as much as was possible. Especially when she'd learned that Mrs Harman was in a private nursing home. That, however, had only lasted for three weeks. Word was that she was an intolerable patient, and the main reason she had discharged herself was because she wasn't allowed to smoke cigarettes while lying in bed.

As far as was known now, Mrs Harman was at home. Attended during the day by a female nurse, while a male nurse took over for night-time duty. Charles spent the best part of every weekend up at Ashford Manor, and of course there must still be some staff employed in that house, but Jane had learned never to ask questions.

It had been exactly as Christine had predicted. Charles's only comments when urged to think of his own life had been, 'One does not desert a sinking ship.'

There had been one disastrous day when even Miss Christy had been moved to phone Charles at his office in London and urge him to come home.

Once again the police had been involved. The day nurse, for reasons of her own, had taken it into her head to walk to the village, apparently leaving her patient alone in that big rambling house. Burglars had broken in, even going so far as to ransack Frieda's bedroom while she lay helpless, watching them help themselves to most of her jewellery.

The men hadn't hurt her, only threatened her. But naturally the poor woman had been absolutely terrified. And it seemed that Charles was the only one who could calm her.

Much to his mother's annoyance, he had slept over at the Manor for three days after that incident. Jane grinned as she remembered how the whole household had breathed a sigh of relief when he had returned home. 'God forbid he should tie himself completely to that woman again,' had been Christine's anguished cry.

Jane had felt for her. How many times even she had asked herself, 'Oh why doesn't he break away from Mrs Harman for good?' She had never found an answer.

There wasn't one to find.

Just lately she had begun to question her own feelings where Mr Charles was concerned and she'd had to tell herself to keep her thoughts to herself.

Towards Miss Christine and of course Mrs Rogers she still felt so much gratitude and was never embarrassed when either one of them showed their affection for her. But lately with Mr Charles it was different. True, she felt sorry for him. But then so did every member of the staff. But it's me that comes into the closest contact with him, she was thinking. And she would have to deal with it.

Some time ago, she had been putting his freshly ironed shirts away in his tallboy when he had come back unexpectedly into his room. She had thought he had left the house. Suddenly she had felt self-conscious at the nearness of this handsome man with his thick blond hair and those blue eyes. He looked so manly. So well groomed, wearing his City clothes, a well-cut suit, crisp white shirt and dark-blue tie. And yet there were times when he looked and acted like a sad young boy. No wonder she had let silly girlish notions get the better of her.

Mary had started walking out with a lad from the village. He could be seen from the windows, waiting at the gate on

Mary's afternoon off. There had been a suggestion that Jane make up a foursome with another lad. The idea hadn't appealed to her. Her life was good. There probably would come the day when she might think about having a young man; even getting married might be on the cards, because a family of her own would be wonderful. But that day was a long way off.

She finished her cocoa and got slowly to her feet. It was time she was in her bed.

As she walked up the stairs, she sensed that life for Mr Charles had become very complicated. She had no idea why she should feel that somehow that fact was going to have a great effect on her own life.

If it were true, what was she supposed to do about it?

Her feelings were too mixed up for her to answer that.

Chapter Nineteen

JANE WOKE EARLY on Christmas morning and knew the whole holiday was going to be a great success. Mrs Wilson had been up half the night, and the smell of roasting turkey and pork filled the air. Beside Mrs Rogers, there were two other house guests: Dorothy and Richard Stuart, who, Jane knew, had been largely instrumental in securing a place for her at Winchelsea Lodge all those years ago.

Jane had been asked if she wanted to spend most of the time upstairs or below stairs with the other staff, Miss Christine not having quite so much need for her while Elsie Rogers was there. Jane was pleased to be given the choice and gladly said she would like to be with the three girls.

With breakfast over, they all trooped upstairs: Mr and Mrs Wilson, Mary, Sarah, Daisy and Jane.

Christine and Charles were standing in the main hall near to the huge Christmas tree, waiting for them. Elsie Rogers stood beside them looking very pleased with herself.

'We wish you all a very happy Christmas and we'd like

you each to have a gift. If you'd distribute these, please, Mr Wilson,' Charles said, smiling broadly.

Mr Wilson took his work very seriously and made a formal thank-you speech before giving everyone a small box with a name tag attached to it, and a festively wrapped parcel from Mrs Rogers.

No one opened their presents until they were back in the kitchen.

All four girls had each been given two half-sovereigns.

'Are they real gold?' Daisy asked, absolutely astounded at her employer's generosity.

'Course they are,' three voices assured her.

The girls' parcels were quickly unwrapped to reveal hand-knitted cardigans which Jane knew from experience Mrs Rogers would have bought at a church sale of work. They were all very nice. Jane really liked hers; it was a rich Oxford blue, with a pattern down each side in cable stitch and leather-covered buttons that did up to the neck. She held it up to her face, feeling the softness and the warmth of the wool.

A glance was exchanged between Mr and Mrs Wilson, who marvelled that the girl who had come to this house wearing a terrible dress and boots that were a couple of sizes too big for her, and looking as if she had been really ill, could have changed so much. About nine months ago, that was all it was. But what a change. Now she had blossomed, her cheeks had filled out, and yes, she was a poised and lovely young woman.

Mr and Mrs Wilson opened their parcels, and their faces showed they were more than pleased with what Mrs Rogers had bought for them. For him there was a sleeveless pullover, and for Cook a huge crocheted shawl. Their boxes containing money they put aside to open later in the privacy of their own house.

Mary, Sarah and Jane were allowed to accompany the five adults from upstairs to the special Christmas church service. Daisy remained behind to help Mrs Wilson. Once they were all back, it was time to serve lunch.

'I still think it should be called dinner,' Mary whispered to Jane as they followed Mr Wilson up to the dining room, each carrying a huge tureen.

Now it was late evening. Everyone had eaten their fill and Mrs Wilson had covered the kitchen table with a chenille cloth, placing a bowl of fruit in the centre and another bowl filled with brazils and walnuts to the side of it.

'Pull the curtains, one of you,' Cook called out. 'And you others sort out the board games and bring them to the table. With the cold buffet supper we've laid out in the dining room, I don't think they'll be wanting much more upstairs tonight if I'm any judge, so perhaps Mr Wilson will relax his rules for once and pour us all a drink.'

Mr Wilson nodded his head and gave his wife one of his rare smiles, saying, 'After all, it is Christmas.'

Jane went to the window and stood looking up into the garden. It was a bright starry night with signs that there was going to be a heavy frost. A few days ago there had been the mention of a white Christmas, but no snow had fallen yet.

She was about to pull the curtains when she saw Mr Charles. He must have fetched his car out from the garage earlier. She watched as he now stowed several parcels on the back seat, then got in behind the wheel, started the engine and put the car into gear. The wheels rolled forward across the gravel.

Even today he has to leave his family and go to her, was the first thought that came to her mind. Then she hastily told herself, not that it's got anything to do with you.

It had been a wonderful day. One Jane told herself she would remember for the rest of her life. Mr and Mrs Wilson couldn't have been nicer if they were the parents of the four girls.

They had all eaten exactly the same dinner as their employers: turkey with bacon rolls and sauages, leg of pork with crisp crackling, roast potatoes, buttered sprouts and baby parsnips, bread sauce and cranberry jelly, home-made, of course. And best of all, at least to Jane, had been the gravy! Dark and rich, made from all the juices from the bottom of the roasting pans, just as Mrs Wilson always did it, but today she had added wine. It had been gorgeous!

The pudding had been made weeks and weeks before, from candied peel, currants, sultanas, almonds and plump raisins. Daisy had moaned about having been given the job of stoning the fruit. It had also fallen to her to grate the huge lumps of suet that the butcher had delivered especially. Being the tweeny in a big house was hard at times.

Of course the pudding had to be eaten with brandy butter and clotted cream. And as if it were her consolation prize, Daisy had screamed with delight when she had discovered not one but two silver threepenny pieces in her portion.

'I shan't spend my silver joeys,' she had quietly stated. 'I shall take them home and give them to my mum, 'cos they're supposed to be lucky, aren't they?'

'They are indeed,' Mr Wilson assured her, thinking to himself how little it took to please this young lass.

Now they were playing games: snakes and ladders, ludo, housey-housey, draughts and shove-halfpenny. Jovial laughter and lots of teasing of each other was probably helped along by the fact that all four girls had been given a glass of port and lemon. It had certainly brought the roses to their cheeks.

'Time for a break,' Mr Wison declared as he got up to shovel more coal on to the fire, sending sparks flying up the chimney. And now there was more food being placed on the table, and what was this that was coming out of the larder? Funny hats, and a box of crackers for the girls to pull. Sausage rolls were going into the oven, and mince pies. It was like a real family children's party.

But finally Mr Wilson said it was time he took one last look upstairs to see if anything was needed, and that the girls should go to their beds.

They got up from the table, now littered with coloured paper from the crackers, jokes and riddles which had caused so much laughter as they had been read aloud, nutshells, and tangerine peel. Mary led the way. As they went, they each in turn paused to stoop and kiss Mrs Wilson's plump cheek and thank her and her husband for having given them such a happy Christmas Day.

There were only two days left of the old year. In the small sitting room, in front of a roaring log fire, Jane had been listening attentively to Elsie Rogers for the past half-hour. Now she said, in a low, thoughtful voice, 'So what you've found out is that both my mother and Wally Simmonds did apply for passports, and also made an application to be considered as emigrants to Australia.'

Elsie nodded. 'But as I have already told you, the trail went cold from there.'

'So what happened? Can we find out if they ever went or not?'

'I don't know.' Elsie gave a slight shrug of her shoulders. 'Despite all my efforts I truly don't have any idea.'

'But why would they apply and then do nothing about it?'

Elsie shook her head. 'I haven't a clue, Jane. I want to help you find your mother, you know I do, but I don't as yet know what my next step will be. They both went to Australia House, that much I have established, but from that point I can't find any trace of either of them. I'm baffled, truly I am.'

Jane sighed and took a sip from the cup of tea in front of her. Then she leaned back in the chair, and glancing round the room said quietly, 'Last night I couldn't sleep. I suppose I dozed off and on, but mostly my mind was wandering way back, trying to remember things.'

'And did you think of anything that would help?'

'Not about my mother leaving Mickey, though from what I do remember she would have had good cause. To my mind she was always terrified of him. No, the clearest pictures that came to mind were of me being in hospital. Whenever I woke up or cried because I was hurting, my mother always seemed to be there beside my bed. She would hold my hand, smooth my hair back from my face.'

There was a heavy silence between them. Eventually, Jane looked at Elsie earnestly, and said, 'She kept telling me how much she loved me.'

'We both know that is true, Jane. And I know full well that giving you up was the only thing she could do at that time. She had no other option.'

'I tell myself that over and over again, and I do my best to believe it. But if that was the way it was, why did she never keep in touch with me? Not even one birthday card in all these years! Why, Mrs Rogers? Why?'

All the feelings that Elsie had ever had towards Jane now rushed to the fore. She wanted to take her into her arms, tell her she would dearly love to be looked upon as her mother, but at the same time she knew it would be of no use.

It had been a privilege to be part of Jane's life, but the need to find her real mother was so great. Jane's big blue eyes were brimming with tears and her face was so bleak that Elsie's heart went out to her.

She swallowed hard. 'I don't know, Jane, she must have had her reasons. I'm sure it wasn't because she didn't want to.'

Jane's thoughts were rushing around in her head and she bit her lip before asking, 'Do you think she may be dead?'

'No, not for a moment do I think your mother is dead, but there's one sure way to find out. Somerset House is the next place I will check; it's where a register of births, marriages and deaths, for the whole of Great Britain is kept. It's a proper mine of information. And while I'm there I'll check if your mother obtained a divorce from Michael Jeffrey; that's if they keep records of divorces, I'm not sure about that.' She certainly would have had sufficient grounds, Elsie thought grimly. 'Can't think why I didn't think of going there before now,' she added out loud.

'Where is this Somerset House?' Jane asked eagerly.

'In London, between Victoria Embankment and the Strand. As soon as I can get up to town I shall spend some time there. We'll find your mother, Jane. Just be patient and bear in mind that it might take some time. But in the end we shall find her. You'll see.'

'I'd like to drink a toast to that,' Jane said, doing her best to smile as she raised her teacup.

'Me too,' Elsie agreed, 'even if it is only in tea, but come the day and we'll change it to champagne and that's a promise. Meanwhile, my dear, remember there are a great number of people who do love you, and I hope you know that I head the list.'

Jane leaned forward and took Elsie's hand between both of hers.

She was too full to speak.

Besides, words were not necessary.

There was a long-established bond between these two.

It was the second week in January before Elsie Rogers was able to get to London. She took a taxi from outside the railway station, and as she walked through the massive doors of Somerset House she found herself in the records office itself. Everywhere she looked there were stacks and stacks of ledgers lined up on shelves. What a daunting task if one had to search through that lot, she muttered to herself as she made her way to the main desk.

The officer in charge was a handsome man who wore his uniform well. He smiled as he said, 'Good morning, ma'am, sorry but I have to check the contents of your handbag.'

This didn't take long, and when he had finished Elsie said to him, 'Please can you tell me how I go about finding out if a person's death has been recorded.'

The officer directed her to an enquiry desk where two clerks were standing ready to be of assistance. Briefly, Elsie told one of them the reason for her being there.

'Have you any idea of the date when the death might have occurred?' this capable young woman asked.

'Well, yes.' Elsie hesitated. 'I know she was alive and well early in 1921.'

'Well, as we are only just into 1929, you only have to search through eight years, which shouldn't take you too long. Alternatively you may pay for a search fee and have the work done for you if time is of the essence.' Having said that, the young woman handed a pamphlet across the counter, saying, 'This tells you how to use the Public Search Room.'

'May I ask another question?' Elsie was feeling a bit bewildered by her surroundings.

'Yes, of course. I'm here to help in any way I can.'

Elsie nodded her thanks, then hesitantly said, 'If there is no record of this person's death, is it possible to discover if her marriage has been dissolved, and if so whether she has remarried?'

'Yes, though that would be in a different set of records, Marriages and Births. I'll get you another pamphlet.'

Elsie thanked her, but because she still looked so worried, the clerk said, 'To save time, why don't you go and have a cup of tea, read through both pamphlets and then decide if you are going to do the search yourself. It really is not too difficult. All ledgers are clearly dated, four books for the four quarters of each year, and they're alphabetical.'

Elsie acted on that good advice.

Whilst sipping her coffee she was talking to herself. Looking for a record of Jane's mother's death is just going to be a wild-goose chase. She is such a young woman, only about fifteen or sixteen years older than Jane. I'm quite sure she is not dead and I don't want to stay here all day, searching through endless ledgers. I so rarely get a whole day to myself and never up in London. So I know what I'm going to do, I'm going to pay the search fee, let someone else find the information for me, and I'm going sight-seeing.

When she came back to the enquiry desk, she bided her time, determined to see the young woman who had helped her earlier.

'I've decided to pay the search fee, please, but I do have one or two more questions. Is that all right?'

The young woman nodded her head. 'Yes, of course, fire away.'

'This lady I am trying to trace may have gone abroad to live. You wouldn't have her death recorded if it had taken place outside of England, would you?'

'Oh yes we would. Wherever a British subject dies, the death is eventually recorded here. The information comes through all of the British embassies around the world.'

'I see.'

'It's really quite straightforward,' the clerk went on. 'If your friend's name is not in one of the registers, then she is not dead. She is still alive.'

Elsie gaped at the clerk. 'Thank you very much for your help.' Still she hesitated.

'Was there another problem?' the clerk asked.

'Well, sort of . . . It's like this. If the lady I am looking for is not dead, she is probably living with an old friend. They would have liked to marry, I'm pretty sure of that, but the lady, when I last heard of her, was still married to another man.'

The clerk laughed. 'Don't sound so embarrassed, your problem is not unusual. We do have records of divorce actions. We could probably find the answers you're seeking, which from what you asked me earlier I presume will include whether or not the lady in question has remarried.'

Elsie breathed a sigh of relief before laughingly saying, 'You're a mind-reader. I would like you to make all three searches for me, please.'

'So . . .' The clerk drew a notepad towards her, picked up a pencil and said, 'First we have to affirm that the lady is still alive. Secondly whether she has been granted a divorce, and thirdly whether she has remarried.' Having written all that down, she raised her head and asked, 'Can you give me the lady's full name? And it would help if you can supply her last known address.'

This was no problem. Having reread Jane's case notes, Elsie knew the address in Tooting off by heart, and the exact date when she had last spoken to Jane's mother.

When all details were down on paper to the satisfaction of the lady clerk, Elsie took her purse from her handbag and with trembling fingers drew forth a note. 'How much will the search cost?' she enquired.

'It will be three separate searches and the fee will be seven and sixpence for each search, making a total of one pound two and sixpence.'

Laying the pound note down on the counter, Elsie searched in her purse for a half-crown to add to it.

'That's fine,' the young lady said, picking up the money, 'I'll just get you a receipt.'

A few moments only passed and the official receipt was in Elsie's hand.

'Will you be calling back for the information or would you like the search set out in detail and posted on to you?'

'Posted on would suit me better, please. Here's my address,' Elsie said, handing one of her business cards across the counter.

The clerk raised her eyebrows as she read the information on the card. 'You should have said you were involved in social work for the law courts. I'm sure one of my superiors would have gladly helped you at no cost.'

Elsie smiled softly. 'Please, don't worry, what I'm doing today is for my own personal reasons and I am truly grateful for your help.'

Feeling very relieved, the clerk held out her hand. 'I hope the search will bring forth all the information that you are seeking and that the outcome will be good.'

'So do I,' Elsie murmured as she turned away.

So do I.

Chapter Twenty

JANE HAD BEEN sitting sewing, only half listening to what Charles was saying to his mother. But when he raised his voice, sounding annoyed, she sat up and began to take notice.

'I never gave it another thought until I checked my diary last night,' he scowled. 'Bit of a nuisance but I'll have to ring the telephone exchange and ask them to put the engineers off.'

'I'm sorry,' Christine murmured without much enthusiasm. 'But my arrangements were made ages ago.'

'That's true,' Jane said beneath her breath. Mr and Mrs Stuart had offered some time since to travel up to Moorfields eye hospital with Christine. That fact had niggled Jane quite a lot. Not that she wasn't glad that Miss Christine was going to have a specialist examine her eyes once more and maybe, just maybe, hold out a little hope that some improvement could be made. It was more that she felt she wasn't needed.

And that fact worried her a great deal.

I should be going to London with Miss Christy. That's

what I get paid for! But she couldn't possibly put her thoughts into words. She just had to accept her mistress' decision.

She stood up. 'I don't mean to interfere, Mr Charles, but if it is only a case of someone being on the premises to let the telephone engineers in and stay there while they work, I'll willingly go there, if you'd like me to.'

Why had she made that offer? Pushing herself forward like that. She wasn't as shy as she used to be, but she wasn't normally forward either.

Charles was obviously taken back slightly by her offer. But he recovered quickly and with a serious look on his face said, 'If you are sure you wouldn't mind, I would appreciate it.' Then quickly he added, 'They don't give an exact time, so you might be there some time.'

Jane smiled. 'I'm sure I'll find a book to read.'

Christine said she thought it was a good idea. 'Be a change of scenery for you, Jane.'

'Well, if you're sure.' Charles turned to face her. 'If you could be ready by a quarter to eight on Wednesday morning, I'll drop you off at the cottage before I catch my train to town.'

By twenty minutes to eight on Wednesday morning, Jane was waiting in the main hall.

Charles parked his car at the foot of the steps, got out, came round to the passenger side and held open the door. He looked at her, just a quick glance, smiled slightly and said, 'All right, just push my briefcase down on to the floor.'

Before they were out of the drive, he leaned over and reached into the glove compartment, his forearm accidentally brushing across her knee. Jane felt the colour flood her cheeks. She had never been this close to him before. One eye on the road, he felt in the compartment and took out a Foyle's bookshop bag. 'I bought you a book yesterday just to make sure you won't be bored,' he said, dropping the bag into her lap.

'Oh, thank you.' Jane nodded, thinking how kind and thoughtful he was.

'I hope you like my choice.'

She withdrew the book and read the title: *Jane Eyre*. 'That's great,' she told him, smiling.

'Not a very nice day,' he remarked, glancing quickly up at the sky as he stopped the car at the end of a country lane. 'It's the last one. Far End is the name of the property. Bit isolated, one reason I've decided to have the telephone installed. You have brought something to eat?' he asked, nodding at the basket she had placed between her feet.

'Did you think Mrs Wilson would let me go hungry?'

'No,' he laughed. 'Plenty of tea and coffee in the kitchen. Did you remember to bring fresh milk?'

'Mr Charles! I'm only going to be here for a day at most. I shall be fine. You'd better get going or you'll miss your train.'

From his wallet he took out a business card and handed it to her. His office address was printed there, along with a telephone number. 'If they do manage to get me connected, give me a ring, and if I don't hear from you I shall pick you up this evening. With any luck I should be able to catch an early train. Be back five to five thirty, all right?'

'Yes,' she said. 'I've told you, I shall be fine.'

She stood by a hedge and watched him back up and drive off towards Rye railway station. Then a biting wind made her tug her hat down securely. It's really pretty here, she was thinking as she walked alongside a stream which ran on the opposite side of the lane. Further along she passed a row of six terraced houses. Then there were several yards of shrubs and trees with fields beyond on both sides of the lane before she came to the detached property known as Far End.

Her first impression was that it was just like an illustration from a child's story-book. Thatched roof, small leaded lattice windows, dark oak front door with heavy studded iron bars. A front garden with stepping stones. Shiny shrubs that were green and leafy despite the fact that it was still only early February.

She took a deep breath, swung open the garden gate and walked up the gravel path. She glanced around to see if anyone was about.

There was no one. She could have been in a world all of her own. It was so quiet. All she could see was sheep in a field, but as she put the key into the lock she noticed a blackbird sitting on a fence looking as if he were watching her. Then she heard the sound of pigeons cooing softly, although she couldn't spot them. She decided they were playing it safe and staying warm under the eaves.

The minute she stepped inside the cottage a smile settled on Jane's face. First glance said beautiful. Charming. There were silk-shaded wall lights and she switched them on. The hall was decorated in soft greyish blue and all the paintwork was gleaming white. She opened the door on the left, obviously a dining room. The table was an antique with brass claw feet and the chairs were covered in pearl-grey velvet, There was an open fireplace with an oak surround, and a basket of logs stood in the hearth.

Moving across the hall, she entered the front sitting room. Fascinated, she walked slowly round. If Mrs Harman had lived here, a fact of which Jane was aware, then all traces of her had been removed. This was a gentleman's retreat.

Certain things in the room were worn, even a little shabby, but the impression she got was one of leather and brass fittings. Two deep armchairs in a burgundy-coloured leather stood one each side of the fireplace. Peeping further she looked into a kind of alcove which made the room an L-shape. Oh yes, this was Mr Charles's retreat all right. One huge leather-topped desk and a swivel captain's chair, almost a replica of the one he used in his room at Adelaide House. There was a pipe rack on the wall and to her amazement a dog's basket in the far corner. A basket for a very large dog, by the look of it.

There were no dogs kept at Adelaide House, though Jane had often seen Charles set off across the fields with a labrador in tow, but that dog, Calum, belonged to one of the gardeners.

Strange! If she could summon up enough courage, she would like to ask him about that. After setting her packed lunch out in the small but very neat kitchen, Jane decided it was in order for her to look upstairs. Though as she trod the narrow carpeted stairs she smiled to herself and said aloud, 'Curiosity killed the cat!'

There were three bedrooms, although one was little more than a box room. Adequate, clean and tidy, but lacking a woman's touch was what she decided. The bathroom was tiny, and a big old-fashioned tub on feet took up most of the space. The washbasin was big, with heavy brass taps, and a wooden shelf above held everything a gentleman needed for shaving and grooming himself. Two white bath towels hung from a brass rail, not very tidily. Jane took them down, shook them, refolded them and placed them back over the rail. From a hook behind the door hung a gentleman's paisley dressing gown.

Halfway down the stairs she stopped on the landing and

perched herself on the wide windowsill. From this window she could see the outline of Rye's girls' school. The years she had spent there had not been unhappy and she smiled as memories came flooding back. When she had first gone there there had been no lighting at all in the school. If it got dark too early in the winter, the headmistress would pop her head round the door of each classroom and ask the teacher to allow the pupils to go home early. The excitement when electricity had been installed had been great, and that had only been a couple of years before she had left.

They had been taught that Rye was one of five ancient ports on the south coast of England lying opposite France. And the fact that it was so near to Winchelsea had been marvellous. Many a happy picnic the Matron of Winchelsea Lodge had prepared for the girls in her charge to eat on the beach there.

Jane sent up a silent prayer of thanks.

Her life to begin with had been rough. Very rough. She had lived in terror of Mick Jeffrey, knowing that no matter what she did, she could never please him. But since she had been taken away from him, life had not been so bad. The only blight had been the loss of her mother and Tommy. It had meant the loss of her whole family really, because as far as she knew she had no one else. Still, the years here in this area could have been a thousand times worse, and she had so much to be thankful for. Her time in the home had come to an end, as was inevitable, and again she had found that life on your own could be rough, even terrifying. Then look what had happened! She had met some bad people, but on the other hand she had meet some really good folk. And to have landed up as companion to Miss Christy was almost unbelievable when you compared the way she lived now to what her life might have been if she had stayed and found work in London.

The door bell ringing broke into Jane's thoughts, and she slipped off her seat and ran down the stairs to open the door to two energetic-looking young men.

One was dressed in blue overalls; the other had his hands stuck deep into the pockets of his short thick double-breasted jacket.

'Miss Dennison?' the younger of the two asked politely. 'All the outside work has been carried out; we only have to make the connection and install the apparatus.'

'No,' Jane stammered, 'I'm Miss Jeffrey, but I was expecting you, please come in.'

'We shan't bother you for long,' he said, stepping over the threshold and laying down his tool kit, while the other young man looked around before placing a shiny black telephone on its own stand on to the hall table. 'This is the model Mr Dennison ordered. He particularly stated he did not want a wall-mounted version.'

Jane smiled at him warmly, liking them both. 'It's a pretty horrible day out there. Would you men like a cup of tea?'

'Yes please,' they answered in unison.

By the time Jane returned to the hall carrying a tray, there was every sign that the work was well under way. A cardboard reel of white-covered cable was being slowly unwound and the second workman was fitting it to the wainscoting with funny-shaped little clips.

As she poured the tea, the older of the two men said, 'This is good of you. We appreciate it.'

Jane said nothing, but smiled softly and went back to sit in the kitchen. She could hear the low murmur of their voices but when, about half an hour later, the shrill ring of the telephone rang through the cottage, she almost dropped her book. The loud sound seemed an intrusion to the peace and quietness. It was obvious the engineer was talking to the main exchange. 'Yes, all right, we'll make the adjustment if you'll ring back in two minutes,' she heard him say.

She was ready for the second ringing and walked out into the hall as one of the men picked up the receiver. After a few short words he replaced the phone on its stand, picked up a clipboard and asked Jane if she would sign on the line that he was pointing to. 'Just to say that the work has been carried out and checked,' he grinned at her.

It was still early when they left, and Jane wondered what she should do now.

She didn't know anything about the buses, and anyway, with Miss Christine away in London, there was no urgent reason for her to return to Adelaide House. She unlocked and pushed open the back door that led out from the kitchen and went outside, across the gravelled footpath and on to the grass, which was bordered with shrubs. At the far end, almost hidden by trees, was a shed. She lifted the latch, had a good look round and found a pair of clippers lying on the bench. Within minutes she had cut a small bouquet of various evergreens. She looked towards the pastures that lay a few hundred yards away but decided the wind was too bitter for her to attempt a long walk. She turned around and headed back towards the house.

Rummaging in the cupboards beneath the sink, she found two yellow dusters and a tin of mansion polish. From a shelf in the pantry she took down a golden-coloured ceramic vase.

For more than an hour she hummed as she dusted and polished the front room. Her last task was the tidying of a magazine rack and the setting of the vase, which now held water and her glossy greenery, on to the centre of a side table. Was it her imagination, or did the vase of leafy branches bring an earthy garden smell into the room? They certainly looked good. Autumn colours, even though that season was long past, and Jane couldn't help but wonder how it would be to live in this lovely old cottage come the spring and then the summer.

The light was going, it would soon be dark. Back in the kitchen she washed the two dusters and hung them in the pantry to dry, put away the polish, filled the kettle and was just about to strike a match to light the gas when she heard a key being placed into the lock of the front door.

She stood in the doorway and watched Charles take off his overcoat. 'Would you like a cup of tea?' she asked quietly.

'Yes, I would, Jane, thank you.'

Her face coloured up. She could feel it. She hadn't done anything wrong, but she felt guilty. Turning quickly, she went and busied herself with the making of a pot of tea.

'Where would you like it, Mr Charles?' she called out when it was ready and a tray was laid.

'I'm in the den,' he called back, 'so we'll have it in here, shall we?'

The den was what she had been thinking of as the front room. She pushed open the door and set the tray down, and was about to go when Charles put out a hand to halt her.

'I can see you've been busy in here. I didn't expect you to clean up, but it is appreciated and the foliage looks great, alters the room, makes it looks lived in. Thank you, Jane.' Then he glanced at the tray. 'Oh, I say, come now, Jane, what must you think of me? Please, fetch another cup and join me.'

Again she felt the colour rise in her cheeks as she hurried back to the kitchen. She rinsed her hands, splashing cold water against her face, and only when she had dried herself and felt more composed did she do as he had asked.

He had lit the gas fire and the warm glow was welcoming. He had also set the two leather armchairs nearer to the fire, and the small table with the tea-tray on was standing between them. Jane had no option but to sit down and pour out the tea for each of them.

'Did you have a good day?' she asked, desperately wanting to break what was to her an awkward silence.

'Yes, I did. Clients were pretty reasonable today.'

'What is it you do exactly? I mean, I know it is office work.'

He laughed. 'I prepare the accounts for very large firms.'

Jane wasn't at all sure what that entailed.

'How about you? What did you do with yourself? I saw the telephone in the hall; were the men here for long?'

Jane hadn't expected him to be interested in her doings. She hesitated for a moment. 'Oh, first off I started reading my book, and then the workmen arrived. I made them tea, talked to them for a while and cleared up the hallway when they'd gone. Then I had a walk around your garden.'

'Why didn't you phone me when they had finished? They tested the line with the exchange, surely?'

'Yes, they did. But . . . if your secretary or someone else had answered, who would I have said was calling?'

He put his cup down on to the tray and turned his head until he was looking directly at her. 'Why, Miss Jeffrey, of course.'

She didn't attempt to answer him because suddenly she felt very sad. I'm not Miss Jeffrey, not really, she was saying to herself. Mickey Jeffrey was not my father. So who exactly am I? What name am I supposed to go by?

She noticed Charles's cup was almost empty. She got up,

tipped the dregs into a slop bowl and refilled the cup from the pot.

Charles said nothing for a moment. Then, 'It's almost a year since you came to my mother; have you been happy?'

'Oh yes.' She looked across the space to where Charles Dennison was sitting and stopped to consider how to put her feelings into words. Finally, with her voice very low, she told him, 'I could never have dreamed of a life such as I have now.'

'You were in a children's home for a number of years, weren't you?'

'Yes, for about half of my life. From the time when I was eight until I was sixteen.'

'However did you come to be sent away? Eight years in a home!' he remarked sadly. He had led such a sheltered life he couldn't imagine such a thing. It was beyond his comprehension. 'Were you taken away because your parents ill-treated you?'

'Not my mother. She was a saint. It was my . . . well, I now know he was not my father, but he was married to my mother and he resented the fact that he had to provide for me.'

'You mean he hit you?'

Jane hung her head. 'Whenever he felt like it. I hated the fact that my mother never stopped him, but now I am older I realize that there would have been severe consequences for her if she had. As it was, he didn't treat her very kindly. She did her best.'

Charles looked dismayed. 'To be turfed out like that! I can't begin to imagine a life without one's family.'

Jane smiled at him then. 'I was lucky. Largely due to Mrs Rogers. Everyone who lived in Winchelsea Lodge became my family.'

Charles studied Jane's face for a moment. There certainly was a vast difference in this young lady compared to the thin mite she had been when first she came to be his mother's companion. But he decided that the main difference was that Jane had learned to smile. Really smile. Such a lovely smile that it lit up her face.

Thoughtfully he said, 'Well, I'm glad you came to us. I've told you before, my mother rates you really highly.' He stood up and drank the last of his tea. 'We should be making a move. I've spoken to Wilson to let him know there will be only the two of us for dinner. I just have one call to make.'

Jane packed the cups and saucers on to the tray as she listened to him ask the operator for a number, using his new telephone for the first time. She felt bewildered. She had supposed that while Miss Christine was away she would eat her meals in the kitchen with the three other girls. Now he was taking it for granted that she'd eat with him in the dining room. She was used to having her evening meal with him, but only ever when his mother was there also.

During the short journey home scarely a word passed between them.

When Charles stopped the car she was out of it before he had time to come round and open the passenger door. Once inside the house, she went straight upstairs to her room, undressed and had a good wash. What should she wear? It wasn't as if she normally wore a uniform as Mary and Sarah did, but then she never dressed for dinner either, normally just freshening up by changing her skirt or her blouse.

It didn't seem proper, just her and Mr Charles eating together. Such familiarity couldn't be right. Should she object? And if so, how did she go about it?

Too late.

She desended the stairs to find that the table in the dining room was laid for two and Charles was waiting by the fire-place, one arm resting along the marble mantel-shelf.

'Come on in,' he called as she hovered in the doorway. 'I'll pour you a drink, you have certainly earned it.'

He walked to the centre of the room and handed her a glass of sherry. Then, returning to the hearth, he picked up his own glass and raised it. 'To better communications now that I have my own telephone,' he grinned.

Jane said nothing, but smiled and raised her glass a little before taking a small sip.

She was almost praying that Miss Christine wouldn't remain in London for too long. Her being alone with Mr Charles felt funny.

It was almost more than she knew how to cope with.

Chapter Twenty-One

As JANE PICKED up the letter that lay on her side plate, her heart was in her mouth. 'Who on earth would be writing to me?' she muttered.

Christine Dennison smiled to herself and said, 'There's only one way of finding out, Jane. Open it quickly before your breakfast gets cold.'

Jane pulled the single sheet of lined paper from the envelope. It looked as if it had been torn from an exercise book. She glanced quickly at the bottom and was perplexed to see the printed capital letters stating that it was from Hannah and John Watkins. She had to rack her brains, but as she read the note she realized that they were Nancy's neighbours, the ones who lived opposite her in Selkirk Road.

Their letter was short and to the point.

Dear Jane,
    Nancy Briggs is ill. We do our best but she needs someone to help her. She won't thank us for telling

you but we hope we are doing the right thing.

Yours respectfully,

Hannah and John Watkins

P.S. We found out where you work from one of the letters you wrote her.

Christine watched the colour drain from Jane's face. 'That letter has to contain bad news,' she commented. 'Is there anything that I can do to help?'

Jane handed her the letter.

Beside Christine's plate lay the silver-handled magnifying glass that she now used since an operation on her right eye had proved partially successful.

'Oh Jane, I am so sorry. If your dear friend Nancy needs you then there is no two ways about it, of course you must go today.'

Jane made a feeble attempt at protesting but in her heart she knew she had to get to Tooting very quickly.

'I'll have Brownlow fetch the car round and run you to the station as soon as you are ready,' Christine said kindly.

'But your post?' Jane nodded towards the pile of unopened letters that lay in front of Christine.

'Don't let it worry you. I'll read what I can, and anything to do with business that needs answering I shall pass on to Charles. Now eat your breakfast and then go and get yourself ready.'

Jane pondered on her position in this household. She had come here as companion to Miss Christine, but in the time that she had been here her role had changed considerably. Miss Christine was fond of saying that she was indispensable. Well, there had never been a job that she had refused to do, and she had learned so much. Sometimes she believed she must be the luckiest girl in the whole world. But she must never forget that when she had been lonely and very afraid it had been Nancy who had been there for her, even going so far as to offer her a home. Now it was her turn to repay some of Nancy's kindness.

Twenty minutes later, as Jane was leaving the dining room, Christine called after her, 'Don't forget to pack a case. You won't be able to sort Nancy out and come back tonight.'

It was that thought that was worrying Jane.

What if Nancy were desperately ill and she had to stay with her for a long time?

She couldn't bear to think along those lines. She just felt an urgent need to be there, as Nancy had always been there for her when she needed help.

Once settled in a corner seat of the train, Jane wished it would travel faster. Under different circumstances she would have been thrilled by the journey, for it was the second week in May and all the trees in the orchards that could be seen from the window of the train were covered in the most beautiful blossom. The sun was shining, the blue sky was cloudless and it would be easy to imagine that the whole world was wonderful.

Only it wasn't. Was it?

The last eighteen months had been good for Jane, just as the whole of the time she had been living with the Dennisons had been. But living with educated people, she had learned a lot. It was 1930 and the country seemed to be in a trou-bled state. Miss Christine always insisted that they listen to the BBC news on the wireless, and from what they had gathered, the United States of America was in a worse state than England was. If that were possible.

With so many men unemployed, things had gone from

bad to worse. On the first of this month there had been a great demonstration in Hyde Park in London. It wasn't only the fact that men had no jobs and so couldn't provide proper housing or clothing for their families; it had got to the stage when they couldn't even feed them. Hunger marches had been organized.

Last week, with the help of Mrs Wilson, Miss Christy had had Mary, Daisy and Jane down in the kitchen helping to pack food parcels, which were later collected and handed out to what Christine described as patient queues of unemployed men. So many men were out of work, tramping miles in a fruitless search for a job. Younger men were enlisting in the army as a way of helping to support their parents and themselves.

Sarah had left Adelaide House because her father had got a job up north and she had gone with her family. That had been nine months ago, and Jane often wondered whether it had been a good move. Sarah never wrote, so they had no means of knowing. Miss Christine had decided not to replace her.

Thinking about Sarah and her family made Jane feel a little envious. However her father's job had turned out, and whatever their circumstances, at least they were together as a family. Mrs Rogers' efforts to find my mother haven't been very successful, she thought sadly to herself.

In fact all the trouble that she had gone to had turned up nothing at all.

The only fact that the searches from Somerset House had proved was that Alice was still alive.

As to her having been divorced and remarried, there were no records to show that either event had taken place. It was as if Mrs Rogers had come up against a brick wall.

She had been so kind when telling Jane that awful news,

going to great lengths to explain how difficult it would have
been for Alice. As the law stood, for a woman to petition
for a divorce was barely an option. It seemed, in the main,
that only men were allowed that right. Unless of course if
the woman in question should be wealthy. That altered the
situation considerably, Elsie Rogers had said wryly; it made
all the difference because money talked all languages.

Mrs Rogers had promised not to give up searching, but
Jane thought it was useless to pursue the matter any further.
At least they had tried, though.

It seemed as if Alice had just wanted to disappear, and
if that were the truth then she had certainly covered her
tracks well. Jane sighed sadly and told herself to stop going
over old ground. Today Nancy had to be her number one
concern, and she was dreading what she was going to find
when she stepped into Nancy's house.

The journey seemed to have taken for ever. But at last she
was in Tooting.

Women were bustling along carrying shopping bags over
their arms and dragging children with them. The rag-and-
bone man came trundling his barrow round the corner as
Jane turned into Selkirk Road, and the ice men were deliv-
ering great blocks of ice to the pie and eel shop. Nothing
much had altered.

Hannah Watkins was standing on her doorstep, and when
she saw Jane she quickly crossed the road and stood outside
Nancy's house, waiting for her.

''Allo, luv,' she greeted Jane. 'I 'ope we didn't get you in
no trouble, writing t' yer like that.'

'No, it's all right, I am very grateful that you let me know.
How is Nancy?'

This kind woman sighed as she stared at Jane. Everyone

in the area was struggling to get by, and there wasn't a soul in the whole street who wasn't saddened by the fact that Nancy Briggs was not getting any better. But there was only so much that any of them could do. Hannah herself was was finding it a great strain caring for her husband and five children, more so since Christmas, when her John had been thrown out of work.

'She seems t' be a bit better this morning,' she lied. 'She's such a nice woman, it must be a terrible worry for 'er lying there not knowing if 'er rent's going t' get paid.'

Fear clutched at Jane's heart and she felt terrible. She knew Nancy had never been well off. She took in washing and did a couple of mornings' work in the big houses up near Wandsworth Common, but as to a regular income, Jane had never asked.

Christ almighty! How could I have been so selfish. She had to swallow hard before saying, 'Well, I'd best get inside and let Nancy know that I'm here now.'

'All right, luv, We've tied her key t' a bit of string since she's bin taken ill so's the neighbours can get in, like. Just put yer 'and in and pull it through the letter box.'

'Thank you very much, Mrs Watkins, I'll see you again.'

'Yeah, I'll pop in later,' she said.

Jane let herself in, walked down the passage and into the kitchen cum living room. She took off her jacket and hung it behind the door, then turned to survey the room.

My God! What a difference to when she was last here. In spite of the bright spring sunshine outside, this room felt cold and damp. The grey ashes in the grate looked as if they hadn't been raked over for days. There was crumpled clothes on two chairs, and looking through to the scullery she saw dirty dishes lined up on the wooden draining board.

Guilt was nagging away at her as she took herself upstairs.

With a hand that was shaking she turned the handle and went into Nancy's front bedroom. Here she was surprised. The room was neat and tidy; in fact it looked quite homely. There were even a few flowers in a jar at the side of the bed. Nancy lay propped up in the big double bed, her arms folded across what had once been an ample bosom. It would have been hard to say who looked the more surprised.

With tears stinging the backs of her eyes, Nancy struggled to sit up. 'My, but you're a sight for sore eyes,' she said. 'You're the last person I expected.'

Jane flew to the side of the bed and, leaning forward, wrapped her arms around her dear friend. She could feel Nancy's shoulder blades sticking through her skin; she must have lost an awful lot of weight. 'Why on earth didn't you let me know you weren't well?' she muttered, unable to stop her own tears.

'Why would I be worrying you? An' I'll 'ave t' be finding out who let on. I bet it was Hannah. Still, I suppose she means well. Anyway, now you are 'ere will yer stop yer blabbering, you're making me nightdress all wet, and please, Jane, make me a decent cup of tea.'

That speech had been an effort. Nancy flopped back against her pillows, and it was then that Jane noticed the blue tinge to her face.

Straighting herself up, she made an effort to smile and said, 'I'll be as quick as I can.'

'Oh pet, you don't know how pleased I am t' see you, an' as for being quick, I ain't going nowhere, so take yer time.'

Downstairs Jane got two clean cups and saucers out from the bottom of the dresser, and laid a tin tray with a milk jug and sugar basin while she waited for the kettle to boil. It would seem that the neighbours had done their best in making sure that Nancy's bedroom was kept clean and tidy, but she wrinkled her nose as she looked around downstairs. Still, these women had their own affairs to take care of. She fell to wondering if Nancy had any family, and if so whether any of them were still living. She knew Nancy had been married because she was Mrs Briggs, but whether or not she had had any children she didn't know. It had never seemed that it was her right to pry.

Jane went back upstairs with the tea and Nancy drank hers slowly but gratefully. When she had finished, Jane wiped her face and hands for her, using the cold water that stood in the jug on the marble-topped washstand. 'When you've had a nice sleep I'll bring up some hot water and give you a good wash. Is there anything particular that you fancy for your dinner?'

'Not really.' Nancy shook her head and it tore at Jane's heartstrings to see that her hair was all grey and so very thin that in places she was almost bald. 'A drop of soup might be nice. Can't seem to manage solids, they won't stay down.'

'Right. And I'll do you some really creamy mashed potato to go with the soup,' Jane told her, wishing with all her heart that she was nearer to Mrs Wilson and her plentiful kitchen. At the thought of the motherly cook, Jane felt a moment of longing, wondering whether she would be able to cope on her own.

'That'll be smashing,' Nancy said, smiling gratefully. 'But don't you go doing too much and making yourself late getting back. We don't want you losing that lovely job of yours, do we?'

'I'm on a week's holiday,' Jane lied. 'Miss Christine said it was about time I took one.'

'That's nice.' Nancy's eyelids were drooping as Jane crept from the room.

The front door was opening as Jane came down the stairs, and Hannah Watkins followed her through into the kitchen.

'It can't 'ave been nice for yer seeing Nancy in such a bad way, an' we guessed yer would want to stay a while, so t' save yer the trouble of going shopping straight off we've gathered together a few bits and pieces.'

'Oh, Mrs Watkins, that is very kind of you,' Jane replied as Hannah opened the brown paper bag she was carrying and tipped the contents out on to the table.

'It's not much, but we're all in the same boat really. That tin of corned beef came from Jenny at the corner shop, an' she put in a pint of fresh milk. Mavis next door put in that packet of Edwards desiccated tomato soup powder. I bought yer some potatoes and a few carrots, an' Stan, whose garden backs on this one, gave two fresh eggs, 'cos he keeps chickens.' Having explained all that, Hannah dived into her pocket and pulled out a handful of pennies, smiling as she said, 'An' the men had a whip-round. It's only coppers but they said it would make sure that you'd got some pennies for the gas meter.'

God! That flung Jane's memory back into the past and that first awful week she had spent on her own in that top room of Mrs Forrester's house.

For a moment she was unable to speak. She was full of gratitude that her own life was now so good, and at the same time overwhelmed and even ashamed that these good folk who were scraping along as best as they could to keep body and soul together were still more than willing to help each other.

Taking a deep breath she said, 'Thank you, Hannah, and please thank all the neighbours. But truly there is no need to worry any longer. I'll stay with Nancy for as long as she needs me.'

When Mrs Watkins had gone, the truth of what she had just said struck Jane full force. Of course she had meant it. She would stay. But would it mean that she would lose her job? She shook her head hard.

There was no choice. None whatsoever.

Some time later, having watched Nancy struggle with a few spoons of soup and potato and then fall back heavily against the pillows and close her eyes, she decided she would let her be. Come back later and wash her and remake the bed.

She closed the door quietly.

With a terrible feeling of fear and dread, she tidied the living room, raked out the cold ashes from the grate and laid a fire ready to be lit later. Then she put dirty clothes out to be washed, did the washing-up and scrubbed the scullery floor. Outside, she cleaned the lavatory pan with Vim and scrubbed the wooden seat, then swept the yard. From time to time she went upstairs to listen outside Nancy's bedroom door. As she worked she couldn't help making comparisons.

Her own way of life was so different to what these poor folk had to deal with. She thought about the delicate clothes that she washed and ironed for Miss Christine. The car that was there whenever they needed it. The wonderful meals that Mrs Wilson prepared day in day out. Even afternoon tea served on white lace-edged cloths and bone china.

All were expressions of wealth and by and large taken for granted. But now she was really seeing how the other half lived and how her own life could so easily have been spent in this part of London. 'I have so much to be grateful for,' she said aloud as she poured yet another kettle of hot water into the enamel bowl and began rubbing a nightdress of Nancy's with a bar of yellow Sunlight soap.

It was almost dusk by the time she had finished. Taking a box of matches with her, Jane climbed the stairs, but before she could put match to the gas mantle she stood by the side of the bed staring down at her dear friend. She felt so utterly useless. And she blamed herself for not having known that Nancy was so ill. Tears burnt the backs of her eyes and the lump in her throat threatened to choke her.

Nancy's head was slumped on her chest, and terrible sobbing sounds came from her mouth. She was crying in her sleep.

Kneeling at the side of the bed, Jane touched her arm lightly.

'Nancy, I'm here, shall I make some tea and we'll have it together?'

Nancy's eyes opened and she stared at Jane, bewildered, frightened. 'Jane . . . ?'

'Yes, I'm here. You must have been dreaming.'

'Yeah . . .' She shuddered.

'Nancy, it's all right. I *am* here and I shall stay for as long as you need me. Truly I will.' She held her friend's face between her palms, covering the weatherbeaten cheeks with kisses. 'You're going to be all right. You'll soon be feeling better.'

'You're staying the night?' Nancy asked, disbelief sounding in her voice.

'For as many days and nights as you need me.' Jane patted her shoulders and back, soothing her as if she were a terrified child.

'Never felt so rough that I've 'ad t' stay in bed before,' Nancy muttered. 'Me legs are so bad it don't feel as if I'll ever be able to walk again.'

'You will,' Jane told her, rubbing the space between her bony shoulder blades. 'You will.'

'Jane, I'd give anything t' be able t' get up an' cook you a nice tea. Never wanted you t' see me like this.' Her words slurred drowsily.

'Ssh,' Jane murmured. 'I'm going down now to make us that cuppa.' She straightened up to go, but suddenly Nancy put out her arms. Jane went into them and they hugged, each comforting the other.

'I've not 'ad a bad life an' you're not to upset yerself over me.'

'Oh, Nancy,' were the only words Jane could bring herelf to say.

As she walked to the door she tossed her head as if to throw off the doubts and insecurities that were filling her mind.

She paused and looked back, and Nancy raised her head and smiled.

Jane spent a restless night in the single bedroom, remembering how much happier she and Nancy had been when she last stayed here for the night. Three times she got up when she heard Nancy coughing. The doctor had left some brown pills and a bottle of what looked like red syrup. Nancy said he wasn't due to come again and Jane at once sensed that it was because she could not afford his fee. Well, we'll see about that! she declared to herself. Probably it would be around five shillings, or with any luck only half a crown. Thank God she'd had the sense to bring her post office savings book with her. She had saved up three pounds, eight shillings and ninepence, and first thing in the morning she was going to withdraw two pounds of it. Then before she went shopping she was going to call in at the surgery in Garrett Lane and she wouldn't leave until she'd had a good talk with that doctor. Somebody had to tell her what was wrong with Nancy and why nothing was being done about it. Surely if she was that ill she should be in hospital.

At last it began to get light.

Jane peeped round the door and sighed with relief that Nancy appeared to be sleeping peacefully. Treading softly, she made her way downstairs. In the scullery she filled the tin kettle, and when it boiled she poured half of the water over a teaspoon of tealeaves in the brown pot. Having drunk two cups of tea, she poured what water remained in the kettle into an enamel bowl, and stood naked at the stone sink and washed herself from head to foot.

Later, Nancy did her best to act as her usual cheerful self as Jane carefully washed and dried her, gently combed her hair and finally, with difficulty, got her to sit on a chair at the side of the bed.

She had found a pair of clean sheets and two white pillow-cases in the cupboard on the landing. As she furled the first sheet open there was a strong smell of lavender, and Jane smiled, thinking to herself that Nancy must have bought the lavender from the gypsies who regularly called at the houses in all the back streets. Lucky lavender, the gypsies always insisted it was. Well, it hadn't brought Nancy much luck.

'Come on, you old lazy-bones, let's get you back in bed,' Jane said as she lifted Nancy's legs and then straighted the pillows behind her head. 'Now, how about a nice boiled egg and soldiers? I'll bring it up and we'll have breakfast together, but then I have to go out for a little while. Will you be all right or shall I ask Hannah to come and sit with you?'

'Jane, luv, I'll be fine, but I don't really want an egg.'

'What you want an' what you're going to get is two entirely different things,' Jane told her, doing her best to laugh.

Over breakfast they discussed, in a rambling kind of way,

what they were going to do over the next few days. From her handbag Jane brought out a notepad and pencil and began to make her shopping list. Post office first. Doctor second. Try and catch a milkman and ask him to leave a pint each morning because all Nancy seemed to use was tinned condensed milk. Thank God the lady at the corner shop had sent a pint yesterday, but Jane had used a lot of that for the mashed potatoes. Loaf of bread and half a pound of butter. What about dinner? Wait until I see what's in the shops, she decided. Fish might be good for Nancy, a nice fillet of plaice done in the oven in milk and butter the way Mrs Wilson often cooks them. Oh, and I must get a letter-card while I'm in the post office because I have to write to Miss Christine. I'll get two or maybe three, then I can keep her posted as to what is happening.

Friday morning in Tooting Broadway seemed busier than Rye on a market day. People crowded the pavements with baskets, prams and pushchairs, stood in groups chatting, took their turn at market stalls, in the fishmonger's and the grocer's, all the while exchanging snippets of gossip and family news. Jane listened and laughed to herself as women lowered their voices to tell of the goings-on in certain families. This was an entirely different world to the one in which she lived.

She had been out a lot longer than she had intended and it was a quarter to eleven when, burdened with a bulging shopping bag and a brown paper carrier, she made her way to Hannah Watkins' house and knocked on the door.

'Jane! Come in, luv, I've just made a cup of tea.'

'No, I won't stop, I've left Nancy on her own too long as it is.'

'I've been over and Mavis from next door has popped in. Nancy's all right an' we see you've washed 'er an' seen to 'er bed. So come on in, you look as if you could do with a cuppa.'

In the narrow hallway, Jane dumped her shopping and took off her short coat. She had barely time to ease herself on to a chair before Hannah was standing in front of her holding out a mug of tea. 'There you are. Yer'll feel better after this.'

Jane sipped the strong tea, afraid to speak, because tears were not far away.

'There's something yer want to tell me, isn't there, Jane?'

When no reply was forthcoming, Hannah again urged, 'Come on, spit it out. You didn't knock on my door for nothing.'

Jane couldn't help herself. The words came out in a rush. 'The doctor said they can't send Nancy to hospital because there is nothing anyone can do for her. He said her kidneys are failing and it is only a question of time. He didn't try to offer any hope,' she said bitterly.

Hannah took the mug of tea out of Jane's hand and placed it on the table. Then she turned and folded Jane into her arms. 'We all know that, Jane,' she said, her voice ringing with sympathy. 'And we've all done our best. Jenny from up the corner shop even bought two officers from the Salvation Army down here to see Nancy and they offered 'er a place in one of their 'omes. Nancy would 'ave none of it. I'll die in me own bed, is what she told them. In a way I'm sorry we let you know. She never wanted us to.'

Jane sniffed away her tears. 'I'm grateful that you did. I couldn't have lived with myself if she'd gone and I'd never lifted a finger to help.'

'Well, that's as may be. You're 'ere now and you just remember you're not alone. Call on anyone in the whole street, day or night, and fer Nancy Briggs there's not a soul that wouldn't come running. Now drink yer tea and I'll come over the road with yer.'

And after that there didn't seem the need to say any more.

Chapter Twenty-Two

IT WAS TEN o'clock in the morning of the first of June when Nancy Briggs died.

She died, as she had wanted to, in her own bed in the house in which she had been born.

Three days previously she had seemed free of pain and had asked Jane to stop reading to her and to listen to what she had to say.

Slowly she had told Jane things that had amazed her.

Her affairs were all in order, and in a tin box in the cupboard under the stairs were all the papers that would be necessary for her to be given a decent burial.

She also painfully related the story of her early life.

She had only been married six months when her husband left her for another woman. Jane's heart had ached as Nancy had said, 'I was pregnant at the time. I had a son, a perfect little boy, born in this very room, only he was stillborn.'

Jane's head was lowered, cupped in her hands, her elbows resting on the edge of the bed as she listened.

Nancy placed her hand on Jane's thick golden hair and there had been a long silence, only broken when Nancy said, 'I took your mother under my wing when that bugger Mickey Jeffrey brought her to live in this street. Then you were born and you brought me more joy than I can tell you. I could 'ave done murder for what that man did t' yer mum, an' as fer what he did to you . . .' She struggled to sit up. 'If there's any justice at all in this world, that sod will be made to pay.'

The effort of the telling had proved too much. Nancy had slept for most of the rest of the day, and somehow Jane had known that the end was not going to be long after that.

The morning had started off wonderfully.

Jane had come into the bedroom and laid down the tin tray on the bedside table, and then gone to draw back the curtains and let the early sunshine in.

'Lovely morning, Nancy,' she had called. 'And it's the first day of June.'

They had each drunk a cup of tea. Nancy said she did not want anything to eat, and so Jane set about making her clean and comfortable.

Finally Nancy lay quietly, her head on the raised pillows, and just as Jane thought she was going to go to sleep she suddenly opened her eyes and smiled.

'Be 'appy, luv,' she said quietly, then gave what sounded like a long-drawn-out sigh.

'I'm happy to be with you. You know that, Nancy, don't you? Don't you?' Jane repeated, but she knew even as she raised her voice that Nancy wasn't going to say anything else.

Nancy lay quietly, looking for all the world as if she'd

gone to sleep. Her eyes were closed and she looked oh so peaceful.

Jane leant across the bed, kissed Nancy's forehead and let her tears drop on to the cheeks of her dearest friend.

Then she pulled the curtains shut and slowly went downstairs.

For the next hour Jane cried softly to herself until she had no tears left.

The sound of the front door being opened startled her and she hastily got to her feet, went out into the scullery and washed her face and hands beneath the running coldwater tap.

'It's only me, Hannah,' the call came from the kitchen.

Jane buried her face in the rough hand towel and took several deep breaths before saying, 'It's all over, Hannah. Nancy died about an hour ago.'

Hannah frowned. 'You're quite sure, are you?'

Jane swallowed painfully and nodded. 'I'm sure. Quite certain. You can go up, she looks very peaceful,' she said, her voice a hoarse whisper.

Hannah did not take up the offer. She said gruffly, 'We ought to notify the undertakers. They'll see to everything. Would you like me t' go an' fetch my John? It's only weeks since he buried his mother, he'll know exactly what t' do.'

'Yes please,' Jane managed to say.

The local undertaker took everything in his stride. Nancy's death was no surprise to him. 'Mrs Briggs came in to see us about three months ago,' he told Jane. 'Soon after Christmas it was. Told us she had an insurance policy that would cover everything. Very precise, she was. Even chose what hymns were to be sung. God rest her soul.'

Jane looked at Hannah Watkins and they both had to smile. They were imagining Nancy placing the order for her own funeral and thinking to themselves, God help the man if he gets it wrong!

Later that day Jane screwed up courage and went to use the public phone box that stood in the post office. She heaved a sigh of relief when she heard Mr Wilson's familiar voice. She pressed the button, heard her two pennies fall and began to talk. Not very clearly but in short sentences, she managed to convey that Nancy had died. Now she had the funeral to see to and was it all right for her to stay on here in Tooting until it was all over?

'Jane, slow down.' She almost dropped the receiver. The voice speaking now was that of Miss Christine. 'Jane, are you there? I am on the other line.'

'Yes, Miss Christine. I'm here.'

'Dear Jane. We are all thinking about you. Of course you must stay until after the funeral, and if there is anything that you need or that we can do, you have only to ask us. Do you hear me?'

'Yes, Miss Christine. Thank you. But Nancy left everything in order. Though I . . .'

'Jane, what is it?'

'I was wondering . . .' Again she couldn't get the words out. 'If it is all right . . . do I still have a job?'

'Oh Jane,' Christine murmured sadly. Then, as if talking to herself, she said quietly, 'We've let you down badly. Left you to cope. Now as soon as you are ready to come home you ring again and Brownlow will come and fetch you.'

'Oh miss, there isn't any need for that!'

'Just listen, Jane, and do as I tell you. We've all missed you. Me especially. And whereas I wouldn't have dreamed of encroaching all the time your friend needed you, now that you've done all that you can do you *must* come home. Promise me you will ring again soon.'

'Yes,' Jane replied, 'I will.' But she stood holding the telephone receiver against her cheek for a while before replacing it.

Miss Christine had twice referred to Adelaide House as 'home'. Oh, that was music to her ears. At last she had a place where she belonged!

Jane had asked that both Mr and Mrs Watkins be present when she unearthed the tin box from under the stairs.

The three of them sat around Nancy's table, over which Jane had laid a gingham tablecloth, and watched as, at her request, John Watkins tipped the contents out.

There wasn't a great deal. A birth certificate which showed that Nancy had been born in the year 1869. God, she was only sixty-one years old! Jane had thought of her as being much older. There was no marriage certificate. Jane made no comment on that fact. More than likely Nancy had burned it, wanting only to erase all memory of that painful time.

There were two assurance policies. One with the Prudential, taken out by Nancy's father and changed to Nancy's name on his death. It had been fourpence per week from the week she was born. Sum insured, fifty pounds, plus bonuses payable on death. The other policy was with the Royal Britannia Assurance company, the proposer being Nancy herself. It had been taken out at the turn of the century, 1900, the premium being one shilling a week. Sum assured, three hundred and fifty pounds.

John Watkins gasped. So did Jane. Hannah, feet ever firmly on the ground, muttered, 'How in hell's name did she manage to pay a shilling a week?'

The only other thing was a flat jeweller's box which sadly looked very much the worse for wear. 'It must have been in the water at some time,' John said, turning the box over in his hands. 'These are water marks.'

'Open it up,' his wife urged.

A sheet of notepaper lay inside the lid, and John passed this to Jane. The box contained only two things: a very ornate cameo brooch and a gold locket and chain.

'I'd better read the letter,' John suggested, quickly adding, 'It looks more like a will.' He cleared his throat and began.

'"To whom it may concern. I have no wordly goods other than what is in this tin box. The two policies should see me buried. Any cash left over is to be given to the Salvation Army, please."'

Jane smiled to herself at the 'please'.

'"The two pieces of jewellery are for Jane Jeffrey, and I state now that had I been able I would have adopted her right from when she was a baby. The rest of my wordly goods I leave to Jane to do with as she thinks fit."'

It was signed 'Nancy Louise Briggs', and two more signatures showed that she had got two people to witness this written will.

Jane's face coloured up. She needed no telling what she would find if and when she opened the locket. She had no intention of doing this until she was safely on her own.

It was a perfect June morning. Nancy lay peacefully in her coffin, which rested on trestles in her front parlour. Friends and close neighbours popped in to see her for the last time. Every window in every house in the street had its curtains closed tight.

Outside on the pavement lay a wreath that had been bought with subscriptions from local shopkeepers. There were small bunches of wild flowers picked by schoolchildren who Nancy had many a time fussed over. There was a sheaf of white lilies intertwined with green fern sent by Christine and Charles Dennison, and by the kerbstone stood a basket of summer blooms embedded in moss. This was from Jane. She had stood in the shop at the Broadway and watched the young lady florist skilfully make it.

Now the men were taking their caps off. The hearse had arrived. Two men dressed in black removed their top hats as they came into the house, closing the door of the front room behind them.

'They're screwing the lid down now,' Mavis from next door whispered to Hannah.

On the shoulders of six strong men, Nancy was borne from her home and out into Selkirk Road. The black-plumed horses stood stock still as her coffin was lowered to rest inside the carriage, which had glass windows on each side. Flowers and wreaths were arranged.

Jane, Mr and Mrs Watkins and Mavis got into the only car that had been provided. Men and women slowly fell in behind to walk the short distance to the church.

The wooden pews were filled with all sorts of people, some of whom had known Nancy for the whole of her life. Jane and the main mourners took their places at the front of the church, and everyone stood as the coffin was carried in.

The young vicar stood silent as folk blew their noses and some cried into their handkerchiefs.

'"I am the resurrection and the life, saith the Lord, he that believeth in me, though he were dead, yet shall he live . . ."

'Please turn to hymn number twenty-four.'

And they sang 'The Old Rugged Cross'.

Then Nancy's doctor read a few verses from the twenty-third psalm. Then there were prayers and a minute or two of silence, during which Jane did her best not to cry. She was thinking of the moment she had opened the locket. It contained a faded photograph of a new-born baby, and a few strands of dark hair. Poor dear Nancy.

Finally they sang 'Abide With me'.

Then Nancy was being carried to her final resting place.

By the graveside, an elderly woman dressed entirely in black touched Jane's arm. 'It makes it all so final, doesn't it?'

Jane looked bewildered.

'Death, I mean.'

'Oh yes. It's final all right,' Jane quietly agreed.

Afterwards, back at the house, neighbours crowded in. Jane, with a lot of help, had done her best. Out in the kitchen all had been previously prepared. The big table had been laid with a white cloth and the local bakery had provided almost everything. Their fee was to be added to the cost of the funeral, so Jane had been informed by the undertaker.

There were sandwiches of cheese and pickle, fish paste and tomato; bridge rolls topped with boiled ham; spring onions and celery in tall glass vases. To finish off there were Victoria sponge cakes filled with raspberry jam, and two large fruit cakes; or for the not so sweet-toothed there was cheese and biscuits. For the children of the street there was jelly and blancmange. To many the sight of so much food had their eyes popping.

They drank to Nancy. Not much choice there! Tea or brown ale.

By the time the table was almost cleared, one and all agreed that Nancy had had a good send-off and that she had done her friends and neighbours right proud.

Jane drew Hannah to one side.

'I shall be leaving here first thing in the morning.'

'Oh pet, I shall be right sorry to see yer go.'

'Well, I shall miss you too, Hannah. I couldn't have got through all of this without your help, and indeed everyone else's too.'

'What's 'appening about the 'ouse, d'yer know?'

'Yes,' Jane smiled. 'The rent will all be paid up and I have arranged for the Salvation Army to collect most of Nancy's belongings. But I have told them that if there are any clothes of Nancy's or any pieces of furniture that you, or any of Nancy's friends, could make good use of, then you are to have them.'

'Really?' Hannah queried in disbelief.

'Yes, really. And when I go in the morning I will take the key off of the string and bring it over to you. The rent is paid for another week and the Salvation Army ladies won't be coming until after that. So you have plenty of time to sort through, and if you would pack up the things you don't want ready to be collected, I would be grateful.'

'Oh Jane. You suddenly sound so old and so organized. Come here and let me give you a hug.'

Tears were still never far away, and Jane went into Hannah's arms and rested her head on her shoulder thankfully.

It was true. She not only sounded older; she was older. This past month had certainly aged her. Still, she had learned a lot. The main thing being that you didn't need money to have good friends.

This part of London where she had been born certainly didn't have many advantages at the moment. Men with no jobs, children bare-footed, their mothers going hungry themselves in order to put food into their bellies.

Life could be so cruel, thought Jane. But to have friends

around you such as Nancy had had must serve to make it a little easier.

She knew now from her own experience that these Londoners were worth their weight in gold.

Chapter Twenty-Three

FOUR MONTHS HAD passed since Jane had returned to Adelaide House. It was a Thursday morning, the first week in October. Miss Christine was getting herself changed because in an hour's time Brownlow was going to drive them into Hastings. Jane was in the garden, gathering flowers for the sitting room. There were still a few roses and the first Michaelmas daisies, as well as some beautiful bright chrysanthemums. The bunch grew in her hands and the scent of the blossoms was gorgeous.

She heard the telephone ring in the house and paused a moment. Mr Wilson would more than likely answer it. But it went on ringing, so she hurried across the grass and through the side door into the hall.

'Adelaide House,' she said into the mouthpiece.

'This is Mr Thomas, the butcher. That's you, isn't it, Jane? I think I'd be better off having a word with Mr Wilson. Is he about?'

'Yes, I'll fetch him for you if you hold the line.' Jane laid the bunch of flowers carefully down on the hall table and turned to see Mr Wilson coming down the stairs. 'Mr Thomas wants a word with you.' She smiled as she handed over the telephone.

She had never really got over the relief of being back in this beautiful house. The autumn sun was pouring through the landing windows as she walked slowly across the hall, and for the umpteenth time she thought what a wonderful place this was.

'Oh, what a bloody mess!' she heard Mr Wilson roar.

He never, ever swore. What on earth could have gone wrong? She stood rooted to the spot.

'Yes, yes.' Mr Wilson was nodding his head. 'Yes, you're right, she should have been looked after better. Never had much time for the lady myself, but now's not the time to air one's views. Yes, I'll let Miss Christy know and she'll have someone notify Mr Charles as soon as possible. No, no, you did right. Absolutely. Thank you. I'm sure Miss Christy or her son will be in touch with you.'

He replaced the telephone and stood tapping his foot. It wasn't like Mr Wilson to let anything upset his serene manner. But that conversation had! The expression on his face was hard to fathom, but Jane was thinking that it was one of deep regret.

Jane didn't need any telling. Something was wrong. Very wrong. She walked to the door, taking deep breaths. The day was crisp and clear, autumn was in the air and she smelt smoke from the gardener's mound of burning leaves.

Jane shuddered. Whatever Mr Thomas had said to Mr Wilson, it had shaken him really badly. And she'd be willing to guess that it had something to do with Mrs Harman. Suddenly she didn't like her own thoughts. Ten to one it will be more trouble, she said softly to herself.

Over the weekend, Mr Charles had taken the last of the

soft fruits down to Mrs Harman. He had also taken a blackberry and apple pie that Mrs Wilson had made especially. Time had eased everyone's feelings, and if asked they would all agree that sympathy was uppermost in their minds where Frieda Harman was concerned. Money was no problem, that was one thing to be thankful for. Right from the start she had been looked after by a trained nurse, several in fact, because none of them seemed to stay very long.

The fact was that she wasn't an easy person to live with. A troublesome patient, was how the nurses put it. Poor Miss Christine worried over her. It wasn't her problem, but as she said, who else's was it? Who was there to care for the poor woman except Charles? And the burden on him was growing greater by the day. The way things were going, it seemed inevitable that Mrs Harman would have to spend the rest of her life in a home. There just didn't seem to be any other alternative.

Jane had turned, ready to set about arranging her flowers, when she saw Christine coming through the hall, looking, as always, immaculate, but frowning heavily. 'There you are, Jane, I feel we shouldn't be involved in what has happened, but . . .'

'It's Mrs Harman, isn't it?'

For a moment Christine closed her eyes and swayed a little. 'Burglars have got into the house again and this time it sounds as if Frieda has been badly hurt.' She paused and then whispered, 'God help us.' It was a plea, a prayer from the heart, but whether that prayer would be answered remained to be seen.

'Oh . . .' Jane's hands covered her mouth. Who would have thought that burglars would go back a second time? Poor Mrs Harman! With her being unable to move she must have been terrified. For it to happen once was bad enough, but twice!

'Jane, I feel I should go to her, what do you think? I'll ring Charles first, see what he has to say.'

Jane knew, and so did his mother, what he would say.

Brownlow pulled the car to a halt in front of Ashford Manor. As Jane helped Christine to get out of the car, she could feel her trembling. It was the shock of seeing two policemen on the steps. With them was a young woman dressed in a navy-blue suit with a crisp white blouse beneath. The young lady came towards them and introduced herself as PC Howard.

'If you are a police constable, surely you should be in uniform?' Jane had never heard Christine speak so sharply.

'On these kind of cases, ma'am, we try to be as informal as possible. It is only recently that the force has asked for volunteers to work in plain clothes so that invalids and disabled people such as Mrs Harman can feel more at ease.'

'That's good,' Christine murmured. 'Shall we go in? I understand Mrs Harman has been hurt. Is she very bad?'

'Yes, I'm afraid she is. The doctor and a police officer are with her now. The night nurse is badly shaken and I was just about to go and talk to her.' Then, as an afterthought, she added, 'She may prefer it if you were to be present.'

As they walked up the front steps, Christine began to talk, more to herself, certainly not to anyone in particular.

'Years ago this was a fine old house. Mr Harman employed more than twice as many servants as my father did. There was a cook, two kitchen maids and a tweeny, a butler, a footman, two grooms and an endless number of stable lads. Mr Harman had a valet of his own, the mistress had her lady's maid and a housekeeper was in overall charge. How times change! And they were such good times. All gone so horribly wrong.'

Jane made no comment, nor did the constable, who had walked on ahead.

The moment they stepped across the threshold on to the deep-pile carpet of the huge sitting room, Jane could feel the tension.

Two females and one male sat in a group near the spacious bay window. All three wore nurse's uniform. The man, tall and thin, stood up and came towards them.

'I am Keith Johnson. All this happened before Miss Russell and myself arrived. We can't tell you anything. If Mrs Harman needs us then we should be allowed to go and attend to her, and if not, is it possible for us to leave?'

PC Howard cast a disapproving glance over Nurse Johnson, who held his head high and returned the look. 'Mrs Harman is receiving medical attention, and no, you may not leave. I would like to talk to all three of you informally, just for the moment, and then my colleagues will take your formal statements later on, if that is all right.'

Keith Johnson nodded his head and sat down.

PC Howard lowered her voice and spoke kindly. 'Nurse Ryan, this is Mrs Dennison and Miss Jeffrey. They are well known to Mrs Harman.' Then, turning to Christine, the constable explained, 'This is Martha Ryan, she was the nurse on night duty. She had the misfortune to open the door to the intruders.'

Both Christine and Jane made sympathetic noises.

'Miss Ryan, do you feel well enough to tell us exactly what happened?'

'I have already told the two policemen. I did so as soon as they arrived,' Martha Ryan said quietly as she stood up.

This night nurse was a tall, stately and overbearing figure

with steel-grey hair wound up into a bun at the back of her head. It was not so neat-looking at the moment. Great wisps of hair had been torn loose from the bun, and there was a deep cut above her right eye which had already been attended to by the application of iodine, causing a nasty-looking yellow stain on her forehead. The bib of her starched apron was badly torn and there was a streak of dried blood running from her elbow to her hand.

'Where do you want me to begin?' she asked in a gruff voice.

PC Howard smiled gently. 'Let's all sit down and get comfortable. The doctor will be coming down soon, I hope, and he'll let us know how Mrs Harman is. Meanwhile, as I said, it's all very informal.'

'Well,' Martha Ryan began, 'the door bell rang and I was pleased because I thought that for once my colleagues had arrived early. Though I did think it was a bit strange because the time was only twenty minutes to eight. I had lifted Mrs Harman out of her bed and got her sitting in a chair. That's no problem because she weighs barely seven stone. I went to the doorway, then I looked back and asked her if she'd be all right. She nodded her head, even smiled at me, and I told her I would only be a few minutes and that I'd give her her medication when I came back.

'As I was running down the stairs I heard the bell ring again, and this time they must have kept their finger on it. "All right, all right, I'm coming," I shouted. No sooner had I got the door open than a heavy fist poked me hard in the chest, and a big, broad-shouldered man shouted at me, "Why's it take so long to open a bloody door?" He was wearing a woollen mask that covered the whole of his head, with slits cut out for the eyes, nose and mouth. He was yelling loudly all the time, pushing me backwards into the hall. I couldn't understand a word, he was incoherent with rage. There were two other men, though not as big as the first man, each wearing the same kind of woolly face mask. "Calm down, Tony," one of them urged, because he was still shouting and poking at me. He'd formed his hard, bony fingers into a fist and believe you me, every poke hurt like hell. I must be black and blue.' She shuddered and crossed her arms over her chest as if to protect herself.

'I asked him what it was he wanted, though I guessed it was money and any valuables that they could lay their hands on. All he said was . . .' and she made a brave attempt to grin, '"Not you, luv, that's fer sure. Just tell us, is the missus still bed-bound in the front bedroom?" That's when I knew they had been here before. But this time I knew they meant business. They weren't going away empty-handed.

'I knew it would be useless to lie, so I just said yes. Then he asked where the safe was, and when I didn't answer he said, "An' don't try saying there ain't one, 'cos we know damn well there is." I suppose it was stupid of me, but I retorted that if he already knew then he didn't need to ask me.

'That's when the smallest, skinny man found his voice. "Yer saucy bitch," he shouted at the same time as he lashed out at me. His arm might have been thin but it felt like a rod of iron, and the blow knocked me down. As I went to get up, I slipped on the parquet flooring and lay stretched out. That's when this skinny one started to kick me.

'Up until now the third man had taken no part in all of this and I got the feeling that he was much older than the others. Suddenly, though, as I was struggling to get up on to my knees, it was he that dealt me a terrible blow which caught the side of my head. Then he had a fistful of my hair and he was dragging me across the hall.

'The big man turned his back, yanked off his woolly mask and without turning round passed it to his mate, who let go of my hair and tugged the mask over my head, back to front, so that I couldn't see anything at all. My hands were tied behind my back and my ankles were roped together. Then I was practically thrown into the hall cupboard, the door was closed and I heard the key being turned in the lock. Some time passed before I heard their footsteps going up the stairs.'

The silence that followed was unbearable. At least it was to Jane. She leaned towards her employer and whispered, 'Aren't there any full-time staff employed here now?'

'I don't think so. Only a daily cleaner, as far as I know.' Christine sounded puzzled by the question.

Jane felt it was time for her to be bold. 'I think everyone could do with a cup of tea or coffee, don't you, Miss Christine? If someone would point me in the direction of the kitchen, I will make myself useful.'

Christine, who was feeling that the situation in this house today was more than she knew how to cope with, smiled to herself. Her young Jane had certainly come out of her shell since having had to cope with the death of her dear friend Nancy.

'Jane, I think that would be an excellent idea, if the police officer has no objections.'

'None whatsoever,' PC Howard quickly replied. 'I think everyone will be glad of a drink.'

It was more than an hour later before a kindly police sergeant came to talk to Christine and finally tell her that it was all right for her to go upstairs and see Mrs Harman.

Jane opened the bedroom door and stood back to allow Christine to enter first.

The sight of Frieda Harman, head laid back against a pile of snowy-white pillows, her face a mass of bruises, one eye badly swollen, and dried blood around her nose, was enough to make even a grown man cry. Keith Johnson stepped away from the bed and motioned for the two ladies to come forward.

'I'll bring a chair for each of you,' he said, keeping his voice low. Dr Haines said it will do Mrs Harman good to talk, so if it's all right I'll leave you alone with her for a while and go and see how my colleagues are faring.'

'Nurse Russell is preparing some lunch, but Nurse Ryan has been seen by the doctor and is now on her way home. PC Howard has gone in the police car with her,' Jane told him.

'I'm glad to hear that. The poor woman bore the brunt of those men's cruelty,' Christine said in a voice that trembled.

Keith Johnson nodded his head. 'Can't think what we'll do about the night shift. Martha certainly won't be up to it. Dr Haines is insisting that Mrs Harman be taken into hospital, or failing that a private nursing home, but not one of us has been able to convince her that it would be for the best.'

'Please don't talk about me as if I weren't here.' Frieda Harman was struggling to sit up, then her gaze rested on Christine and she looked amazed. 'Oh, you are the last person I expected to come to my aid, Christine. It is so good of you,' she said, but managing to sound as if she didn't want to be beholden to anyone.

'Now, Frieda, don't let's have any of that silly talk.' Christine was doing her best to speak firmly and show that she was in control of the situation. 'We can't believe what you have been put through, but I'm here now and Jane is with me, and we won't leave until you are feeling heaps better.'

'Then you'll be here for a very long time,' Frieda answered obstinately.

Nurse Johnson looked at Christine and raised his eyebrows, but Christine smiled and said, 'You go downstairs and have a little break. We'll be fine here, and if we should need you we'll ring the bell.'

'Hmm,' Frieda sniffed. 'You can ring the bell until your arm aches, but they'll only come when it suits them.'

Christine pulled her chair close to the side of the bed while Jane looked around for something to do. She decided that the flowers and plants which stood on the windowsill could do with a bit of attention.

'Would you like me to sit here quietly, or would it help to tell me what happened?' Christine asked Frieda, her voice full of sympathy.

'Please keep me company. I just can't fathom why those men came back for a second time. Would you be a dear and not tell Charles that I was so frightened?'

'Why ever not? I would have been terrified. Your poor face, it takes some believing that men will stoop so low.'

Frieda had begun to cry softly, and the tears were trickling slowly down her cheeks. Christine took a clean handkerchief from her pocket and gently wiped them away.

'I don't deserve for you to be so good to me. Don't you blame me for messing up Charles's life?' Frieda's voice held a plea.

'Shh, shh, that's water under the bridge. It's cost you dearly.'

Frieda sighed. 'You don't know how true that is. When Nurse Ryan was washing me this morning I was looking out over the garden wishing that the bottom half of my body still worked. I thought how I'd love to be out there today, feeling the frosty autumn air on my face, seeing the trees turning a golden russet colour, knowing the ground would soon be covered with fallen leaves. I haven't been out of this house since the accident, apart from a short stay in a nursing home, which mostly certainly was not for me! I know it's my own fault. Charles always offers. And the do-gooders would be only too willing to push me out in a basket bed-chair. Show me off as a freak. Let folk look and say, quite rightly, that I deserved what has happened to me. No thanks. I prefer to stay here in the safety of my own home.' Her hand went up to touch her face and she winced. 'Only it's not very safe now, is it?' she said sadly.

Christine took her hand between both of hers and soothed her as best she could.

It was a while before Mrs Harman spoke again.

'You know, Christine, when that bedroom door burst open and those three darkly clad men burst into the room, all I could think was, not again! I was so frightened I wanted to die. Yes, I did. There and then I wanted to end it all. Then I realized that I wasn't entirely helpless. Nurse Ryan had got me out of bed, I was sitting in a chair and I could reach the telephone which was standing on the bedside table. And that's exactly what I did. Or more precisely what I tried to do.

'Wham! The biggest of the men moved like lightning. He had my arm in a vice-like grip and dragged it up and behind my back. How it wasn't broken I'll never know. That's when I started to scream, and the skinny man grabbed a linen hand towel, rolled it into a ball and did his best to stuff it into my mouth. I wasn't going to let him off scot-free, so I raked the back of his hands with my fingernails, and I'm not sorry to say I drew blood. Didn't do me much good, though. He said I was a right bitch, slapped me around the face and head and didn't stop until blood spurted from my nose.'

'Oh Frieda! You have been so brave. You really have. Now soon you are going to have some lunch and then you must sleep. You must be worn to a frazzle.'

'Sleep is all I seem to do these days, Christine.' And having said that, she smiled.

'What are you smiling at?' Christine felt the need to ask.

'It was something the police sergeant said to his mate when he didn't think I was listening.'

'Oh, and what was it he said?'

'He murmured that I could so easily have been murdered, and then he added, "But we'll have a hard job proving it".'

Christine looked so shocked that Frieda quickly said, 'Don't worry, it didn't happen.'

Jane who had heard everything, looked across at Mrs Harman's badly bruised face and thought what a plucky little thing she was. Aloud she said, 'Why don't I go down and see if your lunch is ready, and I'm sure Miss Christy could do with another cup of tea. I know I could.'

She was glad to get out of the room. Going down the grand staircase, she couldn't help thinking to herself that the matter of Mrs Harman's safety from now on was going to take a month of Sundays to sort out.

With a note of wisdom she muttered, 'And I don't envy Mr Charles his part in all of this. Not one jot I don't!'

Chapter Twenty-Four

CHRISTINE DENNISON SIGHED heavily as she replaced the telephone receiver. Charles had been on the line again asking her advice. She had no idea what to say to him.

It was a fortnight since the burglars had broken into Ashford Manor for the second time, and in the whole of those two weeks Charles's life had been put on hold. He hadn't been to the office and he had not been home.

His plea, over and over again, was that he could not leave Frieda.

As a woman Christine appreciated that. She herself felt nothing but admiration for Mrs Harman and the way she had tried to stand up to those bully boys. But as a mother, well, that was an entirely different story. How could her son be expected to be in constant attendance on a severely disabled woman? He had his business to consider and his own life to lead. Though never in a million years would she voice these thoughts out loud.

Frieda was adamant that she couldn't be left alone. And that was understandable. On the other hand, there was not a nurse who was willing to undertake the night duty in Ashford Manor. Even the day nurses had stated that they would not attend Mrs Harman unless there was another person in the house who could take responsibility for the patient.

Friends, well-meaning ones at that, had tried to persuade Frieda that she must consider long-term nursing in a residential care home. She would have none of it.

The clergyman had tried, as had her own doctor and a specialist he had brought down from London to examine her. All to no avail. She'd thrown her heavy silver-backed hairbrush at Charles when he had tried to reason with her.

Now Charles was begging Christine to tell him what to do.

He didn't ask my opinion when he first took up with her, and she not that much younger than I am, was what Christine was thinking, and her thoughts were full of regret.

Regret that Frieda Harman had seen fit to leave her husband and in the process had ruined the life of her own daughter and Christine's son.

Not that Charles was blameless. Far from it. He had bought a house and set up home with her. Infatuated by the fact that an older woman had found him attractive, he hadn't stopped to think of what the consequences would be. Now he was paying the price.

And now I'm thinking spiteful thoughts, and that won't help anyone, she chided herself. 'I've almost forgotten what peace of mind is,' she said out loud. 'What do they say? No peace for the wicked, eh? Though what I've done to deserve this load of trouble, I just don't know.'

The day that Charles did come home to fetch a change of clothing, Jane thought her heart would break. He came upon her so suddenly, so quietly, that she didn't hear him approach. She had been brushing the shoulders of Miss Christine's coat and was reaching up to hang it in the wardrobe.

She looked round to see him standing there, so tall and splendid, and as always when she set eyes on him she felt a jolt of genuine pleasure.

'Have you come back home to stay?' she asked.

He was looking at her and smiling gently. 'Afraid not. At the moment it is not possible.' His face looked sad for a moment, then he said, 'I think you, of all people, understand why I have to stay at Ashford Manor, don't you, Jane?'

She nodded. 'Yes.' Her voice was no more than a whisper. 'Yes, I do understand. But . . . your mother worries so . . .' She couldn't bring herself to tell him how she felt he was wasting his life.

He forced a cheerful laugh. 'Oh Jane, there is no need for either of you to worry about me. I haven't thanked you for going to the Manor with my mother. That day must have been pretty awful for both of you. I did appreciate it and I still do, the way you care so well for her.'

Jane felt a lump in her throat so big that she couldn't answer.

'I have to stay at the Manor all the time Mrs Harman needs me,' he said softly, coming further into the room to stand very close to her and take her hands in his.

'Do your best to stop Mother worrying, won't you?'

'Yes, yes, I will.' There was a tremor in her voice and she found she had to blink away tears.

'Jane?' He put his arms around her, lowered his head and leaned his cheek against her hair.

Her heart was pounding against her ribs. Surely he could hear it?

'Oh Jane,' he murmured, over and over again.

She was overwhelmed with love for him!

The full realization shot through her.

It shouldn't be happening. She worked in this household. She might be treated as one of the family, but for all that she was a paid employee. Yet she couldn't help it, no matter what. She knew that she loved this man deeply. Maybe she had done so from the moment when she first set eyes on him. The first sort of love she'd felt was because he was kind to her. It had grown because he noticed her. Made time for her. Let her feel she belonged. This was real love.

Nothing could ever come of it. She was well aware of that. She wasn't in the same class as he was. No matter. Whatever turns her life took, what she felt for this man at this moment in time would never, ever change.

It was as if he read her thoughts, for against her hair he whispered softly, 'Oh Jane, why was I ever so foolish? Why did I rush in head first? I am so weak compared to you. You're so young. You've had a hard life and yet you have come through it all because you're so strong, so positive, so sensible about everything.'

Jane pressed her lips together to stop them from trembling. Against his shoulder, she shook her head, not trusting herself to speak. If she were to say one word, just one word, then she was so afraid that her feelings would come pouring out.

Charles's feelings were much the same.

His infatuation with an older woman had trapped him. At the moment he felt that he would be shackled to Frieda for life.

Only now, as he put Jane from him and walked from the room, did he realize where his true feelings lay. He wanted to tell Jane of the fierceness of his love for her, but that wouldn't be fair on her.

Week after week Charles continued to live at Ashford Manor, indulging Frieda's every whim.

'He's resigned himself to the fact that he has no get-out,' Christine told Jane after he had come to lunch one day. 'It's as if he is taking all the blame on his shoulders, as if . . . he's trying to make amends for the fact that her husband and her daughter have washed their hands of her. He regards taking care of Mrs Harman as his duty.' She sighed heavily before adding, 'Which I suppose is true, really. I just don't want to admit it, even to myself.'

'I think you're right,' Jane said quietly. 'We haven't seen much of him since that second burglary, but he seems changed. Very subdued. Not at all the same Mr Charles as when I first came here.'

'I agree wholeheartedly with you, Jane, and yet . . . he's softer. That's a funny word, but I can't think of another way to put it. He cares so much for me, and for you too, Jane, You know that, don't you?'

'Oh Miss Christy, he's always been kind to me.' She felt her face reddening. She wished she could read Christine's thoughts. Would she approve of her son liking me? she wondered. Or of me loving her son? Never. It just wasn't possible. There would always be that great difference between master and servant.

She realized that her love for Charles had been there for a long time, but it was a true, unselfish love, and because of who he was, she would never, ever tell Charles how very much she loved him.

Chapter Twenty-Five

'NINETEEN TOMORROW, EH, Jane?' Elsie Rogers smiled across the breakfast table, then sat back and studied Jane's face. You've done well, she thought, but what she said was, 'I was more than pleased to receive Christine's invitation to spend New Year's Eve here, because I have a special birthday present for you this year.'

'Really?' Jane sounded excited

'Yes, really, though it isn't a present as such, more of an outing.'

Jane looked at Christine, and with a laugh in her voice asked, 'Did you know about this? And are you coming too?'

Christine grinned. 'The answer to the first part of your question is yes, and to the second part no.'

Jane swivelled round in her chair.

'Jane, be still and listen to me,' Elsie ordered. 'Some very old friends of mine, Betty and Bert Smith, run the café in Tooting Market. I have come to know them well over the years, and whenever I am in south London I usually drop in on them, have a cup of tea and a chat.

About a month ago that is exactly what I did.

'They have six children, only one of them a girl, and she works in the Royal London Hospital in Whitechapel. She's not a nurse; a ward-maid I think is how they described her. When I saw Betty and Bert they had just returned from a weekend break. Their daughter had treated them to tickets for a West End show and on the Sunday morning they decided to pay a visit to Petticoat Lane. And here's the coincidence. They overheard a stall-holder asking for the market manager, and the reply was that Wally Simmonds was attending to a bit of business over in Middlesex Street. Bert made himself known and established that it was the same Wally Simmonds they had known so well when he too lived in Tooting and was market manager there.'

Jane's eyes were wide and her mouth had dropped open. 'Did they know if my mother was with him?' she asked timidly.

'Whoa, hold your horses, Jane,' Elsie cried. 'I didn't want to appear too eager. However, Bert did tell me that he'd learned that Wally was living in one of the little streets near Spitalfields and that he'd now got a wife and a little boy.'

Jane looked perplexed. 'But you said there was no record of them having got married.'

'My thoughts exactly. But at present we have no way of knowing if the lady referred to as his wife *is* your mother. Then it came to me. Just because it is being said that Wally Simmonds has a wife doesn't necessarily mean it's the truth. They could be living together. Your mother might even have changed her name to Simmonds by deed poll.'

Jane put her elbows on the table and rested her head on her hands. Thoughts were whirling round and round in her head. Had her mother been living in the East End of London all this time? Was she with Wally Simmonds? Someone had said he had a wife and small son. Did that mean her mother had had another baby?

Elsie and Christine had discreetly left the room, leaving her on her own with her thoughts. Memories. She was dragging them up.

Her dear little brother Tommy. He'd died and she had never even known that he was ill. Her father had never picked on him. Only on her.

Since Nancy had enlightened her, she knew the reason for that.

Another man had fathered her. Mickey Jeffrey had never been her father and he had looked on her as being nothing but a burden.

But her mother had loved her. She knew that much without a doubt. And her mum had been so beautiful. Nancy had often told her that she had her mother's colouring. Fair clear skin. Big sparkling blue eyes and thick straight dark-golden hair that was so long when she took the pins out at night that it hung well past her shoulders.

That was how she remembered her mother.

But there still was, and always had been, that one question: if her Mother had loved her so much, why had she not kept in touch?

Why?

Jane had never found an answer to that question. Only her mother could give her that answer. If and when she and Mrs Rogers ever found her.

Was the fact that Elsie had stumbled on the whereabouts of Wally Simmonds going to make any difference? Would it bring her face to face with her mother?

Her thoughts were interrupted.

'Bit cold outside, but as it's the last day of the old year, Christine and I thought we'd go for a short walk. How about wrapping up well and coming with us?' Elsie Rogers urged. And when no reply was forthcoming from Jane, she asked softly, 'Are you all right?'

Unable to speak, Jane still didn't answer. She took her time, sat up straighter and wiped her eyes with her handkerchief.

'I wish I knew why she didn't contact me,' she mumbled. 'Up until today I thought we would never find her, but now I feel we might. And Mrs Rogers, I just want to ask her why.'

Elsie came closer and put her arm around Jane's shoulders. 'I think this is the break we've been waiting for. We thought your mother might have gone abroad, but maybe all this time she and Wally Simmonds haven't been too far away. They say plant a tree in a forest and you'll never find it. Perhaps that's the way Wally was thinking. Move from south London into the East End. Who would ever think of looking there? And after all, markets are what he knew about, and he had to earn a living. Oh, and by the way, Jane, I think now you're all grown up that it is time you stopped calling me Mrs Rogers and made it Elsie'

Jane managed a smile. 'Got it all worked out, haven't you . . . Elsie?'

They both laughed, and Elsie said, 'Yes. I think this is what we've been waiting for. We're going to find your mother now, you'll see.'

Jane couldn't bring herself to sound that confident, so she just nodded her head.

'Right then, my birthday present to you, Jane, is a trip up to London on Sunday and a visit to Petticoat Lane. How does that sound? Or, if you want to be a real cockney, you just call it "the Lane".'

'Oh, I do. I've discovered that Londoners have hearts of gold.' Jane smiled properly for the first time since the beginning of this conversation.

It was a real smile that lit up her whole face and made those blue eyes of hers twinkle.

'Put your hand through my arm and hold on tight.' Elsie grinned at Jane, who was standing stock still, gazing at the sea of people and the great mass of stalls that stretched away as far as the eye could see.

'It's only on Sunday mornings that it's like this,' Elsie said, laughing. 'It's when the Lane comes alive and offers what must be one of the most colourful scenes in London. Just listen to the spiel the stall-holders are shouting to gather the crowds around them. It's almost as good as going to the music hall. It's the atmosphere, hard to explain, but I don't think you'd find it anywhere else in the world.'

Jane agreed with every word, her eyes popping out of her head. Surely there wasn't a mortal thing that you couldn't buy in this market, and according to the stall-holders most of them were giving the merchandise away, or at least selling it at a loss! Suddenly they were facing a row of stalls that sold food, and folk were standing on the pavement, even in the middle of the road, eating strange delicacies off small china dishes.

'Stay there.' Elsie pushed Jane up against a lamp-post. 'And don't move. Here, hold on to my bag. I've got my purse and I'm going to get you a real treat.'

It was some minutes before Elsie came back holding a cardboard tray in front of her which held four of these china dishes. 'Come on now, which d'you fancy trying first?'

Having said that Elsie burst out laughing, for to see the look on Jane's face was something else. It was a cross between horror and utter disbelief.

'What on earth are they?' Jane managed to ask.

'Well, the ones that look like snails are whelks. Gorgeous,

but need a lot of chewing. Those in jelly are absolutely delicious. They're known as jellied eels. You have to spit the bones out, though, mind. The small ones are cockles, another kind of shellfish. I've put plenty of pepper and vinegar on them. And the last ones are hot grilled sprats, tiny fish dipped in batter. Tuck in,' Elsie urged.

To Jane's amazement she found she actually liked the food – at least the three that she tried, she did, and especially the jellied eels. The whelks she just could not bring herself to place in her mouth. Though she laughed fit to bust as she watched Elsie chewing away at what she was convinced was a snail.

It seemed that Londoners never stopped eating on a Sunday morning. Loaded down with parcels and bags, men, women and loads of small children munched away at saveloys, hot faggots and even pigs' trotters. There was steaming pea soup being sold by the mugful. Elsie said they couldn't go home without taking something for Christine and the staff, and so she bought gingerbread, muffins and crumpets, and for Mr Wilson there had to be hot chestnuts and salted peanuts.

'But they'll be cold by the time we get back,' Jane protested.

'Oh, never fear, Mrs Wilson will pop them straight on to her hot range, and her husband won't be getting them all to himself, never fear. Now choose yourself a present for your birthday, anything that takes your fancy, and then you and I are going to make a beeline for the market manager's office.'

Wally Simmonds was in his office, and rose to his feet as Mrs Rogers ushered Jane through the door. He looked what he was: a self-assured, thick-set, good-looking man in his early thirties with a weatherbeaten face, dark-brown eyes and a cheerful smile.

Jane had no recollection of ever having seen him before. But it was eleven years since she had, and she'd only been a little girl at the time.

'What can I do for you ladies?'

Jane jumped in feet first. 'I'd like to talk to you about my mother,' she said quietly.

Wally Simmonds looked startled. 'Hang on a minute. I didn't get your names.'

'I'm Elsie Rogers,' said the older woman, extending her hand to him. 'And this is Jane Jeffrey. I suppose you could say she is my ward, since I've been partly responsible for her since she was eight years old.'

Wally glanced from Mrs Rogers to Jane and, having heaved a great sigh, addressed the girl. 'When did you last see your mother? Can you remember that?'

'Vividly,' Jane answered without hesitating. 'It was the last time she came to the hospital, and it was eleven years ago.'

'And since?'

Jane didn't know how to answer that, and Mrs Rogers took over, briefly telling Wally how the Guardians of the Poor had found Jane a place at Winchelsea Lodge, where she had remained until her sixteenth birthday.

'I see.' Wally sat back in his chair, his face showing just how troubled he was. Slowly he stood up and came round from behind his desk. He pulled two metal chairs from a stack that stood in the corner and urged them both to sit down. 'Because this is going to take some time,' he said, shaking his head as if to clear it before he really started to talk. 'I'm not sure how much you know, Jane? About Tommy, for instance?'

Jane raised her head and looked straight at him before

saying quietly, 'When I first went back to Tooting and found Nancy again, she told me everything that had gone on since I'd been taken away. She said that Tommy had died and that . . .' Jane hesitated and swallowed hard. 'Mickey Jeffrey was not my father.' She couldn't go on. Her eyes filled with tears.

Wally took over. 'I found your mother lying on the floor in her kitchen. I thought at first that he had killed her. She was white, white as a sheet, with blood oozing from a great gash in the side of her head. I called an ambulance, but it took twenty minutes to get there. She was taken to Wandsworth Infirmary and two days later they transferred her to Belmont. Said she had suffered brain damage. She was there a long time, and to put it bluntly, the doctors said she had gone out of her mind.'

Jane gave a gasp of horror, but eventually managed to ask, 'How long before she got better?'

'Several months,' he answered quietly.

Jane's eyes were riveted on Wally Simmonds. 'What happened to my little brother, Tommy? And to my . . . father?'

'I don't rightly know. At least not all the details. The police were after Mickey but he'd scarpered, and as far as I know it were neighbours that took Tommy in.'

'So what happened when my mum did come out of hospital?'

'Oh, she came back to Selkirk Road but she was very frail, and trying to look after Tommy on her own wasn't easy. Then Tommy dying was the last straw. It hit her so hard. Set her back no end. I did what I could for her.' He looked away into the distance as if remembering was killing him, and it was in barely a whisper that he murmured, 'For a while Alice believed she had buried not only Tommy but her little girl as well.'

Jane's eyes were brimming with tears. 'Mr Simmonds, are you saying my mother became ill again?'

He nodded his head. 'Yes, very ill. To be fair, Mickey felt the death of young Tommy. It was a great blow to him. He was calm enough at the funeral and indeed during the church service, but back at the house he really let his temper get the better of him and that's when he laid into your mother. She was in Belmont a second time.' He hesitated and turned to look at Elsie Rogers. Almost apologetically he added, 'For a while she lost her mind completely.'

The heavy silence was unbearable. And when Wally spoke again it was to Jane.

'Your mother's illness started because Mickey Jeffrey practically bashed her brains in,' he said bitterly. 'Then the fact that she had lost you and then Tommy unhinged her. She convinced herself she had nothing left to live for.'

'Didn't she even bother to find out where I'd been taken?'

'Yes, she did when she first came home from Belmont, but she hadn't much stamina and all the London associations swore they had no knowledge of your whereabouts. After the second bout in Belmont, she didn't know where she was or what she was doing half the time.'

Suddenly he stood up and spoke with a marked determination. 'Jane, I am so pleased to see you, truly I am, but you couldn't have picked a worse day. Sundays are a nightmare for me.' He looked at his watch. 'I've stacks of paperwork to get through, and in another hour or so I have to be out there in the Lane. By-laws and regulations as to how the clean-up proceeds are all down to me. Can we meet up later? I'll try and give you more information.'

'I want to see my mother,' Jane cut in aggressively.

'I know you do, and of course you shall, but I have to prepare her. We can't just spring you on her. Believe me,

Jane, it's been her life's ambition to find you. She'll be over the moon, I promise you, but you have to give me time.'

Elsie felt sorry for the man. He was all at sixes and sevens.

'We could go to a hotel, have some tea, if you could meet us before we catch our train. Would that be all right?' Elsie asked.

He gave a sigh of relief. 'That's a jolly good idea. I'll call you a cab and you wait at the Great Western Hotel. I'll delegate most of my jobs and be with you as soon as I can.'

It was early evening when Wally Simmonds shook hands with Elsie Rogers and very cautiously put his arms around Jane to give her a gentle hug. 'It will be fine,' he whispered. 'Your mother will be reborn. Mind you, I am going to have to break it to her gently, so be patient, Jane. I promise you and she will meet up soon.'

'Well, Mr Simmonds was really nice and very helpful,' Elsie said as she and Jane settled back in opposite window seats in the train. 'But you don't remember him, do you?'

'Not really. I wish I did.' Jane sighed. 'I suppose it was all a long time ago.'

'Does it matter? Think about it, Jane. It came across to me that that man has stuck to your mother through thick and thin. It's obvious that he really loves her. Try and do as he asked, be patient. I'm sure he'll tell us a whole lot more when he's had time to get over the shock of you turning up.'

Jane felt she had no option.

Was she pleased with the way the meeting had gone? In some ways, yes. On the other hand, she was heartbroken to learn that her mother had been so very ill.

I just can't wait to meet her, she cried inwardly as she closed her eyes and listened to the steady drumming of the train wheels on the railway tracks.

Chapter Twenty-Six

THE TELEPHONE CALL came ten days later.

Christine and Jane were sitting in the garden room having coffee and going over their notes on the upcoming events which were held regularly in the church hall when Mr Wilson came calmly into the room.

'Excuse me, you have a phone call, Jane. It's Mrs Rogers.'

Christine and Jane exchanged smiling glances, and Jane got up quickly.

A few seconds later she was saying, 'Hello, Elsie, have you had news?'

'Yes, I have. I had to be in London so I took a chance and telephoned Mr Simmonds. We met for lunch. You don't mind, do you, Jane?'

'No, no, of course not, but please go on. When am I going to meet my mother?'

'As soon as you like now. Mr Simmonds has prepared her.'

'Elsie, we didn't ask if he was married to my mother.'

'Well, no. Not at that first meeting we didn't. I told him

how we searched the records at Somerset House, and he apologized. They learned Mr Jeffrey was in prison and Mr Simmonds paid him a visit but was unable to persuade him to divorce Alice. Apparently they tried very hard, but it all got a bit messy, so they decided to take the quiet course and move away. Mainly because of your mother's illness. Least said soonest mended kind of thing. They did change her name by deed poll and they never mention the fact to anyone. Alice is, and has been for a long time, to all intents and purposes Mrs Simmonds.'

'Oh Elsie, thank you, thank you so much. May I ask you one question?'

'Of course, fire away.'

'Have they got a little boy?'

'Jane, I'm going to leave some things for your mother to tell you herself. I think that's best.'

There was a lengthy silence until Jane said, 'Now that I know my mother is only a few miles away, I feel strange.'

'Do you mean about meeting her?' Elsie asked, sounding worried.

'Yes.'

'Are you frightened?'

'Yes, a bit.'

'You'll be fine, I promise you. You'll see.'

Jane only hoped that she was right.

It was with her heart in her mouth that Jane walked up the pathway of a small house in a dull street. So many similar streets, surrounded by ugly, grimy buildings. Homes where folk struggled against the dirt and poverty to keep their families close-knit. But since having to cope with Nancy's death, she knew that nothing altered the warmth and good humour of these Londoners.

The house was not as big as Nancy's had been. It was, though, still in the kind of terrace where neighbours would help each other. This particular row were well kept, with clean white lace curtains at the windows and the doorsteps regularly hearthstoned.

Now Jane was facing the brown-painted front door, her hand on the black knocker, and her nerve almost failed her. Taking a deep breath, she banged it once and then stood back to wait.

The door was opened almost instantly by a lovely-looking woman with deep-golden hair, who was dressed in a tweed skirt and a pale-blue jumper covered by a wide white apron. Jane stared into the blue eyes that were gazing into hers, and a warmth such as she had never felt before surged through her body. She had no doubt whatsoever that this was her mother.

They continued to stare at each other for what seemed ages, both at a loss for words, until finally Jane gave a great sigh. It was a sigh of relief, as if she were thankful to have come to the end of a long, long journey.

And indeed that was exactly what it was. It was suddenly all Jane could do not to burst into tears. The relief of suddenly finding her mother again was fantastic, marvellous! It might be that now, at last, she would feel wanted again.

Finally it was Alice who opened her arms wide and said, 'Oh Janey come here,' and when she held Jane tight she started to softly murmur, 'Oh thank you, God, thank you. My beloved little girl. How I've longed for this moment. You'll never know. You'll never know.'

It was a long time before they separated. Neither could find the words they so badly wanted to say.

Then Jane brushed away her tears and said, 'Oh Mum. You really are my mother.'

And Alice was saying, 'Is it really you, luv? At long last. Is it true?'

Tears were trickling down their faces as once again they came together and held on to each other tightly.

They broke apart again and Alice began to sob as though her heart were breaking.

'I've waited eleven years for this day. There have been times when I've given up hope of ever seeing you again. Times when I was convinced you had died.'

Mother and daughter stood for a long time in the narrow passageway, holding on to each other as they shed their tears of sorrow and joy. Sorrow for all the years they'd spent apart, for all the heartaches they'd suffered, for all the things they'd missed doing together. And joy that at last they were reunited.

They sat together on a small sofa in the front room, a tray of tea and biscuits on the table in front of them. Neither of them had touched the biscuits. They held hands. Couldn't take their eyes off each other. Their faces sometimes showed wonderment, even astonishment. Alice shook her head, did her best to swallow the lump in her throat that was choking her, and in little more than a whisper began to talk.

'I never came to terms with losing you, but I had to let you go. Mickey was so cruel and there were times I feared he might kill you. Yet I felt so guilty. I *was* guilty. It was my fault, I should have stood up to him more. Wally said Nancy told you he wasn't your father.'

Jane nodded. 'Dear Nancy, she was such a good friend to me.'

'To me too. Always,' Alice said. 'I was so sorry when Wally came home and told me that she'd died. I ought to have kept in touch, but there were times when I . . . when I wasn't exactly with it.'

'Oh Mum, stop blaming yourself. Nancy told me what a terrible life Mickey led you from the very beginning.'

'Not only me, you too, luv. I thought he was being so kind when he offered to marry me. I convinced myself he would take care of me and my baby. The only other option was to have you put up for adoption, and I didn't want that. He turned out to be a nasty man. A cruel one at that. When he'd put you in the hospital and I agreed to let you go into a home I felt it was for the best. I truly believed that if you stayed with me, one day he would end up killing you. I thought about you every day, Janey. Wondered if you hated me. The times I've wished I could put the clock back.'

Jane rubbed her thumb over and over the back of her mother's hand, all the while staring into those beautiful blue eyes. 'I know, Mum, I know. You did what you thought was the best for me.'

'And you never felt hatred for me?'

'No. I never hated you. But I have to admit there were times when I yearned for some answers. I was always wondering about you, wondering why you didn't write to me, why you didn't want me. Wondering if you did love me.'

'Oh darling, don't say that,' Alice pleaded. 'I went mad with worry and that is the truth. Being in Belmont was no picnic. It was a terrible place. A place for lost souls.'

Jane bent over and fished around in her handbag until she found a clean handkerchief, and then she blew her nose hard.

'Mum, I am so sorry you suffered such nightmares. More so because the place I went to was very nice really. I should have left there when I was fourteen but they let me stay on for another two years, and I learnt such a lot. All that was because Mrs Rogers took me under her wing. Have you heard about her?'

'Yes. Wally told me he had lunch with her. And since my memory has become clearer, I do remember her being some sort of a social worker when you were in the hospital.'

'She's a bit more than that, Mum. She lost her husband in the war and devoted her life to helping children. She has a great influence within the law courts. You'll like her, Mum.'

'I think I shall. I got a long letter from her after she'd had that meeting with Wally, and she seemed nice.'

'Oh Mum, she is. From the day I left the hospital she's been my friend. She's gone to such lengths to find you for me. She even went to Somerset House to see if you were still alive and if you and Mickey had been divorced.'

'I know. Wally told me all about that. I'm glad you had someone you could turn to. I need to tell you, Jane, Wally and I aren't married.'

'I know, Mum, it makes no difference. Wally explained the details to Elsie.'

'Oh.' Alice sounded so sad. 'Divorce for someone like me, with no money, was an impossibility. Changing my name was the next best thing. Wally is a good man, an honourable man. He did it legally to make sure his surname was on your little brother's birth certificate.'

'Really, Mum? I still have a brother?'

'Yes, luv, you do. Sadly not Tommy, as you know. But he's a little beaut. Andrew we've called him. Wally's taken him out so as to give us some time together. They should be back soon.'

'I can't believe it! I have a family again,' Jane exclaimed, her face lighting up.

Alice wiped her eyes and smiled broadly. 'The one thing you haven't told me is how you've fared since you left the children's home. What kind of a job have you got? Where are you living?'

'That's a tall order, Mum, and if I started at the beginning it would be a very long story. But it will keep. All you need to know for now is that I've fallen on my feet.' She paused, leaned across and gently kissed her mother's soft cheek. 'After all, we'll have loads of time together from now on.'

There was the sound of the front door being opened and running footsteps in the hall. Jane swung her head round as the door burst open. She saw an adorable, chubby, dark-eyed little boy wearing a red and white woolly hat on the back of his head. He pulled his hat off to reveal a mop of unruly dark curls.

Jane stared at him in amazement. She couldn't take her eyes off him. The boy hesitated for a moment, then flung himself at Alice, who wrapped her arms around him and covered his face with kisses.

'We've bin playing football with a load of kids an' Daddy fell over,' he gleefully told his mother. Alice whispered something in his ear and he turned around to stare at Jane.

'Hallo, Andrew,' she said. 'My name's Jane.'

The small boy giggled, but said nothing.

Wally Simmonds put his head around the door then came further into the room, a look of immense relief spreading across his face.

'You two getting along all right, then?'

'Like a house on fire,' Alice told him, beaming. 'Like a house on fire.'

Having nodded his head in approval, Wally turned and without any warning pulled Jane to her feet and into his arms, and hugged her tightly.

Seconds passed before he said quietly, 'Now at last my

Alice can really start to live again. She'll have two children and peace of mind from now on.'

When he let her go, Jane found herself really liking this big man. He had one of the kindest and nicest faces she had ever seen, and his smile was warm as he studied her. With her voice full of emotion Jane managed to say to him, 'Thank you for taking such good care of my mum.'

Then she felt a tug at her skirt. A chubby face with enormous brown eyes was staring up at her. Suddenly the little boy grinned, showing a deep dimple, and asked, 'Don't yer want t' hug me? Mummy said you would.'

'Oh you little darling,' Jane cried, sweeping him up into her arms. 'You've no idea how much I want to.'

And in her mind she was saying, no idea at all. I can't believe this is happening. At last!

Chapter Twenty-Seven

'GOOD MORNING, MR Wilson. Is my mother up and about yet?'

Jane heard Charles's voice in the hall, and her heart began to pound. She finished addressing the envelope for the letter she had just written to the League of Friends on behalf of Miss Christine, and then made her way out into the hall.

Charles was speaking on the telephone. She watched him in silence, wondering why she felt something was terribly wrong. It was more than just a premonition, and she shuddered at the thought of what had brought Charles to the house so early in the morning.

Charles replaced the receiver and stood looking at it for a moment or two. After a bit he turned to Mr Wilson and said quietly, 'Mrs Harman is dead.' Then he walked across the hall and made his way slowly upstairs.

He found his mother in her bedroom. He tapped at the half-open door, and when she called, 'Come in,' he took a deep breath and entered the room. Seated at her dressing table, Christine wore an elegant swans-down-trimmed silk dressing gown over a lacy nightgown, and fur-trimmed mules on her feet. She had brushed her hair until it shone and she sat with it hanging loosely over her shoulders.

His eyes met his mother's in the looking-glass.

'What brings you here so early in the day?' Christine smiled as she asked the question, but at the same time there was a note of apprehension in her voice.

Charles was reluctant to answer, but it had to be done.

'I'm sorry, Mother, disturbing you so early. Frieda is dead. Last night in her sleep. I found her this morning when I took her her early-morning cup of tea. I telephoned the doctor straight away but I knew she was dead.'

He paused, and on his face was an expression of such sadness, anguish and regret that Christine felt her heart would break. What could she do? There ought to be something at a time like this. But there wasn't anything.

For a while a silence lay between them, and Christine could think of no suitable words to break it.

Then Charles shook his head. 'Oh God, it's difficult to tell you the rest.'

Christine felt fear clutch at her heart, and Charles sensed it. He placed a hand on her shoulder and said, 'Mother, you are sure to find out sooner or later, and better you hear it from me. The doctor fears that Frieda might have taken an overdose of her tablets.'

Christine was stunned. 'How sad,' she managed to say at last. 'Is he certain?'

'No. Not exactly.'

'Well, how would she have got hold of the tablets? I thought there was a nurse always in charge of her medication.'

'There is. Or rather there was. I didn't detect anything wrong. I sat with her until very late last night, and when I did go to bed she was fast asleep. Peacefully. She hadn't complained of any pain or of feeling ill. It doesn't feel right. Maybe I just don't want to believe it.'

Christine sighed and pulled her dressing gown more tightly around her body. 'I still can't fathom out how she could have had enough tablets to kill herself. Where the hell would she have got them from?'

'Oh Mother! That's exactly what I asked the doctor. He thinks she must have saved them up, one or two at a time. Hid them, probably. We won't know until after the inquest. But I don't believe it.'

'I am so sorry, Charles.'

'I know you are, Mother. Oh God, it's so difficult to take in.'

'Charles, go downstairs and have some hot coffee. I'll be down in about a quarter of an hour.'

'Yes, all right.'

She wanted to tell her son not to worry, but realized that would be a daft thing to say. Her innermost thoughts were best kept to herself as well, because if the truth be known, she was thinking that at least now the poor woman was out of her misery. No more suffering.

Hopefully Frieda had found peace at last.

It took two whole weeks before the verdict was given as natural causes.

'She went to sleep and didn't wake up. You must try your hardest to be grateful for that much, Charles,' his mother urged. 'I know it feels as if your world has collapsed around you, and you must be devastated, but Frieda had suffered so much. Now she is at peace.'

Charles, who had been moved by his mother's words,

exclaimed, 'I know you're right, but it doesn't make me feel any better.'

The day after the verdict, Charles sought Christine out again and attempted to explain the situation.

'I've been staying at my own cottage since the day Frieda died,' he began. 'I thought it better. With her gone, legally I was trespassing.'

Oh dear God, Christine thought wildly. If it's not one thing it's another. Aloud she said, 'Why on earth haven't you come home?'

'Mother I'm a grown man, I must take the consequences for my own actions, not keep running home to you. What I do have to tell you . . . it's hard . . .'

She waited, not saying a word.

Charles took a deep breath before saying, 'I'm not allowed to attend the funeral, and neither are you.'

Christine hung her head. This was not entirely a surprise, but nevertheless it hurt. Mr Harman and his daughter had flown home, which was entirely the right thing to happen. All arrangements for the funeral were in his hands. And who could blame him for not wanting any member of the Dennison family anywhere near him. After all, Ashford Manor was still his property.

'You wanted to go?' she timidly suggested.

'Yes, yes, I did.'

'You sound uncertain.'

'Oh Mother, didn't you intend to be there?'

'I don't know. If I did attend I would only have sat at the back of the church. On the other hand, I'd probably have made some excuse.'

When her son made no reply, she said, 'Darling, you have

to put all of this behind you now. You didn't desert Frieda, you did your best. You can't go on punishing yourself for the rest of your life. You must get back to work. See all your friends.'

'As always, I know you are right, Mother, and I will make the effort, I promise.'

But Christine remained doubtful. To all outward appearances, her son was coping. But as his mother she knew that Frieda Harman's death had hit him badly. He was still blaming himself for so much, and if he didn't set about pulling himself together he might never come to terms with all that had happened.

'Why don't you go away for a while?' she pressed him. 'There's really no reason why you shouldn't. I don't want you to go, of course I don't, but I do feel it would be for the best.'

'What about you, Mother? I feel I should be around for you.'

She did her best to laugh. 'A few weeks without you around won't kill me. Besides, I have Jane, and since my last operation I am able to see fairly well with that eye. I try to be independent.'

'Mother you do remarkably well. And regarding Jane . . .' He hesitated. 'You don't think she will want to leave you now that she has found her mother?'

Christine sighed softly. 'The thought has entered my head, I won't say it hasn't. I know she's very excited. Really happy, I can tell, and that's only natural. But as for leaving me, I don't think so. I hope not. In any case, she would give me plenty of warning, never fear. Do you want to know something? I can't imagine my life without Jane, can you?'

Charles felt his cheeks flush up. How badly he wanted to say, no, I can't, and I hope I never have to.

But now was not the time.

'A few weeks away will give you breathing space. You would feel altogether better for it,' and this time Christine's words were said with some force behind them.

And so Charles was persuaded. 'All right, I'll go somewhere,' he said, and smiled, relieved that the decision had been made for him.

When he came home he would come back to Adelaide House, to comfort and warmth, where love abounded freely and he could revel in the sensation of having shed his worries and paid for his folly. He would be able to begin to live again, as his mother had so rightly put it.

He had one great hope: that when he did return, Jane would still be here taking care of his mother.

If she was, then he knew his heart would be filled with gratitude and he would have high hopes for the future.

Chapter Twenty-Eight

THREE MONTHS PASSED before Charles returned home. It was, the first week in July. The sun was shining, the gardens were a blaze of colour and the grass was like green velvet as it stretched away in the distance to the lake.

The house was quiet, not a soul about, but there were flowers on the hall table which stood near to the main staircase, and the usual pile of letters waiting to be taken to the post.

Charles picked up the top one, instantly recognizing Jane's small neat handwriting. He smiled, paused for a moment, and then, when nobody appeared, started across the hall and on towards the door of the garden room. This stood open, and across the room, near the open French doors, he saw Jane, sitting sewing. It was without a doubt the most lovely sight he could have wished for.

There she was, no longer the young, timid girl she had been when she first came to be his mother's companion, but transformed into a beautiful young lady, dressed in a long, full-skirted blue-printed cotton dress which was set off by a plain blue short-sleeved linen jacket. Her dark-golden hair was her crowning glory.

She *was* beautiful.

Charles whispered her name. Jane turned her head, and for a moment her lovely clear blue eyes stared at him in disbelief. Then she put her sewing aside and stood up murmuring, 'Mr Charles.'

At that moment Christine appeared, perfectly groomed as always, wearing a sage-green linen dress with a matching soft silk scarf tucked into the neck and a contrasting cardigan draped around her shoulders. Her make-up was slight but perfect, her perfume flowery.

'Charles,' she exclaimed in delight. 'We've missed you. I thought you were never coming home.'

'Oh Mother, I've missed you too.' He crossed the space between them quickly, stooped, took her into his arms and kissed her on both cheeks.

'You've never written, not one letter,' she rebuked him.

'I know. I had a lot of thinking to do.'

Jane felt that she had to leave the room because she so badly wanted to show Charles how glad she was to see him, and she knew that was not possible. The truth was, she no longer thought of Charles as her employer's son. To her now he was a lovely man. A man she had lost her heart to. Although recently she had accepted the fact that while she truly did love Charles, there was nothing she could do about it.

'Shall I fetch coffee for you both?' she asked.

'That would be nice, Jane,' Charles said softly.

'You make that for the three of us,' Christine said firmly. 'I don't want you asking me endless questions as to where Charles has been or what he's been up to.' She smiled directly at Jane and added quietly, 'Fetch the coffee by all means, but then come and sit down with us and hear Charles's news first-hand.'

Jane felt gratitude flood through her. She so badly wanted to be included yet did not feel she should intrude on his homecoming. Miss Christy was so kind and thoughtful.

Seeing Jane hesitate, Christine added, 'Charles wants you here, I know he does, and we all want our mid-morning coffee, so . . .'

Jane smiled her thanks, not daring to let her gaze rest on Charles.

When she came back with the coffee tray, Charles was breaking the seal on a bottle of brandy. There were three glasses on the table. While Jane poured the coffee, he opened the bottle and poured a measure into each glass.

'To Charles's homecoming and future happiness,' Christine said as she touched her glass to her son's and then to Jane's.

For some reason those words made Jane's heart leap, because Christine was smiling at her in a knowing way as she said them.

They drank their coffee, at ease with each other. Charles was not looking at Jane, but she knew he was aware of her nearness even though he was gazing down the garden.

Christine began asking questions. Where had he been? Whom had he seen? Was he going back to the office? Would he prefer another bedroom for a change or was he content to use his old room?

Their glasses were empty, the coffee drunk.

'I'd better have a word with Mrs Wilson about there being one extra for lunch,' Christine said, rising to her feet.

Jane knew it was an excuse. Mrs Wilson was well aware that Charles was home. Was Christine deliberately leaving the pair of them on their own? Did she know about their feelings? She wasn't at all sure how her employer would react if she did. There had been times and a few words said that had encouraged her to believe that Christine might approve. But what if she was wrong?

When Christine had left the room, the silence lay unbroken. Jane almost wished the floor would open up and swallow her. Had she presumed too much? What had given her the right to think that Charles could ever care for her as she did for him?

He was staring at her so intently she didn't know what to do. It was as if he wanted to stamp an impression of her into his mind.

Was it a vain hope that he did care for her? Jane asked herself. And the only answer she could come up with was that she would have to be patient and let things run a natural course.

Jane had Andrew on her lap and was reading him a story. She heard the knock at the door but took no notice, giving her full attention to her half-brother, who had taken his thumb out of his mouth and was asking, 'Just how big is a giant, Jane?'

'Oh, ever so ever so big,' she told him.

'Even bigger than my Daddy?' he badly wanted to know.

Jane held her head up. It couldn't be! She had heard his voice in the passageway but could not bring herself to believe it.

Then, 'Mister Charles,' she gasped, feeling her face flush a bright red as her mother ushered him into the kitchen. She set Andrew down and rubbed her hands down the sides of her dress. They stood staring at each other while Alice picked Andrew up and quietly left the room, closing the door behind her.

What on earth was Charles Dennison doing in her mother's East End house? She had to swallow a couple of times before she eventually managed to string some words together. 'Mr Charles, won't you . . . sit down,' she murmured, dragging an upright wooden chair forward.

But he continued to stand, just looking at her. 'Oh Jane,' he said at last. 'When my mother told me it was your day off I wormed this address out of her. She said she was sure you'd be here with your family.' He went quiet for a moment and then almost shyly added, 'And I wanted to be with you as well. I knew I had the right house as soon as your mother opened the door. You two are so very much alike. I hope you aren't cross that I've turned up.'

She looked down at the floor, feeling awkward and unsure, only able to murmur, 'Oh Mr Charles.'

The kitchen was so small that he was able to cover the space between them in two strides. Then he put his hands gently on her shoulders, sighed and said, 'Jane, don't you think it is about time we talked? Perhaps we should start off by telling each other exactly how we feel. And please let's drop the Mister, eh?'

She looked around the room and felt the lack of space. The whole house was so very different to what he was used to. She loved this little house, loved coming here. The black-leaded grate, each side of which hung brasses, gleamed bright. The faded cretonne curtains, the wooden dresser with its mismatched sets of china, the threadbare rugs, none of it mattered. Here she was part of a family. Her very own family. She loved and was loved in return. But Charles Dennison would never fit in here. He shouldn't have come.

Charles sensed her embarrassment. There was no need for it. He had to find a way to tell her how he felt.

From the moment he had stepped over the doorstep, the

house had appealed to him. He thought back over the extra-ordinary chain of events that had brought him here. The harsh early years that Jane had suffered. His mother's dear friend Elsie Rogers had taken her under her wing, secured a place for her in a decent children's home. But in all the eight years she'd remained there she had had no link with anyone she could claim as her own relation. She had been turned out into what she had found to be a cruel world at the age of sixteen. Left to fend entirely for herself. Until, thank God, Elsie had brought her to be his mother's right hand. For that was what she had turned out to be.

And then, what a wonderful climax. With a great deal of help from Elsie Rogers, Jane had found her mother. And that had led to so much more: a stepfather who loved her, and a little boy who she could call her brother. She was no longer alone. She had a family of her own.

Would that make any difference to what he was intend-ing to ask her?

He rued the day that he had let his heart rule his head, because his disastrous affair with Frieda had caused heartache for so many people. He had known for certain soon after he had met Jane that what he had felt for the older woman was not love. The day he had had the tele-phone installed in his cottage had marked the first stirring of his feelings for Jane, even though she had been like a frightened newly born colt whenever he held out a hand to her.

After that evening there had been no going back, although he had not allowed his feelings to show. He had a duty to Frieda and he hoped he had not transgressed in any way while she was alive. After her death, just to be near Jane had been impossible. He hadn't been able to think straight. At that point in time the last thing he needed was another emotional involvement. He had had to get away. Sort out his priorities. But always at the back of his mind had been the strong hope that Jane would still be there when he got back. He had isolated himself from everything and everybody that was familiar. Now he was home, and there were no doubts left in his mind.

He had come here today with his heart in his mouth. In the taxi which he had taken from the station, he had passed dirty, bleak buildings covered in bird droppings. Several pubs, and grey-roofed factories, and the endless rows of terraced houses with not a sign of a tree or a bush. In the main these houses seemed to open directly on to the pavement.

He knew his life had been a privileged one, but he had to convince Jane that nothing that had gone before really mattered.

'Jane,' he began, his voice sounding very serious, 'I want you to listen to me.' And when she turned to look at him he added, 'Just listen.'

'All right, I'm listening,' she told him.

'This shouldn't come as a surprise to you. I love you. I think I always have, from the very first time I saw you, because even then I wanted to protect you. Never let anyone hurt you ever again. I want us to be together. For the moment, how about you just agree that we can have a real commitment? But that would only be the beginning, because when we have spent time together and you can form a true opinion of me . . . well, I will know the time has come for us to be married.'

Jane realized that her eyes were filling with tears. She began to search in her pocket for her handkerchief. 'But . . . Charles, your world is so very different from mine. You can't be sure . . .'

'I *am* sure. Never more so. Because one thing is really certain, and that is that you mean the world to me. While I was away I went through a dark and painful time, only bearable when I was at last able to forgive myself for all the heartaches I had caused others. I can't turn the clock back, no more than you or even your mother can, but we can look to the future. Life for both of us might never be the same as it was, but it can be different, and I know that as long as we are together it could be good. I have given so much thought to this, and I honestly cannot imagine an existence without you.'

Jane, having at last found her handkerchief, now blew her nose.

Suddenly she felt very humble. 'Oh Charles, if only you knew just how long I have loved you, but whatever would your mother and your friends say?'

'Hush, my love . . .' Then his lips touched hers in a kiss so tender she could not believe it.

After a while he released her and she shrugged helplessly. 'I really don't think anything could possibly come of this, Charles. We couldn't . . . it wouldn't be right.'

'Why ever not, Jane?' His tone was gentle but she could see the hurt in his eyes. 'I promise I would take care of you, do my utmost to make you happy. You've just said you have loved me for a very long time. Did you mean it? Really mean it?'

Suddenly she was overcome with shyness and stammered, 'Of course I meant it, that's what's so awful. Ever since I first came to Adelaide House and you were so kind to me, I used to long for you to come home.'

'Oh Jane, whatever can I do to convince you that we shall have a future together?' he said, touching her face with the tips of his fingers.

Jane took a step backwards. 'Have you thought what your friends, your business partners, not to mention your mother, might say if you were to tell them that you were thinking of marrying me?'

Slowly and deliberately he placed his hands on her shoulders and looked into her eyes. 'Do you really think I care about what people might say? Whatever happens, you are the one person I want to spend the rest of my life with. I don't want you to answer me today. I want us to spend time together. Enjoy each other's company, really get to know each other's likes and dislikes. And then one day soon I shall do the whole thing properly. I shall get down on one knee, produce a diamond ring from my waistcoat pocket and ask, Jane, will you marry me. Please?'

She couldn't resist the look on his face. She burst out laughing, stretched out a hand and ruffled his hair.

He seized the opportunity and pulled her tightly into his arms. They overbalanced and, arms and legs entwined, fell to the floor, the pair of them laughing fit to bust.

Alice Simmonds, shelling peas in the scullery, heard their laughter, and from her heart she sent up a prayer of thanks that fortune was at last smiling on her daughter.

Chapter Twenty-Nine

'WILL I DO?' Jane asked, sweeping into the big lounge with an uncharacteristic flourish and giving Charles and Christine a twirl, the cream chiffon folds of her very first long evening dress swirling around her ankles.

'Beautiful, really beautiful,' Charles murmured. He too was looking very smart, in a dinner jacket with a crisp white dress shirt, his fair hair sleeked back, giving him a distinguished air.

'You look mighty fine yourself,' Jane smiled, her face specially made up for the occasion, hair piled high in a sophisticated style that had taken her ages to get right. She turned her gaze to Christine. 'Perfection,' she murmured. 'The only other word I can think of is sleek.'

'That describes you exactly, Mother, it really does,' Charles added.

Christine did look as if she had been poured into the tight-fitting golden dress. Around her shoulders she wore a fine stole that looked like a floating spider's web.

'I feel very honoured to have two such beautiful ladies for my companions tonight,' Charles said.

They were going to a hotel in Folkestone to a charity dinner in aid of an association for the disabled of which Charles was a member of the committee. It was a first for Jane and it had taken a lot of persuasion from both Charles and his mother to get her to agree to attend the function with them.

Life was like that lately!

There had been so many firsts. It was as if she had gained entry to an entirely different world. From the day that Charles had first put in an appearance at her mother's house, he had been as good as his word. They had spent hours together, walking across the Romney Marshes, lunching at the weekends in quaint country pubs. Some Saturdays, when Charles hadn't to go up to town, they spent the day in Folkestone, mixing with families on the beach, watching children build sandcastles and run in and out of the shallow waves, the boys dressed only in shorts, their chests bare, the girls with their dresses tucked safely into the waistbands of their knickers, children and adults alike licking their ice creams and running with balloons or kites on the end of long strings. It was an easy, happy companionship.

At other times, Charles took Jane and Christine to race meetings. Oh the excitement! Placing bets with the funny-looking man who wore a bowler hat and had a cigar sticking out from the side of his mouth even when he was talking. He was known as Honest Jack, the bookie.

Wonder of wonders, Jane, on Charles's advice, had laid out half a crown each way on a horse called Nice and Easy. It had come home first at ten to one and she had collected one pound eleven shillings and threepence plus her own stake money back.

They also spent quiet times. Times when Charles encouraged Jane to talk, always proving himself to be a good listener. He astutely made a mental note of everything she told him. Later, alone in his room, he would transfer his own thoughts down on to paper, the written word often making his heart ache just as it had done when listening to the telling from Jane.

Not all their outings or walks were in the south of England.

They had become regular visitors to the East End of London. Some Saturday afternoons Alice particularly loved. She had her Janey all to herself, while Wally, Charles and Andrew went off to watch a football match. When Arsenal, known locally as the Gunners, were playing a home match at Highbury, nothing would have kept them away. Even though Charles's business partners teased him that football was played with the wrong-shaped ball, the fever of being amongst the crowds that gathered at Highbury soon captured Charles as a fan.

When Charles Dennison had made his first appearance on her doorstep, Alice hadn't known what to do. It had taken her ages to really feel at ease in his company. Not his fault, bless him, she would say, just her leftover fearfulness from having spent time in a mental institution. Now she would watch them set off with tears of joy running down her cheeks. Her big burly husband, Wally; Charles, who, against all the odds, seemed to fit in with her family with such ease; and Andrew, with his beautiful happy little face with its high forehead, plump cheeks and dimpled chin, so unmistakably like Wally. The two men would swing Andrew along, his feet barely touching the ground, and Alice would turn and go inside the small house that was her pride and joy, to spend several hours alone with her lovely daughter. God had been good!

There had been times when she had felt she had been

entirely forsaken, not only by people but by God himself.

Not now, Alice Simmonds would say to herself on many occasions; now my cup is so full it runneth over.

Jane couldn't believe that the only doubts about the two of them getting married had come from her mother and Wally Simmonds rather than from Charles's family.

It would be like mixing oil and water, according to Alice. And as much as she wanted her lovely Janey to have the top brick off the chimney stack, she felt she had to voice her fears. They were together in the scullery, washing up the coffee cups, when Alice felt she had to voice her fears. She dug her fingers into the palm of her hand, then, heaving a great sigh, pulled the plug from the sink. As the soapy water drained away, she wished her fears could disappear just as easily.

Alice's face wore a serious expression as she squarely faced her daughter.

'Jane, no one wants you to be happy more than I do. But think about it. You both come from different worlds. Charles has always been treated as someone special. He's been waited on, given opportunities, never actually wanted for anything. In fact you could say he has been spoilt from birth.'

'Oh Mum,' Janey cried out in anguish. 'Keep that up and you'll have me convinced that I should run a mile from him, that it could never work between us.'

'Now I never said that,' Alice protested. 'I'm just pointing out what problems may crop up. I know from what you tell me how good Charles's mother has been to you, but . . . marrying her son? I don't know. Still, answer me one thing before we put our coats on and go for a walk: do you really love Charles?'

Jane felt her cheeks flush and again she cried, 'Oh Mum!

I thought it showed. From my first days at Adelaide House I was happy, but never more so than when Charles was at home. He was kindness itself right from the start and I truly believed that I was grateful to him, nothing more. But I missed him more each time he went away. My heart ached for him during the awful troubled times he went through, and I longed to comfort him. Until one day the realization dawned on me that I was in love with him. I kept it to myself. My love for him was precious and no one could take it away from me. I was fully aware at the time that nothing could come of it: as you so rightly say, I came from an entirely different background, but that didn't stop me from loving him, even though in my wildest dreams I never thought his feelings for me would ever amount to more than friendliness.'

Jane paused and took a deep breath before saying, 'So, Mother, to answer your question, yes, I do love Charles, with all my heart.'

'That's all I wanted to know.' Alice smiled broadly. 'They say love conquers all.'

It was days later, when out walking across the fields, that Jane again screwed up courage to broach the subject with Charles.

'You really mean,' she asked him for the umpteenth time, 'that it was your mother who urged you to propose to me?'

'Yes, yes, yes,' Charles said, hugging her. 'She approves wholeheartedly of you. Ask her yourself. She will tell you that she has looked upon you as a daughter for a long time.'

'Yes, but I didn't think . . .'

'Well,' he said modestly, 'anything that makes me happy is all right by my mother. I may have lapsed for a while, but by and large I've always been her golden boy. Truly,' he added seriously, 'if Mother had chosen you herself she couldn't be more happy. She loves you dearly. She never treated you as a servant even at the beginning, did she?'

'No, she never did,' Jane quietly admitted, on the verge of tears. She put her arms around his neck and kissed his cheek, trying to imagine how her life would be from now on. The most lovely thing of all was that she wouldn't have to stifle her feelings for Charles. She could let the whole world see how much she loved him if she wanted to. And she did want to!

'Charles, oh Charles,' she whispered against his cheek, 'I do love you so.'

On the first Saturday of the new year they were married quietly in the old church in Rye. It was to have been only their immediate families present. However, Jane could not believe how many folk were seated in the pews as she walked down the aisle on Wally Simmonds' arm. It was a testament to Jane's popularity.

The bride's family were in the front row on the left, her mother and her brother Andrew, together with Elsie Rogers and the Matron from Winchelsea Lodge, while Christine and her distant relatives plus many friends were seated on the right-hand side. With her heart so full she thought it would burst, Alice watched her daughter become a married woman. She had been completely overwhelmed as she'd watched her Janey being escorted through the church on Wally's arm. She was sure there had never been a more beautiful bride.

Jane wore a simple high-necked, full-skirted, long-sleeved white silk bridal gown, but because of the bitterly cold weather and a threat of snow, a red velvet cloak was draped around her shoulders. On her deep-golden hair, which had been professionally dressed that morning, she wore a triple crown of snowdrops intertwined with seed pearls.

The sight of Jane taking her place next to Charles at the altar, and the loving look he gave her, had been almost too much for Alice, and the tears spilled down her cheeks. She blew her nose and managed to control her emotions until she heard Jane's voice, soft but firm, saying, 'I will.'

After that Alice saw everything through a haze, and only pulled herself together when they were outside the church once again, being formed into small groups for the photographer.

Christine Dennison held a generous reception at Adelaide House, where everyone seemed entirely at ease. Wally Simmonds saw Alice and Christine deep in conversation, and he was grateful that two women from entirely different walks of life should be at ease with each other so quickly.

His glance went across the room to where Mrs Wilson was smiling as she helped her husband to carry in more food. Earlier in the week she had spoken to him freely, told him not to worry and assured him that the wedding would go off without a hitch. But it was the words that this homely, kind and wise woman had added that had set his mind as rest: 'If ever I saw a man in love with a girl, then that's Charles Dennison. Take my word, this time he's got it right, and he's a lucky beggar, 'cos there aren't many like our Jane about.' When he had repeated the words to Alice, her heart had swelled with pride.

The time went too quickly. 'We should go upstairs to change,' Charles said, tucking Jane's hand through his arm, and added, 'I can't wait to take my wife off on our honeymoon.' They wandered through the guests saying their thank-yous until they came to Christine, Alice and Elsie Rogers.

Jane had a job to find the words, but eventually she murmured, 'I owe it all to you three.'

The look of love on the faces of these three ladies as they each gazed at the newly married couple was enough to pull at anyone's heartstrings.

It had been an absolutely wonderful happy day.

But Charles was determined that it was not to be the end of the celebrations.

He had planned for weeks now. Studied for hours the notes he had made after the lengthy talks he'd had with Jane. It might still take him some time to pull it off, but he was determined that the minute they got back from their honeymoon he was going to do his damnedest to put his plan into action.

Chapter Thirty

'WHATEVER MADE YOU think of doing this?' Jane stared at her husband, her face showing a whole range of emotions.

It was the last Monday in February and the invitations Charles had sent out had stated that it was to be 'A buffet luncheon, and a time to meet and mingle with old friends.' He had arranged everything down to the last detail, Monday being the rest day for most of the London market traders.

Jane stood beside Charles, her eyes wide with amazement, as her stepfather proudly introduced his workmates and their wives to the newly-weds. Their voices were loud and rough but their pleasure at being here was evident. It took quite some time for all the introductions to be made, and Jane wasn't sorry when Wally suggested that he and Charles should fetch drinks from the bar. To say that she felt bewildered would be putting it mildly.

'You all right, love? You look pale.' Alice looked at her daughter with concern.

Jane shrugged. 'I'm fine, Mum, just a little overwhelmed.

Can't believe that Charles thought of putting this do on all by himself.'

'Well, I know for a fact that he did. Even his mother wasn't in on it until the last moment. He said he wanted a do in London so that all our neighbours and friends could be invited. After all, we didn't invite many friends to your wedding.'

Jane looked across the huge hall and watched her mother-in-law throw back her head and laugh heartily. The woman Christine was talking to was large and heavy-breasted with bleached hair and quite a lot of make-up. But when Wally had introduced her, he had also told Jane that she was one of the hardest workers for unprivileged children in the whole of the city.

Christine, as usual, was perfectly groomed, looking better than a lot of woman half her age. She seemed entirely at ease with these Londoners.

Charles came back with a tray of drinks, but Jane felt at odds with him. She really couldn't fathom the reason he had set up this luncheon. There was an undercurrent of tension between her and her mother, and Christine was staying well away from her. Something was going on and no one seemed prepared to tell her what it was

They sipped their drinks in silence, watching a good number of children running round the hall. Jane spotted Andrew in a line of kiddies. Each had their arms around the waist of the one in front and they were singing at the top of their voices. Andrew broke free, crossed to her side of the hall and stopped in front of his big sister.

'Good 'ere, ain't it, Jane?'

'Yes, it is. Are you having a good time?'

'Not 'alf,' said Andrew. 'You see the girl that was in front of me, well, 'er name is Bessie an' 'er dad works in a circus an' Uncle Charlie an' me Dad said they're gonna take all of us t' see the show. That'll be great, won't it? See yer.'

Andrew was laughing as he sped off, and his laughter was infectious. Jane shook her head but she was smiling! All that had been said without Andrew pausing once for breath, and suddenly Charles had become Uncle Charlie. Oh well, she grinned to herself, this certainly was a different world, but it had to be a case of when in Rome . . .

It came to her mind that there was nothing of their mother in Andrew; he was the spitting image of his dad, he even had a dimple in his chin like Wally. Well, she decided, if he grew up to be as good-looking as Wally, with the same kind and generous nature, he wouldn't want for friends.

Charles left the group of men to whom he had been talking and moved to be beside Jane. He kissed her cheek and said, 'I'll only be a few minutes.' Then, turning, he called to Wally, 'Would you like to give me a hand? I think the cars have just drawn up.'

'Cars? What cars?'

Moving quickly to where her mother stood, Jane asked, 'Mum, do you know something I don't?'

Alice didn't answer. Instead she changed the subject. 'Charles really did do his homework. He's a good man, you know, so stop worrying and enjoy the day.'

A hush settled and a group of people that Jane could not place came across the floor and stood rather awkwardly in a sort of line-up.

'Ladies and gentlemen,' Charles shouted, and as the hall grew silent he spoke. 'Today I want to say thank you to many people who were kind to my wife when she most needed friends. I wanted Jane to be able to meet them again in order to be able to say her own thank-yous. But I also wanted those kind folk who befriended her when she was alone in London to see how well she has coped over the years. I needed to let them know that their kind-hearted gestures were appreciated.'

The first couple to stand in front of Jane were Mr and Mrs Forrester. Jane's arms were flung wide; she needed no reminding that her first landlady and her husband had nursed her when she had been so ill. 'Friends for ever,' she murmured as they hugged her.

Elsie Rogers had joined the group and was now saying, 'You won't remember, Jane, but this is Sister Walker from the hospital where I first met you.' She lowered her voice and added, 'She and her nurses clubbed together and bought you a winter coat.'

'Oh, what can I say . . .'

'Nothing, my dear, you were a delightful child, badly in need of some loving care. My Christian name is Glenis, and I am really pleased to have been invited here today. It isn't often one gets the chance to meet up with old patients.'

It was Jane's mother who took hold of Glenis's arm and led her towards the buffet, saying as they went, 'I remember you well. It was me who suggested Charles should invite you. You were kindness itself when I needed it most. To agree to have my small daughter taken into care was the hardest decision I ever had to make, and God knows I paid dearly for it.'

Glenis squeezed Alice's arm. 'You had no option at the time and you were very brave. Besides, us being here today to celebrate just goes to prove that the ends have certainly justified the means.'

'Thank you,' was all that Alice could bring herself to say. But those words from this kind nursing sister meant a great deal to her.

Suddenly there was a whole group of smiling faces, and Jane gazed at them all in amazement.

'Oh my, where do I start?' she exclaimed. Dorothy and Richard Stuart, who had been largely responsible for obtaining a place for Jane at Winchelsea Lodge, hugged her in turn, murmuring how pleased they were to be here today.

They then stepped aside so that Ted Grimshaw and his wife Maggie might have their say. 'You look a bit different today t' what you did when we first met,' Ted told her with a twinkle in his eye, and Jane's heart lurched as she looked again at this bluff, red-faced man who had played such a big part in her life for eight years. And she had to swallow hard as she kissed Maggie, remembering the many times she had been given a fairy cake or a sweet pastry straight from the oven by this homely wife of his.

Next, 'Oh Connie, my very first friend in the home!' Jane held her at arm's length. 'You're no longer fat and cuddly, and what happened to the pigtails?'

'You may well ask, an' I'd like t' know how come you've turned into such a graceful lady.'

'Perhaps it was all those cold-water washes,' Jane said as she gave this dear girl another big hug.

Connie was grinning like mad as she made way for Matron.

Tall and smart, Lillian Cooper, still smiling and finding time for her girls, stood in front of Jane and eyed her from top to toe. 'You are a credit to us,' she said softly. 'But then I always knew you would be.'

'I am so pleased to see you. Matron.' Jane told her, reluctant to let go of her hand, thinking how loath she had been to leave the safety of Winchelsea Lodge and the secure protection Matron had provided during all those years when she had felt she had no other family.

'And I you, Jane. As it's a party, maybe you could call me Lillian?' They both laughed and held each other close. Each one had memories that spanned those eight years.

Then came, Nellie Matthews, the cook who had taught Jane so much, especially in those two extra years that she had been allowed to stay on at Winchelsea Lodge. And now Patrick and Emma Carter were watching her with open mouths, utter disbelief showing on their faces.

'My, my,' Emma tutted at last. 'What a difference! I've never forgotten the day you were brought into our work-room. Such a little mite. Patrick reckoned you were over-awed by all the countryside and animals and that was why you'd lost your tongue.'

'Well, t' be sure it was true, wasn't it? Plucked from London and set down miles from home, what else did you expect of the lass?' Patrick asked, though not expecting to be given an answer.

'You certainly don't need me to find you clothing now,' Emma grinned. 'No one would describe you as a lost London lass today,' she murmured as she took in every detail of Jane's expensive beige suit. 'I couldn't be more pleased if you were my own daughter.'

'Oh, Emma, once you and Patrick took me in hand I became a well-turned-out child. You worked wonders for so many of us. You really did.'

'Not in the footwear department,' Patrick said, staring at Jane's tan-coloured leather court shoes. 'Never shod any of you well.'

'We helped a little there,' a gruff voice put in. 'Better introduce ourselves.'

But before the man could say anything more, Jane laughed heartily. How could she forget! She had practically fallen into this stout, jolly man's café when the sole of her shoe had parted company with its uppers. She'd eaten steak and kidney pudding with loads of vegetables, and apple pie and custard and a large mug of tea, all for the princely sum of one and tuppence!

Then there was his wife, Harriet, as thin as ever, wearing a great big smile. 'Sid's 'ere,' she said, pushing her brother forward. He was still a thin, weedy-looking man, but as before when he smiled his face was transformed, so much so that Jane had felt at ease with him from the moment they had met.

'An 'ow long did yer brown button-up boots last yer, gal?' Sid asked, a grin splitting his face from ear to ear.

'For a very long time,' Jane promptly told him as she grabbed hold of his hand. 'Largely due to the good polishing you gave them, I think. You'll never know, Sid, how many times I thanked you for those boots.'

'And 'ow about my thick socks that yer went off with?' Jack teased her.

'They were my lifesavers,' Jane replied seriously. 'And so were those meals you so generously provided for me.' Then she looked into the faces of these three ordinary working folk and quietly told them, 'I have never forgotten what you did for me. Those days were so bitterly cold and I felt utterly alone and unwanted by anyone. You truly were lifesavers to me.'

'Now, now, no tears t'day,' Harriet rebuked her. 'You ain't getting away with feeling sorry fer yerself. Looks t' me like you've 'it the jackpot with that good-looking 'usband of yours. You wanna know something? You're lucky you caught him before he paid us a visit, 'cos I knew the minute he set foot in our café that if he'd been footloose an' fancy-free, I'd 'ave upped sticks an' made off with him meself.'

'Oh! You would 'ave, would yer?'

Jane turned her head and stared in utter astonishment. It was Charles who had spoken, and she didn't know whether to laugh out loud or not. It was unbelievable to hear her Charles speaking with a cockney accent.

He came nearer and put his arms around Harriet's shoulders, then, looking first at his wife and then at the ring of onlookers, he smiled broadly and said loudly, 'Harriet, after you had served me with that Irish stew and dumplings I was yours to command, But . . .' He paused, giving his words a dramatic effect. 'It was that jam roly-poly that did it, and if only yer ole man wasn't a damn sight heavier than me I'd 'ave gorn off with yer there an' then.'

The silence that followed held for half a second, and then the whole room erupted into loud laughter. Mr Charles hadn't only invited cockneys to his luncheon do, he'd become one of them!

Jane looked from one to another, all these folk who had befriended her in more ways than one! It was beyond her, the lengths Charles must have gone to to find them all! The only person who was missing was Nancy.

Yet Jane had the strange feeling that she wasn't that far away. In fact she could hear her loud laughter and knew she'd be saying, 'See, gal, didn't I always tell yer that life's a gamble? And it seems t' me that one way an' another you backed a winner.'

This day was turning out to be something else! It was such a kind thing for Charles to have done. When this last group of people had been in her life she had been a lost soul. And that was no exaggeration. A poor mite indeed.

Now she was different, with a name that was her own. Not the name of some man who had married her mother but had not been her father. She was Jane Dennison now. A new person, a new woman in more ways than one.

She felt Charles take her hand and was so grateful that he had come into her life. That he had fallen in love with her had been something she could only have dreamed about.

Nothing that she or her mother had suffered in the past could be wiped out. But she could look to the future with high hopes. She had a mother and a father, because Wally Simmonds was that and more to her now. She had the dearest little brother. A mother-in-law who loved her and for whom she would go to the ends of the earth if needs be. And she had Charles.

What more could she possibly want?

Children of their own in the future? Please God.

Jane felt Charles put pressure on her hand. 'Stop daydreaming and come and enjoy the day. Stacked over there on those long tables is some of London's finest food. So, Mrs Dennison, shall we partake?'

When everyone had eaten their fill, a three-piece band was set up on the stage and a gentleman took a seat at the piano and struck a chord while the musicians took up their instruments. The music and the fun was about to begin.

The pianist was an elderly man but his nimble fingers flew over the keys and many guests were heard to say, 'Old Alf can really make that piano talk.' It was true, and he knew which songs to play to get the crowd going. He started off with a wartime tune, 'Tipperary', then moved on to songs from the music halls in the twenties. Marie Lloyd had died in 1922 but her songs and her reputation lived on, and these East Enders knew all the words!

'It's crowded, isn't it?' Christine smiled as she pushed her way through the mass of people to stand beside Jane.

'Yes,' Jane agreed. 'I still can't believe how Charles found all these folk and set this party up without me even knowing.'

'Well, besides finding everyone who had befriended you, I think he wanted to do something for your mother and Wally. They didn't invite many friends to your wedding and Charles saw this as a way to rectify that.'

Jane didn't answer, and Christine wasn't at all sure as to what she was thinking, so she said, 'The band is good, don't you think? But it's the pianist who's the real star. He knows exactly what songs to play to get the crowd in the party mood. I'm finding it a joy to watch all these people enjoying themselves.'

Jane was still feeling a little apprehensive. East Enders and what Christine would describe as the country set were certainly rubbing shoulders today.

Suddenly she looked at her mother-in-law and they both burst out laughing. A whole group of women had linked arms and gone to stand in the centre of the floor, where they were belting out 'Goodbye Sally I Must Leave You'. Hardly had they finished than the band struck up with the Charleston. This hugely popular dance had cut across all social boundaries, and these Londoners were enthusiastically giving it their all. Soon the pianist took over again, and this time he was playing black and white minstrel songs.

A hush fell over the audience as four of Wally's workmates walked on to the stage. Their faces had been blackened and white chalk used to draw a wide rim around their lips. The lights in the hall were lowered, and the men stepped forward and knelt down. No one spoke; even the children were quiet as the men put their heart and soul into an emotional rendering of 'Mammy, I'd walk a Million Miles'.

When the lights went up again, Wally turned to see his wife wiping tears from her eyes. 'Come on, you soppy beggar,' he laughed. 'There's no need for tears today.'

'I know, but it's because everyone is so happy that I'm afraid,' Alice said softly.

'Afraid! Of what?' Wally couldn't keep the disbelief from sounding in his voice.

'Everything is going so well. I can't help wondering if it can last.' Her voice now held a plea.

With a great show of tenderness, Wally took her into his arms. 'Alice, my love,' he whispered against her hair, 'you've known your share of dark days, and there isn't anyone here today who deserves happiness more than you and Jane. It might be hard for you to believe it, but trust me, you have Jane now, and she has you. Charles won't be taking her away from you. He worships her, anyone can see that, and if the pair of them are as happy as you and I have been, well, they won't go far wrong.'

Alice swallowed hard before wrapping her arms around Wally's neck. 'You're a good man, and I was so lucky when you took me on.'

'It takes two,' he smiled. 'And your daughter and Charles were made for each other, so will you please dry your eyes and come and dance with me.'

Alice took the handkerchief he offered and dabbed at her eyes. For a few minutes they watched as their young son held hands with a pretty curly-haired little girl and did his best to dance her around the edge of the floor as the band played a slow waltz. Meanwhile everyone clapped while Jane and Charles had the centre of the floor to themselves and eyes only for each other.

Alice looked up at her tall husband and managed a grin. 'I just love a happy ending, and those two coming together really is unbelievable.'

The rest of the day was so enjoyable, as Jane reminisced with old friends and danced with Wally's mates, who called her 'darling' and held her in a way that Charles's business partners would never dream of doing. There was no offence meant and none taken. They were proud, down-to-earth men who earned a living in the best way they knew how. Their wives were hard-working women to whom family meant everything, and they had taken Jane and Charles to their hearts.

Several times her eyes met those of her husband, and the unspoken message was *I love you*.

Jane felt safe and secure.

As the day drew to a close, she was thinking that she had the best of two worlds. Her own family, who lived in the East End of London, a place where she knew that she and Charles would always find a warm welcome. And their own beautiful cottage in Rye where they could close the front door and she could have Charles entirely to herself. And where Christine, who loved them both dearly, lived close by.

There was, in fact, absolutely nothing Jane would have changed about her life as it was now. As far as she was concerned, it was perfect.

Time Will Tell

BOOK ONE

LONDON, 1944

Chapter One

THE TALL TREES that lined the borders of Wimbledon Common were bursting with new life as the early spring sunshine streamed through their branches and a young girl with flame-coloured hair walked with her soldier boyfriend. Strolling over the thick grass, she slipped her hand into his. He smiled, whispered in her ear, and they both laughed. The lovers went to sit on a park bench looking out over a pond to eat their corned-beef sandwiches and sip bottled shandy. Later, as they kissed goodbye outside the Fox and Hounds, where she worked as a barmaid, passers-by sighed sadly for them. It was nearing the end of February 1944. Life was hard, and the war seemed unending. How much time had the youngsters had together? How long would it be before the young man would have to report back to his regiment?

Joan went through the double doors, across the saloon bar and into the comfortable sitting room that lay beyond. It was only a matter of minutes before she was confiding tearfully to her boss, Poppy Benson, that she was in love with Matt and terrified because he'd be on the move any day now. Eighteen-year-old Joan Harvey's life was anything but routine. And Mathew Pearson, the twenty year old born and bred in the East End of London had long realized his life would be far from normal as long as this war continued.

'I know it's your day off, but why don't you go and wash your face and come down to the bar for a drink?' Poppy suggested kindly. 'It's almost closing time, and you can give Bob a hand with clearing the tables if you like, take your mind off things.'

'All right,' Joan agreed quickly. 'I'll be down in a few minutes.'

Poppy and Bob Benson were really good to her. They had given her a cosy bedroom so that on the days she did work she lived-in rather than having to travel home in the black-out when the pub closed at half past ten. Although her home was only down in Haydons Road, Merton Park, a fifteen-minute bus ride, her parents would never have agreed to their eighteen-year-old daughter working if it had meant she'd be out late at night. True, the air raids had lessened somewhat, but in these terrible days you never knew what to expect.

She went slowly up the broad staircase of the beautiful old public house. Once inside her room, she took off her coat and hung it in the wardrobe, then stood before the black iron fireplace and leant forward towards the mirror that hung over the mantelshelf. She stared at her reflection: her hair was her crowning glory, and today her cheeks were pink from the sharp fresh air. Over a slim black skirt she was wearing an emerald green jumper, which emphasized her bright green eyes.

Oh, why can't we have more time together? She sighed.

Like everyone else she wished this rotten war would end but never more so than since she had met twenty-year-old Matt Pearson. She hadn't realized that you could love someone so much. He made her feel so special. To remember the way he had kissed her and run his hands over her breasts made her blush. Why had he singled her out? There had been dozens of pretty girls in the dance hall where they'd met. She giggled at that. No matter where she went her hair made her stand out from the crowd. She used to hate it when she was at school: Copper knob, Ginger, Red-roots were only a few of the names she'd been called. Now she didn't mind her mop so much. The colour had darkened a little, though it was still thick and uncontrollable. It had a life of its own, was what her mother said – speaking from experience because it was from she that Joan had inherited her colouring. Matt said he adored her hair, so that was all right.

They had been meeting for six months now. He had taken her to meet his family and she had liked them very much. Bit rough and ready, she had thought at first, until she found that all folk who lived in the East End of London spoke in the way they did. They were open and friendly – well, they were if they took to you – And they seemed to take to me, she told herself.

But now Matt was probably going away. No, that wasn't true. There was no 'probably' about it. He *would* be going away.

Just a week ago she had given in to him. No, *that* wasn't entirely true either. They had both wanted what had happened, had been carried away by their emotions. Matt had told her that he wanted them to be married before he was posted. 'I'll get a special licence,' he had insisted.

Joan wasn't sure that that was what she wanted. It had all been so quick.

But the minute she had first set eyes on Mathew Pearson she had gasped. He was every girl's idea of the tall dark handsome man they all wished would come into their lives. He stood six feet three inches tall, had short thick dark hair, big brown eyes, and broad shoulders. But it was the way he smiled at her that turned her legs to jelly. 'How can you talk about us getting married when you know full well you've got to go away soon?' she had asked.

'I've been dead lucky so far. I was almost sixteen when the war started and although me dad got me a good job in the timber yards I knew I'd be called up sooner or later. Me mates were just the same. We all knew we wouldn't escape. So, it's live for the day, ain't it? Has to be, or don't you agree?'

For a moment Joan had looked thoughtful. 'I was thirteen coming up fourteen, still at school, but I wanted to join the Wrens so badly. All my dad said was, "Over my dead body."'

'I should think so too.' Matt had been shocked to think that this gorgeous girl should want to be in the forces. Bad enough that the lads had to go without involving young girls.

Joan had been pampered from the Christmas Day on which she had been born in 1925. Her mother had been only eighteen herself at the time, and her grandmother the same age when she had given birth to her daughter, Joan's mother, so they all lived in a young, lively environment. Both women were petite and attractive, and looked younger than their age. With her mum and her nan, as she called her grandmother, still trim and smartly dressed, spending evenings working up west in clubs and often out dancing,

Joan had always been a daddy's girl. And if he failed to give her the attention she sought there was always Pops, her grandfather. He and Nan lived only four doors up the street.

Joan herself was a mixture: small-boned like her mother and grandmother, with their colouring of hair, she was also blessed with her father's kind, loving nature.

Having brushed her hair and tied it back with a wide velvet band, Joan gazed at her reflection in the mirror and said, 'I'll give Bob and Poppy a hand, then I'll catch the bus and go home for the night. Have a good talk with me dad. See what he has t' say about me getting married.'

With that, she went downstairs and into the main bar.

'Are you coming up to Rainbow Corner on Saturday night?' Peggy Watson asked casually, as she watched Joan, her best friend, bring two handfuls of empty glasses and set them down on one of the mats that protected the counter.

'I don't know. Depends on whether Poppy wants me to work or not.'

'Well,' Peggy answered slowly, 'if you can't make it then we could always go on Sunday afternoon. The girls where I work all say it's full of Yanks and Canadians for the after-noon tea-dances.'

'Good idea.' Joan laughed. Then, seeing her boss making a disapproving grimace, she added, 'The Yanks are smash-ing dancers. They're out to enjoy life when they get the chance. They're lonely, miles away from home, and glad to have a bit of fun now an' again. Can't see no harm in that.'

'Thought you were dead serious about Matt. Only minutes ago you were crying yer eyes out cos you feared he was going to be sent overseas,' Poppy said, polishing a pint glass so hard it was a wonder it didn't break in her hand.

Joan didn't answer, but Peggy did. 'You want her to live

the life of a nun just cos she's got a steady boyfriend, do yer? What I mean t' say is, you're only young once an' God alone knows what's gonna happen before this ruddy war comes to an end.'

Poppy looked across at her husband, who had just finished serving a group of businessmen. He shrugged his shoulders. He had a lot of time for young Joan Harvey. She was a good clean girl, worked hard and was always polite. His own thoughts were that she was far too young to get too tangled up with any man. She should be living her life to the full. This war had been hard on the young folk, made them grow up too fast. They were never going to retrieve the lost years of their youth. However, he had more sense than to voice his thoughts – he didn't want to upset his wife, who had a right old temper when she got going. So, very quietly, he said, 'Won't hurt for the lasses to have a bit of a dance, especially if it's an afternoon do. The Yanks must feel just as bad as our lads about being away from home, and the war can't go on for ever. There has t' be an end to it sooner or later and then things will all get back to normal.'

Poppy sniffed. 'It's not *after* the war I'm worried about. It's *now*. These Yanks have more money than our lads and they're not slow in flashing it about. It's turning the girls' heads an' – you mark my words – there'll be a lot of tears shed an' some heartaches when it's time for them to go home.'

Joan felt all this was getting out of hand. All she and Peggy were considering was whether they should go up west at the weekend or not. It wouldn't be the first time they'd been, and she admitted to herself that she'd always had a wonderful time. You could say that the Americans were a bit brassy, but on the other hand they were kind, too, attentive, great dancers, and they acted like gentlemen. At least, the ones she had met had. They didn't all look like Clark Gable – of course they didn't – but their uniforms were smashing, kind of elegant compared with the rough material of the British soldiers' battle-dress, and that made a big difference when they took you in their arms if the band played a slow waltz.

They didn't shout like the men in the East End pubs did either. Now Joan's thoughts made her grin as she remembered the first time Matt had taken her with his family to their local for a drink. Talk about noise! You couldn't hear yourself think. Their laughter was so loud it had covered the sound of the ack-ack guns down on the embankment. And when a man finished a game of darts on a quick double everyone in the bar went mad. And there had been a lot of crude remarks flying about. She knew she was being unfair to Matt's family but there was no getting away from it: a night out in the East End didn't compare with an afternoon tea-dance at the London Palais. She liked to dance with the Americans. There wasn't a girl in her right mind who would say different, but . . . she loved Matt. Quite honestly, though, she did wish he'd act a bit more gentle, like. There again, every girl they passed in the street envied her because, whatever else you might say about Matt Pearson, he was so good-looking.

'Well, let's leave it for now,' Joan said eventually. 'Maybe I'll have some news to tell you after I've been home this afternoon and talked to me dad.'

'What sort of news?' Peggy's curiosity got the better of her.

'I'm not going to say any more now cos I'm nowhere near sure myself. Wait till I've been home and got things sorted in my own mind.'

'All right,' Peggy answered, with a lop-sided smile. 'I'll pop in tomorrow in my lunchtime. 'Bye for now.'

'I'll walk t' the door with you,' Joan said, linking arms with her friend. 'I wasn't trying to be mysterious, I just want to have a chat with me dad before I decide anything.'

'That's all right.' Peggy smiled again good-naturedly. 'But think about Sunday. It'll be a bit of a laugh, an' if we hang around here Sundays can be a bit of a drag.'

'I will,' Joan called, as Peggy ran off. She thought, There's nothing feminine about those trousers and that duffel coat she wears all week, but it's hardly her fault she quickly chided herself, thinking it can't be any fun working in that factory. Weekends were a different story, though: when you saw Peggy dressed and made up no one would believe she was the same girl. God knew where she got the makeup from and the sheer stockings, let alone the clothing coupons, but Joan didn't ask any questions and that way they stayed good friends.

As soon as Joan put her key in the front door she felt that luck was on her side.

Her father opened the living-room door and stared up the hallway. At the sight of his daughter his face broke into a smile. 'I was just thinking about you, pet, and here you are in the flesh.' Big man that he was, he cleared the space between them in three strides, flung his arms around her and hugged her so tight her feet were lifted from the floor.

How lovely she is, Bill Harvey thought, kissing the top of her head. 'You smell of fresh flowers,' he told her, setting her down and leading the way.

'You in all on your own, Dad?' Joan asked, taking off her coat and laying it over the back of a chair.

'Yeah, I'm all you're gonna get this afternoon. Your mother

an' yer nan are doing a high tea in the Co-op hall. Some bigwig died and apparently it's a funeral on a grand scale so the mourners have to be fed.'

They looked at each other and burst out laughing. Joan recovered first. 'With a bit of luck, Dad, there'll be some boiled ham left over an' you and Pops will get it for yer tea. Beats me that with all the rationing there's always something going to provide for weddings and funerals.'

'Well,' her father said, 'that's the way of the world today. Some blokes have escaped being called up and are making a packet on the black-market. Supply and demand, that's how it is, an' probably how it always will be.'

'Ah, well. Have we got any tea?'

'Yes, yer mum got half a pound this morning. It's in the caddy an' the kettle's on out in the scullery. I was just about to make meself a cuppa when I heard you come in.'

'I'll do it, Dad, you set the cups out. And, Dad, I'm ever so pleased that you're on yer own cos I want to have a talk with you about me and Matt.'

Her father watched her disappear into the scullery and his heart sank. She was still his little girl and he didn't want to lose her. It had been six months and more since she had started going out with that Mathew Pearson, and he knew a lot more about that relationship than he had ever let on.

Bill Harvey worked in the smelting works at Colliers Wood, a reserved occupation. Because it was wartime the furnaces were never allowed to go out so a three-shift system was in place. Six until two was the morning shift, two until ten was the middle shift and ten at night until six a.m. was the night shift. If he was coming off work at ten or just going to sign on, it was a dead cert that he'd catch a glimpse of the pair of them. Time after time he'd had to curb his temper for there they'd be, strolling around in the blackout, with their arms entwined and practically eating each other. He didn't need to follow them: he knew full well they'd be heading for the park and the shelter of the trees.

Joan came back, carrying the teapot. With one look at her father's face she could guess what he'd been thinking. Her dad was well over six foot tall in his stockinged feet. His face was kind, open, with big blue eyes, a wide forehead and a friendly mouth. He had a thick shock of hair that, sad to say, was very grey. To Joan he always looked as if he had just had a good wash for his rosy cheeks usually glowed. Wholesome, that was how she would describe her dad.

They sat at each side of the table with a steaming cup of tea set beside them. Eventually Joan brought herself to say, 'Dad, Matt thinks the Army will be making a big push soon and his regiment will be sent to France. Kind of a second front is what the boys are calling it and, well . . . he wants us t' get married before he goes.' She brought out the last sentence in a rush.

Bill Harvey sighed inwardly. He wasn't a bit surprised. Girls as young as sixteen were rushing into marriage without a thought to the future. Half of them were doing it for the Army marriage allowance. Mind you, he'd been twenty-two when he'd married Daphne, but she had been only seventeen, barely turned eighteen when Joan was born, so he was hardly in a position to preach to his daughter. Nevertheless, he'd give his right arm to stop her from diving into marriage with this Matt Pearson. Although he looked like what every girl must dream of, there was something about him that stuck in Bill's gullet. Beneath that smooth surface he was a cocky bugger – he was as sure of that as he ever could be. He rested his elbows on the table and stared at his daughter. She had an odd, dreamy look on her face. All right, the lad made her happy. He'd give him that much.

'Do you love him?' he asked.

'Um,' she whispered, 'of course I do.'

'There's no of course about it,' he answered sternly. 'I think I'd better have a talk to him before we decide anything. In fact, it should be him to come to me, if not to ask permission – that would be too old-fashioned for you youngsters today – at least to put me in the picture as regards his plans for you.'

That statement frightened Joan a bit. 'Before you talk to Matt, hadn't we better tell Mum?' She paused. 'And we hadn't better leave Nan an' Pops in the dark else there'll be hell to pay.'

'Hold yer horses. At the moment there's nothing to tell anyone.' He leant across, took her hand and kissed her gently and lovingly.

'I'll talk to your mother and if anything is to be decided then the decisions will be made by both of us. I'll have a chat with her tonight, you leave it all to me. You know, Joanie, we both love you dearly, and all we want is for you to be happy.'

'I know, Dad, I know, but what if Matt does get sent away soon?'

Her father's lip trembled. He wanted to ask her some point-blank questions but he hadn't the heart for it. She was still his baby girl. How could he bring himself to ask if there was any particular reason that she and Matt should be marrying in such haste. Had he made her pregnant? He clenched his fists. I'll kill him if he has! He took two very deep breaths. But it takes two. She was all dreamy-eyed when she spoke his name, so it didn't seem as if he had forced her. Oh, for goodness sake! he chided himself. He probably hasn't got further than a few kisses. Anyway, he'd leave it for now until Daffy came home.

Daffy by name but not by nature. Oh, no! His wife had her head set squarely on her shoulders and if anyone could talk some sense into Joan then it would be her mother.

Changing the subject quickly, feeling a right coward, he said, 'I know where your mother's hidden some biscuits, chocolate ones. You sit still and I'll fetch them and we'll have ourselves a real treat.'

'You're the best dad in the whole world,' she called after him, which served to make him feel even more inadequate. He stood still for a moment and covered his eyes with his hands. Great changes were taking place in his daughter's life, changes he didn't like, but somehow he felt he had no power to stop them.

Chapter Two

IT WAS THE first Sunday in March, and the weather had certainly changed for the worse. There was cold rain and a bitter wind that went right through to the bone, as Peggy and Joan got off the bus at Piccadilly Circus. Scarves tied tightly over their hair, they tucked their heads low and ran. Once inside the dance hall, they each let out a satisfied sigh. This was a different world. There might be a war going on outside but here they could forget it for a time. They checked their coats into the cloakroom, spent fifteen minutes in the posh ladies' room titivating their hair and makeup, then came out and stood at the edge of the dance floor.

A few minutes later they looked at each other and grinned. This place was something else: gilt paint, red-velvet seating, and the lighting made for romance, soft and subdued. Blue cigarette smoke wreathed up to the high ceiling while a dazzling mirror-ball sent its reflections darting here and there. At the far end was a stage and a snazzily dressed band were playing all the latest tunes. They couldn't wait to get on the smashing sprung floor. There were loads of servicemen: Navy lads with their white dicky-fronts and well-scrubbed blue and white wide collars, and the Brylcreem boys from the RAF in their special blue uniforms. The poor old Tommies in their serviceable khaki battle-dress looked like the poor relations, and both girls felt a little sorry for them – more so today because the place was swarming with American soldiers, who were stealing the show: they danced with so much energy, jitterbugging in a way that you'd never see in a local dance-hall.

'Would you like to dance, ma'am?' Two lean young men stood before them.

'We'd love to,' Peggy answered for the pair of them, giving the two American soldiers a wide smile.

They allowed themselves to be led on to the floor as the band struck up a quickstep.

It was fantastic, the music was so fast. Within seconds Joan was beaming up into the tanned face of her young man, who was so far from home. 'My name's Hank,' he said loudly, as he led her expertly, following the beat. Suddenly the tempo changed and he asked, 'Can you jitterbug?' Not waiting for her to reply, he pushed her in the direction he wanted her to go and they were off. Joan glanced across the floor to where Peggy was sliding between the legs of her partner and laughed. This was wonderful! Ducking underneath Hank's outstretched arm, grinning as his feet seemed to move like lightning. His arms circled her waist and he had her high in the air one minute then down so low that her hair almost touched the floor the next. Turning this way and that without a break in his own steps. By the time the music stopped Joan fell against him and, for a brief moment, the lad held her close. 'I'll see you to your chair and then I'll fetch us both a drink,' he said.

He was as good as his word, as was his mate. They found a vacant table and asked the girls for permission to sit down with them. Both Joan and Peggy had asked for orange juice and neither of the lads had queried that. Joan's thoughts went immediately to what any of Mathew's relations would have said: 'I ain't going to the bar to ask fer no bloody orange juice. You 'ave a proper drink or go without.'

The juice was refreshing and by the time the band-leader announced the next dance, both girls were raring to go.

'Waltz, then, is it?' Hank asked Joan, while the other young man, who had introduced himself as Greg, stood and held out his arms to Peggy.

'So dreamy,' Peggy mouthed, as the two couples danced close.

The pattern continued: there were several more lively jitterbugs, and even a well-executed fox-trot, but neither gave a thought to changing their partners. Then, far too soon, it was announced that the next dance would be the last waltz and the band struck up 'Who's Taking You Home Tonight'. Joan felt a shiver run down her back as Hank let go of her hand and stroked her long hair. 'I've been wanting to do that all night,' he told her. 'I have a young sister, she's only ten, and she has ginger hair, though it's nowhere near as dark as yours.'

He sighed, and Joan suddenly felt sad. 'Mine used to be more red, and I expect your sister's hair will darken as she gets older.'

'Yeah, you're probably right.' Then, very quickly, he began to twirl her round and round as though to eradicate the memory from his mind.

The lights were brighter suddenly: the dance was over. 'Do you and your friend live within walking distance?' It was Greg, the taller of the two lads, who asked.

'No,' Peggy answered quickly. 'We get the tube, we'll be all right.'

'We can't allow that, not two young ladies out on their own in the blackout.' Greg glanced across at Hank, who nodded. 'We'll flag you down a cab.'

'You'll do no such thing,' Joan said indignantly. 'It would cost the earth. Besides, you'd never get a taxi driver to take a fare out of the West End – they haven't the petrol.'

Both girls had their coats on and were tying their scarves over their heads. Peggy produced a torch from her pocket and switched it on. 'See? We'll be fine. Me dad managed to get two new batteries yesterday.'

Hank whistled under his breath. 'Self-sufficient, eh? But, torch or no torch, we're seeing you to the underground station and safely on to your train.'

Greg linked his arm with Peggy's and smiled down at her. 'It's the least we can do. We've had the pleasure of your company all evening and it wouldn't be right to abandon you now.'

'Come on, then.' Hank had his arm across Joan's shoulders as they made for the exit sign.

Once outside they all stood stock still. There was total darkness, not a star in the black sky. It took a few seconds for their eyes to adjust, then Peggy switched on her torch and handed it to Greg, reminding him to keep it pointed downwards.

'Right,' he said to Hank, who still had his arm around Joan. 'Keep close to us – we don't want to have to send a search party out for you.'

They stumbled along, two in front and two behind, the torch held well down just showing where they could safely put a foot forward. In only a matter of minutes they had reached the tube station at Piccadilly Circus. Black metal shades covered each lightbulb set into the tiled walls of the station, with a small slit cut into the covering base allowing just enough light to show through to enable passengers to reach the moving staircase in safety.

'We'll come down on to the platform with you,' Hank stated assertively.

Peggy tripped as she set her foot on the fast-moving step but Greg's arm was immediately round her, holding her close to his chest, and Joan smiled to herself. Had the trip been deliberate? If it had, who could blame Peggy? There were so few occasions when they had the company of young men, these days, and this evening had been so nice. Suddenly she thought of Matt: maybe she should feel guilty. Then again, it wasn't the kind of evening he would have enjoyed. Come to think of it, he had taken her to many places – the pictures, the theatre, dog-racing, to watch him play darts in the pub, and he had promised her visits to the speedway once the war was over because he was motorbike mad – but he had never mentioned dancing. Perhaps he couldn't dance! She didn't like that thought and hastily brushed it away. All young people loved to dance.

The train was coming through the tunnel as they reached the platform. A little clumsily Hank took Joan in his arms and put his lips on hers. It was not a passionate kiss, just sweet and gentle.

The train came to a noisy halt and the doors slid open. ''Bye, Joan. Maybe we'll meet again. You take care.' Hank's voice was little more than a whisper.

Greg was calling out his thanks, saying what a wonderful evening they had had.

Joan and Peggy stood side by side as the doors closed and they both waved to the two American soldiers standing on the station. Then they moved slowly down the train. As they each found a seat Peggy declared loudly, 'Bloody war.'

It was a sentiment with which Joan, and everyone else in the carriage, come to that, was in full agreement.

Chapter Three

JOAN DIDN'T NEED telling that these next few days were going to be vastly different from any she had ever spent in her life before.

Matt had been given seven days' leave. He had suggested that she came home with him and spent the best part of the week with his family. That way he wouldn't be torn in two as to where he should be. Reluctantly Joan had asked Poppy and Bob if she could have the time off.

Poppy had laughed her head off. 'He's under pressure from his family, my love. You mark my words. And if you don't go, well . . .'

'Poor sod, I know the feeling,' Bob added. "Tis only natural that his mother wants to have him around especially if the rumours are true that his regiment might be posted soon. I'd take a bet, though, he being the healthy bloke he is, he'd rather shack up somewhere with you.'

'Bob!' Poppy screamed at him. 'That's no way t' talk to Joan.'

Joan grinned. Two days ago, Matt had had a couple of hours off and turned up at the pub just as they were finishing the lunchtime session. They had spent the entire time in the wooded part of the common. 'Amorous' was the only word she could think of to describe Matt during the whole of that time. His passion had been such that she had ended up feeling grateful that it was daylight and that quite a few people were about.

Her own family's reaction to her going to stay with Matt's family hadn't been enthusiastic and it had taken a lot of persuasion on her part to get her mum and dad to agree. Matt's home was in Whitechapel, a district of east London in the borough of Stepney. The best way to get there was on a District line train, which, luckily enough, left from their local station at Wimbledon.

As always, these days, the train quickly became crowded. Many servicemen were returning from leave, their kit-bags slung into the string racks in every compartment. A young woman with three children boarded at Putney Bridge, and Matt jumped to his feet offering his seat. He bent low and whispered to Joan, who got up to allow the three children to squeeze into her seat.

There were so many people already squashed into the corridor that Matt had a job to find a space for them to stand. Not that he cared. His arm was already round Joan's waist to hold her steady, and when a sudden jolt threw her hard against his chest he laughed. 'We'll tell my lot we're gonna get married an' when I bring you back 'ome I'll tell your dad straight we don't intend to wait any longer,' he told her firmly, his big brown eyes showing how eager he was.

His grip on her was so tight that Joan was glad when at

last he bent down, picked up her small attaché case and said, 'Next station's ours.'

God! Joan was surprised, or perhaps a better word was shocked. She had been to visit Matt's family twice before but each time he had borrowed his brother's car and taken her door to door. Even when she had been taken to their local pub for a drink they had still driven there and she hadn't taken much notice of the area. Now, standing on the wide platform, she couldn't take in all that she was seeing. So many servicemen. So many different uniforms. Such crowds.

They emerged into a street that was busy, dusty and full of people. And the noise! It was deafening.

'Hold my arm,' Matt urged. 'We're gonna get on a tram. It's only a few stops.'

They surged forward, with half a dozen other would-be passengers, into the middle of the road to board the tram that clanged its way through lorries and cars. On each side of the road, in front of a good many shops, there was a never-ending open market. Joan lived in London herself but until now she had had no idea how vast the difference was between south London and the East End. As they made their way to the pavement she could see the beauty and the magnitude of Tower Bridge. It made her feel that she came from a different world.

'Everywhere is so busy,' she mumbled, as they walked down a side turning.

Matt was so happy to be back in his home surroundings that he didn't notice her discomfiture. 'Yeah, it's always like this, day an' night,' was all he said.

On her two short previous visits Joan had got out of the car and gone straight into the house. Now she was aware of her surroundings. A young woman came towards them pushing a shabby old pram full of babies, lots of children were in the road, and it sounded to Joan as if they were squabbling and fighting rather than playing games. A side road led off and, as they turned into it, Joan took note of a public house on one corner and a corner shop right opposite.

Matt's home was in the middle of a row of terraced houses. It was exactly the same as all the others, with a small fenced-in front garden and a path that led up to a dark-brown-painted front door. A bow window was on the ground floor and two flat windows above.

Matt opened the wooden gate. Amy Pearson, his mother, was hard at work scrubbing her top step. A sacking apron was tied around her skirt, a dark green jersey covered her bosom, and over her wiry grey hair was a flat cap, which she was wearing back to front to enable her to see what she was doing.

She looked up, smiling broadly, as Matt and Joan, doing their best to avoid the soapy water that was running down the path, gingerly stepped their way towards her. ''Allo, son. I wasn't expecting you till this afternoon. Give us an 'and t' get up,' she said.

Suddenly two young lads came tearing up the passage-way to the front door. 'It's our Matt. Wotcher, Matt, 'ow long yer 'ome for?' They fell upon him and pulled him into the house, both talking at once and leaving his mum and Joan to follow them.

'These are my sister's kids,' Matt told her, by way of intro-duction, once they were inside the cosy living room. 'This is Teddy,' he said, waving at the older one, whom Joan thought to be about ten, 'and this is Jack.'

Then, before he could tell her anything else, his mother
cut in, 'It's that little 'un you 'ave t' watch out for. I know
'e looks like an angel but, believe me, love, 'e's a right little
terror.'

'This is Joan,' Matt finally told them.

The younger boy certainly was a lovely child, hair so thick
and blond it didn't look natural, and blue eyes that would
tear the heart out of you. He looked up at Joan and gave
her the sweetest smile before saying. 'You're his tart,
ain'tcher?'

Matt's mother moved with speed that belied her bulk.
She had removed the sacking apron from around her waist
and now she flicked it so hard at the child that Joan winced.
'Yer little brat! One day that mouth of yours will get you
into trouble. Go on, get upstairs, both of yer, an' don't come
down till I say yer can.

'Sorry about that,' Amy said. 'Their mother works in a
factory canteen and I suppose I've let them get away with
murder. Still, they're back t' school tomorrow, thank God.
I expect you're ready for a cup o' tea, ain't yer?' She was
fat and smiling, with the same big brown eyes that had
endeared her to Matt, and Joan felt that in spite of the way
she spoke, she could really come to like this woman.

Soon they were drinking tea and eating home-made rock
cakes in the homely kitchen. Then Joan couldn't believe her
ears: Amy was telling Matt that his father and two of his
brothers were going to be in the pub about now and were
expecting him to join them. Matt got to his feet, bent over
and kissed her. 'Shan't be too long,' he said.

'Can't I come with you?' she asked.

'Later on ternight I'll take yer for a drink, but right now
me dad an' me brothers are waiting for me. Mum'll look

after yer, won't yer, Mum? See yer later.' Then, as he reached
the door, he called back over his shoulder, 'By the way,
Mum, we're gonna get married. I'm gonna get a special
licence. Now's yer chance to 'ave a good old natter, sort
things out between yer.'

Joan wanted to say that they hadn't really settled anything.
When he'd previously spoken about getting a special licence,
she hadn't taken him seriously. Now he seemed so different. From the minute he'd walked into this house he'd
become a different person. He'd even slipped into their way
of talking, which she'd never noticed before. Well, not so
much anyhow.

'He always does that when he comes home on leave.'

Amy's voice made her jump. 'Does what?'

'Goes for a drink with his dad. Lot of his mates'll be in
the Blind Beggar about this time of day. If you've finished
yer tea I'll show yer round. Won't take long, there ain't that
much t' see.'

Joan was upset. He had brought her here, dumped her
the minute they arrived and told his mother they were getting
married when nothing had been agreed between them. Some
cheek he had!

'I'd better show yer the lavvy first. It's out in the yard –
expect you're dying t' spend a penny.' It was true, she was.
But, my God, this was embarrassing. Here she was, sitting
on a wooden seat of a toilet in a shed in an outside backyard with Matt's mother standing outside the door.

The house was small, two rooms and a scullery downstairs, and just two rooms above. The biggest bedroom was
furnished quite nicely. In place of honour stood a wide
double bed with brass rails top and bottom. There was a
tall chest of drawers, which had brass handles, two wicker

armchairs, painted green and gold, and a marble-topped washstand, which held an enormous china bowl and jug. Placed beside this on the floor Joan was amazed to see two big china chamberpots, each sporting the same floral pattern as the washing bowl.

'Jug's 'alf full of cold water if yer feel like a wash,' Amy offered, and before Joan had a chance to reply she added, 'You can sleep in 'ere with me. Ernie, me ole man, can kip downstairs in the middle room with Matt while you're 'ere.'

Joan hadn't given a thought until then as to where she would be sleeping, but now she was expected to share that big bed with his mother!

What with one thing and another being sprung on her Joan was getting more and more mad by the minute.

When Matt came back from the pub, bringing his mates as well as several members of his family, the house was so crowded she didn't have a chance to speak to him on his own. There were his two brothers with their wives, a sister, the mother of Teddy and Jack, and an unmarried sister. Joan got the feeling they were all there to inspect her. Everyone was talking so loudly, telling her how bad the air-raids had been and how glad they were that, for the time being, they seemed to have eased off. Crates of beer had been brought in and, as soon as it got dark, someone said that Mr Clarke had managed to get hold of a few boxes of fish and would be frying tonight. In a flash Amy had her purse out, and the youngsters were sent to fetch fish and chips for everyone. It was a noisy but happy evening. Joan heard songs that she'd never heard before. Then, still without having had Matt to herself, she was being guided up the narrow staircase. There didn't seem any point in protesing so she found herself lying beside Amy in a big feather bed that was far more comfortable than she had imagined.

'You'll meet me other daughter termorrow. She'll be round with 'er kids,' Amy said happily, already half asleep.

Joan sighed. She felt out of her depth. Whatever had she let herself in for? Just have to wait and see, won't I? she thought, as she turned on her side and snuggled down. I'll tell Matt in the morning I'm not staying, she decided, as she plumped up her pillow, hoping and praying for a good night's sleep.

But next morning Amy was standing beside the bed holding out a tin tray with a cup of tea and two slices of bread and butter, saying, 'Sorry there ain't any biscuits. Joe up at the corner shop had quite a few in this week but cos I ain't got no points left for this month he wouldn't let me 'ave any. He'll regret that – you see if 'e don't! There won't always be a war going on.'

Joan smiled at Amy's threat.

'I've brought you Ernie's dressing-gown. It's almost new, he never wears it, and I thought you'd be glad of it, if you want t' come downstairs to the lavvy. And yer can bring a kettle of hot water back up 'ere so's you can wash – be better than down in the scullery.'

'Thanks,' Joan said, appreciating the kind thought. 'I'll come down as soon as I've drunk my tea.'

As the day went on, Joan came to the conclusion that it was the busiest and noisiest she had spent in her whole life. As she soon discovered, Amy was determined to show her their part of London and, at the same time, give her neighbours and friends an eyeful of Matt's posh girlfriend, was how she put it.

Joan did her best to tell Matt that she would rather spend the day with him but he wasn't having that. 'We'll 'ave all the time in the world t' be together when we've tied the knot,' he said, following her up the stairs when she went to fetch her coat.

'No, we won't,' she protested. 'You said yourself your regiment won't be in England for much longer. And you had no right to tell your parents we're getting married before we've settled anything.'

Matt pulled her close and began kissing her face, then her ear and her neck. 'I'd like to spend the entire day on that big bed making love to you, but I can't see me mum standing for that, so suppose I'll just 'ave to be patient. Anyway me dad's coming down the town 'all with me while you're out with me mum. We're gonna get the licence and that means by this time next week we could really be Mr an' Mrs. Just think about it, Joanie, it'll be perfectly legal for us to stay in bed all day long if we want to.' Matt's eyes were half closed as he squeezed her breasts. 'God,' he murmured. 'I've got t' get yer to meself some time today or I'm gonna go mad.'

'Joan, are yer ready? If we don't get off pretty sharpish all the best fruit an' veg will be gone, not to mention the size of the queues there'll be at the offal shop.' Amy's voice, coming from the foot of the stairs, sounded like thunder.

'I'll have to go,' Joan said, and Matt grinned. 'You better 'ad, else she'll be up 'ere like a dose of salts and she'll whack me round the 'ead – not for what I've done but for what I've been thinking I'd like t' do. She's nobody's fool is me mum.'

So Amy and Joan set off for the market.

Much of the area they walked through was ugly and sordid, with slums, the like of which Joan had never imagined. And the bomb damage was beyond belief: whole streets had been razed to the ground. But it was strange: suddenly they would come to an area that was delightful, even beautiful.

The colour and life of the market had Joan laughing as she listened to the barrow-boys spouting off about their wares. Wimbledon had a market on Saturday mornings but it bore no comparison to this one. Offal and fish were not rationed and it stood to reason that more people stood in line outside these shops to have something decent for their dinner that day. 'Blast,' Amy muttered, as from the other side of the road she watched a man with a white apron and a straw boater on his head pull down one of the shop shutters by means of a long pole. Then, 'Come on,' she ordered, grabbing hold of Joan's arm, 'we might just be lucky.'

The fact that the fishmonger was shouting that he was closing because he'd sold out did nothing to deter Amy Pearson. She marched into the shop, set down her bag amongst the sawdust on the floor and folded her arms across her ample bosom. 'Bet yer got a nice little parcel left to take along to Miss High an' Mighty Morrison,' she said, so quietly that Joan wasn't sure that she'd heard right. 'Saved any for yer wife, 'ave yer?'

The fishmonger's face flared bright red and he took such a deep breath he looked ready to explode. Without a word, he placed the pole he was still holding against the wall and walked through to the back of the shop.

Amy winked at Joan as they waited.

'There y'are, Mrs Pearson. Four 'errings, best I can do,' the fishmonger told her, holding them out for her inspection.

'That's very kind of you,' Amy told him sweetly. 'But do me a favour, will yer, and tell me what I'd do with four little fish among my lot? You know 'ow big me 'usband is and me boys are even bigger . . . all employed on war work and Matt's 'ome on leave from 'Is Majesty's forces. They deserve a bit better than that, don't yer think?'

Joan looked at her in amazement. What was she implying? Her words, though spoken softly, sounded sinister.

The fishmonger sighed heavily. 'How many were you thinking of feeding today, Mrs Pearson?'

'Oh, only me own family but most of me lads would eat two of them little 'errings an' still say their bellies were empty, not to mention me old man.'

'All right, all right,' he said, turning so quickly that Joan felt he was now just anxious to be rid of them.

Joan couldn't help it, she wanted to laugh, the satisfied grin on Amy's face as they waited had to be seen to be believed. 'You're the bane of my life, you know that, don't yer, Mrs Pearson?' He pushed two newspaper-wrapped parcels into her shopping basket. 'There's eight 'errings and a couple of codlings. Give us three bob and let me tell you I'm a fool ter meself.'

'Course you are,' Amy agreed, and added softly, 'All sins carry a price.'

Over the next few days Joan became aware that London had many different sides to it. Not much housework seemed to get done, but no one could blame Amy for that. She seemed to spend most of her time providing enormous meals for everyone who cared to step over her doorstep. Joan grew accustomed to the family and laughed to herself when Teddy and Jack warned her to make herself scarce when their gran was in a roaring temper because Granddad had come home drunk.

The wedding was often discussed and everyone, young and old alike, seemed to want to put in their two-pennyworth.

Amy was all for going to the church and seeing if the vicar could do a rush job as Matt only had a few more days' leave. At this Joan was terrified. Get married without her mum and dad being there? And what about Nan and Pops? She'd never dare go home again!

For once Matt showed some consideration for her. 'Suddenly feeling all religious, are we?' he asked his mother. All he got for his pains was a swift smack round the head.

Then came her last day. Half of Whitechapel seemed to be crammed into Amy's terraced house. At least, that's how it seemed to Joan. Still, she had come to realize that they were genuine folk, kind, warm-hearted and generous. If they took to you you'd made a friend for life; cross any one of them and God help you. These East Enders certainly knew how to stick together. They had come to wish her and Matt the best of everything, and hoped to be at their wedding.

Joan smiled and kept her tongue between her teeth. If this wedding was to take place, she knew full well that it would be when and where *her* family arranged it. She was their only child, after all. But she wasn't brave enough to say as much. Instead she bade Matt's mother and father a fond farewell and thanked them for having her. 'Any time, my love,' Amy told her, squeezing her to her bosom. 'Just cos Matt ain't around don't mean you can't come and pay us a visit, so I'm telling you now, don't you dare become a stranger.'

Joan was touched. Maybe she would come up to the East

End to see Amy after Matt had been posted. That brought her up sharp. More than likely she'll be your mother-in-law by then, she thought, as she let go of Matt's arm and turned at the corner of the road to give a final wave.

Chapter Four

JOAN WAS SITTING in a corner of the kitchen, alone with her thoughts. I'll have to tell them, she thought. There's been so much talk already and still nothing has been decided. But this is a different kettle of fish, and there's no getting away from it.

Matt had brought her home three weeks ago and he had faced up to her father honestly and squarely. But Bill Harvey was his own man and no one swayed him easily: special licence or not, there was going to be no wedding until he and Daphne had settled in their own minds that it was what their daughter wanted. That had been his decision and no one could shake him. 'There is plenty of time,' he kept repeating.

Matt had returned to his regiment a sad young man.

Ten days had passed before Joan had seen him again, and then he had been down to take her out over the weekend. It was as they came out of the Odeon cinema at Shannon's Corner and went across to the Duke of Cambridge public house that she resolved to tell him.

It was warm and crowded in the pub, and the smell of beer and tobacco smoke was somehow welcoming even if it didn't make the telling any easier.

'There's an empty table over there,' Matt said, pointing a finger. 'You go and sit down and I'll get us a drink.'

It's as if he knows what's coming, Joan thought, as Matt set down a pint of beer for himself and a brandy for her. 'Not often a pub has spirits, these days, but the barman offered so I accepted. It's the uniform that does it, I expect.'

Joan took a sip and found it warming as it went down into her stomach. 'Matt . . .' she started, her forehead puckered with the effort of trying to find the right words to tell him '. . . about us getting married. I think I can get my dad to agree now if you still want to.'

He took a long drink from his pint, saying nothing.

'Matt . . .' she tried again . . . 'I'm pregnant. I've known for some time. I really am.'

He didn't smile, he didn't speak, he just set his glass down on to the table and drew her close to his side. 'That settles it. Now, I'll tell you what we're gonna do,' he said, sounding determined. 'First we'll finish our drink, then I'm taking you home and I'm coming into the house to talk to your father. I'm gonna tell him that some time tomorrow, depending on when I can get out of barracks, we're going down to your nearest register office, show them the licence I already have and get a date for us to be married.' Seeing the forlorn look on her face he added quickly, 'You know how much I love you, Joan, and I'm over the moon about the baby. And you're not to worry, I'll look after you.'

Surprise and pleasure at the way he had taken her news

had bucked her up no end. 'Well, that sounds lovely,' she said, smiling at him. 'But you may not be able to get the time off.'

Matt had told her to leave everything to him. He would see the padre, get him on their side, and he had no doubt that his commanding officer could wangle him a few days' compassionate leave.

The best-laid plans of mice and men do go astray.

When they had burst into the house, arms linked, faces glowing, it was to find no one at home. Matt had stayed with her as long as he could but finally had to leave. He didn't want to overstay his pass, especially as he was about to ask a favour.

It was very late that night when her mother and father came home, bringing her nan in with them.

'Where have you been?' Joan cried, but the sadness on all their faces made her lower her voice. 'Whatever's happened? Tell me!'

'It's Pops,' her father said, reaching for her hand. 'He had a heart-attack.'

Turning to face her nan, Joan said softly, 'Oh, Nan, he is going to be all right, isn't he?'

Her mother wrapped her arms around her and told her that Pops had died.

There were things that had to be done, or so they told her. That's why they had all gone out early this morning and she was on her own. Joan was frightened, over-whelmed by sadness. The more she thought about her predicament, the more she felt as if she were wading through a sea of mud. Matt would probably turn up here again soon, full of beans and acting larger than life. She would have to tell him to calm down and urge him to say nothing. She just couldn't let him talk to her father, not at a time like this.

Poor dear Pops. He'd loved her so much. And she him. She'd been so privileged to have had him while she was growing up. It had been like having two fathers – two loving fathers, who had not only loved her but spoilt her. Dear God, she was going to have to grow up now! Soon she was going to be a mother. 'Oh, Pops,' she murmured, as the tears trickled down her face.

When the doorbell rang, Joan got quickly to her feet. At least Matt had arrived before her parents had got back, which would give her time to tell him her sad news.

There he was, arms spread wide and laughing. 'Everything's sorted. You're never gonna believe our luck, darling.'

This burst from him before Joan had a chance to say a word. The sight and sound of his joviality annoyed her, and she greeted him curtly. It wasn't his fault that Pops had died – she knew that – but she just couldn't help herself. 'Hold on, Matt,' she said, pushing him away as he tried to take her in his arms. 'Come on inside. Something very sad has happened.'

Once in the kitchen he removed his cap and demanded that she tell him whatever it was without beating about the bush.

Joan did just that.

'I'm sorry, really I am, but we're still going to get married,' he said. It was a statement, a decision: there was no doubt about it.

Joan began to worry. 'We can't tell my mum and dad now, not with all the trouble they've got – and my poor nan, what would she say?'

It was at that moment that the door opened.

'Hello, Matt.' Daphne was the first to speak.

But, sensing that something was not quite right, Bill Harvey faced the young soldier squarely. 'You're not here this morning just on the off-chance, are you?' he asked quietly.

'No, I'm not,' Matt agreed. 'And I'm sorry the timing is all wrong but I do need t' talk to you about Joan and me getting married,' he said, stubbornly.

'I'll put the kettle on,' Daphne mumbled, and she went with her mother to the scullery.

Hester Burton had lived long enough to have learnt a few facts of life. As she watched her daughter go to the sink she murmured, 'Hear of a death and you hear of a birth.'

Daphne turned and stared at her mother. 'What are you on about, Mum?'

'Our Joanie's pregnant. That's what this young man is here about. Not that I'm surprised. I was going to say something to you days ago, but I thought I'd wait till she came back from visiting his folk. You only have to look at her to tell.'

'Mother, you can't be right! She's as thin as a rake.'

'I'm not talking about her showing. Just look in her eyes – you'll know then, right enough.'

'My God!' Daphne clutched at the sink for support. Talk about history repeating itself. She and her mother might have been eighteen when they had given birth but at least they had been married. There had been no hanky-panky before the wedding in those days. It's this damn war that's sending so many girls off the rails, she thought.

'I've laid the tray but I think you'd better put a bottle of the hard stuff out as well.' Hester was staying remarkably cool, considering. 'I'm not sure who's going to need it most, our Bill or that young lad.'

The atmosphere was tense when Hester put her head round the door and asked if it was all right to bring in the tea. Bill just nodded.

Joan was too tired, too stunned by her father's angry outburst to argue any further.

'By the look on the faces of you two you don't need any telling,' Bill said to his wife, and then, much more softly, he said to his mother-in-law, 'At least Matt wants t' do right by her. So, whatever we decide we'll keep it quiet. Well, quiet as possible. Let Pops's funeral be our first concern. I'm just grateful that we managed to get the death certificate and suchlike this morning. We'll have this cuppa and then I'll go back to the undertaker's with you, Hetty, and get a date set.'

Matt cleared his throat. 'Mr Harvey, would it be all right if I take Joan down to the register office this afternoon?'

'Register office?' Joan's mother was appalled.

Her husband gave her a look that silenced her. Then, sternly, he said, 'We can hardly have a church wedding and all the frills, now, can we?'

'I suppose not.'

She looked so forlorn that Joan got up, stood behind her and put her arms round her mother's shoulders. 'I'm sorry, Mum.'

Daphne Harvey wasn't an emotional person: she had always believed that what would be would be. Today, however, she was truly moved, and Joan, unable to stem her tears, had taken her arms from her mother's shoulders and was fumbling for a handkerchief.

'Come here, baby,' Daphne urged, wrapping her close in a tight hug. 'It's a very sad day for all of us but it will all work out for the best in the end, you'll see. Just think what Pops would have said. A baby! Another for him to spoil.'

'Yes,' Joan rubbed at her eyes with her sopping wet hanky, 'but he's not here, is he?'

'He'll be watching over you, wherever he is. You can be sure of that,' her grandmother said.

'I wish I was as sure as you are, Nan. I'm going to miss Pops so much.'

'We all are, pet,' her grandmother admitted sadly.

Daphne felt that things were getting out of hand, and although she was furious with Matt Pearson for having taken advantage of her daughter, she felt just a tinge of sympathy for him as he stood against the wall, ignored by everyone. She said, 'We've to make the best of a bad job and now we know that Joan is pregnant, her and Mathew should get married.' Then, looking across at her husband, she added, 'The sooner the better. It'll be all for the best, don't you agree?'

Her husband bit hard on his bottom lip, then muttered, 'I don't know, I just don't know.'

Daphne picked up the teapot and pushed past him to go into the scullery, leaving him staring at nothing, deep in thought. Then he shifted his gaze to rest on the young man attired in soldier's uniform, knowing that more than likely he would be sent miles away in the not too distant future. All for the best indeed! Yet what else could he do? He felt he had no option but to agree.

At two o'clock, Joan and Matt stood side by side in the register office, and she watched while he explained the circumstances and produced the licence he had applied for in a different area.

'You still have to give seventy-two hours' notice,' the elderly lady clerk informed him. 'We have a free slot at eleven o'clock on Friday morning.'

Matt thanked her warmly. In twenty minutes the whole thing had been set up and he felt a sight better for knowing that.

The next three days passed in a haze.

No one had much enthusiasm for the wedding preparations. Joan was to be a bride on Friday, but on the following Monday they were to bury her grandfather.

What about a honeymoon? Matt asked himself. I suppose that idea goes down the drain. He didn't feel able to ask Joan's father if they could slip away and not attend the funeral.

Then it was their wedding day. Joan looked lovely in a pale blue dress with a loose-fitting coat, both made of silk and embroidered along the cuffs and neckline. Clothing coupons had been begged from all the neighbours, and Sadie Bowman, who owned a dress salon at Wimbledon Broadway, had come to the house bringing three outfits for Joan to choose from. Poppy and Bob Benson had had to be told the news, and they had come up trumps. Indeed, the hat Joan was wearing belonged to Poppy. It had been retrimmed with artificial white daisies and loaned to the bride for the day.

Few were there to see them get wed. To Joan's disappointment her nan had said she wasn't up to it so on her side she had her mum and dad, her best friend Peggy and Poppy. Bob felt it wasn't possible for the two of them to leave the pub.

There were even fewer folk to be with Matt. He had managed to slip away and fill his family in on all that had happened. He still couldn't believe the way his mother had reacted to the news that he was getting married. Down in the south, in a register office, and no ding-dong afterwards? 'Least said soonest mended,' his mother was fond of saying, but that certainly hadn't applied on this occasion. She'd had plenty to say.

'Made her pregnant!' she screamed. If he'd murdered her she couldn't have sounded more scandalized. She practically threw him out of the house, and threatened never to speak to him again.

So, on that May morning the only person Matt had to stand up for him was one army mate. However, at the last minute, to his delight and relief, his eldest brother Stan had turned up.

It wasn't exactly the brightest of wedding days.

It wasn't until she and Matt were alone in her grandmother's house that evening that Joan fully realized that she was married. Matt had been as pleased as punch when Hester had offered her house to them for the weekend, saying she would be fine staying along the road with Bill and Daphne. 'It was very kind and thoughtful of yer nan,' Matt was saying, as he lifted a cloth off the cold refreshments she had set out for their supper. He only wished to God that Joan would cheer up a bit. He'd had it in his mind to take her to Southend or even down to Brighton for the few days he'd got left but they had the funeral looming over them. Still, they had a whole house to themselves and a big double bed upstairs. Things could be a lot worse, he said to himself, as he opened a bottle of sparkling wine. A whole lot worse in fact!

Joan's family had left them discreetly alone, assuming that they were only too glad to be together and it should have been a marvellous time, but it wasn't, and Matt was thoroughly disappointed. By the time he woke up on the second morning of what was supposed to be his honeymoon he was well and truly browned off. They'd made love a couple of times or, more to the point, *he* had made all the running. For all the feeling Joan had shown him, he might just as well have turned on his side and gone to sleep.

Later they took a bus ride up to Wimbledon Common and went into the pub to have a drink with Bill and Poppy, and Bob got on well with Matt. After a while they made their way home, in what Matt hoped was a happier frame of mind.

After a quiet lunch Matt led her upstairs. Loving and gentle though he was, he simply could not rouse her. Suddenly she burst into tears, and he pulled her close to his chest and let her sob her heart out. 'This is supposed t' be our honeymoon,' she mumbled. 'You'll be saying soon you wished you'd never married me. I am sorry.'

'Never mind,' he soothed. 'It's only t' be expected, what with the thought of us having to go to yer granddad's funeral tomorrow an' all.'

'*Are* you sorry you married me, Matt?'

''Course I ain't,' he declared. 'After all, I know what you can be like, remember? Just think, I've got that kind of loving to look forward to for the rest of me life now that I've made an honest woman of you.'

They lay together under the eiderdown and talked. 'It's just unfortunate that death got mingled up with our wedding plans. But think, Joan, despite losing your granddad and having to put up with all the miseries and shortages of this flipping war we've still had this time together, and I know some of me mates would have given their right arm for as much. By the time this war's over we'll look back on this and laugh. We'll have all our lives before us then, just the two of us, an' we'll plan our future together.'

Joan raised herself up on her elbow and stared down into her husband's face. 'Wait a minute! I think you're forgetting something. Not so much of the two of us! There'll be three of us by then.'

'Crikey, yes.' He laughed. 'And if it drags on for much longer and I get regular leave, who knows? We'll probably be on our way to making our own football team, time I get demobbed.'

'Bit ambitious, aren't you?' She giggled, feeling much better as she snuggled up to his bare chest.

'You'll get through it,' Matt told her softly, as she took delivery of yet another wreath.

Joan was doing her best to stay steady and composed, standing beside Matt to open the front door to what seemed an endless number of mourners. Her nan was weeping, her father constantly blowing his nose. Only Daphne was doing her bit, handing out glasses of sherry to the ladies and whisky to the men. Joan thought her mother looked older today, dressed in black, a neat little hat perched on her bright hair. You could tell she'd been crying, even though her face was covered by a thin black veil.

In church the vicar had had plenty of good things to say about Pops. He was well known and liked, having lived in the same road from the day he and Hester had got married. Everyone was thankful that the service at the graveside was brief: with the rain coming down in torrents, it was bleak and cold out there among the weatherbeaten headstones, even under an umbrella. Back at the house all the relatives, friends and neighbours had eaten ham salad with hot boiled potatoes, nibbled cake and drunk tea from a range of borrowed cups. Then they said their tearful goodbyes.

Soon only Hester, Bill, Daphne, Joan and Matt were left in the kitchen.

'I'll 'ave t' get going now,' Matt whispered to Joan, taking his battle-dress down from the hook in the hall.

Joan felt she didn't have the energy to get out of the chair. An awful numbing fatigue had engulfed her but somehow she had to make the effort.

'If you're going to the station with Matt, I'll come with you,' Bill Harvey said, looking at his daughter. 'Breath of fresh air will do me good.' He was thinking that she didn't look well enough to walk back on her own.

Matt guessed what he had in mind and was grateful. Joan got to her feet and slipped her arms into her coat, which Matt was holding. It was as if she was going through the motions like a child.

'Thank God the rain has stopped,' Matt murmured, as the three of them set off.

Standing on the platform Joan clung to Matt, dry-eyed, which worried him more than if she had shed floods of tears. 'I'll be back as soon as I can. It won't be long. I promise.' He kissed her gently, and pushed her towards her father. Then he shook hands with Bill, who was thinking how easy it was to make a promise: who, in times like these, could promise anything?

Joan and her father stood side by side, watching the guard slam the carriage doors and wave his green flag. The train looked awful: grey with dust, its windows criss-crossed with sticky tape to prevent flying splinters if and when a bomb dropped close. Joan tucked her hand through her father's arm and sighed. 'Everything, no matter where you look, is so shabby,' she said.

'I'm going to buy us both a drink,' Bill decided. 'Give your mother and nan time to clear up a bit.' Doing his best to smile, he walked her across to the station bar and ordered a pint for himself and a brandy for Joan.

'Sorry, we've no spirits whatsoever,' the stout barmaid told him.

'Pity. We've just come from a funeral and my daughter could use a pick-me-up,' Bill answered her.

'Truly, we haven't a drop.' Then, almost as an afterthought she turned to look at Joan and said, 'How about a nice drop of port? That'd warm you up.'

'Yes.' Joan managed a weak smile. 'Yes, please, that would be nice.'

It was warm and crowded in the bar and they made their way over to stand against the wall.

'Cheer up, my love,' Bill said, wiping the froth from his mouth on the back of his hand. 'Things will work out for you an' Matt, you'll see.'

'I suppose so,' Joan answered, sounding unconvinced.

'We'll find you a nice place to live, somewhere near to your mother an' me,' he promised. 'You'll stay with us, of course, but you can spend your time making a nice home for Matt and the baby so that it's all ready by the time this wretched war is over.' Then he chided himself. What had he thought when he'd heard Matt make her a promise? Now he, too, was doing the same thing, telling her they'd find her a place of her own. With all the bombing, streets and streets of houses flattened to the ground, he'd have to admit that it would be virtually impossible.

Matt's thoughts were much the same, as he listened to the iron wheels going clickety-clack on the railway track. Over and over again he had wondered how to get them a place of their own. More so now Joan was expecting and . . . boy, oh, boy, she's my wife, Mrs Mathew Pearson. Funny that, not a single soul had mentioned it. What a wedding! They had had a few flowers and a cake of sorts, but no presents, no telegrams wishing them well. No one had thrown confetti and, more to the point, his parents hadn't been there. Poor Joan, she must feel cheated. Maybe not at this moment, but there would come a time. Oh, yes, that was a safe bet. The time would come when she would realize that their wedding day had been a sham: nothing to look back on, no mementoes, not even a photograph of the bride and groom. God! His mother had been right: they'd look back on that day and have a great many regrets.

We'll do it all over again, when this bloody war is over. Now he was making a promise to himself and, God willing, it was one he would keep. And it won't be in the south or in no ruddy register office. Wait till I see me mum again. I'm going t' let her know how right she was, and how bad things were, and that this time I'll let her make all the arrangements. He was laughing to himself now: if his mother had her way there would be a right ding-dong. Well, that would be fine by him. Let the whole of the East End turn up, he wouldn't care, because next time he was going to make sure that Joan had the works.

And to make sure his mum was happy, he'd see to it that it was the biggest and noisiest ding-dong Whitechapel had ever seen.

Chapter Five

BEING A MARRIED woman didn't change Joan's life to any great extent. She still lived at home, still worked at the Fox and Hounds and slept there when she was doing a late shift.

Was she happy? Was she looking forward to having the baby? These were questions she constantly asked herself. As for being a good mother, she felt far from confident about that, although she put on a brave face, especially when her nan was around.

Matt and his brigade were now in what he described as a holding unit out at Hassocks, not far from the south coast. First off he had suggested that Joan come and stay down there in one of the local pubs so that they could meet, even if it was only for an hour at a time, but Bill Harvey was dead against that idea. He felt that quite soon now the war was going to change, and that most of the troops left in England would be on the move. You only had to listen to the wireless or read the papers, he said, to get the feeling that something was about to take place. Hoardings all over the place had been scrawled with the demand 'Second Front Now'.

'The last thing we want is for you to be stranded in some out-of-the-way village when the baby is born,' was how he stated his case.

'But I'm only four months gone,' had been Joan's reply. But in her heart she knew her father was right: she didn't want to be in a pub or a bed-and-breakfast guest-house where she wouldn't know anyone or have anything to do, except wait and hope that she might be able to spend a little time with Matt.

Instead she wrote long letters to him. She told him how her nan was knitting and sewing enough clothes for four babies. How her mother thought that Joanie being pregnant had been a Godsend to Hester. 'She misses my granddad like mad, but at least she's thrilled to think that very soon there will be a baby in the house. Neighbours, too, are very kind. Old Granny Wallace, you know her, lives on the corner opposite the paper shop, well, she's crocheting a shawl for us which my mum says will do for the christening. It's already half finished and she has shown it to me. I can't believe how lovely it is. So fine and delicate. It makes you wonder how the old lady can see to do such work, and as to where she found the silk and the wool, well, my mother says I am not to ask.'

One thing really did please Joan, and that was that Matt wrote to her just as regularly as she did to him. He always wanted to know if she was keeping well, and telling her how proud he was that they were going to be parents. His last letter, though, had frightened her. It was as if he was warning her about something: 'Joan, dear,' he wrote, 'please do me a favour and go up and see my mum and dad. They may have grandchildren already but they really are pleased about our news. Well, me mum is now that she has got used to the idea and, as I see it, you two did get on really well in the short time you stayed with her.'

It wasn't much to ask, Joan decided, and she had been feeling a bit guilty because she had never been in touch with Amy Pearson since she had spent those few days with her. And Amy had gone out of her way to make her welcome.

London was proving too much for Joan. The train ride from Wimbledon hadn't been too bad – folk still had time to help a pregnant woman. However, as she stood surveying the crowds she decided that getting on to a tram was going to be far too difficult and that for once she was going to be extravagant and take a taxi. She got out at the top of the road – she didn't want Matt's family to think she was showing off – and walked slowly down it towards the house. She was feeling lonely, because the last time she had been here Matt had been with her, and even a bit miserable, not knowing what kind of a reception she would get. She raised her head at the sound of running feet. It was the two boys, Teddy and Jack.

''Allo, Joan, come t' see our gran, 'ave yer?' Teddy asked, giving her a cheeky grin.

Before she could answer little Jack piped up, 'Cos she ain't in. She's gone to a jumble sale with me mum an' our aunt Laura.'

Now Joan didn't know what to do. She looked at the children. Both of them looked as if they could do with a good wash. Their hair hadn't been combed. Teddy's jacket was patched and threadbare and the short trousers Jack was wearing were miles too big for him. Yet for all that they both seemed as happy as a pair of larks and as fit as fleas.

'Never mind,' Teddy said kindly, 'the front door's open an' I'll come indoors an' make yer a nice cuppa tea.'

Joan could have kissed him. As she worked her way down the cluttered hallway she had to step over two little girls, whose names she didn't know, and she couldn't remember if she'd seen them before or not. 'They're our cousins,' Jack informed her. 'Our aunt Laura's their mum.'

Teddy plumped up the cushions in the big old armchair set nearest to the scrubbed-topped kitchen table saying, 'Sit in me granddad's chair. I won't be long with the tea.' Then, grabbing his young brother by the arm, he spoke quickly: 'You can set the cups out and see if there's any bread in the bin an' if there is get it out an' the marge an' the jam – that's if there's any of that either.'

Joan had to smother a smile. He was really trying: she was getting the right royal treatment.

Teddy came back with a quart bottle half full of milk and set it down on the table. 'Can't find no sugar,' he said, shaking his head.

'Not to worry,' Joan told him, 'all my family gave up taking sugar in their tea soon after the war started. Just as well, cos it's like gold-dust now, isn't it?'

Young Jack was doing his best to set out the tea things, but every now and then he paused to dart a mischievous grin at Joan from under his long fair eyelashes. Soon Teddy was pouring tea from the big brown teapot into what she supposed must be one of their grandmother's best cups.

Needing to talk, Joan asked Teddy, 'How come you two are still in London? I thought that all children were evacuated about three years ago when the air-raids were so heavy.'

'We was.' This forthright statement had come from Jack.

'What do you mean, you was?' She grinned at the small boy.

For a moment there was silence in the room. Then Teddy said, very softly, 'It was awful. They put labels on us, tied them on with string, and put us all on a train, an' when we got there they separated us. Bruvvers an' sisters, it didn't matter to them, they didn't care. Jack was only a little tiddler an' the last thing me mum said t' me was I 'ad to keep 'old of him an' look after him. I couldn't. They took 'im away. Them people didn't like us an' we didn't like them. All the kids in our street came 'ome once I let me mum know what was going on.'

'Yeah, an' when we come, me mum said we ain't got t' go away no more.' Jack sounded as if he'd scored a victory.

As she listened Joan felt that Jack was old beyond his years. They both were, come to that. She sighed inwardly. Poor kids! Despite the terrors of indiscriminate bombing they had made up their own minds that there was no place like home and that no foster-parents could make up for their own mothers and fathers.

'What the 'ell is going on in 'ere?' Amy pushed open the kitchen door and beamed with delight when she spied Joan.

'I made tea for 'er,' Teddy said proudly.

'Yeah, an' I laid the table, but I couldn't find anything t' put on the bread,' Jack added.

Watching Joan try to suppress her amusement, Amy Pearson said, 'By God, it's good t' see yer, gal. Sorry I wasn't in. We've been to see what we could get in the way of clothes over at the church 'all. Me two girls 'ave stopped off t' do a bit of shopping. They'll bring in something an' I'll soon 'ave a meal on the go.'

Then flopping her heavy body down on to a chair she grumbled, 'If only me blinking legs wouldn't swell up so much I'd be able to get out an' about a bit more. Still, we've done all right today. Got a load of stuff for the kids and ain't 'ad to part with a single coupon.' So saying she tipped a sackful of clothes out on to the rug that lay in front of the fireplace.

Most of the jerseys, shirts and even a few pretty little dresses seemed clean and in good repair to Joan, who was flabbergasted when Amy, smiling broadly, said, 'Whole lot cost me one and tenpence.'

'You're having me on, Amy. You must have paid out more than that.'

'Gawd's truth, love, and if I'd known you were 'ere I'd 'ave been first in the queue for the baby clothes. Still, I'll keep me eyes peeled. How much longer, d'yer know?'

'The end of November, the clinic reckons, but they can't be sure, can they?'

Amy Pearson threw back her head and let out a great belly laugh. 'I didn't need no clinic to tell me no date. It were my Ernie! If he were passionate in a certain kind of way I marked it off on the calendar an', sure as eggs is eggs, it turned out right every time. Better watch out for our Mathew. Who knows? He might take after his ole man.'

The expression on Joan's face set Amy off again. And she was still laughing and clutching her sides when her two daughters came back each carrying a basket of shopping.

'Oh, it's our Matt's wife.' Bertha greeted Joan with a smile. 'What brings you 'ere?'

'Well, I haven't been in touch, and I thought it was about time I came an' thanked your mum for having me to stay when Matt was on leave last time.'

'Never got invited to the wedding, did we?' Laura's voice held a touch of harshness.

'No, I'm sorry. Wasn't much of a wedding because my granddad died and we had to bury him two days after we got married.'

'Oh, we never knew nothing about that, did we, Mum?'

'Well, as a matter of fact Matt did write to yer dad an' me at the time but, you know, I was feeling well out of sorts with the pair of them so I kept quiet. Still, that's water under the bridge now, an' as Matt says this war can't last for ever an' then he swears he's gonna show us.'

Joan was wondering what her mother-in-law meant by 'show' them when Bertha cut in, 'As long as you're all right, love, and the baby arrives safe an' sound, what does it matter 'ow yer got wed?'

Joan felt a debt of gratitude to the mother of the two boys, who had worked their charm on her. Even the children had their hearts in the right place. They were all loyal to each other and to the family. At that moment she felt she might have ended up with far less loving folk than Matt's lot.

'Any luck?' Amy asked her two daughters, changing the subject.

'Not too bad, I suppose,' Laura answered, smiling at Joan for the first time. 'We won't be able to produce a feast but we can run to sausages and mash if that'll suit you?'

Joan felt it was up to her to answer and she said, 'That would be a treat, but only if you're sure there's enough to go round cos I can easily get a meal when I get home.'

Bertha and Laura were unpacking their baskets and placing the shopping on to the table, but at this they stopped, turned their heads and stared at their sister-in-law. 'Send you 'ome with nothing inside yer? Yer don't know our mum very well yet, do yer?' was what Bertha said.

'I'm glad it's sausages for me dinner, I like them best. You will an' all, Joan. They're luvverly.' This statement, from young Jack, had them all laughing.

'Mind you,' his grandmother remarked, 'Gawd above knows what goes inter sausages today. Gone are the times when you could say whether you wanted pork or beef. Still, if you stopped to think about 'alf of what we've ate since this war started you'd never sleep nights.'

'Oh, Mother, give over, and get that big frying-pan going before you put all of us off our meal.' Bertha reached into a paper bag and produced two sticky buns. 'Take these out to the passage, one each for the girls, and tell them dinner won't be long,' she said to Teddy. Jack's eyebrows were raised but before he had a chance to complain his mother was holding out two more buns. 'Now, would I leave you an' Teddy out?' She grinned. 'You'd make me life a misery for the rest of the day if I did, I know that for a fact.'

Then Bertha licked her fingers, pushed her permed hair back from her forehead and apologized that there weren't any buns for the adults.

'Never mind,' Laura sounded apologetic too, 'I'll make a fresh pot of tea an' we did manage to get a packet of short-cake biscuits. We can 'ave them with a cuppa while the potatoes are cooking.'

Joan was glad suddenly that she had made the effort and come up to Whitechapel. It wasn't possible to feel down in the dumps – not with children playing with their dolls out in the hallway, two cheeky lads munching away at sticky buns and three women who were willing to accept her as Matt's wife, even if they had never been invited to the wedding. All in all she had a very pleasant day.

Matt's two sisters came with her to the railway station where they kissed her and said they hoped to see her again soon. If only there hadn't been a war, she was thinking, as she settled into a corner seat of the carriage, maybe she and Matt would have settled down in one of those little terraced houses and their baby would have loads of cousins to play with. But, there again, if it hadn't been for the war and Matt being in the Army, the chances are they never would have met. It was no good thinking of what might have been, she scolded herself, trying to be sensible. There *was* a war and there was nothing she could do about it. But, oh, how she wished that she and Matt could be together. She missed him so much, and more so today, having been in his home and he not there. Nothing had gone right from the moment her granddad had died. If only she and Matt could have had a honeymoon. Just a short while away somewhere on their own. All the way home, she thought of what a difference that would have made, no matter how hard she tried to think of other things.

Chapter Six

SEVERAL THINGS WERE worrying Joan. First, the doctor at the clinic hadn't thought it advisable for her to have her baby at home. Second, the two hospitals in their locality, the Wilson just up the green from the Cricketer's at Mitcham, and the Nelson Hospital at Merton Park had no maternity facilities. The doctor had decided that she would reserve a place for Mrs Joan Pearson at Epsom Hospital in Surrey. A determined woman, she hadn't bothered to ask Joan how she felt about it.

'Epsom!' her father had exclaimed. 'That's ruddy miles away! An' how are we supposed to get you there? What if we should have an air-raid at the same time?'

He was a darling, was her dad. He had got his post-office savings book out straight away, scanned it carefully and declared that, his finances being rather good, his first grand-child was going to be born in a private nursing-home.

He had been as good as his word. Her dad had gone off on his own and God alone knew how many inquiries he

had made or how many nursing-homes he had visited. Then
came the day when he was home grinning like a Cheshire
cat. 'I've found the very place. No, don't start having a go
at me,' he said, ignoring Joan but facing his wife and his
mother-in-law squarely. 'I've not committed myself or Joan
to anything as yet, but I'll tell you this, here an' now, you
can walk the streets of London till your feet are raw and
you won't find a cleaner, more organized private place for
our Joanie to have her baby than the Haven nursing-home.'

The three generations looked at each other and had a job
to control their amusement. Fancy, a great big bloke like
Bill Harvey traipsing in and out of different nursing-homes
telling the proprietor that he wanted only the best for his
daughter and his first grandchild.

'And what's more,' he went on, 'I've made an appointment for all four of us to go and see the place tomorrow
afternoon.'

Three o'clock sharp, and they were there, standing on a
grassy verge that overlooked the railway line in Wimbledon.
The Haven, a large, detached, double-fronted building,
stood behind them. Hester, Daphne and Joan had all made
a great effort, and Bill was well aware that he had three
well-turned-out attractive women with him as he opened
the large iron gate and let them into the attractive grounds
in which the nursing-home stood.

It was the first time Joan had been inside a hospital, and
as she walked down the corridor, which smelt of disinfectant and floor polish, she felt frightened.

'Good afternoon, Mr Harvey. This is your daughter, I
presume.'

Bill made all the introductions and by then Joan was feeling more relaxed.

One of the reasons that Grace Medwin had made such a success of her chosen career was that she had developed the ability to summarize a situation quickly and thereby put folk at ease. 'You'd like to see over the place,' she turned her attention to Joan, 'so we'll start with the day room, and by the time we've finished our tour I'm sure you will all be ready for some tea.'

Mrs Medwin looked and sounded like a very superior person, and the clothes she wore were both expensive and practical. The jacket of her navy blue suit covered a white cotton blouse with pin-tucks that ran straight from the points of her starched collar to the nursing belt that was buckled around her waist. Her light brown hair hung, shining and clean, to her shoulders, and her clear-skinned face was devoid of makeup. 'I am a qualified midwife,' she said to Joan, who was gazing in amazement at the comfortable lounge and the beautiful gardens that lay beyond. Then, turning to Bill, she said, 'I'd like to put your mind at rest on one score. You see that drab brick building over to your left, the one that has the steep slope leading down to its double doors?' Bill stepped nearer to the french windows, looked and nodded. 'That is our reinforced air-raid shelter, which is equipped to handle any emergency. Let's hope we shall have no need of it since the air-raids have, thankfully, become a thing of the past.'

Bill almost said, 'I wouldn't put my money on it,' but thought better, and Mrs Medwin went on, 'We always have at least two porters on duty, day and night. If need be, they can push trolleys down there so that our young mothers can rest easily and have their babies delivered in safety.'

Almost reluctantly Joan's mother and grandmother walked forward to take a look.

'Next I will show you the bedrooms. Every mother has a room to herself and a cot for the baby is positioned by the side of the bed, though we do have a nursery for the odd occasion when Baby may be a bit restless and Mother needs her sleep. We have three resident midwives and two doctors on call for emergencies. Do you have your own doctor,' she asked Joan, 'or have you just been attending a clinic?'

'I've been seeing the lady doctor at the clinic quite regularly,' Joan said. 'Is that all right?'

'Perfectly,' Mrs Medwin answered, as she threw open the door to a bedroom. It had pretty curtains at the windows and a high bed stood in the centre, covered with a snow-white bedspread and a mound of pillows. A large, well-padded armchair was set to look out over the gardens and a low chair with an upholstered high back was set beside a cot adorned with yellow-dotted white muslin frills. Two lovely teddy bears sat side by side on the window-sill. One bear had a pale blue silk bow-tie and the other's was pink.

'I don't think we need to show you the labour ward or the delivery room yet,' Mrs Medwin said softly to Joan. 'I think there will be time enough for that later.'

The tour ended in Mrs Medwin's sitting room, a charming room that, again, spoke of the good taste of the owner of this nursing-home. While the elders ate scones and jam and drank their tea, Joan was thinking that her father's decision to book her into this place had not only been a kind and generous act but a wise one too. She hadn't exactly been looking forward to giving birth. Once she had her baby in her arms everything would be wonderful but the actual birth terrified her. Knowing that she would be in safe hands here made all the difference. She suddenly felt optimistic, as if something marvellous was just about to happen.

She couldn't wait to get home and write a letter to Matt, telling him all about the arrangements her dad had made.

Mrs Medwin wasn't the only one to make the wrong assumption that raids from German planes were no longer a serious threat. When summer arrived so did the planes – in a more frightening form: flying bombs, planes with no pilots. Mostly there was no time to sound the warning sirens. The population of England, and London in particular, stood still in broad daylight, watching helplessly. There was no defence against these planes, which were clearly visible, with flames shooting out of the tail. While the engine could be heard you were safe, but the minute it cut out the silence struck terror into the bravest heart. Young and old alike prayed, Please, God, don't let it come down here. Then the engine would cut out and the plane would dive, dropping like a stone, exploding on a hospital, a school, on a shop, factory or playing-field. The massacre was horrifying.

During the first few days in June everyone was living on a knife's edge. The news on the wireless hinted at happenings yet gave no real information. The weather report was awful: strong winds, heavy rain and rough seas.

Then came the breakthrough: the weather had improved so the second front had been launched. Every household had the wireless constantly tuned in.

American, British and Canadian troops landed on the coast of Normandy on 6 June under General Eisenhower and General Montgomery. Allied planners had kept the Germans guessing as to where the actual landing would take place, which meant that they had had no choice but to position major defences along the whole of the northern coast of France. Casualties were still high, and Normandy suffered heavy damage in the battles that followed. Once the Allied beachheads had been established, the build-up of troops, tanks and artillery was rapid. The German defences were breached and Allied forces broke through into the Normandy countryside.

Day by day the mood of the British people grew lighter. Maybe, just maybe, the end of this terrible war was in sight. One evening, the reader of the nine o'clock news sounded triumphant: a great bonus of the D-Day landings was that Allied troops had discovered and overrun the launching sites of the flying bombs.

As the news improved the long bright days of summer boosted everyone's morale. Even letters from Matt arrived more regularly. During the time when he had not been able to write, Joan had worried herself sick. She knew she had been grumpy, difficult to live with, but as Daphne said to Bill, "'Tis only t' be expected. She's put on such a lot of weight, can't go dancing, and when me an' her gran took her t' the pictures the other night we had to get up an' come out before the end of the film. She just couldn't get comfortable. Fidget, fidget all the time, till the folk behind us complained.'

'I wish she'd give up her job,' her father said. 'Serving behind a bar is not what a pregnant girl should be doing.'

'Oh, give over, Bill. She's only doing three days a week an' no late turns. Bob an' Poppy won't let no harm come to her, and it does get her out of the house and lets her meet people.'

'Yeah, I know all that, but she still has to serve a lot of men and I don't think she should be doing that. Not in her condition.'

Daphne struggled to hold her temper in check. 'She not your little girl any more, she's a married woman, and if she wants to work it's not up to us to stop her. It takes her mind off things and keeps her going.'

'She's so young,' Bill protested.

That made Daphne laugh. 'Not so young that she hasn't found out how many beans make five. Anyway, she'll have to give up working soon, so why not let her make the most of it while she's able?'

'Suppose I don't have any choice in the matter, do I? But with Matt away and not much likelihood of him getting leave before the baby's born, I still feel responsible for her.'

'She'll be fine, you'll see, and you'll be a granddad before you know it.' Daphne grinned. 'Then you'll have two to worry about.'

One afternoon when she got home and found not one letter from Matt but two Joan's heart missed a beat. Her gran was out, doing her bit for the war effort (three afternoons a week she helped out at the Wilson hospital), and her mum was busy making pastry. Daphne shook the flour off her hands and moaned about the shortage of decent margarine and the fact that they hadn't seen a fresh egg for the last three weeks. 'This ruddy dried egg's no flipping good for baking, and as for the marge it's more like cart grease than stuff you're supposed to put on bread.'

'Never mind, Mum. You still manage to turn out real good pies, and the cakes you make don't hang about, do they?'

Daphne laughed. 'I said as much t' yer father on Sunday afternoon when he said that there wasn't much jam in the sponge. Know what he said? "You eat anything if you're hungry enough."'

'Oh, Mum, you know darn well he was teasing you.'

'Yeah, I know, but cooking doesn't give me the pleasure it used to. Anyway, why are you sitting there staring at your letters? Why don't you open them, see what Matt has to say?'

'I'll make us a cup of tea first,' Joan answered, thinking that she'd rather be on her own to read them.

Having gone through the motions, she set a cup down on the far end of the table to where her mother was working, saying, 'Drink it while it's hot, Mum. I'm going to take mine upstairs, maybe rest my legs for a bit.'

Daphne sighed heavily. Joan was such a good-hearted girl, but she tired so easily these days. She was getting so big too – maybe she was carrying twins. This should be such a happy time, but instead Matt was far away and Joan was doing her best to put on a brave face even when she didn't feel so great. Daphne found herself hoping that Matt would prove a good husband and father. Got to get this ruddy war over first and then perhaps he and thousands more of the young men who had been snatched away from their families would be given the chance to prove themselves. They might only have been boys when they were called up but it was a ten to one bet that those lucky enough to come home would be a lot older and certainly a lot wiser.

Upstairs Joan found it pleasant in her bedroom, even though the window-panes were covered with the inevitable sticky tape. She wondered what it would be like when the war ended and all the boarding and this horrible brown tape was stripped off. Homes, hospitals, workplaces and public transport would once again be allowed to let in the daylight. Wouldn't it be nice not to have to shut out the sunlight during the day and black out all the windows every evening? Joan turned down the counterpane, lay on the bed and tucked the eiderdown over her legs.

The first letter had been written three weeks ago and was very short, merely asking if she was keeping well, and saying that he hadn't time to write to his mum and dad and would she let them know that he was all right? He had ended by saying he loved her very much.

The second letter was, oh, so different: 'I do miss you, Joan, and how I wish I were going to be with you when our baby is born,' was how it began. A warm glow spread through her, she closed her eyes and hugged her pillow. Oh, Matt, you don't wish that half as much as I do. They seemed to have had such a short while together and she hadn't been very nice to him directly after the wedding. Losing Pops like that hadn't helped. If only Matt had been given more leave. And if only they hadn't been so headstrong they wouldn't have had to have such a rushed wedding. She read on. 'I love you so much, and just you wait and see, Joan, we'll have a home of our own as soon as we can and, like you reminded me, there will be three of us, and like I told you then, we'll do our best to see that our first baby is not our last. Just keep on loving me, please.'

Tears welled up in her eyes, she placed her two hands over the bulge in her stomach and sighed. This blinking rotten war, the separations it caused, the loneliness, the loss of young men's lives, to say nothing of all the civilians that were being killed in the air-raids. It seemed as if there was no end to it. Surely it couldn't go on for much longer.

'Oh, Matt,' she cried, burying her face in the pillow so that her mother wouldn't hear her sobs.

Later she went into the bathroom, rinsed her face and

hands under the cold tap and went downstairs to help her mother prepare their evening meal. Her dad came home, bringing her a rare bar of milk chocolate, and her nan, who joined them most days for her dinner, showed her yet another matinée coat she had made for the baby. But, through all their efforts at cheerful conversation, Joan's thoughts were miles away with her husband. Before she went to bed that night she had decided that she really should go up to Whitechapel again.

Chapter Seven

TIME HAD PASSED so quickly, yet the days now seemed to drag. Joan didn't know what to do with herself. She was bored. As soon as August had come, her father had insisted she give up her job and stay at home. In herself she felt remarkably well. Every day she went for a walk. Sometimes she took the bus up to Wimbledon Hill, sat for a while on the common then went into the pub to see Poppy and Bob. But she felt useless: there wasn't a thing she was allowed to do at home – both her mum and her nan were treating her as if she were the only woman in the world waiting to give birth.

Breakfast was over, and Joan was in the house on her own. She stood looking out of the window. It was now the last week in October and the weather looked good, but she knew it wouldn't be very warm even though the sun was shining.

She was considering her options. Yesterday she had received a parcel that contained gifts not only from Amy, her mother-in-law, but also from Laura and Bertha, her two sisters-in-law. They had sent some lovely things for the baby, and although she was grateful she felt guilty. She had written quite regularly to Amy, never omitting to let her know when she received a letter from Matt, but she had failed to keep her promise and pay them a visit.

'I'll go today,' she declared. 'In fact, I'll go right now.' She knew that if she waited until her mother or her nan came back from doing the shopping they would have a hundred and one reasons why she shouldn't travel. 'You're nearing yer time, only three or four weeks to go . . . You must be mad – the doctor at the Haven told you only last week that you should take things easy now.'

When she got outside it was colder than she'd thought so, very rashly, Joan flagged down a taxi that happened to be passing. 'Wimbledon station, please.' She smiled at the driver. Once there he climbed down from his cab, opened the door and helped Joan to alight. That thoughtful gesture was only the first she encountered on her journey. Folk smiled at her, made sure she had a seat both on the train and on the tram. The jungle of London's back streets were showing signs of being war-torn, but she was very glad she had made the effort she decided as she walked slowly down the road towards her mother-in-law's house.

The street door stood wide open and Joan called loudly, 'Anyone at home?'

''Allo, Joan, my love.' Amy sounded surprised but pleased as she heaved her great bulk up the passage. 'Christ,' she said, eyeing Joan from top to toe, 'you ain't 'alf a size, but you look marvellous.'

And she was right. Despite the cold weather, Joan

bloomed with health. Her skin glowed, her fine cheekbones had a lot more flesh on them, and her long auburn hair, tucked into a French pleat at the back and piled high on top, shone like amber gold.

'And rationing hasn't made you any thinner,' Joan teased, as she kissed Amy's cheek.

'Aw, Gor blimey, don't you start! I 'ave enough of that from my lot – an' any'ow, should you be 'ere? I take it you've travelled on yer own.'

'Don't you get on to me,' Joan pleaded. 'I made my mind up on the spur of the moment cos if I'd waited to tell my mum I know she would have kicked up ructions. Besides, I wanted to see you all to say thanks for the parcel. I'm not an invalid, you know.' The look that Joan gave Amy defied her to say otherwise.

In spite of her misgivings Amy had to smile: Joan's determination was something else. 'Anyway, let's get you inside, the kettle's on.'

Now it was Joan's turn to smile. When wasn't the kettle on in this house?

As she walked through the kitchen door the heat hit her. What a lovely sight! The fire was roaring away, the darting flames reflected in the big mirror that hung on the opposite wall. Then Joan stood still and stared. The gas jet was alight, but that was the only means of light. The window was boarded over with planks. 'Whatever happened?' she asked, nodding towards the window.

'Laundry at the back of us got a direct hit from one of them doodlebugs an' we caught a lot of the blast.' Seeing the look of horror on Joan's face, Amy said quickly, 'We're the lucky ones. No one in the street has any glass left but no one was killed. It was 'alf past eight in the morning, girls 'ad just started work. Wasn't anyone got out alive. Had a mass funeral. Terrible, it was.'

This was said so sadly that Joan couldn't think of a reply – nothing would sound right in the face of such a disaster.

When Matt's two sisters came in Amy and Joan were munching hot toast and drinking tea from giant mugs. 'We're going shopping down Chapel Street market if you feel up t' coming with us,' Laura announced. 'Word was down the corner shop that there's not only fish about but some decent rabbits as well.'

'It's half past twelve now so I don't suppose we'll be long,' Bertha said, smiling at Joan. 'Be nice to 'ave yer company, catch up on all your news.'

'Well, make sure you don't keep 'er out too long,' their mother instructed. 'She'll 'ave to catch an early train back or else 'er folks'll be worrying themselves sick.'

The three young women set off. They had barely got among the stalls when Joan was knocked flying. She had seen the three children on skates riding round and round in a circle but hadn't been quick enough to get out of their way as they made a spurt to dash off. All her insides went taut. I don't know which way to turn, was her last thought as she felt her feet leave the ground. She wanted to be sick. 'Oh, my back,' she murmured, as Bertha and Laura bent over her. The young boy who had bashed into her kept saying how sorry he was.

Joan was trying hard to sit up, gasping for air.

'I wouldn't try t' move 'er,' one burly stall-holder advised.

'No, I'll go in t' the butcher's an' get them to phone for an ambulance,' his mate called.

The ambulancemen were kindness itself, and Bertha went with her to the hospital while Laura did their shopping before making her way home to tell her mother what had happened. All kinds of thoughts were buzzing through Joan's head. Was her baby all right? She dreaded to think what her parents and her nan were going to say.

The ambulanceman looked at her and grabbed a bowl. Just in time. To Joan's embarrassment, she was violently sick.

'How badly is she hurt?' Fear was making Daphne raise her voice.

'Please,' the staff nurse begged, 'Mr and Mrs Harvey, sit down and try to calm yourselves. Your daughter has been well looked after and at the moment she is sleeping. I'll try to get a doctor or sister to come and have a word with you.' Sensing that the mother of Mrs Pearson might prove difficult she allowed no argument: with a swish of her starched uniform she turned quickly and left the office.

Bill Harvey was afraid, of course he was, and he fully agreed that Joan had done a daft thing in coming up to London when she was so near to having her baby. Having said that, he began to feel that if his wife didn't give over and stay quiet for a few minutes he would cheerfully strangle her.

The news that Joan was in hospital had knocked them both for six and it hadn't done Hester much good either. Bill was glad that he had managed to get her to stay at home: she had convinced herself that Joan was going to lose the baby and she was the last person he wanted around at this moment. He was having enough trouble with Daphne.

They'd got to the hospital in record time, thanks to his neighbour's offer to run them up in his van. A policeman had come to the house with the news that Joan had had an accident in Chapel Street market, and from the moment he had left Daphne had gone on and on: 'That daughter of ours hasn't got the sense she was born with. Fancy going off like that! Just a scribbled note to say where she'd gone and that she'd be back some time tonight. And what about those in-laws of hers? What sort of people are they? We wouldn't know cos we've never been given the opportunity to meet them. What were they thinking of, dragging our girl round markets in her condition?'

Bill was just about to threaten his wife that if she didn't shut up . . . when, thank God, the nurse was back, and with her a sister in a dark navy blue uniform, and a wide winged starched headdress. The sister smiled, but the smile only reached her lips, not her eyes in which there was no friendliness. 'As far as the doctor can tell at the moment, your daughter has suffered no ill effects from her fall.' Stern was the only way to describe her tone. 'She has a few bumps and bruises and a very nasty headache, for which she has been given something, and my nurse has already told you she is sleeping peacefully.'

Daphne was taken aback. It was like looking at and listening to a headmistress.

It was Bill who said softly, 'Two questions, please, Sister. Is the baby going to be all right and may we take our daughter home?'

Ignoring the first question the woman spat out, 'Certainly not. A pregnant woman is knocked down by boys on skates and you think she doesn't need careful monitoring?' Not waiting for Bill's reply she hurried on, 'Mrs Pearson will be kept in for at least forty-eight hours. You may take a peep at her before you leave and Nurse will give you a list of our visiting hours, which we adhere to strictly. Only two visitors allowed at any one time at the patient's bedside.' With that she was gone, and for a full minute you could have cut the silence with a knife.

The nurse moved first. With a kindly gesture she touched Daphne's arm, looked across at Bill and nodded towards the doorway, saying, 'If you'd like to come with me.'

It was coming up to five o'clock in the evening and two men in brown overalls were walking the long ward placing the wooden blackout boards against every window. Joan had been settled in the first bed. 'Just so that we may keep an eye on her from the office,' the nurse explained, and then, as if she felt she needed to comfort them in some way, she added, 'Come back tomorrow. She'll be awake then, and you'll be able to see for yourselves that she's all right. I'll leave you to have five minutes with her now.'

As he stared down at his daughter Bill felt choked, but he managed to murmur, 'Thank you.'

'She don't look all right to me,' Daphne said.

Because her voice was shaky Bill answered her gently. 'Please, love, leave it for now. Let her sleep. Tomorrow everything will seem better.'

'You don't know that,' she mumbled. 'If she has to be in hospital why can't it be nearer home? Oh, I can't just go away and leave her here.'

Bill felt exactly the same way. He leant over the bed. Joan's face was deathly white but there wasn't a mark on it, which he thought must be a good sign. Her hair looked a bit untidy, and against the whiteness of the pillows it was a deep chestnut. He wanted to tell her she looked a proper copper knob. He wanted to tell her that he'd lift her up in his arms and take her home. He wanted to tell her that he'd booked a place for her to have the baby in a lovely nursing-home near to where they lived, and that he didn't want to go away and leave her here in this long drab-looking ward of a big London hospital. But he couldn't tell her anything. All he could do was gently stroke a few strands of her hair back from her forehead and place his lips there in a soft kiss. Joan never stirred.

Her mother did the same. Only she, too, felt so helpless she couldn't control the tears that were trickling down her cheeks. She was praying to God that her daughter would be all right, as her husband put his arm around her shoulders and led her away.

When Bill and Daphne got back from the hospital it seemed as if half the street was gathered in her living room, keeping Hester company and all anxious for news of Joan.

Next day, at three o'clock sharp, Joan's parents and her grandmother were waiting in the corridor outside the ward that Joan was in. A very young nurse removed the screens that covered the glass doors from the inside and bolted the two doors back against the wall.

'Two visitors only to each bed, and the bell will ring at ten minutes to four to warn you that visiting time ends at four o'clock.' She was a pretty girl and her words were recited in a sing-song voice, evidently she was tired of repeating them day after day.

'Only one hour's visiting time?' Hester was appalled.

'You go on in with Daffy first,' Bill insisted. He wasn't going to incur his mother-in-law's wrath by telling her she had to wait out here in the corridor.

'Oh, my darling, you look so much better.' Daphne's face

was wreathed in smiles when she saw that her daughter was sitting up, propped by a mound of pillows, and looking hardly affected at all by her fall.

Hester was a different matter. She stepped forward to kiss Joan and burst into tears.

'Don't get so upset,' Joan implored, wriggling to get herself comfortable in the narrow bed. 'I'm fine, Nan, really I am. Doctor said another twenty-four hours to be on the safe side and then I can come home.'

'Oh, my love,' Hester sniffed, 'whatever got into you? Going off like that! The sooner we get you home where we can keep an eye on you the better. I'm not going to let you out of my sight till that baby's born.'

Joan sighed inwardly. What have I let myself in for? she wondered. There was something she had to ask her father. She hoped against hope that she'd be able to get him on his own because the request she was going to make wouldn't please her mother and it would upset her nan even more.

'Tea or a glass of milk?' a rosy-faced ward orderly asked Joan, as her two visitors sat one each side of the bed.

'Tea, please, no sugar.'

'One or two slices of bread, an' would you like jam or fish-paste?'

'One slice, please, and a little jam.'

'Is that all they give you for your tea?' Hester sounded indignant and Joan wasn't sorry when her mother suggested they walk down to the hospital shop and buy her a bottle of orange squash. 'We'll send your dad in to keep you company while we're gone.'

Thank God for that, Joan thought, then smiled broadly as she watched him step inside the ward and come to the side of her bed.

'And how's my old sleepyhead?' he asked, taking both her hands between his own. 'You didn't even open an eye when we were here yesterday.'

'Oh, Dad, I am sorry I've been so much trouble, and now while we're on our own I want to ask you a favour.'

'Pet, you're not to upset yourself, and whatever it is if I can do it you know full well I will.'

'Dad . . . . there's an hour's visiting tonight, isn't there?'

'Yes. Why? Are you worried we won't come back?'

'No, Dad, that's not it at all. I can't tell Mum or Nan but Staff Nurse said that Matt's sisters rang up and when they were told you were visiting me this afternoon they said they'd come and bring their mum to see me tonight. They're ever so worried, Dad. I think they blame themselves for taking me to the market when they were only being kind.'

Her dad patted her hand. 'Don't fuss yourself. I understand, truly I do. I'll think of something to tell your mother. We won't come tonight but we'll be back tomorrow, hopefully to take you home with us.'

'Oh, Dad, you're great, you really are.' Joan sighed with relief. It was difficult playing peacemaker with both sets of parents.

'Well, I've got a great daughter, and I can't wait to see whether you're going to present me with a granddaughter or a grandson. I'm so pleased you'll be having the baby at the Haven. Their visiting rules are a lot less strict, so Mrs Medwin tells me.'

Joan breathed another sigh, laid her head back against the pillow and closed her eyes. She was surprised at how tired she felt.

'I brought you two magazines and a tin of fruit drops,'

her father whispered, as the warning bell sounded. 'I'd better go now and let your mum an' your nan come in to say goodbye.' Then he put his arm across the top of the pillow and told her, 'I'll be here to fetch you tomorrow. We all love you – you know that, don't you? Get some rest now.'

Joan sat up to put her arms around her father's neck. It was a touching moment, when neither of them could say a word.

It was much the same when her mum and her nan gave her a cuddle, and as Joan watched them wave goodbye she was telling herself she was a lucky young woman to have such a caring family.

It was close on midnight, and Joan hadn't been able to get to sleep. She had refused the nurse's offer to ring a doctor and ask permission for her to have a sleeping pill. It was difficult to turn over: the great swelling of her stomach kept the bedclothes high, and although she had heard several of the other patients complain of how cold the ward was she was sweating profusely and the pain in her back was driving her mad.

'Here, I've brought you a cup of milky Horlicks. It might help you sleep.' It was the same two nurses on duty as on the previous night, and this one in particular seemed very friendly.

'Thanks ever so much, but I think I need to go to the toilet before I drink it.' Joan had already pushed back the bedclothes when the nurse said, 'Stay where you are, I'll get a bedpan.'

'No, please, I think I need to do more than just wee and I can't go on a bedpan, really I can't. Please, let me get to the toilet.'

'Well,' the nurse sounded reluctant, 'I'll fetch a wheel-chair. Wait just a minute.'

Joan felt so thankful as she waited. Bedpans were horrible. Turning back the top sheet still further she swung her legs over the side of the bed as the nurse reappeared with the chair. Her feet touched the cold floor and she stood up only to gasp in amazement. A terrific pain had settled in her lower back and she was wetting herself. She had no control – the wee was running everywhere around her feet. 'Oh, I'm so sorry,' she murmured, as it ran down her legs and splashed on to the wooden floor. Never could she remember having felt so embarrassed.

The kindly nurse grinned. 'Not to worry but I'd better get you back into bed and alert the maternity unit. Your waters have just broken.'

'What?' No one had warned her of anything like this. 'Does that mean that the baby's coming?'

Now they were joined by the second night nurse. 'Not as easily as all that, I wouldn't think, but by this time tomorrow I'd say your baby will be a few hours old.' They were laying dry towels on the bed and lifting Joan's legs back up.

'I can't have my baby, not here,' she moaned. 'I'm booked into a nursing-home – my dad's paying for it all. Oh, please, can't I go home?'

The nurses looked at each other and laughed. 'You've left it a bit late for that,' they said. 'You have no say in the matter now. He or she has decided it's time to come into this world and you can't stop it. So, be a good girl, we'll have the porters here with a trolley and you'll be whisked off to the mother-and-baby unit.'

Joan didn't get a chance to answer because she was doubled up in pain.

It wasn't until an hour later that the full extent of what the doctor was telling her sank in: 'I'd say another couple of hours then the labour pains will increase and you'll be ready to give birth. Would you like a hot drink now?'

The pain would increase? She'd never be able to stand it. Whatever had she done to deserve this?

She was in a small, very shiny clinical room, which they told her was the labour ward. A doctor and a midwife had placed cold instruments on her swollen tummy and listened to the baby's heartbeat, or so they'd told her. The bed she lay on was very high, and more than once she'd been afraid that, as the pains came and went, she would fall off. This was a nightmare, nothing short of a living nightmare. What was she doing here? Did her mum and dad know what was happening? What about Matt? Several children, he'd said he wanted. Well, *he* could have them! If he thought for one moment that she was ever going to put herself through all this again he couldn't be more wrong.

Oh, oh, oh. She bit her bottom lip until it bled. Where is everybody? How can they come and look and say, 'You're doing fine, Mrs Pearson,' then go away and leave me all on my own? After all the trouble to which her father had gone in finding the Haven nursing-home! Now here she was, miles from home, in a place where no one seemed to have any time for her. Her dad would be upset about this. Oh, it wasn't fair. Somebody, anybody, help me. Please help me. Her hair was lank and wet and she was sweating like a pig. She smelt horrible. I know I do, she told herself, wiping her face on the corner of the sheet.

'I'm the senior midwife in this hospital, Mrs Pearson. This is your first baby, isn't it?'

A stoutish nurse was leaning over the bed, and Joan

thought she'd never been more glad to see anyone in her whole life. 'Yes,' she said, through gritted teeth, as yet another pain tore through her. Reaching out she grabbed the midwife's hand and, like a small child, she pleaded, 'Please, don't leave me on my own. I'm frightened, I'm not supposed to be here . . .' She doubled up her knees, dug her fingers into the arm of this nurse and just yelled. It was unbearable – her voice was now one long terrifying scream.

'All right, Mrs Pearson, all right. Just be a good girl and try to relax. Baby is just telling us it's time to begin work.' The midwife moved to the end of the bed, and as she did so the door opened and a doctor and another nurse came into the room.

There was a hurried discussion. Joan caught the words 'First baby, very large, mother has small pelvis.' Now there were other sounds. A trolley was dragged across the floor. A machine was placed near the bed. The doctor put on a face mask. 'Bend your knees up, Mrs Pearson,' he ordered, pulling a long metal arm that held a strong electric light down from the ceiling. He switched it on and manoeuvred it into position so that the beam would be directed between Joan's legs.

From that moment on Joan lost all sense of time. She ached from head to toe. She was sopping wet, yet her mouth was as dry as a bone – oh, she'd give the world for a drink. The pains were coming more frequently now, and each one left her feeling shattered.

'Push,' she was ordered, time and again. 'Almost there, great big push this time.'

'We've got the head, come on, push.'

'Well done, Mrs Pearson. You have a lovely baby boy.'

Again she caught snatches of their whispering: 'Still bleeding heavily, badly torn. I'll have to put in a few stitches.'

Joan heaved a huge sigh, but didn't get the chance to tell them she wanted to hold her baby, because at that moment there was an awful roaring sound, followed by an almighty thump. The bed on which she was lying felt as if it rose up then fell down heavily. The whole room seemed to rock as instruments rattled to the floor. The blackout board clattered down from the window – it sounded as if it were raining broken glass. Then all the lights went out.

The doctor swore loudly and even the midwife let out a scream. All Joan could think was that if it was a bomb it must have landed very close to this hospital, and she prayed as she never had before that she and her baby would soon be safely at home. She wanted her parents, she wanted her nan, and most of all she wanted and needed Matt. At the same time she was asking, Why, oh why did I come to the East End? It was so dark and there didn't seemed to be enough air: she was fighting for breath. She felt, rather than saw, the doctor lean over her, his voice reassuring as he said, 'Everything is under control, Mrs Pearson. The nurses are fetching torches, everything is fine. I'm going to give you an injection. You'll be able to have a little sleep while I clean you up.'

'But I haven't even seen my baby yet,' she protested.

She felt a scratch on the back of her hand and then she was falling. It was dark, oh, so very dark, and the ground was a long, long way down. Then she was oblivious to everything.

London was experiencing another type of bombing, this time from huge rockets, and such were the explosions that they caused deadly damage and the blast was felt for miles around. Patients were being brought into the hospital. Bodies were being transported to the morgues, and rumours were adding fuel to the fires.

It was 2 November 1944. In the early hours of the morning, amid all the turmoil of London's first rocket raid Joan Pearson had given birth to her first baby, a boy. The nursing staff were clearing up, the baby had already been washed and taken to the nursery. Joan had received four stitches to her insides, and was now lying unconscious on a trolley, waiting for a porter to take her back to the ward.

The midwife was filling in her notes when she looked up as the other nurse remarked, 'No wonder she was so frightened. She's only eighteen, nineteen on Christmas Day, according to her notes.'

'That's if she lives that long,' came the blunt reply.

Startled, the homely midwife looked up. 'She's not that bad, a bit torn about but that's because the baby was so big, nigh on nine pounds.'

'I didn't mean it like that,' the nurse added quickly. 'Who knows how many of us will be here to see Christmas? By the look of the bodies they're taking downstairs I'd say Hitler really has thought up something terrifying for us this time. From what the air-raid wardens are saying, we're not going to get any warning from these rocket-type bombs.'

'Oh, come on, lass. Don't start thinking along those lines. Best thing to do is live your life from day to day.'

'That's all very well, but if there's no telling when or where these new bombs are coming over then it stands to reason we aren't going to have any defence against them, doesn't it?'

The older midwife stared at the young nurse. What an attitude to adopt. Oh dear. She sighed sadly to herself. This war had an awful lot to answer for. It was certainly putting old heads on young shoulders.

Chapter Eight

JOAN LAID HER baby son down in her father's armchair, looked round the room at all the smiling faces there to welcome her, and decided she was never going to leave home again. At least, not for a very long time. Tears of happiness welled in her eyes. This was the first time she had felt safe since the blast from the rocket that had exploded so near to where she lay in hospital.

They say that in the wake of evil good can follow. Well, it certainly had in this case.

She had her darling baby son. He was gorgeous. Round chubby face, a dimple in his chin where the angels had kissed him. Fat little hands, long fingers each with a perfectly formed pink nail. Not very much hair but what there was showed signs of being dark like his father's. Skin like silk. Each time Joan guided his little mouth to her nipple and held him close to her breast her wonderment knew no bounds. He was perfect. Warm, soft, sweet-smelling, oh, she was so lucky. Hard to believe that she and Matt had made this tiny human being.

Everyone argued about what name he was to be given. Hester had said, 'Call him Edward after your grandfather,' but that didn't seem fair to Matt or his family.

William, Daphne wanted, 'After your dad,' she pleaded. Peggy Watson had suggested Geoffrey or Stuart – Sees too many films, does my friend Peggy, Joan had decided. In the end she had learnt from her mother-in-law that Matt's father's second name was James, and as her own father was named William James, she made the decision herself. Pushing the lovely high perambulator that had been Hester's gift she had set off for the council offices. Taking the baby in with her – she couldn't bear to leave him outside in his pram – she waited her turn. James Mathew Pearson, she registered him.

So the days passed. She wrote proudly to Matt, every letter giving him the tiniest scrap of information as to how his son was doing. She still missed him terribly, was wishing they could go to the pictures together or up on the common, arguing over who was going to push the pram. He was missing so much. Jamie, as everyone seemed to call him, now gurgled, looked at his own fingers and wiggled his toes when at bath-time she tickled the soles of his tiny feet. Matt wrote when he could. The end of the war which had seemed so close in June, had not come about. People were disheartened again.

The rockets were different from anything anyone had remotely imagined. Reports were that they could be launched from anywhere and that they travelled at 3,600 miles per hour – several times the speed of sound. Once launched they could not be intercepted and arrived without warning. There was even talk of children being evacuated from London again.

Christmas was upon them. Shortages made decent presents almost impossible, but parcels were sent and exchanged between Matt's family and Joan's, although as yet Amy had not seen her new grandson.

Joan had to admit that theirs had been a happy Christmas Day. Just watching her father lying flat on his stomach holding up toys and shaking rattles to make Jamie smile, not to mention the silly faces he pulled, was enough to make her, her mother and Nan, sigh with contentment. Though the awful thought was always in everyone's mind: how many more Christmases would be spent with families separated, young men, sons and fathers in different parts of the world?

On Christmas night, before Joan lay down to sleep, she had added a postscript to the letter she'd written earlier that day: 'Roll on peacetime and we can be a proper family with a home of our own, please, God.'

Days later, when Mathew Pearson received that letter, he had to turn away from his mates – He was a soldier, fighting for his country. At that moment all he wanted was to be with his Joan, and to look down on his baby son. Even perhaps to hold him. The writing on the letter was blurred now because his eyes were brimming with tears.

One week later it was New Year's day: 1 January 1945. Still the war dragged on. Matt had written that there was a slight possibility he'd get seven days' leave, and ever since Joan had lived on that hope.

For reasons best known to the British Army, no leave was granted at that time. The days were dark and bitterly cold; even the weather seemed as if it were against everyone. There was a terrible shortage of coal, and one Monday morning,

Elizabeth Waite

when Bill Harvey was on a later shift, he declared that he was borrowing a barrow from the corner shop to go up to the coal yards at Tooting Junction with two mates in the hope that they would be allowed to buy a few sackfuls.

Three hours passed, then Joan, Daphne and Hester heard a commotion out in the street. Running to the front door, Joan turned and called, 'Come on out here, Mum! This you've got to see!'

Mother and daughter plus several female neighbours fell about laughing. 'Talk about the Black and White Minstrels,' one cheeky young housewife yelled from across the road.

Joan's dad was walking down the front path of old Granny Seymour's house, folding up a dusty coal-sack as he came. He looked every inch a cross between a chimney-sweep and a coal-miner just up from the pits, and his two mates were just as bad. Between them they had a wheel-barrow, an old pram that had a wobbly wheel, and what looked liked a bicycle with a home-made side-car attached to it. All three vehicles were loaded with half-filled sacks of coal. Well, there was as much dust as actual coal. Three more houses received a quick delivery, two where just a single elderly person lived, and the third was the home of a young mother with three children whose husband was away in the Army. When all this was finished, and the men prepared to take the remaining sacks into their own homes, a roar of thanks and applause went up from those who had been watching.

Inside the Harvey household poor Bill was dispatched to the scullery and told to strip all his clothes off. Daphne was adamant that she wasn't having him traipsing through her house shedding coal-dust.

'It's all right, Dad,' Joan laughed, 'I'll run you a bath, but

I'll have to bring you up a couple of kettles of hot water cos the fire's been nearly out and the back boiler hasn't been able to heat the water.'

Bill didn't find that funny: he ached in every limb, had coal-dust in every pore, and all the thanks he was getting for having trudged all the way to Tooting Junction and back was a cold bath!

The weeks did pass. Spring was a certainty, and suddenly the day started with the sound of raised, joyful voices. It was 8 May and on all sides could be heard, 'THE WAR IS OVER. Really it is. No, I'm not making it up.' It was difficult for people to comprehend that the day they had waited for so long had finally arrived.

'Germany has surrendered unconditionally.' The words echoed again and again, and folk everywhere sent up silent prayers of thanks.

Bonfires were lit and allowed to burn all night. Who cared now if the flames could be seen from the sky? For the first time in six years, folk felt they were entitled to laugh, sing, shout and cry with relief. Many thanked God that their menfolk had come safely through this awful war and would soon be coming home.

For others it was a sad time, a time to mourn again the loved ones they had lost, men *and* women who would never again walk into their homes. No amount of celebration could ease the pain of those folk.

Now came the demolition. Unsafe buildings had to be razed to the ground. Some whole streets had to be totally pulled down. All this left ugly bare sites throughout the length and breadth of the country, and a great shortage of houses for married men returning home from the forces. The joyful part was the removal of boarding from all the window-frames and hundred of sandbags being taken away from the outside of buildings.

Ten months passed before Matt finally got leave, but at last he was coming home to his son, who was already sixteen months old.

On this bitterly cold day in March, dressed in her winter coat, with a navy blue velvet collar, her hair freshly washed and set, Joan paced the platform of Wimbledon station in a fever. She was longing to see her husband again, yet terrified as to how they would react to each other after so long a separation. Should she have brought Jamie with her? Would Mathew be cross because she hadn't? How would Jamie react to a father who was a stranger to him?

Whistles and bursts of steam heralded the train's arrival.

She saw him! His head and shoulders were hanging out of the carriage window.

The train came into the station and shuddered to a halt. Throwing caution to the wind she ran. The moment they neared each other he dropped his kit-bag and she was safe, held close in his strong, muscular arms.

'Oh, Joanie,' he murmured, 'I've longed for this moment for so long.'

Regardless of the crowds heading for the barriers, the WVS women who were manning the tea-wagons, the train guard and the porters, they stood clinging to each other. This was their moment and they savoured it to the full.

When at last Matt released her, Joan cried, 'I still can't believe it.' Putting out a hand she touched the lean lines of his face. 'It really is you, Matt.' Suddenly she felt shy. This man, she knew, was a very different person from the easy-going lad Mathew Pearson had been the last time she saw him.

Then again she was different too: a young girl who hadn't really known her own mind when he'd left her, now a mother. 'Let's go home, Matt,' she said, with a sob in her voice.

It was another four months before Matt was finally released from the Army, and during all that time Joan stayed on at her parents' home. When Matt was on leave, it was far from the ideal situation, and worse when it looked like becoming permanent. Sleeping with Jamie in a cot beside their own bed in a room next door to her parents', Joan was embarrassed by Matt's passionate lovemaking. 'These walls are paper thin,' she would complain, which Matt would have ignored but not Joan.

That was only one of the problems that stared them in the face. Civvy Street wasn't all that men returning home had imagined it would be. Matt, like hundreds more, needed a job. His preference was to be in the East End of London, to be near to and work with his brothers, his father and his mates. And for him that was no problem: his old manager eagerly offered him his job back in the timber yards. There was also an offer, secured by his father, from the Port of London, and yet another came through his eldest brother Stan, who was employed on Butler's private riverside wharf.

There were no such offers of employment floating around Merton Park and Wimbledon where they were living, not by Matt's choice.

The final offer came from Matt's mother. She had had a word with the landlord and he had a two-bedroomed house coming vacant in Bull Yard at the end of the week. After she'd made this important announcement, there had been a dramatic pause and then, with all eyes on her, Amy had burst out, 'I've paid him a month's rent in advance, got him t' give me a rent book with Matt's name on it. Did it before 'e 'ad a chance to change his mind. Wasn't gonna let the bugger slip off the 'ook if he got a better offer. That much yer can forget about. Never did get round to giving the pair of yer a wedding present so me an' yer dad went 'alf each an' that'll give yer a bit of time to get on yer feet before you 'ave to start paying rent.'

Sitting in her mother-in-law's living room, which was crowded with various members of the family and Jamie on the lino being petted and fussed over by half a dozen kids, Joan did not know what to think, let alone say. To *her* the offer was a death knell. 'Why, that's marvellous, Mum. Bull Yard, that's not ten minutes from 'ere. You've saved our bacon,' Matt cried. Then, to Joan's dismay, he added, 'Joan's pregnant again an' we couldn't 'ave stayed in her folks' house much longer. Bad enough with one baby, never mind two.'

Joan felt herself flush a deep red. If looks could have killed, at that moment Mathew would have been stone dead. Bad enough that he was thrilled his mother had rented them a house, never mind that it was in an area she had no wish to live in, that it was miles away from her friends and family – and, what's more, that it was a place she had never set eyes on. She'd never been inside the front door and here was Matt accepting the offer and being grateful. And to top it he had blurted out that she was pregnant again. She hadn't even told her parents yet, or her nan.

She thought they had had problems before, but now they were really beginning.

Ten days later, a stern-faced Bill Harvey stood out in the street beside a tearful Daphne and Hester, and watched as

Jamie was handed up to Joan. Matt had hired an open-backed truck, which was now loaded with odd items of secondhand furniture, rolls of linoleum, several rugs, boxes of china, cooking utensils and a hamper packed with bed-linen. 'At least they've got the basic necessities,' Hester said to her daughter.

Daphne was lost for words. She had spent the last three days helping Joan to clean and decorate the small terraced house in Bull Yard, which was now to become her daughter's home. The whole area was appalling. At least, in her opinion it was.

Nearby, whole families lived on barges on the Thames, more children than you could count, scraggy-looking dogs and cats, and the adults, as well as the kiddies, looked none too clean. Was that the type of child Jamie was going to grow up with? Go to school with? If, indeed, those families ever sent their children to school. And that wasn't the worst of it: Bull Yard was narrow and dark, with houses only on one side of the road while on the opposite side stood a huge warehouse. From the windows of the house her daughter would be living in, you looked out on nothing but a great wall of sooty bricks. The most terrifying sight, although she had to admit it was magnificent, was a giant passenger liner at the bottom of the yard. At least, the ship's middle section was visible above the brick wall that formed the end of Bull Yard. It straddled the whole width of the Yard. The great ship was in dry dock, towering over the small houses and the children playing in the street. At least three of her decks and two mighty funnels were visible from Joan's doorstep.

Matt didn't give two hoots that his in-laws disapproved of his taking Joan and the baby to live in the East End of London. 'We have our own front door, our own bedroom and, most important, plenty of privacy,' he told her repeatedly, always giving her a cheeky grin.

Joan did her best to settle down in her new surroundings – at least, she thought she did. Matt didn't agree. Only this morning, before Stan had picked him up to go to work, Matt had yelled that she didn't put herself about enough and didn't mix with his family as much as she should.

Left on her own at only seven o'clock in the morning, another long, lonely day stretched out in front of her. Closing the front door behind him, Joan ran her fingers through her hair, then went back to the kitchen to clear away the breakfast things. She felt miserable and frustrated. She knew the rows were partly her own fault, but her idea of a good weekend was not going from pub to pub, watching the men play darts or snooker and listening to the women gossip. In her whole life she had not felt quite as she did now, so agitated with her temper on such a tight rein. Normally she was calm, in control.

But her world had never been turned upside down before. Only weeks to go and she would have another baby to care for, and that meant more washing. There was nowhere to hang a washing line, except out in the street, and Joan couldn't bring herself to do that.

With a heavy sigh, she poured boiling water from the kettle into a bowl and began to wash up. Thank God Jamie was blessed with a sunny disposition and a cheerful personality. For one so young he was great company. Funny thing was, Matt didn't take much notice of him. All he ever said was it would be great when he could take him to the speedway and to football matches. 'And to pubs,' was what Joan always felt tempted to add. Maybe she should feel grateful that she was about to have another baby: he or she would be company for Jamie. But money was so short, or at least it was for household goods, baby clothes and things like that.

Matt gave her five pounds a week, and that wasn't too bad as far as food went – she had to make sure there was plenty on the table or there would have been ructions. But there was never any money left over, at least not where she was concerned, at any rate. Friday night, Saturday and Sunday Matt spent freely, and to give him his due she could have had anything she asked for when they went out, just so long as it came in a glass and was handed over the bar of one of the numerous public houses that the Pearson family and their mates seemed to spend half their lives in.

By the time she was heavy with this second baby Joan was listless. She had tried to change a good many things in her day-to-day life but it was useless. She would just have to put up with it, was the conclusion she had reached. She no longer hoped that Matt would change, for she'd realized that that was like asking for the top brick off the chimney.

Her first daughter was born in the same hospital as Jamie, just six days after Jamie's second birthday. Less than five months later when she realized that she was pregnant once more Joan gave up worrying. She got by, taking each day as it came, coping with whatever life threw at her. But only just.

Her second daughter was born at home, in the upstairs front bedroom with only an elderly midwife in attendance. After that birth, to the horror of her parents and her grandmother, she let herself go. She hadn't argued when her in-laws suggested that the first girl be given the posh name of Margaret, although she had thought that inevitably she would be called Maggie. And Joan had been right. She hadn't protested either when the midwife had declared her second girl as sweet as a rose, and Matt had decided that that should be her name.

She kept the children clean and tidy, no complaints there, and she cooked good, hearty meals and kept the house as clean as possible against all the odds of London dirt and grime. As to herself, it was as if she had given up all hope of ever having a better life.

The funny thing was, Matt adored his two daughters. They were lovely little girls, as alike as two peas in a pod, so pretty with light auburn hair and the same colouring and beautiful skin as Joan, her mother and grandmother still boasted. They had cherubic faces, covered in freckles, and were always laughing and into mischief. They were certainly their daddy's girls, and Matt spoilt them rotten.

Jamie was different: very protective of his sisters but quieter in every respect. He was doing well at school. His teachers were pleased with his work, and Joan was thrilled with his reports.

Matt wasn't: he believed he should be out and about, roughing it with other boys, even getting into trouble around the dockyards. That was what boys did, not sit hour after hour with their nose stuck in a book. Matt never looked at a book, and the fact that Jamie liked to read was becoming an obsession with his father.

Joan often thought that at times Matt made life so difficult.

Of course, looking back she had known there were two sides to his character when she married him. To say he was outspoken would be putting it mildly. And he had to have everything his way, no matter what. If his brothers were going to the pub, then Matt went with them. Nothing was allowed to stand in his way, especially if there was a darts match to be played.

On a day when she wasn't feeling too washed out, Joan would tell herself that, when all was said and done, Matt was a good husband and she could have done worse. Oh, yes, as her mother-in-law was fond of telling her when she complained, much worse.

So the time went on and as a family they muddled through, until Jamie came to sit his eleven-plus examination. The boy tried so hard. He could please most people but hardly ever his father. He did go to football matches with his dad and every single week to the speedway. He was enthusiastic about motorbikes but not nearly as keen as Matt.

Joan listened to their conversations and her heart ached for her son. Matt taunted him, she didn't know why. His mind was set on Jamie leaving school at the earliest possible age and going to work with one of his uncles or with himself. Schooling got you nowhere, was Matt's view and he wouldn't change it for anyone. Good, hard work was what paid dividends, according to him, and despite all Joan's pleading, he would never give Jamie any encouragement when it came to academic subjects.

Ah, well, she sighed, trying hard to put it out of her mind, if things don't alter, they'll stay as they are.

Chapter Nine

THERE WERE TIMES when Joan felt the whole world was changing around her yet, try as she would, her life never did, from one year's end to the next. Well, not for the better, it didn't. There had been that letter from the council, which had arrived more than a month ago stating that the houses in Bull Yard were due for demolition and that they would be advised as to where the tenants were to be relocated.

Not rehoused! Oh, no. Relocated, as if they were pieces of machinery.

Matt said houses in Bull Yard were nothing whatsoever to do with the council, to burn the letter and not to worry about it. She couldn't help but worry, and more so since her next-door neighbours on both sides had told her about their visit to the town hall.

'Definitely going to be in one of the new blocks of flats up near the Angel, Islington,' was what Doris Shepherd insisted she'd been told, while on the other hand May Brown said her information had been along the same lines but in a different area. Either way, Joan dreaded to think how she was going to cope in any of these new high-rise blocks of flats. How could she keep an eye on her children if they were playing out on the street and she was indoors up several flights of stairs? Her sisters-in-law had thrown in their opinion. According to them, she and Matt should count themselves lucky that they'd probably be getting a three-bedroom flat with a proper bathroom and a modern kitchen.

An indoor lavatory would be a dream come true. So would a nice bathroom – now she had to drag the tin bath in from the yard. Apart from those two factors, though, Joan was convinced that if they were rehoused in any one of those horrible cement columns with windows, it would be a change, all right, but a change for the worse. Still it had been quite a while since the letter had arrived, so it was still a case of wait and see.

As usual, at this time in the morning, she was alone. Jamie had left home at a quarter past eight – he liked to get to school early – and the two girls had left home at twenty to nine because the junior school they went to was only a five-minute walk from the house. She was bored. How long would it take her to make the beds and put a duster round the rooms? And then what?

How often she wished she had a reason every day to leave this dismal house – to go out to work. Any job would do, just so long as it brought her into contact with people. People who would talk about something other than what was on sale up the market or which pub they were all going to on Saturday evening. Besides the company, a little cash she could call her own wouldn't go amiss.

What had Matt to say when she broached this subject? 'You can forget it! No wife of mine is going out to work.

A woman should be at home, looking after the kids and keeping the place nice.' He should have added, 'And have my dinner on the table at whatever time I tell you I want it, and a clean shirt and jacket laid out on the bed on the nights I play snooker or darts.'

Matt had been like a dog with a bone. He just wouldn't let the matter drop. 'I can just hear my mates talking among themselves, sniggering behind my back cos my wife 'as t' work to help support my kids.'

'You and I both know that's not the reason I'd like to go out to work,' she had pleaded.

'Maybe not, Joan, but I'm telling yer, that's what they'll think. Just you remember that I'm the man in this house and I pay for the food that goes on our table, and I make the decisions, not you.'

She had tried so hard to stand her ground with Matt, asking, 'Why does it matter what people think?'

'Leave it. I don't want to 'ear another word.' And with that he had brought his fist down on the table so hard that all the dishes had rattled.

She had been too frightened to pursue the matter any further, but that didn't stop her from thinking that because Matt had married her he had no right to control her, as he seemed to believe. In the end she had given in: arguing with him was like bashing her head against a brick wall.

So much was happening outside her little world. Every time she picked up a paper or saw the news at the cinema she wished she could be a part of it all. Take television: Matt had gone spare when she suggested they might rent one, yet if folk were to be believed you could sit in your own home and watch a film, see big dance bands and hear plays. There was talk of major sports such as football being televised. If that came about then Matt would be first in the queue. Another thing: telephones in private houses weren't rare now – her own mum and dad had one. She'd have to live a long time before one would be installed in this house. Asking for a new pair of curtains was like asking for the crown jewels, never mind a telephone.

Slowly she climbed the narrow flight of stairs. These walls hadn't seen a coat of paint in all the ten years they'd lived here. Matt's view on that was that there was a major crack running right through the middle wall of the house and that things were best left untouched. Ah, well, nobody had everything they wanted in this life.

Maggie and Rosie had both been cross with her last week because she wouldn't buy them each an Elvis Presley record. She'd never heard of him until Laura, her sister-in-law, explained that he was a truck-driver in America who had shot to fame and become the king of rock 'n' roll. Needless to say, Matt had given in to the girls. He'd bought records for both girls, and now Joan knew the words of both songs off by heart, because the girls played them endlessly.

She began by pulling the bedclothes off the twin beds in the room the girls shared. She wished they had a garden, instead of just a yard that was only slightly bigger than the shed that housed the lavatory. Oh, well, it would get her out of the house if she took the sheets up to the wash-house. At least other women would be there to talk to.

Stripping the cases off the pillows her eye caught sight of a poster on the wall of Princess Margaret. The girls always reckoned they had been named Margaret and Rose because they were the two names given to the Princess. It wasn't true. At the time the thought had never entered her head. Nevertheless she did not disillusion her daughters, rather she encouraged them to follow the life of Princess Margaret and, indeed, the whole of the Royal Family. Gazing again at the picture, which had been cut from a magazine, she felt sad for Princess Margaret. She and that Group Captain Peter Townsend had appeared to be so much in love with one another. Now it was all off. The announcement had come on the wireless: the Princess had decided not to marry him because he was divorced. Such a shame. Joan felt she had been pressured into making that decision and not for the first time wondered why individuals weren't allowed to make up their own minds.

With the upstairs two bedrooms sorted, she came down, her arms full of dirty sheets, which she dumped in the passage. Now to see to Jamie's bed. She couldn't say bedroom cos the poor boy didn't have one. Until Rosie was born, when Maggie had slept in the big bedroom with Matt and herself, Jamie had had the other. With the coming of Rosie, Matt had decided that two beds in the small room was best for the girls, and Jamie got a Put-U-Up in the front room.

As Joan pushed open the door she smiled to herself: she was proud of this room. It was one battle with Matt she had won. The focal point of the room was the fireplace and she made sure that every Sunday a fire was lit in the hearth and they had their Sunday tea in there and spent the evening in comfort. Six days a week was quite enough to live in the kitchen. Matt had argued that most folk lit a fire in the front room only on high days and holidays. The tiled surround was surmounted by a heavy wooden mantelpiece. On this stood a small clock, two brass candlesticks and a framed photograph of each of the three children. The hearth was protected by a heavy brass fender, her pride and joy. She cleaned it regularly every Friday and it glittered like gold in the dancing flames of the fire. Two brown corded-velvet armchairs stood at each side of the fireplace, and the brown and fawn tweedy-looking settee was placed beneath the window. This was what served, when folded down, as a bed for Jamie.

He was a good lad: he never failed to leave the room fairly tidy.

The minute his father left the house of a morning, at about seven o'clock, Jamie was up, washing and dressing in the scullery. His clothes were kept in half of the wardrobe that held hers and she had managed to find him a tiny chest of drawers, which just about fitted against the wall of the small landing. It wasn't the best of situations but, as always, Matt disputed that his son was hard-done-by. As a young lad himself, he'd had to share a bed with two of his brothers and he considered Jamie lucky to have a bed to himself.

Looking up the passage to the front door Joan saw that some post was lying on the mat. Postman must have been late today, she thought, bending to pick it up. One letter was for Mr M. Pearson, probably setting a date for yet another darts match, and there was a postcard from her mother, which she read at a glance. 'Coming up to visit you tomorrow. Bringing your nan with me. Expect us about 11 o'clock. Love, Mum.'

That set her brain ticking over. Whatever could it mean? How many times had her parents been to visit them since they'd lived in this house? Three, maybe four times at most. She went home, as she still referred to it in her own mind, as often as she could, always taking the children with her. Never once had Matt accompanied her. God, she could remember the time when the children had had half-term and once during the long summer holidays when she had dared to suggest that she and the children spend a couple of weeks down at Merton Park and that Matt could come and stay at weekends. She might just as well have been suggesting that they fly to the moon, for all the notice Matt took of her. Her place was here, in the home that *he* provided. And nothing she'd been able to think of had shifted him.

Well, this certainly was giving her something to think about now.

She popped the card into her bag, packed the laundry into the special sack she kept for that purpose, changed her shoes, donned her coat and set off for the wash-house, which was in the next street. On one corner of Bull Yard there stood a big red pillarbox and on the opposite corner there was a metal rubbish bin.

The thought came into her head, Get rid of that card.

Why should I? she questioned herself. Because if, for any reason, Matt should find it and read it, he would want some answers and want them quick. It was ten to one he'd convince himself something was going on that he should know about. She wouldn't be able to tell him a thing because she had nothing to tell. She couldn't fathom why her mum and her nan were coming up to visit her, but Matt wouldn't take that for gospel truth and he'd more than likely finish up belting her round the head again. He was becoming too fond of doing that and the last blow had given her a headache that lasted for days. So, having reasoned all that out with herself, Joan crossed to the other side of the street, propped the sack of bed-linen against the wall, took the postcard out of her handbag and tore it into strips. With a slight smile she pushed the pieces down into the litter-bin. Time enough to tell Matt after the visit. Then she would swear her life away that it had been a total surprise, them coming to see her after all this time. Well, it was, wasn't it? She didn't tell lies. Well, maybe white ones when it suited her.

It had turned half past eleven. I stayed too long chatting, Joan was saying to herself, as she hurried down Bull Yard carrying her sack of damp washing. The girls will be home for their lunch soon and I meant to iron a load of this washing before then. Jamie always had his mid-day meal at school and Matt at work, so she and the girls only had a snack and she cooked the main dinner at night.

Having finished laying the table for three, Joan set the big pan of soup nearer to the hot-plate of the range and began to cut thick slices from the new loaf of bread she had bought at the Jewish bakery. Nobody made bread better than Mr Isaacs did. She grinned and smothered butter on a slice and munched it contentedly. She heard the front door bang open and two voices calling, 'Mum, Mum, there's a man here says he wants to talk to you.'

Maggie and Rosie came flying down the passage and flung themselves at their mother. Joan bent down, kissed the tops of their heads and hugged them both to her. Then she raised her face and smiled at the gentleman standing on her top step. He was tall, well-built and, with the heavy overcoat he was wearing, broad-shouldered. Very masculine, she decided. He wore a trilby hat, which he removed, showing blond hair, a fair complexion and friendly grey eyes.

'Mrs Pearson?' he asked.

'Yes.'

'Mr Stevens, your housing officer.' He smiled, holding

out his hand for Joan to shake, which she did, without enthusiasm. 'We don't have a housing officer,' she told him firmly. 'All these houses in Bull Yard are privately owned.'

'Not any more.' He shook his head to emphasize what he was telling her. 'Several properties in this area have been acquired by the council under a compulsory-purchase act and are now due to be demolished.'

'Oh, yes, and where does that leave us?'

'We have a duty to rehouse every tenant. You were sent a letter laying out all the facts and offering further information and advice if you cared to visit the town hall.'

'We did get the letter but my husband said at the time that we were protected by our landlord.'

'Well, Mrs Pearson, your husband has got it wrong.'

Quick as a flash, Joan flung at him, 'Come back when he's home and try telling *him* that! Anyway, I haven't the time to chat to you now. I have to give my girls their meal and get them back to school.'

She was half-way to closing the street door when he thrust out his arm and said, 'Just one minute and then I'll leave you. The point of my being here now is to invite you to view a few of the flats that we shall be offering you as alternative accommodation. Sorry it's such short notice, but if you wish to take me up on the offer could you be outside Whitechapel Underground station at two thirty this afternoon? A colleague and I will be there to meet a group of you.'

Well, that was a turn-up for the books!

Joan still hadn't made up her mind if she was going. It was as she stood at her front gate, seeing the girls off back to school, that it was made up for her. Doris Shepherd opened her front door and called, 'Shall we walk up together?' And when Joan didn't answer straight away, she added, 'You are gonna come along and see what's on offer? I thought it was just as well for some of us t' be nosy. May Brown isn't in, she's working today, so I'll 'ave t' tell her about this Mr Stevens ternight.' She looked at Joan urgently and repeated, 'You are gonna come?'

'Yes, all right, Doris, I'll walk up there with you. Give me a shout when you're ready t' go.'

The Whitechapel Road, with its wide pavements, still delighted Joan. She had never got used to the traders, their stalls and their barrows. They whipped fruit from the stall to the scales and into a paper bag all in one swift movement. Vegetables were ladled up in a brass scoop, weighed, and shot straight into the customer's shopping bag. No dithering as to the cost. These men had been brought up on mental arithmetic. 'That lot'll cost yer five an' six, me ole darlin'. Six bob? 'Old on, I'll get yer a tanner change.'

After all this time their chatter still made her smile.

When they arrived at the tube station Mr Stevens was there. Only three women besides themselves had bothered to turn up, and Mr Stevens introduced his assistant as Marie Wilkinson. She looked to be in her early twenties, and had long dark hair tied back in a plait.

'What are you going t' do if we don't like any of the places you're offering? We could refuse to move, you know,' Doris Shepherd asked as they reached the entrance of the first block of flats they were about to view.

Without any hesitation the young woman snapped, 'We'd apply for an order to evict you.'

'Well, thanks a bunch.'

And all four other women joined Doris in her condemnation.

'That's great that is.'

'Take what you offer or else.'

'Never mind what we want, just chuck us out in the streets.'

'Big-hearted – is that what they call you, Miss, down at the town hall?'

'Now, now, ladies, please, Miss Wilkinson was merely pointing out that we must find somewhere to suit each and every one of you.' Mr Stevens had his job cut out, trying to be a peacemaker.

The foyer of the flats smelt of new paint. Already several families were living there but they had only been moved in recently, according to Mr Stevens.

Joan looked across at Doris and knew they shared a sense of dismay. There was a clutter of toys. Two bicycles and a pushchair that had lost a wheel lay side by side, and a sack of rubbish had burst, spilling empty baked-bean tins and wet newspaper over the floor. But it was the walls that were so appalling: somebody had written in bright red wobbly letters every swear word you could think of and the name of a girl who apparently gave her favours for free.

'What are you going to do about that?' one woman asked, pointing to the graffiti on the walls.

'We're not sure yet,' Mr Stevens answered, keeping his voice low.

'Typical council attitude,' the woman said, tossing her head.

They split into two groups to ride up in the lift to the seventh floor.

There Miss Wilkinson put a key into a lock and flung open the door on to an empty set of rooms. The view from the wide, uncurtained windows was fantastic: out over the rooftops of London, and in the distance the mighty Thames winding its way ever onwards. The kitchen had cupboards fitted to the walls, and in a corner stood a shiny but tinny-looking gas-stove. 'Cost a fortune to feed the meter and cook by that thing,' a woman said, nodding in disgust.

The bathroom! And, oh, the toilet! Sheer joy. Three bedrooms. Jamie would get a room of his own. Joan was almost convinced. Tempted for sure.

The door to the flat had been left open, and Miss Wilkinson could be heard arguing with a group of boys who had been standing on the landing when they had arrived.

'And who the fucking 'ell is gonna make us do it?' the lads were jeering at her.

Joan took a step backwards, while Doris Shepherd went forward and was peering down over the railings of the balcony. 'Blimey, it's a damn long way down. I've got four kids. What am I supposed t' do with them if we lived up here?' she asked of no one in particular.

'Chuck 'em over the bloody balcony if they git on yer nerves, missus,' grinned the tallest of the five lads.

'Yeah, then yer can always go down and scrape 'em up like a load of strawberry jam,' his mate volunteered.

Mr Stevens wasn't at all pleased at the way things were going, and he wasn't surprised when the oldest woman in the group said, 'I've seen more than enough for one day, thank you very much. If you can't come up with something better than these flats then I'll stay where I am, compulsory-purchase order or not. Wild horses wouldn't drag me from my little house to live 'alf-way up to the sky with nothing but riff-raff for neighbours.'

A set of heads nodded agreement as the group walked towards the lift.

'I'll see you back at the office,' Marie Wilkinson called to Mr Stevens as, without so much as a goodbye, she ran off, dodging between the groups of children playing hopscotch outside the entrance to the flats.

Doris and Joan both shook Mr Stevens's hand. If anything, they felt sorry for him: he was only trying to do his job. Blooming difficult job it was an' all, they agreed, as they set off to walk home.

'I've got a feeling we haven't seen the last of him,' Joan muttered sadly.

'No. You're probably right,' Doris reluctantly concurred.

Chapter Ten

JOAN HAD BEEN up since the crack of dawn. She had even walked the short distance to school with her two girls. It was a lovely day, considering it was late October, sunny but bitterly cold. One of those days that so often occur in the autumn, just before winter sets in.

In her kitchen all was ready for her mum and her nan. The air was fragrant with the smell of freshly baked pies, and on the dresser she had set two fruit cakes to cool before she took them out of the tins. She had filled one of the pies with Bramley apples and the smell of cloves and cinnamon was strong.

She was washing and drying all of her cooking utensils. It was still only ten o'clock and she wasn't expecting her visitors until after eleven so she glanced up in surprise when she heard the front door open. Her mother walked in, followed by her nan. God, they were a sight for sore eyes! They both looked as if they'd just stepped out of a band-box. Smart and trim down to the last detail, they could easily have passed for sisters rather than mother and daughter.

'You're nice an' early,' Joan said to her mother, as she threw her arms about her. 'Hallo, Nan. Cor, don't you look posh! New winter coat, is it? Come on over to the fire, take your coats off. I'll make a pot of tea.'

'Joan,' her mother laughed, 'will you please stop talking for a minute and give us a chance to get inside the door?'

The kettle was hissing and steaming on the range, as it always was in winter, and Joan spooned tea into her enamel teapot, then filled it with boiling water. She placed it on the table beside a tray she had already set with her best cups and saucers, seated herself and looked across to where her mother and her nan were now sitting, one each side of the fire.

'I suppose Dad's working,' she said. Then, without waiting for a reply, she pressed on, 'I'm dying to know what's brought you two up to see me.'

Daphne flushed, but she did not reply since this trip and the reason for it had been her mother's idea. Not that she hadn't gone along with it. She had. Wholeheartedly.

'I'm about to poke my nose into your business,' Hester volunteered. 'I've been worried sick since you wrote and told us you were probably going to have to get out of this house and be rehoused in a flat. I want you to know that I can get you a house in Morden.'

'I see.' Joan sat up straighter and stared hard at her grandmother. All kinds of thoughts were buzzing around in her head. Morden, in Surrey, was near to where her parents lived and such a nice place. It would be like living in the country. She then sighed the deepest of sighs and murmured, 'Matt would never go for it.'

'You haven't heard what I've got to say. I want you to listen to me,' Hester said, leaning forward, fixing her eyes on Joan's.

'All right,' Joan said, putting her cup down on the saucer, instantly aware of her nan's stern tone.

'We, your mum an' dad as well as myself, feel you're facing a serious problem and it's about time you let us help you. It came about like this. A young woman I've worked with up at the hospital for some time now told me she was taking her mother to live with her for reasons that I won't go into now. She also said she was putting her mother's house on the market but was complaining at how much of the sale price would get eaten up in the estate agent's fee and how much better it would be if she could find a private buyer. That's when the idea came to me. It would solve all your problems.'

'Problems?' Joan's voice was little more than a whisper. 'We've not got more than most.'

'Come on, now, Joan, don't play dumb with me. You've let yourself go downhill badly these past few years, which is one signal that everything is not exactly right. And we don't see anywhere near enough of you and the children.'

Joan noticed her nan did not include Matt.

'Nan, we've no money to buy a house.'

'I've nowhere near finished telling you why I've come here today, so please, Joan, be patient. When your grandfather died he hadn't made a will. He hadn't got a lot of savings but he did have a lump sum due from his employers and quite a hefty amount from an insurance policy. I also draw a pension from his firm. I don't go out to work because I need the money. I do it to get me out of the house and to meet people.'

Joan smiled, knowing exactly what her nan meant.

'I want you to have some of your granddad's money. It's what he would have wanted, and you know that's true. I got this young friend of mine to invite me home to meet her mother. The youngsters are not selling her house just to get the money. I made sure of that. She'd only be moving a few streets away, still near enough to visit her friends, and the money from the sale of her house is going to go towards building a self-contained apartment on the back of her daughter's house. The mother won't feel so lonely, she'll have her own place still, and an income from the money remaining from the sale.'

Hester paused for breath and Daphne moved her chair away from the fire, saying, 'I've soon got warm in here. Is there any more tea left in that pot?'

Joan jumped to her feet. 'Oh, Mum, I am sorry. I've been so intent on what Nan's been saying that I've not offered you anything to eat.'

Daphne waved away her protests. 'I'll see to the tea and you hear your gran out. Time enough then for you to feed us.'

Hester took a deep breath. 'The asking price for this house is eight hundred pounds.' She had to stop talking because Joan had gasped so loudly. 'Sounds a lot, doesn't it? But, as a gift from your granddad, we could pay one hundred pounds down, and from what I've learnt, the repayments over fifteen or twenty years would be about four pounds twelve shillings a month. Also out of your granddad's money I would be able to pay all your legal fees and the removal costs.'

'Oh, Nan! You make it all sound so easy. But where would Matt get a job? That was the main reason we had to come and live in the East End in the first place.'

'Things are different now. Your dad has made enquiries and the best and quickest way would be for Matt to keep his job and get the tube straight up from Morden station.'

'If only it were that simple.' Joan felt tears burn the backs of her eyes. 'I'll see about some lunch now. The girls will be in any minute – they didn't want to go to school this morning when I told them you were coming.'

'How about Jamie? Will he be coming home?' Hester asked hopefully.

'No, he's got further to come so he has school dinners.'

Between them Daphne and Joan soon had the table laid. Potatoes and a saucepan of mixed pot-herbs had been slowly simmering on the back of the range, and in the slow oven to the side there was a golden-topped steak and kidney pie. Daphne was stirring the gravy when the door burst open and Rosie ran into the kitchen, followed more sedately by Maggie.

'You did come, Gran, you an' all, Nan,' Rosie yelled, throwing her school hat and scarf on a chair. Her coat followed, and she flung herself at Hester.

Maggie, who was taking off her own coat, said, 'I can't believe you've both come. Wish Granddad was here too.' She kissed them both in turn.

Daphne looked at her two lovely granddaughters and her heart ached. They were growing up so quickly and what her mother had said was true: they didn't see them very often, and when Joan did bring them down to Merton Park they were never allowed to stay for a few days.

Hester's thoughts were running along the same lines. There were four generations of females in this kitchen. Maggie was nine with huge green eyes like her mother's and bright red-gold hair. Her sister, seven-year-old Rosie, was a bit of a scatterbrain, but her winning smiles and fanciful chatter endeared her to everyone. In fact, we all have the same colouring, the same build and the same friendly nature, she was thinking, as she looked from one to the other.

Now she was praying hard. She had spent a few sleepless nights, pondering whether or not it was right for her to interfere in Joan and Matt's lives. Pops had settled the question for her. Oh, yes, if she said that aloud to anyone they would have thought she was mad because, of course, he was dead. But there was times, especially when she needed him, that he was never far away and talk to him she did. Out loud at times. She spent so many hours on her own. She was lucky, and she realized it only too well, to have Daphne and Bill living only doors away, but she didn't impose and when she wanted advice she felt somehow that it was Pops who gave it to her. And despite all the arguments that Matt would put up, she was going to do her damnedest to see that Joan and her lovely children didn't end up in a tenement flat.

After a happy, jolly lunchtime, Daphne and Hester walked the two girls back to school. There were hugs and kisses at the gate, promises that they would see them soon. 'Your granddad has sent you and Jamie some pocket money, and we'll leave it with your mum,' their gran called after them.

Maggie stopped dead in her tracks, turned and came back. 'Aren't you going to be here this afternoon when we get home?'

Daphne shook her head. 'No, love, we're going to get the train before the rush-hour starts. Besides, it gets dark so early and your granddad would start to worry if we weren't home when he gets in from work.'

Maggie looked thoughtful for a moment. 'I see.' She reached up and planted another kiss on Daphne's cheek. 'That one's for Granddad. Tell him we all love him.'

Daphne was too choked to answer. She nodded and waved at Rosie, who was standing still, waiting for her sister.

Time was getting short, and Hester felt she still hadn't made her point. They were hardly inside the house before she began again. 'Would you like to hear about the house, Joan?'

Joan laid aside the tea-towel she had been using to dry the lunchtime dishes, and turned to face her nan. 'What would be the point? I'm sure it must be a nice house but what chance do I have of ever getting out of here and going to live in Surrey?'

'If Pops were here, d'you know what he would say?'

Joan shook her head.

'Don't be such a pessimist, that's what he'd say. He'd also tell you that in this life, if you want something bad enough and you try hard enough, you'll get it in the end.'

'Sounds lovely when you say it, Nan. But how do I convince Matt – and, more to the point, his family? Because believe you me, Nan, the Pearson family will have a great deal to say about whether or not their beloved Matt moves away to the other side of the river.'

'We'll cross that bridge when we come to it,' Hester said, knowing she was beginning to sound cross. 'Now, listen, these houses I'm talking about were built not long before the war started. This one in particular is very close to Ravensbury Park. It has three bedrooms, well, two fair-size ones and a box room, which is still big enough for a single bed, a bathroom and a separate toilet all on the first floor. Downstairs there's a sitting room, a dining room, and a big kitchen. Half-way up the stairs, there's a window and on the window-sill my friend's mother had a beautiful trailing plant. There was a light, airy feeling about the whole of the house. It had a happy atmosphere. But,' and here Hester paused and stared straight at Joan, 'I've saved the best bit till last. There's a long back garden, which borders on to the park. The lady has most of it laid to grass but there's rose bushes and two trees down at the bottom.'

'Oh, Nan,' Joan moaned, 'how I wish!' But what she was asking herself was, could I convince Matt? She was sure he could afford the monthly repayments on this house. He was better off than he let on to her. She was convinced of that.

Immediately after they had come to live in Bull Yard he had gone to work with his brother Stan, and eventually, after talking about it for ages, they had set up on their own. He no longer worked in the timber yards and he had given the dockyards a try but working with his father hadn't suited him at all well. Stan did most of the costing and the paper-work while, as far as she could make out because Pearson men did not discuss business with their womenfolk, Matt acted as the foreman when they were busy with local projects.

Joan smiled at her nan. 'Seems ever so strange that I got your postcard yesterday saying you were coming today and yesterday afternoon I went to view a flat.'

'Oh, Joan,' her mother exclaimed sadly, 'so it's come about, even though Matt said they wouldn't be able to get you out of this house.'

'Afraid so, Mum. A council officer called here yesterday morning and when Doris Shepherd, from next door, and I told him these were privately owned houses he soon put us right. Said there had been a compulsory-purchase order on most of the properties around here. Clearance of the whole site was how he put it.'

'And how was the flat?' Hester asked.

Joan resisted the urge to swear. 'Nothing wrong with the flat – the inside could be made into a very nice home. Trouble was the area, the kind of people who are already living there, and the fact that the one we were shown was on the seventh floor and there were five more floors above that.'

'Oh, my Lord!' Hester gasped, striving not to show how horrified she was. 'Tell you what, bring the children down for the day on Saturday. We'll leave them with your father and I'll ask my friend if her mother will let you look over the house. See what you think of it. Then we'll see what we can do.'

Can you work a miracle? was what Joan was wondering, as she walked back home from seeing her mum and her nan board a tram to take them to the railway station.

She was so lost in thought that she almost jumped out of her skin when she walked into her kitchen and saw her mother-in-law and her sister-in-law seated at her kitchen table. 'Hallo, Amy, Bertha,' she said.

'Knew the key was on a string so we let ourselves in when Doris next door said you'd gone to the tram stop with your mum and your nan,' Amy told her.

Well, I'll be blowed. Everyone knows everybody else's business around here before it even happens, Joan thought, as she made tea for her second lot of visitors. Setting out her best cups again Joan placed what was left of the cakes she had made in the centre of the table, picked up a long-bladed knife and cut some slices. 'They're both recipes that you've given me over the years, Amy, but I never think my cakes turn out as well as yours do.' She smiled as she slid two slices on to pretty plates and set one in front of Bertha and the other for Amy.

First sipping her tea then nibbling her cake, Amy nodded in approval before she said, 'We 'eard you'd been to view a flat yesterday. Is that's why yer mum came up today?'

Once again Joan was astounded. Talk about bush telegraph!

'How could my mum possibly know that I went to see a flat?'

'They're on the telephone, aren't they?'

'Yes, but I hardly ever phone them.'

'So why did they come? 'Tain't often they do.'

Joan knew her mother-in-law had her trapped. She couldn't think of a plausible story on the spur of the moment, and she could hardly tell her to mind her own business. 'My nan has a friend who has a house for sale and she thought it might do for Matt and me. It has three bedrooms so it would be ideal for the children.'

'And I suppose this 'ouse is on the other side of the river, near to your parents?' Amy retorted swiftly.

'What difference does that make?' Joan protested indignantly.

Amy pretended to sigh. 'Matt is an East-End boy, his work is here. What would he do if he lived down south?'

Joan's temper was rising, though she was striving to keep it under control. 'There are such things as trains and buses, but that's not the point you're trying to make, is it, Amy?'

The air was heavy with silence. Joan shot a glance at Bertha, who merely shrugged her shoulders.

She had another try. 'You mean Matt wouldn't be able to make constant visits to you or go out night after night with his brothers and their mates. Well, think about me for a change. I've had to put up with being so far away from my folk ever since we got married.'

Amy shook her head. 'You don't understand, lass. That's the way of it in our working-class world. The men work 'ard, take care of all the bills and see that there's always plenty of grub on the table. In return for that you surely can't begrudge them a few pints, a game of darts or snooker, a laugh or two in male company?'

'No, of course I don't. But there are times when I would like to go out with my husband. Do things together. Take the children to see my parents a bit more often.'

'But Matt offers yer to come out every weekend and you used to. Now you don't. Too rowdy for you, are we?'

Joan's face tightened in annoyance, and she spoke the next words in haste. 'What I would like is to be allowed to get a job. Do something useful, meet people and have a bit of money to call my own.'

'Do what? My sons would never agree to their wives going out to work!' Amy exclaimed, sounding horrified. 'It would make Matt feel less of a man. Whatever would people think? I think it's downright terrible that you should even think of such a thing. Matt works 'ard. Neither you nor his three kids go short. You ought to think about appreciating him a bit more.'

Joan stared at her mother-in-law in utter astonishment. This was 1955 and she was talking as if they were still in the Dark Ages. What she almost yelled in reply was, 'I don't give a damn what people think!' Instead she bit back the words and took a deep breath.

Suddenly she felt she was fighting a losing battle. She had often thought that Amy regarded her as standoffish, even a snob, but what could she do about it? True, she came from a different background, but she had done her best to adapt herself to their way of life. Oh, I have, I have, she was saying over and over in her mind, but a damn lot of good it seems to have done me. She turned to look at Bertha. Now, she had always been her friend. Both she and Laura had been kind to her. You could say they had initiated her into the ways of the East End. It wasn't their fault that she hadn't knuckled down and acted as if she had been born there. She and Bertha now exchanged a knowing glance.

Joan jumped to her feet and made sure she was smiling when she looked at Amy and said, 'I'll make a fresh brew, shall I?'

She felt relieved when Amy shot her an answering grin, which let her know that she had had her say and as long as Joan took her words to heart they could go on being friends.

Well, it was all to the good to let her think she had won the day . . . But she can talk till she's blue in the face! I'm still going to do whatever it takes to make Matt come round to my way of thinking. Moving to Surrey *had* to be a good move for all of them.

This was one time when she was going to have things done her way or she'd know the reason why.

Chapter Eleven

JOAN WAS TERRIFIED. She and Matt were standing in the entrance to Manor Park Court, which was another block of flats they had gone to view. Only yards away men and boys were fighting, their voices loud in anger, fists flying, language disgusting. She had the feeling that Matt was about to dash forward to help what looked like a woman lying on the floor surrounded by not only burly-looking men but several teenage boys, who were leaving the fighting to the men but were kicking the woman's body.

Matt pushed Joan backwards but then she screamed: knives were flashing. 'Christ, this is getting positively dangerous,' she heard Matt mutter. The sound of sirens filled the air, blue lights were flashing, and from every direction police cars were screeching to a halt.

Matt stopped dead. He turned, grabbed her arm and hissed into her ear, 'For Christ's sake, let's get out of here.'

Her feet barely touched the ground as he propelled her along. Within minutes they were outside a pub and for once

Matt walked past the public bar and pushed open the door to the saloon. He practically pushed Joan down on to a seat and said, 'What do you want? Beer or a short?'

Joan did her best to smile. 'I think I need a whisky tonight, please, Matt.'

He returned with a tray that held two double whiskies, a dry ginger for Joan and a pint of beer for himself. He flopped down beside her and lit a cigarette. He drew heavily on it, letting the smoke go deep into his lungs, then tossed a third of the whisky down his throat before taking a sip of his beer.

Not a word had passed between them when the double doors were pushed open and three men made for the bar. Joan didn't know where to look. One – he was hardly more than a boy – had blood streaming from a cut to the side of his head. A second man was holding out his hands to his mates, both fists bloody. The third man was smartly dressed and had obviously not been involved in the fight, but as he glanced towards where she and Matt were sitting Joan was scared. The fierce look in his eyes sent a chill right through her.

It was Saturday night, and all Joan could think now was, I shouldn't be here, I should have gone home today. Gone with my nan to view that house.

Matt had put a stop to her plans. He wouldn't even let her finish telling him the details of the house. The very next morning, at seven o'clock, Mr Stevens, the housing officer, had again appeared on their doorstep. The long and short of his visit was a declaration that he had been ordered to deliver in person. It stated quite plainly that all tenants had until 21 January 1956 to relocate into alternative housing or face being evicted on to the streets. Mr Stevens had also handed Matt three addresses of flats from which he could take his choice.

Faced with such an ultimatum Matt agreed they would have to start looking at whatever was on offer. On Saturday evening he had grudgingly agreed to go with her and view the first of the three addresses on the list.

For days afterwards Joan asked herself if that fight and the police raid had been a lucky break. Depends on which side of the fence you were standing, she would answer, feeling grateful at the same time.

It was Matt who broke the silence. 'Could 'ave got me brains bashed in there, couldn't I? If the villains hadn't have copped me one it's dead sure the coppers would 'ave.'

Joan didn't answer. Her insides were still wobbly and she was having a job keeping her hands from trembling.

'Was the flat you and Mrs Shepherd looked at just as bad?' he ventured.

Joan shrugged. 'What d'you mean, "just as bad"? We haven't yet looked at anywhere else. I told you, the flat itself was all right. Very nice, in fact, but it was on the seventh floor and there were gangs of lads hanging about. Anyway, that one isn't on the list Mr Stevens gave you so I suppose it's gone.'

'Oh, yeah, had a queue lining up for it I've no doubt.'

Joan was irritated by his sarcastic tone. 'The one we were about to see just now was on the eighth floor.'

Matt raised his eyebrows. 'All I can say is it's a jolly good job we weren't stuck up there when the police arrived. Bloody council! You'd think that for families with kids they'd come up with something better than a flat in a skyscraper block. They've no right to chuck us out of our houses then treat us as if we're nothing. Damn town-hall wallies, they always were full of bullshit.'

Matt was spoiling for a fight, and Joan didn't know what to say. If she dared to tell him it wasn't her fault, he'd only come back with 'Then whose bloody fault is it?' Because say what you like, plead all you like, there was no way that Matt was going to accept that the blame for any of this might be laid at his door.

Then, out of the blue, his attitude changed. 'Drink up, love. I'll get us another drink, and then I think I'd better have a talk with you.'

She drained the remains of her whisky and dry ginger and for once did not argue. She felt she could well use another drink.

Matt came back, set down the drinks then looked at his watch. 'I'm supposed to be meeting Stan and a client at the Flying Horse at six but it's ten past now so I think I'll give him a quick ring t' tell him I'm not gonna be able t' make it. I'll be back in a minute.' He made for the telephone box, which he'd said the barman had told him was outside in one of the corridors. He was letting his brother down to stay with her! Wonders would never cease. Why had his mood changed so rapidly? What was he going to talk to her about? Couldn't be anything to do with the Pearson family or the whole lot of them would be here to join in the discussion.

Both of them were shaken by what had happened at the block of flats. As Matt had said, fights on a Saturday night were nothing out of the ordinary when the pubs were turning out, but so early in the evening and in an area where the council expected folk with children to live, oh, no, that's not on. And the fact that it wasn't a bloke on the receiving end but a woman! No way did a gang of blokes set about one woman. That wasn't on either.

Joan soon began to realize that it was warm in this pub.

She pulled off her woollen scarf and unbuttoned her coat, then settled back to wait for Matt.

When he returned, he took a long drink of his beer, lit another cigarette and said, 'Tell me some more about this house your nan was on about.'

Had she heard right? Don't be sarcastic, she chided herself, and don't make it any harder for him than it already is. 'It sounded nice, and there was a garden,' she replied, giving him a little smile.

'Can't live in a garden.'

'No, but be great for the kids, and just to have somewhere to hang my washing out. You could grow a whole load of vegetables.'

Matt made a face. 'Hmm, that's what you think. Plenty of barrow-boys sell veg without me breaking my back digging for hours on end.' He drew on his Woodbine, blew out the smoke, then flashed her one of his cheeky grins. 'Had a talk with Stan this dinner-time. He reckons I'm a jammy bugger and that I'd be daft not to go for your nan's offer.'

Joan was silent for a moment. She was too busy sending up a silent prayer of thanks for brother Stan. Then she said, 'Really? He's the last person I'd have thought would encourage you to move away from the East End.'

'Yeah, me too. Thought he was taking the mick at first. Then when I realized he was serious I put up all sorts of reasons why the whole idea was sheer madness.'

'Tell me, Matt, what were those reasons?' Joan was sorry the minute the words were out of her mouth. She didn't want to hear all his negative arguments. She should have kept her mouth shut.

'How the 'ell I was gonna get to an' from work for a

start?' He smiled at the despondent look on her face. Then, to Joan's amazement, he threw back his head and gave a great belly laugh. Minutes passed before he said, 'Guess what his answer was. Go on, take a guess.'

'Same as my dad said, I suppose. Use the Underground. The house is only about five minutes' walk from Morden station.'

Matt was still laughing. 'Never in yer life! "Buy yerself a car, yer great big dope," is what he yelled at me.'

Talk about surprises! This evening was turning out to be something else! First off she was having a drink with her husband, just the two of them. No Pearson clan, where the men grouped on one side of the bar, the women on the other. And they were actually talking to each other. Just the two of them. No Amy to put in her two-pennyworth. *And* they were smiling. *And,* best of all, there was hope!

Suddenly Joan was laughing fit to bust.

'Now what's tickled you?' Matt asked, thinking it was a long time since he had seen his wife look so happy and, more to the point, she looked so nice tonight. She'd taken pains over what she wore and her hair, which these days was usually just dragged back and tied with a piece of tape, was shiny clean and piled up high in a tight bunch of curls.

'Sounds as if things might be going to get better and better,' Joan said, still smiling. 'Not only are you asking about the house but now you're considering buying a car.'

''Old yer 'orses,' Matt told her sternly. He wasn't about to give in that easily. If, and it was still a big if, anything was to come of Hester's proposition then at least it had to seem that the final decision had been his. He'd make damn sure of that! He wasn't going to let all the womenfolk believe they had ordered him to change his way of life. 'I ain't said anything was gonna 'appen. Not yet I 'aven't.'

Joan kept quiet. All right, he was making out that he was chastising her but only mildly.

Now he was on his feet, empty glasses in his hand. 'Do you want another drink?' His voice was quite soft.

'No more for me, my head's swimming already.'

Matt made for the bar, and she could hear him whistling under his breath. The evening that had begun so disastrously was turning out to be . . . oh, she couldn't find words to explain it even to herself. Matt had been adamant. No, he wouldn't move, especially not south of the river, and nothing she could say or do would shift him. Now listen to him! Oh, if only it could come about.

Most of it would be down to her nan and Pops. Mustn't forget Pops. How she wished she could still run to him, tell him how grateful she was. And how much she still missed him. She hadn't had her last surprise of the day.

'I'll finish this drink and then I'll take you home. We're not bothering to look at any flats tonight,' Matt said, giving her a kind of sheepish look. 'But before we leave 'ere I want yer t' do something for me.'

'Oh, yeah?' she answered, grinning cheekily.

'Behave yerself, Joan,' he muttered, but even he couldn't keep the grin off his face.

Pushing a handful of coppers towards her he said, 'Go and phone your mum an' dad. Tell them I'm gonna borrow a car an' bring you and the kids down for the day termorrer. Ask 'em if that'll be all right.'

Well, if he'd said he was going to sprouts wings and fly she couldn't have been more surprised. 'Oh, Matt,' she muttered, throwing her arms around him, 'I don't know how to say thank you.'

His mouth twitched and he burst out laughing. 'I'll show you a way later,' he whispered in her ear.

The time was getting on and by now most of the seats in the bar were taken. Several customers were looking at the pair of them as if they'd gone mad. Joan picked up the pennies and went to make that oh-so-important telephone call. Then a sudden thought hit her. So hard it was like a bolt out of the blue.

If events did turn out favourably, and she, Matt and children ended up living in Morden, Surrey, what would her mother-in-law have to say about it all?

She shook her head hard. Didn't bear thinking about.

Later, going home with Matt, she was aware that the events of this evening had encouraged him to have second thoughts about Hester's kind suggestion. That and his brother Stan's sensible comments. All being well, in the not too distant future, her life should take a turn for the better. Right until the moment they reached their front door she kept her fingers crossed.

BOOK TWO

MORDEN, SURREY, 1964

Chapter Twelve

'FLAMING JUNE' WAS absolutely the right description for it and into the second week the weather was glorious. It was going to be another long, sunny weekend, the kind that made you want to stay outdoors for ever, Joan was thinking. She glanced over to where her two daughters were sitting on the lawn eating their midday snack. They could still almost pass for twins and were so like her, except that their golden reddish hair was nowhere near as unruly as hers. She felt so lucky. She had everything anyone could ask for: a husband she loved, and who loved her, a safe, secure life, and three wonderful children. What a difference moving out of the East End had made, but where had all the years gone?

Her beloved Jamie would be twenty in November, and in the same month Meg (as Margaret had preferred to be called, rather than Maggie, since she started working in a solicitor's office) would be eighteen, while young Rosie had turned sixteen and was working for the Water Board. Those two girls were absolute gems. And just sitting there watching them on this Saturday morning she could feel the strength of the bond between them. Another blessing was that they both adored their big brother.

This house in which they lived, thanks to her nan, wasn't elaborate, but it was roomy and comfortable, in a nice area. Hardly a day passed that she didn't count her blessings and feel grateful. How different all their lives might have been if they had moved into a flat in one of those high-rise tenements when they were evicted from Bull Yard.

As her mum and dad, who were now frequent visitors, were fond of saying, she had turned this house into a lovely home. Her reward was that Jamie and the girls brought their friends home. She had overheard one girl ask whether their mum would mind them coming without notice and Rosie's answer had been, 'Oh, no, our Mum's OK,' which was high praise from a sixteen-year-old.

Jamie, having got himself eight O levels and three A levels, was at university. That was one thing she and Matt still disagreed on. According to Matt, Jamie should be out in the world earning his own living. Her one big fear was that their son would give in to his father's complaints and leave university before he had his degree in economics. Still, Matt had given way on quite a few things, even going so far as to buy Jamie a motorbike on his eighteenth birthday. She smiled, remembering how frightened she'd been the first time he had roared up the road on it. If anything were to happen to him she didn't know what she would do. She said a prayer for his safety every time he left the house to ride that bike. She couldn't begin to imagine life without him.

She loved her girls with every fibre of her being but, she had to be honest, Jamie was the light of her life. She shuddered, remembering the night he had been born. The memories had never dimmed. Both she and her baby could so easily have been killed. Her labour had been long and hard. She had never felt so lonely. So cheated. Because, of course, if things had gone according to the plans her father had made, Jamie would have been born in a quiet nursing-home in Wimbledon, not in a London hospital so near to where a German rocket had landed. But in the end, they were both safe and he was perfect.

Maybe it was because of the danger they had shared that night that they were so close. It still startled her sometimes when he walked into the house. He was so strikingly good-looking, so mature, at six foot two not quite as tall as his father, with Matt's dark hair, and the most gorgeous big blue eyes. She'd wondered about that when he had been born because her own eyes were green and Matt's a deep brown. 'Most babies have blue eyes to begin with,' one of the nurses had told her. 'They change colour later on.' Jamie's never had. He was always on the go, thinking ahead to what he wanted to do next, yet always thoughtful of others. And Joan was particularly pleased about the bond that had grown between her father and her son.

Jamie had been eleven years old when they had moved to Morden and until then had not known his grandfather well. Now it was a different story. When Jamie played rugby, Bill Harvey was on the touchline. They went swimming together and Joan often thought that her father would have given the world to be young enough to own a motorbike and roar off into the wind beside his grandson. Fishing was another sore point with Matt: 'Sheer waste of time. Asking to catch yer death of cold. So boring, sitting silent on a riverbank for hours on end,' he would say, and those were only a few of the arguments he threw at his father-in-law and his son. But nothing, least of all the weather, deterred Bill or Jamie. Fishing was high on their list of priorities.

It was a shame, really, that Matt didn't spend more time with Jamie, while he would go to the ends of the earth for his two girls. He spoilt them both rotten and always had, right from the beginning. As her nan was fond of telling her, that was the way it always was. Fathers spoil their daughters and each and every mother thinks her son is a gift from God, especially if he happens to be an only son. If that was true then Joan was no exception.

Matt was working this morning, which was unusual for him on a Saturday. He said that, more than likely, he would be home this afternoon but that this evening he was playing darts. She wished that Matt didn't spend so many Saturday nights in the East End, but she never argued the point: it was a chance for him to relax and catch up with what all his family were doing. She knew she'd be more than welcome to join him but doing the round of the pubs still didn't appeal to her.

As it was so warm, Joan was thinking about making a picnic dinner, with a few hot dishes and some salad they could eat in the garden. She'd have it ready early just in case Matt came home. 'What are you two planning to do with the rest of the day?' she called across to her daughters.

'Haven't quite decided,' Meg answered.

'Tennis first. We've promised to play doubles,' Rosie reminded her sister. 'Then I'd like to go swimming.'

'Rather you than me.' Their mother smiled. 'At least, the tennis bit. It's too hot. Who's making up the foursome?'

'Mary and Linsey. Their dad said he'd drive us to the

courts, and then I expect he'll have a drink in the club-house while we play. He'll take us to the baths too.' Meg offered the information with a knowing look.

'It's kind of Mr Chapman to run all you girls here, there and everywhere. I don't know him all that well but I've always had the feeling he's a nice man,' Joan said.

'It gives him something to do,' Rosie said, sounding like a thoughtless kid.

'How do you know he's nothing more important to do with his time?' Joan was quite shocked.

'Oh, Mum,' Meg exclaimed, 'you know very well his wife went off with another man.'

But that had happened over two years ago, Joan remembered. At the time it had come as quite a shock because everyone had thought of the Chapmans as an ideal happy family. Since then everyone who knew of the situation had been impressed by how well John Chapman had coped with his two daughters, and how much he did with them.

There had been just one time when he had admitted to Matt that it wasn't easy. He made no secret of the fact that he had loved his wife deeply and had been badly hurt when the truth came to light that she'd been seeing this other fellow for more than two years before she left him.

Linsey was the same age as Meg, and Mary was just a year younger than Rosie.

'Mary says she wishes her dad would find himself another ladyfriend,' Rosie piped up.

'Well, I've never heard her say anything of the sort,' Meg rebuked her sister. 'Her dad likes taking them both out and about and he's always pleased for us to join them.'

'Well, I think you two are very lucky,' their mother told them as she stood up, leaving her book on the garden table, and collected the empty glasses. 'I'm going indoors to make another jug of lemonade.'

'Mum,' Meg called after her, 'which weekend did you say Jamie would be coming home?'

'Not for three weeks yet. He said he's trying to swot up for the summer exams.'

'Oh, that's a pity. Linsey's having a party a fortnight today and I was hoping Jamie would be home and perhaps bring a friend with him.'

'Well, he'll phone tomorrow. You know he always does on Sundays. Talk to him about it then.'

As Joan neared the house the phone rang. She hurried through the kitchen to answer it, placing the empty glasses on the draining-board as she went.

'It's only me,' Matt said, as she lifted the receiver. 'Shan't 'ave time to come 'ome. Big match tonight, starts early, so I'll grab a bite at me mother's. I'm sorry, love. Still, you've got the girls for company. Why don't you go to the pictures with them?'

Joan wasn't surprised that he wasn't going to come home, and she certainly wasn't going to debate whether girls of sixteen and nearly eighteen would want to go out with their mother on a Saturday evening. Instead she said quietly, 'It's all right. Hope your team wins the darts match. But before you go, Matt, will you please do something for me? Make sure you remind your mother that we've booked the Crown for Jamie and Meg's birthday do, and ask her to let the rest of the family know.' She heard Matt sigh heavily. 'Oh, for God's sake, Joan, it's months away. Even I'm getting tired of hearing you go on an' on about it.'

'All right, all right, but make sure you tell your mum. I'll be up to see her next Sunday, not tomorrow, a week from tomorrow, and I'll give her all the details then.'

'Yeah, I'll tell her, an' if it'll make you 'appy I'll check with Stan just t' make sure he's got the date OK.'

'Thanks, Matt.'

'See yer later, then. Don't wait up if you're ready for bed cos I'm sure to be late.'

'Is that Dad?' Rosie yelled, her face lighting up as she ran through the hall.

'Yes,' Joan said, handing the phone to her youngest daughter, knowing she'd want to chat to her dad.

As she walked to the kitchen and set about squeezing a couple of lemons Joan was in a thoughtful mood. For a year after they had moved out of the East End, relations between herself and her mother-in-law had been strained, to say the least. Amy Pearson, the respectable, warm, kind-hearted mother of six, dependable, honest and generous to a fault, was stubborn as a mule.

There were times when Joan had to feel sorry for her, probably because it was Matt and she who had started the ball rolling and put the idea in the heads of his brothers and sisters. Whatever the reason, only two of Amy's children, Stan and Bertha, now lived within walking distance of the family home. Added to that, in 1958 Matt's father had died suddenly of a severe heart-attack. It had all left Amy feeling lonely and, perhaps, unwanted. Laura and her tribe had moved to Southend, and although she got a train up to Fenchurch Street station and called in on her mother from time to time, Bertha had confided to Joan that Amy had not set eyes on either of Laura's children from the day they had moved out of London.

The same could not be said of Joan's children. Thankfully

she had no problems on that score. Jamie thought the world of his gran and whenever he was in London he never failed to call in and see her. As for Meg and Rosie, she had taken them regularly to visit their gran. When Joan planned river trips, outings to Greenwich or to the Tower – the girls loved the Beefeaters – and to the museums she always asked Amy if she wanted to accompany them. Sometimes she did, if not too much walking was involved. However, if her legs were playing her up they'd set off without her, knowing that by the time they got back Amy would have a feast of a tea all ready for them.

Now shrieks of merriment were coming from upstairs as her two girls got ready for an energetic afternoon. Joan liked weekends best when Jamie came home and brought a couple of mates with him. They were precious days. The house really came alive: the lads would be boisterous, and they teased the girls unmercifully, but their laughter was good to hear.

She was about to go back out into the garden, carrying a tray of clean glasses, the jug of lemonade and a plate of butter shortbread she had made earlier that day when Meg came down the stairs, followed by Rosie. Meg looked particularly grown-up, in her pleated white tennis skirt, a pale blue jumper, with a V-neck and short sleeves, and her shoulder-length hair loose and shiny. She had grown into a real beauty.

Her eyes turned to Rosie, her baby, but there was nothing babyish about her today. Oh, why did they have to grow up so quickly? Rosie was wearing white linen shorts, a pink top and a little bit of makeup but she still looked clean, healthy and young. 'Well! You've both gone to a lot of trouble. Meeting someone special, are you?'

'Depends if there's four good-looking guys at the tennis club this afternoon.' Meg grinned. 'There's four of us so it's a case of take one, take us all.'

'Are you coming back for your dinner?' Joan asked.

'Not unless you want us to. Mr Chapman said we could eat at his house or maybe he'd treat us all to fish an' chips.'

'Oh.' Joan saw a lonely evening stretching before her, but before she had a chance to reply they heard a car draw up outside the house and the sound of a horn. Both girls kissed her, picked up their tennis racquets and raced off.

'Hey, wait a minute! What about these bags? I suppose they hold your swimming things, don't they?'

'Oh, yes, ta, Mum.'

'It's very kind of you to give up your time like this,' Joan said to John Chapman, as she leant through the driver's window.

'My pleasure,' he assured her. 'And please don't worry, I'll make sure they're all right and I'll have them home by, say, nine o'clock. Is that all right by you?'

'Yes, that's fine, thanks again.' She straightened up and stepped back, and all four girls waved as the car moved off.

It was just two thirty.

Joan walked slowly into the house. She felt lonely. It was stupid: she was a grown woman and she couldn't keep her children tied to her apron-strings for ever. And there was nothing stopping her from going up to London and spending the evening with her husband and his mates. Except that she didn't like sitting in a pub for hours on end.

In the months that followed there wasn't time for any of them to think about much except the coming double birthday party. There were days when tempers flared and Joan felt she had an enormous task in trying to please both adults and children. And that wasn't counting Matt. Londoners were renowned for their parties, and over the years Joan had attended quite a few hosted by the Pearsons. This was the first one she had organized on her own. For several reasons she had felt compelled to do it. On 2 November Jamie was to be twenty years old. No longer a teenager. Six days later, on the eighth, Meg would be eighteen and, these days, folk tended to regard that as coming-of-age. When she had first suggested the idea of a double party to their father, Matt had been as defeatist as ever. 'Ten t' one they'll both want another do when they really do come of age! Wait till Jamie is twenty-one – you'll see! And our Maggie will be just as eager for another party in three years' time,' he had declared.

Joan had pushed that thought to the back of her mind and gone ahead.

Now the day had dawned.

The room they had hired ran the full length of all three bars that were open to the public down below. A special bar, with two barmen, had been set up for this evening and Matt had placed a generous amount of money with the land-lord of the Crown so that all drinks were free to their guests. He and Joan had also had the forethought to book several rooms in and about the pub for those who were too tired or drunk to travel home that night.

Fifty-four relations and friends had sat down to a four-course meal, and now they were on to the speeches. First, Matt had stood up and praised his children to the high heavens, even going so far as to thank their mother for all her devotion over the years. Brother Stan made a point of thanking Joan for all the hard work and effort that he knew had gone into making this evening such a great success.

Then Amy was on her feet. Wonder upon wonders, she had something she needed to say. ''Andsome is as 'andsome does,' she declared. 'Well, I think you'd go a long way to find a better-looking lad than our Jamie and a kinder one, come to that. I'm not going to tell yer that I always agreed with the way his mother was bringing him up cos I didn't. Bit posh, like, for me, giving him big ideas, getting above his station and looking down on us as 'is relations. Now, I'm telling all of you, I was wrong. Yes, you can snigger, and laugh all yer like, cos I know what you're all thinking. It's gotta be a first, Amy Pearson admitting that she was in the wrong. But I freely admit I was. Our Jamie 'as turned out a smasher, an' I for one am dead proud of him. For all his schooling he's not a snob. Turns up on my doorstep, brings his mates as well, ain't ashamed of me or of where I live, and eats my bread-pudding like it's going out of fashion. And his sisters are all right an' all. The pair of them 'ave always had time for their old gran, so I'd like to take this chance and give a vote of thanks to their mother, my daughter-in-law. She's done a damn good job.'

It was impossible to say who was the most embarrassed, Jamie or his mother, yet when they looked at each other their pride was apparent. Praise from Amy Pearson was something that not many people received.

Matt asked his father-in-law if he wanted to say a few words, but Bill Harvey shook his head and smiled broadly. 'How on earth could I follow your mother? Leave it be. Amy was the star turn tonight.' That brought forth not only laughter but a standing ovation, which Amy had *not* bargained for.

Now the hall was filling up with extra young friends who had been invited for the evening, and the revelling began. Unrestrained by their elders, the youngsters took to the floor and the singing and dancing continued until midnight.

'I reckon we ought t' meet 'ere for a drink at lunchtime,' Stan said, beaming round at members of his family. 'One for the road to round off this smashing weekend.'

There was a general nodding of agreement as everyone moved towards the door.

Matt stood where he was with his arm round his wife. 'Did you see the girls and lads that went off with our three? Suppose they're all going to kip down at our place.'

'You don't mind, do you? But I expect you're right, we'll probably have to step over bodies lying on the floor when we get in. But it all went off very well, don't you think?'

'Oh, not bad,' he teased her, and then grew serious. 'You've done a fine job, in more ways than one. Even me mother said you 'ave.'

They were both still laughing when he added, 'Come on, let's go 'ome.'

Chapter Thirteen

JOAN FELT AS though her life had been transformed. Christmas had been a wonderful time with just her, Matt and the children, and not once had Matt shown he was restless. On Boxing Day they had gone to her parents, and Matt had been the life and soul of the party. Even Hester said it had been a joy to have him around. They had spent the weekend in the East End, staying at Amy's house and having one evening with Bertha and her family, and the other at Stan's.

Now it was January, a new year, a new beginning.

Jamie had got himself a part-time job, of which his father heartily approved, because his grant didn't stretch to cover his expenses. He came home as often as he could and Joan teased him that the main reason was to show off his beloved motorbike. Both Meg and Rosie worked locally, sometimes popping in at lunchtime for a snack, and she had the feeling that Rosie had a boyfriend. In fact, it was more than a feeling. She knew. Rosie was taking so much time and care over her hair, her makeup and her appearance that it was obvious she was trying to impress someone special.

Meg had been courting for some while now but had only brought Brian Clarke home regularly since the night of her birthday party. There were days now when she'd say, 'I won't be in for dinner tonight,' and her father would tease her. Joan wondered how long it would be before they announced their engagement. Not too long, she hoped, and smiled to herself at the thought of making her daughter's wedding dress with the help of her mother and, of course, her nan.

Brian worked for Macdonald and Partners, chartered accountants, whose offices were housed in the same block where Meg worked. It seemed he had a good job, which mattered to Matt. Joan didn't mind what he did for a living, as long as he was fit and healthy and would make Meg happy.

Joan had the front door open, her purse was in the bottom of the shopping basket and she had pulled on her gloves then flung the end of her long scarf over her left shoulder. These January winds were biting cold. She was wondering what meat to buy for dinner that evening and was about to close the door when the shrill ring of the telephone made her hesitate. Should she answer it? It was probably one of the women from the Guild who would want to chat for half an hour and she hadn't the time to waste. But she decided she had better find out who it was.

'Mrs Pearson?'

'Yes.' Joan felt a little apprehensive: she didn't recognize the voice.

'Is your husband at home?'

What the hell had that got to do with this frosty-sounding woman on the other end of the line? 'No, he isn't at the moment. Can I help you?'

'I'm Miss Reid, secretary to Mr Clive Richardson, who would like to have a word with you. Will you hold the line, please?'

Really, this was ridiculous! Who was this Mr Richardson and what could he possibly want with her?

She didn't have long to wait before she found out.

'Good morning, Mrs Pearson. I am a partner in the firm of Richardson and Bentley, solicitors and commissioners for oaths. Would it be possible to make an appointment to see you and your husband? I will come to your house, if that is all right with you. You tell me when it would be convenient.'

The voice was educated but Joan still felt . . . She couldn't put it into words. 'Would you mind telling me what this is about?'

'Nothing for you to worry about, Mrs Pearson. I do want to reassure you on that score. But it is not anything we should discuss over the telephone. I'm sorry.'

'I can give you my husband's business number. Perhaps you should call him.'

'I know I'm treading on eggshells but I really do have to meet both of you face to face. You could come here to this office, in High Holborn, but I do urge you to let me visit you at home in the first instance. It would be better all round. Just say what day is best for you.'

In the first instance? A sense of urgency came over Joan. She had to find out what this was all about so she said promptly, 'Tomorrow morning, I'll ask my husband to go in to work at a later time, so come as early as you like.'

'Shall we say nine thirty, then?'

'Yes, that will be fine,' Joan murmured. By then the girls would have left for work.

'Thank you, Mrs Pearson. Goodbye.'

Joan did her shopping slowly. Her mind was muzzy, almost as if she had had too much to drink the night before. The man had been nice, very polite. But why all the mystery? The day dragged and she couldn't settle to anything. She made herself another cup of coffee, the second since she had got back from the shops. She could phone Matt at work, but what good would that do? He'd worry just as much as she was. Probably a whole lot more. And he would demand answers – probably look up the address of Richardson and Bentley and go tearing up there making a scene.

Suddenly she frowned. What if Matt was in trouble? Had he and Stan got into money difficulties?

Never had she been so relieved as when she heard her husband's key in the lock of the front door that evening.

She didn't give him time to get his overcoat off, just blurted out the essential parts of the telephone conversation in disjointed sentences.

'Oh, for God's sake,' Matt protested, 'the bloke's 'aving you on. Collecting for some charity or other, I bet.'

'Well, it didn't sound anything like that t' me,' Joan said. 'Honest, Matt, he sounded really serious. I can't tell you why cos I don't know myself but he frightened me. It was nothing he said, it was just a feeling I got that it wasn't good news he was coming to see us about.'

Matt laughed. 'Well, I'll make short shrift of him. I'll

give him just five minutes and then he'll be out of that door a damn sight quicker than he came in. Come on, love, I'll pour us both a drink so put it out of yer mind till termorrow.'

Easier said than done, Joan thought, as she tossed and turned in bed that night.

Clive Richardson rang the doorbell on the dot of nine thirty. He was about five foot ten inches tall, immaculate in his navy blue Crombie overcoat with his briefcase in his hand. Matt towered five inches above him as they shook hands.

'Thank you for allowing me to come to your home,' he said pleasantly, as Joan took his coat and Matt pointed him to an armchair.

'Just tell us why you felt it was so important,' Matt said, in what, for him, was quite a courteous tone.

Mr Richardson set his briefcase across his knees, clicked open the lock, took out three or four typewritten pages and was about to speak when Matt said, 'I might as well tell you, if this is anything to do with business I won't take kindly to you involving my wife. So let's 'ave it out in the open. Does she need to stay in the room or not?'

Clive Richardson sighed. He hadn't expected this to be easy. 'Mr Pearson,' he began, 'I am here as a lawyer, not an investigator. This is a very personal matter that concerns both of you. I know you will find it painful and I can't help wishing that this particular job had fallen to someone else. So as I can think of no way with which to soften the blow I will get to the point.'

Joan was really frightened now. Her eyes were fixed on the stranger.

'We have taken instruction from a firm in the United States of America who are representing a family whose son was born in a hospital in Whitechapel during the early hours of the second of November 1944. You also have a son, I believe, born in the same hospital round about the same time on the same day. Is that correct?'

Joan's hands flew to her mouth. She still had no idea why the man was sitting in her front room: all she knew was it concerned Jamie and the man had said his news would be painful.

'Yes, that's right,' Matt answered, his voice rising. 'What the hell 'as that t' do with an American family?'

Matt would have gone on, swearing like a trooper more than likely, but suddenly he realized that this solicitor was having a hard time. The man was tense: his knuckles were white as he gripped the handle of his briefcase. He was about to offer him a shot of whisky or maybe a brandy but decided this matter had to be got to the bottom of before a drink of any kind was brought out.

Clive Richardson looked from one to the other then back to Matt. 'I am so sorry. I have never, in all the years I have been in practice, had to deal with anything even approaching this. The American family in question had a family crisis. A relative needed a blood transfusion and it was only then that it came to light that their son, whom they had raised for nearly twenty years, was not their own flesh and blood. Wheels were set in motion. Hospital records were checked and it was discovered that a German rocket had been launched that night which fell close to the hospital in which this mother had given birth to her baby. The blast was so great that it caused windows of this hospital to be blown in and the electricity to fail.'

Clive Richardson paused. He could not bear to look at Joan, whose face was deathly white, but he knew he had to press on.

'During the chaos that followed two newborn babies were taken to the nursery.' He paused and swallowed. 'There is reason to believe that a mistake was made and that these two babies, both male, were wrongly tagged.'

Joan was drawing in great gulps of air. She felt sick.

Matt jumped up from the settee where he had been sitting next to her. 'What? What the bloody 'ell are you going on about? After all these years you expect us t' believe a cock-an'-bull story like that? Get out. Go on, take yer damn papers and get out of our house.'

All kinds of emotions were ripping through Joan. She was so angry with this man that if she had had any weapon in her hand she felt she would have struck him with it. How dare he come here to tell her that maybe Jamie wasn't her son! For that was what he was trying to say, wasn't it?

She was his mother. She'd breastfed him, nursed him for hours on end, cared for him through measles, mumps, chicken-pox and every other ailment kids get. Did he really believe I wouldn't have known he was someone else's child? My God! She was so angry. But, more than that, she was desperately afraid.

'Wait.' Just the one word came out of her mouth, and even that was a dry, harsh sound.

'Take your time, Mrs Pearson,' Clive Richardson said. 'Ask me any questions you like. If I have the answers I'll tell you, and if not I shall do my best to find them.'

By now tears were burning her eyes. Impatiently she brushed them away. 'I don't believe one word you said, and whoever sent you here is wicked. No, more than wicked. They must be downright evil to think up such a story. But before you go, tell me just one thing. What was an American woman doing having her baby in Whitechapel in 1944?'

She shuddered, and Matt was by her side in an instant. 'It's all right, love. We'll get to the bottom of this rubbish and, by God, I'll see some bugger pays for starting this rumour.'

'Oh, Matt, what if we have to tell Jamie?'

Even burly, street-wise Matt was appalled at the very thought, and the anguish that came through as his wife spoke those few terrible words was something he wouldn't forget if he lived to be a hundred. He couldn't let this happen. If it was true it would kill Joan. But it wasn't true. It couldn't be, because if it was the consequences would be too awful even to think about. Gently he pushed Joan back on to the settee and looked at the intruder.

His mood changed abruptly. Whoever had thought up this scam, Clive Richardson was in no way to blame: the poor man looked green around the gills. 'I'll stick the coffee-pot on and get the brandy bottle,' he muttered, and made for the door.

Silence hung heavy between Joan and the solicitor, and it wasn't broken until all three were sipping coffee. Both men had tossed down their brandy in one gulp. Joan hated the taste but she had drunk hers too.

'Mrs Pearson, perhaps you'll let me answer your question now.'

Almost apologetic, Joan said, 'I didn't think you knew the reason.'

'I have to tell you, the research has been thorough. The

mother was not an American. She was a London girl married to an American soldier. After her baby boy was born she lived with her parents in Stepney for two years.'

He waited, allowing that information to sink in, before explaining further. 'Many thousands of American soldiers had fallen in love with British girls. Some eventually married them and in 1946 they became known as GI brides when transatlantic liners took them to their new homes in the USA. That is what happened in this case. For some of the brides the experience was less desirable than they had expected. Fortunately for this mother, the father of her child came from a good family and until now it would seem that life has been good to both her and her husband. Very good indeed, from what we've been led to believe. They have two more children.'

Joan was startled to find herself becoming interested in what Clive Richardson was saying. Quickly she covered her ears with her hands. 'I don't want to hear about them. Not their names or where they live or what they do for a living. Nothing. Do you hear me? They, them, their kids, *I don't want to know.*'

'I agree,' Matt shouted. 'You can't just come here out of the blue and tell us the son we've had for twenty-odd years is not our son. Things like that don't 'appen.' His voice was hoarse and his cheeks were flaming. 'It's enough to scare the life out of my wife.'

'I just can't apologize enough,' Clive Richardson said quietly, 'but it did happen. The law firm we have taken our orders from have made extensive investigations and so have we. Without a doubt we have established that there were just two male infants born that night within minutes of each other. What happened after their birth was a tragic accident, one which came about because of the war. With broken glass and falling debris in the hospital, plus the fact that the electricity had failed, a mistake was made and at whose door the blame is to be laid is very uncertain to say the least.'

Matt was having a job to breathe now. His hands were knotted into tight fists. Trying hard to control his temper he got to his feet and said, 'That's enough, Mr Richardson. My wife has told you, and I'm telling you now, we don't want to hear any more.'

Now Mr Richardson looked tense again. 'There is a simple way for us to get at the truth.'

'Oh, yeah? Pay them off! Is that what this 'as been all about? Cos if it is I'll see the buggers damned first,' Matt yelled at him.

'That is not what I am suggesting. All you need to do is have a blood test, you, Mrs Pearson and your son. The results would be conclusive.'

Matt went mad. 'Oh, he's *our* son again now, is he? Thanks for bloody nothing. If you think we're going up to the university where our boy is to drag him out and say, "Oh, come on 'ome, son, cos we're all gonna get a blood test t' make sure you know just who your parents are," then I'm telling you, man, you're barking up the wrong tree.'

Mr Richardson shook his head sadly. 'The other family could insist. They could apply to the courts for an order.'

Joan covered her mouth with her handkerchief and ran out into the kitchen. Bending low over the sink she vomited until there was nothing left to bring up. Her heart was hammering, her head spinning. What was the object of all this? What did this American family want? Did they expect to exchange sons? How ridiculous. Would they have to tell Jamie he had to go and live in America then wait for a replacement to walk through the door?

She'd never be able to broach this subject with him. How could she? Where would she begin? Tell him that he wasn't and never had been her son? She couldn't begin to imagine the look on his face – and as to what his reaction would be . . . Dear God, it was a living nightmare.

Matt appeared in the doorway. 'You all right, love?' Then he added, 'Silly blooming question cos you're not. I'm gonna tell this bloke to leave now and then you can go an' 'ave a lie down.'

Minutes later as Matt held the front door wide open, Clive Richardson gave him a long, sorrowful look. 'Goodbye, Mr Pearson. I am sorry your wife is so upset, but I have to say you have not seen the last of me. This matter will have to be thrashed out. With or without your permission.'

As Matt closed the door he was striving to convince himself that he would be able to sort this out. Nobody could just walk into their house with a story such as the one Clive Richardson had come up with and be allowed to get away with it. Look what it had done to Joan already! If he didn't put a stop to it straight away it would turn their whole lives upside down. At that moment he caught sight of his reflection in the hall mirror. 'Jesus Christ, by the look of me I've aged ten years this morning,' he muttered to himself. 'It feels like it an' all!'

Before going in to comfort his wife he had to stand still and take several deep breaths. What could he possibly say to ease her mind? Somehow he had to find words that would make her feel less afraid. But how? He couldn't even convince himself that the facts that had been laid out for them were untrue.

The sad part was that in his heart he knew only too well that Clive Richardson had just spoken the truth.

They certainly hadn't heard or seen the last of him.

Chapter Fourteen

JOAN WAS SITTING in her bedroom, staring out of the window. Her hands were clenched in her lap and her head ached. Jamie would be home this morning and somehow she was going to have to tell him about Richardson and Bentley, solicitors, and why they were now deeply involved in their lives.

On Christmas Day she had turned thirty-nine. Before Clive Richardson had paid them a visit she would have said she didn't look her age. Like her mother and grandmother she kept herself trim and smart, but these past weeks had aged her. It had taken Richardson and Bentley a great deal of effort to persuade Matt and her to submit to blood tests. Now over the weekend they had suggested that, on some pretext or other, they get their son to do the same.

With that thought foremost in her mind Joan sighed. This was such a dreadful situation. How was Jamie going to feel to be told that maybe she wasn't his mother or Matt his father? They were not going to be able to put it off any longer. If they didn't persuade him to take a blood test while he was at home, the solicitors had threatened that they would deal with him personally.

Joan got to her feet and pressed her head against the window-pane, her eyes now too blurred with tears to see anything outside, her shoulders shaking.

She was sick with worry. Matt was, too, and not just with worry but with rage. His temper got worse every day. He had refused to be there when she spoke to Jamie and there was no reasoning with him.

She heard the motorbike before she saw him. She didn't move, just listened as he parked it, let himself into the house and went from room to room. Finally, from the foot of the stairs, she heard him call, 'Isn't anyone at home? Mum, are you upstairs?'

She came out of the room, rubbing hard at her face with her handkerchief. Then she smiled. 'Oh, Jamie, it is good to see you. I'll come down, make some coffee and get you something to eat.'

Her foot was only on the first tread when he reached her. 'Hugs and my kiss first,' he declared, wrapping his arms around her and practically lifting her feet off the floor. 'Oh, Mum, it's going to be a great weekend. I've invited David and Ken to come for the day on Sunday, hope that's all right. Where is everyone? Oh, the girls are at work I suppose?'

'Wait, wait,' his mother implored him. 'Let's go downstairs and you can get those outdoor clothes off while I make the coffee and then we'll talk.'

Jamie turned and walked slowly down to the hall. He waited until his mother was standing beside him, then, staring into her eyes, he said, 'Something's wrong. You've been crying. Come on, Mum, tell me, what's the matter?'

I can't tell him, Joan thought. No, I can't do it. His father should be here. He should be the one to tell him. He won't, though, will he? And it'll be a thousand times worse if strangers get him to one side and say calmly, 'Your parents are not who you thought they were. They're a different couple altogether. They don't even live in this country.'

Jamie felt the tension. It alarmed him. 'Whatever is it? Has Meg or Rosie had an accident? It's not Dad, is it?'

'No, Jamie, nothing like that. Please, let's go into the kitchen. Perhaps if we have a hot drink I'll find it easier to tell you.'

Jamie sighed heavily. 'All right. I'll get my things off while you put the kettle on, and then I want to know whatever it is.'

Like a robot, she set about doing everything just right. Cups, saucers, sugar-bowl, jug of cream from the fridge. 'Are you starving?' she asked.

'No, Mum. Just coffee will be fine.'

When they were seated opposite each other she poured coffee into each of their cups. Jamie added two spoonfuls of brown sugar and dribbled cream over the back of his teaspoon watching it make an ever-increasing circle on top of his coffee. 'You're not well, are you, Mum? Have you been to the doctor's?'

He sounded so concerned that her heart ached even more. 'I'm all right, truly I am, but I want you to listen to what I have to tell you,' she began, trying to keep her voice steady. 'You've heard me tell you often enough about the night you were born, haven't you?'

'Gosh, yes. I've even told that story myself. We were lucky to come through that night, so you've always impressed on me.'

'That's very true. It was an awful night. That German rocket caused so much destruction, and what followed in the hospital was chaos.'

Jamie was holding his cup in both hands and had been sipping his coffee. Now, very precisely, he lowered the cup to the saucer. Then he raised his head and looked straight into Joan's eyes, and said, 'Get to the point, Mum.'

She sighed softly. 'I suppose I better had.'

Jamie kept his eyes on her. It broke her heart just looking into them. Such beautiful eyes, not green like hers, not brown like Matt's, but a deep, deep blue.

'Two boy babies were born that night,' she whispered. 'You were one of them. The other mother was married to an American soldier and when her baby son was two years old she went to the USA to live. Recently your father and I have had a visit from a firm of solicitors acting for an American family who have reason to believe that in all the hectic goings-on in the hospital the night you were born there was a mix-up.'

Jamie didn't move. The silence just went on and on. Eventually he cleared his throat. 'If you're trying to say what I think you are, then something is terribly wrong.'

'Don't I know it?' she muttered, and burst into tears. She reached across the table and took his hand between both of hers. 'Oh, Jamie, I'd give the world for this not to be happening. The solicitors have practically forced your father and me to take a blood test. They said they'd get a court order if we didn't agree. And now they want you to do the same.'

'Mum, stop crying, please. That's no problem. I'll do as they ask and surely that will prove conclusively that they're barking up the wrong tree. Now, try and be calm and start at the beginning. Wait. First tell me what Dad had to say about this.'

Joan wiped her eyes and even managed a laugh. 'Can't you guess? "Load of old cobblers!" He said it must be a scam to get money out of him. He'd get to the bottom of this, he said, and when he did he'd commit murder. If anyone could even think that he didn't know his own son after twenty years then they ought to be locked up in a lunatic asylum.'

'Good old Dad. Now tell me everything, right from the beginning. Please.'

Slowly, and as calmly as she could, Joan went back to that first telephone call, how she had felt apprehensive right from that very moment. She told him the events in the order they had taken place.

Jamie looked shattered. 'It's so crazy. Can it be true? Perhaps Dad is right and someone hopes to gain from this, though it's hard to see how.'

'Well, according to Clive Richardson, the lad in America has been proved beyond all doubt not to be the other couple's son.'

'Even so, what is it they want? Do you know the name of this family? Their circumstances?'

'We have been told that they have two other children and that the family is pretty well off. All the main details I wouldn't listen to. I don't want to know who they are, where they live or anything about the lives they lead.'

She couldn't add that at the back of her mind was the awful thought that if she were to listen to all the facts about this family she might have to admit that they had been bringing up a son to whom she had given birth. That would mean she believed their claim. Never in a million years was she even going to give half a thought to the idea that this dearest boy, who was sitting opposite her now, was not her own flesh and blood. She cringed inwardly at the thought. He was the light of her life. After all the intimate details of bringing up a child to manhood, you just didn't take as gospel the words of a solicitor who came along and to put it bluntly said, 'Oh, sorry, but you've had the wrong boy right from the start. Please change over with a family that lives thousands of miles away in America.'

What about this American family? How had they felt when a simple blood test apparently proved beyond doubt that their son, whom they also had brought up for twenty years, was *not* their own boy? Had they stopped loving him? Did they really want to make an exchange now? Or perhaps, since they were well off, they thought they could entice Jamie to become part of their family, thereby gaining another son while she and Matt lost out. Could folk really be that cruel?

What if she and Matt had found out first? I wouldn't have told a soul! Least I don't think I would have. What good would it have done? Just bring heartaches all round. Why had they engaged an English firm to sort this matter out? As yet, no one had said what they hoped to achieve by getting at the truth.

Jamie refilled their coffee cups. Then he said, 'I rather fancy we're going to have to listen to a lot more facts whether we want to or not, before this farce can be brought to an end.'

Joan drew in a long breath. 'Son, are you saying that this could turn out to be rubbish?'

'Probably. It's too ridiculous to be true. You'd have known over all these years if I wasn't the son you gave birth to. Wouldn't you?'

'Oh, Jamie, that's exactly what I've been saying all along – when you cut your first tooth, took your first steps on your first birthday because we'd bought you a wooden horse on wheels. You grabbed the handle, stood up and tottered along the narrow passage we had in our house at the time. Every illness. The worst was when you had whooping-cough – I hardly had you out of my arms for days and days because that cough racked your little body so much.' She ended on a sob and when she could bring herself to look at her son she saw that he was crying. She got to her feet, came around the table and drew him into her arms. Holding each other tightly, her head buried in his chest, they shed tears that came right from the heart.

They didn't hear Matt come home. Quietly he opened the door to the kitchen. The sight of his wife and son clinging together, both crying their hearts out, met his eyes. If he had the rotten person responsible for this in his house right now he would kill the bastard. 'With my bare hands I would, and bugger the consequences,' he muttered.

It took a minute or two for him to control his temper. When he spoke his voice was filled with emotion. 'I guess you've told him. I've brought a drop of brandy for us. I'm sure you two need it.' Then he watched his son break free of his mother, swipe the tears from his eyes and turn to face him.

'I know, lad, I should 'ave been 'ere.' He opened his arms and, without hesitating, Jamie went into them. 'I'm so sorry, son.' Now there were tears running down the cheeks of Matt Pearson, a sight his wife had never seen in all the years she had been married to him. Moving his big hands gently up and down Jamie's back, his father whispered, 'We'll get this bloody mess sorted. You take the test – that'll show 'em.

You're a Pearson through an' through, an' I'm not gonna 've anyone tell me different.'

'I'm sorry, too, Dad. I shouldn't be crying like this – but to come home and hear that solicitors are saying my real parents are in America! Well . . . How could they do that to their own son? What must that lad be feeling like? Don't they want him any more now they've found out he's the wrong blood group?'

'God knows, son!' Matt's heart was doing somersaults. Jamie's shoulders were heaving and sobs were racking his body. 'Go on, son, get it out of yer system. It's not a sin for a man to cry. Jesus Christ, I saw enough men cry when I was in the Army during the war.'

Four days later, long drawn out days. Some spent mostly in silence, others when they talked until their heads ached, going over and over every single detail. Now Joan, Matt and Jamie sat facing a doctor, who was sitting behind his desk.

The doctor turned his gaze away from the three to look out of the window to where ambulances were unloading patients. He wasn't sure whether it was worse to have to tell parents that a child had died or to give them the information he was about to impart. Never had he come across such a case before. It did happen, he knew, he'd heard of such cases, but after twenty years for such a thing to come to light! A catastrophe, nothing less, for each and every person involved.

Matt was the first to break the unbearable silence. 'Doctor, we'd rather you just spat it out. You 've got the results there in front of you, 'aven't you?'

The doctor was a young man and he was considering how to be kind, how to wrap it up in some way. He picked up a fountain pen and twiddled it between his fingers, lifted a paperweight. Then he took a deep breath and let it out slowly.

'You have to tell us one way or another,' Joan said.

'Yes, I'm afraid I must.' His voice was barely more than a whisper. 'I have the results of the blood taken from all three of you now. I am so sorry, but they do prove that James cannot be your son.'

This must be what they mean when they say, 'It hasn't registered yet,' Joan thought, as she sat in Matt's car staring at the back of her son's and her husband's heads. But the terrible truth had been admitted at last.

Jamie was not her son. Neither was Matt his father. Inside her head a voice was screaming, *What are we going to do? What are we going to do?* She wasn't shedding tears. She had none left to shed.

Chapter Fifteen

JOAN SHIVERED AS she pulled the string through the letter-box, found the key on the end and used it to open the front door of her mother-in-law's house. She walked down the narrow passageway, the smell of Mansion polish in her nostrils. When she pushed open the kitchen door the warm aroma of baking filled the air.

'Good God above!' Amy Pearson cried, appearing from the scullery dusting flour from her hands and running them down the front of her spotless white overall. 'You're a sight for sore eyes an' no mistake. But what's brought you 'ere? Oh, never mind, I'm that pleased t' see yer. I'll put the kettle on.'

Joan gave her a grateful look. 'I asked Matt what days you were home.'

'Well, he got it right for once. Sit yerself down, I'll see to the tea.'

Amy lifted the big black kettle from the hob and went into the scullery.

Joan took off her coat, sat down and looked around the familiar room. What a change! Over the past two years Amy had become a different woman. She had got herself a job down at the local police station. Three mornings a week she did an early shift cooking breakfast for the constables. At first she had been the butt of her sons' jokes. But she had shown them! Proved herself no end. Having something to do, meeting people and feeling wanted had made all the difference in the world to her. When most of her family had moved away it had shattered Amy. Living alone had left her feeling not exactly unwanted but un-needed. For a brief moment Joan smiled to herself, remembering all the arguments her mother-in-law had put up when she herself had wanted to get a job. Still, that was water under the bridge now. Everything and everyone seemed to have changed lately.

This kitchen was so . . . 'homely' was the word that sprang to Joan's mind. The same scrubbed table dominated the centre of the room but now it was covered with a dark green chenille cloth edged with long tassels. A cut-glass bowl filled with fresh fruit stood in the middle. Two fairly new armchairs were at either side of the fireplace, comfortable-looking with plump cushions and lace-edged linen headrests. The cooking range was well blackleaded, as it always had been even when the house had been crowded with adults and children. The mantelpiece was full of china knick-knacks, which Joan knew had been presents from her children when they were growing up. There was a memory in each and every one. This morning the fire burnt brightly and the brass fender shone. The big dresser still held an enormous amount of china and some of the huge old meat dishes, which Joan felt must be valuable.

Amy came back carrying a tray. She had set out her best cups and saucers and a plate of warm rock cakes. 'This is a surprise,' she said, and set the tray on the table. 'Don't very often get t' see you of a weekday. Though, if I tell the truth, I 'ave been 'alf lookin' for yer t' turn up.'

Joan flushed. 'So Matt has told you?'

'Not much,' said Amy quickly. 'He was in such a state the night he stayed 'ere. I blamed our Stan for letting him drink so much. He just needed someone t' talk to. I expect you do as well. My 'eart went out t' the pair of you when Matt told me. Mind you, it were only the bare bones of the matter he went on about and I didn't ask no questions. It weren't for me t' do that. You knew where I was if you wanted t' tell me, an' now you're 'ere it goes without saying that anything I can do to 'elp, you only 'ave t' say the word.'

'Oh, Amy,' Joan whimpered. Her mouth was dry and her hands were shaking.

'There, there,' Amy soothed her. 'Drink yer tea. It'll all come out in the wash and someone will 'ave t' pay for this mistake.'

'Amy, there is no mistake. It has been proved now that our Jamie does not have our blood group but he is a match for this American family and the same goes for the lad that they have had since birth.'

A few minutes passed before Amy spoke. 'Joan, I am so sorry for you and our Matt. Whatever can I advise you to do?'

'Nothing. There's nothing anyone can say or do that will alter the situation in any way whatsoever. We have to face it. The truth is that a mistake was made in 1944 and now two families have to face up to that fact.'

'Oh, God, what's this doing to our Jamie?' Amy fumbled for her handkerchief. Then she turned to Joan almost beseeching her, 'We won't lose 'im, will we?'

'I've asked myself the same question over and over again. I couldn't bear it if we did.'

'Can yer tell me how he's taken it?' Amy asked, tears running down her cheeks.

'I can't fathom him out.' Joan sighed. 'Even when there's just him and me he won't talk about it. When I move around his eyes never leave me. It's queer. Everything about Jamie at the moment seems queer.'

'Oh, this is all so dreadful. 'Ave this other family been in touch with you and Matt?'

'No, that's the strange part of it all. Mr Richardson, he's the solicitor that first contacted us, gave a letter to Jamie which was supposedly from the American family his firm are acting for. Jamie has never mentioned it. Whether he read it, destroyed it or if he's just put it away somewhere safe, I just don't know. I did ask him if it were a nice letter but he ignored me.'

Silence hung heavy between Amy and Joan. They were both at a loss for words. Then, more to herself than to Joan, Amy mumbled, 'What I can't make out is why they did it. What in hell's name are they after?'

'Me too,' Joan confessed. 'Listening to the men in posh suits, which is how Matt describes them, you'd think it was me and Matt that had done this family a terrible injustice. Wronged them something terrible. There's never a mention that the same tragedy has affected us too.'

'What about this other lad, the one that's supposed to be yours? Have they written to you about him, or has he contacted you?'

'No. According to what we've been told he's doing well and is truly considered their son.' Joan hesitated. 'Amy . . . that's partly my own fault. I refused to listen when the solicitors went on about who this family are, where they live and how prosperous they are. I felt . . . I can't find the words to describe it. I dunno, but if I can get anyone to understand I think it'll be you. I can't seem to get through to my own mum. She's too upset at the thought of losing Jamie.'

'Come 'ere.' Amy was on her feet. She had lost some weight since she'd been working but still had plump arms and a soft bosom. Pulling Joan close she patted her back as if she were a small child. Minutes later when they'd wiped away their tears, she said, very seriously, 'Joan, take your time. Tell me, if you can, just what's going through your mind. Maybe together we can get it sorted and if not, well, they do say a trouble shared is a trouble halved.'

'It's this feeling,' Joan began slowly, 'and if I let it take over then I'll be lost. If I let myself wholeheartedly believe that Jamie is not the baby I gave birth to, no longer anything to do with me, that he belongs on the other side of the ocean, then I don't want to go on living and that's hardly fair on Meg and Rosie. Nor on Matt, I suppose. But he gets so angry if I try to talk to him. If I were to listen to details of this family, how they live their daily lives and so forth, my imagination would have something to go on and I'm afraid it would run away with me. Would Jamie be better off with them? I keep asking myself that question. Could they give him much more than we can? They say that America is the land of milk and honey. Are Matt and I depriving him of things that should rightfully be his?'

'Joan, I do understand,' Amy said softly. 'I ain't never 'ad

much t' give my lot but there's always been love. Every brick
in this 'ouse can vouch for that. So, you listen t' me.
Remember the party you gave just before Christmas?'

Joan half smiled and nodded.

'We couldn't 'ave known then that this bombshell was
going to drop on you and Matt, could we? Course we didn't.
But, looking back, it's as if I did 'ave that knowledge. I got
t' me feet and I told everyone that there wasn't a bit of
snobbery in our Jamie. He was our lad and he loved each
and every one of us. Even his old gran who still lived in a
two-up-an'-two-down 'ouse with a lavatory out in the backyard. But did he mind? Never in yer life. He came t' see
me cos he wanted to, *and* he brought his posh, well-dressed
mates with him. And it wasn't t' take the mickey out of me
neither. I never knew when they were coming, they just took
me as they found me. Those lads came time an' time again
and they never failed t' kiss me goodbye. So, I'm saying t'
yer now, gal, you're misjudging that son of yours. Yes, I said
it and I mean it. In your heart he's your son, he knows it,
an' you an' Matt knows it. And don't you dare try an' tell
me that Maggie and Rosie 'ave altered one iota in their feelings towards their brother. No blood test can wipe away
twenty years of love and affection from bloody good parents.
I don't care what no blooming doctor or solicitor has to
say.'

'Oh, Amy, you're a tonic, you really are. I got up this
morning and felt I'd go mad if I didn't talk to someone.
Just couldn't wait to get on the train and come an' see
you.'

'Well, you're 'ere now. You can stay all day, can't you?'

'Yes, I'll take you out for a bit of lunch, if you like,' Joan
answered, sniffing away her tears.

'No, I've got plenty in the 'ouse. Now, if we go through this together we'll not only feel a whole lot better, we might even come up with an answer to what we can do about it.'

Joan doubted that. Hadn't she gone over and over it through the long hours of the night, from the very moment Clive Richardson had dropped it on them?

''Ow about a bacon sarnie? I've become a dab 'and at frying rashers, an' if they're good enough for the local coppers they ought t' suit you, my lady.'

Joan set a determined smile on her face. 'I mean it, Amy, you're better than a dose of salts. I'd love a sarnie. I'll come out and help you.'

'Where's Jamie now?' Amy asked, snipping the rind off half a dozen rashers of back bacon.

'He's gone back to university. He phoned us on Sunday, just as he always does, but he seemed so, well, distant. Meg and Rosie spoke to him – they're the only ones who don't seem to think this is a disaster. They were laughing fit to bust when they put the phone down.'

'There yer are, then. Those girls know he's their brother. He's loved them, teased them and looked out for them since the day they were born and no solicitor is gonna change that.'

'I heard them telling my dad much the same thing. Amy, you wouldn't believe how cut up he is over all this.'

'I can guess, love. I've seen the pair of them together. To your dad, Jamie's the son he never had and, being a grandfather, he's got time to devote to him. It takes some believing for all of us. Things like this only 'appen in books and plays and then not to ordinary folk. You said yer mum was taking it badly, what about Hester?'

'I couldn't bring myself to tell her. Left that to my dad.

Poor old Nan. She'll be seventy-five this year and she could have done without this shock.'

'Couldn't we all?' Amy muttered. 'Especially you an' Matt.' She was busy at the frying-pan. She'd laid out four thick slices of bread on a dish and said, 'Spread them for me, will you, love? You can 'ave butter or dripping, whichever yer prefer. It's pork dripping, lots of thick jelly on the bottom. I'll 'ave that – put plenty of salt an' pepper on it for me.'

Soon they were seated at each side of the fire. 'I'd forgotten just how good a bacon sandwich can be.' Joan smiled, munching away.

'I'm just so glad you decided t' come up 'ere today,' Amy said.

'So am I,' Joan answered. She stared out of the window. 'There are times when I feel guilty. I should be thinking about this other lad, the one that's supposed to be my son. How does he feel about me and Matt? But then I think, No, it's not true. Jamie's ours. It's not fair. We've been good parents. Why, oh, why did this have to be brought out into the open? What we didn't know wasn't hurting anyone.'

Poor Amy didn't know what to say or do. She frowned, then murmured, 'The whole thing is a right old cock-up.'

In spite of everything Joan had to smile. Trust Amy to call a spade a spade. Because if you went right back to the night that these two baby boys had been born that's where the trouble was started. And to coin Amy's phrase it had certainly turned out to be a right cock-up.

Later, on the way home, Joan was telling herself how much better she felt for having paid a visit to her mother-in-law. Rough and ready Amy might be, but she was the salt of the earth. She hadn't been able to solve any of their problems but just being with her, feeling the warmth of her love, had gone a long way to helping Joan feel that she hadn't got to cope all on her own.

Chapter Sixteen

In spite of her misgivings, Joan opened a padded envelope which had been forwarded to her by Clive Richardson, and took out what was obviously a wallet containing photographs. She placed it to one side without looking inside. Then she withdrew the letter. There were six pages, handwritten.

Breathing heavily she sat back in her chair and started to read.

3021 16th Avenue
Circle west
Kingston 32405
New York, USA

Dear Joan,
All things considered, I think we have to be on first-name terms, don't you? I have had more time to get my head around this situation, so I do know what

you are going through. Mixed-up feelings, eh? Where
to lay the blame? Asking, 'How can anyone have
done this to me?' Telling yourself over and over again
that you'll die if they take your son away from you.
I've spent the sleepless nights. Cried buckets of
tears. Blamed everyone and anyone. And still have
no answers.

The whole thing is so crazy. Think about it. We
must have seen each other in that hospital. Said
good-morning, maybe good-night. Looked at each
other's baby and admired, even maybe discussed
feeding problems. I do remember my breasts were
very sore and someone gave me a loan of a tube of
soothing cream. Could well have been you.

For nearly two years after having my baby I lived
with my mother, only a tram ride away from where
our babies were born. I understand you lived near
Wimbledon.

Then in 1946 I came to the States. What a journey that was! If the mix-up had taken place during
the voyage I could have understood. We GI brides
were jammed into cabins with tiered bunks, but the
babies were put into one huge nursery with Army
nurses to take care of them. Thank God Peter was
going on for two years old and I was able to keep
him with me. My mother chose the name Peter,
after my father who had died when I was very
young, though immediately we arrived in America
my in-laws called him Junior, and I'm afraid that has
stuck.

One thing I have come to be grateful for is that
both of our baby boys went to a decent loving

family. Mr Richardson has not only written to me, we've spoken a few times on the telephone. I wanted to know everything about you and your husband and was so pleased and, yes, relieved to be told that you were kind, loving people and that James is such a nice young man. It was a great comfort to learn that you both love him dearly, as we do Peter. Things could have been so very different. Especially for me.

I left my home, family and friends and brought my small son to live with strangers thousands of miles away. It wasn't easy at first. I was desperately homesick. But in so many ways I was extremely lucky. For a great number of the English brides, coming here was a disaster. My new family were well-off, but the conditions some young women encountered were truly bad. Some brides found their new home to be little more than a wooden shack, miles from anywhere and with none of the amenities we'd all taken for granted back home. Almost all toilets were outside and running water was not laid on because of the distance to run the pipes – all water had to be drawn from a well. However, on the other hand, food was so plentiful. After the British rationing almost every meal was like a banquet. But, like so many more war-time brides, I was so homesick, I felt so lonely – day in, day out, I longed to be back in the East End of London. I missed the Thames and the busy life of the river. I missed the London voices, the Cockney accent. That sounds silly, doesn't it? But it's true. The American way of speaking took a long time to get used to.

I had more babies and that helped.

When I became pregnant again my husband, Joe, was really happy and not only his parents but all his relations (and there are plenty to contend with) seemed to take to me from then on. I have to say, though, I still felt so much closer to Peter. Not only was he my first-born, he was a reminder of London. My Cockney lad. Though you'd never think so to hear him speak. Junior won't have it. Likes to be told stories of England, but to him that is all they are, stories. He is an all-American boy, according to him and his father. Which is only natural, I suppose. He *has* grown up here, has experienced all the good things that America has to offer, been part of a large family whereas I was an only child.

Peter was eight years old, and Joe and I had had two more children, both girls, before my mother came over to visit us. It was her reaction to how we lived that set me thinking. Mum went on and on about grey British skies, the cold climate and how the damp English chill got right through to her bones. Our American home is very large and warm inside, and the sun shines outside, or at least it did while she was here. My memories of London had been rose-coloured. Her stories of poor housing and not too many jobs had me realizing how lucky I was and what a wonderful chance Joe had given me and Peter. Not far from where we live is a tourist area. Peter and three of his cousins worked there one summer, when they were all about fourteen years old. Their fathers teach them from an early age that it is good to work. Peter enjoyed talking to British visitors and I suspect he boasted that he had been born in London.

He does say that, at some stage in his life, he would like to have a vacation in England. Now to the hard part.

How does Peter feel about you and your husband? I can't honestly answer that. He has always had a quick temper but since he has grown up it would take a hell of a lot to make him lose it. Since learning about his blood group he's been very quiet. Makes no comment. When questioned he gives no answers. We shall have to give it time.

How about James? Does he want to hear about us? Perhaps visit? How do you feel? Would you like to visit?

Writing this letter is probably the hardest thing I have ever had to do. But, then, it's doubtful that there has ever been a more heartbreaking situation.

If you will let me I'd like to keep in touch. We could write to each other about how we feel, about our sons, tell it as it happens. Don't know about you, though I'm pretty sure it must be the same, my heart aches just looking at Peter. For the first time in twenty years I do not know what to say to him. Joe feels the same. He said it is like walking on eggshells.

I hope you give it a try.

Put your feelings down on paper and send me a letter. Has to be better than doing everything through a law firm.

If you cannot bring yourself to write to me I will try to understand.

With all best wishes,

Yours,

Beryl Piviteaux.

PS

Peter is six foot two inches tall. Has dark hair with reddish tints, which the family have always said he got from his Polish grandfather. Big brown eyes. Is very intelligent. Kind and loving. Adores his two sisters.

When Joan had finished the letter her head was spinning. So many similarities! We both seem to have the same kind of feelings. Now I'm so mixed-up. One minute I didn't want to know, wasn't the least bit interested in that family. Now I feel guilty: this other mother wanted, *needed*, to know everything and anything about the boy to whom she had given birth. She wanted the truth, never mind how much it would hurt. I'm a coward, burying my head in the sand, telling myself that what I didn't know couldn't hurt me, instead of facing the fact that everything now had to be brought out into the open.

She folded the letter carefully and put it back in the envelope. She couldn't bring herself to look at the photos. Not yet. Not by herself. She'd wait until Matt came home and perhaps they could look at them together. Sighing again she scolded herself 'For God's sake, go and do something and stop feeling so sorry for yourself.'

Long past midnight Joan was still awake, turning things over and over in her mind. Matt had phoned to say he wasn't coming home that night. Very early business meeting on site in the morning, he said. He was spending the night at his mother's. Pity, she'd so badly wanted to share the letter with him. She couldn't show it to the girls. Not yet. Not before their father had been given a chance to read it.

She slipped out of bed, pulled on her dressing-gown, pushed her feet into her slippers and went downstairs. A cup of cocoa was in order, she decided. Waiting for the milk to come to the boil, her mind was on Beryl Piviteaux. For so long she had done her best to block out her and her family completely but now her attitude had changed. It had to! Wilfully disregarding this American family was no longer an option.

Like herself, Beryl had brought up a son for twenty years, had loved and cherished him, planned with such hopes for his future, which must seem so unsettled now. God alone knew, she and Jamie were close but Beryl had clung to Peter like a lifeline. She had been uprooted from the East End of London and transported to live thousands of miles away, in the midst of strangers, a totally different way of life. Joe, the husband, was among his own kith and kin but whom had that poor lass had to turn to in those early years? Was it any wonder that Peter was the love of her life? What had she called him in her letter? Her Cockney lad!

Bet she didn't even voice that thought out loud, not too often anyway. Not to all his American relatives. An all American boy is how his father saw him. As for Joe's family, seems they changed his name to Junior as soon as he arrived in the States. None of it could have been easy for Beryl.

The sound of the milk boiling over brought Joan's thoughts back to the present. She made her cocoa, wiped up the spilt milk from the top of the stove and sat down at the table. She sipped at her drink.

Jamie, my beautiful, gorgeous Jamie, isn't really mine! And poor Beryl's thoughts must be running along the same lines.

Again her mind returned to the similarities between them. She and Beryl were both only children. They had both given birth to one son and two daughters . . . God, what a mess! There was so much she wanted to say to Jamie. She wanted him to know that nothing would change, that he was still her son, Matt was still his father, Meg and Rosie were still his sisters, but how could she put into words things that she now knew were not true?

She folded her arms on the table and her head went down. Now she didn't bother to brush away her tears. She was crying not only for herself but for her girls, for Matt, her parents and even Hester, who stubbornly refused to accept the truth. She cried for the American family, and in particular Beryl, the mother who had brought up Peter, the baby to whom Joan had given birth.

'God help us all,' she murmured, then stayed still and truly wept for a long, long time.

Upstairs Meg turned over her pillow because it was damp with her tears. Her heart was thumping. She had heard her mother get up and go downstairs, had wondered whether to go after her and decided against it. What comfort could she offer? So much that had once seemed steadfast had changed.

Jamie was quiet, still loving, but distant. Was he frightened? Apprehensive as to who he was and where he belonged? He must feel as if the bottom had fallen out of his world. God knew, she would do anything to help her brother but what could she do? She was at a loss to know which way to turn.

Rosie had been distraught when Jamie had phoned to say he wouldn't be able to get home for a few weeks. 'He's gonna stay away! He's not going to come home any more!' she had sobbed. 'All because someone has told him he's not really our brother.'

It had taken Meg ages to soothe her, to reassure her sister that nothing would alter, that Jamie *was* their brother and *always* would be. She was now asking herself a question: who was going to reassure her?

Chapter Seventeen

HAVING SAID GOODBYE to his mates Jamie Pearson hurried out of the café. It was a quarter past two, he hadn't been home for three weeks and he wanted to be back in time for the family evening meal. As he walked to where his motorbike was parked he was wishing he didn't feel so nervous. For weeks now he had been saying to himself, I don't want to belong to another family. Couldn't anyone understand that he didn't? That he was more than happy being James Pearson? He had parents and grandparents who adored him and two sisters for whom he would go to the ends of the earth. Why in hell had someone had to come along and demand that he take that blood test?

He wasn't stupid. He knew it had to be true: he hadn't been brought into this world or fathered by the couple he'd always known as his mother and his father.

That was now a proven fact.

The amount of tests that had been done, nothing had

been left to chance. As the saying goes, if you wait long enough the truth *will* out.

But why now, after all these years?

To come barging into their home to tell *his* mother that the baby she'd given birth to was really in America. How many times had he been told the story of the night he'd been born. It was a miracle really that anyone in that hospital had survived and if – no, not if – a mix-up *had* occurred, no one could be blamed, not with all the chaos that must have been going on that night. Patients and staff alike must have been terrified.

As far as he could gather from the private talks he'd had with Clive Richardson, the other lad had led a good life. The parents seemed OK, loved their son and had provided well for him, so why on earth had they stirred up this hornets' nest? They had found out the truth by accident. Until then, no one had had any doubts or been unhappy within the families so why not leave well alone? He was certainly not bemoaning the fact that he should have been brought up in the USA. He'd been given every chance in life within a good, caring family and now he'd give the world not to have learnt that he didn't really belong to them.

What a mess! I'm James, known to everyone as Jamie, not Peter, with Polish ancestors. He climbed on to his bike, put on his helmet, tightened the straps beneath his chin, then sat for a while just staring into space. How could he look at his mother, knowing that he had no real claim to her? Until he had left home to go to university he could never remember a night when she hadn't kissed him good-night. As for his dad! They didn't always see eye to eye, especially on education, he was the rough and ready type who earned his living by sweat and toil, but that took nothing away from his good nature. In so many ways he was exactly like his mother, dear old Gran, the salt of the earth. She was the kind of person of whom you knew every little fault but loved them just the same.

Thinking of his dad brought back a memory that hurt. It was when they'd come out into the fresh air, having been told the results of the tests. Matt had been livid. Before they got into the car he had put his arms around Jamie, saying, 'You're my boy, aren't you? Always have been and always will be, and no damn stranger is gonna tell me different.'

It had taken a great effort on his part to get the words out but he had said, 'Of course I am, Dad.'

If only it could have been the truth!

It had been even worse with his granddad. They'd always been such good mates and now to be told that he was no relation was more than the old chap could take.

'This won't do,' Jamie muttered aloud. 'Staying away from home isn't going to solve anything. Besides, I miss them. Every single one of them.'

He kick-started the bike, the engine roared into life and he was away.

He was more than half-way home when the skies opened up and the rain fell in torrents. He shook his head to clear the water from his visor, and took his eyes off the road, just for a second. Then as he gripped his handlebars even tighter, he saw it. Too late. He leant right over to the left, hoping to take the bike swiftly to the near-side of the road and avoid the huge lorry negotiating the bend but it clipped his right leg and he went into a spin, skidding and slithering on the wet surface. The noise was deafening. He had no idea where it was coming from or where he was going. Then suddenly there was silence. At least, for Jamie there was.

Cars stopped, people got out and ran. One man shouted, 'I'll phone for an ambulance.'

'Won't do the bloke on the bike much good,' said someone.

A middle-aged man approached, saying he was a doctor. Two burly-looking workmen heaved Jamie's bike out of the way. The lad appeared to be unconscious, but having found a pulse the doctor spoke quietly and calmly: 'The ambulance will be here in a minute, son. Squeeze my hand if you can hear what I'm saying.'

There was no response.

One onlooker offered to remove Jamie's helmet.

The doctor raised his head, and very determinedly said, 'No, leave it until the ambulancemen arrive. They'll know better what to do.' He felt helpless. The lad was lying awkwardly with one leg twisted. There was a lot of blood on the road where he lay, and they wouldn't know what was wrong with his head until they could see more. The lorry driver had been lucky: apart from having had a nasty shock he appeared to be all right.

'Good God, they're taking for ever, aren't they?' said one of the men who had helped to move the bike.

'It just seems like that,' the doctor answered.

Then they heard the wail of the sirens, and finally the ambulance was there.

One ambulanceman knelt to check that there was still a pulse, and the other said, 'Best to get a drip into his arm,' to the doctor, who was cutting through the sleeve of

Jamie's leather jacket. Then, very carefully, the two ambulancemen slowly removed Jamie's helmet and gently strapped padded boards and what looked like soft square pillows under his head and around his face, which was covered in blood.

Within twenty minutes the ambulance had sped off, its sirens screaming.

By the time the six o'clock television news had finished, Joan was worried. Jamie was always home by about four thirty, five o'clock at the latest. She had done a roast, even though it was a Saturday, because it was the one meal Jamie said the university never had on the menu and it was still his favourite. All the vegetables were dished up, the joint of beef was on the side waiting for Matt to carve it and the Yorkshire pudding batter was ready to go into the oven. She liked the puddings to cook while they were eating their starter; then she could carry them straight to the table and show off just how much they had risen.

Meg was sitting on the settee talking to her boyfriend, Brian Clarke. He had been invited to join them for dinner because Meg had said she didn't want to go out this evening as Jamie would be home. Rosie was sitting on the floor, her head resting against her father's knees. Everything seemed set for a happy family evening. Matt had brought some beer and a bottle of brandy home with him, which said a lot about how he felt to be seeing Jamie again. As a rule it took a lot to keep Matt at home on a Saturday evening: he was usually in the East End, touring the pubs with his brothers.

'It's foul out there,' he said, doing his best to calm Joan down, who was pacing back and forth to the window. 'Jamie's bound to be taking it carefully.'

By seven o'clock even he was worried.

Joan was just deciding that she had better feed them all and put Jamie's dinner in the hot cupboard to keep warm when the doorbell rang. She assumed it would be one of the lads with whom Rosie usually went to the community hall on a Saturday evening. As she was the only one on her feet she hurried to the front door. The sight of a policeman in uniform left her speechless and frightened.

'Mrs Pearson?'

'Yes.' It came out as a whisper, and fear gripped her.

'May I come in?' he asked, removing his helmet and undoing his drenched cape. 'I'll leave this in the porch, if that's all right,' he said. He wiped his feet on the doormat as Joan stepped aside.

'What's going on? What's 'appened?' Matt had appeared in the hallway. 'It's our boy, isn't it?' he asked, looking directly at the constable and placing a protective arm around his wife's shoulders.

'Yes, sir. I'm sorry to tell you that your son has been in an accident.'

'Oh, my God.' All the colour drained from Joan's face. 'Is he alive? Please tell us.'

'Yes, he is, but he was still unconscious when the ambulance got him to Kingston Hospital.'

'Kingston?' Matt queried. 'Then he wasn't too far from home. Can you tell us what happened – and how is he?'

'I know nothing of the accident, sir. I've only been told that your son has been seriously hurt and that you should get to the hospital.'

'Dear God,' Joan cried. 'What does "seriously hurt" mean? Just how bad is he?'

The constable looked uncomfortable. 'I'm sorry I can't

tell you more, I only know what I've been told. I've given you the message as it was given to me. I really think you should be getting to the hospital.'

'You're right,' Matt said, taking charge. 'I'll see you out then I'll get the car out of the garage. Thank you for coming. Yours is not an enviable job at a time like this.'

'I hope you get some good news when you arrive at the hospital. Goodnight, Mrs Pearson, goodnight, sir.' The policeman fixed his cape round his shoulders and headed out into the night.

Tears were streaming down Meg and Rosie's faces when their parents came back into the room. They had heard enough to know that their brother had been involved in a road accident and was now in hospital.

Matt was shoving his arms into his raincoat when he turned to Brian, saying, 'You'll stay 'ere with the girls till we get back, won't you?'

'Course I will, Mr Pearson, don't worry about them.'

'You'll ring as soon as you know anything, won't you, Dad?' Meg's voice was full of fear. Matt swallowed the lump that was nearly choking him and hugged his daughters in turn. 'The minute we know anything I'll be on that phone. Meg, you serve up the dinner – go on, never mind shaking your head, yer mother's gone to a lot of trouble and you three have to eat.' He turned to Brian. 'Give your folks a ring and tell them what's 'appened. They won't mind if you stay, will they?'

'Course they won't, Mr Pearson. I'll be here until you get back. And I do hope that you get some good news when you arrive at the hospital.'

Matt patted the lad's shoulder. 'Thanks, son,' he murmured, and headed for the door.

Joan pulled the belt of her coat tightly round her waist, tugged on her hat, pushed her handbag under one arm, kissed Meg, hugged Rosie, nodded to Brian and flew out after him.

Moments later they were on the way to Kingston. All the way Joan was praying, Please, God, let Jamie be all right, please don't take him from us.

Matt found a parking space near to the emergency entrance and together they ran into the building. The casualty area was ablaze with lights, and lots of people were sitting waiting, some with bandaged arms or legs. Further down was a corridor with a placard over the entrance that read, 'Treatment Area'. Matt took Joan's elbow and steered her towards the reception desk. His voice was gruff as he gave their names and asked to be directed to whichever ward his son had been taken to.

Joan's face was grey and she was trembling. The desk clerk felt sorry for her as she checked the surname and called a senior nurse. The nursing sister was efficient, yet her eyes showed that she cared as she led them both into a small private office. She made sure that they were sitting down before she began to speak. 'Your son has been taken straight to the operating theatre. He has a severe head injury. The doctors have decided to wait for a specialist. If you'd like to stay in here, where's it's quiet, one of them will come and talk to you both. He will be able to tell you more.' She went on, but Joan knew she wasn't taking in what was being said.

The sister left the room and shortly afterwards a middle-aged woman in a green overall came in bearing a tray of tea. Matt thanked her and took charge. He poured it out, then, remembering that he had once been told sweet tea was good for shock he ladled three heaped spoonfuls into one cup and stirred it well before handing it to Joan. She had taken several sips before she could bring herself to ask, 'Did the sister say that Jamie's head injury was serious?'

'Yes, she did,' he told her. 'She also said that if the surgeon does go ahead and operate it will take three to four hours, maybe longer. We just have to be patient and try not to panic.'

'I wish they'd let us see him,' Joan murmured softly. So many thoughts were going round and round in her head. Would her son end up brain-damaged? Would he die on the operating table before she had a chance to tell him she loved him? To let him know that no matter what any solicitors, doctors or members of that American family wrote or said to her he was, and always would be, her son, her one and only son. Oh, dear God, please, please, spare him. Don't take him from us. Not like this.

Matt felt at a loss. He could see that Joan was torturing herself. He took a deep breath. 'You just 'ave t' believe he'll pull through. Our Jamie's a tough nut, he won't give in, you'll see. Come on, love, drink yer tea.'

Joan was grateful that Matt was there. What if he'd been off on his usual Saturday-night binge with his brothers?

'I'm just going to find a telephone and ring the girls. I won't be long. You'll be all right? Though what the 'ell I'm going t' say t' them God only knows.' He left her and all Joan could think of was that her Jamie was lying on an operating table and the hospital staff wouldn't let her go to him.

Later, hand in hand, she and Matt walked the corridors and went outside to stand in the covered walkway feeling the cold air of the dark night. The rain continued to pour down relentlessly. When they returned, the sister approached them again. 'Mr Pearson, one of the doctors would like to see you both.'

'May we see our son now?' Joan's request was more of a plea.

'Just a little longer, Mrs Pearson. The doctor waiting for you will explain your son's condition. Give you all the details, well, as far as he is able.'

Joan turned quickly to stare at Matt and he was alarmed by the terrified look on her face. She hesitated, seemed unable to move, to put one foot in front of the other.

Matt grasped her arm. 'Come on. At least we'll know what's going on.'

They made their way down the corridor to where the doctor stood waiting. The very sight of him had Joan trembling from head to foot. He was still wearing what she took to be a surgical gown and a funny crumpled cap on his head. A mask had been pushed down to hang round his neck.

'Is our boy all right?' Joan blurted out. She had to know. Was Jamie alive and if so in what state?

The doctor directed his reply to Matt. 'Mr Pearson, your son has come through the operation. He's a well-built lad, strong constitution, which is all in his favour. His leg was broken, and he's suffered some internal bleeding. It's the head injury that was the problem, and we've done all we can for the time being. Now it's just a question of waiting. With such a head injury many a lad would not have made it this far. But James has, and that has to be a good sign, though I have to add there's a long way to go yet.'

'Thank you,' Matt said gruffly, holding out his hand to shake the doctor's. 'Will we be able to see him?'

'We'd rather he wasn't disturbed. We're going to keep him where we can monitor everything. Later on, maybe in the morning, he'll be transferred to a side ward.' He turned to Joan, who was staring into space, and wondered if she had taken in any of what he had said. 'Our main concern at the moment is his breathing, but that's to be expected with this type of injury. You can just take a peep at him. Don't be afraid of the tubes – he'll look so much better when you come back tomorrow.' The last sentence was spoken without conviction.

Nothing that anyone had said had prepared either Joan or Matt for what they saw when they went into the recovery room where Jamie lay. There was a breathing tube in his throat, and more tubes and machines seemed to be attached to all parts of the bed. His head was swathed in bandages. The small part of his face that was visible was so battered that Joan wasn't even sure it was Jamie who was lying there.

Matt was sobbing openly, but Joan took a deep breath and bent over Jamie, gently stroking his hand, which lay on top of the sheet. All she could think of was the night he'd been born. Both of them could so easily have died that night, but she had had him now for twenty glorious years. He was one of the best things that had ever happened to her. But suddenly everything was going wrong. How was it possible that so much could change so quickly? First to be told that he wasn't the boy to whom she had given birth and now this accident. Would he go out of her life for ever now? That couldn't happen. She wouldn't let it. He had to come home, be part of their lives. A big part: play pranks on his sisters, tease them, shout at them; leave his bedroom in such a mess that she would shout at him. I'll never have a go at you again, no matter what mess you make, she vowed silently. Just wake up and be well. Come back to us. Bring your girlfriends home, let me see you get married and have the joy of holding grandchildren who look just like you did as a baby.

Matt wiped his eyes and put out a hand to his wife. 'I'm going to take you 'ome now. We both need to get some rest and, anyway, the girls will be waiting up. We'll come back first thing in the morning.'

'All right.' She touched Jamie's hand.

Matt took his wife's arm and gently led her out of that strange, silent room. He helped her on with her coat and held her tight for several minutes. As he slowly released her he saw such deep sadness in her eyes that it frightened him. Never in all the years they had been together had he seen her suffering as she was at this moment.

'He doesn't deserve this,' Joan whispered.

Matt nodded but stayed silent. To himself he was agreeing, but he was also thinking that if everyone got their just deserts in life then where would we be?

Without thinking about it he found himself praying silently. Please, God, spare my son. I'll never ask for another thing if just this once you listen to me. I've not been the best of husbands but I can't stand to see my Joan suffer like this. And as to losing our son, it doesn't bear thinking about. Please let him pull through.

'How's Jamie?' Meg asked before they had set foot inside the door.

'Pretty poorly,' Matt told her. Then, doing his best to smile at his daughters, he added, 'But he's going to be OK. One of the doctors who helped operate on him said he's come through remarkably well. Now we have to wait and see.'

'I'm going to make us all some tea,' Rosie said.

Joan gave her a hug. Rosie was always so kind-hearted and thoughtful.

'I've left the car in the drive,' Matt said to Brian. 'I'll run you home.'

'If it's all the same to you, Mr Pearson, I'd like to stay here. I can kip down on your big sofa. I've already told my parents that I'd more than likely stay the night.'

Matt remembered something. 'Have you kids eaten anything?'

'Yes,' Meg answered softly. 'I dished up the dinner. Can I get you and Mum something, even if it's just a sandwich?'

'No, darling,' Joan answered quickly. She felt that food would choke her.

'Do you want anything, Dad?'

He shook his head. It wasn't fair: he should be looking after his family but he couldn't protect any of them from this.

Rosie's face was full of sadness. 'Our Jamie will be all right, won't he, Dad?'

Poor Matt. This was more than he could bear. It was as though an icy hand was touching his heart. He looked away from her. He couldn't lie to her and he didn't know the answer so he said nothing. Rosie stood beside him for a minute, then knelt down, placed her arms around his neck and cried. Yet somehow Matt felt comforted.

He heard Meg yawn. 'Come on, let's get you all to bed. Tomorrow everything will seem better.' He glanced across the room to where his wife was laying out a pillow and a blanket for Brian's makeshift bed. All tomorrows were uncertain, he thought, but none more so than this one.

Chapter Eighteen

By TEN O'CLOCK on Sunday morning Joan and Matt were back at the hospital. For two hours they had sat in uncomfortable chairs in the waiting room. They hadn't been told much except that Jamie was holding his own, and so far they had not been allowed to see him. It didn't make sense to Joan, and Matt was getting more than a little irritated. It was a relief when, at last, a sister came and said the doctor had finished his rounds and would like to talk to them.

His first statement hit Joan like a fist in the face. Jamie's condition was so severe that he would have to stay in hospital for some time. But he had survived the operation well. It would be several days before they would know how complete his recovery would be.

Oh, my God! Joan's hands shook.

Matt wanted to put questions to the surgeon who had done the operation, but was told that was not possible.

Sister beckoned a young nurse and asked her to take them

along to spend a little time with Jamie, who had been moved into a side ward.

Joan stood beside the bed. She didn't dare look at Matt.

If anything, Jamie looked worse than he had last night. The top half of his face was free of bandages and both eyes were badly bruised. She clutched Matt's hand. Someone brought a chair and she sat down beside the bed.

Matt sat next to her, and his heart ached as he listened to his wife talking softly to their boy. 'Meg and Rosie send you all their love. Rosie said she got you that book you wanted from the library. Your dad is here . . . We both love you so much. Everyone does. We haven't told your gran yet. Can you imagine if she comes here to visit you?' Joan gave a foolish laugh, which she smothered. 'Knowing Amy, she'll want to take over. Only she can really take care of her Jamie. That's what she'll tell them.'

Hysterical laughter and tears were getting mixed as Joan continued to whisper, her face close to Jamie's bandaged head, without so much as a flicker of recognition from the still figure in the bed.

It was early afternoon when Matt went home. He had done his best to persuade Joan to go with him, but there was no budging her and the nurses said it was all right for her to stay. He said he would see that the girls were OK, have a bath, change his clothes and come back for her at about six o'clock.

Later, a young nurse suggested that Joan have a break. 'I'll walk with you, show you where the canteen is,' she offered. All the way there she chatted about how big and strong James was, and how that would help in his recovery.

'I can't see any of his hair,' Joan remarked, more to herself than to the nurse.

'That's because his head has been shaved.'

Once inside the cafeteria the nurse got Joan a cup of coffee and a packet of biscuits, then left her. Joan didn't hear anyone approach the table until she felt a hand on her shoulder. Looking up she saw John Chapman. He was the picture of health, wearing a dark grey suit and a crisp white shirt.

'Mary and Linsey told me the sad news. They've been to your house this morning and Meg and Rosie explained where you were, but they said Matt was with you.'

'He was. He's not long left, gone to see if the girls are all right.'

'Have you seen Jamie today?'

She nodded.

'How was he?'

Joan shrugged. 'Hard to tell. He hasn't come round yet.'

'Jamie's a strong lad. I'm sure he'll be all right.'

'Yeah. Maybe. Everyone keeps telling me he will be,' she said.

'You've drunk your coffee, but weren't you supposed to eat the biscuits?'

Joan tried to smile. 'They're too dry, they'd stick in my throat. Besides, I'm not the least bit hungry.' Then, changing the subject, she asked, 'What are you doing here on a Sunday afternoon?'

'Visiting a colleague. I've brought him a book. He's upstairs. Had a heart-attack, not allowed to get up. Now, tell me, when did you last eat?'

'I'm all right. Really. I just don't think I could eat just now.'

'You're going to have to try,' he told her, quietly but firmly. 'Come on, on your feet. Come to the counter and choose something hot. It need only be something light.'

Joan sighed. 'OK,' she said reluctantly.

At the counter he took a tray, leant forward and spoke quietly to a motherly woman, who was arranging an assortment of food. Then, turning to Joan, he smiled. 'You have a choice, poached egg on toast or scrambled egg.'

'A poached egg would be fine, thank you.'

'I'll bring it over to you when it's ready,' the assistant said.

John thanked her, then ushered Joan to a table, before going back to the counters. 'Don't know about you,' he said, 'but too much coffee makes me thirsty so I've bought tea for us both. You going to be mother?'

He chatted, Joan half listened, and then her meal was brought to her. It didn't seem right to her to be sitting here, eating hot food, talking to a neighbour with whom she had never been over-friendly. Jamie was lying unconscious, her girls were at home with no Sunday dinner, and Matt was having a hard job to cope with life at the moment. She managed to eat the egg and most of the toast, then laid down her knife and fork and thanked him.

John's quiet voice droned on as if in the far distance. She never realized her head had dropped forward and she had dozed off.

It was some time later when she woke with a start to find Matt watching her. There was no sign of John Chapman.

Matt looked at her for a long moment, not sure what to say to her, then glanced at his watch. He'd been to see Jamie. There was no change: he was in a deep coma. This was all too much for Matt: he needed a pint. In fact he needed several pints. What with the girls inconsolable, he was at his wits' end.

'Come on, Joan,' he pleaded, reaching a hand across the

table. 'I'll come with you to say goodnight to Jamie and then I'll take you home. You'll be all right with Meg and Rosie, won't you?'

'I don't understand,' she answered, rubbing the sleep from her eyes. 'Where are you going?'

'To see my mother. She must be very cut up about all this.'

Joan knew there was more to it than he was letting on. What he wanted was to go drinking with his brothers. Well, who could blame him? She wanted to ask him if he'd be home that night, but it would be late before he even got to his mother's and she knew what the answer would be.

It was ten o'clock on the Monday morning as Joan stood in her kitchen, trying to decide what to do next. She had come downstairs at seven and rung the hospital. Jamie was comfortable, whatever that meant, otherwise no change. She had been right in her assumption that Matt would stay up in the East End. He had probably had so much to drink that he would have been incapable of driving home. Like a zombie, she had made a pot of tea and taken a cup up to each of the girls' bedrooms, standing awhile gazing at their faces, which looked so peaceful while asleep. An early-morning kiss and cuddle had been a good start to the day. The three had breakfasted together, just cornflakes and toast, and she had promised to have a good dinner ready for them when they got home that evening. At the doorstep Rosie had turned back. The pitiful look on her young face made Joan's heart turn over. 'Mum,' she said, 'today please ask when we can visit Jamie.' Meg was nodding.

'I will. I promise. I do tell him all the time that you ask about him and send him your love.'

'But you said he can't hear what you're saying.' Rosie was on the verge of tears.

'We can't be sure of that,' her mother insisted. 'According to the staff nurse who was on duty last night, he might be able to hear everything. Perhaps it's just a matter of time until he responds.'

Rosie looked at her as she absorbed what her mother had said, then she asked another awkward question. 'Why didn't Dad come home last night?'

'By the time he got to your gran's it must have been late and I guess he went with your uncles for a drink. He's just as cut up about Jamie as we are. I think it's probably done him some good to stay over and talk to his brothers.'

'Oh.' Rosie looked relieved.

Meg guessed what her mother was feeling. She had already spoken to her about visiting Jamie and Joan's answer had been frank: 'Try to keep Rosie off the subject as much as you can, sweetheart, because we can't let her see Jamie at the moment. I'd rather you waited a bit as well, really.'

'Just tell me about him, please, Mum.'

'Well, for a start he has no hair. His head and more than half his face are covered in bandages. What would frighten her most is all the tubes and machines. When he's a bit better . . . when he comes round . . . we'll take her then.' That's what she had said, but Meg knew that even as her mother spoke she was fighting tears and praying that it would soon be the truth.

It was with a sigh of relief that Joan had closed the front door behind them. Now she had washed and dressed and was undecided whether to go straight to the hospital or wait until the morning rounds had taken place.

She had tried to concentrate on jobs to be done – rooms

to be tidied, washing put to soak, vegetables prepared for dinner that night, all the little things that still had to be coped with despite the trouble that had come so unexpectedly into their lives.

The ringing of the front doorbell startled her. She opened the door to find John Chapman on her doorstep. 'Good morning,' he said. 'I just wanted to offer my services in any way that might be of help.'

'Oh.' Joan was taken aback. This was so unexpected. 'That's very kind of you.'

'I know you don't drive so if you need a lift to the hospital at any time you've only to ask. I am a writer, I work from home so am freely available. Or perhaps you'd like me to keep an eye on the girls at the weekend. It would be no bother, you know. They get on well with Linsey and Mary.'

Joan stepped back. 'Would you like to come in for a minute?' It was the least she could offer since he was so kind.

'I owe you an apology,' she said, once they were seated at the kitchen table. 'You were kind enough to buy me a meal yesterday and I repaid you by falling asleep.'

He threw back his head and laughed. 'I felt guilty leaving you. You didn't look at all comfortable but it seemed such a pity to wake you. You needed the rest, you were exhausted, and I couldn't stay. I had to get back to get my girls' tea. Not that they couldn't have fended for themselves but I'd told them I wouldn't be long.'

'I did feel better for that sleep, and Matt was there when I woke up.'

Without asking, Joan set out two cups, cream and sugar, and lit the gas beneath the coffee-pot. Then she said, 'You cope very well on your own with your daughters. My two are full of praise for you. I'm just afraid that they take advantage, you running them about as you do.'

'Never think that,' he said sounding stern, but he was smiling as he said it. 'It's a pleasure, really it is. I'd do anything for my two and your two are good company, all of them being around the same age.'

'Must have been very difficult at first, coping on your own,' Joan remarked.

'In one way you could say that, but then again it was a great relief when my wife finally made the break. Everyone seemed to know what was going on except me. Even at the beginning you couldn't have said we had a good marriage.' He paused, as if deep in thought. 'Though out of it came Linsey and Mary, and for those two I shall always be grateful to my ex-wife. They fill my life.'

Joan remembered what Rosie had said on the day he had picked them up for tennis: that his daughters wished he'd find another ladyfriend. Joan felt sorry for him: he was an attractive man, kind-hearted and thoughtful. 'Now your girls are almost off your hands maybe you will meet someone else,' she ventured sympathetically.

'No, I don't think so. I get stuck into my work so I'm happy enough, and as long as my girls are too, that's all I ask.'

Joan poured coffee for them both. He took his black with no sugar. Joan helped herself to cream and sugar.

'Are you going to the hospital this morning?' he asked.

'Not yet. I'm going to see my parents and my nan. Then I expect my dad will go with me to see Jamie.'

'Oh, I didn't realize your folk lived nearby but, come to think of it, I have seen them here on several occasions, and Meg and Rosie often speak of them.'

'They're only at Merton Park. I can get a bus from the main road.'

John Chapman drained his cup, stood up and said, 'No need for that. My car is outside. If you're ready I'll willingly take you.'

Joan hesitated. She had been hoping that Matt would have rung by now. Of course she could phone him at the office but ten to one she would only get the girl who worked there. As it was Monday morning Matt and Stan would be out touring the sites, setting the men on for the week. The offer of a lift was pleasing: she didn't feel like standing about waiting for a bus and she could always ring Matt when she got to her mum's. 'I'll be five or ten minutes, if you're sure you don't mind.'

'Of course I don't. I'll wash the cups while you're getting yourself ready.'

Joan was touched, and didn't know what more to say than, 'Thank you.'

Not a word passed between them until the car was caught in traffic at South Wimbledon.

'You turn right here, then take the second left,' Joan directed him.

Within minutes they were outside the house. John switched off the engine, got out of the car, came round to her side and held open the door. 'Now, don't forget, if you need me just ring. I wrote my number down and left it on your hall table, though I'm pretty sure that either of your girls could have given it to you.' He grinned. 'They ring my two often enough.'

As soon as she was safely on the pavement he waved and drove away.

She had thanked him again, but it didn't feel enough.

She was pondering: was John Chapman a thoroughly nice man, a real gentleman? Or was he just a little bit smarmy?

Don't be so unkind, she chided herself. It's probably that I'm used to Matt. A rough diamond if ever there was one. But smarmy? No. Never. You couldn't use that word to describe Matt.

Chapter Nineteen

HER DAD OPENED the front door. Both Daphne and Hester were out. Bill Harvey held out his arms, and Joan rushed into them. 'Am I glad to see you,' Bill said, and he kissed the top of her head. Once he had her settled in an armchair beside the fire he bent down and took a good look at his daughter. He was appalled: the dark circles under her eyes looked terrible. 'Have you phoned the hospital this morning?' he asked.

'Yes, about seven o'clock.'

'And?'

Suddenly she couldn't find the words. Bill watched as she tried to hold back the tears. 'They said there was no change but that Jamie had had a comfortable night.'

'Has Matt gone to work?'

'I don't know. He didn't come home last night.' She had spoken without thinking.

Bill straightened up and patted her shoulder.

Joan sensed that her father was angry with Matt. 'What

with all that has happened already since Christmas, I don't think Matt can face much more,' she said quietly, not daring to voice what was really going through her mind.

'Oh? And what about you? Are your shoulders so much broader than his?'

'Please, Dad, you mustn't judge Matt. He really cares about Jamie, honestly he does. He just doesn't know how to handle it all.'

'And you do? You can carry all the burden on your own? Doesn't it make you angry that he's not here with you?'

Joan sighed. 'He never left me all Saturday night, and all day yesterday he stayed at the hospital. I think he felt he just had to get a break. If there was anything he could do . . . He feels so . . . helpless, I suppose.'

'I'll come to the hospital with you this morning. We'll leave a note for your mum to tell her where we've gone.'

The first person they saw when they got out of the car was Matt. He was standing outside the main entrance. He came running as soon as he spotted them. 'I was trying to make up my mind what to do. I went in to work this morning just to set things straight in the office, then I phoned home and got no answer so I came on here. I've been to the ward. Sister said there had been no change since last night and that the doctor would talk to us as soon as the ward rounds were finished.' He took Joan's arm and squeezed it, then turned to Bill. 'Bloody bad business all round, ain't it?'

Joan sighed. He had said nothing about not having come home last night and yet, in a way, she felt sorry for him.

Those were Bill's sentiments too: Matt looked spruce enough, well turned-out, clean-shaven, his short thick dark hair was neat and tidy yet somehow his spirit had been broken.

Later, the three stood in a group and listened to what the surgeon had to say: 'There has been no sign of an improvement in your son and we need to operate again.' Joan would have liked to put so many questions to this stocky, broad-shouldered man, who held her son's life in his hands. Instead she listened quietly as he talked to Matt and her father, and a few minutes later Matt was signing the necessary papers. 'We can see Jamie now for a little while. They won't be operating until later on today,' Matt told them, doing his best to smile.

Her father and Matt looked awkward as they sat side by side beside the bed opposite Joan.

She was leaning across the bed, holding Jamie's hand and talking softly to him. Now and again she stroked his arm. It seemed a long, long while, and it was something of a relief when a nurse quietly told them they must leave as it was time to prepare James for surgery.

The surgeon had said that he did not know how long the operation would take, which in itself was frightening. What were they looking for? Would they be able to repair the damage inside his head? All three were trying hard not to think of what might happen in the operating theatre.

They came outside into the damp, miserable April day and stood like three lost souls. 'I suggest we all go home to your mother,' Bill said quietly. 'She'll be only too glad to see you both, and she'll want to feed you. Besides, it will relieve your nan's mind if she hears first hand from you that Jamie's holding his own.'

Joan looked up sharply. 'Are you suggesting that we lie to her?'

'No, of course not,' Bill assured her. 'Jamie *is* holding his own so far, and we've got to hang on to that.'

'Good idea,' Matt said. 'I'll leave my car here if you'll run us back later on, Bill. But while you're getting yours out I'll pop back inside, let the ward sister know where we'll be if they need to telephone us.'

It was a long afternoon. After a tearful welcome from Daphne and Hester they had struggled to eat a late lunch but had little to say to each other. Hester started to reminisce once or twice about Jamie and the girls when they were small, but Joan couldn't bring herself to join in. Most of the time she sat quietly, lost in thought, wondering how she was going to answer Beryl Piviteaux's letter.

Matt was watching the clock, half hoping that the telephone would ring but dreading the thought that it might be bad news. At half past five he got to his feet. By then he and Joan looked as if they couldn't take much more. 'Come on, Joan,' he said. 'We'd best get back to the hospital. D'you mind running us there, Bill?'

'Course not. I'll just get my keys.'

First Daphne and then Hester held Joan long and hard. 'We'll be praying,' her mother said, as they stood on the doorstep. 'You'll ring straight away if there's any news?'

Joan nodded, tempted to say, 'Don't get your hopes up too high.'

When they arrived at the intensive care unit the sister said, 'James hasn't been brought back up yet,' so once again they sat in the waiting room.

It began to get dark outside and it started to rain again, spitting and splashing against the uncurtained windows, making them both feel grateful at least that they were inside in the dry.

The same stocky doctor came in to them at a quarter to seven.

'How did it go?' Matt leapt to his feet and stared down into the eyes of the shorter man.

The doctor smiled. 'We're all very hopeful. It went better than we expected.'

Matt was getting tired of that word hopeful. 'Please, would you mind explaining that in plain words,' he said.

'During the night we were worried about James. There was too much pressure in his skull from when his head hit the ground. We have succeeded in relieving most of that and now we feel there's every reason to believe that your son will make a full recovery.'

Joan wanted to stand up and thank him, but her legs wouldn't support her. She just sat there, saying silently over and over again, thank you, God.

The doctor was still talking to Matt. Most of their conversation went over Joan's head until she heard him say, 'It's a question of waiting now to see how he does and, of course, how long he remains in the coma.'

'You mean, he still won't come round and talk to us?' Matt was dismayed.

'Mr Pearson, the kind of injury your son sustained requires patience. Only time will give us all the answers we need.'

Matt sighed heavily and the surgeon turned to look down at Joan. 'Your son really is holding his own, Mrs Pearson,' he said gently. 'He's not out of danger yet but he's come though this second operation really well and that is an encouraging sign. For the next twenty-four hours we're going to keep him on strong medication. I suggest you both go home and get some rest. I promise we'll call you if there is any news.'

He shook hands with them and left. Matt and Joan looked

as if they had had the stuffing knocked out of them. 'If only there was something we could do,' Matt said miserably.

Joan raised her head and asked the question that had been niggling at the back of her mind since seven o'clock that morning. 'Matt, why didn't you come home last night?'

'I had too much t' drink so I stayed at my mother's,' he answered calmly.

'No, you didn't,' she said, without raising her voice. 'I telephoned Amy as soon as I got out of bed this morning because I was worried about you.'

'Does it matter?' he queried gruffly. 'I had a few too many. I was with Stan.'

'Yes, I know you went drinking with your brother, but he left you just after eleven o'clock.'

'What is this?' Matt's face had turned a deep red and there was an expression in his eyes that she hadn't seen for ages. Sheer rage was what she was looking at. 'Did you ring round all of the family just t' check on me?'

'No,' Joan answered. 'While I was talking to your mum, Stan walked in and he hedged, just said he'd get you to ring me as soon as you walked into the office. But you didn't ring, did you? I couldn't help wondering who you did spend the night with.'

Half of her wanted to push it further and ask, 'What about all the other Saturday nights you've spent away from home? Were you at your mother's, as you always said you were?' But now was not the time. All she said was, 'Maybe you'd like to tell me about it sometime,' in little more than a whisper. Matt looked away and didn't answer.

Slowly she got to her feet. 'Shall we go home? The girls will be worried.'

Chapter Twenty

JOAN WAS LISTENING to Matt tell Meg and Rosie what had taken place at the hospital that day. Their brother, he explained, had suffered a severe head injury. The first operation had not quite done the trick so today the surgeons had performed a second. 'Now all we have to do is wait for Jamie to come round, and by the time he's recovered from two lots of surgery he's going to be fine.'

The girls had prepared a meal and Matt opened a bottle of port, telling them that one glass would make them all sleep better. Somehow they passed the time until Meg and Rosie said they were going up to bed.

Joan went to the foot of the stairs with her girls, kissing them both in turn and saying, 'Goodnight, my darlings, try to get a good night's sleep. God bless you both.'

Rosie hesitated on the third stair. 'Mum,' her voice trembled, 'is it true that our Jamie's going to be all right? An' if it is, can I come with you to see him tomorrow?'

Meg looked her mother straight in the eye, and her face

showed that she, too, would like an answer to that same question.

'Well, my pet, the surgeon did say we all had to show a great deal of patience. Jamie is still in a coma but they're now sure it's only a matter of time and then . . .' Then what? She didn't know herself so how could she tell her girls? 'I will promise you one thing. The moment they say it's all right for Jamie to have visitors you two will be the first.'

Rosie looked doubtful and Meg put her arm around her sister and said, 'Come into my bed for a little while. Bring a book and we'll keep the light on and read together.'

Back in the sitting room Matt had his legs stretched out and was reading the paper.

'You shouldn't have told the girls that,' she said, more loudly than she had meant to. There were so many questions she wanted to ask him and now that the girls had gone to bed she could begin.

'Told them what?' he asked angrily. He knew that he was going to have to face up to the fact that Joan had caught him on the hop.

'You told them that Jamie was going to be fine. We don't know that for sure.'

'Oh, for Christ's sake! Now you're splitting hairs. That surgeon said our son has a good chance of making a full recovery. What more do you want? A bloody guarantee? Our girls are going through hell. They love Jamie t' bits. What was I supposed t' tell them, eh? Go on, answer me. What d'yer want me t' tell them? If it 'elps them through this it can't be bad, and if the worst comes t' the worst, well, we'll all 'ave t' face that, if an' when it 'appens.'

He was shaking with temper, and Joan couldn't stop herself saying, 'Feeling guilty, are you?'

'And what's that supposed t' mean?' he yelled. He hated the way this conversation was going, but he knew he was cornered.

'I was merely asking about last night. So far you still haven't said where you spent it.'

'It's got bugger all t' do with you.' He hadn't meant to say that, but there was no turning away now.

'Oh, Matt, I think it's got everything to do with me. Many a Saturday you take yourself off and I've never questioned where you go or who you're with, but this time you deliberately lied to me.'

'I've asked you t' come often enough but you just don't like drinking in pubs.' Matt was seeking any excuse he could think of.

'This wasn't a Saturday night it was Sunday, and the pubs close at ten o'clock. You said you were at your mother's, and by chance I found out you weren't, so is it too difficult to tell me who you spent the night with?' Joan was finding it hard to control her own temper.

'All right. OK. So you found out. You sure you want t' know the ins an' outs?'

Joan had thought she knew what his answer was going to be, but this outright admission knocked her for six. She had been hoping he would deny everything, come up with some plausible excuse. She hadn't wanted it to be true. But now he'd told her it was. It had to be faced.

'How long, Matt?'

He didn't answer her.

'Tell me, please. Has it been a regular thing? Who is she? Do we know each other?'

'I'm not going into all the ruddy details with you, Joan, so just leave it, will you?'

'No. I need a few answers. I think you owe me that much. Is it just a fling or has it been going on for a long time? Maybe all these years since we moved away from the East End.'

Matt sat down and stared at her. 'I should have put a stop to it ages ago,' he said, sounding confused.

'Is it serious, then?' Joan didn't want to know but felt compelled to ask.

For a long time he didn't answer. 'No, it isn't. Not on my part it isn't, but how can I make you believe that?'

'What d'you mean, "ages ago"? So it has been a long-term thing? And I'm asking you again, who is she and do I know her?'

'It began when we first moved here. I missed me mates and I missed the pub life. Then I put a stop to it. It only started up again when Clive Richardson appeared on our doorstep.'

'If it's a she, how can you say it was because you missed your mates?'

'Well, she used to get in the pubs I used with me mates. She was always on her own. Her 'usband was killed on the docks. I felt sorry for her. She was left with four kids.'

'I can't take this in,' Joan said slowly. 'First you say you took up with her again when you found out that Jamie was not your true son. Some way to get yerself over that shock, I must say. Then you're telling me she's a woman with four kids, so how come she could afford to go drinking on Saturday nights in the same pubs that you and your brothers used? What kind of a woman is she?'

'She's not a bad woman. She copes as best she can. She's not as intelligent as you but she always speaks highly of you.'

'God Almighty, so it is someone I know!'

'Yes.' For the first time Matt looked sheepish. 'Doris Shepherd, our next-door neighbour when we lived in Bull Yard. She got put into one of those high-rise flats and . . . I don't know . . . I guess I've always felt sorry for her. She needed a bit of comfort . . . someone t' talk to more than anything else. I did stop seeing her ages ago, more than three years, but then, well, I was almost out of my mind thinking we was going to lose Jamie.'

'Stop it. Just stop it, please.' Joan felt that if he said another word she'd kill him. She was asking herself why had she been so stupid. Out every weekend with his brothers! Those oh-so-important darts matches that meant he had to stay the night away from home.

Matt was watching her carefully. He ran his hand through his thick hair. 'In a way I'm glad it's all out in the open.'

For the life of her Joan couldn't understand why it had happened. Maybe if the other woman had been some London high-flyer, someone well groomed and sophisticated, even someone who was really beautiful, but Doris Shepherd! She had had four kids even when they lived next door to her. They must be all grown-up by now. She couldn't take it all in. Too much had happened.

'I'll knock it off. I swear t' God I will. Look,' he held out his hands, 'I don't expect you t' understand and certainly not forgive me. But listen t' me. Please, Joan, give me a chance. Let's concentrate on helping our girls to cope and praying that Jamie will come through with flying colours. Then perhaps you'll believe me when I say I will deal with this.'

Joan remained silent.

'I can't figure myself out,' Matt said, breaking the silence and making Joan jump.

'I'd made the break all that time ago, and you weren't hurt cos you were none the wiser. Then this bloody affair with the American family cropped up and I went to pieces. It was the daftest thing I've ever done in my life. Joan, can you believe me, please? I know I sound pathetic but I am sorry. I really regret going back to her.'

Tears were glistening in Joan's eyes as she and Matt looked at each other across the room.

'You deserve better than me,' he said, so quietly that Joan burst into tears. 'Can I make you a cup of tea?' He didn't know what else to say.

Through her tears Joan was smiling. To her knowledge Matt had never made a cup of tea in his life. 'Yes, please,' she murmured.

Twenty minutes later they were seated at the kitchen table and Joan was sipping quite a decent cup of tea.

'Joan . . . I do love you. I know it will take time for . . . I'm sorry,' he said softly, and made no move to stop her when she got to her feet.

'I'm whacked,' she told him. 'I have to go to bed.' Then she picked up her cup of tea and went out of the room.

Upstairs she closed the bedroom door and turned the key in the lock, then sat on the edge of her bed and finished her tea.

This year was a third of the way through. It would be May soon, springtime. New life, new beginnings. Could life throw anything else at her? She had had to face the truth that her dearly beloved son was not hers at all. Then that same lad had almost got himself killed and was by no means out of the woods. To top it all she had learnt that her husband had been having an affair, for a very long time, with a woman who had four children. All in all that didn't say much for her, did it? As she climbed into bed she was praying that 1965 wouldn't hold any more unpleasant surprises.

It was some time later that she heard Matt's unsteady footsteps as he came up the stairs. She listened as he turned the door-handle. Then came a terrific thud as he kicked at the door, then a string of swear words. He had been drinking. Since she had come up to bed he must have hit the bottle hard. Even when he moved from the landing the noise didn't stop. Downstairs he was banging about like a madman. She hoped against hope that the girls would have the sense to stay in their room; certainly their father must have woken them up. Only someone stone deaf could have slept through the racket he was making.

Joan knew what was biting him: she hadn't acted in the way he had wanted and expected her to. She hadn't crawled, hadn't said she understood or that she would forgive and forget, hadn't fallen into his arms or pleaded with him to go on loving her. In other words he had come off worst and because of that *he* felt hard done by and had let his temper get the better of him. What had been his main excuse? The fact that so much had happened, especially dealing with the solicitors over who were Jamie's rightful parents.

He couldn't take any more? What about *me*? He was always drumming into her that women were the weaker sex. Finally the noise lessened, the house was quiet, and Joan, exhausted, fell into a deep sleep.

Chapter Twenty-One

JOAN LOOKED DOWN at her son. He looked better, or was it her imagination? He still hadn't opened his eyes or said a word. Now and again he seemed restless, as if he was struggling to come out of the coma, and the nurses kept telling her that that was a good sign.

She leant back in her chair and stretched her arms above her head. She was trying to decide whether to go to the cafeteria for a hot drink, or whether to go home and make dinner for the girls.

The clock on the wall of this single room showed it was just coming up to two o'clock. It was Thursday, she reminded herself. Tomorrow would be the start of another weekend, and she shuddered to think what might happen.

She hadn't seen Matt since that awful Monday night. She had come downstairs on the Tuesday morning to find the living room a shambles and Matt gone. How could he do this, with Jamie still so ill? Every day she had gone through the motions of seeing the girls off to work then spending as much time as she could at the hospital. Now it was as if she didn't have the energy to get to her feet.

A nurse came out from behind her glass partition and said quietly, 'The front office have just rung through. Your mother-in-law is in Reception and would like to talk to you.'

'Oh.' Joan was flummoxed. Amy? Here? She'd made the journey? 'Sorry,' she stammered, trying to smile. 'I was just making up my mind to have a break, thank you.'

My God, look at the change in her, Amy thought, as she watched Joan come down the corridor. 'How's Jamie?' she asked. 'And you? How are you? I just had t' come.'

Joan felt Amy's arms wrap round her and she sighed. 'I don't know what you're doing here but, Amy, I was never more pleased to see anyone in my whole life. Jamie seems a bit better but actually there's no change. He doesn't even open his eyes.'

The two were feeling awkward now. Joan patted Amy's shoulder and broke free. 'We can't talk here, not with all this hustle an' bustle going on. I was about to go and have something to drink so shall we save all the questions till we're sitting down?'

'Those words are sheer magic,' Amy declared. 'One, me feet are killing me, and two, I could murder a cup of tea.'

Joan linked her arm through her mother-in-law's and felt Amy pull her close and squeeze her tight. It felt safe and comfortable as they walked along slowly together. When there was a sticky bun and a cup of tea in front of them it was Amy who opened the conversation. 'You must 'ave a 'undred an' one questions you want t' ask me. First off, I expect you wanna know 'ave I seen Matt. Well, the answer is no, I 'aven't. But I 'ave kept tabs on him an' he's been with our Stan for the past three days. He knows what I'll 'ave t' say t' him an' he's steering well clear of me.'

Joan shook her head. 'Did you know about Doris Shepherd?'

'Well, when you first moved away I suspected it, but I buried me 'ead in the sand, so t' speak. It wasn't none of my business. Stan dropped 'ints from time t' time. Always said his brother was a bloody fool. Besides, what could I 'ave done? Matt's a grown man. Honest t' God, though, I'd no idea it 'ad started up again.'

'Matt told me it was only since Clive Richardson came on the scene and we've had all this trouble with blood tests and the knowledge that Jamie wasn't our true son.'

'Yeah, Stan said he was using that as an excuse.' Amy sighed. 'Don't make my son much of a man, does it? But I never knew. Not this time. And that's the gospel truth. I'd 'ave torn him off a strip or two, leaving you at a time like this and for what? A woman older than 'imself with four grown-up children. I never even 'ad a suspicion, not until Stan came t' me this morning an' said Matt had been on a binge for three days now and he didn't know what t' do about it. How come you suddenly found out what was going on?'

'It was when I phoned you last Monday morning and asked to speak to Matt. You said he wasn't there, then Stan arrived and sounded so guilty, doing his best to cover Matt's tracks. I knew Matt hadn't been with him either.'

'Oh, Joan, what a mess.' Amy gulped some tea, then went on, 'I don't want the two of you t' split up. These last four months must 'ave been a ruddy nightmare for yer an' I'd give me right arm t' be able to do something t' help. I keep asking meself, what is there that anyone can do?' Her words ended on a sob.

'I know, Amy, I know.' Joan was sorry to see her so upset but she was glad too that she was with her.

Amy took a handkerchief from her big handbag and blew her nose. 'I'll admit that first off I thought you were a bit uppity for our Matt. Then I could see what a good mother you were, and there came a time when you let yerself go an' I began t' think Matt was dragging you down. Then yer bucked up, wanted to get a job an' make something of yerself and . . . well, I wasn't much 'elp, was I? Didn't want yer to move away from the East End either, didn't think it was right at all. But time 'as proved me wrong. Admitted as much at Meg an' Jamie's party, in front of everybody, didn't I?'

Joan was feeling calmer now, and smiled hesitantly. 'Yes, you did, Amy. At least I always knew where I stood with you.'

Amy shook herself. 'Now tell me the truth. How is Jamie?'

'About the same, as I said. Eat your bun, then we'll go back together and you can see for yourself.'

The staff nurse met them at the doorway. Joan introduced her mother-in-law, and the nurse said, 'I'll fetch another chair.' When Joan and Amy were seated side by side she told them, 'The doctors looked in while you were away, and they seemed satisfied with Jamie's progress.'

Joan wanted to ask, 'What progress?' but said only, 'Thank you.'

Poor Amy was crying quietly, upset to see her dear Jamie's face under all the bandages.

'His colour is ever so much better this last couple of days,' Joan whispered, 'and he's resting ever so much more peacefully.' She took Jamie's hand as she always did, and began talking to him softly. 'Your gran's here. She's come on her own. You ought to feel honoured, young man. Gran never leaves the East End unless 'tis for a very good reason. I haven't asked her yet but I'm hoping I can persuade her to come home with me and stay a few days. Then she'll be able to visit you again tomorrow.'

Suddenly there was a movement. The sheet that covered Jamie had lifted a little. Joan wondered if she had imagined it. She glanced at Amy, and from the look on her face knew she had seen it too. They turned their gaze back to Jamie, and he gave a shuddering sigh. Joan got up quickly and went towards the glass partition. The nurse met her halfway.

'He moved, well, not so much moved as sighed then settled down again.' Joan's voice was little more than a whisper.

'Would you mind waiting outside? I'll have to call Sister. She'll check his blood pressure and . . .' The nurse never finished the sentence. Joan and Amy were outside in the corridor and the door to the room where Jamie lay was firmly shut.

Amy looked angry. 'Why did she push us out like that?'

'Amy,' Joan said firmly, 'try to be patient. I've had to do a lot of waiting around. The sister will let us back in as soon as they've checked Jamie.'

Two doctors came, and it was some time before Joan and Amy were told they could return to his side. 'Your son is slowly coming out of the coma,' one doctor said, with a slow smile. Three nurses were standing at the end of the bed, whispering and watching.

'Thank you, thank you,' Joan muttered to no one in particular. Jamie's eyes were still closed but his breathing seemed different. She didn't know. She felt sure of only one thing and that was that there had been a real danger that Jamie would leave them. He had been so close to death but he had returned to her. Now he looked so peaceful. It was only a matter of time and, please, God, he would open his eyes and say, 'Hallo, Mum.'

She felt more peaceful than she had since the moment the policeman had called at the house to tell them that Jamie had had an accident. They had been given back their son. There was no mistake about it, and she would never, as long as she lived, stop thanking God for the reprieve.

Amy was crying unashamedly but they were different tears from those she had shed when she had first set eyes on Jamie's still figure lying in that bed.

As Joan and her mother-in-law left the hospital to go home, they were both struck by the power of prayer. Neither could put it into words but they would freely admit, sometime in the future, that there hadn't been a day go by since Jamie had crashed his motorbike that they hadn't prayed.

Joan was so grateful she felt light and happy. The misery and the anger she felt about Matt and his affair with Doris Shepherd didn't matter any more. She'd find the strength to deal with that somehow. It was impossible to explain, or to describe, but it was as if she'd been given an inner strength. Right now she was looking forward to telling Meg and Rosie that, any day now, they could visit their brother.

Chapter Twenty-Two

OVER THE WEEKEND, Joan felt as though her life had taken a turn for the better. Amy was still with them, much to the delight of Meg and Rosie, both of whom had now seen Jamie. And Joan no longer felt as if disaster loomed every time the telephone rang.

This morning, Sunday, she'd had a bath, washed and set her hair and had taken time to decide what to wear. She and Amy were going to the hospital after an early lunch, and then her father had offered to run Amy home. Despite all her protests Bill Harvey had been adamant. He wasn't going to allow Amy to travel back to the East End by train and then bus.

Yesterday Joan had taken Amy shopping, bought her a blouse, a pair of stockings, some knickers and a comfortable pair of shoes, because her mother-in-law hadn't come prepared to stay a few days. It was an outing they had both enjoyed and they had avoided all mention of Matt. Joan was aware that the girls had asked questions of their grandma but she didn't know what had transpired and she hadn't asked. It was sufficient for her to see that the girls had accepted some explanation of why their father was not at home. She herself had talked to them about Jamie and how his recovery would be a long-drawn-out business. Both girls had hugged her before she set off with their gran for the hospital.

The small room in which Jamie lay no longer seemed depressing: the screens around his bed had been removed and bright sunshine streamed in through the window. Both Joan and Amy looked and felt so much happier. True, Jamie had not come fully out of the coma yet but they were no longer terrified that he might die. And just seeing the sunshine made everyone feel so much better.

They hadn't been there long when Matt arrived. Told by the sister in charge that his son had turned the corner, he stood at the foot of the bed and let the tears trickle down his cheeks.

Amy knew it was a shock for him to find her there and her presence wasn't making it any easier for him to talk to Joan. She made a quick decision. 'Why don't the pair of you go for a walk? I'll sit with Jamie. There's a few things I'd like to tell him an' it's better done without either of you being here, whether he can hear me or not.'

Silently Joan thanked her for her tact, and said, 'All right, we'll have a cup of tea, then you can get yourself one when we come back.'

They left the room. Matt was feeling awkward. Joan was angry with him, he could see that from her face, and she had every right to be.

The cafeteria was packed. Sunday was a popular day for visitors at any hospital, and this one was no different. There were no empty seats, and children were running around chattering loudly.

'Shall we skip the tea and walk round the grounds?' Joan suggested.

Matt agreed, and soon they had found a bench on which to sit. It really was a glorious day: spring flowers were in bloom and the grass looked so green. Matt leant forward, his hands clasped between his knees. Without looking at Joan he said, 'Don't suppose there's much use in me saying sorry, is there?'

'Depends on what you're saying sorry for,' Joan replied sharply. 'If it's because you got found out, then don't bother.'

Matt straightened up. He looked grim. 'You shouldn't 'ave 'ad t' deal with this on top of everything else,' he muttered.

'You're damn right I shouldn't. But my husband had to find comfort away from home because too many worries were being thrown at him and he couldn't cope.'

'I deserved that,' Matt said bleakly.

'Would you like t' know what's really eating me?' Joan didn't wait for him to reply. 'The worst thing for me is that I was so blind. I would have sworn on our children's lives that we had a good marriage. Talk about deluding myself!' She shook her head. 'Been a proper fool, haven't I? You and Doris Shepherd must have laughed your heads off. Every weekend I stayed at home while you went off with her, an' I swallowed every story you told me. Special darts matches. Work to be seen to. Anything and everything I believed. Oh, I know it was my fault in the beginning that I wouldn't go on pub crawls with you but why couldn't you have stayed home sometimes and come on picnics with me an' the girls or taken them swimming or anywhere else they wanted to

go? You love them so much, you'd do anything for them –
that's what you're always saying, isn't it? Just goes to show
how cheap your talk is.'

Joan's voice had risen. Other people were walking in the
grounds and several heads had turned in their direction.

'I never thought of you as a fool, Joan,' Matt protested,
his voice low.

'Easy to say that now,' she said. 'I bet Doris Shepherd
did. She's been having the time of her life at my expense.'

Matt looked nervous. 'Are you going to tell me now what
you want to do about it?'

'Isn't that up to you and your ladyfriend?' Joan was trying
to be flippant. 'You probably can't wait to go back and live
in the East End. I bet you'll love it, living in a high-rise flat.
Might have a problem parking your car, though. Be quite
a change for you, won't it? By the way, are you coming to
the house today to fetch your clothes?'

'Are you throwing me out?' He sounded surprised that
she would dare even to suggest such a thing.

She smiled. It was a bitter smile. 'You really are amazing! You know that, Matt? You take the biscuit.'

'I never had any intention of leaving you,' he said stubbornly. 'You and the kids are my whole life.'

'Oh, I see. You want to have your cake and eat it too. You
don't want your image damaged, you still want to be seen
as a good father, head of a happy household. Doris is just
a bit on the side, is she? I wonder if she looks at it like that.
Perhaps I'll pay her a visit. Then she'll be able to tell me
her side of the story.'

By the look on Matt's face he was on the point of bursting a blood vessel. He ran a finger round the inside of his
shirt collar and took a deep breath. 'There's no need to start

being nasty. I've said I'm sorry and I mean it. It wouldn't 'ave 'appened if we 'adn't 'ad to go through all that flipping palaver over Jamie.'

'That's a fine excuse. Tailor-made for you. But if you think that's going to get you off the hook you've another think coming. Tell me about the first time. What's your excuse for starting the affair in the first place?'

Matt made no answer.

Joan pressed him. 'Come on, give me a reason. We'd moved to a lovely house, a nice area, and the children were all doing well. I thought I was the luckiest woman alive. Never dreamt you were going back to the East End to sleep with another woman.'

'It wasn't like that,' he hissed. 'Doris was lonely. She'd come into the pub where me an' me brothers were 'aving a drink, always on her own. It started, I suppose, cos I bought her a drink.'

'Oh.' Joan's voice was pitched high again. 'Her services to you in bed was her way of repayment, was it? Where the hell were all her kids when this was going on?'

Matt clenched his fists. 'I never thought you could be so nasty.'

'And I never thought that every weekend you were two-timing me,' she retorted.

Matt's anger was getting the better of him. 'Why you're 'aving to rake over old coals I can't fathom out. It 'ad been over between me an' Doris for years until I got knocked back with the news that my son belonged to a family in America.'

'So, I'm to understand that the pressure of finding out that we'd been bringing up the wrong boy for twenty years is what upset you. Drove you into sleeping with another woman. Or should I say drove you *back* to sleeping with her. Well, let me tell you here and now, Matt. That knowledge didn't do me much good either. What if I'd started an affair? I could have asked the milkman in, given him a coffee or something and asked him to comfort me.'

'Now you're being bloody ridiculous,' he snapped.

'Oh, I see. What's sauce for the gander doesn't apply to the goose?' Angry tears stung her eyes and she felt as though she might explode, but by now they both knew they were not going to solve anything sitting arguing in the grounds of Kingston Hospital, where their son still lay in the intensive care unit.

'Come on, Joan. Shall we call a truce for today? Let's go back and let my mother go for a cup of tea.' He was trying his best to keep his temper under control.

It was hard for him, she was well aware of that, and his suggestion was reasonable, but Joan was still too angry and she was about to tell him to get lost when he spoke again. 'Besides, Jamie might open his eyes soon. You wouldn't want to miss that, would you?'

She looked up at him and her heart ached. He was still so good-looking, his big brown eyes looked so sad and when he was . . . his normal self, she still loved him to bits. Right this moment if Doris Shepherd had appeared she would have killed her stone dead. I would share most things with someone less well-off than I am, but share my husband? *Never.*

'So, what you're saying is, we shelve . . . this rotten business and not talk about it till later?'

'If you think you can manage that, well, yes, please,' he mumbled, knowing he was asking a lot.

They got to their feet and walked back down the path,

which had such pretty flower borders. Joan wanted to ask Matt a hundred and one questions, the first of which was whether he was going to stay at home tonight. But she couldn't bring herself to do this. She didn't want to argue with him any more. There must be plenty more that hadn't been brought out into the open, such as Doris Shepherd's feelings in all this. More than likely she wanted to hang on to Matt. After all, she was on her own and it would seem that Matt had been showing her a good time. And what about Matt? He'd said he was sorry but he hadn't said he was going to put a stop to it, had he? Would she still want him if he did?

That was a difficult question to answer. When Jamie came round, and it might be any time now, thank God, he shouldn't be burdened with the fact that his mother and father were living separate lives. Dear Jesus, the lad still had to sort out in his head what he wanted to do about the Piviteaux family as well as struggle to become fit and well again.

Why, Matt? Why? I need you, Meg and Rosie need you, and most of all Jamie needs you. And what do you do? Go to pieces and go off with another woman. Comfort you, did she? Did sleeping with her feel good? She clenched her fists and held them close to her sides. Thank God there were people about or she might have done something she'd be sorry for. And knowing Matt and his temper, she might have come off worst.

They had reached the entrance. Matt held open the door for her, and as she passed him, she paused and stared into his eyes. She thought he looked angry, sad, even confused. She felt all of those things and more. Her husband had betrayed her and she had a right to be furious; she had been for days now, even though so far she had managed to keep

herself under control. At this moment she was almost longing for him to reach out and take her into his arms. Why?
After the way he had treated her? Because she was frightened,
lonely, and tired of trying to cope with so many troubles.

When they got home Joan was surprised that Matt offered
to lay the table. The girls were out but they had left a note
saying they'd be back by six thirty, and as it was almost that
now she set about making a huge salad and putting a
saucepan of new potatoes on to boil. Obviously Matt was
taking it for granted that he would eat with them.

The front door opened with a bang. The girls had seen
their father's car in the drive. Both Meg and Rosie threw
themselves at him and he lavished hugs and kisses on them.
Just watching them tore at Joan's heart. How could he go
off and leave them? They might be classed as grown-up but
they were still their babies. Mine *and* Matt's.

It was a proper family meal, Amy at one end of the table,
Matt at the other. It was Matt who carved the piece of
gammon Joan had boiled earlier on in the day before going
to see Jamie.

'Will you be here in the morning, Dad?' Rosie piped up.
No one else in the room would have dared asked that
question.

He looked lovingly at his younger daughter, gave her one
of his wonderful smiles and said, 'I will see you some time
tomorrow but, right now, when we've had our fruit and ice-
cream, I'm going to drive yer gran home. It's been a long
day for all of us.'

Joan protested, 'But my dad's coming over at eight o'clock.
He's going to take Amy home. We arranged it yesterday.'

'Yeah, I know,' Matt said sheepishly. 'Mum told me. While

we were at the hospital I phoned Bill, let him know that I was here an' that I'd take me mum home.'

'Oh . . . I see,' Joan stammered. He'd found a good excuse to go back to the East End again tonight then.

'I really do need to pick up some papers an' see a bloke in the City first thing tomorrow morning. I've let things slide a bit this past week.' Matt kept his eyes on his plate as he made that statement.

And whose bloody fault is that? Joan was tempted to cry out, but instead she said, 'Amy's got a few parcels upstairs, if you'd like to fetch them down for her.'

It was a sad little group who stood in the doorway and watched as Matt drove away with his mother beside him in the passenger seat.

'You and Dad are really mad at each other, aren't you?' It was Rosie again who popped that question.

Joan stared at her two girls, still so alike in looks, flawless skin and red-gold hair that set them apart in any crowd. In temperament, though, there was a vast difference between them. Meg was wise, tactful and understanding, while Rosie jumped in feet first, thinking only after the words had been said. God give me strength, Joan prayed. This younger daughter of mine dashes in where angels would fear to tread. 'Not really,' she lied. She couldn't face telling her girls the complete truth. 'Your father has a heavy workload on at the moment.'

Meg caught hold of Rosie's hand and said, 'Let's make Mum a nice cup of tea. We'll leave the washing-up till later. You go and put your feet up, Mum, and switch the telly on. We'll bring the tea in as soon as it's ready.'

For once Joan did as she was told and sighed with relief as she sank down into one of the big armchairs.

Rosie had always been the inquisitive one but this was the first time, as far as she could remember, that she had ever lied to her. For the time being, she told herself, it had been the right thing to do. She had no idea what future there was for her and Matt, so how could she tell the girls? Take one day at a time, she told herself. That's all you can do.

Chapter Twenty-Three

JOAN WAS IN a raging temper. It was bad enough what Matt was doing to her but he had lied to the girls, to Rosie in particular, and that was unforgivable. Four days had gone by since he had taken his mother home and promised he would be back the next day. Not only had he not put in an appearance, he hadn't even had the guts to pick up the telephone.

She had continued to spend a good deal of her time at the hospital while the girls were at work, but she missed Matt. She missed having him to talk to, missed his arms around her, and at night their double bed seemed so big and empty with no one for her to cuddle up to. At times she let her imagination run away with her. She couldn't help it. In her mind's eye she would see Matt being tender and loving to Doris Shepherd, see them in bed together, and it was more than she could bear. You shouldn't punish yourself like this, she told herself repeatedly, to no avail. In the corridors of the hospital, in the cafeteria, everywhere she looked, it seemed that there were couples. Old and young alike, everyone had someone except her. Some were celebrating good news, maybe the birth of a baby, others were consoling each other. Who did she have to turn to?

As if in answer to her own question the front doorbell rang. She was in two minds as to whether to answer it or not, then got up and walked down the hall. When she opened the door, John Chapman was leaning against the porch looking immaculate, his fawn trousers creased like a knife's edge, white shirt unbuttoned at the neck and a Prince of Wales checked jacket. His feet shod in slip-on casual shoes of the softest beige leather. Cautiously he held out a bunch of spring flowers, which Joan took at the same time stepping aside and saying 'You'd better come in.'

Hardly a word passed between them until Joan set two cups of black coffee on to the table and turned to take a jug of cream out of the fridge.

'Rosie spent last evening at my place,' John said. 'She came in with Mary, saying that Linsey had gone to the pictures with Meg and Brian Clarke and another lad.'

'Oh, she didn't tell me where she'd been.'

'Tell me if I'm butting in where I'm not wanted but she seemed upset. Said her father wasn't living at home any more.'

Joan was about to protest when the thought came to her that Rosie had spoken the truth. What answer could she make? None, she decided.

'This has been a very bad time for you, hasn't it?'

Joan gazed at him. 'Do you know more than you're letting on?'

John Chapman sighed. 'Kids talk among themselves and I did hear the bare bones about Jamie and the possible mix-up of the babies when he was born. Then came his accident. It can't have been easy for either you or Matt.'

Joan studied his face for a full minute. Was she right to trust him? 'Oh, there was certainly a mix-up at the time I gave birth to Jamie. It has been proved beyond doubt. I keep telling myself it had nothing to do with Jamie being knocked off his motorbike but at times I'm not so sure. He could have had his mind on other things when he came round that bend.'

'And Matt? Hit him for six. Can't blame him for that.'

'After twenty-one years of being married to him I can blame him for a whole host of things.' Joan was on the verge of tears. She hadn't meant to unburden herself to this charming man but, oh, God, she needed to talk to someone. Somehow she didn't feel she could tell her family how things were between her and Matt.

'Have a good cry if it helps,' John said. 'I know something of what you're going through.' He reached across the table and she smiled as his fingers touched hers just for a moment. 'Would you let me take you out for lunch?'

Joan looked bewildered.

'Sorry,' John said. 'Shouldn't have blurted it out like that. I know you go to the hospital every afternoon, Rosie told me your routine. I just thought a light lunch somewhere quiet might do you good. That's if you can put up with my company for that long.'

Joan kept her eyes down and didn't answer.

'Go on, get yourself ready,' he said, sounding as if he wouldn't take no for an answer. 'I know a restaurant where they have a wonderful garden and we can eat outside. It's a gorgeous day.'

* * *

He was right. The sun was warm, the sky was blue and the raised patio on which they were having lunch looked out over well-kept lawns and flowering shrubs. She could hear the peaceful sound of trickling water from two nearby fountains. And for the moment she was feeling better. Without thinking, she touched his face, saying, 'You really are very thoughtful.'

He put down his knife and fork and gave her a look she had never seen on Matt's face. It made her realize suddenly what a limited life she had been leading.

His hand was on her hair, which was not as unruly as it had been when she was young. Still a deep copper colour, she wore it high and smooth in the front and twirled into a neat French pleat at the back. 'You're beautiful. You could pass for a Greek goddess,' he teased.

Joan blushed. 'Now I know you're mad. Whoever heard of a goddess with red hair?'

He raised her hand to his lips and kissed her fingers, laughing. She felt the years roll away and she was young again. Of course she didn't believe a word he was saying but, by Jove, it had done her wounded pride a power of good.

It was just as well that a waiter appeared to remove their plates and John ordered coffee for them both. She shook her head thoughtfully. Things had been getting out of hand. But it had been nice to be told that she was beautiful and, yes, desirable. He might not have said that but his eyes had told her so quite plainly.

'I'll drive you straight to the hospital,' he offered, when they had drunk their second cup of coffee. It was an offer for which Joan was immensely grateful, yet part of her longed to linger in the peaceful garden where the birds were singing, the air was fragrant and she had no need to make decisions.

Her common sense rose to the surface. This was a dream world. The real world lay beyond this garden and she had no option but to go and face it.

Outside the hospital John Chapman opened the car door and helped her out. He kissed her cheek. 'You know where I am if you need me,' he said, holding her hand longer than was necessary. 'I'll see you tomorrow,' he added huskily.

Joan was wondering what he meant by that. She didn't trust herself to speak, nor did she wait to see him drive away. She merely nodded and made her way into the everyday life of a busy hospital.

'Mrs Pearson, James has regained consciousness.'

Joan stared at the staff nurse in disbelief. 'Oh, my God! And I wasn't here. I should have been.'

'It's all right, Mrs Pearson, really it is. He's sleeping so peacefully now.'

Joan smiled up at her and murmured her thanks. Then she took her seat beside her son's bed. She sat quietly for a time, then told him how pleased his sisters had been to see him and of all the celebrations they were planning for when he came home. She told him that the weather was glorious, and of how pretty all the flower-beds were looking, when suddenly Jamie opened his eyes, and moved his head slowly towards his mother. When his lips parted slightly and he half smiled she couldn't see it because she was blinded by tears.

The nurse, who had watched the whole time, handed Joan a paper tissue. 'Wipe your eyes,' she ordered. 'This is no time for crying. You've been through so much, a truly devoted mother.'

Jamie did not move again that afternoon, but nothing

could take away the joy Joan felt as she sat quietly watching him, holding his hand. Her heart was light as she kissed him goodbye and said, 'I'll be here again tomorrow morning.'

She called in to tell her parents and her nan the wonderful news, and as soon as she reached home she picked up the telephone and rang her mother-in-law. 'He smiled at me, he really did! He hears me, Amy! Now I know he does,' she told her, still sounding so excited.

Poor Amy was sobbing at the other end of the line, so thankful to hear the good news yet half afraid to let her hopes get too high.

'Amy, I really should phone Matt. He would want to know, don't you think?'

'Aw, pet, yer know he would, but if yer asking me where he is an' 'ow can yer contact him I honestly ain't got a clue.'

'Amy, please, surely he's been in to see you.'

'I swear on all I 'old dear 'e ain't never set a foot in this 'ouse since 'e dropped me off at the door when 'e brought me 'ome from your place. Stan ain't mentioned 'im an' I ain't asked. Best thing I can suggest is that you ring our Stan.'

Joan moaned softly, which broke Amy's heart. That bloody son of mine, she said to herself, needs someone t' tell 'im a few 'ome truths an', by God, I'll let me tongue rip the minute I set eyes on 'im.

Aloud she said, 'I'll do the rounds of the pubs. Someone must know where 'e's 'anging out. And if I find 'im I'll make sure 'e rings you. That's a promise.'

With that Joan had to be satisfied.

For the rest of the week she went into the hospital twice a day. Every day Jamie stirred a little more, but he never spoke. However, there were signs that he understood what was being said to him. He would move his head, open his eyes, squeeze her hand and even moan occasionally.

John Chapman called at the house with offers of a lift or was outside the hospital waiting to take her home in the early evening.

There was still no sign of Matt.

The weekend came again, and the girls were out with their friends when Joan opened the front door to see John striding up the drive. 'You look fantastic.' He stared at her in open admiration. She was wearing a sleeveless cream linen dress, with a jade green cardigan around her shoulders. Jade green went so well with her dark green eyes. With her hair piled up on top and high-heeled court shoes she looked a lot taller than she was. 'You must be feeling better,' he said. 'May I offer you a lift?'

'Why, thank you, kind sir.' Joan laughed as she got into his car, and he headed towards Kingston Hospital.

On arrival he didn't drive off but got out of the car and walked her slowly to the entrance. 'Will you have a meal with me later?' he asked softly. 'It has to be better than going home to an empty house. I'll be here waiting at about six.'

Suddenly she felt shy, and she was taken aback as he lowered his head and gently laid his lips on hers. They stood together, staring into each other's eyes, until he straightened up and murmured, 'I'll be here when you come out.'

Joan opened the door to the side ward and the colour rose in her cheeks. Matt was sitting beside the bed and Jamie's hand was between both of his. She glanced at Jamie and saw his head move. He was turning it slowly towards her, and she was thrilled by how quickly he had known she had come into the room. Joan caught her breath: her son was doing his best to lift his head from the pillow.

She covered the distance between them in three strides. Matt let go of Jamie's hand and got to his feet. Side by side they stood while Jamie smiled a real smile that took in both of them. Joan put down her handbag and drew nearer to him. 'Jamie . . . you look so much better. We're both here . . . your dad and me. It's OK, you're back with us . . . you are, aren't you?' She was speaking very softly as she stroked his hand. Then it happened. Jamie squeezed her hand and held out his other hand to his father, which Matt took and held tightly. Neither of them moved for several seconds. Then Joan looked at Matt and each saw that the other was crying.

They spent the next two hours talking quietly about Meg and Rosie. Matt asked if Brian Clarke was still seeing Meg. 'Very much so,' Joan told him, adding, 'I think you will soon have the expense of a wedding, the way things are going there.'

'Where 'ave all the years gone?' Matt murmured, half to himself. 'Doesn't seem possible that all our kids are grown-up.'

'No, it doesn't,' Joan agreed.

Jamie had slipped back into sleep, and Matt leant over the bed to kiss his son's forehead. Then he looked long and hard at his wife. 'As miracles go I'd say we've been granted one,' he said.

At that moment Joan would have given a lot for him to hold her close. She was thinking of all the years they had had together, blessed with three children, and how lucky they had been. Only right now they did not have each other. There was such a distance between them she didn't even know where he was living, let alone who with.

Matt looked at his watch. 'I have to be going. If you need to get in touch, ring Stan. He'll get a message to me.'

Joan looked at him in amazement. 'I think we need to talk right now.'

'No, sorry, Joan,' he muttered, having the grace to look guilty.

'What? You haven't seen the girls. You broke a promise to Rosie and now you turn up out of the blue and say it doesn't suit you to stay. You're pushing your luck a bit too far, Matt.'

Before she had finished, Matt was at the door. 'I'll be in touch, give my love t' the girls.'

If Joan had been at home she would have grabbed the nearest heavy object and thrown it at his head. Instead, she had no option but to watch as the door closed behind him and she was left with an unbelievable heavy silence and a great number of unanswered questions. The next few hours were some of the worst she had ever sat through. She felt so utterly alone. As the time drew near for her to leave she comforted herself that John Chapman would be waiting outside for her. Life has been treating me very unfairly, she was saying to herself. Surely I'm entitled to a break now and again. But was she just trying to get her own back on Matt? 'I don't know what to do or what to feel,' she muttered, as she bent over the bed and kissed her son goodbye.

John was as good as his word. He jumped out of his car as soon as he saw her, settled her into the passenger seat and headed for Epsom. 'I've reserved a table for two at the Chequers. We'll have time for a drink before dinner,' he told her quietly.

It was the most lovely hotel she had ever been in, and she felt special and spoilt as she headed for the ladies' powder room. She washed her hands, repaired her makeup and ran a comb through the front of her hair, then pushed the pins into the back pleat more securely. As she approached John stood up. He had chosen a table set in a bay window that looked out over the famous racecourse and drinks were waiting, a sherry for her and a lager for himself.

The head waiter brought them each a huge menu from which John chose smoked salmon for both of them as a starter. For the main course he ordered roast rib of beef, and Joan decided on breast of chicken in white wine. When a waiter came to tell them their table was ready in the dining room Joan had another surprise: a band was playing and the tables were set around the edge of a small dance-floor. Much later she gasped at the sight of the sweet trolley.

It was a marvellous dinner, an enchanting place, and John's attentive company, with a few glasses of wine, went a long way to smoothing her ruffled feathers caused by the fact that Matt had walked away from her without offering so much as the vaguest excuse. After coffee they danced, and Joan was only too aware of how close his body was to hers. She had tried to tell him she hadn't danced in years but he was in no mood to take no for an answer. It didn't matter in the least. He was a terrific dancer and she only had to go where he led.

They left the hotel at ten o'clock, Joan smiling like a Cheshire cat. 'This evening has done wonders for me,' she said. 'I just don't have the words to thank you.'

'We'll do it again soon.' He grinned.

John's footsteps were light as he walked her to her front door. Joan reached up to give him a thank-you peck on the cheek but that wasn't what he had in mind. He took the key from her and unlocked the door. 'May I come in?' he asked.

Joan stepped back and looked up to see that two bedrooms were showing lights. 'Better not. The girls are home, and as soon as they hear me come in they'll be flying down the stairs.'

It was as if he hadn't heard her. He stepped inside. The hall was in darkness. 'I'd better put the light on,' she muttered, but got no further. He had pulled her to him. They just stood there, in the dark, kissing, he touching her body as if he had waited all his life for this. Joan's mind was in a whirl. This shouldn't be happening, but didn't she want it too? Oh, yes. Very much so!

She wanted him to prove to her that she was desirable. She was human, she had needs and desires, and hadn't Matt betrayed her? Not just now but, as she had recently found out, many times over the years? The knowledge had hurt because she'd thought that they had such a good marriage.

John was caressing her with his lips, allowing his hands to roam over her whole body until she was almost moaning with pleasure.

'Mum, is that you?' Meg's voice floated down the stairs as a door was flung open and light streamed out.

'I love you,' John whispered, his voice throbbing, as Joan stepped away, tugging frantically to straighten her dress.

She found the light switch, snapped it on and gazed up at her elder daughter, who was looking over the banister rail. 'It's all right, Meg. Mr Chapman is with me, he took me for a meal. I'll be up to see you and Rosie in just a minute.'

'I do love you,' John whispered, as he kissed the top of her head and made for the door. 'I'll see you tomorrow.'

The door closed behind him with a click and Joan let out all her breath in a long gasp as she leant against the wall.

I must be mad, she was telling herself. Supposing the girls had caught her and John? What kind of explanation would she have been able to give them? That she was merely getting her own back on their father for what he had done to her? Of course not. That wouldn't have been the truth. Not the whole truth, anyway. Suddenly she couldn't stop smiling. It had been a fantastic feeling. Raw passion. Something that hadn't stirred in her for a long time. Oh, she and Matt still made love, but it hadn't aroused her like John Chapman had tonight for many a long day. She had felt wanted, special, the one and only lady in his life.

She kicked off her shoes and made for the stairs, then stopped. She had better stop trying to analyze her feelings where John Chapman was concerned or she may find herself getting in beyond her depth.

Chapter Twenty-Four

IT WAS BARELY ten o'clock when Joan opened the door to John. 'I think we have some unfinished business,' he whispered, as he took her in his arms. 'I love you so much, I haven't slept a wink all night.'

They stood together swaying as they kissed and touched each other. 'You're incredible,' he told her, as he undid the buttons of her blouse, murmuring 'Oh, Joan,' as he caressed her. Then they slowly climbed the stairs and she led him into her bedroom.

Her clothes fell away and she watched as he undressed. Then he lifted her gently on to the bed, and began to move his lips over her breasts. Their coming together was powerful, an explosion of need, until they lay spent in each other's arms, stunned by the force of what had happened.

'If the girls hadn't been at home when we got back last night I wouldn't have had to spend a sleepless night. Joan, you are great, and, oh, how I needed you,' he whispered.

She laughed with pleasure. 'It's amazing, isn't it?' she

pondered. 'We've been neighbours for years and never really known each other and now . . .'

'We're lovers.' He finished the sentence for her. 'We've found each other and from now on we can fill a need whenever the mood takes us.'

Joan was shaken by what he had said so casually. A moment ago they had been like passionate young lovers, barely able to tear themselves apart but now a warning bell rang in her head. He began telling her of places he would take her to, but Joan was only half listening. Later he said, 'This is a waste of time! I can't stand having you in my arms and not making love to you.'

Joan wriggled free and sat up. 'John, I don't know whether Matt and I will get divorced or not.'

'What the hell's that got to do with us being together?' he asked. 'Lie down again, my darling, and let me prove to you once more how much I love you.'

She swung her legs over the side of the bed. 'John, you are the most romantic man I've ever known, and your kindness to me has been a Godsend, but I think that what you and I want are two different things. I'm going down to make some coffee. The bathroom is the second door on the left. There are clean towels in there.'

Downstairs she washed and dressed. Her mind was working overtime and she couldn't believe how naïve she had been, acting like a rich man's mistress one minute and then, when the penny dropped that she was being used, she had reverted to being a housewife, telling him that there were clean towels in the bathroom. How would she ever look him in the face again?

She didn't wait long to find out.

He breezed into the kitchen, beaming. 'Too much for you,

was it? Wore you out, did I? It can only get better, I promise you. Next time we'll take it steady.'

'John, sit down.' Joan placed a cup of coffee on the table. 'I've only got ginger biscuits,' she added, matter-of-factly.

He roared with laughter. 'Well, I suppose there's always a first. Is that all I merit? A ginger biscuit? Come on, Joan, I can understand that you're feeling guilty but you shouldn't be. You're being silly . . . I love you.'

The amazing thing was he probably did, at this point in time, but it would never be a lasting love.

Joan sat down and sipped her coffee. She couldn't get her thoughts into any kind of order but she knew, without a doubt, that she was right. She had been feeling lonely, betrayed, unwanted, even, and John Chapman was a slick, charming man.

'You were just as hungry for me as I was for you,' he said, doing his best to tease her into a better frame of mind. 'As things stand, I'd say we're both free and there is nothing to stop us from indulging ourselves whenever the fancy takes us. Is there?' he asked hopefully.

Joan took a deep breath, then leant close to him and, almost in a whisper, said, 'To you I'm just a roll in the hay.'

He smiled wickedly at her. 'Is there anything wrong with that?'

'Not to your way of thinking obviously,' she said, but then she had to laugh. After all, it was she who had read his intentions wrongly. Like some starry-eyed school-kid, she had thought of him as a knight in shining armour coming to her aid when she most needed it.

He smiled. 'I was really hurt when my wife went off with another man and I vowed then I'd never let a woman get that close to me. I live for my two girls, and I love them very much. I'd never think of marrying again, but that doesn't alter the fact that I have my needs and when I meet someone who feels the same way, well . . .'

Joan couldn't argue with that. He had never promised her anything different.

John had been watching the different emotions flit across her face and felt sorry for her. Things could have been so great between them, given half a chance, but he could see that was never going to be. Joan Pearson was what he would term a good woman.

'I'd say it's game, set and match,' he said, and smiled. Then he looked serious. 'If it's any consolation to you, Joan, if I were thinking of taking a second wife I'd hope and pray that it would be someone as good and kind as you.'

'You don't have to say things like that, you did nothing to mislead me. It was my own fault.'

'Well, stop feeling so guilty. Shall I tell you what I think?' Joan made no reply, so he went on, 'You and Matt have gone through a terrible time just lately, but it will get better. I promise you it will. I can't see you two getting divorced. I hope you won't for the sake of your three children. I hope you manage to work things out.' He saw that her eyes were brimming with tears and it was all he could do to stop himself taking her into his arms. Instead he said, 'I have to go soon but before I do could you bring yourself to give me another cup of coffee and this time I would like a little cream or even milk, I can't stand black coffee.'

She looked straight at him. He smiled, looking mischievous and she found herself laughing at him. 'I think I can manage that.'

Just then the telephone rang.

Joan lifted the receiver but before she had the chance to

say anything she heard Matt's voice. 'I'm coming down to the hospital this afternoon. Shall I come to the house first and we go together?'

'Matt.' Joan hesitated. 'All right. What time will you be here?'

'Is two o'clock all right with you?'

'Yes, I'll be ready.' She heard a click and the line went dead.

'There you are,' John exclaimed. 'I'm so glad your boy's out of the woods and that now his father is beginning to see sense. It's time I faded into the background. Will you do one thing for me, Joan?'

'If I can.' She felt awkward.

'Don't go around feeling you've got to wear sackcloth and ashes. Don't ever let the girls get an inkling of what has been between us. They're great friends with my two and I wouldn't want that to change. We haven't become an item, much as I would have liked it,' he said ruefully. 'You've let me know that once was enough, so let's leave it at that.'

'I'll do my best,' Joan said thoughtfully.

'You'll do as I asked,' John corrected her gently. 'Confession might be good for you, but it would hurt a good many others and they'd end up hating us both. That's not what you want, is it?'

She swallowed hard, before saying, 'No, it isn't. I'll do as you say.'

At the door John bent his head and kissed her cheek.

She watched as he strode off down the drive. She was sure that his last words had been sincere and she knew she would miss him. She thought about the times they had spent together. He had been good to her. She hadn't read the situation right but neither had he for he hadn't truly got to know her – but, then, perhaps she didn't really know herself. But since John Chapman had come into her life, some deep change had taken place within her.

She leant against the wall, closed her eyes, and remembered almost every moment she had shared with him. His kisses. How he'd . . . She shuddered, feeling shame and remorse and now, above all else, guilt. How could she have allowed it to happen just because Matt had treated her so badly? Two wrongs never made a right She began to cry – bitter, reproachful tears. What had possessed her? What if the girls were to find out? That must never happen.

Never!

Chapter Twenty-Five

I WONDER WHY we're all so nervous, Joan thought, as she looked at Matt's twitching lips. Meg and Rosie were sitting in the living room. Both girls had taken great pains over their appearance for today they were going to the hospital as a family to fetch Jamie home.

'Do calm down,' Matt said. 'I promise you everything will be all right.'

How she wished she could believe him. A new relationship, different from any that had gone before, now existed between herself and Matt. He had asked, no, pleaded to be allowed to come home.

She had taken days to come to a decision. It had been as if she was carrying a heavy secret, and she had wished she had someone to talk to, to tell them about John Chapman. Friends were out of the question, and her mum and dad, even nan, wouldn't understand. So often she had come near to telephoning John. Yet she resisted the temptation. Life was already too complicated.

Did she want Matt back in her life? She hated him for the way he had deceived her with Doris Shepherd, but the answer was yes. She had had visions of living without him, and she hadn't liked the prospect. The feeling of loss would always be there. And he had been a good provider and a damn good father. The girls loved him so, and Jamie too. How could they bring Jamie home to a divided house? Hadn't he enough to cope with without them adding coals to the fire?

Over the past weeks they had all gone through a traumatic experience and now the end was in sight. They had so much to be grateful for.

Jamie was coming home. Although it would take time for him to be one hundred per cent fit again, they could thank God that he had not suffered any permanent brain damage.

There was still the matter of the Piviteaux family to be faced. What the outcome of that would eventually be only time would tell. Jamie would have to decide for himself. A small consolation had to be that they lived in America. Had they been in England contact would have been inevitable, and God knew what the result would have been.

Meanwhile, she had written twice to Beryl Piviteaux, the first time telling her that Jamie had been in an accident. However, in her second letter Beryl had sounded so kind and thoughtful that Joan was quite sure that, were they to meet, they would instantly become friends. But, Beryl's son Peter had been quite the opposite. A note from him, included in the letter, had been coldly polite. He had said in no uncertain terms that he was an American citizen and had no wish for ties in England.

Deep in her heart Joan couldn't blame him. And she reckoned that Jamie's views would run along the same lines as

Peter's. Given the choice she would have liked to wipe the slate clean, as though those blood tests had never taken place.

As for herself, she couldn't be a normal person or she would be longing to visit that family, to clasp in her arms the son to whom she had given birth to. On the other hand, could she ever have wiped away all the years she had nurtured Jamie? Put into her arms when only hours old, all the love, yes and heart-breaks, derived from various experiences only a mother would know about.

The short letter she had written to Peter had been one of the hardest tasks she had ever had to tackle. She hoped that she had been kind and considerate, and certainly felt that she had paved the way, should he ever change his mind. It must be awful for that poor lad. It wasn't fair on any of them and she shook her head in disbelief. A simple ordinary mistake made in the throes of a terrible air-raid over London and now, even after all these years, the repercussions were affecting so many lives.

'I'll get the car out,' Matt said briskly. 'They said we could pick him up as soon as the doctors had finished their rounds.' He picked up his keys and strode towards the door.

'Matt,' Joan's voice held a plea, 'we have so much to talk over with Jamie. I'm scared. What if he decides he wants to go to America? What'll we do then?'

Matt came back to where she stood and, very gently, put his arm round her shoulders. 'We decided to take one day at a time. "What if" never solved anything. All we can do is wait an' see. Come on, now, there's a good girl. You've been so brave all along and now we're all going to fetch our Jamie home.'

* * *

Jamie had been home for four days and the atmosphere was tense to say the least. His friends had dropped in, some making the journey from the university as soon as they heard that he had been discharged from hospital. Trouble was, he tired so easily. Though Joan felt that that was not at the root of what was troubling him.

So far not a word had been said about the blood tests. Both Daphne and Hester had to be persuaded to stop trying to spoil him. Meg and Rosie were reluctant to go to work – they wanted to be near their brother. It was as if they were half afraid that he might just go to America and they would never see him again. Jamie seemed more at ease with his father and his grandfather than he did with his womenfolk. With Matt the talk was of rugby and football, and Matt promised to get tickets for any match Jamie wanted to see as soon as he felt fit enough to face the crowds. Bill Harvey walked as if a great weight had been lifted from his shoulders. His beloved grandson was home, and at the first opportunity the pair of them were going fishing.

Joan woke with a start and struggled to sit up. Glancing at the bedside clock she saw it was a quarter to four. Matt hadn't stirred: he lay beside her, dead to the world. Things were so much better between them: they had talked for hours, and he had told her of how he had rented a bed-sitting room and literally drunk himself stupid in the days when he had disappeared. It had been a Salvation Army officer who had straightened him out. 'By the time he had finished with me I realized that the most important thing in this world was my wife and my family,' he had told her, with such frankness that Joan had cried as she listened to him say those words. 'I never thought for one moment you'd 'ave me back,' he had added later.

Now she was wide awake and she had to make sure nothing had happened to Jamie. Standing by his bed she looked down at his dear face, seeing it in the dim light that came from the landing. Her love for him was so great it made her whole body ache. How could anyone believe that they could take him away from her? No mother in her right mind would give up her son to a family that had never set eyes on him from the day he was born. She turned on tiptoe, about to go back to bed.

'Mum, I'm not asleep, stay with me, please.'

She drew his bedroom chair nearer, sat down and took his hand.

'I don't want to go to America and I don't want that family to come here.'

'Ssh, Jamie. Nobody's going to make you do anything you don't want to.'

'But before I went into hospital you said I'd have to meet them sometime.'

Joan considered. 'I think that what I said was that naturally they would want to meet you some time in the future. But you are an adult. There is no question of anyone forcing you to do something you don't want to do.'

'Dad said I'll never have to meet them. Granddad says the same.'

Joan had to stifle a little laugh. Both Matt and her dad were finding it hard to accept. Her two men were like small boys: neither would admit that it was true, and that worried her a great deal: there was no getting away from the facts and sooner or later they would have to admit it.

'You don't want to meet this family, do you, Mum?'

It took her a minute or two to compose an answer to that. 'No, I don't,' she told him sadly, 'but I can feel for that mother. Her situation is no different from mine. If she and I were to meet then I'm sure we could become good friends. But if she wanted to take you away from me then I would end up wishing her in hell.'

'What about the other boy? Peter Piviteaux. Dad said he's Polish.'

'That's not exactly true. His great-grandparents were Polish, but he says he's one hundred per cent an American boy and wants nothing to do with being English.'

'*He* told you that?'

'Well, that's the gist of a letter he wrote me.'

'Well, that's that, then,' Jamie said. 'He's happy where he is, and I certainly don't want to be uprooted. You've never known any son other than me, and that woman has had that lad all his life, so why, in God's name, did they start this investigation in the first place?'

'How many times have your father and I asked ourselves that very same question?' Joan said ruefully.

Jamie raised himself up on his elbows and looked gravely at his mother. 'Mum, do you and Dad still think of me as your son?'

The question broke her heart. 'Oh, Jamie! Do you really have to ask?'

'I know how Dad feels. He has never admitted that any of this was true right from the beginning, but . . . well, it must be harder for you and that worries me.'

She was surprised how well Jamie had summed up the situation.

'This lad who wrote to you, he really is the lad you gave birth to, isn't he?'

'Oh, don't, Jamie, please. You aren't doing me any good and you're torturing yourself.'

'Well, aren't you curious about what he looks like? Don't you feel the need to go and meet him?'

She sighed heavily. 'In a sense, yes, I do. I wonder about all of those things but have you looked at it from his mother's point of view?'

'You are his mother.'

She heard the break in his voice and felt she had to sort this out here and now, at least to a certain degree. 'If you feel so strongly about that, Jamie, then you have to admit that Beryl Piviteaux is your mother.'

The look he gave her tore at her heart, and the lump in her throat threatened to choke her. It was a while before she felt calm enough to speak again. 'Jamie, you can't have it both ways. Have you thought that Beryl might be just as frightened as I am that she'll lose the lad she has thought of all these years as her son?'

He made no answer.

'From the letters she has written to me I know she regards Peter as her son, just as much as I do you. Nevertheless each of us gave birth to a son that another woman has reared. I like to think that when Mr and Mrs Piviteaux were made aware of the mix-up one of their first reactions was to make sure that you had gone to a safe and happy home. I know if I had been told first that would have been my main concern.'

Still Jamie made no reply.

'Try to see it from Beryl's point of view. The fact that she feels the need to see you has nothing to do with her loving Peter, and were I to agree to see him at some time in the future it wouldn't alter my feelings for you, not by the tiniest scrap. I just can't put into words what you mean to me, Jamie. You'll just have to be content when I tell you I wouldn't swop you for all the tea in China. You *are* my son and I love you dearly. I just don't know how to put it more clearly than that.'

Jamie looked at her, his eyes brimming. 'Thanks for telling me, Mum.'

'Right, now you try to go back to sleep. We'll talk again in the morning. In fact, I'm going to get your father and granddad to have a word with you. If they can't convince you, well, we'll see.'

Back in bed Joan lay awake. During the past few weeks her mind had been centred on getting Jamie well enough to come home. Practically all thoughts of the Piviteaux family had been pushed to the back of her mind. Now there would be a lot more soul-searching before she came up with answers that would be fair to all concerned. Right now she felt too tired to think straight.

Chapter Twenty-Six

DAY BY DAY Jamie got stronger. In the middle of the third week since his homecoming Joan watched as he and her father set off on a fishing trip.

'I've made some coffee,' Matt said, as she came back into the kitchen. 'You're going to feel lost today, aren't you? Can't 'ave you left in the 'ouse all on your own. How d'you feel about coming up to town with me? You could spend some time with my mum, or I can drop you off in Haydons Road. I bet your mum and Hetty would be more than pleased to see you.'

'I think I'd like to go to my mum's,' Joan said. 'It won't take me long to get ready.'

'Sit down and drink your coffee first. I'm in no great hurry. Stan an' I are going after a new contract but we 'aven't got t' see the bloke till this afternoon.'

They sat in silence for a while until Joan murmured, 'I hope my dad manages to talk some sense into our Jamie.'

Matt put his cup down. 'Aw, Joan, you're not starting all

that again, are you? I've asked you time an' time again, for God's sake leave the boy alone.'

'That's the trouble. He's not a boy, he's a grown man,' Joan muttered.

'All the more reason to let him make his own decisions in his own good time,' Matt answered sharply.

Joan gave a deep sigh. 'You don't help, you know that, don't you? He's had a letter from Beryl, which he hasn't even let me read.'

'Quite right too. It's got nothing t' do with you.'

'How the hell can you say that? It's tearing me apart. Of course that family want to meet Jamie, they have a right to. Especially Beryl. They've suggested that if we don't want to visit them they will come to England but so far I haven't answered that letter cos I just don't know what to say.'

Matt got to his feet, his eyes blazing. 'Is there no end t' this bloody nightmare? How many times d'you want telling? Jamie wants nothing whatsoever t' do with them. He's our son and he lives 'ere with us an' as far as I'm concerned that's the end of the matter.'

'Oh, Matt, please. You don't help when you tell him things like that. You deny the facts and on top of that you won't let Jamie face reality.'

He brushed past her. 'You'll be telling me next that you can't wait to see that Peter, an' a fat lot of good that would do. Well, I'm not wasting any more time arguing with you about something that can so easily be settled. I've told you, let Clive Richardson write to Mrs Piviteaux and tell them to get lost. Now, if you're coming with me let's see you smile. Come on, you can go over it a dozen times with yer mum, if yer like, an' I dare say yer nan will want to throw her two-pennyworth in – that'll cheer you up – but just leave me out of it. I've said all I've got t' say.'

Joan was in two minds as to whether or not she should continue to argue with him. She decided not to today, but she was thoughtful as she made her way upstairs to get ready. When alone she freely admitted to herself that she would dearly love to meet the son to whom she had given birth. It did hurt, in a funny sort of way, that Peter had said in his letter that he wanted no contact with her. Oh, he hadn't been rude, but neither had he gone out of his way to spare her feelings. However, she still felt that at some point in the future it would be nice to meet him face to face. In no way did that alter the fact that she loved Jamie with all her heart. But what woman wouldn't be curious, if she found herself in this awful situation?

There were times when her heart ached for both Jamie and Peter. After more than twenty years to be told that the family that had loved and cherished you for the whole of your life was in no way related to you! It was enough to send any young man off the tracks. Each day that went by it became more apparent that both lads would prefer to forget that the truth had ever come to light. And who could blame them for that?

She could feel for Beryl, of course she could. But again there were times when she could cheerfully strangle her. All right, it wasn't her fault that a blood test had proved Peter was not her son and God alone knew how she must have felt when faced with that. But there were two ways of looking at this. One, she and her husband could have kept the information to themselves and not run the risk of losing Peter, whom they so obviously loved, or two, delve deeply and cause distress that, in the end, might turn to bitterness.

If the tables had been turned what would she and Matt have done? She had considered that question several times and, as always, she could not decide what her answer would have been.

Heaving a great sigh, she put the finishing touches to her makeup, picked up her handbag and made her way downstairs. Thank God she was going to spend the day with her mum and her nan. They would not be able to come up with a magic answer to all these problems but at least they would listen, rather than dismissing the matter out of hand as Matt did.

Matt stopped the car at the corner of the road in Merton Park. 'I'll be back about six, take you out for a meal, if you like. Just the two of us.'

In some ways life was improving. Only rarely did Matt suggest that the two of them had a meal out, but he was making more of an effort now. 'That would be a nice change,' she answered quickly, hoping he hadn't been able to read her thoughts.

'Remember to phone the girls and let them know we'll be eating out. Jamie won't mind staying on for the evening with his granddad an' we can pick him up later.'

'Yes, all right, I'll see to it.'

Matt leant across and kissed her cheek. 'See you t'night, then.'

Joan stood on the pavement, and within seconds the car was out of sight. She was thinking how grateful she was that Doris Shepherd was in the past. If it weren't for this American family business, life would be sweet. Matt was so much more considerate: he didn't take her half as much for granted as he used to. Thoughts of John Chapman came to her. He had helped her over a trying period and, though she now knew him to be an unreliable gadabout, she could smile as she remembered how charming he had been. And what a marvellous dancer! But all that was a dream world. Everyday life wasn't like that.

She looked about her as she walked down the road to the house she still regarded as her home. The corner shop was no longer there: three new houses had been built where it had once stood. In fact, nothing looked quite the same and she felt a bit sad until she reached her parents' front door, its paintwork bright as ever. It was such a comfort to take the key, with which she had never parted, from her handbag and open the door.

The smell of baking came from the kitchen. The door to the front room was open and the midsummer sunshine flickered on the wallpaper. There was no fire in the grate today but a huge bowl of ferns and dried flowers stood in the hearth. Photographs stood on the piano and on the mantelshelf. Taking pride of place was one of herself and Matt, and another of them both with the three children.

Feelings of love and security rose in Joan as she turned to see her mother standing waiting, arms outstretched. 'I heard the door open an' I guessed it was you. How are you, love? Yer dad said he thought it was more than likely you'd come over for the day so I started baking early. I've got the kettle on an' your nan will be in any moment now. I'd bet my last shilling she's seen you arrive.'

Joan was laughing. 'Give me time to get in the house, Mum. You go on as if someone has wound you up.'

'Good God, do I really?'

'I'm only teasing. I'm so darned glad to be here I don't care if you go on at me non-stop all day.'

'It's only me.' Hester's voice echoed down the hall.

'Told you so.' Daphne grinned.

'Oh, Nan, you look perky as ever,' Joan said.

'Come on, you two. I've got t' see to me oven,' Daphne urged, as she edged past.

Later as they sat around the kitchen table eating hot buttered scones, Joan said, 'I feel tons better already. What would I do if I didn't have you two to turn to?'

It was then, as she looked at these two dear faces, that the dam burst. She had merely meant to outline the reasons why she was still worried about Jamie and to listen to any advice they cared to offer her. But instead she found herself pouring it all out to them as she had poured out her troubles as a little girl, in the days when her nan and her mother were still full of beans and spent a lot of their time gadding about in dance halls. They listened to the torrent of words in silence, their green eyes attentive and concerned. 'Don't you see, Mum? With Matt and Dad refusing to face the facts and, more to the point, encouraging Jamie to do the same, it's like bashing my head against a brick wall. I haven't got a chance in hell of getting Jamie to answer Beryl's letter. And as for getting him to agree to meeting her, not a ghost of a chance!'

'But why didn't you tell us all this before now?' Daphne asked quietly. 'Did you think we wouldn't understand, or at least find a way to try to help?'

'Well, Mum, *you* might have tried to influence Jamie but . . . well, Nan, you're a bit like Matt and me dad. You've done your best to close your eyes and ears right from the beginning.'

'Just because I didn't much like the sound of those people in America doesn't mean I don't want to get things sorted out.' Hester sounded offended.

'No, I know you mean well, Nan, but you said quite frankly that you found the story of a mix-up at birth unbelievable, and you told Jamie that even if they did find out because of a blood test that the two babies had been given to the wrong parents they should have left it at that. That's what good parents would have done, you said, not taken the matter this far.'

'That,' said Hetty calmly, 'is still my opinion. Jamie is a serious young man, but he is also bright, decent, loving, and when it comes to the crunch he'll do what he feels to be right, no matter what you, I or anyone else has to say.'

'Clive Richardson has spoken to Beryl and her husband Joe several times, and he thinks they come across as nice, kind people,' Joan told her.

'Does he, indeed?'

'Yes. He was quite sure that they wanted what was best for everyone.'

Daphne chipped in, 'Well, the best for us on this side of the ocean is to forget we ever heard of them.'

'Oh, Mum! Not you too! Talking like that isn't going to help,' Joan rebuked her mother. Then turning to her nan, she said, 'If I were to be given three wishes, all of them would run along the same lines. I'd give the world to turn the clock back. And I keep asking myself, Why the hell didn't they just keep quiet about the blood test? But on the other hand I have to keep telling myself that Mr and Mrs Piviteaux started this investigation for all the right reasons. They appear to be quite prosperous, own a long-standing family business and somehow I do believe their main concern was to find out if their true son was healthy and well-cared-for. I can understand that. Can't you?'

'Yes, of course I can.' Hester was quick to establish that.

'But they could have achieved that by being much more discreet. Instead, what have they done? Churned up a right old hornet's nest and, from what I can make out, left two troubled young lads on the way.' Suddenly she felt she had been too outspoken and that now was the time to become the peacemaker. She added, 'Perhaps we ought to pray for a miracle. You know, something along the lines that the two lads meet and become the best of friends.'

'Oh, Nan,' Joan cried in despair, 'don't you think I've done my fair share of praying these last few weeks? Anyway, happy-ever-after only happens in fairy stories and this is real life.'

'No, it doesn't. Not always,' Hester replied. 'Happy endings happen every day somewhere in the world. If there's one thing I've learnt during my lifetime it is that if you have enough faith you can, as they say, move mountains. I prayed that Jamie, my great-grandson, would get well and come out of that hospital without the accident having affected his brain, and my prayers were answered.'

'Oh, Nan, we all said that prayer over and over again.'

'So, like I said, all our prayers were answered.'

'So now you're telling me that maybe an angel of the Lord could come down from heaven to sort out this horrible mess not only to our complete satisfaction but to give joy and peace of mind to the Piviteaux family as well.'

Hester sat up straight. 'And why not? Stranger things have been known to happen. There's no need for you to be flippant. As your granddad used to say, the Lord works in mysterious ways his wonders to perform. I shall pray for guidance – and for everyone concerned, come to that.' Then, getting to her feet, she added, 'About time we cleared this table and sorted out what we're going to do with the rest of the day. It isn't very often we get you to ourselves, Joan, so while I wash these cups you think about what you'd like to do.'

Daphne managed to get Joan on her own and, smiling broadly, told her, 'When your nan says she'll pray that the outcome of all this will see everyone happy, what she really means is she wants our Jamie to be just that for as long as he lives and that the Piviteaux family will remain where they are and get on with their own lives.'

Joan put out a hand to her mother. 'I don't care if it's an angel or the Lord Himself who's going to intervene. I just hope somebody comes up with an answer soon. All I really want, Mum, is for our lives to be normal again.'

Hester had overheard this last remark as she carried a tray out into the scullery, and thought, So do I. But I've got a feeling it's going to get worse before it gets better.

Chapter Twenty-Seven

DURING THE LOVELY summer months they all seemed to have reached an uneasy truce. As he had long been doing anyway, Matt refused to utter one word on the matter of the Piviteaux family. Jamie had gone from strength to strength: his skin was tanned, he looked fit and healthy and, more to the point, he was fun to be with. The only fly in the ointment was that he agreed with his father and grandfather that it was quite in order to ignore the American couple who were insisting that he was their rightful son. Joan's problem became harder.

Beryl had telephoned her, twice, which she had kept to herself.

Weeks went by. In spite of all her nan's promises, neither an angel nor the Lord Himself put in an appearance to help find an answer to satisfy everyone.

With the days now drawing in, the main topic of conversation in the Pearson household was that Jamie would be twenty-one in November, and all three females felt that if they kept on at Matt long and hard enough he would give in to their way of thinking.

'All right, all right,' he protested one evening, as they sat around the dinner table. Then to Joan, he said, 'I told you last year that they'd both want another do. Our children think I'm made of money.'

Joan had to raise her voice to be heard because Meg, Rosie and Jamie were rolling about in fits of laughter. 'Meg was quite content with her eighteenth,' she assured him, 'but we all feel Jamie's birthday this year is extra special an' not only because he's to be twenty-one.'

Matt glanced across at his wife. He knew what she was saying: first that they were lucky to have Jamie as he had been so ill, and second, that they had weathered the storm of his parentage. It had been a mutual decision that he would remain at home for the rest of the year, and would start work in the City from the first week in January. He hadn't lost out though. The university had recognised that his work had shown that he would have gained a degree had he not missed so much time because of his head injury and they had conferred a degree on him, a fact that had delighted Jamie and made the whole family really proud of him.

'I give in,' Matt muttered, doing his best not to laugh. 'What with your parents, not to mention Hetty and the way she's been going on, an' my old lady, you'd think there'd never been a lad reach the ripe old age of twenty-one before.' Seeing the wide grin on Jamie's face, Matt added, 'Think yerself lucky, my lad. It were 1944 when I 'ad my twenty-first an' not a soul offered t' do a damn thing about it.'

'You were in the Army an' there was a war on,' Joan protested.

'Exactly. That's the point I'm trying t' make.'

'Oh, come on, Dad,' Meg objected. 'You haven't done so badly since. Can we have Jamie's do at the same place? The Crown at Morden?'

'That would be smashing, Dad,' Rosie said. 'And while you're about it, you could book it for me too cos I'll be eighteen soon.'

'The Lord save us! I'll 'ave to see about robbing a bank,' their father said, turning away so that his children wouldn't see he was grinning.

'Tell us the old, old story,' Jamie sang, and as Joan got to her feet and began to clear the table she felt as though her heart was bursting. It had been such a happy meal. The children could wrap Matt round their little fingers. It was as if each and every member of this family realized that they had come close to losing so much. Matt could have lost all of them if he'd stayed away any longer, and the girls could have lost their brother if the tide had gone the wrong way.

And as to her own behaviour, she couldn't believe how gullible she had been where John Chapman was concerned. She had believed everything he told her and had wallowed in the attention he lavished on her because at that time she had felt the need to be wanted.

Having found out about Matt and Doris Shepherd she had been hurt much more than she had been willing to admit and taking up with John Chapman had been her way of getting back at Matt. But now she would readily agree, two wrongs don't make a right. In the end it was love, even with all the trials and tribulations over the years, the love they all felt for one another had held them together and helped them to weather the storm. For that she would be eternally grateful.

* * *

It was Monday afternoon, a nice windy day, and Joan had got two lines of washing dry. She was humming to herself as she stood in the kitchen doing the ironing.

When the telephone rang she put down the iron on its stand and went into the hall to answer it. She picked up the receiver and heard a female voice say, 'Joan?'

'Yes, who's speaking?' she asked, though the voice was familiar.

'Oh, sorry, it's me, Beryl. Beryl Piviteaux. I hope I'm not disturbing you.'

Joan's heart missed a beat. Not again! Why did she keep ringing? Joan knew the answer to that one. The poor woman was hoping that, just once, Jamie might answer the phone or at least someone might persuade him to talk to her.

'No, you're not disturbing me, Beryl. I'm the only one in the house at the moment.'

'Oh, I was hoping . . .'

'Yes, I guessed as much. Believe me, Beryl, I have tried to get Jamie to ring you, really I have. I don't know what else I can do.' Then, feeling that she shouldn't be bearing the brunt of all this, let alone made to feel so guilty all the time, she added, 'Surely it's no surprise to you the way he's behaving? After all, Peter's treating me no differently. He wrote quite openly that he wanted nothing to do with me or Matt – or Britain, come to that.'

There was an awkward silence. Then, her voice breaking, Beryl said, 'I have written twice to James. It bothers me that he won't admit who I am, or that Joe is his real father. It doesn't seem to count so much with you. It's as if you put it to one side . . . as if you don't care.'

'That's not fair,' Joan shouted. 'I have to deal with my husband and my parents who flatly refuse even to consider

that Jamie doesn't belong to this family. I console myself
that he has been mine from the moment he was born, and
still is. I thought it would be the same for you. But it isn't,
is it? You seem to want to lay claim to both of them.'

'Please, Joan, don't let us quarrel. The reason for this call
is to tell you we're coming to England.'

'What? Really?' Oh my God!

'Yes, really, we're all coming.'

'Who exactly?'

'My husband, myself, our two girls and Peter.'

'Peter? Has he agreed? Does he want to come?'

'He hasn't been given a choice. He's coming. His father
and I agree he has to meet you.'

Joan didn't know what to say. The boy to whom she had
given birth was coming here. Suddenly she was afraid. Was
she pleased that at last she would meet him? If she was
offered a hundred pounds she wouldn't be able to answer
that question. And Beryl must be feeling the same way,
because faced with the family being here, in England, Jamie
would have no option. He would have to meet his real
mother.

When Joan remained silent, Beryl spoke abruptly. 'How
it will all turn out I dread to think, but at least we will see
their reaction face to face. We'll arrive about the sixth or
seventh of November, staying at an hotel in Chingford.'

'Chingford?' Joan was having a job to take it all in.

'Yes. My mother moved out of London some years ago.
She has a small flat in a block near Epping Forest. She
found this hotel for us, the Ridgeway. It's only ten miles
from London, about twenty minutes on the train, so she
tells us. It should be convenient all round.'

Joan couldn't think of a word to say.

'Joan, are you still there?'

'Yes,' she muttered.

'I'll write you our full itinerary. I won't telephone any more as it's not always easy to get a connection and it is rather expensive, nor will I write to Jamie again. At least I've given you time to prepare him for this. So, we'll see what happens when we meet. 'Bye, Joan.'

The telephone clicked. Slowly Joan replaced her receiver.

She stood stock still. What now? How on earth was she going to tell her family that they had to come to Chingford or London or wherever to meet the family that had invaded their lives to such an extent that she didn't know what to do for the best. Matt, her parents and Jamie wouldn't want anything to do with the American family. They'd refuse outright even to consider meeting them. That was a dead certainty. What could she do about Jamie? Would it make any difference whatever she said? She had pleaded enough in the past to no avail. She could try to assure him, once again, how much he really meant to her and Matt. Ask him to give it a go. Be reasonable. That was a laugh for starters. From the day that Clive Richardson had come into their lives all reason had flown out of the window.

What about Meg and Rosie? How would they react? They probably wouldn't mind, they might think this visit was a great lark, even look forward to meeting the other family. As long as it didn't jeopardize their relationship with their beloved Jamie.

Her legs felt heavy and her heart was aching as she walked back to the kitchen. Why on earth did Beryl have to keep digging away at a problem that was far better left to sort itself out? She took a lot of understanding, did Beryl Piviteaux. She had said that she wanted to keep Peter as her son. She had brought him up all these years and the bond was too strong to break now. 'That is exactly the way I feel about Jamie,' Joan said aloud.

So what was the problem?

Was it just curiosity? Aching to find out how her real son had fared in these past twenty-odd years? Did she not realize that a meeting might go terribly wrong? Even if they did all meet face to face, eventually. Who's to say how it would turn out? Would it help matters if the boys hated each other? A sudden thought struck Joan, and the horror of it caused her to catch her breath so hard that she had to grab hold of the back of a chair to stop herself from falling. On the second of November both Peter Piviteaux and their own Jamie would be twenty-one years old! How could they have a celebration birthday party for Jamie knowing full well that within a few days they were going to force him to meet with the family that were claiming him as their own.

'Mum, are you all right?'

Joan shook her head, took a deep breath and waited a second for the colour to come back into her cheeks. Such had been the shock of her realization that she hadn't heard Jamie come in.

'Yes, son, sorry about that, it was only I felt a little dizzy.'

Jamie went to the sink and fetched a glass of cold water. 'Here,' he held the glass to her lips and she could see the concern in his eyes. 'Drink this slowly and then you can tell me what upset you cos by the look of you something has.'

Joan made a decision. He would be the first one she would tell. After all, it would affect him the most.

'Please Jamie, I want you to be patient and listen carefully to what I have to tell you.'

He sighed heavily. He knew that what was coming had

to be about the Piviteaux family. 'All right, Mum. I promise I won't say a word until you finish. What's happened now?'

Joan began with the ringing of the telephone and continued until she had related the whole of Beryl's conversation.

Jamie had been very tolerant, listening, taking in every word and not showing her how annoyed he was that once again that family had upset his mother. There was a brief silence, then, without raising his voice he began to repeat what were to him the bare facts of the whole matter.

'Mother, as I've repeatedly told you, I believe that the facts my blood tests turned up are true. Tests such as they were don't lie. But they haven't altered my feelings as to who I am and where I want to be. Not in the slightest. If the American family were hoping for a different reaction then I'm sorry. A mistake was made all those years ago and although that fact has now come to light in my book it's too later for it to be put right. That is my firm opinion.'

He paused and took a deep breath.

'I'm grown up, old enough to make my own decisions. They cannot come into my life just because they want me to know that my ancestors were Polish and are now one hundred per cent all-Americans. I am not interested.' He went to where his mother was sitting, bent down and took one of her hands between both of his.

'If you want the whole truth, Mum, I think fate, if that's what you want to call it, dealt me a great hand. I am James Pearson, have been since the day I was born, and as far as I'm concerned nobody is going to convince me otherwise. My parents are Mathew and Joan Pearson and I've two great sisters, grandparents and even a great-grandmother. My whole family love me and I dearly love each and every one of them.'

What could she say to that? What could she do about it?

She got to her feet, too choked with emotion to speak as her son hugged her close.

Later as they sat opposite each other drinking a cup of coffee Joan asked herself another question: What did she want to do about it?

Nothing, if she were truthful. Jamie's words had meant everything to her. In every sense that mattered he was her son.

Chapter Twenty-Eight

SEPTEMBER AND OCTOBER had given them an Indian summer, but now it was different. The first few days of November had been bitterly cold, and winter was about to settle in good and proper.

Joan didn't like that prospect any more than she did the proposed visit of the Piviteaux family. From the moment she had taken that phone call from Beryl, she hadn't had a moment's peace. Trying to convince her family that it would be in the best interests of them all to meet the Americans and get it over and done with had been the hardest task she had ever had to tackle.

Meg, Rosie, her parents, even Hester and Amy had come round to her way of thinking, but Matt and Jamie were still dead against it, and for the first time Jamie and his grandfather were at loggerheads. It had been a unanimous decision to postpone Jamie's twenty-first birthday party.

Beryl's mother had telephoned and introduced herself as Eileen Fowler. She had been kind and chatty, so Joan had no qualms about meeting her. Between them they had reached an agreement that the best way for everyone to meet for the first time would be in normal circumstances rather than in a hotel. Joan had invited them all to lunch on their first Sunday in England. She sighed and shook her head at the thought of it.

Christ knows how I let myself in for that, she thought. Would the whole day end up in ructions? Common sense told her she had had no choice. It was a bloody awful necessity that she had to get through. She would have to pull herself together and get on with making this family feel welcome.

She heard Matt and Jamie come downstairs and went into the hall. 'Where are you two off to?'

'Out,' Matt answered, surly.

'We're going for a walk,' Jamie told her.

His voice and the way he was standing, with his chin thrust out and hands in his pockets, infuriated her and Joan felt she couldn't take much more. 'I think the pair of you are acting very badly. The least you could do would be to sit down and talk to me properly. We've only a couple of days to go before they arrive and I'm getting no help from either of you.'

Matt flushed. Clearly he was angry. 'You invited them here, you deal with it.'

'That's the way I feel,' Jamie put in. 'How many more times must I tell you? I don't want an American woman fawning all over me telling me she's my mother.'

Joan felt it was time she stood up for herself. She was fed up to her back teeth with carrying the can all the time. 'Your mother was English, born and bred in the East End of London,' she flung at him.

'Really?' he said sarcastically. 'I thought you were born in Wimbledon, and if you insist on me meeting her on Sunday that is exactly what I shall tell her.'

Matt was frowning. He had never heard Jamie speak to his mother like that. He put his hand on his son's arm. 'Take your coat off, son, and come into the living room.' Turning to Joan he managed a smile. 'Go put the kettle on, love. Make us some tea and we'll 'ave a talk.'

There was a good fire burning in the grate, and the room was comfortable and cheerful. It was a whole lot better than arguing out in the hall. They were each drinking their tea. Jamie had retreated into silence: not a hostile silence but a melancholy one. Joan felt she had to start the conversation or they'd sit here all day. She took a deep breath, then said, 'Jamie, and you, Matt, I do wish you'd see things from my point of view. I could certainly do with a bit of help from somebody.'

'Oh, come off it,' Matt exclaimed crossly. 'You've got your mum and dad an' my mum all agreeing with you, what more d'you want?'

Joan sighed. 'They're not in this house. It's me who has to deal with all the animosity and it's not fair. This mix-up, or whatever you want to call it, was not of my making yet I seem to be getting the blame from all sides. Have either of you ever stopped to think about how I feel about it all?' She paused, and both Matt and Jamie had the grace to look guilty. 'I know it hasn't been easy for you, Jamie. Believe me, if I could wipe it all away I would. But, for once, just listen to me. This family has travelled all the way from America, and if I hadn't agreed that they could come here they wouldn't have just gone away. You'd better believe that because it's the truth. Would you rather that they followed you? Talked to you in the street? Besides, they've had the same trouble with their son. He doesn't want to know me. Has that ever struck you? I feel obliged to meet him, even if it is the one and only time. I honestly believe the best way to satisfy everyone is to let them visit us quietly here in our own home. That way, please, God, it will be over and done with.'

Joan felt such pity tug at her heartstrings as she watched Jamie look at his father. My God, he really is frightened, she thought. What on earth could she say or do that would absolutely reassure this loving, kind young man that he really did belong with them? How could he possibly, even for a minute, think she would allow another lad to come into her life and destroy all the ties that had taken years to grow between a mother and her son?

'Mum, I'm sorry, it's just that . . .' Tears weren't far away.

Matt took charge. 'All right, gal. I'll go along with 'aving them 'ere on Sunday, if that's what will make it easier for you.'

Joan sighed again, but this time it was a sigh of heartfelt thanks.

Now everyone was pulling their weight. Of course it was to be no ordinary Sunday lunch. Beryl and Joe Piviteaux were bringing Beryl's mother so that made six of them. Bill and Daphne would be bringing Hester so that was three more. And no one in their right mind would think of leaving out Grandma Pearson. Amy would never let them forget it if they did! So with us five I make that fifteen, Joan mused, as she made yet another list. Luckily, there were folding wooden doors between the living room and the front room, and although the dining table wasn't anywhere near big enough for fifteen a smaller one could be tucked on to the end. A sheet would have to serve as an undercloth with two fancy ones on top. Bill had promised to lend some chairs.

What to give them to eat? Did Americans like our kind of food?

'Give them good old roast beef,' Matt had said, 'and if it's not t' their liking they can always leave it.'

Joan had ordered the meat from her regular butcher, and when he had assumed that it was for a celebration dinner for Jamie's twenty-first she hadn't put him right. What he didn't know he couldn't gossip about to all his other customers. Hester had offered to make two apple pies on the Saturday so that they would only need warming through. Daphne had suggested that not everybody would fancy pastry after a big meal so her contribution was to be two bowls of sherry trifle, and with a good assortment of cheeses to follow that ought to fit the bill. Meg and Rosie were to do the vegetables on the Saturday, so all that remained now for Joan to worry over was whether or not to offer a starter and if so what? She was still pondering on this when the telephone rang.

She had hardly lifted the receiver when Amy's voice boomed down the line. 'It's only me, love. I just wanted to know if there's anything I can bring with me for the week-end an' don't forget to sort a few jobs out for me. Can't do with sitting about on me backside for hours on end.'

'Oh, Amy,' Joan laughed, 'I'm so glad you're going to be here. I'm dreading long silences when nobody knows what to say or where to look.'

'Don't let it bovver yer, love. I'll 'ave a thing or two t' say if they upset our Jamie.'

'Don't be rotten,' Joan scolded. 'Perhaps you can help me

out, though, because I can't think what to give them to start the meal off. I did consider soup but that seems a bit ordinary. Any suggestions?'

'Well, before Matt picks me up on Saturday morning I could nip down Petticoat Lane. There's always the herring sellers. Come to that, if you don't want roll-mops, 'ow about smoked/mackerel, or a couple of crabs?'

'All a bit messy,' Joan said.

'Could always bring three or four pints of winkles, give 'em all a pin an' let them 'elp themselves.'

Joan had to hold the phone away from her ear because Amy's bawdy laughter was deafening. Even so she herself was giggling helplessly. She doubted very much if the Americans had even heard of winkles let alone eaten them. And the very idea of asking her guests to sit there with a pin, picking the tiny worm-like pieces of fish out of each shell, well, only Matt's mum would even think of such a thing.

'Amy, you've given me an idea. If you would bring a couple of nice dressed crabs and some fair-size prawns, I'll make seafood salads.'

'Okay, love. Yer wouldn't like some cockles and whelks just to add a bit of taste, would yer?'

'No, I wouldn't, an' just you remember t' be on your best behaviour over the weekend. You will, won't you?' Joan begged.

'Course I will. If that Beryl an' 'er mother were born and lived in the East End then I'm 'ome an' dry for someone t' talk to, ain't I?'

As she put the phone down Joan thought, The Americans are going to love you.

* * *

Everyone was attempting to keep busy, except Matt, who was reading the Sunday paper. 'For Christ's sake sit down an' get a grip on yerself,' he said, as Joan went over once more to gaze out of the window.

'I'm all right,' she answered, twiddling with a bowl of flowers. When he tut-tutted she dropped her hands to her side. 'Oh, how I wish today was all over. My mum and yours wouldn't let me near the kitchen and my nan has dusted and polished everything in sight. I don't know what to do with myself. God, why did Meg and Rosie have to go out? If they're not back when the Piviteauxs arrive I'll kill them. And Jamie wouldn't open his door when I called to him.'

She was working herself up into such a state that Matt was about to pour her a stiff drink when the two girls burst in. 'Dad, you'd better come. We think they've arrived. A car has drawn up on the opposite side of the road with hire-car plates.'

From that moment on Joan could not have said what happened or in what order. Suddenly there was a semi-circle of tanned-looking people standing in her hallway. Two girls in the front, both dark-haired and blue-eyed, were introducing themselves to Meg and Rosie as Karen and Betsy. Beryl Piviteaux was a short, good-looking woman, who in her early years must have been a natural blonde. Now the colour was fading and she could only be described as plump, though the suit she wore was well cut and fashionable. Now, looking at her smiling, good-natured face, Joan came to the conclusion that she was a happy lady.

The two mothers stood staring at each other, both near to tears. Suddenly they both spoke.

'Where is Peter?'

'Where is James?'

Joan turned round to Jamie, who stood against the far wall. In a low voice she said, 'Come and meet everyone, Jamie.'

Beryl was doing the same thing, almost dragging her tall son from where he stood behind his father. 'This is Peter,' she said.

Then both women had their arms around each other.

It was Matt who said, 'Come on, come on, give these folk a chance to get inside the house. They must be dying for a drink.'

Beryl and Joan broke apart, each fumbling for handkerchieves.

Hester, Daphne and Amy saved the day. They were taking hats and coats, ushering everyone into the living room down the end nearest to where the grate was filled with crackling logs. Bill Harvey was making small-talk and asking everyone what they'd like to drink. Beryl's mother was of the same age and type as Amy, and there was no hanging back between the two of them from the word go.

By the time Joan had wiped her eyes and got her breath back Joe Piviteaux and Matt had a glass in their hand and were acting as if they were old buddies. Now she could take a good long look at Peter, the lad to whom she had given birth.

He stood well over six feet tall, far taller than Joe Piviteaux, had big dark brown eyes like Matt's and his dark hair held the reddish tints of Joan's family. Their eyes met, then the lad's fell away. He looked so uncomfortable and clearly he had nothing to say to her.

She glanced at Jamie. He looked even worse.

Beryl was doing her best to engage him in conversation, and Joan felt sorry for her. And she had noticed that Jamie had taken his clear blue eyes and dark hair from Joe Piviteaux. In fact, he bore a distinct likeness to his natural father.

'I hope you're all hungry,' Joan said, making an effort to lighten the atmosphere.

'You must have gone to a whole lot of trouble,' Beryl answered, glancing at the long dinner table. Her face was very pale and Joan placed a hand on her elbow and led her to a chair. Matt offered a glass and urged Beryl to drink. 'It's port with just a dash of brandy to settle you down. Just sip it slowly.'

Jamie couldn't take his eyes off his mother. His insides were raging. His mum and this other woman were getting on like a house on fire. Doesn't my mother remember why this family is here? Anyway today, if nothing else, was all his mother's fault. Why had she had to ask them here? She could have stopped them if she'd tried hard enough. Their Peter was downright rude. He was standing with his back to everyone just staring out of the window. It had been a shock to see him. He was so tall, just like Matt, and there was no question that he had the colouring of the Harvey family. He'd seen his granddad's reaction as he'd compared faces, and when he looked at Nan he knew that she, too, had accepted the resemblance. He didn't like Peter. The quicker they get him and his family out of our house the better I'll like it, he cried silently. Besides, just look at Mr Piviteaux! Such dark hair even on the back of his hands and when he spoke there was no mistaking he was an American.

Then Beryl was on her feet again and crossing the room to where he was standing. She put out a hand and, automatically, he took a step backwards. Surely to God she wasn't going to kiss him – or, even worse, put her arms round him and start to cry. His heart was thumping against his ribs and he was thinking that he'd give anything in the world to be able to get out of the front door and start running.

'I'm sorry, James,' was all she said, awkwardly, and this time she made no attempt to touch him. She was making him feel even more uncomfortable, if that were possible. She merely stared at him, with such a sorrowful expression that as she turned and walked away he found to his surprise that he felt sorry for her.

Amy had come into the room to clear space on the sideboard for the vegetables but seeing her beloved Jamie looking so sad and forlorn she went to him. Resisting the urge to wrap him in her arms and hold him close – that would never do, not today, they might both just end up in a flood of tears – she whispered, 'Head up, Jamie! Get through this meal and we'll soon 'ave everything back to normal.'

'Oh, Gran, I wish you meant that,' he said, keeping his voice low.

'Course I bloody mean it. Every word. Come on, lad, show them what a man you are, a Pearson and proud of it.'

Joe Piviteaux was looking at him, though trying not to. He felt his gran pat his back, so he straightened up, did his best to smile and, seeing that Matt was dispensing more drinks, he made a beeline for him and asked, 'Can I give you a hand, Dad?'

'Will you all please sit at the table.' To Joan's surprise, Hester had given the command. She was certainly rising to the occasion!

Matt went to the head where his mother had placed a large dish that held the big joint of roast beef.

'Please, do sit down,' Joan urged, because no one had moved. 'Sit anywhere you like.'

The Piviteaux family arranged themselves down one side of the table and the Pearsons, in the main, sat facing them. Joan's head was spinning as she watched everyone toy with the first course, over which she had taken such trouble. Matt endeavoured to make jokes as he carved the beef, and it was a relief when Amy and Daphne got to their feet and passed round the plates, telling everyone to help themselves to vegetables.

Having this lot here was a terrible mistake, Joan thought. Jamie and Matt had been right. But I meant well. She was crying inside. When Peter bothered to raise his head he just glared at her, as if she had done him a terrible wrong. She knew he was having a hard job to curb his tongue. But if he did let loose, what would he say? Come to that, what would Jamie say to his real mother? It was worse than a funeral party.

Amy did her best to break the awful silence. 'You two lads 'ave come of age now. Did you 'ave a party for your twenty-first, Peter?'

He looked across at her, his eyes asking, What the hell has it got to do with you? He merely shook his head.

'We're having the neighbours and Peter's friends round when we get home,' Beryl answered for him.

They were laying their knives and forks down on their plates. No one could say a hearty meal had been eaten by all! The apple pies and trifles were brought in and Matt carried the cheese from the sideboard.

Joan got to her feet. 'Where are you going, dear?' her mother asked, the concern showing on her face.

She had to gulp back the tears. 'To make the coffee.'

Jamie watched her leave the room and there was hatred in his heart for the strangers who were sitting around the table. Why, oh, why had things been allowed to go this far? If only that American doctor had kept his damned mouth shut. If only they had accepted the truth but kept it to themselves. That's what Joe and Beryl should have done if they truly loved Peter. Instead look at the trouble they had caused. Every single person in this room was all twisted up and nobody had a clue how to sort it all out. There wasn't going to be a happy ending, and there was no use pretending there was.

The women seemed to be getting on better than the men. The older ones were in the kitchen doing the washing-up and talking away nineteen to the dozen. Joan and Beryl were clearing the table and folding cloths. The four girls had taken themselves upstairs because Meg had suggested they might like to freshen up and at the same time take a look at their bedrooms. If the truth be told, both Meg and Rosie loved listening to eighteen-year-old Karen and fifteen-year-old Betsy, and they wanted to know a whole lot more about life in America.

As Joan had watched them all climb the stairs she had wished so hard that the two lads had also formed such a quick and easy friendship. In the circumstances, though, that was an impossible wish. Amy came in, carrying a loaded tray of clean cutlery. She was smiling broadly.

'What's cheered you up?' Joan had to ask, even though she dreaded hearing the answer.

'It's all right, love, nobody ain't killed anyone.' Then, throwing her head back and roaring with laughter, she added, 'At least, not yet they ain't.'

Joan looked at Beryl and they, too, started to laugh.

'Oh, Amy, now I know I'm home. Listening to you I

hadn't realized how much I missed the East End. You're a gem, you really are,' Beryl said spontaneously.

'Glad yer think so, love.' Amy grinned. 'But you'd better 'ave a good look round while you're 'ere cos there ain't much of the old London left standing. Yer mum 'as been telling me 'ow glad she is she moved out t' Chingford. She's invited me to go an' see 'er place, an' I told her if she wants to breathe in the smoke again there's only me left in the 'ouse an' she'd be more than welcome to stay with me.'

Good Lord! Joan stared at her mother-in-law in amazement. There was no side to her. How did she do it? Most people would describe Amy as being rough and ready and yet she got on well with everyone and everybody loved her.

'Where have the men got to?' Joan asked.

Amy's grin widened. 'They've taken themselves down the garden, would you believe it?'

'But it's freezing cold,' Joan protested.

'Well, they obviously thought the atmosphere in 'ere wasn't exactly warm.'

'From the kitchen could yer see what they were doing?'

'Yeah. Matt and yer dad took Mr Piviteaux into the shed. The two boys were down beyond yer big apple tree. They 'adn't come to blows the last time I looked.'

By four o'clock it was getting dark as they all stood in the front garden saying goodbye. All the women hugged each other, the men shook hands and the four girls kissed. Only Peter and Jamie had nothing to say.

'Let's get their reaction tomorrow, after they've slept on it,' Joe Piviteaux said wisely. 'We've a while to go before we return to the States. We'll ring you – maybe we could meet up in London. Would you show us some of the sights? In particular I want to show my kids the place where I met their mother and the district where we did our courting.' He guffawed and Beryl blushed. 'But for today, well, we're mighty grateful, even if we haven't expressed ourselves very well.'

Matt assured him they had been more than welcome and both he and Joan made noncommittal noises as regards meeting again.

Once the car had turned the corner they all trooped back indoors.

'I'll see about getting us some tea,' Daphne said, 'since nobody ate much dinner.'

'I don't want any, Gran. I'm going to my room.'

Jamie had spoken quietly and Joan's heart ached for him. She'd take a bet that it wouldn't be much different for Beryl. She doubted that Peter would have much to say on the journey back to their hotel.

They had somehow got through the first meeting, but had anything been achieved? Somehow she felt more undermined than before. And as for both Jamie and Peter, their minds must be in a terrible whirl. She would pray hard tonight. But exactly what would she pray for? Guidance for them all?

Chapter Twenty-Nine

JAMIE FELT HE had tossed and turned long enough. At two o'clock that morning he had gone downstairs, drunk a glass of milk and munched his way through a pile of cheese and biscuits. Even after that he still hadn't been able to sleep. He switched on his bedside light and saw it was a quarter to five. His mind was made up. Argue and turn it over as much as you like, when you boiled it all down it was himself and Peter Piviteaux who were most affected by this strange turn of events. But it had gone on too long. True, both his mother and Peter's had been shaken to the very core. How about the fathers? Matt took refuge in bad temper, making out that he disbelieved the whole damn caboodle from start to finish. That fact had Jamie loving him even more. At least he hadn't wrung his hands in despair and whined. Outright, with no hesitation, he had maintained that Jamie was his son and that was an end of the matter. Out in the garden yesterday Jamie had heard him say to Joe Piviteaux that he was his one and only son born on 2 November 1944 and he didn't care if folk wanted to talk to him till they were blue in the face it wouldn't alter his opinion one iota. Jamie had felt so proud. If Peter hadn't been watching him he'd have gone and thrown his arms around his dad and more than likely bawled like a baby.

It was just after that that Peter had said grudgingly, 'My dad feels the same way, I know he does.'

If that were true then it was only the women who were pursuing the matter. And he knew his mother hadn't been the instigator. That left only Beryl Piviteaux! When he had said to Peter that Beryl was to blame for the current situation they had practically come to blows. Then, reluctantly, Peter had added, 'You don't know the half of it. You don't have Polish relations and scores of ancestors clamouring away at you about their forefathers. None of you has the slightest idea what my mother has had to put up with. They just keep on to her. And at me.'

At that Jamie almost found himself feeling sorry for Peter.

Now, an awful thought came into his head. Were Peter's grandparents letting him think that if he was not of their blood they wanted nothing more to do with him? Straight on top of that came another thought. If those grandparents were such sticklers for their own bloodline, were they setting out to claim Jamie? If that was their aim, they were going to be disappointed.

It was about time he did something about all this, he decided, and climbed out of bed. He washed and brushed his teeth, then dressed. He folded some trousers, two shirts, underwear, socks and a few handkerchiefs, then added a washing pouch and put them all into the bag he used for his rugby kit. Money. He took ten pounds out of his drawer, then remembered his birthday money. God bless his aunts and uncles.

The house was still, but it wouldn't be long before his father was up and about. By the telephone in the hall he found his mother's address book. He turned the pages quickly and found the address and phone number of the Ridgeway hotel where the Piviteauxs were staying. He propped up the short note he had written, then pulled on his winter coat, wound a long scarf around his neck, opened the front door and closed it quietly behind him. He set off at a trot towards Morden station.

The warmth and the familiar smell of the Underground was comforting. Even at this early hour the train was fairly full and he looked around at the workers setting off on a Monday morning to begin the week. Come the new year, he would be joining them. The City held out good prospects for him and he had been looking forward to the opportunity that had been offered him. But, thank God, there were still a few weeks left before he had to think about it and hopefully by then he would have sorted out the mess that had been dumped on his family.

He came out into the hustle and bustle of Stockwell station, walked a few yards and turned left into South Lambeth Road. There he waited for a bus and when it came he climbed the stairs which gave him a jolly good view of the River Thames as the bus drove over Vauxhall Bridge. This reminded him of his days of sight-seeing with his mates on trips which had mostly ended up with them all paying a visit to his Gran Pearson. God, she could be a funny lady! But she had a heart of gold and there was never a person he had met that would dispute that fact.

The bus pulled into Victoria station. Suddenly he was very hungry. Except for the cheese and biscuits he'd eaten at two o'clock that morning he had hadn't a proper meal since Saturday. He wasn't going to waste his money on the posh cafeteria. His dad had taught him better than that. He made his way to the transport café behind the station.

Having put away a huge breakfast he decided it was time to make that telephone call. Less than an hour later the two young men were boarding a fast train bound for the West Country.

'I always did have a passion for travelling light,' Peter said, as he stowed his bag on the luggage rack.

'Did you leave a note for your parents?' Jamie asked

'Yes, I did. It wasn't the smartest thing I've ever done, running out on them like that, but what you said made sense.'

'I'm feeling guilty,' Jamie admitted, 'but I do believe it's up to us to have a few days away and decide what we think should happen.'

For the first time since he had heard the name James Pearson, Peter realized they were in the same boat, and it made sense for the two of them to be allies, not enemies. It was unthinkable to both young men that their lives should be turned upside down because of a mistake that had taken place over twenty years ago.

As the train pulled out of London they settled back in the corner seats of the carriage and their eyes met. Each could almost read the other's thoughts. Until now there had been little comfort in the situation and as time went on and nothing was resolved it was tearing their mothers apart. Would they be able to come up with an answer? They'd have to wait and see.

Jamie spoke first. 'I've no idea how we're going to carry on for the next few days, but whatever conclusion we come to, it won't be a victory for one of us and defeat for the other. How can it be?'

'I know what you're saying. But us clearing out of the way for the time being was a brilliant idea and at least it will give us a chance to . . . I don't know, certainly not find an answer to which everyone will agree.' Peter heaved a desperate sigh.

Jamie shook his head. 'Not a chance in hell of us doing that! Nothing short of a miracle would work now. But just because neither of us liked the sound of belonging to another family doesn't mean we don't care. I'd give the world to be able to ease the heartache both our mothers have been suffering.'

'The trouble with each of us is that we're pretty settled in the life that has been allotted to us and . . .' For the first time since they had met, Peter smiled '. . . well, James, we might even become buddies. You never know, do you? Just before we left the States my dad was telling us how he and Mom managed to grab a few days' honeymoon in Corn Wall.' He pronounced it as two separate words. His smile broadened. 'Wonder what made you think of us going to the West Country? Anyway, here we are, on our way there. We might even enjoy ourselves,' he said. That's if we don't end up coming to blows, he added to himself.

Meanwhile both mothers had found the notes and had arranged to meet. 'I can't believe it,' Beryl said, in the tea lounge of the Grosvenor Hotel at Victoria station that afternoon.

'No, but I was quite relieved when you rang and said Peter had gone off with Jamie. All Jamie's note told us was that he was going to telephone Peter.'

'I know what you mean,' Beryl said. 'While I sat here on my own waiting for you, I've been making mental notes of every single thing I wanted to tell you. And I imagined that it was going to be terribly difficult, and found myself searching for the right words and the best way to say them. But then you came through the door looking just as worried as I felt. My mind went blank. Now I've come to the conclusion that we both want exactly the same thing where our boys are concerned.'

'Oh, Beryl,' Joan cried, 'I've been so afraid of hurting or upsetting you that I've held back from telling you what was really in my heart.'

'Well, maybe the boys going off like this will prove to be a Godsend. Let's hope they come back friends. What did Matt have to say?'

'Much the same as your Joe did, I guess,' Joan replied.

'Yeah, well, I'm more than happy to shut my ears to that. Leave Peter and Jamie to get on with it. Now, I'm going to order coffee for myself and I guess it will be tea for you.'

Two days later Peter and Jamie, dressed in suitable winter clothing and heavy shoes, were sitting on a rock eating sandwiches. In all directions the moors looked bleak, but there were small shaggy ponies who were tame enough to nuzzle their hands and chew the crusts of bread they held out to them. They had spent their first night in an hotel in Truro, but on the advice of a hall porter had taken a bus out to Portreath, a fishing village nestled at the foot of breathtaking hills. They had taken two single bedrooms in a pub, with the offer of a hearty breakfast, a packed lunch and an evening dinner all inclusive for seven nights at twelve pounds each.

'We should at least send a postcard to our folks,' Peter muttered, as he crunched into an apple.

'No, I don't agree,' Jamie answered quickly. 'The post-mark would give away our whereabouts and we'd have the whole place swarming with relatives before we'd be able to turn round.' They laughed.

They were having a great time. The days were good, if bitterly cold, with whippy, freezing winds and an angry grey sea. Their evenings, perhaps, were the best of all. News of their presence had spread through the village, and the pub's evening trade was so good as a result that the landlord and his missus were thinking of asking the lads to stay on a bit longer.

With the curtains drawn and a fire blazing, the small bar was packed. The boys, who had had a hard job to get used to the thick Cornish accent, were not surprised to learn that Cornwall had once had its own language. But if they liked to listen to the locals, Peter's Americanisms and Jamie's London accent held the villagers spellbound.

The boys were told of how the area had been an important centre because of its tin and copper mines, but when the talk turned to the military activity that had gone on in the surrounding countryside during the latter years of the war they sat up straight and began to take notice.

''Tis true, lad.' The landlord came out from behind the bar. 'Quite a few Americans were here. Very inconspicuous at first, they were, but as time went on our narrow cobbled streets rang with the tramping of Army boots. Barbed-wire barriers were everywhere, certainly along the coastline. And many a night there was a jeep parked outside here.'

His missus wasn't going to be outdone. 'I could tell ee a tale or two,' she said to Peter. 'Further over the headland it's rugged country an' that's where they put the Nissen huts that became an American base.' She would have liked to tell him about the dance she went to up there. It had been a night she'd never forget. But one look at her husband's face and she decided against it.

'I was in the Home Guard,' one white-haired old gentleman quavered.

'Home Guard? Sorry, would you explain, please, sir?' Peter asked.

'Well, some of us had to defend our shores. At first, when we were formed in 1940, I suppose we were a laughing-stock. No weapons, only pitchforks and suchlike, but we drilled till we were dead on our feet, and as time went on we were well equipped. We'd have put up a good show if Hitler had sent his troops to invade us.'

'I'm sure you would have, sir,' Peter answered politely, even though he was having great trouble in taking in the fact that men had been doing their best to defend the shores of England with little more than garden tools in 1940.

He was so glad that Jamie had made that telephone call suggesting that they take off together. The funny thing was, though, that they hadn't even begun to discuss the situation. They'd spoken of everything under the sun but that. It was as if they were two old mates who had met up and decided to have a break in different surroundings. And of all the places to find himself! Portreath in Corn Wall!

It was so small, quaint, like nothing he could have imagined. He found himself wishing that he could invite James to visit America. How he'd gasp if they had a vacation up in the log cabin that the family used for holidays. Boy, he'd have to agree that was some beautiful country.

Here the narrow streets of the town were empty and quiet, except when a fishing-boat put into the harbour to land its catch. He could hardly believe that he was sitting here, in this pub that was a warren of stone-flagged passages, ceilings so low that he already had one lovely bruise on his forehead to show for it, and being made to feel so welcome, almost as if he and Jamie were long-lost sons.

He fell to wondering what these good down-to-earth folk would have to say if he and Jamie were to tell them their story. Hey, you guys, he's really the American, Peter Piviteaux, although he believes he's a Limey. And I'm the English one who should be going by the name of James Pearson. My father was an American soldier who came to these parts early in 1944 to spend a few days of wedded bliss, but quite recently we've learnt that man is really Jamie's father. Not mine! Surely they'd never be able to grasp those facts. He and Jamie were having a hard enough job as it was!

One of the women customers stooped to pile more logs on to the fire from the basket that lay in the hearth. 'Here, let me do that for you, ma'am.' Peter was on his feet in an instant.

Straightening up the woman looked at him, thinking what lovely manners he had. Then she turned her gaze to Jamie, a real English gentleman. She felt she'd love to dig deep into their friendship. There had to be more to these two than met the eye – God above, it was November and not the time of year to come sightseeing.

She thanked Peter, and asked, 'Haven't you got any tales to tell *us*? We'd love to know what's brought two big lads like you to our part of the country in the dead of winter.'

At this the boys stifled their laughter and did their best to dodge the question.

Much later when they were saying goodnight they came to the conclusion that the locals' way of life was different from anything either of them had experienced. The men seemed so elderly and so small, and there was hardly one among them whose hair had not turned grey. Take the governor of the pub: he wore an old jersey, and of an evening he'd take off his shoes and put on carpet slippers. You'd never believe he was the owner of the place. As for the other men, their hands were rough and horny – they might lead their lives at a slow pace but they worked hard.

Next morning, washed and dressed before eight o'clock, Jamie glanced out of the window and was surprised to see that Peter was already outside, standing by the big stone wall that surrounded the public house, staring out to sea. He hastened down to join him.

'I was trying to decide what we should do today.' Peter gave him a cheery welcome. 'Although it's hardly light yet, I just know the sun is going to come out. I've been standing here imagining what a difference that will make to this place.'

They both gazed out to sea. Today it glowed with different colours. Over the rocks and seaweed that lay near to shore the water was dark. Far out, where a fleet of small fishing-boats were battling their way across the waves it became almost green. There was hardly any wind yet the sea was never still, swelling and dipping, constantly rolling.

Both boys were deep in thought until Jamie spoke: 'I think today we had better see if we can come up with some answers, don't you, Peter?'

'Yeah. Okay.' Then, as if thinking aloud, he said, 'My life was carefully planned. I had everything. Yes, and I took it all for granted. Now I wonder after all these years why a bolt out of the blue has been directed at my family. It has caused my mother such anxiety that I felt I could cheerfully kill the doctor who had laid the true facts bare. And to top that, she had my grandparents to contend with and they've convinced her somehow that she's an utter failure. It doesn't seem to count that she has two lovely daughters besides me.'

Jamie felt closer to him at that moment than ever before. 'I know what you're saying. I, too, wanted to lash out at someone when the proven facts were laid out for me. I blamed your parents for not keeping it to themselves. Then on my way home from university I had an accident. Got knocked off my motorbike. They tell me I hovered between life and death for some time. I do know that during those long days and nights my mother was never far away. I sensed her presence. She and my family willed me to live. All that time, the question of whether Joan and Matt Pearson were my true parents was irrelevant. So the answer, whatever it is, is no longer of any real importance.'

For one long moment they stared at each other. Then simultaneously they held out a hand, and grasped each other's.

'Something weird going on out there. Come an' look, me dear,' the landlord urged his life. She saw the two big lads holding each other in what she later described to her customers as a great big bear hug.

She would have been even more amazed had she heard the American and the Londoner swear to regard each other as a brother for as long as they should live.

'I'm ravenous,' Peter declared. 'Shall we go in for breakfast?'

'Yes, and I don't know about you but I feel as if a huge weight has been lifted off my shoulders.'

'Do you think we should make tracks for London?' Peter asked.

The very thought of it filled Jamie with dismay. 'What difference is a few more days going to make? Let's make the most of it, have a real holiday.'

Peter felt filled with the same need to stay on here in Portreath because there were so many more places for them to see and he was already making a mental list.

The time went all too quickly. They spent a few queasy hours out with the local fishermen, with an added thrill of seeing a shoal of mackerel being hauled aboard while the seagulls filled the sky with their screams. They tramped for miles finding yet more villages with maze-like narrow lanes. They found it pleasant to be alone. All the hurt and anger had been wiped away. They hoped that the same could be said for both sets of parents. Soon they would have to go back and face the music. But still, for a little while longer, they had each other's company.

One day they found a gift shop, filled with the sort of rubbish that tourists rushed to buy. Its windows were dusty and the door was closed.

'You boys looking to buy a present for your womenfolk?'

They turned to stare at a stout man in a leather apron. 'There be a factory down there.' He pointed with a gnarled finger. 'No rubbish, mind, handmade woollen garments finished off neatly on machines. Take a look. Won't cost yer nothing.' They were speechless but managed to nod their thanks.

They set their feet in the direction he had pointed. God, the way was steep, the road so narrow that there was no space for a pavement and the small whitewashed houses had steep granite steps up to their old oak front doors. Surely the man was wrong. No factory could exist in such a place. Where were the tall chimneys, Jamie wondered as he thought about the East End of London where his gran lived.

In a crooked corner they found it: a beautiful double-fronted cottage. A huge wooden board that had been painted bright blue was fixed to the stout wall: 'Shetland Wool Cottage Industry'.

As they stood there the door was opened by a little woman with rosy cheeks. 'I'm Mrs Benbridge. Come in.'

The boys looked at each other. Obviously she was a lady of few words.

Five young women sat working at a bench and when the ten eyes were turned on them the boys felt embarrassed.

Mrs Benbridge pushed back the mob cap she wore and scratched her head. 'For your mothers? Jumper or cardigan?' She pointed to a glass display cabinet.

The boys shifted their feet. The garments looked very nice, and it wouldn't be a bad idea to buy presents for Beryl and Joan, but what about size – and colour?

Peter was the first to recover and, using all his charm, he said, 'May we see one of each please, ma'am, and may we rely on your good judgement to advise us on size?' The approving sigh that rose from the girls as they stared at their American visitor was loud, and Mrs Benbridge quickly stared her condemnation.

Several items were brought forth and laid on top of the cabinet. They were indeed of the finest wool and skilfully hand-embroidered. Jamie whispered, 'Shall I buy one for Beryl and you buy one for Joan?'

'What a good idea.'

Mrs Benbridge snorted in disapproval. 'These cardigans are more suitable for your mothers. I'm sure they are sophisticated ladies.'

Peter couldn't bring himself to answer. This woman thought they were referring to their girlfriends. Good job she wasn't aware of the full story or she'd probably have forty fits.

Jamie came to the rescue. 'Joan and Beryl *are* our mothers,' he told her. 'I would like a blue cardigan, please, for Beryl. She's quite short and a little on the plump side.'

Before the poor woman could regain her composure, Peter said, 'And mine will be for Joan, who is tallish and has the most lovely red hair, so I think perhaps the green would suit her best.'

Still without a word Mrs Benbridge sorted through her stock and finally laid out two very fine cardigans in what appeared to be the right sizes. 'They be one pound ten shillings and sixpence each, and sixpence extra if you'd like them packed in a gift box.'

Both boys murmured, 'Yes, please.'

As they left the shop, each with a neatly packed box under one arm, they turned in the doorway and winked at the row of girls, who had stopped working and were craning their necks, following their every move, wishing to God that it was time for them to go home so that they could rush out and at least speak to these two gorgeous-looking young men, the likes of which they didn't often get to see in Cornwall.

Bags slung over their shoulders, the lads stood still and looked back. Half of Portreath must have gathered this morning to bid them farewell.

'Us'll never forget ye,' was what they had been told over and over again.

'And as long as we live we're never going to forget our time here,' Peter said, as they went towards the bus stop.

'Nor the good it has done us,' Jamie answered.

Chapter Thirty

IT WASN'T A good day to be arriving in London. The spell
of good weather had broken. The railway station was heavy
with smoke and it was bitterly cold, the roads treacherous
with ice. Having spent the last seven days entirely in each
other's company, now came the time for parting. The
comradeship Peter and Jamie had experienced over the past
seven days could not have been imagined when they had
first met.

'So,' Peter grinned, 'I guess we'll be meeting up again in
the next few days.'

'Sure to be,' Jamie agreed. 'The whole family will want
to compare notes. Oh, by the way . . .' He pulled his bag
from his shoulder and took out the cardigan he had bought
for Beryl.

Peter did the same. 'I've put a short message on the gift
tag for Joan.'

'Me, too, for Beryl. Wonder what they'll make of us buying
them a gift?'

'Floods of tears is my guess.'

'Yeah, but I bet you anything you like they'll wear them when we meet, just so they can compare with each other.'

'That's a safe bet, Jamie boy. Probably see you tomorrow, till then take care.'

'You too, Peter.' It wasn't enough. They had become too close.

Then Peter's long arms came round Jamie's lean frame and they hugged before going their separate ways.

Joan was looking out of the bay window when she saw Jamie coming up the drive. He hadn't noticed her. She rose to her feet. He looked well, very fit. She walked out into the hall and opened the front door.

She listened to the frosty grass scrunching under the soles of his shoes, and then he saw her. His face broke into a wide grin. She flew down the steps and he rushed towards her. His hand was in the air giving her a thumbs-up and he was laughing. Thank God for that! Jamie was home.

When they were settled with a cup of tea in front of them, Joan asked, 'Are you all right?'

'Did you think I wouldn't be?'

'No. But it was a bit of a long shot, you two going off like that. We didn't know for sure, until Joe phoned your father, that Peter had agreed to go with you. And we were worried sick. We had no idea where you were.'

'We got a train to Cornwall. We thought it best not to tell you our whereabouts. I'm sorry, Mum.'

'I'm sorry, too, son, we all are. None of us handled that first meeting very well.'

'I felt I had to get away and was pretty sure Peter felt the same way. Very fortunate we did what we did, the way things have turned out.'

'You sure about that? How does Peter feel?'

'Well, he's sent you a present. I'll fetch it and I suggest you read the message on the gift tag.'

When Joan had the wrapping paper off and the box open she exclaimed in delight, 'Oh, this is a really lovely cardigan! I've never seen one like it before.'

'Mum, you still haven't read what Peter has written on the card.'

Jamie watched in silence as his mother read the message and wasn't at all surprised when he saw tears spring to her eyes. It was some minutes before she was able to speak and when she did it sounded like a moan. 'Oh . . . isn't that lovely.'

The card said, 'To Joan, I hope we get to know each other a whole lot better in the future. With love, Peter.'

The words were very much the same as he had written for Beryl. He was about to mention this to his mother when she coloured and asked, 'What about Beryl? I wouldn't offend her for the world.'

'It's all right, Mum, really it is,' he reassured her. 'I bought one for her. Hers is blue and I wrote her a card too.'

'Oh, Jamie, bless you, bless you both. You must have wise heads on your shoulders, the pair of you. Us adults could have gone on wrangling for days and getting nowhere. You two lads take yourselves off to the West Country and it seems to me you've managed to become the best of friends. I hope it lasts.'

Jamie looked into his mother's eyes. 'Mum, that's one thing I can promise you. No matter what, Peter and I have agreed to be friends.'

He still had nagging feelings as to what *might* have happened but now they were pushed to the back of his mind. Between Peter and himself they had laid to rest a lot of the anguish. But the very shock of it all would never be forgotten. All those weeks when the possibility had hovered over him that the parents he had known all his life might now want to reject him. The very thought of him not having Joan for his mother had made him physically sick. And as for Matt! A giant of a man that everyone thought twice about crossing. He remembered his early days at school when he'd been bullied and he'd asked his father to meet him at the school gates one afternoon. He had deliberately hung back and come through the playground with the older boys that were troubling him. Seeing Matt, he had said real loudly, 'Come and meet my dad.' One look at the great hulk of Matt Pearson and those boys had never bothered him again. In fact they had gone out of their way to be his friend. And the beauty of it was that Matt had grasped the situation at a glance, although Jamie hadn't uttered one word of complaint. 'Well done, son,' his father had said to him, laughing, well aware his presence at the school gate had been put to good use. Praise from his father had been music to his young ears. All those years he had kissed Joan goodnight and hugged Matt. Of course they were his parents. Hadn't Matt carried him high on his shoulders when the crowds at a football match had been overwhelming?

These past seven days had been an eye-opener. The talking that had gone on between Peter and himself had not been for anyone else's ears. They had confided things to each other that they had barely been able to admit to themselves. With the calm that had followed had come acceptance. It was a strange tale that could so easily have ended up being a tragedy for two families. Not that it was perfect even now: that was asking for the impossible. But Peter and himself had come to the conclusion that they were the main characters in this drama, and if they could behave in a reasonable way perhaps they could prevent much of the heartache, or at least ease it a little. They had both grasped that in this life there were so many forms of love. Which made it a dangerous commodity for mere humans to cope with.

How long they had sat there Joan couldn't tell. She had watched the different expressions flit across Jamie's face and didn't need telling that her son had grown up a lot in the week he had been away from home. He certainly wasn't the angry tormented young man that had walked out of the house so early one morning. She hoped with all her heart that Beryl was having the same thoughts about Peter. Maybe there was hope for all of them yet.

Chapter Thirty-One

A TRUCE HAD been called between both families. Maybe it was more than just a truce. Time would tell.

During the evening of the day their sons had returned from Cornwall Joan had spent nearly an hour talking to Beryl on the phone. Neither of them had an inkling of what had taken place during those seven days, yet each knew that the outcome was good.

As Joan was about to replace the receiver Beryl mentioned the cardigans.

'What did you think when you were given yours?' she asked Joan.

'Overjoyed is the only word that comes to mind. It was such a surprise.'

'That's exactly how I felt. I want to wear it and yet I don't. I almost feel like having it put in a glass case to keep it safe for ever and ever.'

Joan laughed. 'That's not a bad idea. Imagine if we're lucky enough in the future to have grandchildren and we try to tell them the whole story. We could produce our gifts as evidence.'

'Dear Jesus,' Beryl said softly, 'I hadn't given a thought to grandchildren. As time goes on this mix-up is going to become quite a family legend, isn't it? Still, I suppose we just have to say, sufficient unto the day.'

At that moment Joan could easily have lost her temper. Pity you didn't think of that and keep the facts to yourself when you first got the results of that blood test, is what she had to stop herself from saying. No one could turn the clock back. At least everyone was on better terms than when the Piviteauxs had first arrived in England. That was something to be grateful for.

Long afterwards, when it was all over, Joan would remember the hectic remaining days that the Piviteaux family spent in England.

They had done the whole London scene on their own, but Daphne and Bill invited them for an evening meal. Considering how badly the Sunday lunch had turned out, Joan thought it was brave of her parents to make another attempt. She need not have worried. The Piviteauxs seemed different, relaxed. Indeed, they kept the conversation going non-stop.

Joe sounded like a tour guide as he described their visit to St Paul's Cathedral, starting with the fact that it was at the top of Ludgate Hill, in the heart of the city. It was only as Joan listened to how the monks had 365 stairs to climb in order to reach the dome, a fact that she had been well aware of since her school days, that she suddenly realized that this family were really interested in English history. Then Karen and Betsy were telling of their visit to the Tower of London. There was the most beautiful chapel in there, the likes of which they had never seen, they declared, and yet the place had been used as a prison. A fact that they found hard to believe.

Jamie, smiling broadly, told them that in the first place it had been used as a palace but was still most famous as a prison. And when Betsy raved about the crown jewels, again it was Jamie who told her that the Towers that housed the jewels were built much later. From there, they had gone on to Tower Gate on Tower Hill and Betsy had everyone in fits of laughter as she shuddered whilst telling of the poor souls that had been hung there. They still had to see Buckingham Palace, the Changing of the Guard and Windsor Castle, and when Beryl asked Joan to go to Windsor with them, she agreed happily.

My feet are killing me, Joan was muttering to herself and was as pleased as punch when she heard Peter urging his father to let up a bit and take them all for some refreshments.

'OK, son, we'll take a break,' Joe answered, taking his wife's arm and heading for the nearest café.

Take a break! God help us, Joan was thinking as she gratefully sipped a steaming cup of coffee. The flag above Windsor Castle was flying at half mast, signifying that the Royal Family were not in residence. That meant that the State Apartments, round tower, stables, Saint George's Chapel and the Albert Memorial Chapel were all open to the public. And Joe had made sure that they had done the lot!

Their last day had arrived. Their flight was booked for six p.m., which meant they didn't have to be at Heathrow airport until four thirty.

Matt had booked a luncheon for the Piviteauxs and the Pearsons. He had also invited Beryl's mother. They would all meet up at the Goring Hotel at twelve thirty, and two cars had been ordered for two thirty to take everyone to the airport.

Matt was indeed a wise man. His choice of the Goring had been a good one. Everything about the building, the staff and the décor reflected the best of the British way of life. As Matt had become more prosperous in his business dealings, he had taken Joan there for a meal, and once they had stayed the night there after the theatre. Everything about the hotel had impressed Joan, and now it was having the same effect on Joe and Beryl.

'Old-world splendour,' Joe had stated, as Matt ordered drinks from an immaculate waiter.

'Will you have them in the main lounge or on the enclosed terrace, sir?' the waiter asked.

'Oh, the terrace, I think,' Matt told him: the elegant windows of the terrace overlooked the beautiful garden.

'Wow,' Joe exclaimed loudly, 'this place is something else.'

And so it was. It was only a few minutes from Victoria station yet it was like going back in time; stepping out of a cab one could leave behind the hustle and the bustle of London town. Dressed in the distinctive uniform of a great family hotel, a porter would open the taxi door and welcome you to the Goring Hotel. And from that moment it was personal attention down to the finest detail.

As they were a party of eleven, they were served in a private dining room It was a spacious room yet cosy. The meal was excellent, the service discreet and professional. When it was time for them to leave Joe Piviteaux was beside himself, shaking hands with everyone in the entrance hall and saying, 'We sure as hell ain't got anything like this in the States. Fantastic! Not like an hotel, more like a family house that belongs to an important aristocrat. And to have been made so welcome!' These Americans certainly hadn't the reserve for which the British were so well known. One young man, attired in morning dress, thanked Joe for his compliments.

'Don't know how you Brits do it,' Joe had answered.

'Sir, when your name is above the door you try that much harder,' the young man said, smiling.

'Your family own this hotel?' Joe spluttered.

'My great-grandfather opened it in 1910 as the first hotel in the world to have a private bathroom and central heating in every bedroom.' What could Joe say to that? Except to make a firm promise to return.

The drivers had already warned them that out at the airport there was a 'right pea-souper'. And they weren't wrong. The cars had crawled the last few miles because the fog was so dense. However, it wouldn't have mattered if they had arrived late, because the flight was delayed. Nevertheless it wasn't long after they had checked in their baggage before the passengers were being called into a departure lounge. Since this was beyond Passport Control, folk seeing off their friends and relatives were not allowed to enter.

The final moment had arrived. Both families formed a line to say goodbye. Everyone was hugging someone, and the girls were clinging to each other, promising not to lose touch.

Peter stood in front of Joan. She bit her lip as she watched him struggle with his emotions, willing him to put his arms around her. Come on, please, just this once, she begged him silently. Don't go without touching me. Suddenly he moved, and once he had taken that final step that brought him so close to her she held out her arms and he came into them. She was really holding him in her arms! In that moment, the touching of mother and son, she felt many things. She couldn't have explained the feeling, but she simply knew that a bond *did* exist between them and that from that moment some kind of seal had been set on their future relationship.

Beryl had been taking her leave of Jamie. Joan hadn't seen what had taken place between them, but as they looked at each other, she knew.

Both mothers understood that they would have to tread warily, but they also knew that their new bond was permanent.

Matt and Joe were clasping hands, Joan and Beryl were crying, Beryl's mother was cuddling her granddaughters. Only Peter and Jamie seemed quiet.

'Wipe your eyes, you two,' Joe ordered Beryl and Joan. 'We have to go.'

'We could go up to the observation area and watch your plane take off if it weren't for this damn fog,' Matt said.

'Never mind. When you all come to the States we'll show you what sunshine is. We'll go up to the cabin, do a bit of fishing, or even down to Florida.'

Meg and Rosie pricked up their ears. The Pearsons go to America? It was something to think about.

Then, gently and without haste, Beryl kissed Joan and whispered, 'So far, so good.'

BOOK THREE

ASHTEAD, SURREY, 1980

Chapter Thirty-Two

MATT DROVE HIS new Ford Granada slowly along the empty country lane. It was the beginning of May, a spring day with bright sunshine and clear blue skies. The trees were heavy with blossom while the hedges were green with fresh leaves. Away in the distance he could see a lone farmhouse and flocks of sheep. Over the past few weeks he had travelled this road daily and had often stopped the car to watch the lambs nestling up to their mothers' thick fleece.

Hopefully it was the promise of things to come. Sunshine always made everyone feel better.

Well wrapped up in the passenger seat, Joan was thinking how wonderful it was to be away from the hospital and all its smells of disinfectant. She thought that she had never seen the countryside look so beautiful

Matt turned his head and smiled at her. Ahead stood the wooden fence that fronted their long ranch-style bungalow, which Matt had had built for her four years ago. She leant forward, gazing at the clumps of spring flowers, remembering when the girls had planted bulbs beneath the trees and in scattered clumps over the lawn. She felt so happy. The white gates were open. Matt drove through them and drew the car to a stop at the front of the house. He opened his door, got out and came round to the passenger side. 'Come on, my love, we're 'ome.' He held out a hand to assist her and watched as she winced with pain. She had been so ill he'd thought they were going to lose her, but she had refused to go into a convalescent home, for which he was glad. She would be far better off at home. He would see that she had everything she needed. And when she was well enough he was going to take her on an extended holiday, maybe a cruise. That was if he could persuade her to be away from the children for any length of time. Children? They were all grown-up and some even had children of their own.

'Shall I carry you in?' he asked.

'I'll be fine,' she said softly. 'Oh, Matt, it feels so good to be home.'

'Well, at least take my arm. Everything's ready for you, loads of pillows on the settee. Mrs Simmonds has been a Godsend while you've been away. I'd be the first t' admit I never wanted t' 'ave a char-lady in the 'ouse, knowing all our business an' gossiping to 'alf the village, but she's turned out trumps.'

The first door in the wide hall was open and a well-banked-up fire burned in the grate. Joan went into the sitting room and sat down. Matt propped pillows behind her head and carefully lifted her legs up from the floor. She let her shoulders sink back and sighed with relief. She was home.

As soon as she felt a bit stronger she was going to walk

this bungalow from one end to the other. She had never got over feeling how lucky she was to have such a wonderful home. When Matt had first shown her the plans she had cried, 'God, I'll need a bike to get from one end of the hall to the other!' Now she loved every inch of it. The three bedrooms, the dining room, this lovely sitting room, and it had an office too for Matt, which kept him happy and out from under her feet.

The kitchen was something else. It had taken her weeks to get the hang of using the Aga, but now she wouldn't be without it. There were two bathrooms and many was the time she'd lain soaking in deep, sweet-scented water, thinking of how she'd had to wash all three of her children in a tin bath in front of the fire when they'd lived in Bull Yard.

It truly was a grand bungalow and lying here she could see beyond the windows to her garden, showing off all its springtime beauty.

'I'm just going to the car to fetch your case in,' Matt said, bending over her and planting a soft kiss on her forehead. 'Then you can tell me what you'd like to eat.'

'Oh, Matt, there's only one thing I'm longing for.'

'Well, tell me what it is an' if it's possible I'll see that yer get it.'

'A decent cup of tea.'

'You're something else, you are, Joan. You know that, don't you?' he laughed. 'I'll have a pot beside you just as quick as I can get the kettle to boil.'

While he was gone she took a good look around the room. There were several get-well cards on the sideboard as well as the host she had received while she had been in hospital. She hadn't realized they had so many friends.

Everything was fine. Mrs Simmonds was indeed a treasure. Left to Matt her house plants would surely have shrivelled up for want of a drop of water, but all their leaves were shiny and green. Nothing had changed. This was a beautiful room.

Matt came back carrying a loaded tray, which he set down on a side table. He should have looked awkward, a big man like him, handling bone china, but he didn't. So much had happened over the years and her husband was a different man from the one he had been in the early stages of their marriage.

Life had been good to them in so many ways. And yet, some regrets? Of course there were. Whoever said that life was going to be easy?

He placed another table near her so that she could easily reach her tea. Then he sliced a Victoria sponge, sandwiched together with thick cream and early strawberries. Placing a small wedge on a plate he ordered, 'I've been told to see you eat that. Mrs Simmonds came early this morning just to make it for you. Her way of saying welcome home, I guess.'

Joan did as she was told, savouring the lightness of the sponge and the sweet taste of early English strawberries. She drained her cup and smiled as she held it out for Matt to refill. By God, the hot tea tasted good. How come it didn't bear any resemblance to what was handed out from the hospital trolley? Matt's expression was serious as he took it from her. He was so relieved to have her home again. They'd had their share of rough times and right now all he wanted was to look after her and see some colour come back into her cheeks.

Joan was thinking what she would have liked to do now

was walk through the whole of this bungalow. Open every door, inspect each bedroom, because she knew some of the children had stayed here during the three weeks she had been away. She would know by their perfume which girl it was that had occupied which room. She wanted to touch her furniture, to see the curtains she had so carefully chosen. To make sure that everything was still as she had left it. She knew it was a daft idea but she had come so near to never coming home she needed reassurance that nothing had changed.

Matt piled logs on to the fire and the dry kindling flared and crackled, sending flames high up into the chimney.

Joan felt blissfully warm and cosy. She really was home. If only she didn't feel so tired. She knew why it was. Only too well. The doctor had said it was imperative that she had an hysterectomy, then all would be well. It hadn't been that simple. Not for her it hadn't. She was fifty-five years old and after the operation she had haemorrhaged. She had suffered such a blood loss that she had had transfusions and was kept in hospital much longer than she had expected. Now she felt weary. But it was a different kind of weariness to what she had felt as she lay in that long ward.

In hospital she had never had a peaceful night's sleep. So much was always going on even during the night: admissions, trolleys being wheeled along the corridors. Then there was that poor soul in the next bed who was always crying. During the time she'd been there Joan had come to realize the woman had never had a visitor and she had felt so sorry for her. Now she looked across to where Matt was sitting and as he smiled at her she felt his love flow across the room. She had so much to be grateful for. The last fifteen years had turned out so well. It was unbelievable, really. It was as if she had two families. And she knew Beryl Piviteaux would say the same.

Now they each had one son in America and another in England. Over the years it had given both families experiences that otherwise they would never have known.

'Joan,' Matt said, as he came to her side, 'I'm just going to switch on the electric blanket and then I'm going to see that you get undressed and into bed.'

'Oh, Matt, I'm so comfortable here.'

'Never mind that. You know what they said before you left the hospital: at least another week in bed before you start putting your feet to the ground.'

'All right. I do feel as if I need a good sleep, but what am I going to do lying there for another seven days?'

'You've got several new books the girls brought you. You can't have read them all.'

'No, I haven't read even one. A look at the daily paper was about all I managed. There was never enough peace and quiet in the hospital for me to settle down to a good read.'

'Well, now's your chance,' Matt told her, sounding masterful.

A sudden thought came to Joan. Yes, she felt she could easily sleep the rest of today away, and probably all of the night as well. But tomorrow she'd ask Matt to bring her six special books into the bedroom for her; they'd keep her happy and contented. They weren't scrapbooks, more a record of what her three children had achieved and how their lives had become entwined with the three Piviteaux children's. They regarded Peter, Karen and Betsy as their extended family, and as far as it had been possible she'd kept a kind of diary on all three of them as well as her own three. Now she and Matt saw more of Karen than Beryl and Joe did.

I shall go through each one slowly and carefully, she promised herself.

She was beginning to feel stronger and certainly much more optimistic.

Chapter Thirty-Three

JOAN WAS GOOD at sitting in silence while others liked to keep up a lively source of conversation. She didn't dislike her own company and she was actually looking forward to a few hours on her own today.

Matt was worried because Mrs Simmonds was taking her granddaughter to the dentist and wouldn't be coming to work, and he had had a phone call from Stan saying that he was needed at a meeting.

'Matt,' Joan pleaded, 'just get yourself ready and go. I'll be fine, honestly I will.'

'Well, if you're sure. I 'ave rather left Stan t' carry the can these last few weeks but I'll be 'ome no later than four o'clock.'

'Stop fussing,' was what Joan felt like screaming at him, as he checked that she had plenty to drink near her bedside.

'I've made you a salmon sandwich and I've cut all the crusts off and there's plenty of fruit if you fancy it. Are you sure you can get along to the kitchen all right on your own?'

'Matt, I go to the bathroom, don't I? I'll be fine.'

He put his arms around her shoulders and kissed her, reminding her of how it had been when they had both been young and so much in love. In spite of all their setbacks, it wasn't so very different today. They just took life at a slower pace. She watched as he shrugged himself into his jacket. At fifty-seven he was still a sight for sore eyes, his movements quick, his hair still dark, though showing grey around the sides, and the big brown eyes that flashed with the same smile that had captivated her when they had first met. By any standards Matt was a fine-looking man.

She had been home now for three days and he hadn't allowed her to lift a finger. To tell the truth she had slept most of the time.

The minute she heard his car drive away she threw back the bedclothes and put her feet into her slippers. Then, with her dressing-gown wrapped around her, she headed for the third bedroom, which overlooked the front garden. From the inside shelf of an oak tallboy she took down two parcels, one labelled 'The Pearsons' and the other 'The Piviteauxs'. She smoothed her hand over the cover of the second and replaced it on the shelf. I'll get to you lot later. Then, tucking the other set of books under her arm, she made her way back to bed.

Minutes later with her pillows arranged behind her back and a bedjacket tucked round her shoulders, she opened the first volume. It bore the title 'James Pearson'. She turned to the first page. The date was January 1965 and it was a record of the first visit to their house in Morden of Clive Richardson, followed by a catalogue of the events that had swiftly followed in those troubled times. She skimmed through these pages. She didn't want to dwell on that dark period of their lives. It was the happier days she was after. Then she came to a page headed 'Our Holiday'. She smiled. That was when they had returned the Piviteauxs' visit.

It had taken two years after Joe, Beryl and their family had returned home for Matt to agree that they should go to America. But at last they had managed it. That had been some holiday. So much had been packed into such a few weeks.

Beryl and she had become the closest of friends, because of the love they both had for their children. And both she and Matt felt a great affection for Joe too. He was such a considerate man, and he'd been a tower of strength to Beryl through all the sorting out of Peter and Jamie.

The seeds that had been sown during those three happy weeks had been nurtured and had grown. Almost on their first day in the States, Karen had introduced Jamie to Pamela, her best friend. Within two years the pair were married. Joan felt lucky that they had decided to live in England. They had a beautiful house in Chelsea, not far from Albert Bridge. Their firstborn was a son, named Matthew, much to Matt's delight. Eighteen months later their daughter Beryl had arrived. That had sent the phone lines crazy across the Atlantic.

When Hester, Jamie's great-grandmother had died, everyone had been devastated and none more so than Grandma Pearson. The funeral had taken place the same week as Amy had received notice that her house was due for demolition. The council welfare officer had suggested that she go to live in a council-run home. Amy had had other ideas. And loudly and firmly let everyone know her objections.

Joan laid down the book, took a long drink of her lemon-barley water and smiled to herself. She remembered it as if it were yesterday. Matt had taken it for granted that his mother would make her home with them, and Joan would gladly have gone along with that arrangement.

Amy's response had been to the point. 'If you think that I'm comin' 'ere to be buried alive in Surrey you've got another think coming. Where would I do me shopping? Ain't a decent market for miles. No. I was born in London an' in London I'm gonna die. Whether the council like it or not. But it won't be with a load of white-'aired old folk that spend two-thirds of the day dozin' an' if they do wake up long enough to feed their faces they dribble 'alf of it down their clothes. I know cos I've been to visit a few of me friends what 'ave got shoved into them places.'

Joan chuckled. Amy hadn't altered even now. At the ripe age of eighty-nine she wouldn't let anyone consider her old. Tears came to her eyes as she read of the kind way in which Jamie and Pamela had acted. The solution? A granny-annexe had been built on to their house, and to this day Amy reigned there like the Queen Mum. As she said, she only had to get on a bus and cross the bridge and she was near enough into her part of London.

Joan chuckled. When she and Matt had first been married she'd had the occasional set-to with her mother-in-law, but over the years a great affection had developed between her and this large jolly warm-hearted woman. A woman who had taught her that love could still exist despite the traumas that life threw at you. She loved it when Amy honoured them with her presence for a few days. Her larger-than-life figure filled the house, her bellowing laughter, her spoiling of the little ones, her witticisms which made them all laugh.

Funny when you came to think about it: Jamie had always been Amy's favourite. Not that she didn't love Meg and

Rosie, but Jamie had been to university and was now holding down a successful job in the City. You might have thought he would have outgrown his gran but nothing was further from the truth. He was very proud of her. And not only of Amy, Joan thought. He had never abandoned any of the family he had grown up with. He was wont to say that he had just spread some of his family across the Atlantic which was great when it come to holiday time. As for sharing his love, Jamie had proved that he had more than most to give.

Remarkable really that such a catastrophe had brought so many people together. At least every other weekend Pamela and he would bring Mathew and little Beryl to see her and Matt. At this thought Joan looked out of her bedroom window. The sun was shining, and it wouldn't be long now before it was warm enough for them all to have barbecues in the garden.

Soon after she and Matt had moved here, Matt had built a brick fireplace for the barbecue in a sheltered spot at the far side of their garden. He had come home from America determined that they would have one built in their 'backyard', as Joe Piviteaux would say. For the past three years it had been put to good use, with everyone sitting outside to eat, the adults at one table and the children at another, the sound of laughter filling the garden. When it got dark, Matt always lit candles in tall narrow glasses to prevent them being blown out by the breeze.

She hadn't made any entries in these books for some time now, but soon she would take up her pen again. She had only to sit back and listen when the children were talking and she would hear how their lives were proceeding.

Joan sometimes thought that of all her children Meg needed her most. She certainly led a much more ordinary life than her brother or sister, yet it seemed fraught with complications.

She opened the book on her eldest daughter and was surprised to see a photograph taken at Meg's wedding lying between the pages. She hadn't remembered placing it there. Such a carefree, happy couple they looked, Meg and Brian.

Meg had married her faithful Brian Clarke and had two children, John and Josie. They still lived within a short distance of the Pearsons' old house in Morden. She and Brian had a good lifestyle. He was now a partner in the same firm of chartered accountants that he had started out with, Macdonald and Partners.

It was the children who caused the trouble – though when they stayed here neither Matt nor she had had any complaints – or maybe just one: both children wanted to sit in front of the television set all day. Josie was a sweet girl, but she sucked the end of her pigtail, which annoyed Matt no end, and you couldn't get her to open a book, let alone read one. John wasn't much better: he hated school and all forms of sport. Perhaps the fault didn't lie with the children.

Brian had been lucky with their house. Situated at the top of Wimbledon Hill it had been a vicarage in the past. It was the most lovely old house with a large garden, and Brian employed a gardener-handyman, Harry Evans. As Joan read what she had written she chuckled again. What Matt had said had seemed funny at the time, but sad to say it had turned out to be true.

'That bloody man Evans is so slow I doubt he could catch a cold, and as for 'im producing vegetables, well! If he does get sprouts to grow he'll be too lazy t' pick 'em. Probably believes if he leaves them in the ground long enough they'll grow into cabbages. I was there once when he was supposed to feed the dogs. Know what the lazy bugger did? Put the bowls down and a tin of meat in each, but never opened the tins!'

Of course, the last bit hadn't been true, though it had caused a lot of laughter, because everyone knew Evans.

Joan sighed. Brian and Meg's life read like a depressing saga. Their children were always suffering from some ailment and Meg continually rang home for help. Matt called her 'The Drama Queen'.

It wasn't until the next afternoon that Joan got round to opening the book that told the story of her successful younger daughter's life.

The previous day Matt had been as good as his word, arriving home by three thirty to find Joan propped up in bed, fast asleep, with her book on Meg lying open across her chest. He hadn't disturbed her, merely removed the book and gone to the kitchen to prepare a light dinner for them.

While he stood peeling a few potatoes his mind was centred on Joan. What a woman! What a mother! She kept in close touch with all three of their children, didn't interfere, mind you, but was there if and when any of them needed her. And not only their brood: she'd taken on Peter, Karen and Betsy too. Not that he minded that in the least. His views on the Piviteaux family had changed since he'd spent so much time with them. He himself had come from a big family and the fact that they had all scattered sometimes worried him. The only ones who seemed to care about their mum these days were himself and dear old Stan.

It was different with his children: they were always

coming home for the weekend, and if they weren't they never failed to pick up a phone and chat to their mother. They had all rallied round while she was ill: a fact for which he was eternally grateful. Add to that the American side of it and how close they had all become and it was pretty unbelievable!

Why, some folk would never understand it if you were to sit down and tell the story till you were blue in the face. And though there weren't many folk to whom he would make this admission, he had felt, over the last fifteen years, as though he had two sons. Which, of course, he did.

That reminded him. He'd had a telephone call from Karen while he'd been at the office this afternoon and she'd be coming home next weekend. He would tell Joan when she woke up. Home to Karen Piviteaux was here in Ashtead, or at least while she was working in England. Her own parents heartily approved of this. Bit of a mix-up all round when you thought about it – his Rosie lived in the States now. Matt tossed a peeled potato into the saucepan. No wonder Joan kept books on them all. It was the only way she could keep tabs on them. He had let Joan get out of bed and come out into the lounge to eat their meal. She'd had a wash and brushed her hair and the atmosphere as they sat in front of the fire was relaxing. When Matt had brought in ice-cream and a pot of coffee, Joan had felt a bit guilty because he was waiting on her so much. Later, seated on the settee, nestling back against his broad chest, his arms encircling her, Joan had felt that she was indeed a lucky lady.

Today there was no need to light a fire: the morning was bright with warm sunshine. Unable to resist Joan's pleading that she'd had more than enough of being in bed, Matt had settled her in an armchair from where she had a good view of the garden.

He placed a stout stick beside her chair and said, 'I'm going to be working out there for a while so if you need anything just tap on the glass an' I'll come in. Do you want me to fetch you your books?'

'You're a darling,' she told him.

'Anything for a quiet life,' he retorted. 'Anyway, better make the most of it because we'll probably end up with a house full in a week's time. At least on the Sunday, they'll all be wanting to check up on you. Make sure I'm not ill treating you.'

'Get on with you,' she smiled. 'I'm glad Karen is coming. Do you know if Meg and Brian are?'

'Most probably, more than likely they'll bring some of Evans' wonderful garden produce.' Matt couldn't resist that sarcastic gibe.

Joan gave a little laugh; it was difficult getting Matt to agree that Brian and Meg did their best. All she could do was try and make a joke of it, so she answered sweetly, 'And if they do I'm sure they will be the best we've ever tasted.'

'Hmm, some bloody 'opes you've got.'

Joan squared her shoulders, her voice shaking with laughter. 'Well, you'll be the one that has to cook them.'

Matt had reached the door, then hesitated, turned round, and said, 'That's where you're wrong, my old darling. With a 'ouse full of women and kids I'm going to shut myself in the bedroom with you. But if you insist on getting up and pretending you're well enough to be the hostess then I'll be off down the pub.' He closed the door firmly. Only to open it again and say, 'Use the stick to bang on the window when you feel like a cuppa.'

What a real family man Matt had become. He could be gruff, but the girls could still wind him round their little fingers. These days she did worry about Meg and Brian. Meg didn't help herself. Which made it nigh on impossible for anyone else to offer her help. Funny thing was that she belonged to the Women's Guild and several other clubs, where it seemed she was well able to cope with organizing events and meetings, yet she was scarcely able to control her own two children. Just thinking about Meg was fairly draining and it was with a heavy sigh that she laid down that book and picked up the book about Rosie.

How could two sisters turn out so different? If she had been asked to foretell the future when both her girls were small she would have laid a penny against a pound that Meg would be the more successful of the two. And how wrong she would have been! On leaving school it had been Meg that had landed a job in a solicitor's office while Rosie had been content to be a mere clerk in the offices of the Water Board.

She began to read. Rosie had been nineteen, coming up twenty, when Matt had taken them all to America to stay with the Piviteauxs for three weeks. Against Joan's better judgement, and despite all her protests that Rosie was far too young, Matt had given his permission for Rosie to stay on with the family for another month. From that time on Rosie had been fascinated by the American way of life. If it had been only that, perhaps she would have settled down in the country in which she had been born and, like the rest of the family, been content to go to the States on holiday. However, at the end of her stay when they'd met her at Heathrow airport she had been full of the fact that if the Piviteauxs were allowed to sponsor her and she were to be granted a work permit she had a job waiting for her in New York.

New York!

As Joan read on, and relived those months, she remembered how sad she had felt that her younger child not only wanted to leave home but go and live on the other side of the Atlantic Ocean. How could she or Matt have stopped her? They couldn't.

Rosie had always been a story-teller. Even at school she got high marks for all of her essays, and to be offered a job in a publishing company was the icing on the cake for her.

Joan turned to the pages that told of her own visit to New York just five years ago. She had travelled alone, which would have been unheard of before the war. Matt had insisted she go. He was up to his eyes in contracts and couldn't possibly accompany her.

Joan hugged herself as she recalled those two weeks. The main reason Rosie had so badly wanted her to be there was for the launch of a book she had written to be published by the firm she worked for. The party was held in New York, and Joan wouldn't have missed it for the world. To see her daughter being made so much fuss of and listening to compliments coming from all directions had to be seen to be believed. Today Rosie was a successful author with half a dozen best-sellers to her name.

Betsy Piviteaux was an editor with the same firm, and the girls shared a flat in a building so tall that terror had gripped Joan's heart: whatever would they do if the lift was out of order?

'Mum, it's an elevator, not a lift, and the Americans always have a back-up service,' had been Rosie's reply.

She was so proud of her baby. No matter how old she

was she had been Joan's last-born and therefore would always be her baby. It seemed such a long time since Rosie had been home; seven years, in fact, though she and Matt had been over to stay. And while she had been in hospital the nurses had wheeled the phone-trolley beside her bed so that she could take a call from Rosie. Twice that had happened, and each week a huge bouquet of flowers had been delivered to the ward with a card bearing such loving words from her.

She mustn't complain. She had a wonderful family.

To be honest though, she did worry about Rosie – not in the same way that she worried over Meg – there was no need. The truth was it was more wishful thinking on her part, rather than a cause for concern. It was just that there was never any mention of men in Rosie's life. Everyday workmates, oh, yes! While she had been staying with Rosie she'd been introduced to several handsome young American men. Quite a few of them had seemed to be very much at home in the girls' apartment. When she mentioned it to Matt he always laughed and told her not to be so daft.

Joan hadn't asked questions because what she didn't know supposedly wouldn't hurt her, but she belonged to a generation that attached great importance to marriage. Marriage was the beginning and the end for a well-brought-up young lady. It was all very well for Rosie to have a career, even such a successful one that she'd carved out for herself, but what about the dreams Joan had had of her getting married, looking beautiful in a flowing white dress, walking up the aisle on her father's arm? Didn't Rosie want to have children? It might not matter to her now – she was thirty-two – but her body wouldn't stay young for ever.

It was some time later that Matt opened the sitting-room

door. Joan woke with a start as he laid a hand over hers. 'It's ten to seven. You've been asleep for three hours. I know because I've checked on you three times. Dinner is all ready but I can keep it hot if you'd like to freshen up first.'

Joan stretched her arms. 'Oh, Matt, I'm sorry.'

'Nothing to be sorry for,' he told her. 'Sleep is the best medicine you could have.'

Suddenly she smiled and said, 'Would you like to know something? For the first time in ages I'm hungry.'

'Good. Shall I bring our meal in here or shall we eat in the kitchen?'

'Give me a few minutes in the bathroom and then I'll come out into the kitchen.'

Matt laid his cheek on the top of her head, and they shared a quiet moment, each grateful that they still had each other.

Then she struggled to get out of the chair, moaning, 'If only I didn't feel so weak.'

Matt laughed. 'You always did want to walk before you could run. Will it help if I tell you how much I love you?'

'Yes,' she told him. 'You know it does. It helps a great deal.'

Chapter Thirty-Four

JOAN WAS READING the book on Peter Piviteaux, and promising herself that she would do exactly as Matt had told her and keep her legs up. He had been right: the rest she had had over the past few days had worked wonders. She felt so much better. Peter. It was still a wonder to her that she could feel such deep love for the son to whom she had given birth yet not brought up. It was the same for Beryl where Jamie was concerned and that point alone had both mothers thanking the Lord for the way things had eventually turned out. She had often wondered just what had been the incentive that had made each of them fight so fiercely for the right to keep their sons. They both had two girls and knew full well of the intimacy that existed in a mother's relationship with her daughter. Didn't the well-known saying state that a daughter is a daughter for all of her life but a son is a son until he takes a wife?

And yet isn't there that very special affinity that sparks a mother's fierce love and loyalty to a son? She only knew that of all the many happenings in her life Jamie, from the moment he had been put into her arms, had to be looked upon as the best. And now she regarded Peter as a terrific bonus.

Peter still lived with his family in America, but was no stranger to her and Matt. At the moment he was in Sweden. She knew because he had telephoned her the minute he had been told she was home from hospital. Today the world seemed so small with all the children getting on planes and going places in the way that she and Matt used to catch buses.

The Piviteauxs' company had expanded. She and Matt had been told that it had started out as a dry-cleaning business. Now it offered hotel-, office- and furniture-cleaning on a huge scale. With several members of the family involved, they had won many contracts and employed more than a hundred people. Peter had been chosen to oversee the purchase of new equipment, which would come from several different countries. It was a feather in his cap to be responsible for such expensive items.

'Let me see,' Joan murmured, turning the pages slowly. When she came to the record of his first marriage she sighed. Things hadn't gone all that smoothly for Peter. He had been on holiday with some of his mates, hunting and fishing, staying at the family lodge, when he'd met Abigail. He had found her extremely attractive. The long and short of it was, she'd turned up pregnant three months later claiming that Peter was the father. She wanted him to take her home, face her parents and marry her.

'Home is where?' Beryl had questioned.

'Down south.' And that was about all the information Abigail had offered.

It had not been an easy time for Joe or Beryl. They had shown their disapproval, only to get up next morning to find that the two had gone. They had suggested that Abigail stay with them and get to know them before the pair applied for a marriage licence.

Joan sniffed back tears at the memory of Beryl on the phone asking her advice. Joe had talked long and hard to Matt. 'The greatest gift a parent can give his son is independence,' Joe said, 'and, God knows, I've done my best to give him that.'

Matt had told her afterwards that he could hear the sobs in Joe's voice when he was telling him that Peter had thrown it all away for some little trollop. Beryl had blamed herself. Perhaps they should have been a little less ambitious for him, or even more tolerant of Abigail. But it was all too late. Peter had left with her, and they hadn't an address or a real inkling of where she lived.

Joan searched for and found the two letters she had folded between the pages. They gave an end to this story. One was from Beryl, showing relief, if nothing else, and one from Peter telling her he realized what an idiot he had been. Joan smiled as she read. It hadn't been hard to see things from his point of view. Hadn't they all been young once? Hadn't they all done things they later regretted?

As he was over twenty-one he had had no trouble in obtaining a marriage licence, but the honeymoon period had lasted all of three weeks. The next five months Peter described as unbearable, but he had stayed for the sake of the unborn baby. When the little girl had been born, he said, he had been rooted to the spot. Not that she wasn't the prettiest thing, with huge eyes and thick tight curls, but her skin was coffee-coloured. She was not his daughter.

Poor Peter. He had tried to do right by Abigail but she had made the mistake of thinking he was a simpleton, which of course he most certainly was not.

But thanks to his father he had weathered that storm. Joe had set the wheels in motion and had the marriage annulled. It had taken time for the hurt to heal. It didn't seem fair that so much deceit and trouble should have been heaped on one young man's shoulders.

But again God was Good, the right young lady had come along, and although she and Matt had not made it to the wedding in New York they had been pleasantly rewarded. Peter and his lovely bride, Louise, had come to London for their honeymoon, staying at the Goring Hotel. Twice she and Matt had had a meal with them. Louise was the kind of girl that every mother would want her son to marry, and both she and Matt had loved her from the moment they had met.

Karen's book came next: not that she needed to familiarize herself with what Karen was getting up to because hardly a week went by when she and Matt didn't have the pleasure of her company. Karen had chosen nursing as her career and now specialized in children's welfare. Where better to gain experience than at Great Ormond Street Hospital in London, the most famous of children's hospitals?

Beryl said she had breathed a sigh of relief when Matt had assured her there would always be a bedroom in their house for Karen whenever she had days off and wanted to get out of London. Eighteen months she had been over here now, and Joan would be sorry if and when Karen decided it was time to go home.

Karen was an absolute beauty, always full of energy, turning heads wherever she went. She had come to visit Joan in hospital, wearing black slacks and a white silk blouse with a scarf tucked in at the neck. She was a kind, caring person, like her mother. She talked about several boyfriends but had only ever brought one down to Ashtead for the weekend, a doctor at the hospital where she worked. His name was Alex, a rugged, handsome man in his late thirties. Matt said he looked more like a rugby player than a doctor.

Karen acted calmly and quietly when he was around, which made Joan think she might be serious about him. 'I hope so,' Beryl had said, when they were chatting on the phone. 'After all, she is thirty-four.'

But girls didn't get married so young, these days. In fact, many of them didn't bother to tie the knot at all. They just found themselves a young man, and before they had time to get to know each other they were openly living together.

These were hard times for mothers, especially when the world was their children's oyster and they could take a plane to any country in the world that took their fancy. Getting pregnant out of wedlock was no longer frowned upon. In my day, Joan was thinking, you would have been an absolute outcast, someone dirty and disgusting if you had a baby before you got married. Not today. They talked about having a love-child with their partner! Joan felt she was in an awkward situation and when she voiced her fears to Matt he laughed. Yes he had! Even going so far as to say she was jealous that the Pill hadn't been around when they'd been young. He'd laughed even more when she blushed and called him a cheeky bugger.

Anyway, Karen was coming down on Friday and Joan began to wonder whether she would be bringing Alex with her. Wait and see, she chided herself, and took up the last book, which was all about Betsy.

She couldn't think about Betsy Piviteaux without coupling her with Rosie. They both worked for the same publishing firm and they shared a flat. Or, as they were more apt to say, an apartment. She had shut her eyes to some of their goings-on when she had stayed with them for two weeks. They certainly lived a different life from anything she had known. There were times when she didn't know what to make of either of them. Their moods seemed to change with the weather. This last month they had been in high spirits. Apparently Rosie had been away from New York, on a tour to publicize her latest book and to sign copies. When she came back Betsy was going to tell her that she had everything planned out. It wasn't going to happen until December, six months away, but Betsy was full of it, right down to the last detail. Rosie, she and two male companions were going to spend Christmas in Switzerland. It sounded, from Betsy's account, an enviable way to spend the festive season. But – and it was a big but – by the time December came, would they still be friends with these *male companions*?

Joan laughed and shook her head, saying out loud, 'I don't suppose so.' What it was to be unrestricted! The life that young women could live nowadays was beyond her comprehension. Still, she would be daft to start worrying about what might never happen. As Matt was fond of telling her, 'That would be putting the cart before the horse.'

Chapter Thirty-Five

IT WAS FRIDAY morning and Joan knew something was going on but couldn't put her finger on what it was. Matt seemed always to be answering the telephone or making calls of his own.

This weekend was going to be marvellous, especially tomorrow. Matt was taking her to lunch at the Crown Hotel in Morden. It would be her first real outing since she had been discharged from the hospital. Karen had rung to ask if it would be all right for her to bring Alex home with her so, of course, Matt had said yes and extended the invitation to include them in the special Saturday lunch.

Shortly after three o'clock she watched from the window as Alex and Karen got out of the car. To her surprise they had brought Amy with them.

'You don't mind if I park meself on yer for a few days?' Amy asked, before she'd set foot inside the house.

Karen kissed Joan warmly, offering no explanation as to

why they had her mother-in-law with them. Alex shook her hand, saying how pleased he was that she had been discharged from the hospital, then warned her to take things easy for a while.

Though their evening meal had passed quietly enough Joan sensed that everyone was hiding something from her. She couldn't stand it any longer. As Karen got up and went to the sideboard to pour coffee, she turned to her mother-in-law. 'Amy, are you going to tell me what's going on? Cos I know something is.'

Amy grinned. 'Do you?'

Joan nodded. 'Yes, I can smell you're up to something a mile off.'

'Aye, well,' Amy said, 'you're a clever clogs. But, then, you always have been.'

Joan burst out laughing. 'And for your information I know when you're trying to soft-soap me.'

'Now, would I do a thing like that?'

'You're losing the battle, Amy.' Karen laughed, as she set the tray down on the table.

'Shall I be referee?' Alex asked.

'Oh, I don't think it will come to fisticuffs.' Karen smiled gently at the rugged, well-built man, whose bright blue eyes were telling her that he was happy to be here with her.

'Well,' he pursed his lips, 'I think I should take Matt down to the local for a pint and leave you ladies to sort yourselves out.'

'You've never 'ad a better idea.' Matt got up and came to stand behind Joan's chair. 'You don't mind, do you, dear? We won't be late but if you want to go to bed Karen will see you're all right.'

'Of course not, I'll be fine.' Joan reached up to pat his cheek.

With the two men out of the way, the three women sat over their coffee. It was Amy who broke the silence. 'I'm sorry I didn't get down t' see you while you were in 'ospital, Joan. Me legs were playing me up. But I'm downright pleased t' see yer looking so well. I'd never 'ave forgiven meself if anything 'ad 'appened to you.'

Joan patted her workworn hand. 'Well, nothing did happen to me, did it? As you can see I'm almost as fit as a flea, so you needn't worry. And I really am so pleased that you're here now.' Then quickly, as an afterthought, she added, 'But I still think there's more to this visit than either you or Karen is letting on.'

'You're letting your imagination run away with you,' Karen said, and sprang to her feet. 'I'm going to get your nightdress and dressing-gown and put them in the bathroom. It's time you were tucked up in bed.'

While Karen was out of the room Joan seized her chance. 'Amy, what do you think of Alex?' she asked.

'So far so good. He seems a fine man, not too young. What I did like, having listened t' them talking in the car, was that he doesn't sound t' me as if he's for the social limelight. You know what I mean, London an' all the parties an' goings-on. No, I think he'll suit our Karen cos he's the steady type.'

'Oh, Amy, I'm glad you say that. I feel responsible for Karen, what with her own parents being so far away.'

'Bit like tit-for-tat, ain't it, gal? They keep an eye on our Rosie and you do the same for them with Karen.'

'Keep an eye on them is about all we can do,' Joan muttered, more to herself than to Amy. 'I used to think that by the time they were twenty-one you didn't have to worry about them any more. As it turned out, the real worries started at just about that time. And, these days, it seems to me that they do exactly as they please.'

'My, my.' Amy chuckled. 'Feeling old, are we? Our brood ain't youngsters any more and if that makes you feel yer age, what d'yer think it does t' me?'

'Time for bed. Big day tomorrow,' Karen announced, coming back into the room.

Joan latched on to that. She was even more sure now that something was afoot. Ah, well, better do as she was told and take herself off to bed.

'How does she look to you?' Karen asked Amy, once they were alone.

'Bit thinner, but better than I'd expected, thank God.'

'I just hope tomorrow isn't going to prove too much for her. Do you think we've done the right thing?'

'Aw, pet, course I do. She'll be that 'appy, she'll be over the moon. You wait and see. It will be just the tonic she's needing.'

'I hope to God you're right,' Karen said, beneath her breath, and even to herself it sounded like a prayer.

As it was Saturday lunchtime, the bars of the Crown were busy. Matt had a firm hold on Joan's elbow as he guided her through the customers. Suddenly a voice from behind her was saying, 'I'm so glad to see you again, Mrs Pearson.'

Joan turned her head and smiled. The man who had spoken was the manager, and just seeing him brought back memories of the happy family parties they had held here. 'I'm glad to see you too, Mr Curtis. It's been a while since I was here.' She studied his face: he hadn't aged, with his curly iron-grey hair and tanned complexion. She wondered why he was welcoming her personally. His eyes were bright and twinkling as he turned to Matt and said, 'Everything is ready outside. Shall I lead the way?' His voice was remarkably soothing and he had an old-world charm about him as he offered his arm to Amy.

Two young men held open the double swing doors for them. At the far end of the lawn a marquee had been erected.

'Went up a treat,' Mr Curtis murmured to Matt. 'Always best to be on the safe side in case it rains, though the forecast is good.'

Joan stood still. It was a glorious day with the sun high in the sky, the green grass stretched in front of her to where a brightly coloured marquee had been erected. It was a sight to behold, plastic windows in each side and the opening appeared to be a huge front door. Now she knew her instinct had not been wrong.

She looked at Karen, who merely smiled. Amy's head was turned away.

Joan was feeling bewildered, even a little apprehensive as to what might be going to happen next. Nothing in this world could have prepared her for what did happen. Her younger daughter was coming towards her.

Joan stared in amazement. She tried to go forward but her legs wouldn't move quickly enough. Arms outstretched, Rosie reached her.

'How did you get here?' her mother asked, her voice little more than a croak.

'I swam the Atlantic,' Rosie said, and threw her arms around her mother. 'I love you, Mum,' she whispered.

'My God,' Joan gasped, 'I've missed you so much.'

'Me too, Mummy, and I worried so much while you were in hospital.'

Rosie calling her Mummy after all this time! It tore at Joan's heart. Tears were pouring down her cheeks and Rosie said, 'Oh, please, don't cry, Mum.'

'I'm not crying because I'm upset,' Joan spluttered, 'I'm crying because I'm so happy to see you. Have you got a handkerchief?'

Matt came to her side, holding out his own big white one. 'I've a feeling you're gonna need this even more when you see everyone else that's here to wish you well.' He took her arm, making sure she was close to his side. 'Come on, my darling,' he whispered, 'I just know you're gonna 'ave a happy day. You've nothing to cry about. Nothing at all. Just remember I love you very much and so does everyone else that's here.'

Now she really cried.

Matt stepped aside, letting Rosie lead her mother forward into the centre of the marquee.

Joan was dumbfounded. 'Just look at you all,' she said.

It took ages for everyone to hug her, to tell her how glad they were that she had got over her operation, Jamie and Pamela, Meg and Brian, Matt's brother Stan and his wife Hazel were here. And all her grandchildren were outside in the sunshine enjoying themselves.

Betsy Piviteaux popped out from behind a chair. 'You didn't think I was going to let Rosie swim all that way on her own, did you?'

Then her mum was holding her close, telling her how afraid she'd been that they were going to lose her.

'Not today, Daphne,' Bill Harvey reproached his wife. 'No more tears. This is going to be a good day.' With that he bent his big frame to take his daughter into his arms. 'Love you, Joan. We all do.'

'Love you too, Dad.'

There was a moment's confusion as everybody moved back to the sides of the marquee. Then, once more, Joan just could not believe what she was seeing. Beryl was the first to move, covering the space between them in no time. Joan held her arms out wide, feeling enormous pleasure that her dear friend was here today. And then came Joe: 'Hi, how you doing?' There was no holding back, his strong arms lifted her until her feet were no longer on the ground. 'We couldn't let you guys have a party without us being here, now, could we?'

Beryl's mother kissed her on both cheeks.

The last to appear were Peter and a very pregnant Louise. The hug that Peter gave her seemed to go on for ever. A head came over her shoulder and she twisted round to kiss Louise.

To say the very least it was a lively lunch, and as Joan settled back in an armchair Amy came over to her and said, 'Well, Joan, love, 'ow d'yer feel now?'

'I just don't believe that so many people were that concerned for me that they came all this way to wish me well.'

Amy gave a deep laugh. 'They're all so grateful.'

'What d'you mean, grateful?'

'Well, let's face it, gal. They could 'ave all been gatherin' 'ere dressed in black. Much better t' be 'ere drinkin' yer 'ealth.'

'Oh, Amy! Only you could think of something like that!'

Amy thought it best to keep the rest of her thoughts to herself. Nevertheless she still thought she wasn't far wrong.

Most of the adults had gone off to help amuse the children, and even Meg had offered to organize a game. She seemed so much happier today, Joan thought. Let's hope it lasts, especially for Brian's sake.

She turned her gaze to where Matt was standing just outside the opening of the marquee. Joe Piviteaux was beside him, and the two men seemed to be deep in conversation.

Joan had been so relieved when those two had become friends. The last few years had changed Matt so much. When the truth had come to light about Peter and Jamie he had been rebellious, angry, determined not to face the facts. Now she could see that he and Joe were watching their sons with pride on their faces. Despite the heartache and against the odds they had all survived, and everything had fallen into place.

Now Matt was making his way towards her. 'What are you doing sitting here all on your own?' he asked.

Joan looked up at him standing over her, his eyes twinkling. He took her hands and pulled her to her feet. 'Later on our grandchildren are going to sing a song for us. There are some deckchairs out there if you feel up to it.'

'Yes,' she said softly, 'that will be lovely. But while we're on our own, Matt, I want to say thank you for today. And for so much more. No man could have done more for their wife than you have.'

'Just so long as you're happy. We've come a long way, ain't we? Mine an' Stan's business 'as turned out even better than we 'oped and that pleases me cos I'm able to give you an' the kids so much more. All I want you t' do is get a bit stronger and then I'm taking you off on a long holiday. Will that make you 'appy?'

'I am happy, Matt.'

'Then that's all that matters.'

She sighed. 'Things have turned out so much better than we could ever have imagined, haven't they?'

'You can say that again. We 'ad our rough passages, by God we did, but we weathered them. Right now, though, I think we'd better go outside. Everyone will be worried as to where you are.'

'Oh, do we have to?' Joan asked playfully. 'Can't we just stay here, the two of us?'

'No, we can't. We've family and friends t' see to.' Suddenly he grinned wickedly. 'You could go so far as t' say we've got double trouble cos we've got two families to contend with.'

'I heard that, Matt Pearson, and what goes for you two goes for the two of us!' Joe Piviteaux was smiling broadly as he and Beryl came to stand beside them. Then, with a theatrical flourish, he produced a bottle of champagne from behind his back.

It took a while for Joe to release the cork, but then he was pouring the foaming wine into four glasses. 'Here's to us two sets of parents,' he declared, raising his glass. 'Good health, and may we always be friends.'

'I'll willingly drink to that,' Matt said, 'but I'll add a bit. To Anglo-American relationships.'

All four were laughing as they drank, but when Beryl and Joan looked into each other's eyes they couldn't help but see the glint of tears. Then Beryl said, 'I'll make the next toast.' She raised her glass and, with her eyes fixed on Joan, she said, 'Here's to our two sons.'

The air was so charged with emotion that it was a relief when they heard, 'Oh, so this is where you're all hiding.'

Both women blinked away their tears and smiled as Jamie and Peter came striding towards them. Then, in unison, they said, 'We're just coming, son.'

Chapter Thirty-Six

'THEY DO A pretty good job at the Crown,' Matt said, the next morning, as he stretched out in an armchair. 'And it all went off very well, even if I do say it myself! There's usually someone who gets upset at a family do but this time everyone was remarkably well behaved. All getting older and wiser, I suppose.'

'Trust my husband to take all the credit.' Joan grinned

Joe and Beryl both laughed. It was good to see Joan looking so relaxed, and it was true, Matt had given everyone a great day. They were sitting close together on the settee which was drawn up close to the fire.

Joe and Beryl were staying for a few days with Matt and Joan. Rosie and Betsy had stayed the night with Meg and Brian, and Stan and Hazel with Daphne and Bill. Peter and Louise had gone off with Jamie and Pamela, while Karen and her new friend Alex, with Amy and Beryl's mother, had come home with Joan and Matt. Tomorrow most of the Piviteauxs would be flying back to New York, but today it was open house here in Ashtead.

Joan was thinking that yesterday had been a most wonderful day, and today, with all the family around her in her own home, was the icing on the cake.

'Who'd have thought it, eh? All of us under one roof.' Beryl's voice was soft.

Joan laughed. 'Took time but we got there in the end. I wish my nan was still here to see us all together.'

Amy and Beryl's mother came into the room carrying plates of food. 'Shall we lay the table or just set up a buffet for everyone to help themselves?' Amy asked.

Joan and Beryl grinned. 'Why ask us? You're in charge.'

'Then a buffet it will be. Much less washing-up.' Amy had always been jolly but since having her own flat at Jamie and Pamela's house she had blossomed even more. She loved living there, still so close to the East End and with company on hand if and when she needed it.

'Joan, your mum and dad are here. I've just seen their car pull into the drive,' Karen called from the hall.

Daphne burst into the room, followed by Bill who said to Joan, 'Your mother's thrilled she hasn't got to cook Sunday dinner. And as I haven't had to do all the vegetables here's my contribution.' He held out a cardboard box containing three bottles of white wine and three bottles of red.

'Thanks, Bill.' Matt relieved him of the carton. 'You're a man after me own heart.'

Stan and Hazel followed close behind. 'All right, are you, Joan? Yesterday didn't tire you out too much?'

'No, love, I'm fine.' Joan got up and kissed her sister-in-law. 'I expect there's tea on the go in the kitchen but if you want to join me and Beryl ask Matt to give you a glass.'

'What you two drinking, then?'

They raised their glasses, and Beryl said, 'Try some. It's Bucks Fizz.'

By now a host of women were setting out enough platters of food to feed an army. The doorbell rang and, seconds later, it appeared as if everyone had arrived at the same time. The whole room was in an uproar.

John and Josie, Meg and Brian's two children, with young Matt and his sister Beryl, Jamie and Pamela's two, were all claiming the right to kiss their grandma first.

Meg bent over her mother's shoulder. 'Are you all right, Mum?'

'Never better.' Joan smiled at her elder daughter. Meg looked happier than she had for ages. She was a bit too thin, but her skin was good and she still had a gorgeous head of hair with the reddish tints inherited from the Harveys.

Joan transferred her gaze to Brian as he lowered his head to kiss her hello. This son-in-law of hers was a good man, a bit of a stick-in-the-mud but steady. Just lately she'd had the feeling that he and Meg had weathered their storms, and that much between them had changed for the better. She hoped she was right. Nobody had an easy ride through life.

Pamela bent over Joan and said gently, 'It was a lovely gathering yesterday, and we're all so pleased to see you on the mend.'

Joan touched her daughter-in-law's cheek. If she'd searched the earth she couldn't have found a more loving wife for her beloved Jamie.

Now Louise crouched in front of her and took her hand. They say pregnant women take on a special bloom and it was certainly true where Louise was concerned. She looked so nice in her navy blue maternity dress which had a wide white lace collar.

'Stand up,' Joan urged her. 'You shouldn't be crouched down like that.'

Louise did as she was told but grinned as she said, 'I'm having a baby, I'm not ill.' Her voice was full of happiness as she hugged Joan.

Beryl and Joan looked at each other and raised their eyebrows, what with the children and the adults it was beginning to be confusing. 'Best we stay where we are and let the youngsters get on with it today,' Beryl suggested.

Suddenly Rosie and Betsy clapped their hands and when order was restored they said in unison, 'Grub's up. Come and help yourselves.'

The two mothers looked at each other. Both of their daughters looked stunning. It was easy to see why they set the pulses of their menfriends racing. They were the modern young woman personified, in their tailor-made suits, sheer nylons and high-heeled plain court shoes.

The glance that went between Joan and Beryl was one of understanding and amazement. Everyone in this room loved everyone else. The old were adored by the young. These two women, who at one time might have hated each other, were firm friends. Today it was as if two completely different families had been moulded into one, each member had accepted the inevitable, all happy in their own ways, and glad to be here. The story of their coming together would go down in family history. Their children would tell their own offspring, and so it would live on. No one could have foreseen that what had happened on 2 November 1944 would have brought such heartache and then such joy.

Joan felt Beryl's hand take hers and they looked into each

other's eyes. The rift that might have ruined their lives had been healed. They were confident women with loving families of their own and yet they shared a part of each other's. They reached for their drinks, then raised their glasses in a very personal toast, just for the two of them.

The silent toast was 'To our two sons.'